BLOODY SAM

BLOODY SAM

The Life and Films of
SAM PECKINPAH

by Marshall Fine

DONALD I. FINE, INC.
New York

Library of Congress Cataloging-in-Publication Data

Fine, Marshall, 1950–
Bloody Sam / Marshall Fine.
p.   cm.
Includes bibliographical references (p.   ) and index.
Filmography: p.
ISBN 1-55611-236-X
1. Peckinpah, Sam, 1926–   . I. Title.
PN1998.3.P43F56   1991
791.43′0233′092—dc20   90-56081
                                                      CIP

Manufactured in the United States of America

10 9 8 7 6 5 4 3 2 1

Designed by Irving Perkins Associates

For my parents, Barbara and Irving Fine

A man has to be judged, in the final judgment, not by the depths to which he sinks but by the heights to which he rises.

—OLD SAYING

Contents

PART NINE: 1983–1984

PART TEN: EPILOGUE

Introduction

SMALL PECKINPAH HATED the nickname "Bloody Sam."

As a director of films that blended pure action-adventure and complex morality tales, he was offended at the name's shortsightedness. It reduced his work—some of which took literally years to write, finance and make—to one visceral bit of imagery. While the graphic violence of his films was intended to make a statement, violence itself was not the statement.

More important, the nickname limited him, defining him in a way he had no interest in being defined. The powers that be in Hollywood associated his name with a certain kind of films and couldn't or wouldn't see beyond that to the skill, artistry and vision that went into making those films transcend that kind of categorization.

Like the best of his films, Sam Peckinpah the man defied simplistic analysis. Known as a hard-drinking, hard-living maverick, he was a sensitive and poetic soul who tried to hide that side from the world. Renowned for his tough, unrelenting cinematic action, he felt a kinship with writers such as Tennessee Williams and William Saroyan.

He was, in short, a colorful character, with strengths and weaknesses, bad habits and lovable idiosyncrasies. He was someone, as most of his friends say, with whom it was easy to become quickly and inexorably embroiled. If he liked you and felt you were worth knowing, he pulled you into his world almost instantly, immersing you until you began to see things his way, for better or worse.

Most of the people who knew Sam Peckinpah don't just remember him fondly (or disdainfully)—they remember him vividly. They also each remember him differently, because Peckinpah was a master actor and director in real life. He showed other people what he wanted to or needed to; he rarely showed any two people exactly the same facet of himself. Yet the impression he made was so strong that each is convinced that the Peckinpah he or she knew was the real one.

In some cases, they seem to have a personal stake in promoting their personal image, their Sam Peckinpah. They feel their Sam is the real Sam, someone other than the Sam Peckinpah mythologized in the media. Anything at odds with their particular version must necessarily be wrong.

But Sam Peckinpah was too complex for simple analysis. As truthful as their version may be, it is far from the whole truth. Peckinpah had a powerful personality; once exposed to it, you would be hard-pressed to be objective about it ever again.

He was, in the words of his friend and associate Walter Kelley, the kind of friend "you loved and dreaded at the same time, someone you could have a wonderful lunch with and end up having a fistfight with in the parking lot."

He could be utterly charming and frighteningly cruel, to friends and strangers alike. He brought a rigorous discipline to his work and yet succumbed to his own self-destructive tendencies. His mercurial nature gave rise to rapid mood swings and quirks, from startling generosity to a complete stranger to provocative nastiness to a close friend.

Peckinpah promoted this kind of confusion, reveling in misconceptions about himself, relishing the myths that arose about him as Hollywood's bad boy. Too late, he saw the damage that myths can do in Hollywood, a place where perception is taken for reality.

He started, for example, as an idealistic film director fighting narrow-minded, shortsighted producers who equated artistry with revenues. For his efforts, he developed a reputation as a director who had a problem with authority. As true as that was personally, it wasn't always the case professionally, certainly not when working with a sympathetic producer who understood how to collaborate with him.

As time went on, the battles with producers became such a part of his image that they became de rigueur, an expected part of any movie he was associated with, a part of his myth that he was only too able to oblige. Fueled by alcohol and, later, cocaine, Peckinpah eventually began to play the part of Sam Peckinpah—the Peckinpah that other people seemed to expect. It became a self-fulfilling and self-destructive prophecy.

By the time he had figured this out, it was too late. Out of work, out of favor, he quested after that one script that would turn things around, the Western that would sum up all that he had done right, and excuse what he had squandered. It ultimately was a fruitless quest, because he was looking for the movie that only the mythic version of himself could have made—and that person never existed, except in other people's minds.

I FIRST RAN ACROSS Sam Peckinpah's films as a junior high school student. I turned on the TV one afternoon and found a Western about two aging lawmen: *Ride the High Country.* I was instantly captivated by this story, and surprised at how moved I was by its understated sadness and nobility, and by the performances of Randolph Scott and Joel McCrea.

While in college, I saw *The Wild Bunch* and was overwhelmed by its power and excitement. I made a note of the director's name—Sam Peckinpah—and began to make a point of looking for his films. And was rewarded: *The Ballad of Cable Hogue, Straw Dogs, Junior Bonner.*

By now a committed Peckinpah fan, I watched his work deteriorate through the late 1970s. When he surfaced with *The Osterman Weekend* in 1983, I was saddened at what an unextraordinary film it was. But I always retained a fondness and a fascination for his best work.

I got the idea for this book in 1989. Frustrated by the limitations of daily journalism, I was casting about for a topic for a nonfiction book that would allow me to research, report and write in greater depth and at greater length than a newspaper's Sunday entertainment section could accommodate. Biography appealed to me and I tried to think of someone who would interest me sufficiently to devote a large chunk of time to.

I thought of Peckinpah, because of my background in film criticism and because I could recall no book that examined his life or work. Doing some checking, I found that none existed that looked at his films or the rest of his world with any sense of perspective or objectivity. The only book that resembled a biography, Garner Simmons's *Peckinpah: A Portrait in Montage,* had been published by the University of Texas Press in 1982, before Peckinpah's death, before he had even made his final film. An expanded version of Simmons's master's thesis, it was based on interviews done in the mid-1970s.

For all of its information about the films, it seemed too ready to buy into and embellish the myth of Peckinpah, the lovable hard-drinking maverick. It offered little sense of who Peckinpah was as a person: as a husband, father or friend.

Nor did it offer any sense of perspective about Peckinpah's place in film history during that unique period of the 1960s and 1970s when he was principally active. It was a time of turbulence and change in the movie industry, both as a business and as an art form, with a shifting power base, a changing audience and a radically altered sense of the possibilities of what film could achieve. Peckinpah had contributed to those changes.

I was also spurred by the sense that, as influential as he had been, Sam Peckinpah was being forgotten. An entire generation had been affected by his work—but another generation had come of age since his most fertile period without knowing who he was. They were seeing his influence without being aware of his name.

BIOGRAPHY IS AN IMPRECISE ART, particularly when assessing the life of a man one has never met, more than a half-decade after his death.

I feel fortunate that I had the trust, cooperation and help of so many people who knew Sam Peckinpah so well. My goal was to write a serious and honest book about an imperfect man with a singular vision; their assistance was invaluable. My search for information took me back and forth across the country and to Mexico, as well as by telephone and fax machine to Europe and Indonesia.

I tried to confine myself to primary sources: the people who had known Sam Peckinpah personally. I sought out all known interviews with Peckinpah. I was fortunate in that he was both an inveterate letter- and memo-writer and a pack rat. The archive of his papers at the Academy of Motion Picture Arts and Sciences offered a true treasure trove of material, both about his work and his personal life.

There were some in the Peckinpah network (and believe me, it's a grapevine that still exists, through which news travels fast) who didn't want his memory besmirched by what they considered embarrassing or irrelevant incidents from his life. They were convinced that no good would come from dredging up the dark part of his past along with the glories.

But for every person who refused to talk, there were five or six more who willingly, sometimes painfully, offered to share their memories and other resources to give as complete a picture as possible.

In that sense, I am particularly appreciative of the time and help I received from Kristen Peckinpah, Sam's daughter, and Denver Peckinpah, his brother, the executors of his estate. I also received valuable insight from Sharon Peckinpah Marcus, his daughter; Mathew Peckinpah, his son; Susan Peckinpah, his sister; Marie Selland Taylor, Begonia Palacios and Marcy Blueher Ellis, his ex-wives; Walter Peter, his brother-in-law; and his cousins Bob Peckinpah and Wanda Justice.

Special thanks also to Judy Selland, Gill Dennis, Betty Peckinpah, Bobby Visciglia, Walter Kelley, John Bryson, Peter Falk, Jim Hamilton, Michael Sragow, Don Hyde, Paul Seydor, Richard T. Jameson, Andrew Sarris, David Warner, Martin Lewis, David and Sandy Peckinpah, Juan Jose and Kathy Palacios, L. Q. Jones, Martin Ransohoff, Carol O'Connor, Frank Kowalski, Martin Baum, Joe Bernhard, Blaine Pettitt, Bud Williams, Kip Dellinger, James Coburn, Daniel Melnick, Katy Haber, Seymour Cassel, David Wardlow, Jay Cocks, Jason Robards, Lois O'Connor Robards, Stirling Silliphant, Robin Chambers, William Panzer, Dr. Bob Gray, Gordon Dawson, Robert Culp, Isela Vega, Alex Phillips, Jr., Newt Arnold, R. G. Armstrong and Mort Sahl.

Thanks also to Charles FitzSimons, Theodore Bikel, Joe Swindlehurst, Carolyn Swindlehurst, Dr. Dennis Noteboom, Paul Peterson, Roger Spottiswoode, Kathleen Murphy, Lou Lombardo, Gary Weis, Walon Green, B. W. L. Norton, Gary Combs, Max Bercutt, John Crawford, Lee Pogostin, Mariette Hartley, James Drury, Alan Keller, Camille Fielding, Don Levy, Dave Rawlins, Bill Jenkins, Garth Craven, Kenneth Hyman, Monte Hellman, Rudy Wurlitzer, Anne Thompson, Jules Levy, Alan Sharp, Joe Wizan, Stella Stevens, Arnold Laven, Arthur Lewis, Harry Mark Petrakis, Dan York, Michael Deeley, Norma Fink, Jim Silke, Ted Haworth, Paul Schrader, Cliff Coleman, Max Evans, Charles Champlin, Albert Ruddy, Joe Canutt, James Caan, Stephen Farber, Mike Medavoy, Kent James, Michael Levine, Carol Lanning, Charlton Heston, Graeme Clifford, Pauline Kael, Dub Taylor, Dennis Hopper, John Calley, John Milius, Martin Scorsese, Bill Kenly, Wendy Morris and Marian Billings.

For research support and facilities, I would like to acknowledge Val Almendarez, Howard Prouty and the library staff at the Academy of Motion Picture Arts and Sciences in Beverly Hills; the White Plains Public Library in White Plains, New York; the New York Public Library at Lincoln Center and the Museum of Broadcasting in Manhattan; the Sioux Falls Public Library in Sioux Falls, South Dakota; the Ossining Public Library, Ossining, New York; the Los Angeles County Medical Examiner's office; Dr. Bruce Heckman; Dr. Hugo Kierszenbaum, director of Alcohol Treatment Services, Psychiatric Institute, Westchester County Medical Center; Dr. Emily Stein; Brian Gordon of the San Francisco Film Festival; Beyond Words Professional Word Processing Service; Terry Geeskin and Mary Corliss at the Museum of Modern Art Film Stills Collection; and Judge Peter Lieberman.

I could not have found the time to write this book without the understanding and enthusiasm of my employers at Gannett Westchester Newspapers, specifically my editors: Meryl Harris, Evelyn McCormack and Larry Beaupre.

I also wish to thank my agent, David Vigliano, and the people with whom I have been associated at Donald I. Fine, Inc.: Adam Levison and Donald Fine (who is no relation—honest!).

My work was aided by the friendship, support and assistance of a number of close friends and relatives: my parents; my mother-in-law, Mary Jacobs; George Meding and Lin Loy Chang; Howard Lapides; my aunt, Ruth Sperling; and my siblings, Richard and Julie.

My good friend Jay Straim has listened to me talk endlessly about this project and has been tirelessly supportive.

My oldest friend in the world, Larry Sutin, provided immeasurable guidance and wisdom, as well as the impetus to write this book in the first place.

Finally, and most important, I owe a sizable debt to my wife, Kim Jacobs, and my son, Jacob Fine, who have put up with my demanding schedule throughout this project. They made it possible for me to make this book become a reality. I could not have done it without them and cannot adequately express my thanks.

Prologue

PRODUCTION ON *The Cincinnati Kid* began the first week of December 1964.

A week later, director Sam Peckinpah was out of a job.

He didn't work as a director again for almost two years and didn't have another film released until 1969.

The Cincinnati Kid seemed to embody much of Sam Peckinpah's career, though it was a movie he never got to make. Within the four months of preproduction and the one week of actual shooting, all of the key elements of Peckinpah's life in the movie business came into play.

There were the strenuous clashes with a strong-willed producer that marked so many of his films. There were arguments about the script, the casting and the tone of the picture. There were problems with schedules and budget, marked by the producer's sense that Peckinpah was making the film up as he went along.

And, finally, there was the impact of Peckinpah's often tempestuous personal life—specifically, the effects of his crumbling second marriage to Mexican actress Begonia Palacios, whom he'd met, wooed and married on his previous film, *Major Dundee*. Tormented by his marital woes, Peckinpah was distracted from the work he'd been hired to do.

It was a pattern that was to persist through most of Sam Peckinpah's career. For part of that period, he was able to harness those personal demons and professional antagonism to make several classic films. Ultimately, however, those same forces wound up controlling him, pushing him to a level of self-destruction that finally kept him from reaching his real potential as a director.

IN SEPTEMBER 1964, Peckinpah had been hired by producer Martin Ransohoff to direct *The Cincinnati Kid*, on the basis of his work in the short-lived TV series, "The Westerner," which won him more than one directing job.

1

Peckinpah was in the midst of battles over the editing of his previous film, *Major Dundee,* but those battles had yet to become public.

The Cincinnati Kid would be a film about professional gamblers based on a novel by Richard Jessup. Ransohoff, who was producing the film for MGM, thought Peckinpah's no-nonsense style was perfect for what he wanted to do.

"I felt *Cincinnati Kid* needed a down-to-earth, rough-hewn treatment," Ransohoff says. "I felt Sam was capable not only of that but of getting the humor. He was a man's man and his background was interesting. I liked the fact that he'd been a writer."

Ransohoff's approach to the film had already shifted, based on research that writer Paddy Chayefsky had done while writing the screenplay. The novel was set in modern times and detailed a gambling milieu in and around St. Louis. Chayefsky pictured a kind of mythical existence for these poker players, an almost Arthurian ethic among cardplayers, who venerated the greatest player of them all, Lancey the Man.

But Chayefsky discovered that none of this was true. "Paddy found that there was no Lancey the Man, no honor among cardplayers," Ransohoff says. "Paddy thought there was a mystique. But he did research and found out it was horseshit. He didn't think the entire concept could be based in anything real that he could find."

So Ransohoff and Chayefsky shifted the time scheme, keeping the mystique but setting the story in the 1930s: "If it was going to be sheer entertainment, it was better if we drop back twenty-five or thirty years, which would make it more difficult to criticize," Ransohoff says. "I didn't want to gamble on taking any kind of documentary approach to reality. We were going to do it as pure entertainment. I intended this to be an old-fashioned Western gunfight, but with a deck of cards."

As Peckinpah began preproduction work, disagreements began to crop up with Ransohoff. As Peckinpah recalled the preparations for the film, "I spent about four months on it, none of it pleasant, I might add. We did not see eye to eye, to put it politely. There was a time when it no longer made sense even to meet with him on story conferences."

The disputes ranged from casting to questions of whether to shoot in black and white or color.

"I thought of the story in color," Ransohoff says, "but Sam talked me into black and white. I was extremely concerned and so were the executives at MGM. I wanted a non-docudrama look to the thing. I said, 'It's a peppermint stick.' What I didn't want to do was make a movie based on reality."

Peckinpah won the argument, however: "He was given all the cooperation in the world," Ransohoff says.

The men's casting had not been in question: Steve McQueen, by that point one of the hottest actors in Hollywood, would play the title role and

Spencer Tracy would play Lancey the Man. When Tracy pulled out because of ill health, he was replaced by Edward G. Robinson.

But Peckinpah and Ransohoff quarreled bitterly over the two key women's roles. To play the Kid's girlfriend, Ransohoff wanted to cast an unknown young actress in whom he had an interest: Sharon Tate. "A role like this would be a great way to launch Sharon's career," he says.

Peckinpah was opposed to casting her, based on an unimpressive screen test and the fact that "she bad-mouthed Katharine Hepburn and we had a little tussle," Peckinpah said. Ransohoff says today, "We had tested Sharon. Steve thought she could have been better. She did too." Instead, the role went to Tuesday Weld.

Producer and director clashed again over casting an actress to play Karl Malden's wife, a temptress who repeatedly tries to seduce McQueen. Peckinpah thought Ransohoff's choice for the role, Ann-Margret, was too similar in type to Tuesday Weld. But Ransohoff prevailed, in part because Ann-Margret was also the choice of Bob O'Brien, MGM chairman.

As he worked through the preproduction period during the autumn of 1964, Peckinpah was in the midst of watching his second marriage fall apart. Within three months of returning with him to Los Angeles from Mexico, where they had met on *Major Dundee*, Begonia, frightened by his outbursts of drunken violence and disapproving of his frequent pot smoking, had left him. She returned to Mexico City and initiated divorce proceedings.

"He was immensely anxious about it," says John Calley, who was Ransohoff's partner at the time and went on to be the head of Warner Bros. "He was not the kind of man who could suppress that kind of intensity of feeling. Sam was crazed at the time."

Part of the problem was Peckinpah's drinking, says Martin Baum, who worked with Peckinpah as studio head, then as producer, and finally as his agent. Not that he was drunk when he was working, but Peckinpah's way of coping after working hours was with alcohol, which kept taking its toll long after drunkenness had passed.

"This was a period when Richard Harris, Richard Burton and a whole group of actors were drinking heavily," Baum says. "It was a big thing in the Sixties. Maybe it was supposed to show machismo or irreverence, but it was a curse. It killed Richard Burton. Richard Harris, Peter O'Toole and others quit but Sam didn't stop."

Calley recalls that at one point in preproduction, Peckinpah called him into his office to show him some pictures. The plan was to shoot on location in New Orleans; the stills showed potentially promising locations.

"They're all in L.A.," Peckinpah said, launching into an impassioned argument to shoot the picture in California instead of Louisiana.

"He said he could find no reason to go to New Orleans," Calley says.

"His wife was coming back to L.A. and he was having anxiety about it. Suddenly New Orleans was unacceptable to him."

Eighteen hours later, Calley had another call to come to Peckinpah's office—this one from Steve McQueen. When he got there, McQueen started haranguing him: about the cheap horseshit of not going on location, about his intention only to work with first-class operations, which this obviously was not. Why, McQueen demanded of Calley, were the producers forcing the director to shoot in Los Angeles instead of New Orleans?

"I was so shocked," Calley recalled. "It was so without my experience. Sam had laid it off on us. It was so shocking to me; I couldn't believe it."

It was made even more mortifying by the fact that "we were a rather small production company," Calley says. "McQueen was the biggest star we'd worked with up to that point. We were desperate for it to go well."

Filming started December 1, 1964, on the MGM soundstage, while New Orleans locations were being prepared. Ransohoff, however, had two other pictures in production at the same time: *The Loved One* and *The Sandpiper*. Overseeing them kept him away from Hollywood that week, so Calley was in charge of keeping an eye on *Cincinnati Kid* production.

According to Calley, the first scene Peckinpah shot seemed strange: After Lancey the Man, played by Edward G. Robinson, checks into his hotel, he carries his own bag up a long staircase.

"Wouldn't he take the elevator or use a bellboy?" Calley asked.

"You want to see the sets, don't you?" Peckinpah replied.

"I thought it was weird," Calley says now. "And it got stranger and stranger."

Jim Silke, who spent much of Peckinpah's career as the director's protégé and collaborator, observes, "You had to understand that it was a search. He would make his movie three or four times. Once when he wrote it. Once when he cast it. Once when he was shooting it. And once when he edited it. Everybody does that to a degree but with Sam, it was why he got lost sometimes."

Silke, who had been brought in as dialogue director, recognized early on that the script needed a scene between Rip Torn and Edward G. Robinson on the telephone. Though not long on exposition, it would help establish both of their characters. Peckinpah agreed and Silke wrote one. It was rewritten by Terry Southern, the author of the semiscandalous *Candy*, who had rewritten the script, which had been completed by Ring Lardner, Jr., to give it more humor.

"It was this wonderful Terry Southern script with all the fetishes," Silke says. "He even had a vibrator in there." The setup involved Torn, as a supposedly upstanding family man, lying in a hotel room with a whore and calling up Lancey the Man to challenge him to a card game. The setting—

the hotel, the whores, the sex tools—were to establish the depths of Torn's character's corroded morality.

As Peckinpah shot it over the next two days, however, he manipulated and reworked it, trimming it to the essentials: Torn and the whore (who was either Latino or light-skinned black) in the room. The actress playing the whore was nude but, according to Silke, the camera only photographed her from behind, taking off a fur coat.

L. Q. Jones, an actor who worked on more Peckinpah films than any of the director's stock company of performers, was in the cast. He says the technique—shaping the scene as he shot and reshot it—was vintage Peckinpah.

"He'd tear everything down the first couple of days and then put it back together," Jones says. "He figured out that the way to do it was A) fear, and B) disassociation. He'd try to get you disassociated from your normal way of living and connected to him as the great white father. He'd solve it all. He had the strength to do that. He learned what to do technically, how to control himself and his people."

That approach became his standard modus operandi in years to come, Jones says: Destroy the script, break everything down into small pieces, then reassemble it. The problem later in his career, Jones adds, was that drinking and drugs eventually robbed him of the strength and coherence to carry it out: "As he deteriorated physically, he'd still try to disassociate everything but he couldn't put it together again. He couldn't grasp why, either. The wheels just started to come off."

But Calley didn't see it that way. What he saw was an already erratic director spending three days on a scene with a nude woman. While Peckinpah's intention may have been only to show her naked back, what Calley saw was mounting footage of a nude woman. In 1964 (soon to be 1965, a watershed year for this sort of thing), you simply could not show nudity in an American studio film, let alone a nude scene involving interracial participants.

"I called him in after I saw the dailies and said, 'What are you doing? You're shooting a lot of nudes,' " Calley says. "Sam said, 'It's for my version.' He seemed obsessed. He kept shooting and shooting that scene."

"It was a 'Fuck you' remark," Ransohoff says of Peckinpah's response to Calley. "The essence was 'Script or no, I'm shooting this.' "

L. Q. Jones says, "As Sam saw it, he was being challenged. Someone with a little sense would have backed off. Sam charged ahead."

Silke and Peckinpah subsequently claimed that a production schedule was not published until after three days of shooting, which then showed Peckinpah to be two weeks behind schedule: "It was lies," Silke says now.

Calley says, however, that after four days of shooting, "He was four days behind schedule. We knew he was gifted but we didn't expect he'd make the movie up as he went along. He had spent three nights on one sequence. At that pace, the picture would have been quadruple the budget."

Calley talked to Ransohoff, to MGM executives, to McQueen and McQueen's agent: "McQueen thought Sam was acting weird too," Calley says. "Sometimes you get into a situation that's a nightmare, and you either face it or be passive and let the picture be over budget. There was no telling [if] Sam [would] snap out of it in a week. Did it seem probable? No, it didn't."

Ransohoff was notified and returned to Los Angeles. After Ransohoff looked at the four days' footage, the decision was made to fire Peckinpah on Friday, then shut down until another director was in place. Norman Jewison replaced Peckinpah when production resumed two weeks later.

"I called the head of MGM and said, 'This is going to be expensive,'" Ransohoff says. "'We either shut this down and eat a half-million dollars or we make a picture I'm real concerned about.' I recommended shutting down. O'Brien backed the recommendation to replace Sam."

That Friday, according to L. Q. Jones, who was in the film at that point, "We did a riot scene with one hundred extras. Sam did in one day what it would take a good director five or six days to do. When we finished shooting that day, the cameraman came by and said, 'Did you know they fired Sam?' The crew knew and Sam didn't."

Peckinpah was called in by Ransohoff and Calley. L. Q. Jones says he was out in the hall just before Peckinpah came out afterward and maintains he heard Peckinpah yell, "You can take this picture and shove it up your ass with this desk."

Ransohoff and Calley both remember a short and unemotional meeting, at which Peckinpah and his agent were informed why he was being replaced and that the move was endorsed by McQueen.

"I got one of those Everlast headguards, like boxers wear, as a joke prop for Marty, because Sam had a reputation for fighting," Calley says. "But Sam was reasonable. The meeting lasted ten minutes."

"My guess is he never thought I'd do it," Ransohoff says. "Once that faucet is on, it's hard to shut a company down."

Peckinpah insisted that firing him had always been part of Ransohoff's plan, though he never explained why a producer would purposely inflict a 15 percent increase in the budget on himself just to mistreat a director.

"I had a feeling I would never do the picture, but I didn't really expect to be fired after I got started," Peckinpah said. "But that was just Marty's way. I found out later that no matter what I'd shot . . . I was going to be fired, or shall we say, sandbagged."

In a letter to MGM executive Robert Weitman two days after the firing, Peckinpah wrote: "I feel I was dismissed not for the reasons given by Ransohoff but the fact that he decided, and I believe some time ago, I was not going to make his picture. This may well be true but Ransohoff has known my intentions regarding this picture from the beginning and the only change I made was to go along with his demand to highlight every aspect of sensuality and sexuality through the picture, particularly the relationships between Ann-Margret and Karl Malden, Ann-Margret and Steve McQueen and Ann-Margret and Tuesday Weld. . . . When I brought up my doubts, which I did many times, I was told by Ransohoff, 'Fuck the code. If [Billy] Wilder can get away with what he's doing, we'll go twice as far.' "

(The Wilder reference was to the film *Kiss Me Stupid,* a broad 1964 sex comedy starring Kim Novak and Dean Martin. The film was condemned by the Catholic Church and was released without the seal of approval of the Motion Picture Code.)

Silke recalls being approached by Ransohoff's publicist shortly after Peckinpah was fired and being given a sheaf of clippings of newspaper articles, in which Ransohoff advocated the liberalizing of standards and the use of nudity in contemporary films.

"He told me to advise Sam to sue," Silke says. "Sam's lawyer thought it was all a joke and Sam didn't sue, but he should have."

What it came down to was two strong personalities, each convinced that, eventually, he could bring the other guy around to his way of thinking.

Ransohoff says, "The nude scene was one of a number of reasons Sam was replaced. There was nothing sinister, no motives, no predisposition for firing him. It was simply that he was way out of line. He was shooting stuff we never discussed. I guess he took a calculated risk that he couldn't be replaced. He was wrong."

Producer Daniel Melnick, who would rescue Peckinpah from unemployment a couple of years later, says, "When a director is fired from a picture, it's not something that's done casually. There's an enormous amount of problems and expense involved. It's a step that's not taken capriciously."

Calley adds, "In all my time in the business, I've only shut one other film down—*Reata,* which was being shot by Sam Fuller. The easiest thing usually is to hope to Christ the guy knows what he was doing. But we thought we were in trouble."

The combination of the flap over *Major Dundee* and the problems on *Cincinnati Kid* seemed to sew up Peckinpah's reputation as a problem director. He stood up for himself, but lacked the clout to do more than complain loudly—which was the same as wearing a big sign on his chest that said, "Here comes trouble."

"The Cincinnati Kid was an important picture," says Martin Baum. "He shouldn't have lost it. He would have had a different career."

"I got angry and named names," Peckinpah said. "Then I spent three and a half years without shooting a camera. It was slow death."

Part One

TO 1958

My people were all crazy, just crazy. And they dominated the Valley too.

—SAM PECKINPAH

1

From Peckinpaugh to Peckinpah

SAM PECKINPAH HAD NO INDIAN BLOOD, though he loved to tell people that he did. It was as much a myth as his stories of growing up on a ranch in the mountains outside of Fresno. He invented the life he needed, as though his own life wasn't interesting enough for the person he thought he should be.

The story of Indian blood served its purpose for years. It gave him cachet on the playground as a boy and fit the bill when he was reinventing himself as an adult. It was as though some errant gene drifting down from a clandestine liaison in the distant past would explain—or excuse—his own unpredictability. Perhaps making people believe in a story he concocted about himself made it easier to live with who he really was. He could take some refuge in the fact that he was misunderstood—never mind that he was the one who helped foster the misunderstanding.

Just as likely, it was part of Sam Peckinpah's ongoing effort to edit his past, in the same way he edited and reedited his movies.

"I had a great-aunt Jane who was a full-blooded Paiute," Peckinpah once told an interviewer. "Other than that, I'm a Californian, born and raised here."

There are Peckinpah friends and family members who will tell you that there were Indians in the Peckinpah lineage and others who will deny it categorically. Peckinpah did have an Aunt Jane who was a native American. But Jane Visher was a relative only on paper. As a girl, she was adopted by his grandfather, Charles Peckinpah.

Otherwise, the Peckinpah family was of sturdy European ancestry, descended from George Peter Peckinpaugh, who came to Pennsylvania from Germany's Rhine Valley in 1751, settled in Uniontown, Pennsylvania, and had eleven children.

His tenth child, John Peckinpaugh, moved to Kentucky at the end of the eighteenth century as a teenager, to help settle the territories explored by

Daniel Boone. He married and had five children, including Rice Peckinpaugh, Sam's great-grandfather.

In 1828, Rice, twenty-one, married Elizabeth Edwards, a native Kentuckian. By 1851, Rice and Elizabeth had fourteen children. When news of the California gold rush reached Mercer County, Illinois, where he lived, Rice decided to move to California. He and his family began gathering supplies; they started west in 1852 and reached Sonoma County, California, in October 1853.

Before leaving Illinois, Rice and Elizabeth concluded that the family name had too many letters. After a family conference, it was decided that, in order to save ink and retain the same pronunciation, the name should be shortened by dropping the "u" and "g"—from Peckinpaugh to Peckinpah.

Charles Mortimer Peckinpah was Rice's twelfth child. As he reached adulthood in his new California home, he learned the lumber business and bought his own sawmill in Guerneville, California, only to go broke during a lumber famine in the early 1870s. He apprenticed himself to a wagon maker, then built himself two large wagons and borrowed money to buy a team of mules. He headed to Death Valley, where he hauled borax and built up a stake to relaunch himself in the timber business.

Before he left for Death Valley, he met a young girl named Isabelle Toner, who was born in Scranton, Pennsylvania, in 1866. Smitten with the young redhead, Charles promised that he would come back and marry her.

From Death Valley, Charles and his brothers headed into the mountains of Madera County to establish the Peckinpah Lumber Company on a mountainside that eventually became known as Peckinpah Mountain.

In 1890, Charles married Belle Toner. He was forty-two; she was twenty-four. They had three sons: Edgar Mortimer (known as Mort), born in 1893; David Edward (called Dave), born in 1895; and Charles Lincoln (known as Link), born in 1896. Charles and Belle adopted two girls: Jane Visher and Lena Long, both Sierra Mono Indians.

Bob Peckinpah, one of Link's children, recalls that his grandfather Charles "would babysit for me. I remember him telling me I always had to know where north was. He took me to a movie when I was five or six years old and when we sat down, he said in a loud voice, 'Which way is north? If you don't know, you're going home.' "

Charles and Belle's sons were educated in a one-room schoolhouse at North Fork, where many of their classmates were Indians. When they reached adolescence, Charles hauled lumber down to Fresno and built a house, where Belle and the three boys lived while the boys went to high school. The boys took to telling their new schoolmates that they were part Indian.

Charles Peckinpah and his brothers operated the lumber mills from 1885 to 1904. Charles subsequently tried his hand at a number of businesses, eventually retiring to Fresno, where he died in 1925.

After high school, David Edward Peckinpah, Charles's middle son, wanted to go to law school but didn't have the money. Instead, he found work as a ranch hand on the 4,000-acre spread owned by a prominent Fresno attorney serving his second term as a Democratic congressman—Denver Samuel Church.

Born December 11, 1862, in Folsom, California, Denver Church was the son of a blacksmith. He was named for James William Denver, a former California congressman and Union general in the Civil War, in honor of the Union victory at Antietam.

Denver Church attended Healdsburg College in Sonoma County, where he met Louise Derrek, a girl from Carson City, Nevada, during his senior year; they were married in 1889. They both enrolled at California Medical School in San Francisco but Louise, known as Luttie, became pregnant with their first child, Earle, who was born in 1890. Denver dropped out of medical school, switched to law school and passed the bar in Fresno in 1893. Fern Louise, their second daughter, was born that year.

Denver was appointed an assistant district attorney. He ran for the D.A. job in 1896 and lost. Out of work, and now with a third child, Denver and Louise drifted east to Salt Lake City. But Church earned too little to support the family, and their baby died in the winter of 1897 of tuberculosis. In 1899, barely surviving, he planned to leave the family while he went to Alaska to prospect for gold.

But he was offered an assistant district attorney's job in Fresno. By 1905, he was able to buy a homestead in Crane Valley near Peckinpah Mountain. The next year, Denver Church won election as Fresno County district attorney. He was reelected district attorney in 1910; he ran for Congress in 1912 as a Democrat and won. He moved his family to Washington, and was elected to two subsequent terms.

Dave Peckinpah was a lanky eighteen-year-old, a ranch hand on Denver Church's spread—and one of several hands who were attracted to Church's daughter Fern Louise.

Fern was two years older than Dave. He was lean and straight-backed, standing an inch or two over six feet. She was short and attractive, with long auburn hair. He was direct and gregarious, with brown eyes that could envelop anyone who spoke with him. She was shy, even introverted, more comfortable on the ranch than keeping up appearances in Washington social circles.

She was also spoken for (or so she thought), engaged to a Fresno boy named Bob. She corresponded with him while living in Washington during Denver Church's first congressional term. For whatever reason, Denver

Church disapproved of Bob and strongly opposed Fern's plan to marry him. It was one of the few times that Fern put herself at odds with her father.

Church finally took matters into his own hands. He discreetly threatened Bob with unspecified trouble if he came anywhere near the Church ranch on the agreed-upon date. Church sent Fern a telegram, purportedly from Bob, calling the wedding off. The wedding day came and went; Fern never saw Bob again.

When Church was reelected to Congress in 1914, Fern chose to remain in California. Dave Peckinpah, with his mother's Irish gift for talk, soon began to court her; the courtship lasted a year. They were married in South Fork in December 1915.

Fern never forgot Bob and never forgave Dave for not being him. She also looked down her nose at Dave's backwoods background; she was the daughter of a much-honored attorney and public official. Dave, on the other hand, came from a family of Irish immigrants and lumbermen—and failed lumbermen at that.

"She was very dominated by her father," says Susan Peckinpah, Sam's youngest sister, who was adopted in 1942. "I don't think my father let my mother grow up. Basically, she was afraid of people. Yet she was highly manipulative and extremely bright."

"She was the daughter of a very strong man—the favorite daughter—and she married a strong man," says Marie Selland Taylor, Sam's first wife. "She somehow had to accomplish what she wanted by manipulation. That was the only way she could get what she wanted. All her kids feel they were done in by their mother."

Dave and Fern had a normal relationship in at least one respect: Fern gave birth to their first child, Denver Charles, in September 1916, nine months after the marriage.

Dave was largely self-educated, devouring books as quickly as he could get his hands on them. He yearned to become an attorney and Denver Church admired his ambition. Church pulled strings to get Dave admitted to National University Law School in Washington. Dave went to law school while working as a doorman in the House of Representatives, a job Church also helped him land.

Church had been elected to his third term in Congress in 1916. In the spring of 1917, he was one of fifty congressmen to vote against American intervention in World War I. Stung by the defeat, he returned to Fresno and went into private law practice. In 1919, Dave Peckinpah finished law school and joined his father-in-law's firm.

Denver Church eventually broke up the firm in 1924, when he was elected state superior court judge. Still a popular politician, he sat on the bench until the early 1930s.

In one of his more notorious cases, Church presided over a criminal trial in Fresno Superior Court involving three men who were jointly charged with first-degree burglary of a store. The deputy district attorney made a deal with one of the three defendants to turn state's evidence against his accomplices, in return for a light sentence.

When Judge Church called the case, only two of the three defendants were represented by counsel; the third was the one who was going to testify against his friends. Although this was almost thirty years before the U.S. Supreme Court ruled that defendants were entitled to an attorney, Church believed that fair was fair. So Church instructed the jury that, along with presiding over the case, he would also serve as defense counsel.

He made multiple objections to the deputy district attorney's arguments about evidence that was admissible against his client and, as judge, sustained his own objections. He finally moved to dismiss the case against his client, then accepted the motion and freed the burglar. The jury convicted the other defendants, without the third defendant's testimony.

Denver Church left the bench in the early 1930s to pursue his first love, his cattle ranch. But he quickly went broke, one of thirteen times Church's business acumen betrayed him. So he ran for Congress again in 1932, in an effort to earn money to make his ranch solvent again.

PARENTHOOD DIDN'T AGREE WITH FERN, who simply wasn't interested in baby Denny. "I don't remember my mother ever expressing any physical affection for me," says Denver Peckinpah, now a retired superior court judge. "I spent more time with my grandparents than with my parents. Mom and Dad thought it was great not to have the responsibility of a baby. That carried on for years. I was president of my high school class, valedictorian and had the lead in the school play, all in one fell swoop. My grandparents came. But my folks didn't because they were attending an Exchange Club convention in Reno."

While the Churches were considered acceptable babysitters, the Peckinpah grandparents were not. Fern refused to invite Dave's parents to the house. She went out of her way to make sure that Denny—and, later, Sam and her two adoptive daughters—spent as little time as possible with Charles and Belle Peckinpah.

"My mother successfully isolated Sam and me from my grandparents on our father's side," Denny says. "I still resent that bitterly."

Dave would take the boys up to the mountains, where his brother Link was an assistant supervisor for the Plumas National Forest, to visit Link and his children, Bob and Wanda. Fern Peckinpah would never go with them.

Bob Peckinpah says, "You got the impression that Sam's mother didn't want to share her family with my family and grandparents. She had some peculiar ideas about how important her family was."

"They were a very manipulative bunch of people," says Betty Peckinpah, Denny's wife. "There was an arrogance; the whole family acted like Western royalty."

After Denver Church assumed the bench in 1924, Dave Peckinpah put a new practice together. Even as it started to take off, Fern discovered she was pregnant again.

But it was a problematic pregnancy. The doctors told her that, if she didn't stay in bed, she might lose the baby. So Fern spent eight months flat on her back, developing a bond with the unborn child. That bond would strengthen—and tighten—after the child was born, on February 21, 1925. It was the same year the new baby's grandfather, Charles Peckinpah, died.

They named the new child David Samuel Peckinpah. To avoid confusion with his father, they called him D. Sam. Where Fern had all but ignored Denny, she made little D. Sam her pet.

"Sam was my mother's pride and joy," Denny says. "He could do no wrong in her eyes. No matter what he did, it was forgivable."

(Fern Peckinpah would repeat the same pattern with the two girls she adopted: Fern Lea, adopted six years after Sam was born, and Susan, adopted almost a decade after that. She favored Susan while ignoring Fern Lea. "It's a pretty screwy family," says Kristen Peckinpah, Sam's daughter. "They were like a bunch of only children.")

Sam was a bright, energetic child who quickly took to life on the Church ranch and cabins in Crane Valley and at Bass Lake, where his parents would take him to visit. Sam was exposed to ranch life at an early age: "My earliest memory is of being strapped into a saddle when I was two for a ride up into the high country," he once said.

Sam's father and grandfather would take him hunting, teaching him lessons about the outdoors, about game conservation and killing only as much as he was willing to eat.

"Sam had a lot of respect for Denver Church," says Joe Bernhard, one of Peckinpah's lifelong friends. "When old Denver was eighty-eight, he could still knock a bullet through a silver dollar at ten yards."

In later years, Sam Peckinpah liked to give the impression that those days at the Church ranch told the whole story of his childhood and his upbringing. But Sam was a city kid. It took as much as five hours by car to reach North Fork, so it wasn't a trip that his family made often.

Instead, they lived in Fresno, a relatively sleepy town on the edge of the Sierras. Flat, almost Midwestern in character, Fresno today is the country's raisin capital, a faint mark of distinction that, in 1987, earned laughs in a satirical TV miniseries called, appropriately, "Fresno."

In the 1920s and 1930s, Fresno was a WASPish enclave, without many visible racial minorities. Ethnic minorities were another matter. Fresno, situated several hours south and east of San Francisco, had attracted a sizable contingent of Armenian immigrants, European Jews and Italians.

"The Fresno we were reared in wasn't just a white-oriented or dominated society—it was WASP," recalls Joe Bernhard, a childhood friend of Peckinpah. "The neighborhood I grew up in didn't allow Armenians. There were a few Jews. The prejudice was so intense that nobody was sure who was prejudiced against what. There was no prejudice against blacks because there were no blacks or Mexicans. And yet Fresno was a wide-open town, with $3 whorehouses, dozens of them. There was dice gambling. In the Plantation Club across the street from the police station, there was always fairly heavy gambling."

Dave Peckinpah tried to resist that kind of small-mindedness. Bernhard remembers Dave Peckinpah and Bernhard's father taking heat for protecting the farms of local Japanese residents, who had been taken to internment camps after Pearl Harbor.

As liberal as Dave was, he drew the line somewhere: Susan Peckinpah recalls being forbidden by her father from dating one young man simply because he was Italian.

In his book *A Bicycle Rider in Beverly Hills,* William Saroyan, one of Fresno's most famous sons, wrote:

> "In Fresno the boredom came from poverty, but I am not speaking of material poverty, for no human being needs very much of material things. The boredom came from spiritual poverty. I was starved for ideas, nobody had any first-rate ones to share with me, so I had to try to invent or discover my own."

Fresno was a place Saroyan escaped from, though his memories remained strong: He categorically refused to let the city of Fresno name any building whatsoever after him.

THOUGH AT HOME IN FRESNO, Dave Peckinpah was embarrassed by early court appearances. "The nerve of some people's children," his mother overheard someone say after Dave struggled through a summation in a trial.

A tall, Lincolnesque man, he worked at his speaking style with the same tenacity that had pushed him through law school (where he was a classmate of political columnist Drew Pearson). He gradually became one of Fresno's most prominent attorneys, a liberal Republican with a reputation for helping Armenian clients who'd been rejected by more snobbish firms.

"Dave was a very warm, friendly man with a gentle streak," says Blaine Pettitt, a boyhood friend of Denny Peckinpah's who is now a superior court judge in Fresno. "He was a good orator who used an old-style oratorical approach. I saw him argue cases and he was a dramatic speaker."

Bob Peckinpah says, "He had great success acquitting people. You have to be a dramatic showman to get that done. If Uncle Dave had a trial, I'd go and watch. He always came across as being extremely sincere."

Yet Dave Peckinpah was cowed in his own home. Though his sons grew up calling him "the Boss," Fern was the real power in the family: "We called him the Boss but it was really an exercise in futility as far as the house was concerned because he wasn't the boss—she was," Denny says.

But none of this was ever spoken of explicitly. The Peckinpahs didn't discuss their family life, even among themselves.

"It was difficult to tell what was going on in our family," Susan says. "There were all these choices of what the truth was. If you guessed the truth, you were told it was something else."

Sam was pulled between two poles: his father, whom he loved and respected, and his mother, who pampered and spoiled him. The relationship reached a critical point in the early 1940s, over Dave's desire to run for Congress—and Fern's opposition.

A Democrat had been elected to Congress from what was then California's Ninth District, which included Fresno. Dave Peckinpah, by then a well-known attorney and activist in Republican politics, had never run for office, but was well known in the state. Prominent Republicans in the state—and elsewhere—began to mention Dave's name as a possible candidate for the office.

But Dave Peckinpah declined the invitation to be nominated. Initially, Denny said, he couldn't understand his father's hesitance. He had, after all, served as a doorman in the U.S. House of Representatives during Denver Church's first series of terms in Congress. What could be more satisfying than returning to Congress as a congressman?

The answer, of course, was Fern, who made her own threats to Dave to keep him from accepting the candidacy, going so far as to tell him, "If you do, I'll leave you."

"She wanted only one congressman in the family—and his name was Church," Denny says.

As if to cover her tracks afterward, Fern "started a campaign to convince us that he really didn't want to go, but that she would have liked to," Denny says.

Had Fern not opposed him, Denny speculates, Dave's future (and the country's future, for that matter) might have turned out differently: "My father was a guy who could take over," Denny says. "He had that instinct Reagan had, as far as being a natural-born bullshitter." It's not too great an extrapolation to speculate that David Peckinpah, a California Republican, might have fit on the ticket with Dwight Eisenhower in 1952. Eisenhower could have done worse for a running mate—and did.

It was several years before the angry Sam estranged himself from his mother. But the damage was done—long-term damage in his attitude toward women. Here was the most important man in his life being emasculated by the most important woman. His father was the Boss—and yet he had caved in to a tiny, manipulative little female.

"Sam had a lot of resentment of his mother," says Katy Haber, who was Sam's assistant and companion for most of the 1970s. "He said that, when she died, he was going to piss on his mother's grave. All his love/hate feelings for women were based on his mother."

Dave finally took what he wanted for himself a few years later. In early 1959, there was a vacancy on the California Superior Court in Madera, the next county over from Fresno. Gov. Edmund "Pat" Brown, a Democrat, asked Dave Peckinpah to fill the position. It was a lifelong dream of Dave's to sit on the bench but, again, Fern opposed it.

"He had had a serious heart attack in the 1950s and she used that as an excuse," Susan Peckinpah says. "My father lied to her and said he wouldn't take it, then he did. It was so serious that there was almost a divorce."

"MY FATHER WAS A GENTLE MAN, but he tended to be violent when he was disciplining us kids," Denny says. "Sam learned early on that he could get protection from my mother. So the Boss would backhand Sam and Sam would be flying backward before he even hit him. He'd go flying into a wall and hit the floor. And my mother would say, 'Oh, Dave, you've killed him.' "

Dave and his brothers were all six-footers, long and lean. But Sam got the Church gene: He was short and wiry, small as a boy, only reaching a height of five-foot-nine as an adult. It would be simplistic to attribute the combativeness he carried all his life to frustration at his height, if he hadn't commented on it himself throughout the years.

Sam was a feisty kid, loving but with an easily offended sense of dignity. Even his grandfather wasn't immune: One favorite family story has Denver Church teasing little Sam at the age of three. The lad got so mad that he picked up a pitchfork (which was bigger than he was), chased Church and, ultimately, treed his aged but laughing progenitor.

"Sam was an extremely affectionate kid, but he would fight at the drop of a hat," Denny says. "He wasn't mean, but he was not loath to accept a challenge from Mother, Father or anybody he happened to meet. He was a very independent little guy. If he thought someone was taking advantage of him, he'd go after them."

There were definite rules for being a Peckinpah and a Church. Peckinpah men acted a certain way and treated women a certain way.

"All the men in this family are men's men," says Susan Peckinpah. "They are charming, artistic, bright in their own way. The mystique of the Western man with a six-gun—that was how they patterned themselves. If you took them back a hundred years in time, they'd be more comfortable."

Sharon Peckinpah, Sam's oldest daughter, says, "There was always this undercurrent among the women on my father's side of the family—about how the Peckinpah men thought of women as squaws. That's a very racist thing to say but it really did describe how they expected women to behave. Women were definitely not to assert themselves."

A legal career also seemed to be a given: Denny was placed on a chair to give speeches at family gatherings from the time he was eight or nine. It was considered solid training for the life his family had picked out for him.

SAM WAS A BRIGHT CHILD, who loved reading and tended to keep to himself: "I was very much a loner, very much into what I read and imagined as a kid," he once said. "I used to read a lot, even when working on my grandfather's pack station up in the high country."

Reading, however, was frowned upon by his grandfather, who wanted his grandson to have a rough-and-tumble outdoors upbringing.

Betty Peckinpah recalls, "Sam loved poetry and reading when he was little. He was reading way beyond the level of a young boy. His Grandfather Church hated that. He wanted him to be outside. He'd get on Sam's back for reading."

Young Sam's early penchant for scrapping with his schoolmates got him into trouble, but Fern Peckinpah remained his protector. She would often walk him home from school to keep him out of fights.

Despite her pampering, she would often leave him in Denny's care and the two became extremely close: "I was always a tagalong kid," Peckinpah once said. "We're very much alike and yet completely different."

For all of his schoolyard scuffling, Sam could occasionally play peacemaker. Joe Bernhard remembers a fight he was in when he was five: "I was hitting this son of a bitch—I'd hit him four times for every time he hit me. Everybody was talking at once and this one voice suddenly sounded like it was coming out of the bottom of a well. It was Sam; I swear he was able to do that when he was eight. He says, 'That's enough,' and broke it up. Then he said to me, 'You've got to learn to plant your feet.' "

As Sam grew up, Fern continued to isolate him and Denny from Belle Toner Peckinpah. Sam got to spend time with her in spite of his mother. "I was nine years old," he recalled, "and I was raving about Calamity Jane. [My grandmother] turned and told me, 'She was a dirty, drunken woman and she smelled bad.' I said, 'How do you know?' And she said, 'I saw her and talked to her—and your grandfather spent too much time with her.' "

More often, however, Sam was expected to listen to and, occasionally, participate in the serious-minded discussions about the law and the Bible, the two dominant issues in any family gathering involving his father and Denver Church.

"When I was a kid, I grew up around those people . . . sitting around a dining-room table talking about law and order, truth and justice," Sam recalled. "I suppose I felt like an outsider and I started to question them. I guess I'm still questioning.

"My father believed in the Bible as literature and in the law. He was an authority and we all grew up thinking he could never, ever be wrong about anything. The law and the Bible and Robert Ingersoll were our big dinner-table topics."

Sam spent his winters going to school in Fresno and his summers at North Fork and Bass Lake. He would spend time with the Peckinpah cousins he seldom saw during the year. Link Peckinpah, his uncle, got him a summer job clearing gooseberry bushes in the Plumas National Forest. Cousin Bob Peckinpah, who was a rodeo buff, took him to his first rodeo.

By the time Sam reached high school, he had a reputation both as a fighter and as a strangely solitary figure.

"We were the smallest guys in our class," Joe Bernhard says. "We both were tough. People had to know that if they were going to fuck with you, they were going to have a good fight on their hands."

Don Levy, another high school friend, recalls, "He was a kind of a loner. I liked him because he seemed so unpredictable in a way."

He did it by fighting with anyone who looked at him cross-eyed. After he spent a tumultuous freshman year at Fresno High School, his parents thought his fighting and discipline problems might be solved if young Sam switched schools. He moved to Clovis High School for his sophomore year. More fights. He moved back to Fresno High for his junior year.

"Sam was a little guy and he went out for junior varsity football," Don Levy says. "In practice, we were supposed to run the gauntlet and the big guys would tackle you. Sam just ran headlong as fast and as hard as he could right into the first guy. He blew him away. The coach got on his case but Sam walked away with a little smile."

What was there to do in Fresno for a teenager during the early years of World War II? Very little. Life was centered on the family. What little recreation there was involved driving around in cars and drinking.

Betty Peckinpah says, "He'd drink in high school. It was the only thing to do in that town. The boys all drank too much."

"We all started drinking at fifteen," Joe Bernhard says. "We didn't give a shit about school. We used to steal watermelons, cut the heart out, fill it with vodka and drink it with a straw.''

Dave Peckinpah did what he could to show Sam what it meant to cross the line and break the law. Dave once forced Sam to sit through a statutory rape trial, both to show him how the system worked and to make an impression. When Sam didn't learn his lesson, Dave took it a step further.

Sam later recalled, "I was sixteen and I was driving my Model A. I got some blanks and I was shooting down, with blanks, most of the people I could find on the streets. And, at the same time, with four of my buddies, I stole a red blinker light from a highway project. I got busted. My father came down, took one look at me and said, 'Leave him.' I spent the night in jail.''

Before his senior year, Sam was invited to join one of the more selective fraternities at Fresno High: the Oxford Club. It was a prestige group, and Sam, coming from a prominent Fresno family, was a logical choice. But the hazing that preceded initiation changed his mind.

Betty Peckinpah remembers being awakened at 5 A.M. by a pounding on the door. Denny was on a hunting trip, so she tiptoed to the window and peeked out.

"There was Sam, stark naked, covered with goop and feathers," she remembers. "He was so humiliated, so full of rage and humiliation. It was a high school fraternity prank and they didn't give him his clothes back. It was humiliating for a boy with as much pride as he had.''

Says Joe Bernhard, "Sam went through the whole shit for the Oxford Club. After the initiation, he told them to shove it up their ass.''

His parents enrolled him in the San Rafael Military Academy for his final year of high school. Depending upon who is talking, he was sent to the military academy either at his own request or because his parents felt he needed the discipline.

The former is unlikely; even at that age, Sam Peckinpah had contempt for rules, regulations and anything else that interfered with his quest for a good time. More likely, his frequent fights and run-ins with authority, at school and elsewhere, convinced his parents that he needed an environment that might somehow tame him, or at least teach him respect for the rules.

It was a quick-fix solution to a lifelong character trait. Though he was able to concentrate on schoolwork without the diversions Fresno offered, he still ran afoul of school officials consistently, earning enough demerits to deny him cum laude status when he graduated.

Shortly before his eighteenth birthday, in February 1943, Sam Peckinpah enlisted in the United States Marine Corps; he entered the service upon high school graduation. Peckinpah was assigned to marine training programs, first in Flagstaff, Arizona, then in Lafayette, Louisiana, before attending boot camp at Camp Pendleton in California. Servicemen were allowed to take college classes at nearby schools if their time permitted and Peckinpah did so, at Arizona State College and Louisiana State Teachers College.

Most of the courses, in mathematics and engineering, proved too difficult for Peckinpah. But he couldn't accept his own lack of ability and, briefly, wound up in a base hospital. He later told his first wife, Marie Selland, about the episode.

"He was taking heavy math classes that were not something he took to naturally, in terms of learning," she recalls. "He had to work very hard. From what he said, he ended up in the hospital [from], well, not an extreme breakdown, but a breakdown of sorts. He was physically very sensitive. He would hate it if he heard that, though."

Because he had attended military school and then tested well upon entering the Marines, he was sent to Officer Candidate School at Camp Lejeune in North Carolina. Denny, who was in naval air combat intelligence, saw him from time to time. The culmination of these visits was a joint trip to raise hell in New York before Sam was shipped overseas.

The pair took a hotel room together and hooked up with a mutual friend from Fresno for a couple of nights of drinking and carousing. The brothers got so drunk that Sam missed his bus and was late getting back to Camp Lejeune. As a result, he was drummed out of his OCS class.

"He gave me credit for saving his life," Denny says. "His class graduated two weeks later—and had a 78 percent casualty rate in the first six months."

In mid-1945, Peckinpah's unit was shipped to China: "It never felt like we were an occupying army," he once said. "We were there to take the Japanese out of North China, where they had been since 1937."

Shortly after he arrived, the United States dropped the atomic bomb— first on Hiroshima, then on Nagasaki. The war quickly ended. "I never saw any combat," he said later, "but I was ready to. I was pretty gung ho."

He stayed in China, a country he quickly grew to love. Though there was a truce in the Chinese civil war, the country was still the site of sporadic fighting between the forces of Mao Tse-tung and Chiang Kai-shek.

Peckinpah himself saw no action, though a troop train he was riding on was fired upon by Communist forces. The train sustained casualties; it was Peckinpah's first real exposure to human carnage.

He subsequently would describe the firefight: the way it made him feel as though time had slowed down. He always referred to it as the moment he would call to mind when he began experimenting with slow-motion violence in his films.

There was always some question about who the Communist bullets hit. To one writer, he described the sensation of seeing a Chinese coolie being struck by a sniper's bullet and dying next to him: "One of the longest split seconds of my life," he said.

At another time when he told the story, he was the victim: "I was shot and remember falling down and it was so long. I noticed that time slowed down and so I started making pictures where I slowed down time, because that's the way it is."

Several years later, when asked if he had been shot, he replied enigmatically, "That's what people say."

Peckinpah spent a year in China. He saw the sights, studied Zen, learned a little Mandarin and fell in love with a Chinese girl. Coming from the relatively sheltered world of Fresno, it was all a revelation—as was the attitude of some of his fellow marines toward the Chinese.

He recalled, "Another marine told me—boasted to me—that he'd thrown a Chinese woman down on a concrete platform and raped her, hit her head against the pavement and, after he was done, she didn't move. I'd been practically adopted by a Chinese family. I actually decided I was going to kill him. I went out and stole a gun, a Russian gun, and offered to sell it to him. You know, the souvenir mentality. When I sold it to him, I was going to kill him. Put the barrel of the gun right up under his chin and pull the trigger. The night before our meeting, I saw him standing there completely blind. Permanently blind. He'd drunk some bad whiskey. If it hadn't been for that, I might be in prison today."

Peckinpah's enlistment was up in the summer of 1946. He asked to be discharged in Peking so that he might marry the girl he loved, but the request was denied. Instead, he was shipped back to Los Angeles.

Peckinpah had no firm plans, but he had a strong idea of what he didn't want to do: "Maybe the only thing I knew for certain was that I didn't want to be a lawyer," he said.

Which, of course, was exactly the direction his family was pressuring him to go. Denny had gone into practice with Dave and they were eager to have Sam join them.

"Sam had other ambitions," says Bud Williams, a friend of Denny's and hunting companion of both Peckinpah brothers. "He wanted to be a writer. But he didn't get much support from his family."

Peckinpah enrolled at California State University at Fresno, better known as Fresno State College, in the fall of 1946 "because I had nothing better to do," he said. A flat, tree-lined campus of brick buildings in the middle of what was then farmland, it had an active theater department. Sam gravitated to it, as did a young woman named Marie Selland.

MARIE WAS EIGHTEEN, the oldest daughter of Cecilia Hagedorn Selland and Arthur Selland, who eventually became mayor of Fresno (and for whom Selland Arena in downtown Fresno is named). As she finished high school in Fresno, she knew she wanted to study theater.

She chose Fresno State, which seemed eminently manageable: "It had an interesting little theater department. It was small, but there was always the opportunity to work. Sometimes in a larger school, it takes a couple of years to get to do your own things."

Arthur Selland and Dave Peckinpah were in the Fresno Exchange Club together and Selland admired Dave Peckinpah. Sam Peckinpah was another story: "He was somewhat older and much, much wilder," Marie says. "He was considered a wild boy. I think he drank then. And, as they said in those days, he was fast with girls."

Still, when a friend presented the opportunity for a double date, Marie assented. Her girlfriend was dating Sam, who was a twenty-one-year-old freshman at the time. Marie's blind date would be with Sam's friend.

Marie remembers Sam as "a beautiful young man. He had large eyes, a bony face, a beautiful mouth and chin. He was what I would consider a poetic-looking man."

The date was a smashing success—for Sam and Marie, who ignored their respective dates when they found that they shared a passion for romantic poets, particularly Rupert Brooke. "That's partly why I fell in love with Sam," she says, "because he looked like Rupert Brooke."

The resemblance would have been significantly lessened had he not had a black mustache, which he'd grown in the Marines. Without it, the combination of his slight stature and youthful face made him look like a boy. "When he was twenty-five, he looked fourteen," Don Levy says. "That's why he first grew a mustache. He always wanted to be a macho guy."

A couple of weeks later, Peckinpah and Marie ran into each other at a party and spent the evening dancing and talking together, ignoring their dates. He asked if he could see her again and she agreed.

They dated through the rest of the school year. Sam tagged along to her directing class, eventually enrolling in it himself.

"He got interested in the theater department," Marie recalls, "and jumped right into a directing class. He started taking acting and directing classes and decided to major in theater.

"He was kind of a theatrical person, anyway. The first scene he directed in directing class was astonishing. Everybody was flabbergasted because he was the new kid on the block. The rest of us had been there a couple of years. But he had it. He was really amazing."

Don Levy, who knew Sam only slightly, was also in the theater department at the time. "I just knew him as a kind of unpredictable loner with maybe a little chip on his shoulder. So it came as a surprise to me: This guy had talent."

Peckinpah and Marie quickly became an item—a couple who worked together in the theater department and spent all of their spare time together outside the theater.

"Dating was fun. We were in school together and there was a lot to talk about in terms of the theater department," Marie says. "We had our crowd. It was very romantic. He was the first man I ever had sex with. He was wonderful, very special."

They dated from October 1946 until school let out in the summer of 1947, but Peckinpah resisted whenever Marie would raise the issue of making a commitment to each other. Peckinpah enrolled in a summer-school program in theater in Mexico City; when he left, there was no concrete discussion of future plans together, no mention of marriage.

"We hadn't talked about it when he left," Marie says. "He said, 'I'll be back.' We talked about plans for school in the winter. That was it."

Peckinpah was part of a theater group from Fresno State that spent the summer in a special program at the University of Mexico in Mexico City. Once he got there, however, Peckinpah got restless with the tameness of the university program. He began casting about for something more real, something less academic—and found it in the theater company of Seiki Sano.

Born and reared in Japan, Sano had studied with Stanislavski in Moscow and with Lee Strasberg in New York. He had taken a new technique, the Method, to Mexico and established his own acting laboratory. Peckinpah found his way to Sano's classes and never looked back.

"There were these literary guys at Fresno State, the whole acting group," Joe Bernhard says. "The first week down there, Sam found this Mexican acting group and abandoned his friends. These are Fresno WASP fraternity types and this guy was one of them—and then he just splits."

His Mexican studies ended in September and he headed back to Fresno, driving an old Army jeep he had bought. "He had this old military jeep and he was flat broke," Joe Bernhard says. "He drove the jeep home and would sleep in the fields and bum meals from the *campesinos*."

He got as far as Arizona before the jeep broke down. Peckinpah left it there, wired his family for money and took a train home. Once he reached Fresno, he went home to see his parents, then headed for the Selland house.

He walked in carrying a bolt of red silk, which he'd bought when he was a marine in China. Marie asked what it was for. Peckinpah said, "When a man presents red silk to a woman he loves, it's an engagement. I think we should get married, don't you?"

"I was surprised he wanted to get married," Marie says. "I was very young and very romantic. To have a man appear on the scene with red silk— I loved him very, very much."

They kept the proposal a secret from their parents. Two days later, Peckinpah asked her if she wanted to make the trip to Arizona to retrieve his car. Marie's father gave his permission; her mother was out of town at the time "and she would have said no," Marie says.

The train ride to Arizona was uneventful. They picked up his jeep and headed back. As they drove, Peckinpah looked at her and said, "You know, we could just drive back through Las Vegas and get married."

"In retrospect, I don't know why we thought that was a great idea," she says now.

Marie was nineteen; Peckinpah was twenty-two. They found a justice of the peace—actually, John E. Whipple is listed on the marriage license as an acting justice of the peace of Las Vegas township. The heat was oppressive because it was late summer in the Nevada desert: August 17, 1947. Peckinpah was clad in khaki; Marie was wearing a red peasant blouse and a black skirt. The witnesses were professionals; the marriage license lists them as "Mrs. Myrtle Tate and E. Vaughan." In the midst of the ceremony, a mouse scuttled across the floor.

"Getting married in Las Vegas was dismal," Marie says. "The justice of the peace was very impersonal. It was like having to make something out of it for ourselves. In the midst of this, we both felt, 'Oh God, this is so strange.' "

They went to Los Angeles to visit a friend. "Our honeymoon night was spent in Cucamonga in a motel," Marie says. On the way back to Fresno, they decided to keep their marriage a secret.

As the eldest in the Selland clan, Marie knew her parents dreamt of staging a large wedding in the family home. Her father, a successful businessman who came from a poor family, had shared with Marie his fantasy of seeing her come down the staircase of their house as a bride.

"I was a bit torn because I wanted to please my parents," she says. "At the same time, I didn't want to do something just for them. In the end, we decided maybe we should try to please them and pretend we weren't married."

Back in Fresno, however, the secret wore thin. They both were still living with their parents and felt silly sneaking around. Their original plan was to announce their engagement during the school year and go through a second ceremony. But, after a month, the game lost its novelty.

So the couple arranged a large Sunday breakfast at the Peckinpah ranch just outside of Fresno, for the two families to get to know each other. Dave Peckinpah "was a great breakfast maker," Marie recalls, and whipped up a huge meal. In the midst of it, Peckinpah and Marie announced that they were already married.

"I had a feeling something was up," Arthur Selland said, as his wife began to cry.

Congratulations were passed back and forth. Dave and Fern Peckinpah had a small cabin at the rear of their property, which was offered to the newlyweds for the remainder of the school year.

Peckinpah always got along with Ceil Selland; indeed, he developed a bond with "Mama Ceil" that lasted long after his marriage to Marie had dissolved.

Arthur Selland was another story. Selland was a conservative man, an up-by-the-bootstraps success who considered Peckinpah, with his advantaged background of lawyers and congressmen, to be spoiled.

"He was always very suspicious of Sam," Marie says. "I think my father always had the feeling that Sam was not being quite truthful. He thought he was a spoiled brat. My father had worked all his life in investments. He was suspicious of the fact that Sam had things."

Peckinpah, in turn, thought of his father-in-law as "a Republican, this Babbitt-type," according to Judy Selland, Marie's younger sister. "My father never liked Sam very much," she said. "He was too weird. They never got to know each other. They put each other off so much because of what they represented, in a way."

Selland's mistrust extended to everything from gambling to the family car, exemplified by two incidents that typified their relationship.

On one occasion, Selland and Peckinpah were involved in a poker game with several acquaintances. Peckinpah was an exasperating card player anyway, given to wild hunches and reckless bets. During one hand, he raised the bet until there was a large pot and everyone had dropped out. When the last player folded, Peckinpah cackled victoriously, swept up his winnings and flipped over his hand: not even a pair. Garbage. In a fury, Selland picked up the cards and threw them on the floor, shouting, "Nobody plays poker that way."

In another instance, Marie and Sam were visiting her parents in Fresno one Christmas. On the spur of the moment, Peckinpah needed to go out but didn't have a car. No one was home, so he took Ceil's car without asking. When the Sellands returned, Marie assumed that the absent Sam had been picked up by friends. When they discovered that the car was gone, Arthur Selland called the police and reported it stolen. Peckinpah drove up later and blithely walked in. Selland, normally a taciturn man, blew up at him.

"I remember Papa being so mad because Sam would do such a stupid thing," Judy Selland says. "And Sam was really mad to think that Papa had called the police on him."

Marie entered the marriage with a fairy-tale vision of what their life would be like. "I thought, 'Wonderful, this is perfect. We'll go off into the theater, into the sunset.' I had absolutely no practical ideas of being a wife," Marie says. "Then I found out that that's what Sam expected: a wife."

Peckinpah finished his B.A. in the spring of 1948. He was accepted in the graduate program in theater at the University of Southern California in Los Angeles. He and Marie packed up their few belongings and headed south, with the encouragement of his brother.

If anything, Denny says, the family was relieved that Peckinpah had discovered this passion for theater. For a while, it had seemed that he was unable to figure out what to do with his life. Once he had decided on theater, Denny and others knew it was important for Peckinpah to get out of his hometown to pursue it.

"He was not as much anxious to get out of Fresno as to pursue his career," Bud Williams says. "He couldn't be successful in the business he wanted to be [in] unless he went where the success was."

Through a friend of a friend of a friend, Peckinpah and Marie managed to rent a one-bedroom apartment above a garage, less than two miles from the USC campus. Money was tight: Peckinpah received a V.A. loan from USC and Marie went to work at a department store.

The USC theater department was dominated by students from Los Angeles, who were as focused on the movie industry as on their studies. Peckinpah was in classes with Don Levy, his Fresno acquaintance, and the two became fast friends. Levy lived in a boardinghouse; Marie would pack the two would-be directors sandwiches for lunch each day.

"Everyone else wore dark glasses and silk neckerchieves and talked about getting agents," Levy says. "We were just a couple of hicks from Fresno, but we decided to take the place by storm. We said to each other, 'We're going to show these guys,' and we did."

James Butler, the associate head of the department, took notice of Peckinpah and Levy. He asked Levy to be his assistant director on a production of *Oedipus* and later offered Levy and Peckinpah the chance to present their own program.

They assembled an evening of work by William Saroyan. Peckinpah directed *Hello, Out There,* and Levy did *My Heart's in the Highlands.* They built the scenery themselves, rolling it across the campus to the theater in little red wagons. The student newspaper gave them good reviews.

Though his affection for Saroyan was ingrained, Peckinpah was fascinated by the work of another writer as well: Tennessee Williams. As a project at Fresno State, Peckinpah had cut *The Glass Menagerie* to one hour and directed it. "I learned more about writing from having to cut that than anything I've done since," he once said.

Though Peckinpah never actually said it, Marie always felt that he particularly identified with Tom Wingfield, the hero of *Glass Menagerie.*

"I think there was something of Tom Wingfield in him, though he grew up being well taken care of," she says. "There was always this male expectation in a family full of lawyers: You were a rancher or a lawyer. There was something else in Sam, this dream. He responded to Tom's frustration, the feeling of affection toward his sister and the guilt at leaving her behind. There was a lot he connected with, including the relationship with the mother. There was a poet in him, a real sensitive thing."

Dreams and reality seemed to mesh during the first couple of years of their marriage; life initially seemed idyllic. Peckinpah and Marie would eat out at homey little steak joints and cheap Mexican restaurants near the USC campus, go to see jazz musicians such as Charlie Parker, Shelley Mann and Milt Brown at local clubs—and go to movies.

"We saw *Henry V* and *Hamlet* I don't know how many times," Marie says. "We would talk about movies and he would analyze them. He was a great fan of Olivier and liked Italian and French moviemakers. He loved *Henry V* because he was king and was a hero to his men."

For Peckinpah, life in graduate school seemed perfect: He would finish his class work, write his thesis, get his master's degree and go to work in theater or film. Then Marie became pregnant, giving birth to daughter Sharon in late 1949.

"We both wanted children but we didn't talk much about how it would be," Marie says. "After a while, it became evident: Sam was afraid of having too much to do with the kids. He loved them but he couldn't see himself as their caretaker. He did see me that way. I remember Sam saying about me, 'She's the kind kids and dogs just love.'"

After Sharon's birth, Peckinpah continued his classes, finishing all of his course work by mid-1950. Feeling pressure to support his family, he quit school before completing his thesis and began to look for a job.

His graduate school adviser told him that there was an opening for a director-in-residence at the Huntington Park Civic Theater near Los Angeles. The job didn't pay much, but it would allow the director to choose his own season, do his own casting, direct his own shows and oversee all of the technical aspects as well.

There were more than three dozen other applicants, some from Ivy League schools. When the final selection process was completed, Sam Peckinpah was the new director at Huntington Park.

2

Stage, Screen and Television

FOR HIS FIRST SEASON as director-in-residence at Huntington Park Civic Theater, from September 1950 to April 1951, Sam Peckinpah was paid $500.
For his second season, his pay was raised to $800.

Though his name would later become synonymous with tough-minded
action and bloody movie violence, Peckinpah was content to stage the popular hits at Huntington Park—*Our Town, The Man Who Came to Dinner,
South Pacific.*

"He took the job because he wanted to direct," Marie says. "And he
needed the money. He wanted to be in a position of directing plays more
than making money."

The money was hardly enough. Both sets of parents helped out financially,
so that there would be money to buy things for the baby.

The job gave Peckinpah the opportunity to return to *The Glass Menagerie,*
the Tennessee Williams play that had so fascinated him as an undergraduate.
He cast Marie as Laura, Tom's physically handicapped, emotionally reclusive
sister. Midway through rehearsals, the actress playing Amanda Wingfield
dropped out and Peckinpah recast Marie as the smothering mother.

The symbolism aside, the chance to finally work together was not as
smooth as either had hoped: "It was touchy when the two of us worked
together," Marie says. "I was sensitive to anything he told me. If I didn't
respond to something immediately, he took it personally. I was fearful of
displeasing him."

After a productive season, Peckinpah and Marie had to take jobs for the
summer. They found them at a resort at Florence Lake in the Sierras where
they received minimal wages, along with room and board. Marie worked in
the kitchen and Peckinpah worked on the boats. "It was not his kind of
work," she says, "but it was his kind of place."

In the fall of 1951, they headed back to Huntington Park. Peckinpah got

31

a G.I. loan and they bought a little house in Whittier, near Huntington Park. It was $7,900 with no money down—the middle-American dream.

As Peckinpah directed another season at Huntington Park, Sharon grew from infant to toddler. It became obvious to Marie that her husband liked the idea of being a parent better than the reality of it.

"I don't know why he thought he would be a terrific father, although he was excited about the preparations before the baby came," she says. "After the kids were born, I think it frightened him. He looked at them as something extremely vulnerable, who might fall apart at any moment. He had no experience with children. I'd helped raise my younger brother and sister. Children were not a mystery to me.

"I had to leave him with Sharon when she was six or eight weeks old, so I could go to a doctor's appointment. I came home and all the way up the steps I could hear her screaming. He had set himself up to look like he was dead, lying on the floor. Sharon was in her bassinet, yelling. He had a diaper on her that was a total wreck. He was just beside himself. He had put on this scene, but it was hard for him."

Nor did he take it well when his child fell ill. He himself was a hypochondriac, as liable to suffer from an imagined malady as a real one.

"Our standard joke was that whenever anyone got sick, he immediately got the symptoms," Marie says.

Peckinpah's reaction to fatherhood is understandable, if hard to forgive, considering the times. He was part of the generation that had children before "to parent" became a verb. This was before it became popular for fathers to be the kind of hands-on partners in care-giving they became thirty years later, when the generation to which Peckinpah's children belonged became parents themselves.

For Peckinpah, it seemed perfectly normal to leave the work to Marie. He worked at the theater in the evenings, was home in the mornings and left for the theater in midafternoon. Did he change diapers? "Not if he could get away with it," she says.

After the 1951–52 season at Huntington Park, Peckinpah took a job directing summer stock in Albuquerque, New Mexico. He directed old-fashioned melodramas, emphasizing the corny, stagy values that made them popular with audiences. "There was always a part of Sam that loved real hammy stuff," Marie says. "It's funny all the things he was interested in and then he got into that one mode in movies." Marie served as costume mistress to earn extra money, as well as doing a little acting.

But Peckinpah was restless. He had no interest in returning to Huntington Park, where he was a big—and underpaid—frog in a minuscule pond. There was little future in directing talented amateurs in community-theater productions that were seen mostly by friends, family and neighbors. He had to move someplace where there was room to grow.

So, through a friend, he landed a lowly job at KLAC-TV, Los Angeles's Channel 13. Hired as a stagehand, he was paid $22.50 a week to sweep floors, move scenery and do the least interesting jobs.

"He was doing the most menial jobs at the TV station," Betty Peckinpah says. "He was terribly intelligent, terribly frustrated. He realized he had to go through all the steps. It wasn't a matter of choice."

Peckinpah took the job for its proximity to TV cameras. He wanted to learn the tricks of visualizing through a lens and to get a grasp of editing techniques. He was a constant presence, asking questions, soaking up ideas and storing them for later use.

"It was just for the chance to work around cameramen," Marie says. "[Sam hoped it] would lead to something else. He always talked about work. He was excited, but frustrated too. There wasn't much for him to do there. The station was mostly hucksters selling stuff over the air. But it gave him a chance to try out some things. He learned a lot hanging around other people who knew a little bit about film and video work."

He was able to use the TV studio after hours to complete his master's thesis. He put together a production of Tennessee Williams's one-act play *Portrait of a Madonna,* the work from which Williams later extrapolated *A Streetcar Named Desire.* The half-hour production starred Marie and was staged at a USC theater in early July 1953. About three weeks later, after KLAC had concluded broadcasting for the day at 11 P.M., Peckinpah took over the studio and restaged it for a three-camera TV production, which was filmed on kinescope.

The thesis was called "An Analysis of the Method Used in Producing and Directing a One-Act Play for the Stage and for a Closed-Circuit Television Broadcast." Among his conclusions was the idea that, because TV could only show a portion of the entire stage picture at any given moment, an imaginative use of the camera was needed. When given an entire stage image to choose from, the audience member made the subjective choice for himself of what to watch. On film, each individual shot shaped the work as a whole because the camera dictated the subjective view of the audience.

After Peckinpah went to work at KLAC, he sold the house in Whittier and moved with his family into what amounted to two Quonset huts set end to end, in Latigo Canyon in the hills above Malibu. In 1952, Malibu was still just a remote beachside community far from the action in Hollywood and not yet the pricey show-business enclave it would later become. The area made enough of an impression that Peckinpah eventually named his own company Latigo Productions.

As valuable as the experience at KLAC was, it didn't prevent Peckinpah from establishing early work habits. His mother had taught him early on to question authority (except hers) and he frequently bumped heads with his superiors at the TV station.

According to one oft-repeated story, he was sweeping floors in one studio when Liberace, whose popular national show aired from the station, noticed him. The flamboyant pianist and entertainer had strict standards for his staff: They all wore suits and ties at work. Peckinpah, on the other hand, was wearing what he usually wore: jeans and a work shirt.

"I was fired as a floorsweep on 'The Liberace Show' because I refused to wear a suit," Peckinpah later said.

But there is more than one story about his firing from KLAC. Walter Peter, who married Peckinpah's sister Fern Lea, recalls a later incident. Peckinpah was part of a remote broadcast crew, which would routinely do live commercials from the sales lot of a local Chevrolet dealership. The dealer himself would stand in front of fifty to one hundred cars and make his pitch directly to the camera. Peckinpah's job was to cue the dealer when the remote camera went live.

"Sam hated the job and hated this guy but he needed the work," Peter says. "So this chap was looking at Sam to give him the cue. Sam casually says, 'Oh, we're live.' Here was the camera on this guy scratching his balls and Sam hadn't told him the camera was on. It was beamed all over L.A. Sam was cashiered the next day."

At some point between the Liberace incident and the embarrassing car commercial, Peckinpah went to work for "The Betty White Show" as a prop man. As an experiment, he filmed a sketch from the show. "Everybody said, 'Betty's so funny,'" Marie recalls. "They thought she should do some kind of skits. So somebody wrote something and Sam set up a way of doing a three-camera studio shoot and shot a trial run."

Peckinpah later referred to those as "some experimental films. I made them on my own time and money. Not that they were any good. More like homework, you might say." Still, they were good enough to make KLAC reconsider the way it dealt with prerecorded shows, which were filmed before broadcast.

In 1953, Peckinpah was admitted to the editors' union and landed work as an assistant film editor with CBS News. But, in the first year of his eight-year apprenticeship, Peckinpah had to miss work without giving sufficient notice when Marie went into labor to give birth to their second daughter, Kristen. Peckinpah suddenly was an unemployed father of two.

3

A Gofer Moves In

THERE IS DISAGREEMENT over who put his foot in the door so Sam Peckinpah could slip into the movie business.

One version has his brother, Denny, putting in a good word. Another has his mother mentioning her son's ambitions to a family friend, "Walter's boy —you know, John Huston."

The most persuasive version, however, involves Dave Peckinpah. "Sam's father, in his folksy way, said to Pat Brown, who was the California attorney general, 'Know anyone in Hollywood?' " Marie says. "As it happened, [producer Walter] Wanger had gone to the attorney general to get permission to shoot in a prison."

Brown provided the entrée for Peckinpah to meet Wanger, an independent producer at the time working for Allied Artists. Wanger, who had started his career with Garbo's *Queen Christina* and ended it with Elizabeth Taylor's *Cleopatra,* let Peckinpah sit in his outer office for three days. He eventually introduced him to Don Siegel, who was directing *Riot in Cell Block Eleven.* Siegel hired Peckinpah as a gofer.

The new guy quickly proved his worth when Siegel took the film on location to Folsom Prison. Siegel and his assistants were having a meeting with the warden, who proved particularly thorny regarding requests for access that he considered too dangerous, given the nature of the prison populace.

"I was introduced to the warden as the director of the picture," Siegel recalled years later, "and he continued scribbling on his desk, not looking at me. Finally, he said, without looking up, 'How long are you going to be up here?' I said, 'Sixteen shooting days.' He looked up at me and in a rough voice said, 'You're full of shit.' I said, 'You may have a point but if we get the cooperation we're looking for, we'll do it in sixteen days.' "

The warden went down the line of the rest of the crew, who were assembled in his office. The last man he quizzed was the lowest on the totem pole. When he heard Peckinpah's name, Siegel says, "He looked up sharply and said, 'Are you related to the Peckinpahs in Fresno?' "

When he found out that Peckinpah was part of the family of judges and lawyers, he began treating Peckinpah like a long-lost relative of his own— and the film crew as his extended family.

"We were stunned," Siegel said. "We'd never been exposed to the mystic name of Peckinpah."

Peckinpah subsequently worked on four more films with Siegel: *Private Hell 36, Annapolis Story, Invasion of the Body Snatchers* and *Crime in the Streets*. On most of them, his title was dialogue director, which meant that, along with working with actors to make sure they knew their lines, he served as Siegel's personal assistant.

"Don was a dude from Warner Bros., successful with second-unit and special-effects work," says Ted Haworth, who was production designer for both Siegel and Peckinpah. "He was a humorous, quiet man. Don was creative and yet the most economical director I knew. He taught Sam how to get the best out of people with a minimum of effort."

Peckinpah worked for other directors on other films at Allied Artists, about a dozen pictures in all. But the only movie from that period with which his name is connected (and one of the few that still holds up well) is Siegel's *Invasion of the Body Snatchers,* the 1956 film starring Kevin McCarthy and Dana Wynter. The story of a town in which the residents are being replaced by mindless "pod people" from another planet, it had the Red scare of McCarthyism as its subtext. It was remade (with a new emphasis on the mindless belief in new-age psychological remedies) by director Philip Kaufman in 1978.

Beside serving as dialogue director on *Body Snatchers,* Peckinpah made a brief appearance as Charlie, the town's meter reader (who returns as a pod person). Marie also had a brief role in the film.

Over the years, Peckinpah liked to tell the story about how he rewrote the screenplay for *Body Snatchers*. He gave himself varying amounts of credit, but always made it clear that he had contributed as a writer.

- In a 1964 interview: "Don Siegel and Walter Wanger gave me a chance to rewrite a scene in a picture called *Invasion of the Body Snatchers*. And because of that scene, I did a rewrite on the picture."
- 1969: "I played different parts in *Body Snatchers*. In addition, Don also had me on it as a writer for two weeks."
- 1972: "One of my first film jobs was a rewrite of *Invasion of the Body Snatchers*."

There were other examples as well, one of which finally found its way to Daniel Mainwaring, who actually did write *Invasion of the Body Snatchers*. On September 16, 1969, Mainwaring wrote to Peckinpah and said: "Friends in Europe, including Joe Losey and Pierre Rissient, have been asking how come Sam Peckinpah is claiming credit for the screenplay of *Invasion of the Body Snatchers*. I figured you had been misquoted—as I recall, you served as dialogue coach and possibly added one line. You may not have been guilty, but since in an interview with Aljean Harmetz in the *New York Times* of August 31st you told him [sic] you became a screenwriter with *Body Snatchers*, I can only conclude that you are. Will you desist, or must I have you up for disciplinary action before the Screenwriters Guild? Keep your sticky fingers off my work, good or bad, please."

Peckinpah recanted, but it took him until a 1982 interview with the BBC: "I'd like to clear up that I never did a rewrite on Don Siegel's *Body Snatchers*," he said. "I did a very small polish on one scene."

WHILE PECKINPAH WAS STILL WORKING at Allied Artists, Siegel received an offer in 1955 to get in on the ground floor, as producer and director, of the TV version of one of radio's most popular series: "Gunsmoke." Siegel wasn't interested in television because his movie career was going strong. He also intuited (wrongly) that the series wouldn't work on TV because its star, James Arness, a massive six-foot-six, would seem too invincible to viewers.

But he did suggest the show to his young protégé, Peckinpah, and suggested Peckinpah to the show's producer, Charles Marquis Warren. Peckinpah tried his hand at a script; the process was painful but the result was a success.

"It took me five months of day and night writing to get the first one finished," Peckinpah said later. "It was hell because I hate writing. I suffer the tortures of the damned. I can't sleep and it feels like I'm going to die any minute. Eventually I lock myself away somewhere, out of reach of a gun, and get it on in one big push."

The ordeal seems unusual, considering that he was adapting a preexisting radio script. Maybe it was just the nerves of a perfectionist tackling his first real script. Whatever the reason, he subsequently adapted another dozen "Gunsmoke" scripts, which he said took about eight hours apiece.

"His career at that time was to be a writer," says Ted Haworth, who met Peckinpah on *Body Snatchers* and used to give him a ride home from the set. The "Gunsmoke" scripts also established a pattern that carried on throughout his career: Peckinpah hated to write first drafts. He was at his best rewriting what someone else had started.

PECKINPAH'S THIRD DAUGHTER, Melissa, was born in 1956. By the end of the year, his writing career was flourishing. Beside the "Gunsmoke" episodes he had written, he had had a script produced on "Broken Arrow" and was negotiating to write for "Tales of Wells Fargo," "Blood Brother" and "Have Gun—Will Travel."

Peckinpah found himself spending less and less time at home. When he did come home at night, his daughter Sharon says, "He had an office in the basement. He'd always be down there working on one project or another. He was always writing and writing."

During that period, Peckinpah heard from an old Fresno friend, whom he hadn't seen in several years. Joe Bernhard was living in Watts with a black girlfriend, listening to jazz and trying to be a novelist. Convinced he was going to be the next Faulkner, Bernhard made ends meet by serving as a go-between for young women seeking abortions, earning $50 a day delivering them to the abortionist for whom he worked.

Peckinpah offered him $1.25 an hour to fix up the Latigo Canyon residence for Christmas. As Bernhard worked, Peckinpah would bounce story ideas off him, while the two drank Gallo sherry, which they bought by the gallon.

Peckinpah always made Christmas a special occasion: "Christmases were a real production and they were brilliant," his daughter Sharon says. "I'd go to bed and there would be a tree but no ornaments. The next morning, the whole living room would be transformed. It was magical."

For Christmas 1956, Bernhard recalls, "We had this great dinner, with Don Siegel, Strother Martin [who had starred in "Cooter," one of Peckinpah's best "Gunsmoke" adaptations], Walter and Fern Lea. There was duck, venison. We got drunk on our ass and everybody left, but Sam took my [car] keys away.

"The next morning we both got up with a thirsty hangover. We were fighting over the one can of tomato juice and I said, 'Sam, where's the fucking opener?' He goes to his living room and then I hear him say, 'Joe, come here.' I look and here is this giant orange tongue of flame burning up the canyon."

The Malibu fire of 1956 claimed the Peckinpah home. Peckinpah and Marie got the kids out; Peckinpah managed to salvage a couple of scripts but lost everything else: books, clothes, half-completed treatments and several cats and dogs.

They moved temporarily into a house at Las Flores Beach in Malibu. Though their plan was to rebuild up in the hills, "we liked living on the beach so much that we decided to look for a place to live on the beach," Marie says. Within six months, they found a big red barnlike house in Malibu Colony and moved in.

Life at the beach seemed even more idyllic. The Peckinpah household became the site of regular weekend barbecues and beach parties.

"For three or four years, we went scuba diving every Saturday," recalls Walter Peter, who was one of Peckinpah's best friends. "We'd dive for scallops, clams, fish, abalone. Whatever we were diving for, it was always who could get the biggest abalone or the biggest scallop. He could be like a big kid: water fights, running around the house. Those were happy times; he could relax. That's why he lived at Malibu.

"We used to laugh because he'd invite ten or twenty people over on a Sunday. Fern Lea and I would spend most of our time in the kitchen preparing the food. It used to be a standing joke. We would nibble all evening and Sam would say, 'I'll do the meat.' He loved to serve hot dogs. If you got fed before 10 P.M., it was an act of God. On a Sunday night, when you had to work the next day, that could be tough. So when he'd finally start to cook, we'd say, 'Gotta go.' "

Oddly enough, although he was beginning to make a name for himself writing for television, it wasn't until after the fire that Peckinpah got his family its first TV set.

"The house we rented had one," Sharon says. "He hated the hypnotic quality of TV but he watched it. He thought game shows were fascinating. He'd say, 'Look at all that greed.' He hated the advertising; the censorship on TV was appalling to him. We used to watch his shows—'The Rifleman' and 'The Westerner'—but a lot of times, he wouldn't want to stay in the room. He said he was constantly editing, redoing it in his mind. After a while, it was too much for him."

His professional success, however, seemed to exacerbate the problems he and Marie were beginning to have. He spent more and more time at work. When he was home, he wasn't interested in Marie's concerns about the house or the children.

"With each child, there was a distancing," Marie says. "There was a lot of closeness during birth. The day-to-day caring and parenting, though, somehow seemed to distance the two of us."

Their home at the beach was "where some of our difficulties with each other started to come out," Marie says. "I guess it was because we were living around more people and he was at a point in his career when things were starting to grab on. People were beginning to take notice of his work, his writing. The more that happened, the more tense Sam would become, the more he needed to control me, my movement. He'd go hunting with his brother-in-law and his friends and the directive to me was that I was not to go out at night. I was feeling guilty because supposedly he was worried about me and I was resenting it."

The tension was obvious to the people who knew them. Peckinpah's youngest sister, Susan, remembers visiting them in her teens and finding that "there was always some tension at Sam and Marie's. We did Thanksgiving at their house once and it was a major ordeal."

Walter Peter says, "Sam and Marie at first loved each other very strongly. Sam was doing a lot of TV and was gone a great deal. He'd get home late and that wore Marie thin rather quickly. There were exciting chapters. Sam threw things while we were there. It got a bit warm at times and that's probably what tore them asunder."

Their relationship was born out of a mutual love of the theater, but Peckinpah was the only one who got to pursue his muse. When Marie would complain about not having an outlet for expression, Peckinpah would try to ameliorate the situation by bringing gifts. At one point, he gave her a set of oil paints, encouraging her to take up painting.

Mostly, however, Marie was left to raise the children and keep house, neither of which she did to Sam's satisfaction. Sheltered as a girl, she believed in letting her children take more chances physically—a fact that scared the athletically inclined Peckinpah to death. Nor was she the kind of woman who put particular stock in keeping a well-scrubbed house.

Betty Peckinpah says, "She was a hippie before there were hippies. He was so unconventional himself; he'd do things like come home and make great big tic-tac-toe things on the white walls in black paint or paint big words. And she was an absolutely frightful housekeeper."

Peckinpah's drinking added to the problem. He had always been a drinker, though it wasn't until after the divorce that Marie figured out that he was an alcoholic. She simply knew that when he got home from work in the evening, she needed to get a meal into him as quickly as possible. If she didn't, she faced the consequences of a long evening of his drinking on an empty stomach. Peckinpah would never acknowledge that alcohol was the problem.

"He was the kind of person who needed to eat often," Marie says. "He was real slim. He needed to have little meals during the day. I always had to make sure he had dinner before he got too hungry. I had to make sure he had something to eat before he started drinking too much.

"I don't think I ever realized he was an alcoholic until years later, when we were long since divorced. When we were married, I had a feeling it was almost like a love affair with that booze. It was like a personal thing to me. It was not like a man with a disease [or] a severe problem that had not much to do with me."

Nor did his children understand until they were much older just who they had been dealing with. Sharon recalls reading an article on alcoholism when she was in her early twenties and realizing that the description fit her father. "He was more of a weekend drinker when I was younger," she says. "Gradually, as I became aware of the problem, I noticed he was drinking in the morning, that he was always drinking."

The same delayed realization is true of Kristen: "I was not aware until I was much older. Then I figured out, 'That's what all the rage was. It wasn't my fault.' It was a huge part of his life and you can't ignore it."

Yet there was a kind and compassionate side to him as well, as Marie's sister Judy recalls. Fifteen years younger than Marie, she would visit the couple in Malibu, where Peckinpah would give her books to read (such as Jack Kerouac's *On the Road*) to broaden her horizons. They would take Judy out to dinner and even bought her her first lobster.

"Sam and Marie were a big influence on me," she says. "They were pretty glamorous; their life-style was pretty exotic to me. I looked at what I did through their eyes, to check to be sure it was cool. He opened some doors to me in reading, ways of looking at the world."

When she was fifteen, Judy Selland got pregnant and went to spend some time with the Peckinpahs before entering a home for unwed mothers. Peckinpah went out of his way to make her feel comfortable, even cautioning his neighbors to be nice to her. Her boyfriend wanted to marry her but Judy thought they were too young.

Eventually, however, Peckinpah convinced them that marriage was the best solution. He hosted the wedding at his house, then paid to send them on a honeymoon at a hotel in Santa Barbara, where he treated them to a suite complete with flowers and champagne.

"My parents were horrified because nice girls weren't supposed to get pregnant and I was a nice girl," Judy says. "But Marie and Sam really changed that for me. They made it a special celebration instead of something embarrassing."

But the Jekyll-Hyde aspects of Peckinpah's personality were already apparent: "On the one hand, he could be the most wonderful, fun guy—my father," Sharon says. "And then he'd snap and go into this rage. You didn't want to be around him. It was frightening."

IN EARLY 1957, producer Frank Rosenberg approached Peckinpah with a novel called *The Authentic Death of Hendry Jones*, by Charles Neider, based on the story of Billy the Kid and Pat Garrett. Rosenberg offered Peckinpah scale, about $3,000, to write a screenplay. Peckinpah, who was anxious to write for movies, readily agreed.

He finished the script in six months and turned it in. "It was a damn good script," Peckinpah maintained later. "I told [Rosenberg] to send it to Brando. And damned if he didn't and Brando bought it."

Marlon Brando was coming off an Oscar for *On the Waterfront* and a box-office hit, *The Wild One*. He pushed for—and received—the chance to direct the film himself. He also demanded—and received—extensive rewrites on the script. Convinced that his public didn't want to see him die, Brando had the story reworked so that the Billy the Kid character killed the Pat Garrett figure in the end. Retitled *One-Eyed Jacks*, the film was finally released in 1961.

"I worked with Marlon for three and a half weeks before he fired me," Peckinpah said. "There's two scenes of mine in the picture and I did not receive credit for it."

He added, "Marlon screwed it up. He's a hell of an actor but in those days, he had to end up as a hero, and that's not the point of the story."

Actor James Coburn says that, some years later, Peckinpah told him, "Marlon taught me how to hate."

Despite that setback, Peckinpah was writing constantly for the most popular Western series on TV at that time: "Man Without a Gun," "Trackdown," "Tales of Wells Fargo" and "Tombstone Territory." Having sold five scripts to "Broken Arrow," he finally got the break he sought so desperately: the chance to direct a half-hour of television. It wasn't a movie, but it was a directing credit.

The assignment was the final episode of "Broken Arrow." "They liked the scripts I was doing but the show was going off the air," he said. "Elliot Arnold [the producer] gave me a chance to direct the very last show."

Peckinpah eventually developed a reputation as an exacting, perfectionist director who possessed an iron will. But to hear him talk about those early directing assignments, one would picture him as a hyperactive nerve case who could barely keep his breakfast down when he walked on the set in the morning.

Of that first directing assignment, he later told an interviewer, "There was one scene I must have photographed from at least eighteen angles. I was never so frightened in my life. Don't let anyone kid you. It's bloody murder learning how to direct."

Warming to his theme, he told another interviewer around the same time: "Every time I started a show I would walk on the set, lay out the first three or four shots, then go back to the head and throw up. Then I'd have a milk shake, settle down and make a picture."

A couple of years later, he brought it up to another interviewer: "Christ, it was five years after I started directing before I wasn't throwing up every morning when I walked on the set."

Despite his expanding directing credits, Peckinpah was still known primarily as a writer. As such, he came to the attention of the production company of Jules Levy, Arthur Gardner and Arnold Laven (known collectively as LGL), who were looking for a writer for a screen project.

United Artists had purchased a book, *The Dice of God*, a fictional version of Custer's last stand that focused on one of Custer's battalions that survived Little Big Horn.

"Our program was always to look for undiscovered writers to develop the screenplay, so it was not burdened with a lot of preproduction costs," Laven says. "We tried to catch them early."

Peckinpah's agent submitted a "Gunsmoke" teleplay that impressed Laven. Still, he knew that "Gunsmoke" was derived from radio scripts, so he asked to meet Peckinpah. "He gave me a sense of a guy with a fabulous sureness about him," Laven says. "He was an impressive young man. My partners agreed that Sam was worth giving a try to."

Even as Peckinpah was writing *Dice of God* (which would eventually be made as *The Glory Guys* in the early 1960s), he had finished a script for "Gunsmoke," called "The Turkey Shoot." As he was writing it, Joe Bernhard recalls, Peckinpah said, "I'm sick of all this quick-draw shit. I'm going to write one about a guy with a rifle."

Everyone involved with "The Rifleman" has a different story about who had the original idea for the show. Peckinpah always claimed credit for originating the idea. But Laven and his partner, Jules Levy, both take some —if not all—the credit for the genesis of the show.

According to Peckinpah, he wrote the script, which was subsequently turned down by "Gunsmoke." So he took it to Dick Powell, the former actor who was the highly successful head of Four Star Productions, and sold it to him. Peckinpah made his own participation part of the package.

Levy, however, has a different story: "We had developed a screenplay with Larry Roman. He did a Western and changed the name to 'The Rifleman.' I got the idea for a TV series of a guy with just a rifle. We developed it with another Hollywood writer but it didn't work out. Sam had a short story called 'The Turkey Shoot.' We used it as the basis for the pilot. He got no creation credit because we created the idea. We took it to William Morris and William Morris took it to Four Star. It's inconceivable to me that he took credit. He had a 5 percent interest in the show. If he had created it, he would have had a larger ongoing interest."

Laven tells a slightly different story: " 'The Rifleman' was a title my partner owned. One day Sam was in the office and, in conversation, we told Sam about 'The Rifleman' title. He said he'd already written a teleplay. We read it and it was a good one, about a loner coming out of the wilderness to compete in a turkey shoot. At the end, he's threatened with his life and so he purposely loses."

There are other claims of input into what eventually became "The Sharpshooter," a pilot for "The Rifleman" that aired on "Dick Powell's Zane Grey Theater" in the spring of 1958. Peckinpah's brother, Denver, says that, after the script was rejected by "Gunsmoke" but before it was shown to Levy, Gardner and Laven, Peckinpah let his brother read it. As Denny Peckinpah recalls, the central character was not a rifleman but a riflewoman; they convinced Sam to make the central character a man.

Laven says that, at the time, he was struck by the ending because he felt it

was too unconventional. A Western hero didn't back down simply to save his
own skin. But if the character had a small son and the threat was to the child
rather than the father, it gave him a valid reason to throw the match.

Peckinpah has been quoted as complaining that he was denied creator
credit because Laven came up with the idea of adding the boy. So Laven's
recollection may be the most accurate.

With "The Sharpshooter" nearing production, Peckinpah turned his attention to other writing projects. His goal was to write and direct a movie of
his own so he set to work on a couple of screenplays.

One of them was *Hound Dog Man*, a coming-of-age tale of a boy in the
Old West. Peckinpah lost the chance to direct it—to his old mentor, Don
Siegel, who made an undistinguished hash of it with Carol Lynley, Stuart
Whitman and the pseudo rock 'n' roller Fabian.

THE PILOT FOR "THE RIFLEMAN" was filmed three weeks after Peckinpah finished the script. "The Sharpshooter" aired on "Zane Grey Theater" in the
spring of 1958. ABC-TV found a sponsor for the well-received pilot with
little trouble.

"It was like a hot knife through butter," Laven says, "a very fine script. It
was a downhill shot from the moment Sam delivered the screenplay. And
LGL was in the business of making 'The Rifleman.' "

Peckinpah was given a contract for the first season as the show's story
editor. He would supervise the scripts for the first season's twenty-six shows
and write scripts as well. He would also be able to direct two episodes during
the first season.

But the professional strides he was making seemed only to increase the
problems at home. The added pressure on Peckinpah led him to drink more
and become more abusive to Marie. He was home less—and became increasingly suspicious of his wife.

His life was about to fall apart, even as his career was on the verge of
taking off.

Part Two

1958-1963

It is not a good world. There is no such thing as "they lived happily ever after." It is a good and bad world and how we live depends almost one hundred percent on ourselves.

—SAM PECKINPAH, IN A LETTER TO HIS DAUGHTER SHARON

4

"The Rifleman" and "The Westerner"

"THE RIFLEMAN" WAS ONE OF THE BIG HITS of the 1958–'59 television season, a year when Westerns ruled network television.

From October 1958 through April 1959, seven of the top ten weekly series were Westerns. "The Rifleman" ended its first season as number four; pitted against the much weaker "George Burns Show" and "Arthur Godfrey Show," it was part of a powerful ABC Tuesday night lineup that included the hits "The Life and Legend of Wyatt Earp," "Cheyenne," "Sugarfoot" and "Naked City."

The show's success, Arnold Laven says, was largely due to Peckinpah's creative input. Drawing on his own background—using place names from his boyhood such as the Dunlap Ranch and North Fork—he created a show that departed from the formula of lawmen battling outlaws. He had broken the mold of the quick-draw hero with his central character of Lucas McCain.

Lucas McCain was a widower who carried a specially built Winchester rifle that he could cock and shoot with one hand. He lived near North Fork, New Mexico, with his son Mark. McCain was an anomaly on TV in those days: a family man without a wife, a rancher who knew how to use a gun, a hero of a TV Western who didn't wear a badge (though he could be counted on to back up the town marshal). He had principles and he had speed, but he had no interest in building a reputation for his quickness with a gun. Yet the novelty firearm made him a target for attention from bad elements.

The combination of his gun, his remoteness and the fact that he had to care for a young boy combined to make "The Rifleman" a hit. Toy companies sold versions of his rifle.

Chuck Connors, a one-time athlete who had played second string for both the Boston Celtics and Brooklyn (later Los Angeles) Dodgers, had been making a comfortable living playing flinty-eyed heavies in films such as *Hired Gun* and *The Big Country* with small parts in *Designing Woman* and *Old Yeller*. Suddenly he was one of the biggest stars in television, his squinty look

47

and raspy voice transformed into emblems of upright fortitude and moral principle.

And Peckinpah was suddenly a hot commodity. He had an office on the Four Star lot and was something of a magnet for a group of rising young actors. Among them was Dennis Hopper, who, having filmed *Rebel Without a Cause* and *Giant*, was about to get himself blackballed in Hollywood by tangling with Henry Hathaway on *From Hell to Texas*.

"I used to go to his office with a couple of guys—a whole bunch of us who smoked grass, a tight-knit group," Hopper says. "We were all closet smokers and Sam was one of us. Steve McQueen too, later on. Sam was one of the hip guys around. So we'd go visit him and smoke a joint in his office or walk around the lot smoking a joint. He didn't say a hell of a lot. He had an intense kind of energy but he didn't seem to have a great gift for gab."

Hopper was cast in "The Sharpshooter," which Laven directed. Peckinpah, as the writer, was on the set during production. "He would stand off to the side and tell me stuff," Hopper recalls. "He'd come and take me aside, out of the sight of the director, and tell me stuff about my character."

Actor R. G. Armstrong was also cast in the pilot, playing the town marshal. He had come to Hollywood initially to do films, after appearing in *Cat on a Hot Tin Roof* on Broadway and doing three or four other Broadway plays. A member of the Actors Studio, Armstrong was eager to reestablish himself as a New York actor. When Laven asked him to become a "Rifleman" regular after the pilot went to series, Armstrong turned him down. But Peckinpah remembered him and later made him part of his stock company.

To meet the demand for script ideas, Peckinpah imported his old graduate-school friend Don Levy, who was teaching college drama in northern California.

"At one point, he said, 'I want you to write ten synopses, one paragraph each, to shoot for "The Rifleman," ' " Levy recalls. "I'd think, 'How can I make *Streetcar Named Desire* work here? Or *Death of a Salesman*?' But I got ten and the next day he said, 'Write ten more.' And the next day it was ten more. I wrote thirty of them. He gave them to the producers and Arthur Gardner would grade them, like a class. Whether Sam ever used them, I have no idea."

Though their relationship was mostly professional, Laven regarded Peckinpah as a friend, at least through the beginning of the first season of "The Rifleman." At that point in his career, Peckinpah's drinking was still confined to after hours and weekends. Laven got some inkling of Peckinpah's capacity, however, when they got together to work over a script at Laven's house.

"I had a bottle of Remy Martin brandy that Dore Schary had sent me while I was doing a picture at MGM," Laven says. "It was my prize bottle. I asked Sam if he'd like a drink and he said, 'Do you have any brandy?' I got a little glass and poured him some of the Remy. In the course of going through the thirty pages of teleplay, he continued to help himself. By the time he left at the end of the evening, he had finished the bottle. If it had been another bottle of booze, I would never have noticed. But it was my good bottle of Remy Martin. And it was all gone—in one evening. Yet he showed no evidence that he'd even been drinking."

Peckinpah ran into conflict with Jules Levy when it came time to direct his first episode (he eventually directed four in that first season).

"It took him forever to direct a simple little scene," Levy says. "We had a thirty-page script to shoot each week and needed to shoot ten or eleven pages a day. You had thirty hours to shoot a half-hour show. It took him a half-day to shoot a quarter of a page. I said, 'If you don't get a day's work done, we'll replace you.' When you agree to do something in three days, if the network says you have X number of dollars, you've got to do it within that. But Sam was not concerned."

Laven, who seems more forgiving of Peckinpah's quirks, says, "Sam improvised the use of the camera and changed it. I thought it was awkward, lacking in standard technique that I'd hoped for. There was an awkwardness in the angles."

Apparently, Peckinpah's proficiency increased with subsequent episodes he directed. But all of his episodes had a different tone—a rougher, slightly nastier edge—than the ones directed by Laven and other hired directors.

" 'The Rifleman' was a tough, hard-hitting show, but the violence didn't have that meanness," Laven says. "It had action but the world's violence did not really play a part. There was a reality and meanness to Sam's violence that bothered me. It was overt but not overabundant. It was a little more of that kind of violent violence than was characteristic of any Western in those days. It separated those shows by shadings that went beyond the general flavor of the show."

Johnny Crawford, who played Mark McCain, was eleven during the first season of "The Rifleman." He remembers Peckinpah as "very serious and yet easygoing. He was a little intimidating because he was so serious but I felt comfortable. I wanted to be good because he obviously cared about what he was doing."

While working on "The Rifleman," Peckinpah met actor Robert Culp one day at Four Star Studios. Culp had starred in "Trackdown," a short-lived TV Western, and had developed a reputation for being prickly to work with. Culp was trying to establish himself as a writer as well as an actor and had been to LGL to pitch a script he had written for "The Rifleman."

"I didn't really know Sam but I knew who he was," Culp recalls. "So when I ran into him, he said, 'You wrote something? I want to see it.' I sent it over and the next morning he called me at an ungodly hour and started cussing me out. 'You dumb asshole son of a bitch, etc.' He finished with, 'You sold this to those people. You are never permitted to sell anything to anybody without checking with me first.' And he meant it."

Peckinpah's concept of "The Rifleman" focused on the evolution of the relationship between Lucas and Mark McCain. Peckinpah already had a vision, if somewhat unformed, of the Western genre as a vehicle for depicting the change in the country, from innocence to pragmatism, from idealism to cynicism. Later, his topic would be the times themselves and the men who were affected by the way the West evolved. For now, his metaphor was the education of a boy and his gradual growth into manhood, perhaps prematurely because that was what the forces of the West dictated.

As the show grew rapidly in popularity, however, it became clear to Peckinpah that his vision for developing Mark was at odds with that of the producers. LGL felt the show's appeal lay in keeping Mark a boy; this child would never become father to the man.

Peckinpah made his concerns clear but the producers weren't interested in his idea. So Peckinpah quit after the first season.

"He told me later that he quit because he was disenchanted because the producers didn't want me to grow up on the show," Crawford says. "He thought it was going to be too superficial."

In early 1959, Peckinpah wrote another script for Dick Powell, which aired on "Zane Grey Theater" as "Trouble at Tres Cruces." It was filmed as a pilot for a series to be called "Winchester." Shortly after completing that project, he wrote and directed another pilot, "Klondike," but wasn't happy with the production and left before it became a series.

By the time Peckinpah was ready to quit "The Rifleman," Powell had sold "Winchester" (retitled "The Westerner" because the rights to the title "Winchester" were already taken) to NBC, for the fall of 1960.

"I think Sam would have quit 'The Rifleman' anyway," Laven says. "In his heart, he would have liked the show to be leaner and tougher. You could tell that by looking at 'The Westerner.' If Sam said he was disappointed that we didn't encourage his point of view, he was accurate."

Jules Levy, for one, was not sorry to see him go. "Sam started out as a fairly nice guy who didn't know the time of day," he says. "He was very violent-minded, an angry person for no reason. He had talent as a writer and director but he was impossible. He would do things the hard way and not be concerned about costs or the problems with the studio."

But Laven says, "He was forthright, strong, much easier to get along with than later on. He seized the first opportunity to move forward."

As for Peckinpah's script for *The Glory Guys*, it was produced (with Laven as director) around the same time in 1964 that Peckinpah was shooting *Major Dundee*. LGL had jettisoned the title *The Dice of God* and was calling it *Custer's Last Stand*.

As ill-fated as Custer, the film lost that commercial title when Arthur Krim, head of United Artists (for whom LGL was making the picture), sold the rights to the name *Custer's Last Stand* to Twentieth Century-Fox. Fox had plans for a Fred Zinnemann-directed Custer project that would be the definitive film on the Little Big Horn. (It was never made.)

To the producers' further sorrow, United Artists nixed their notions for casting the re-retitled *The Glory Guys* with two actors who were not yet stars: Lee Marvin and James Coburn. After UA said no, Coburn's career quickly took off when he starred in *Our Man Flint*, while Marvin won the Oscar for his next project, *Cat Ballou*. *The Glory Guys* ended up starring Harve Presnell and Tom Tryon and disappeared under the weight of their big-screen charisma.

"THE WESTERNER" put Sam Peckinpah on the map in many people's minds. Not enough of them, however, were signed up with the A. C. Nielsen Co. to be counted as viewers to give the show a fighting chance.

His work on the short-lived series had farther-reaching effects than anyone could imagine. It eventually led to his directing *The Deadly Companions* and *Ride the High Country*, his first two films, as well as *The Cincinnati Kid*. Critics, fans and friends would refer to it repeatedly as proof of his ability to take the Western genre and give it new depth and reality. Not bad for a series that barely lasted thirteen weeks.

Peckinpah had been hired as producer for "The Westerner," with a scheduled air date of September 1960. He had to postpone some of the writing, however, when the Writers Guild of America staged the longest strike in its history, from Jan. 16–June 22, 1960. With his own series on the schedule, Peckinpah became part of a splinter group of working writers who tried to effect an early resolution to the work stoppage so that their projects could push forward.

Writer Stirling Silliphant, one of the creative forces behind the popular "Route 66," recalls a meeting in which the splinter group, of which he was also part, confronted the WGA negotiating team.

"We were working writers, as opposed to the hundreds of nonworking members who wrote in their spare time, and we felt the committee was being unreasonable," Silliphant says. "They were demanding things we would never get. Sam came to the meeting wearing cowboy boots, a ten-gallon hat, dark glasses, looking lean and mean and fit and tan. He put his feet up on the table, pulled his hat down over his eyes and appeared to fall asleep. The meeting was very heated and I asked a lot of searching questions.

"But they treated me with arrogance: When I would ask the questions, they wouldn't answer them. Peckinpah, looking like a dozing lizard, pushed up his hat, looked at the chief negotiator and said, 'Answer the man's questions or I'll take you outside and beat the living shit out of you.' It made a big impression.

"I saw him one more time at a horrible meeting, where the Guild splintered between those writers who wanted the strike settled and those who wanted to hold out. We were accused of being fat cats who were denying the rights of the common man. They accused us of being fascists and we called them commies. It was brutal. There were fistfights in the parking lot. I was starting down the stairs and I bumped into Sam, who had a roll of quarters in his hand. I said, 'What are you doing?' He said, 'I'm going to knock the first son of a bitch to hell who starts trouble with me tonight.' He didn't hit anyone but what fascinated me [was that] he was ready to."

With the strike finally settled, Peckinpah spent the summer of 1960 writing, directing and otherwise overseeing production of the first thirteen episodes of "The Westerner."

The show was built around Dave Blassingame, a wandering cowboy played by Brian Keith. Blassingame traveled the countryside with a mongrel hound named Brown, getting involved in mildly comic adventures as well as tense ones. His occasional sidekick was a humorously shifty gambler named Burgundy Smith, played by John Dehner.

Peckinpah directed five episodes of the series and wrote or co-wrote four of the scripts. He hired a writer named Bruce Geller, who would eventually go on to produce "Mission: Impossible." Geller wrote three or four of the best "Westerner" comedy scripts, in which the macho world of the cowboys ran foursquare into the uncharted—and always sticky—terrain of women and romance.

(Peckinpah, Geller and producer Bernie Kowalski started a production company of their own, Unit Productions. Geller and Kowalski eventually split in anger with Peckinpah, a not-uncommon occurrence. In a subsequent project they did together, Geller and Kowalski created a particularly odious villain named "Sam Fresno" as a subtle form of revenge.)

Beside Keith and Dehner, Peckinpah drew upon a widening circle of actors, who would be part of his stock company in films: R. G. Armstrong, Warren Oates, Dub Taylor. Taylor says that, even in those early days of Peckinpah's career, he would attempt to bully people to see how far he could push them before they would push back. When dealing with Peckinpah, it was important to stand your ground immediately.

"We had a run-in right at the beginning of 'The Westerner,' " Taylor says. "I had this hat and he said, 'You big son of a bitch, get over here with that hat and take it off.' I said, 'The next time you holler at me, I'll knock your fucking head off. I'm small but I can fight some.' After that we got along fine."

But Peckinpah could also hold back and let people learn lessons for themselves. Robert Culp recalls handling a small part in a "Westerner" episode that called for him to play a scene in which he drunkenly shot it out with Dave Blassingame.

"I said to the prop guy, 'Get me a pint of Scotch,' and the prop guy immediately called Sam, who said, 'Give it to him,' " Culp says. "I tried to time it to be on the hair's edge of drunk. Later, all Sam said was, 'Did you see the dailies?' And it sucked. I was over the edge into blurry and soft. That solidified our relationship as producer and actor."

For the opening episode of "The Westerner," which aired September 30, 1960, Peckinpah chose a show he had directed and co-written, "Jeff." In it, Blassingame goes to retrieve a young woman from Mexico for her father. Her name is Jeff and she is a prostitute, in service to a vicious pimp. Blassingame, who knew her as a child, ends up fighting the pimp and beating him ("Hey, that's against the rules," the pimp cries at one point in the fight, to which Blassingame replies, "This ain't a game"). But Jeff tells Blassingame that she isn't unhappy in her life and would just as soon stay where she is.

The story was one of many Peckinpah had heard during his annual fall hunting trips into the area east and north of Fresno, across the mountains as far as Ely, Nevada. Part of every trip involved stops at the local brothels for drinks and, certainly for Peckinpah and perhaps for his compatriots, a bout with each establishment's whores.

"I can remember sitting on a bar stool in those places until two or three in the morning," says Walter Peter, who was part of the annual hunting trips for two decades. "He was always looking for interesting stories. There was one old crone in Ely who swore she had Teddy Roosevelt as a steady customer."

Peckinpah said he heard the story on which "Jeff" was based from one such hooker, a seventy-five-year-old woman who told him the story of her first love. The next year, Peckinpah returned to the same whorehouse, where the same woman confronted him and said she had heard that he had used her story on TV and felt she was owed something. Peckinpah asked her what she would like.

"I believe I'd like a beer," she said and Peckinpah willingly helped her quench her thirst.

The first episode received a positive review in the trades, with the *Hollywood Reporter* calling it "breathless theater" and "moving poetic drama." Affiliates in less sophisticated markets than Los Angeles and New York, however, received phone calls of complaint from local viewers about what was then controversial subject matter, including the fact that one of the characters used the word "damn" in prime time.

" 'The Westerner' was strictly adult," Arnold Laven says. "That first script did not have a typical ending for an episode in the 1960s. It had an unusual reality and cynicism, more cynical than was done on TV. The sponsor did not want to attach his name. So Sam enhanced his reputation and brought about the demise of the show."

The network cancelled the show after the thirteen episodes had been aired. It was not because of the controversy, however. "The Westerner" was cancelled for a much more mundane reason: low ratings.

"The Westerner" was one of three new shows slotted in at 8:30 P.M. on Fridays. The other two were the instantly successful "Route 66" (which quickly became one of the most popular shows of the period) and "The Flintstones," an animated reworking of "The Honeymooners" (which became one of the first prime-time cartoon series). An adult program in a young person's market, "The Westerner" was off the air by the end of 1960.

Actor James Coburn, who had worked for Peckinpah on a couple of "Rifleman" episodes, recalls running into Peckinpah at MGM while he was directing *Ride the High Country*. Having not seen him in a couple of years, Coburn remarked on how good he thought "The Westerner" had been. Never one to take a compliment graciously, Peckinpah replied, "Yeah, it was too good for television."

5

Personal Problems and *Deadly Companions*

OUT OF THE ASHES OF "THE WESTERNER" would come Peckinpah's first movie: *The Deadly Companions*. But even as he made that significant step professionally, Peckinpah was weathering serious storms in his personal life.

Before "The Westerner" even reached the air, Peckinpah's marriage was in tatters. There was a combination of factors, many of them derived from his preoccupation with his work. When his youngest daughter, Melissa, wound up in the hospital with complications from a childhood illness, Peckinpah refused to visit. "In the end, what made me stop caring about him was that he wouldn't come to the hospital because it made him feel bad," Marie says. "I thought there was no hope for a man who was so self-concerned."

But there were other even more severe problems. Peckinpah's drinking led to scenes with the neighbors—and worse. Kristen was once confronted by a playmate in Malibu Colony who said, "Your daddy threw a chair at my daddy."

She also remembers an argument with a friend who, reaching for an epithet, finally blurted, "You—you—you Peckinpah!"

Robert Culp recalls arriving at Peckinpah's house one afternoon to find Peckinpah and his friend Frank Kowalski slugging it out on the beach behind his house. Kowalski, significantly larger, kept trying to bear-hug Peckinpah into submission, saying, "Sam, I love you," while Peckinpah, saying, "You son of a bitch," wrestled with him until they both fell through a window. Peckinpah had to be taken to the hospital to stitch up a serious cut on his arm.

Marie and Peckinpah separated in early July 1960, after Peckinpah broke her cheekbone in a drunken rage. As with most abusive alcoholics, Peckinpah suffered great remorse. It was not the first time he had struck her, nor was it the last.

"I had a very large black eye," Marie says. "It was pretty terrible. He'd feel so terrible and I'd think, 'He can't possibly do it again.' "

But he did, so she finally took the kids and left, asking him to move out of the house.

"It's strange, but the last few days before you left, you seemed to go further and further away from me," Peckinpah said, in a handwritten letter dated July 4, 1960. "Why did you send me away? Was it because I struck you? Or was it because I had become something you no longer could afford or want to cope with? Do you want to be a wife to me, Marie, and a mother to your children? Can we talk, you and I, sometime when I won't see the fear and uncertainty in you? In your love I want to fight the fear. I want to build that certainty. I want us to be part of each other in a way with an understanding, patience and respect more better [sic] than we have ever had, but it seems that you must want this too."

The next day, he wrote again, in his crabbed, almost indecipherable left-handed scrawl: "The kids need a father, and by that I mean me! I need them. I miss them so damned much it is almost impossible to keep from jumping in the car or plane and finding you.

"I guess it's tough now for me, because I feel so different about things and how I came to realize that I was not completely to blame for what happened. I feel shook up that you feel I'm so unfit to be a father. That I am such a damned brute. I am all of these things to a degree but really feel you have gone too far with your all-inclusive judgment. I know what a fool I was. I also know I had considerable help from you.

"You are not Saint Marie and I am not Mephistopheles. We are Sam and Marie Peckinpah, both with some degree of mortal illness but better I hope to look at each other, judge what must be done and do it with pride in ourselves as individuals and pride and respect for each other.

"Sometimes I think that you feel you can only be an individual at my expense, only by being in opposition to me, hurting me, ignoring me, destroying some part of me and you become a complete person. Maybe you think I feel the same about you. Well, I don't. Not any of it.

"Listen, Marie, I am part of you or I have been part of you and hope and pray to continue, and in putting me down you are putting down part of yourself, not becoming independent. You don't find independence by hurting others. You find it by knowing yourself. Sometimes I think that you want me to be dependent and I'm not a guardian angel brought to provide carte blanche for whatever you want to do.

"I am doing and will continue to destroy the sickness I have carried, evidently for a good many years. How about you? It's strange but this free association kind of writing is a great help. It's full of contradictions, repetitions and considerable honesty. But I'm writing it as if you didn't have a problem and as if you had nothing to do but listen to my problems.

"We have got to quit being strangers. The time is long past. You must talk to me for I have learned how to listen."

Marie says, "We had a trial separation. He got abusive and would drink too much, so I told him to leave. But we had these wonderful getting-togethers. He'd come back and ask forgiveness. As I've grown older and talked to more women, I guess [I've found] this is typical of this kind of man. But I didn't know how to handle it at the time.

"He was a very sensitive man, very extremely, highly sensitive. Which made him wonderful in some ways and extraordinarily cruel as well."

The separation and marital problems caused consternation within the Peckinpah family. Betty Peckinpah recalls Peckinpah's mother being extremely fond of Marie and unforgiving of Sam for letting the marriage collapse. Susan Peckinpah has an opposite memory.

"My mother thought the divorce was Marie's fault," Susan says. "It was the only time I saw my father go down to Los Angeles. I felt Marie was being railroaded but my father was there for Sam."

Sam and Marie tried to reconcile but the tensions could not be resolved. Kristen recalls a couple of family trips between the separation and the divorce that were "fairly disastrous." Sharon, who was about to enter her teens, remembers overhearing them fighting at night, after the kids went to bed. She also remembers a trip she took with him as the marriage began to unravel for the final time.

"He tried to explain to me why he was getting divorced," she says. "He said he was married to a camera and my mother couldn't live with that. He told me—and this was part of his misogyny—she didn't know how to keep house. She was a lousy housekeeper. But so was he. They were both slobs."

He tried to explain the problems to Sharon in a series of letters that fall. In a letter dated October 23, 1960, he wrote: "Sharon, love is respect and concern and, above all else, I think a kind of honesty and the truth is that few people ever find it. Your mother and I never did; [n]either did your grandparents. I think it's something you must do more than look for. It is not a good world. There is no such thing as 'they lived happily ever after.' I would like you to be strong as I hope I am becoming without being hard."

In a subsequent letter, explaining the separation, he wrote: "Everybody, whether it's for work or living, must take some time to be alone or they lose part of themselves, a very important part, the part that they can share with others. This time I'm going to make sure I have more to share with you."

Finally, he tried to articulate the problems in a way that an eleven-year-old girl would understand: "Marriage is what people bring to it, nothing more, and people bring to it themselves, what they are, what they have been taught, how they can learn. I'm afraid, my darling, that your mother and I brought very little to our marriage except our needs to run away from home. Marie and I were children when we married and our love for each other, while very strong, was childish love where taking was more important than giving. Neither of us ever learned how to share anything but problems. Neither of us ever learned how to care about anybody but ourselves, because we never, as children, learned how to care about ourselves."

Peckinpah moved back in. He and Marie went on as husband and wife, shakily, for several more months. Peckinpah, for all his impulses to the contrary—impulses that, a few years later, he would have acted on without a second thought—tried to maintain the semblance of a normal middle-class family. Though he was learning to be part of Hollywood, he was still just a guy from Fresno, a place where divorce was a stigma, rather than the commonplace occurrence it eventually became.

IN NOVEMBER 1960, as both "The Westerner" and Peckinpah's marriage were facing cancellation, yet another tragedy struck: Peckinpah's father, who had been in a Fresno hospital to be treated for a bout of phlebitis, died suddenly of a heart attack.

"He had a blood clot in his leg but was supposed to be okay," recalls Susan, who still lived at home at the time. "While he was in the hospital, I had an unusual conversation with him. He was telling me how important I was to him but that I should listen to my mother because she had things to teach me too. Then he wanted me to go home."

Earlier that month, Dave Peckinpah had gone against Fern's wishes: He had run for election to the superior court judgeship in Madera County to which Governor Pat Brown had appointed him the previous year—and had won easily, over a younger opponent. Fern had opposed the appointment; she was so mad when he accepted that she refused to attend his swearing-in ceremony.

His final year had been a blend of satisfaction in his work and sorrow at the state of his personal life. His time away from the Madera County Courthouse was divided between his bachelor apartment in Madera and the cabin at the rear of his own property to which his wife had banished him when he returned home on weekends.

After his death on November 30, 1960, Dave Peckinpah's four children gathered in what must have been a highly charged atmosphere at the Peckinpah household in Fresno. The expected grief over the death of a beloved patriarch is traumatic enough without adding in the stress of bringing together a family in which the surviving parent has always favored two of her children (Sam and Susan) while expressing virtual antipathy to the other two (Denver and Fern Lea).

Even after Dave's death, Fern Peckinpah still saw her late husband as a competitor with her dead father. Imagine how tautly stretched nerves must have been when Fern summarily banned her children from announcing the time or place for Dave Peckinpah's funeral. Finally, picture the tension and the release when more than 3,000 people showed up for the funeral anyway, to pay their last respects.

It was the kind of drama of human nature pushed to its limit and beyond that became a hallmark of Sam Peckinpah's best work—and it was being acted out in real life.

Aside from bringing her family together for a tense few days, the death of Fern Peckinpah's husband also wrought an interesting change in the new widow.

"My mother was truly a hypochondriac," Susan Peckinpah says, "in clinical terms. She was on a lot of medication and the fact is nothing was wrong with her. After his death, she got healthy."

THE DEADLY COMPANIONS began life as a screenplay, which languished on shelves all over Hollywood for three years. The script had been written by A. S. Fleischman and promoted by producer Charles FitzSimons, his partner. Unable to get any action on it, Fleischman wrote a novelization, which was published with surprising success. The script that the studios previously had turned their noses up at suddenly smelled pretty good.

FitzSimons and Fleischman, together with FitzSimons's sister, actress Maureen O'Hara, formed their own production company, to avoid outside interference. Securing financing from Pathe-America, FitzSimons was able to cast Brian Keith along with O'Hara. "They had just done a movie at Disney Studios called *The Parent Trap*," FitzSimons says. "I knew *Parent Trap* was going to be a big box-office picture. I thought that combination—getting the picture out after *Parent Trap*—would be a presold team and that our picture would do very well."

FitzSimons had not yet hired a director for his package. Keith, coming off "The Westerner," suggested Peckinpah: "It was Brian Keith who got me my first movie-directing break," Peckinpah said. "He'd been signed to star opposite Maureen O'Hara and he persuaded the producer to take me on."

"Peckinpah was not my choice to direct the movie," FitzSimons says. "Brian had a personal pact with Peckinpah that he'd have Peckinpah direct whatever movie he would do immediately after doing the TV series. To get Brian, whom I wanted very, very much, I accepted Peckinpah, based on looking at a number of episodes of 'The Westerner.' It had the right reality quality for what I wanted to do."

The friction that quickly developed between Peckinpah and FitzSimons set a pattern that would affect virtually Peckinpah's entire career. While some disagreements inevitably exist between creative artists (directors) and the people who sponsor them (producers), Peckinpah's loathing for producers eventually became almost reflexive—and not always justified—because of painful encounters early in his career.

Their first meetings were cordial. "He exuded charm," FitzSimons recalls, "because he wanted to do the picture. He had not done a theatrical motion picture. Brian had terrific confidence in him. And Sam was very, very charming."

But Peckinpah's disputes with FitzSimons began almost immediately, out of disagreements about Fleischman's script.

The story centered on a former Union soldier, Yellowleg, who is hunting Turk, the Confederate who tried to scalp him during the Civil War. Yellowleg still carries a bullet in his shoulder from the war, which makes his aim with a pistol erratic. He comes across Turk in a small town and manipulates Turk and a young gunslinger named Billy into teaming up with him to rob the bank in the next town, intending to kill Turk in the process.

Before they can carry out their plan, however, another gang robs it instead. In trying to shoot one of the robbers, Yellowleg's bullet goes astray and kills a small boy, the son of the town's dancehall girl, Kit Tildon. To atone, Yellowleg agrees to drive a wagon carrying the woman and the boy's body across the desert, so that the boy can be buried beside his father's grave in a distant ghost town. Billy and Turk accompany them.

Billy tries to rape Kit and Yellowleg beats him, then forces him to leave. Under cover of darkness, Turk also sneaks away. Yellowleg and Kit continue and Yellowleg's penance is taken to ridiculous lengths: Through various misfortunes, including snakes and Indians, Yellowleg and Kit are reduced to carrying the casket by hand across the desert to the ghost town of Siringo.

There, they are confronted by Turk and Billy, who have gone back to rob the bank and are now hiding out. Yellowleg has his showdown with Turk— but finally stops himself before killing the now-insane villain, letting the forces of justice take control of Turk's fate.

The Deadly Companions is a static, over-serious and downright poky Western. The coincidences and plot conveniences make the story all but unworkable. When it isn't sluggish, it's positively silly. Peckinpah, whose specialty was rewriting the material of others, assumed that FitzSimons was hiring him to perform much-needed surgery on the hackneyed screenplay.

"It was all based on gimmicks," Peckinpah said. "The scarred head, the dead boy being carried across the desert for five days. The one thing I will take credit for doing: At least I kept off [the dead body] enough that we weren't too conscious of it. To do it realistically would, I suppose, have been a lot of fun. You'd have buzzards flying over them and wearing masks and so on."

FitzSimons, however, had time and money invested in the script, as well as loyalty to Fleischman. "I'd spent three years developing this script; I had total confidence in the screenplay," FitzSimons says. When Peckinpah showed up for a meeting with twenty pages of rewrites, FitzSimons rejected Peckinpah's changes out of hand. FitzSimons says, "It didn't create the best auspices for the future."

Peckinpah said, "Every time I'd volunteer anything, he'd tell me to go back in the corner. I wanted to make a picture as best I could. He wanted someone he could push about."

Production began in Old Tucson, Arizona, a setting of old Western buildings maintained for production companies. They also shot on locations in the wilds of Arizona. Shooting started in January 1961; the budget was just over a half-million dollars. The shooting schedule was twenty days—leisurely compared to the three-day schedules Peckinpah had for a half-hour TV show but still hectic for a ninety-minute feature film.

Beside Keith, who was playing Yellowleg, and O'Hara, who played Kit Tildon, the cast included Steve Cochran as Billy, Chill Wills as Turk and, from Peckinpah's future stock company, Strother Martin as the parson in the town of Gila City, where Yellowleg, Billy and Turk go to rob the bank.

FitzSimons was on the set as much as possible, to oversee Peckinpah's work. There was a schedule to be met and FitzSimons wanted to be sure that Peckinpah kept it in mind. "I was in the position that I had to get it made on schedule," FitzSimons says. "I had my own money in it. I had to get that picture made and I had to get it made in twenty days; I did it in nineteen and a half. It was a very tight budget and a terrible struggle."

But FitzSimons couldn't keep his thumb on Peckinpah for the entire shoot. Peckinpah and Brian Keith did what they could to punch up the dialogue to give the picture more depth and believability.

"Brian had sense enough to know we were in trouble with the script," Peckinpah said. "So between us we tried to give the thing some dramatic sense. Consequently, all of his scenes have a certain strength, while those with Miss O'Hara (with whom I was forbidden to talk) come off not at all well. All I can say is this: You think it's bad dialogue, I think it's bad dialogue, but Mr. FitzSimons thought it was excellent dialogue."

FitzSimons resisted various images that Peckinpah felt were necessary to achieve the grittiness he hoped would disguise the script's problems. At one point, one of the remaining horses left to Kit and Yellowleg is threatened by a rattlesnake. Though Yellowleg kills the snake, the horse breaks its leg and has to be killed, leaving them with one animal to cart the corpse.

"He was determined to film the snake getting its head blown off on camera—a harbinger of his career to come!" FitzSimons says. "I tried to explain to him that the physical death of the snake had nothing to do with the scene. But he bugged me and bugged me and bugged me. Just to get rid of the aggravation, I brought in a rattlesnake. I got a sharpshooter and had him blow the head off the snake so Peckinpah could shoot it in close-up. I didn't even use the shot in the finished film." There is, however, a shot of the headless snake flying from the impact of the bullet.

William Clothier, the veteran cinematographer FitzSimons had hired for the film, recalled, "Poor Sam, [FitzSimons] was a goddamn idiot. Peckinpah really had his problems on that one. I was actually told not to cooperate with him. Sam and I understood each other. We had to, with all those idiots running around."

The finished film is a period curiosity, marked by its annoyingly omnipresent music, which highlights virtually every moment with a grating blend of Mexican guitar, accordion and harmonica. Keith, looking perpetually pained, walks through most of the film with gritted teeth, while O'Hara seems to be able to express only two emotions: annoyance and greater annoyance.

The most startling aspect of the film is the ending, which makes little sense. Peckinpah and FitzSimons wrangled over the final showdown, which wound up as a botched version that satisfied neither of them.

The original script called for a shoot-out between Yellowleg and Billy. It was set up by Yellowleg shooting at Turk, who takes off running, pausing only to return fire. Turk climbs up to the tower of an abandoned church and shoots at Yellowleg, whose shoulder injury affects his aim. Billy, Turk's partner throughout the film, steps in front of Yellowleg. He calls him, somewhat unwillingly; there is tension over whether Yellowleg can shoot straight enough to defend himself.

"There's only two horses in this town," Billy says, "and only two of us are riding out." They draw, and Yellowleg kills Billy. He then turns his attention back to Turk—but when he reaches his nemesis, Yellowleg finally realizes that revenge won't salve the wound on his soul that he's been carrying around for all those years. He leaves Turk, now gibbering insanely about his dream to start his own nation and lead a Comanchero army, to the opportunely arriving Gila City posse.

Peckinpah, however, saw Billy as a minor impediment to Yellowleg's thirst for revenge. As he filmed it, Yellowleg strides toward his confrontation with Turk when the flippant Billy casually steps in his way, saying it's time for them to have it out. Before the two of them can formally square off, Yellowleg, who has his gun in his hand, purposely shoots Billy point blank, without breaking stride or pausing to watch him die. "It's a brutal, realistic act," Peckinpah said.

After production was completed in February 1961, Peckinpah made his director's cut of the film and turned it in: "When he showed it to me, I said, 'Well, fine, Sam, I'll probably not leave two splices the way you have them,' " FitzSimons says. "It was just god-awful. I had to devise a whole new ending because of the way Peckinpah shot the scene with Billy."

In FitzSimons's version, which is the way the film still stands, Yellowleg is seen striding purposefully toward his showdown with Turk. Billy stands up to Yellowleg. So far, so good. Then FitzSimons cuts to a shot of Turk in the church tower, firing his gun. Cut back to Billy, apparently shot by Turk, sinking to his knees with a dying look of disbelief (which the audience probably shared) as Yellowleg walks past him.

"It was cut in such a way that it appears the shot comes from Turk, which changed the whole focus of the thing," Peckinpah said. "We had everybody riding off in the sunset, which wasn't my touch. Mr. FitzSimons took over the editing, scrapping my original cut. He then got into such a mess that he had to return to my original pattern."

FitzSimons disagrees: "I tried to bring the picture as closely back to what we intended to make in the first place."

FitzSimons justifies his actions by saying that as the producer who developed the material, he had every right to make it the way he wanted. "I don't believe in the auteur theory of directors. The director, like the cinematographer and the actor, is there to serve that project."

But Peckinpah said later, "I defy anyone to make sense of the ending."

No one tried to. *The Deadly Companions* did little box office in the United States, a fact that FitzSimons blames on the distributor, Pathe-America, which went belly-up before the film had finished its domestic run. Still, if *Deadly Companions* had been an obvious hit, Pathe probably could have found the will to live.

Aside from laying the groundwork for a lifelong hatred for producers, Peckinpah came out of the experience with some respectful reviews. *Variety* called it "an auspicious debut as a director by Sam Peckinpah, a fine TV helmsman," while the *Hollywood Reporter* referred to the director's "genuine feel for drama and film."

The *Los Angeles Times* said, "[Peckinpah] has brought a feel for authenticity . . . [and] an instinct for both cruelty and compassion. Peckinpah may be guilty of excesses and a too-deliberate pace. As a first release, Pathe-America may be surprised to find it has a more artistic than commercial cinema for a starter. In either event, watch Peckinpah."

THE DEADLY COMPANIONS was released in June 1961. Within a short span, Marie gave birth to their fourth child—a son, Mathew—and she and Peckinpah separated for the final time.

Despite the drinking and abuse he had inflicted upon Marie, it was Peckinpah, not Marie, who sought the divorce. He suspected that she had been unfaithful—at one point telling Joe Bernhard that he had walked in on her kissing another man—and hired a private detective to investigate his suspicions.

"He hired a private eye to watch me because he thought I was seeing someone and he suspected correctly," Marie says. "During the end of the marriage, I had a rather brief encounter with somebody who was very nice to me. I wanted someone to be nice to me at that point."

According to Bernhard, the detective produced compromising photographs, and Peckinpah, his male pride stung, filed for divorce.

"It was that whole macho thing: As long as you took care of your wife and kids, you were a man," Joe Bernhard says. "He had his feelings of possessiveness too. It was a patriarchal thing. If a woman betrays you, it's a lot heavier sin than if your best friend betrays you."

Peckinpah himself didn't have a spotless record of fidelity. Aside from his dalliances with prostitutes during his annual hunting trips, there were apparently other flings as well.

"I never had a detective watch, but I'm sure he was unfaithful, just because of intuition at different points," Marie says. "Sometimes you feel those things."

She had her suspicions confirmed after the divorce by an unlikely source: a psychiatrist both she and Peckinpah had seen individually near the end of the marriage, as a last-ditch effort to come to terms with their problems. Though she had never been comfortable with the process of psychotherapy, she returned to the doctor after the divorce to cope with guilt she was feeling.

"I felt Sam was a needy man," she says. "I was very angry with him, I'd lost respect for him but I felt guilty because I wasn't caring for him, so to speak. I was talking to the doctor about some of these issues and the doctor said, 'I don't know why you feel guilty. Don't you know Sam was unfaithful to you?' "

Even that didn't have the desired effect: "He said it to make me look at the whole scene and not waste a lot of my energy feeling guilty. And all I could think was, 'Oh my God, he shouldn't have broken that trust.' "

Peckinpah moved in with Bernhard. Even as he was pursuing his freedom, Peckinpah suddenly took a notion that, because of her romantic activity with other men, Marie was an unfit mother for their children. So he filed a petition to be awarded custody.

"It was funny because he didn't want to take care of them when we were married," Marie says. "Once he took me back to court when I was dating a man. I had a sense of him doing it just to keep me in a state of unsettledness, to put a certain sort of fear in me. I had a hundred people ready to say I was not an unfit mother."

The night before the custody hearing, Peckinpah called Marie, after a lengthy phone conversation with her mother, of whom he was still fond. According to Marie, Cecilia Selland "really read him the riot act. She'd told him he was a spoiled brat." As a result, Peckinpah offered to cancel the whole custody hearing, but Marie refused.

When they got to court the next day, Marie recalls, "The judge looked at him and said, 'I don't understand what this is about. I think you're wasting my time. Mr. Peckinpah, do you spend all your hours after work playing tiddlywinks? I suggest you and your lawyers discuss this in a civilized way and not waste my time.' We never went to court again."

The divorce became final on June 18, 1962. The impact on their children was considerable: "In a divorce, you lose both your parents for a period of time," Kristen says. "They're both so involved in the breakup that it puts another kind of pressure on the day-to-day level."

Kristen recalls her mother going to work as a secretary because of her fear that Peckinpah would cut off support. His support checks would be late on occasion: "Dad would say he was going to pull the rug out from under us," she says. "He was full of threats on a financial level. But sometimes Mom wouldn't remember to pay the bills and the electricity would be turned off. She'd say, 'Didn't I pay that?' One time she got a traffic ticket and forgot to pay it and they took her to jail. When she got out, she said, 'Don't tell your father.' "

Sharon, the oldest child, was the most resentful of the breakup. She would go along for the weekend visits, but says, "Those weekends were pretty riotous. He was drinking a lot and I'd be in charge of taking care of my siblings because I was older."

She finally began refusing to participate in the weekend visits—"Upon which I was sent to a psychiatrist because I didn't want to see my father," she says. "They were having problems and I was acting them out. The psychiatrist finally told them to lay off and let me do what I wanted."

Kristen says, "The only time Mom ever talked about the divorce was to Melissa and me. She said, 'Daddy is going to live someplace else,' and they were getting divorced and that was that. She never talked about it. I didn't know anybody else whose parents were divorced."

The same was true of Mathew Peckinpah, who has no memory of his parents living together. "The hardest part for me was the fact that I didn't have a 'normal' family," he says. "I often felt embarrassed when other kids at school would find out my parents were divorced."

When he moved out of the family house, Peckinpah promised his children that he would do his best to see more of them. His promise came true, to his chagrin. Used to being an absentee father, he found himself forced to spend large, concentrated blocks of time with them and seemed totally unprepared to do it.

Before the divorce, Kristen says, "He wasn't there as a day-to-day thing. He didn't sit down and have dinner with us. When they got divorced, he'd have to sit down and have dinner and he'd go crazy because our table manners weren't good. Mother was very loose and somewhat casual. I think that drove him crazy."

Initially Peckinpah lived at the Holiday House, a hotel on Pacific Coast Highway in Malibu. The weekend visits with his children would commence with a trip to the supermarket: "He would buy everything we wanted," Kristen says. "We were on a fairly tight budget at home so it was exciting. Potato chips, all the stuff Mom wouldn't let us have except if we were sick. Then sometimes we'd go to a toy store and buy toys. One time he bought us oil paints because he wanted us all to have artistic endeavors. That was kind of a blowout. He'd start out, full of 'Okay, we're going to do this' and before the day was over, something would have happened and it would be kind of a brawl. He'd blow up at everyone or one of us. We were like the unwashed masses."

Peckinpah's dissatisfaction with Marie's child-rearing philosophy was symptomatic of problems that had plagued them throughout their marriage. The child of a strict upbringing, Marie rebelled by giving license to her children and herself.

"She was very much a bohemian," says Betty Peckinpah, her sister-in-law. "Sam was brought up in a conventional, clean household where even the brand of chocolate you drank was important. Where you bought your clothes was important. But Marie couldn't have cared less. If she did anything wrong, he drove her to it."

But Kristen recalls at least one conversation with her father in which the emotion of the marital breakup seemed to overcome him.

"We were sitting in the Holiday House in the dark," she says. "Mostly he was talking about all the books Mom had stolen from him. He was sitting there crying, which is terrible when you're a kid. He was talking to me about divorce, saying that he'd never marry again. He said Mom would probably marry someone and I was to call this man Uncle Bill or whatever. The implication was that I wasn't to call anyone else Daddy. He was really upset and I felt bad. But I was a kid; I remember I was very anxious to get outside and go swimming in the pool at the hotel. Not long after that, of course, he had us out to his new house in Point Dume and introduced us to his new wife, Begonia."

Peckinpah and Joe Bernhard found a place together, a large rental house near Point Dume in Malibu surrounded by nests of pelicans, gulls and sandpipers, which they dubbed "the Bird House."

"It was an incredible place for two bachelors on the way up," Bernhard says. "Both of us drank real heavy. Sam had ended thirteen years of marriage and I had split with my lady after four years. We fucked a hell of a lot at the Bird House. I think it was his first adventure with all these long-legged, big-titted women. It was still a macho thing then."

Peckinpah's way of seducing women, Bernhard adds, was the forerunner of what would become known, more than twenty years later, as "the sensitive guy."

"He had the tenderest approach," Bernhard says. "The woman would say, 'I don't want to make it.' He would never pressure them; he'd talk to them instead, and, eventually, they would go to bed with him. Then they'd tell me how understanding and tender he was.

"After the Bird House, he seemed to be antiwomen. He reverted back to the old Madera-Fresno idea. In a lot of ways, Sam was always a North Fork square."

Despite what eventually became his image—the tough, brawling cowboy who feared no man—Kristen remembers Peckinpah as being extremely fearful for his children's safety. For example, he would harp upon the importance of wearing safety belts before they were a standard feature in most American cars.

"He was crazy for us to wear seatbelts and Mom wouldn't put them on us," Kristen says. "My aunt Judy's husband was killed in a car accident and so was my mother's father. Dad would go crazy. He would get very tight-lipped. He tended to lecture a lot."

If drivers in Malibu Colony sped down the streets, Peckinpah would go racing after them, screaming at them to slow down. Sharon recalls, "I can remember wanting to take walks when I was thirteen. He'd be worried about my taking a walk in Malibu because he thought there were gangs of boys. It was this funny duality in him. He expected you to be independent and confident. Then he'd lay this trip on you about how the world was a land mine and you couldn't be too careful."

He was also extremely squeamish about blood, particularly when the carnage was real. Several incidents from that period provide a marked contrast to the image Peckinpah would eventually develop as a result of the violence in his films.

Bernhard remembers sitting and drinking in the Malibu Inn on Pacific Coast Highway in March 1962, watching a prizefight on TV with Peckinpah. The boxers, as it happened, were Emile Griffith and Benny "Kid" Paret. Griffith beat Paret so badly that he died following the fight.

"Sam watched and suddenly said, 'My God, he's killing the guy,' " Bernhard recalls. "I said, 'Yeah, he sure is.' Sam went out of the bar and puked in the parking lot. He couldn't handle it."

Kristen recalls an incident where Mathew accidentally overturned a pot of boiling water on the stove, scalding himself severely. Mathew was rushed to the emergency room "but Dad couldn't drive. He just couldn't. Someone else had to."

Finally, Peckinpah panicked one afternoon while driving to pick up Sharon at a slumber party. Kristen, along for the ride, accidentally slammed her thumb in the door of Peckinpah's Corvette. The resulting cut was severe enough to warrant stitches.

"He had wrapped my thumb in Sharon's nightie and taken me to the emergency room," Kristen says. "And when they started to stitch me up, he started to faint. The nurse put a chair under him when he started to fall."

The macho dad, laid low by the sight of actual blood.

6

Elegy for the *High Country*

IT WAS "THE WESTERNER," DEAD FOR ALMOST A YEAR, that landed Peckinpah the job directing his second film, *Ride the High Country*.

The film's producer, Richard Lyons, was looking for a director and Peckinpah's agent at that time pitched her client, convincing the producer to look at his work on "The Westerner." Not only was Lyons sold; he showed the same episodes to reluctant studio executives at Metro-Goldwyn-Mayer, which was behind the project, and they too agreed that Peckinpah was the man for the film.

The script itself was by an aging alcoholic named N. B. Stone, Jr. Before his deal with MGM had been lined up, Lyons had mentioned his search for a solid script to William Roberts, who shared his office at MGM. Roberts remembered a script a friend of his, Stone, had written several years before. Lyons got a commitment from the studio, based on Roberts's description of the script, only to discover that Stone's screenplay was an incoherent 145-page quagmire. Chagrined, Roberts himself rewrote the script, something the drunken and agoraphobic Stone refused to do.

Based on that version, Lyons was able to sign two semiretired legends of movie Westerns for the two central roles: Joel McCrea and Randolph Scott. The story was about two aging former lawmen, Steve Judd and Gil Westrum, who are hired to guard a gold shipment on its way down from a mountain mining camp in the Sierras to the town below. While one of them sees this as a chance at one more honorable job, the other decides that this is his last opportunity at a big score, even if it means breaking the law. Set in turn-of-the-century California, the film opens with shots of a Western town that is on the cusp between the past—horses—and the future: cars.

McCrea was originally cast as Gil Westrum, the lawman who turns bad, with Scott in the role of Steve Judd, the righteous ex-marshal. Fortuitously, both actors decided they were miscast and, not realizing they both felt the same way, made independent queries of the producer about the possibility of exchanging roles. With a minimum of fuss, the parts were reversed: McCrea would play the upright Judd and Scott would play the shifty Westrum. With his stars in place, Lyons made his offer to Peckinpah, who read the script and accepted the job.

Even as he began casting, Peckinpah started his own rewrite of the script. In later years, he would take credit for drawing upon his own personal knowledge of the area and its history in doing the rewrite; at the time, however, he said, "It's very difficult to write about things you don't know. Those mining sequences and the brothel sequences, for instance, took a great deal of research, but it paid off."

He enlivened the dialogue, adding depth to the characters while infusing bits of his own past into the script. Inadvertently or not, he remolded the central characters into people more familiar to him.

Paul Seydor, a critic who closely analyzed all of Peckinpah's films in his book *Peckinpah: The Western Films* and subsequently became a friend of the director, says, "I think Randolph Scott was the image of himself that Sam wanted to see. And Joel McCrea was a more ideal image of his father."

Peckinpah gave Steve Judd the film's most quoted line, drawing it from discussions about the Bible he remembered hearing his father have around the dinner table. Peckinpah recalled a section of the Gospel of St. Luke, 18:14: "I tell you, this man went down to his house justified rather than the other; for every one that exalteth himself shall be abased; and he that humbleth himself shall be exalted."

Toward the end of the film, Gil Westrum, who is planning to steal the gold and has been trying to determine if Steve Judd will help him, asks Judd, "Do you know what's on the back of a poor man when he dies? The clothes of pride. They're not a bit warmer to him dead than alive. Is that what you want, Steve?"

To which Judd replies, "All I want is to enter my house justified," a line that Peckinpah had heard his father use.

Another line came from Peckinpah's living arrangement with Joe Bernhard, who had a black girlfriend. "She let the word 'peckerwood' slip one time and Sam says, 'What the fuck is that?' " says Bernhard. "She said, 'It's a WASP who hates niggers.' " At the end of *Ride the High Country*, when Gil and Steve goad the Hammond brothers, the film's villains, into a shoot-out, one of the slurs they toss at them, along with "Southern trash," is "peckerwood," perhaps the first time the word had been used in a Hollywood film.

One final Peckinpah touch: In the original script, it was Gil Westrum, newly redeemed by his decision to give up the gold and fight the Hammond brothers, who is killed in the gun battle. Peckinpah knew instinctively that the film would have more poignance if the upright Steve Judd died instead.

To fill the other roles, he began calling on actors with whom he had worked in television. He cast L. Q. Jones, whom he'd met while working for Don Siegel, and Warren Oates, whom he'd directed in "The Rifleman" and "The Westerner," as two of the crazier Hammond brothers; both would become part of Peckinpah's stock company over the years.

So would R. G. Armstrong, who had quit "The Rifleman" to return to theater. He was cast as the father of the heroine, a Bible-thumping farmer with a sadistic streak.

Billy Hammond was a key role, a character who begins as a romantic figure but quickly reveals himself as a backwoods savage. Peckinpah offered it to his friend Robert Culp, who was looking for a chance to break into motion pictures. To his surprise, and Culp's eternal regret, Culp turned it down.

"I didn't want to do it because I was trying to create a career in features and I was fighting to be a leading man," Culp says. "If I'd done that, I would have wound up like Bruce Dern, playing crazies. In terms of mistakes in my life, that was one of mine. He never forgave me. And he never offered me another part. All the people who were part of his stock company were his friends and, as an actor, I was bitter at not being one of them that he called on. It was because I turned him down."

Instead, he offered the role to James Drury, whom he had directed in an episode of "Trackdown" for television a couple of years earlier. "I'd been a contract player at MGM, but this was my first film," Drury says. "I was pleased to be working on it with Joel McCrea and Randolph Scott, together."

Peckinpah cast Ron Starr, a former car salesman, as Heck Longtree, Gil Westrum's impetuous partner. For the role of Elsa, Peckinpah took a chance on a young stage actress who showed up at MGM with her hair cropped short from playing Joan of Arc in Chicago—Mariette Hartley.

Elsa was a part that most of the young contract actresses at MGM hungered after. Though this was a low-budget film (about $800,000), it was obviously a terrific role, with two major stars, semiretired though they might have been. Hartley, on the other hand, came from a relatively sheltered background and admits she didn't even know who Joel McCrea was when she walked in to audition.

"Sam was in this little room, with a cowboy hat and boots and his feet on a desk," Hartley says. "He kept me there reading the entire day. He turned to me at one point and said, 'I think you're wonderful.' "

Peckinpah had her read opposite various young men who were auditioning to play Heck. Though she was flattered, she didn't realize that it was a good sign. She found out she had the part three weeks later and was brought back for a screen test, along with four or five finalists for the role of Heck (including Wayne Rogers).

"I did the screen test in Deborah Kerr's old wig from *Quo Vadis*," she says. "Sam took me aside and said, 'I hate the wig. I think it's shit. Keep your regular hair.' "

As they prepared to leave for the location in the Sierras, Peckinpah took a particular interest in Hartley's costume. Hartley recalls probing the bowels of the MGM wardrobe department for dresses with Peckinpah. Once he found one he liked, he repeatedly sent her back into the dressing room, instructing the studio tailor to pad her chest more fully.

"Sam always liked breasts," she says, "and he wanted me to be larger than I was. He kept adding padding until, in profile, I looked like a busty lady. By the time we finished the afternoon, I literally was walking at a tilt."

It was a relatively low-budget picture for MGM, which had recently gone significantly over budget on the Marlon Brando remake of *Mutiny on the Bounty*, a box-office bust. Peckinpah convinced MGM to let him film the riding sequences on location and took the cast and crew to Mammoth Lake, near Bishop, California. The settings were in the High Sierras; the fictional location of the mining camp was Coarsegold, California. The real Coarsegold was on the other side of the mountains, near Peckinpah Mountain.

Shooting began at the beginning of October 1961. Within four days, a freak snowstorm hit and MGM told Lyons to bring the production back to the MGM lot in Hollywood. MGM pulled the plug without telling Peckinpah; when he arrived to shoot that morning, he was told to get on the bus with the rest of the cast and crew and head back to Los Angeles.

"Literally five miles down the road, the weather was clear," Hartley says. "It just got him in the gut. It was a devastating blow; there was no sense of the amount of money being lost—instead, a dream was being lost. He wanted it to be a true Western and he didn't want to fake it."

Peckinpah began drinking and playing cards on that bus ride back to L.A. Hartley, who had grown up with an alcoholic father, made a remark and Peckinpah turned on her, scalding her with his tongue. "He became what I had experienced with alcoholics—his whole personality changed," she says. "That made me know he was an alcoholic. But there was only that one day that he was drinking on the film. When he wasn't drinking, he was an extraordinary human being."

Back in Hollywood, Peckinpah continued shooting through the end of November 1961, at a variety of spots: the MGM back lot, the Twentieth Century-Fox ranch, Malibu Canyon and Bronson Canyon in Griffith Park. When he had to shoot the mining-camp scenes that called for snow, the location was sprayed with soap foam, which stuck to the canvas tents (cut from sails from *Mutiny on the Bounty*) and turned the ground into a muddy mess.

Peckinpah and cinematographer Lucien Ballard, who had worked together initially in television, did what they could to give the film both beauty and authenticity. Some years later, Ballard was asked by film critic Leonard Maltin about a particularly striking close-up of Joel McCrea at the beginning of the film and said, "Well, that might have been because we couldn't show the water towers and other things in the background at the Metro lot. Everything in this business is a compromise. Chances are we had to do it because of necessity."

As he shot, Peckinpah didn't fill in with much coverage—the method of shooting in which each scene is shot from different angles. Peckinpah tended to edit in his head and in the camera; he knew what he wanted and only shot that (although he still shot large amounts of film). So there wasn't the conventional amount of coverage showing up each day in the screening of the rushes. That led Lyons—or Sol Siegel, head of MGM production (there is some disagreement)—to send Peckinpah a note: "Who do you think you are—John Ford?"

With the exception of being forced to abandon the mountain locations, much of *Ride the High Country* was smooth shooting. Peckinpah fired a few crew members, though nowhere near as many as he would on subsequent films. Otherwise, the actors recall it as a satisfying experience.

"He was innovative, imaginative, always anxious to work with actors on their characters," James Drury says. "He'd get involved in heavy-duty discussions but he didn't overdirect—he'd consult. He had a tremendous amount of respect for McCrea and Scott and they had a lot of respect for him. They were pleased to be working in the picture. At that point, he was a happy man. We knew him at his best and his most likable."

Peckinpah loved to tease Hartley, knowing that she was just naive enough to fall for it. At one point, she wore the wrong socks in a scene that was filmed in a long shot, where her socks would not even be visible.

"Somebody must have tipped him off," Hartley recalls. "From a quarter-mile away, I heard, 'Christ, girl, you wore a different pair of socks!' "

The innocent young actress was convinced that her mistake was an unforgivable one. "That SOB really made me believe I'd ruined the shot because of my socks," she says. "I'm such a patsy. I knew that a lot of contract players wanted the part. He told me, 'If you don't behave, if you're really rotten, I'm going to give your part to Joan Staley.' "

Yet Hartley could tell that the teasing came from affection. "From the day I walked into his office, I felt blessed," she says. "I was very enamored of him. I knew he meant it when he said he thought I was wonderful. I felt I could do exactly what he wanted. He was, in many ways, the successful father I'd never had.

"He was great-looking—handsome, quite small, earthy and boyish and attractive. He had a tendency to fall in love with his leading ladies and I think it happened, although it wasn't a love affair. He'd call during editing to say that the stuff looked wonderful and that he was living with me every day."

The film ranks as one of Peckinpah's four or five best. It established a theme that Peckinpah would return to over and over throughout his career: the man whose time has passed him by, looking for one last opportunity to make the world the way it used to be, when he was at his best.

"Sam made one picture fourteen times," L. Q. Jones says, not quite kidding. "It's about himself, a guy who comes along at a time he doesn't belong. His movies were about men."

There is both wry humor and poignance to Peckinpah's characters in the film. McCrea, as the righteous (but not self-righteous) Judd, is full of self-deprecating wit that can't disguise an unshakable moral integrity. Scott brings a bitter edge to Westrum's constant irony. His wisecracks unwind at a leisurely pace, only to sting as he cracks the whip on each line with exquisite timing.

Although MGM had its own staff editors, Peckinpah was allowed to edit the film with his own editor, Frank Santillo. The two of them came up with a cut in January 1962 that pleased Sol Siegel enormously.

It also pleased one of the major participants—Joel McCrea, who wrote Peckinpah a letter: "It was a pleasure to do a picture with a man who can write, direct and knows the West. I saw the picture at the studio and think everyone connected with it did a good job. I hope the public likes it as well as I do. If so, we have a hit. I'll expect to hear big things about you in the years ahead."

But Joseph Vogel, head of Loews Inc., MGM's parent company at that time, hated the film. According to reports, the only time he screened *Ride the High Country*, he fell asleep during the first reel, snored loudly throughout, then jumped up at the end to proclaim, "That's the worst picture I ever saw!" He fired Siegel and barred Peckinpah from the MGM lot.

"MGM didn't have a lot of confidence in it," Drury recalls. "They didn't put money into publicity and it didn't last in initial release."

Because of Vogel's antipathy, *Ride the High Country* was figuratively buried, put out as the second half of a double feature with either *The Tartars* or *Boys' Night Out*. The film was in the form that Peckinpah wanted it—but it was released in such a way as to guarantee that hardly anyone would see it.

"MGM saw *Ride the High Country* as a low-budget quickie they could throw away in the second halves of summer double features," Peckinpah said later. "If I'd tried to talk to them about the basic theme of the picture, which was salvation and loneliness, they'd have fired me on the spot. Even so, they hated what I'd done and they threw me out."

That the film is still hailed as one of the memorable efforts of 1962 is significant. The major films of the year included *Lawrence of Arabia, To Kill a Mockingbird, Bird Man of Alcatraz, Days of Wine and Roses, The Miracle*

Worker, Whatever Happened to Baby Jane?, The Manchurian Candidate, Lolita, The Longest Day and *The Man Who Shot Liberty Valance.*

Despite MGM's efforts to bury the film, critics found it—and hailed it, while taking MGM to task in the process.

Newsweek: "That Hollywood can't tell the gold from the dross has seldom been so plainly demonstrated. *Ride the High Country,* deemed unworthy of a first-class run, has been gradually leaked—like a secret—to various theaters around the country. When it reached New York last week, *Ride,* a modest, meaningful and faultlessly crafted film, was dumped carelessly as the bottom half of neighborhood double bills, playing in the abysmal company of *The Tartars.* In fact, everything about this picture has the ring of truth, from the unglamorized settings to the flavorful dialogue and the natural acting. *Ride the High Country* is pure gold."

Arthur Knight in *Saturday Review:* "*High Country* is a straight adventure film—no message, no re-creation of an historic incident, not even a particularly 'big' picture. But it works, with a difference. Directed by Sam Peckinpah, the film presents an offbeat and attractive heroine in Mariette Hartley, the pleasure of watching two old pros working comfortably with what is for them unaccustomed material and the most deglamorized version of the West since the old William S. Hart movies."

Time: "Under Sam Peckinpah's tasteful direction it is a minor chef d'oeuvre among Westerns. *Ride the High Country* has a rare honesty of script, performance and theme—that goodness is not a gift but a quest. The Western has always been a stance as well as a story, and when actors with the unforced dignity of McCrea and Scott go, the old breed of Western will go with them."

If the film died a quick death on American screens, it was hailed in Europe, where it was released in 1963 as *Guns in the Afternoon.* It won the top prize at the Belgium Film Festival (over Fellini's *8 1/2*) and the award as best foreign film that year in the Mexican Film Festival in Mexico City. To this day, Drury says, people come up to him and mention it as one of their favorites. "The picture keeps following me around," he says. "People still talk about it all the time. It was a real high point in my career. But you never know how good it is while you're doing it."

Peckinpah got another vote of confidence from McCrea, who wrote to him later in 1962: "Congratulations! As Dick will tell you, business is poor everywhere on most films. But I keep telling him that the important thing is we made a good one! (The cream rises!) Your old friend, Steve Judd."

Other critics also developed a loyalty to the film. Andrew Sarris, at that time the critic for the *Village Voice,* says, "I still like it. I realized there was a revisionist element to it. I like the nobility of it; it was an anti-Western but it was heroic."

The film also caught the attention, some years later, of critic Pauline Kael, who saw it on a double bill in 1966 or 1967 with *Major Dundee,* Peckinpah's next picture. She was so excited by what she had seen that she tracked Peckinpah down at his home in Malibu and called him up, just to tell him how much she liked his work. She became one of his critical champions and a friend for years to come.

As a result of a similar reaction to *Ride the High Country,* another even closer relationship developed. Jim Silke, a young man who was executive art director at Capitol Records and a cinephile, had seen *Ride the High Country* with *Boys' Night Out,* at a drive-in and was so impressed that he decided to interview Peckinpah for *Cinema* magazine, which he had started a year or so earlier.

"I put it together with 'The Westerner,' which I thought was pretty great, and said, 'I've got to interview this guy,' " Silke recalls. "It was the start of a long relationship.

"When I met him the first time, he was a dandy. He had dark black hair and a cigarette holder like FDR. He made an appearance: dark sport coat, brown Levi's. I asked him why he had used two old has-beens and he screamed. He said these guys had the greatest walks in Hollywood. But I hung in with him and he liked that. After that, we kept seeing each other."

Their relationship would quickly turn into friendship and a collaboration that would last the rest of Peckinpah's life.

WITH *RIDE THE HIGH COUNTRY* finished, Peckinpah went back to work for Dick Powell, putting together two shows for his new anthology program, "The Dick Powell Theater."

The first was "Pericles on 31st Street," based on a story by writer Harry Mark Petrakis. It starred Theodore Bikel as a modern-day Pericles, a peanut vendor who stands up to a local political boss. In doing so, he gives the other residents of the slum neighborhood the gumption to follow his example.

Petrakis was a Chicago writer, the author of three books who had never written for television before. Peckinpah had been given the "Pericles" story by Lucien Ballard and had brought Petrakis to Los Angeles to develop the script. Petrakis would drive out to Peckinpah's house in Malibu for writing sessions, where they would talk and eat and write together.

"He'd go over pages of dialogue and draw a red pencil through them," Petrakis says. "He'd say, 'This is great dialogue—but when you've got a camera, you don't need it.' He had a very perceptive sense of how a story could be transposed to film. I didn't feel he was trying to overwhelm me. He loved my story. He wanted its fullest potential realized."

Even working on an hour-long TV show, Peckinpah was a perfectionist, seeking the best from himself and his crew. As a result, schedules often went out the window.

Theodore Bikel recalls, "On the second day of shooting, we were one day behind schedule. He didn't give a damn about schedules; he just cared about the work and the result of the work. It was rather liberating. In TV, you had to be not only good but fast. When he chose to be slow, it was because fast didn't serve the screenplay or his vision of it."

Peckinpah was generous to his collaborators. Bikel mentioned in passing that he had neglected to tell his agent to get him a kinescope of the show. In the days before videocassette recorders, the only copies of a TV show were the filmed 16mm kinescopes; some actors would have contractual clauses ensuring that they received kinescopes of their work.

"Halfway through the shoot, I said, 'Damn it, I like this so much but I forgot to tell my agent to make it part of the deal to get a print of the show.' Sam said, 'I'll get you a kine, but it'll cost you.' I said, 'I'll pay.' He said, 'I don't mean money. It'll cost you an evening with a guitar and two girls.' So we went out and had a terrific meal someplace and then went back to my hotel. We sat and drank and played music and joked. It was very convivial."

Peckinpah's next project for Powell was "The Losers," an updated version of "The Westerner." Written by Bruce Geller, it was moved out of the Old West and set in contemporary times but with the same two principal characters: Dave Blassingame (played this time by Lee Marvin) and Burgundy Smith (now portrayed by Keenan Wynn). The show was a hit; there was serious talk about turning it into a series, something both Wynn and Marvin were willing to commit to.

Western novelist Max Evans, who met Peckinpah around this time, says, "I once accused him of stealing 'The Losers' from two of my novels, *The Rounders* and *The Hi Lo Country*. He said, 'Of course. It just shows what good taste I have.' "

But Dick Powell died suddenly of cancer, leaving Four Star in disarray. His successor at first refused to meet Marvin's price for a "Losers" series; by the time he came around, Marvin had moved on to other projects.

Powell's death squelched another project Peckinpah was working on for "The Dick Powell Theater." This one was a script by Peckinpah's friend Robert Culp, whom Peckinpah had talked into fleshing out a two-page outline.

Titled "The Gunfighter," it was to star Culp and Tuesday Weld. Culp, who had spent a year after the cancellation of "Trackdown" on the state-fair and rodeo circuit doing gun tricks ("I was a drugstore cowboy"), would play a fast-gun champion who goes to a big quick-draw competition in Las Vegas. When he only comes in fifth, he goes berserk, killing police and eventually being killed himself.

"It was the best thing I'd ever written," Culp says. "It was right on the edge and Sam was going to direct it. Then Dick Powell died and that was the end of the series."

It was also the start of a fifteen-year pattern in their relationship. Culp would write scripts, Peckinpah would try to arrange a production to direct— and then the deal would fall through. "In all those years, we never got one thing done together," Culp says. "It was all done for no money and not one word got on screen."

Peckinpah next had a shot at a possible film project at Walt Disney Studios called *Little Britches,* based on a novel by Ralph Moody. Peckinpah wrote a script called *The Boy and the Gunfighter,* dealing with themes similar to those he had tried to examine in "The Rifleman." Despite some enthusiastic meetings with Walt Disney himself, Peckinpah eventually fell out with the producer. "He wanted a rewrite, to bring more children and dogs into it," Peckinpah said after leaving the project.

Peckinpah continued looking for another project. He lived the bachelor life in Malibu, seeing his children on weekends for barbecues and beach parties, usually with his sister Fern Lea, her husband Walter, their children, as well as other friends and their kids.

"I think he never had much faith in being able to deal with [his children]by himself," his ex-wife Marie says. "So he'd always make a situation where there were a lot of other people around."

As his daughter Sharon says, "My father had his priorities: his work, his drinking and then his children came into it. Our welfare was high on his list of priorities but not necessarily seeing us."

By the summer of 1963, Peckinpah was in negotiations to direct his first major motion picture, a Civil War cavalry epic to star Charlton Heston for Columbia Pictures: *Major Dundee.*

A few months earlier, Jim Silke's interview with Peckinpah had been published in his *Cinema* magazine. Among other things, Silke had asked about his favorite films and directors. The list of directors who had most influenced him was headed by Fellini, Kurosawa, Kazan and Ford; his list of favorite films included *Rashomon, Treasure of the Sierra Madre* and *La Strada.*

But Peckinpah couldn't have known how the answers to a handful of Silke's questions would come back to haunt him—both in the decades to come and in the immediate future.

"SILKE: Should a director have full control of the final cut?
"PECKINPAH: It depends upon the director.
"SILKE: How can he get this? What holds him back? How did you get it? Will you insist—perhaps that's the wrong word—will you sometimes work around to it?
"PECKINPAH: One at a time. Let's take how can he get this? What holds him back? Many things hold him back. Usually the fact that

somebody knows more, has more control, more money and considers (and they're very often right) that they have better judgment than he does.

"SILKE: How did you get it?

"PECKINPAH: I was very careful about compromising.

"SILKE: Will you work without final control?

"PECKINPAH: It depends on whom I work for."

Part Three

1963-1968

Now, with the success of Ride the High Country *behind him, Peckinpah is able to make his next film as he wishes. His personal background and, one gathers, his personal taste and vision of life are reasonably congruent with something the industry is used to. So long as his vision does not become too harsh, too flamboyant or too unorthodox, he should be able to work freely and successfully.*

—ERNEST CALLENBACH, FROM "A CONVERSATION WITH SAM PECKINPAH," *Film Quarterly,* Winter 1963–64

7

A "Major" Project

As EARLY AS 1959, PECKINPAH HAD BEEN INVOLVED with the idea for a film based on the James Gould Cozzens novel *Castaway*. A short work, it detailed a few days in the life of a Mr. Lecky, who finds himself alone, like Robinson Crusoe, but in a department store. There evidently has been some cataclysm, for there is no electricity. He forages around until he has created a living space, which he equips with candles, flashlights, camping equipment, canned food—and weapons. The first time he sees another human being, he kills him.

"My plan at present is to begin *Castaway* as soon as I finish *Major Dundee*, which means sometime in May," Peckinpah wrote to producer Samuel X. Abarbanel at the end of September 1963.

But Peckinpah never did make *Castaway*, though he came close on several occasions. He carried a copy of the screenplay around with him for most of his life. When nothing else was in the works, he would pull it out and rewrite it, as a way of resurrecting the dormant project for himself. If all else failed, he figured he could always make *Castaway*.

In the fall of 1963, Peckinpah was about to become a figurative Mr. Lecky: alone, cut off, scrambling to stay alive and not realizing that he was his own worst enemy. It was a period that, in one way or another, lasted for four years. And it began with *Major Dundee*.

In retrospect, it is easy to see *Major Dundee* as doomed from the start. None of the three principal parties involved—Columbia Pictures, the studio that was making the film; Charlton Heston, the film's star; and Peckinpah, the director—agreed what the film was about. But none of them realized this until afterward.

The studio thought it was making a standard cavalry-versus-Indians action film. Heston, on the other hand, wrote in his journal at the time that a lunch with the film's producer, Jerry Bresler, and Columbia brass in June 1963 to discuss the script "seemed to promise a chance to include in the film an honest statement about the Civil War, which has never been seriously treated in film."

Six months later, Heston made another journal entry: "We still haven't isolated exactly what this picture's about . . . maybe because we can't agree or just don't know. It has to be about the Civil War, I'm convinced."

But before the film even started production, Peckinpah was quoted in an interview as saying, "Very simply, it's the story of a strong-minded major who takes it upon himself to run down an Apache predator. Actually, the chase is subordinate to what happens within the man. It's high adventure and I hope a little something else."

Major Dundee grew out of a script outline by Harry Julian Fink. Jerry Bresler, a producer who had worked with Heston on the film *Diamond Head,* had a deal with Columbia and the script treatment by Fink. Using both of them, he was able to convince Heston to sign on.

"The unfinished script appealed to me because of the character," Heston says. "Also, I'd wanted to make a picture about the Civil War, which had not been done. I was still young and naive and thought it could be that."

At that point, Heston was one of the biggest stars in Hollywood, an actor of Biblical proportions based on his larger-than-life performances in *The Ten Commandments, El Cid* and *Ben Hur,* for which he had won the Oscar. He was powerful enough to demand—and receive—director approval on any project.

Bresler had seen and admired *Ride the High Country.* He screened the film for Heston, who says, "It impressed me enormously. I called Sam and said, 'I'd love to work with you.' "

Production was scheduled to begin in October 1963. Peckinpah and Heston moved into an office together at Columbia to begin preproduction, including working on the script.

"The office had a largish central room," Heston recalls. "I'm a pacer during discussions; I walk up and down. So did Sam. One day he called me in and he had put a big strip of masking tape on the carpet. He said, 'You pace this side and I'll pace that side.' "

When Fink completed the first draft, however, it was a sprawling mess, with several different story lines intertwined. Production was put off until January 1964, to give Peckinpah and a new writer, Oscar Saul, a chance to sort it out and put it into better shape.

Even then, when shooting began in Mexico shortly after the beginning of the new year, the script was not complete. As he was trying to master new locations and the logistics of filming a huge action film with hundreds of extras, Peckinpah was trying each night to find the final shape for his film.

The story centers on Major Amos Dundee, a Virginian who fought for the North in the Civil War. Because of his misguided initiative during the Battle of Gettysburg, he has now been reduced to commandant of a prison full of Confederate prisoners in Texas in 1864.

Apaches, led by the bloodthirsty chief Sierra Chariba, wipe out a platoon of Dundee's men and the family whose ranch they have stopped at. The Indians take three white children with them; Dundee decides to give chase. But he lacks the men or the authority to do so. So he recruits Confederate prisoners, including Capt. Ben Tyreen, a former West Point classmate of Dundee's who bears him a longstanding grudge.

They chase the Apache into Mexico, a breach of international law. Though they get the children back, Dundee decides to continue the search for Chariba. But they spend weeks and then months on his trail, with only ambushes and casualties to show for it. Dundee confronts failure after failure, all under the watchful eye of Tyreen.

When Dundee is wounded due to his own carelessness, his men press on without him while he recuperates. Tyreen finally comes back for him and they use their last opportunity to kill Sierra Chariba. They then must face French forces they have antagonized. It is Tyreen who finally saves Dundee's life and sacrifices his own, teaching his former friend and antagonist a lesson about honor and duty as Dundee takes his men back to the United States.

As Dundee, Heston was a given. The role of Tyreen was more of a question mark. Bresler's initial inclination was to hire Richard Harris, the Irish actor who had made a big impression in *This Sporting Life*. When negotiations with Harris hit a snag, Anthony Quinn and Steve McQueen were both considered. Eventually, however, Harris signed on.

Lee Marvin was approached to play Samuel Potts, Dundee's one-armed scout, but turned it down; instead, James Coburn was signed for the role. Michael Anderson, Jr., and Jim Hutton were cast as Dundee's top subordinates; Senta Berger, a German actress, was picked to be the love interest who ultimately leads Dundee astray. To fill out the ranks of Dundee's men, Peckinpah looked to his expanding stock company, which included L. Q. Jones, Warren Oates, R. G. Armstrong, Ben Johnson and Slim Pickens.

Peckinpah had a $3 million budget and a sufficient shooting schedule to film what he thought would be a Western epic. It would be a road picture, booked to play with an intermission and reserved seats.

Despite problems in completing the script, Peckinpah was convinced that this film would be shot and made his way. He got his first inkling that the picture would be problematic shortly before production began.

"Jerry Bresler gave his blessing to what we wanted to do, though when it came time to shoot, he double-crossed us by ordering fifteen days cut from the schedule two days prior to starting," Peckinpah said. "I said what he was asking was impossible, that I would rather leave the picture there and then. To which he replied, 'Look, I'm acting under instructions from New York. Leave it to me, I'll take care of it.' But he never did."

"Dundee was set up to be a film with intermissions," Jim Silke recalls, "but the producers had a shooting schedule for a B film."

Assessments of Bresler's talent as a producer vary. James Coburn calls him "a candy-bar-eating prick." Stuntman Joe Canutt, who worked for Peckinpah on *Major Dundee* and *The Wild Bunch,* says, "Bresler was typical of Columbia: tight and cheap and into nickel-and-diming. Sam wanted to make a David Lean picture on a Jerry Bresler purse. Sure, Lean can sit for six months until the flowers grow. But the result is *Dr. Zhivago* and *Lawrence of Arabia.*"

Heston, on the other hand, recalls Bresler as competent and professional. "He was an extremely able producer," Heston says, "a very pleasant fellow, intelligent, experienced. But you needed something more to deal with Sam."

The entire picture was shot on location. Peckinpah wanted to shoot in New Mexico but Columbia elected to make the picture in Mexico, to save money. Production chores, including much of the costuming, were farmed out to Mexico City's Churubusco Studios in a cost-cutting effort. But the work was shoddy and needed redoing, which inflated the budget.

Peckinpah was a perfectionist, even at this early date. Here was a picture about a cavalry unit hunting Indians for months. Each of the men, including the principals, has to look progressively scruffier as the picture goes on. So Peckinpah insisted that each of them have a range of costumes, from the snappy new uniforms they start in to the torn and tattered remnants they're left with at the end.

It was a point about which Peckinpah occasionally wrangled with his peers and mentors. Director Peter Bogdanovich remembers Peckinpah and John Ford discussing that issue—the look of soldiers who have been in the field. "Sam had a revisionist view of Westerns which was very different from Ford," Bogdanovich recalls. "He was talking to Ford and he said, 'You know, they didn't have these perfectly pressed, picture-perfect uniforms in the cavalry.' Ford said, 'Yeah, but it looks great in color, doesn't it?' "

Heston still sees the decision to begin production without a completed script as one of the gravest errors. In early February 1964, a month after production began, he wrote in his journal, "I spent some time today thinking about the rewrite Sam's done for us on *Major Dundee.* There are holes in it, serious holes, I think. That means either he knows a lot less about scripts than I do . . . or a lot more. I'm perfectly willing to accept the latter premise, but it's a bit spooky just now."

Peckinpah had problems right off the bat with Tom Dawson, head of wardrobe at Columbia, who was in charge of costumes for *Major Dundee.* Unhappy with Dawson's designs and Churubusco's execution, Peckinpah insisted on bringing in Jim Silke to help with design ideas.

Despite Silke's efforts, the wardrobe department was woefully behind. In an effort to bring it up to snuff, Columbia called on Dawson's son, Gordon, who was only a rung or two higher than an apprentice, to go to Mexico City and then on to Durango, Mexico, to help with costumes.

"I was working in the basement at Columbia, aging the clothes," Gordon Dawson says. "One day, I got a call from Columbia, saying, 'You're going to Mexico tomorrow and, by the way, can you smuggle in a Panavision lens?' It was my first important assignment. I was in terror. Sam had already fired half of the department heads. My old man's job was looking shaky. Everyone was scared of Sam. I flew down there, looked around and thought, 'What happened to my life that I wound up here?'" It was a question Dawson would ask himself many times over the years, after becoming part of Peckinpah's inner circle.

Conditions while filming in the wilds of Mexico were, at best, primitive and, at worst, brutal.

"It was the most intense, hardest film I've ever been on, a real medal-earner," James Coburn says. He recalls one location at Chilpancingo where "we were working in the river. The river was a foot deep and the water was red and hot. Along the shore, you couldn't walk through the layer of flies. Everyone was stuck in the honey wagon. You had to be on the set every day, whether you were working or not. You'd sit for weeks with nothing to do. Then you'd do the work great because you were seething in this atmosphere. That contributed to the sense of misery of a group of soldiers going to Mexico to find an Indian."

R. G. Armstrong says, "We thought we wouldn't get out of Mexico alive."

Peckinpah had his own share of wild times. "One night I ended up in this Mexican whorehouse, as I have a habit of doing," he recalled. "And I was drinking. This French guy across from me made some remark and so I went for him. Cleared off the goddamned table, y'know, went right over it. My friend tried to stop me so I caught him on the chin. The French guy had already split so I ran over to the door, broke a goddamned whiskey bottle on the wall, held it in front of me and said, 'All right, who wants it?' Nobody came. So I threw it down, picked up this chair and threw it right across the room at the glass wall and said, 'Is anybody going to try me?' Well, they did. I woke up in the john with this Mexican whore kneeling over me, trying to revive me. They had kicked every single part of my body except my balls. Broke a rib, too."

Peckinpah used his sense of imminent, self-inflicted madness to shape the performances of his actors. That was particularly true of Heston, playing an obsessed man whose twisted notion of revenge was mixed up with a perverse sense of honor. Peckinpah's direction, Heston says, came as much from his own behavior off the set as from things he actually told Heston about Dundee.

"You had to be married to Sam to make a film and I was," Heston says. "What quality the performance has stems from Sam subconsciously imposing Dundee's circumstances on me in shooting. We were constantly on horseback in miserable country in miserable conditions and on into the night, when he would take me drinking in miserable cantinas. You become the guy a little bit. You inhabit his world."

Peckinpah tried to convey images that would inspire his actors, without overintellectualizing what he wanted. Coburn recalls a shouted conversation through the door of the bathroom in his trailer. Peckinpah was coping with a case of the trots while Coburn tried to pry some information about his character out of his director.

"He'd come to my trailer because I had a bathroom," Coburn says. "I asked what the character was about and he said, 'He's dry. Make him drier.' That's really an action word. From that, I immediately got a sense of the dryness in the throat. There's a tendency to try to get comfortable on location but he always made you as uncomfortable as possible. The actor always wants to be confident that the director knows what he's doing but Sam didn't want to know. He wanted to see it and guide it. You'd intellectualize during rehearsal but when it came time to shoot, that went out the window. He created an atmosphere around the film that was so real that you just had to play the character."

Gordon Dawson says, "With Heston, he was very responsive. He was the same with [William] Holden and Edmond O'Brien on *Wild Bunch*. The rest he would make crazy. Jim Hutton he drove nuts on *Dundee*. He treated actors like Preminger did. He was really tough but they loved to work with him. Some people he had to charm and some he had to whip. He knew who was who."

But Bresler was like a gnat swarming around Peckinpah constantly, stinging him about schedules, about costs, about locations. Whatever Peckinpah wanted to do, Bresler wanted to do less.

"Jerry Bresler was a pain in the absolute ass," L. Q. Jones says. "He would purposely antagonize people. He'd go out of his way to say things to cause the studio to get on our case."

"Bresler wanted Sam to direct a script and Sam never worked that way," Coburn says. "The script has to be destroyed for the film to become itself. Sam used the script to guide him through."

Still, says Coburn, Bresler served a purpose for Peckinpah, playing a role that producers would continue to play through much of his career.

"The producer was Sam's greatest challenge," Coburn says. "It gave him something to work against and that was his trip. It kept the conflict of the movie within him. It gave him a challenge to overcome." But, Coburn adds, "Most of the time, he failed."

The company spent a month shooting in Durango, before returning to

Mexico City to shoot a week of interiors at Churubusco Studios. Then it was back into the Mexican countryside, to godforsaken sites such as Tehuixtla and Cuautla, for the bulk of the location work. The tensions escalated as pressure from Bresler and Columbia—to cut costs, to maintain the already truncated shooting schedule—increased.

Some of the delays were, of course, due to Peckinpah's own perfectionism. On the other hand, Peckinpah found himself having to cope with the demands and eccentricities of Richard Harris, an actor who was not averse to playing power games about when he would or wouldn't show up on the set. Much of it was predicated on his own secret sense of the balance of status and power between himself and Heston.

Gordon Dawson recalls, "Harris would say, 'I'm not coming out until he's on his horse.' So we'd have to wait."

"Richard Harris is a bit of a handful," Heston says. "In my journals I said he was a professional Irishman rather than an Irish professional and he got pissed at me."

After *Dundee* wrapped and Heston had gone on to shoot *The Agony and the Ecstasy* in Rome, he read a story about *Dundee* shortly before the opening by gossip columnist Louella Parsons, in which Bresler described Harris as "a cooperative actor." Heston was incensed enough to write to Bresler on June 6, 1964: "Richard is a talented and sincere man, and a delightful companion as well, but cooperative is the last adjective that would occur to me in describing him. In fact, I think I would have to specify that he is the least cooperative actor I've ever worked with. For the seventy-some days we shot, I don't think there were ten when Richard was actually on the set, in wardrobe and makeup, at the hour specified in his call. He consistently was the last principal mounted in shots involving the troop and on at least one occasion in my hearing told one of John's assistants to fuck off when he called him to the set. I think I am being conservative in saying that Richard Harris was personally responsible for a minimum loss of fifteen to twenty minutes of shooting time each day he worked."

Peckinpah responded to Bresler's pressure by driving his cast and crew even harder. Peckinpah sent crew members packing who couldn't meet his pace and demands.

"Sam was a driver but a terrible leader," Heston says. "He was good with actors but Sam was lousy with crew people. There was a dangerous instability in Sam. I'm not saying he was literally crazy, but he was unstable."

When Peckinpah was working, anyone who wasn't helping him clear away obstacles was the enemy. He could be prickly and insulting; when Peckinpah blew up, the only way to survive was to seize the offensive and attack him even more aggressively.

L. Q. Jones recalls filming the Indian ambush on Dundee's troop: "It was a hellacious master shot. At the end, Ben [Johnson] and I were on the outskirts and the Indians were making an escape. We took off after them. We heard, 'Cut'—and then he started in on us: 'You ignorant cocksuckers,' etc., etc. He was on our case and got a little hostile. We rode back to the platform where he was and I started climbing up to kick his ass. I told him he didn't have the talent to direct me to the men's room. The next line should have been, 'You're on the bus,' when he fired me. But it wasn't. You couldn't back off with Sam or he'd be on you like a duck on a june bug."

Peckinpah found he could push too hard on the wrong guy and end up having to eat his words from time to time. James Coburn recalls that, on a later take of the same battle scene, the prop man was supposed to cue the Indians. But he gave the cue too early, ruining an expensive and hard-to-coordinate take.

"Sam was up on the crane and his legs were kicking, he was so mad," Coburn says. "He looked like a spider, shouting, 'Get him off the set, you're fired.' But he couldn't fire him. The guy put all his props in the truck and would have taken off. He said, 'They're my props.' So Sam had to make a compromise. The prop master stayed on the truck and another prop guy moved things from the truck to the set. Sam wasn't allowed on the truck."

Even Heston, who prides himself on his even-tempered approach to his craft, was provoked to go after Peckinpah with a saber. It was late in the day and shooting had almost wrapped. When a picture-perfect sunset presented itself, Peckinpah quickly ordered Heston and his troop to mount up for a shot of them riding down a ridge, silhouetted against the Technicolor sky.

Heston asked Peckinpah whether they should come at a trot or a canter. Peckinpah said, "A trot," then ascended the Chapman crane to get the shot.

When Heston had performed the short ride, he rode up to Peckinpah to ask how it was. "Terrible," Peckinpah said, cursing Heston for bringing his troop down too slowly. Heston reminded him that he had specifically asked for a trot.

"I didn't tell you that. That's a fucking lie, you son of a bitch," Peckinpah shouted.

Heston, who was still about fifty or sixty yards away from Peckinpah, was furious. Without thinking, he drew his sword and, spurring his horse on, charged at Peckinpah. Peckinpah, who had ridden the crane back to ground level, saw death on horseback bearing down on him and screamed at the crane operator, "Up! Up! Take me up!" Though the Chapman crane moved slowly, it lifted him out of Heston's reach just in time, leaving Peckinpah trapped in the little chair high in the air while the furious actor gestured at him with three feet of sharpened steel just below.

"I can't remember ever being so angry on a set," Heston says. "He swore at me and he was lying. Sam is the only person I've ever physically threatened on a set. But people had told me before we started the picture, 'Sam won't quit until he gets you mad at him.' "

Silke readily admits that, for all of Peckinpah's subsequent protestations—about the film he tried to make versus the one Columbia butchered and released—*Major Dundee* was fraught with intrinsic problems: a complex plot, an unsympathetic central character played by an actor who wanted to be liked, a massive cast, impossible logistics.

"*Dundee* was a mess," Silke says. "He was lost on *Dundee*."

Yet Peckinpah couldn't give up. The film was as much his obsession as the ruthless Apache Sierra Chariba was Dundee's. "On *Dundee*," R. G. Armstrong says, "I said, 'Sam this is *Moby Dick* in the West.' Sam said, 'I'm glad someone else recognizes that.'"

But Peckinpah commanded loyalty from his cast and crew because he offered it in return.

"Sam was a charming son of a bitch," Gordon Dawson says. "He'd say, 'It's you and me, partner. There's only ten of us left in the world. I'm five and you're the other five.'"

Peckinpah and Bresler continued to clash over every decision Peckinpah was making: where to shoot, what to shoot, how fast to shoot. Bresler complained consistently about Peckinpah's intransigence. Columbia executives began making visits to the locations, to convince Peckinpah to pick up the pace.

Bresler himself was dividing his attention between two pictures. His other film, *Love Has Many Faces,* a cheap soap opera with Hugh O'Brien and Cliff Robertson playing gigolos chasing Lana Turner, was filming in Acapulco. That Bresler could be so self-righteous without devoting the same kind of blood and sweat to the picture as were Peckinpah and company rankled whenever Bresler would start issuing orders and raising complaints.

"Jerry Bresler was a nice, personable kind of guy—but he was an asshole," R. G. Armstrong says. "Sam told Bresler, 'Get the fuck off my set.' You can't mess with an artist like Sam. This would be his major epic and he knew how to do it."

The more Columbia tried to twist Peckinpah's arm, the more he went his own way. In March 1964, Heston wrote in his journal, "Sam's cold nerve astounds me. With the production brass breathing down his neck, he continues to shoot every shot he feels he needs."

"It gives me the shivers thinking back on the arguments I had with Bresler and the studio," Peckinpah said. "Maybe I should have argued more strongly going in, telling them all in no uncertain terms what sort of film I was after."

As Heston observed later, "There are directors who seem to function well in an atmosphere of continuing crisis. Sam is one. Personally, I can't stand it."

With only a couple of weeks of shooting left, Columbia was ready to take the penultimate step: fire Peckinpah and finish the film with another director. (The ultimate step would have been to pull the plug on the picture, a step that would have cost more than $3 million—a significant amount in 1964.)

Despite his saber-rattling encounter with Peckinpah, Heston was convinced removing Peckinpah would be a mistake. So he stood up for him in a memorable meeting with Mike Frankovich, the head of the studio.

At that point, the picture was, by various estimates, $600,000 to $1 million over budget and two weeks behind schedule. The decision was finally made to remove Peckinpah, shut down for a week, bring in a new director and finish the final two weeks of shooting as quickly as possible.

"I thought Sam was doing a good job, in terms of directing the picture," Heston says. "They were going to fire him and I called the head of the studio and said, 'You have a right to do this but don't do it. It's a bad idea.' I didn't say I'd walk because I wouldn't have. But I muscled Sam on the picture. I said I would be glad to contribute my salary, which I believe was about $200,000, if they would keep him on. I didn't, however, offer my percentage of the gross. But I thought of it as a gesture. And Mike said, 'No, no, Chuck, we couldn't do that. Never mind.' "

Pleased with himself ("because I'm not great at negotiating"), Heston called his agent, Herman Citron, one of the partners in the powerful Chasen Park Citron Agency. Citron was audibly upset at Heston's gesture.

"You're out of your mind," Citron told him. "They'll take the money."

"No, they won't," Heston said. "They said they wouldn't."

Two days later, Citron called Heston: "They changed their mind. They're taking the money."

Hollywood being a town fueled by rumors and gossip, the story of Heston's move quickly made the rounds, until it wound up as a news item in the trade papers. "Do you think this will cause a precedent among other actors?" a reporter asked him.

"Fuck precedent," Heston replied. "Is it going to happen to me again?"

Today, Heston seems chagrined at his own naïveté: "It wasn't my plan to give it back. My plan was to make sure they did not pull the plug on Sam. What prompted me to offer to give back my salary? Stupidity."

Heston never mentioned the act to Peckinpah. But Peckinpah heard and said in a later interview, "It was a very gallant gesture."

Gallant, misguided or both, Heston achieved his desired end: Peckinpah was kept on the picture and given the chance to shoot the final weeks.

As if life wasn't complicated enough for Sam Peckinpah, in the midst of production he fell in love with one of the Mexican actresses he had cast in a supporting role. Even as he was coping with various battlefronts—the production, the producer, the studio—he had to handle his own wildly romantic impulses toward a woman whom he would be involved with for the rest of his life: Begonia Palacios.

"The only time I ever made love to a woman on a picture," Peckinpah said a decade later, "I married her three times."

In 1964, Begonia Palacios was a nineteen-year-old with a burgeoning career in Mexico. She was as popular on stage as on television and had made several films as well. An accomplished dancer and musical performer, she had been working professionally since she was ten.

Peckinpah spotted her in *The Picador of Milago*, a film directed by Pedro Armendariz. Peckinpah decided he wanted to look at her for the role of Linda, the young girl who falls in love with Tim Ryan, the company bugler played by Michael Anderson, Jr.

Having summoned her, however, Peckinpah told her agent Lanca Becker, that Begonia would have to audition for the role, along with several other actresses. Begonia, who was used to being treated like a star—or at least a starlet—was upset at what she considered an affront to her standing in the Mexican show-business community. But Becker kept reminding her, "Here is your opportunity to be a star in the United States."

"He was very handsome," Begonia recalls, "but when I got to him, he doesn't even see me. He said, 'Do you speak English?' I said, 'Not very good.' 'Not very well,' he says. So I hate him even more."

But Peckinpah had Becker bring her to Durango for the beginning of shooting. Ostensibly, this was to give the producers an opportunity to see if she was right for the role. She arrived accompanied by her aunt, who would serve as her duenna. Once there, she found she had been cast as Linda, only to spend the next month waiting to film her first scene.

Gradually, however, Begonia began to notice the director paying attention to her, though indirectly. Glances, looks, brief conversations. Though there was a language barrier, the meaning was clear. "I started to feel maybe Sam was in love with me," Begonia says. "My aunt would say, 'Be careful, I think you're getting in love with this crazy man.'

"He would sit in the sky on his camera, telling the producers not to come there and telling me to hurry up. I started looking at him like a Caesar. I said to myself, 'Okay, Sam, you're going to love me.' But I didn't know what love I was getting."

Peckinpah began to court her, trying to work his way past the defensive perimeter set up by her aunt. "I'm in love with her. I want to tell her I love her," he said, but he was having no luck.

He sent a messenger to Begonia's trailer bearing flowers. The gesture and the gift both moved the impressionable young actress. The flowers were yellow roses, which became Peckinpah's signature gift to women over the years.

(A perfectionist who possessed a surprising amount of arcane knowledge,

Peckinpah had to be aware of the symbolism of yellow roses, which usually represent contentment. But according to *The Folklore and Symbolism of Flowers and Trees*, by Ernst and Johana Lehner (Tudor Publishing, 1960), yellow roses are a symbol of infidelity and jealousy, as well as a bad-luck gift to a woman. Peckinpah no doubt savored the irony of the hidden symbolism of the yellow roses and the joy with which women accepted them, ignorant of their true meaning.)

Peckinpah continued his pursuit of Begonia Palacios, at one point sending a guitarist to her hotel to serenade her with "Cielito Lindo." He hosted a party in her honor and spent the evening holding her hand and gazing into her eyes. "I could only see his eyes and they were very deep," she says. "We forgot about everybody. That was the moment I felt we were really in love."

Begonia's mother was alarmed at the reports she was receiving about her daughter's increasing involvement with the American director, who was twenty years Begonia's senior. Begonia had been on location for two months and had other commitments, including a performance with a Mexican dance troupe at New York's Carnegie Hall. Peckinpah let her leave to fulfill the commitment, then return to complete the film.

Toward the end of the picture, Peckinpah returned to the United States briefly, to defend his job when it was in jeopardy. When he returned, he once again beseeched the glowering aunt to let him speak to Begonia. This time she assented. He took Begonia to his trailer, sat her down and took her hand.

"You have a lot of light," he said. "I love you and I'm not going to let you go. When we finish this picture, can you go to L.A.? I want you to meet my family."

Swept off her feet, Begonia lied to her mother about her destination. She flew to Los Angeles, where Peckinpah and writer Max Evans met her at the airport. They took her luggage to the Bird House, then drove over to introduce her to Walter and Fern Lea Peter. At the door, Peckinpah said, "I present my fiancée."

Almost as an afterthought, he said to Begonia, "Do you want to marry me?" She agreed.

"I knew I would have to forget my position, my station, my mother, my country," she says. "But I wanted to marry him."

Fern Lea, taking the pragmatic side, pointed out, "She's so young and she doesn't speak English." To which Peckinpah replied with a sly smile, "That's okay. I don't speak Spanish."

Begonia's mother's initial response was "You are no longer my daughter." But, in the end, both of Begonia's parents and many of her relatives came to Los Angeles for the wedding, a civil ceremony, in June 1964.

As part of their honeymoon, they made the obligatory trip to Fresno, to introduce Begonia to Sam's mother.

"Sam used to say bad things about her," Begonia says. "He didn't love her because she held his father back. She was very small and beautiful—but she was at him like a mosquito. She didn't like to have him drinking in the house."

They returned to Malibu to start their life together, even as Peckinpah began editing *Major Dundee*.

8

Done in by *Dundee*

IT'S NOT THAT SAM PECKINPAH'S LIFE AND CAREER were a house of cards, waiting to crumble. It just seems that way.

He approached everything as a war: Every battle was a bloody one; every loss took a significant toll on the other facets of his life in equally devastating measure. So the debacle of editing *Major Dundee* and the collapse of the first of his marriages to Begonia Palacios were intricately linked, though neither specifically caused the other.

Having survived the attempted putsch, Peckinpah assumed he would be allowed to cut the picture himself. He envisioned it as the story of one man's battle that turns into an obsession and, eventually, a descent into a personal hell, with a final redemption, thanks to the one man he is most at odds with.

The road shows of the day were, by custom, epic in length. Peckinpah assumed he would have between two and a half and three hours (including intermission) in which to tell his story. He paced the film accordingly, devoting significant sections to scenes that established Dundee's character and his dilemmas, without necessarily advancing the story. They were the connective tissue that explained and motivated everything that came later in the film.

Peckinpah's rough cut ran more than four and a half hours, obviously too long, but intentionally so. In his next cut, he brought it down to three hours, then tightened it to what he considered its optimal length of two hours and forty-four minutes.

"At two hours and forty-four minutes, it was much better than *Ride the High Country*," he said. "It was possibly the best picture I've made in my life."

But Bresler and the Columbia brass were restive. The film seemed too long to them, and they said so. They suggested making cuts before the first preview, then reinstating the excised scenes for a subsequent preview. The director tried to calm their panic in a memo dated September 11, 1964, to

Bresler, Mike Frankovich and Arthur Kramer, another Columbia production executive: "It appeared our general feeling was the film played quite well in two hours and thirty minutes. I certainly believe it does and I believe even more strongly it will play better with certain sequences shortened and two or three very slightly lengthened.

"After running the picture again with Jerry Bresler Monday, August 31, I got the feeling his attitude is to shorten the film regardless of the values I feel are important. I believe very strongly the picture should be previewed at this length with the cuts and added shots I requested included. If they don't work—if they don't play to an audience—we have obviously no choice but to remove them. However, to remove them first, saying, 'We might be able to put them in the second preview,' doesn't quite make sense to me. I believe it can and will be a damn fine motion picture, but I believe the time has now come to put aside the axe with the heavy cutting edge and apply a little tender loving care. I am, of course, anxious to help in any way that I can."

But Peckinpah's entreaties to test the film before cutting it further went unheeded. Three days later, in a letter to his agent, Evarts Ziegler, Peckinpah wrote: "Needless to say I am very disappointed with the way things have been going. The last time I spoke to Bresler was a week ago Monday. Since then I understand nine minutes have been cut out of the film, but I have heard nothing. As I remember from Arthur, Jerry and [you], I was to stay with the cutting. It doesn't appear to be the case now, does it?"

Heston wrote in his journal at one point shortly after shooting was completed, "I get the feeling Bresler would almost be willing to have the film fail, if only to justify misgivings about Sam."

After Peckinpah turned in his final cut, Columbia—with Bresler—trimmed it further, without his input or consent. But they didn't need it; Peckinpah did not have the right to the final cut.

As James Coburn says, "Sam was living under the impression that he had final cut. Sam made a lot of assumptions. That was one of the things that caused problems. He made assumptions and acted on them and created acrimony as a result. It was generated by the need to turn the sword in people who were turning the sword in him."

"The thing is it was too long," Heston says. "In the process of editing a picture, you take out the bad parts so the good parts come closer together. What happened with *Dundee* is it didn't cut well. There was so much to it that it would clearly have to be shorter. I saw Sam's final cut and it was pretty long. *Ben Hur* is longer but it has more good stuff. At that point, Sam was in no position to defend his cut. I'm not certain it was entirely defensible."

There has been extensive discussion about how much was cut out by the studio and who did the cutting. Peckinpah alternately spoke of his cut being

2:41 and 2:44; he railed in print for the rest of his life about Columbia cutting as many as fifty-five minutes out of his movie. How do those figures square?

As his memo states, he had brought it down to 2:30 while he was still editing it for Columbia, but not willingly. If he started with 2:44, that's fourteen minutes lost. The first-run version of the film was 2:14—another sixteen minutes lost. When it was shown in second-run houses, it was less than two hours long—at least another fourteen minutes lost.

The total: forty-four minutes, almost 27 percent of the film's running time.

Not every second of film cut may have been golden, but much of what was lost was crucial to the film's structure and cohesion. All of the scenes that showed Dundee's descent into confusion and dishonor were removed; the final half-hour of the film makes little sense. From the point that Dundee is wounded, the film amounts to little more than a series of strung-together action sequences.

"Where it fails, where it refuses to make sense, lies in the fact that all of Dundee's motivation, the why behind it all, is all gone," Peckinpah said.

Who did the cutting? Peckinpah always blamed Bresler. If Bresler didn't do the actual physical cutting of the film, he was in the position to either order it or stop it from happening.

Bresler, however, denied that the cuts were his. In a 1974 letter to a graduate student researching Peckinpah's career, Bresler claimed that the cuts had been ordered and carried out by Columbia executive Arthur Kramer, behind his back and against his will.

But Bresler was never one to take the blame when he could lay it on someone else. Jim Silke recalls a story about Bresler producing a picture for Harry Cohn, the legendary terrible-tempered mogul who ran Columbia for many years. There were obviously problems with the picture when it was previewed in Palm Springs. On the ride back through the desert, Cohn asked Bresler what had gone wrong. Bresler began assigning blame to everyone he could think of—except himself. Cohn pulled over to the side of the road, forced him to get out and drove away.

So pointing the finger elsewhere would not have been uncharacteristic. Bresler tipped his own hand after Peckinpah wrote to Columbia to excoriate the producer and demand that his directing credit be removed. Bresler responded with a letter on March 15, 1965: "Our biggest argument during the editing of *Major Dundee* was my desire for clarity. *Major Dundee,* inclusive of the footage you claim should not have been cut, was screened for sixty-five people in New York City, executives, exhibitors, district managers and movie-goers. There was unanimity from all that the picture was confusing and, even more important, far too long for either enjoyment or good financial return.

"Your claim that the character concept, mood and meaning had been destroyed by the elimination of eighteen minutes of film is as ridiculous as all your other statements and attitude throughout. It was very obvious from the first day of shooting that you were unaware of character concept or anything else that was practical to the making of *Major Dundee*.

"My own disservice to myself and to those working with me was in not insisting that you as director be removed and replaced, regardless.

"Your inability to work with people, your constant desire to create ill will among your fellow creators and technicians to the disadvantage of the movie is also well documented. Your inexperience, your lack of daily preparation and your failure to seek advice when and where needed showed up on film in each day's work. They are all just part and parcel of a very confused human being.

"I may be the one who will suffer the most but I do not damn you, Sam Peckinpah. I feel sorry for you."

James Coburn recalls walking out of the preview of the studio cut of the film at the Paramount Theater on Hollywood Boulevard and finding Peckinpah standing on the street, a hip flask in his hand.

"He was shaking from rage," Coburn says, "and the bottle slipped and broke. He couldn't say anything. My then wife put her hand on his neck and said, 'It's just a movie.' Sam said, 'It's my fucking life.' "

Peckinpah's daughter Kristen says, "I remember his talking about how they cut it to shreds. He was so upset at the idea that he could make something and then these other people had that power over it. They came in and hacked it away. It was really distressing."

Today, when the average person gets daily doses of entertainment news on television and in the newspapers, a movie in trouble is easily identified as such, long before it is released. But when *Major Dundee* was released in April 1965, the critics could only conclude that the problems rested with the director and they said as much.

One of the first reviews came from James Powers in the *Hollywood Reporter* in March 1965, who called it "bewildering . . . stuck together with almost no continuity. Character changes and development occur without explanation. Not in memory has a major film been such a confusing experience."

Peckinpah responded with a letter to Powers on March 25, 1965, in an effort to set the record straight: "You are absolutely correct. After seeing it at the press screening on February 4, 1965, I didn't know what in hell it was about and I was the director. August 31, 1964 (the last time the studio permitted me to see the film), it was twenty minutes longer and I know it had the makings of a fine motion picture. The film I made is on the cutting-room floor.

"I suppose the people who are responsible for its present shape, Jerry

Bresler, Mike Frankovich and Arthur Kramer, believed they were improving it. But while I appreciate their motives I can only deplore their lack of taste and judgment and bitterly regret the time and work that so many of us spent on the film because, as anyone who has seen the picture knows, it was a total waste."

It was an idealistically self-defeating stand to take. The moral high ground Peckinpah may have commanded was vastly overshadowed by the mountains of the studios. A director who wasn't willing to go along to get along quickly found himself out of work. It was a small, exclusive club; no matter which studio head he pointed the finger at in the trade papers, the rest of them saw it—and figured they wouldn't want to deal with someone so eager to go public with his grievances.

The trade papers weren't the only ones to find *Major Dundee* lacking. Hollis Alpert, of *Saturday Review: "Major Dundee* left me with the impression that I had seen a movie of no distinction whatsoever—crude in its action, composed of remnants and fragments of other Westerns, its plot meandering over a florid landscape of clichés."

Time: "Sam Peckinpah lets *Dundee* ramble so freely that the Apaches are soon lost in subplots."

Newsweek: "Major Dundee is a disaster. There is not even any evident ambition, any apparent effort at anything better. It is almost as if Peckinpah were enjoying his ruin."

As if the *Newsweek* review were not nasty enough, it went on to note: "None of this is the fault of Heston or producer Jerry Bresler." Incensed, Peckinpah dashed off a letter to Osborn Elliott, *Newsweek*'s editor (which he addressed to "Elliot Osborne"): "The review states none of this is the fault of producer Jerry Bresler, and it implies that it is the fault of Sam Peckinpah. I disagree. It is his film and he is responsible for its current condition. My personal failure was, first, signing my contract and, second, believing Bresler when he said the film would have a public preview and that, regardless of the contract, I would be permitted to stay with the cutting of the picture until it was finished.

"If you're interested in facts, you should know that *Major Dundee* was at one point an entirely different film. That film was butchered. Too much of what I helped write and what I filmed is not part of the current film you reviewed."

Today, Heston says, "I don't think the film is a debacle. I've made a lot worse. It's not the film it could have been but I'm not ashamed of it. I would describe the whole production as unstable and highly volatile."

For Peckinpah, however, the experience sharpened his distaste for producers and refined his rebellion toward any type of authority.

Among Hollywood stereotypes, players on each side of the movie-making equation are assigned certain characteristics. The creative players—directors, actors, writers—share the common denominator of artistic egomania. The people on the business side—producers, agents, studio executives—usually are tarred with the sleaze brush. If there is a way to achieve nirvana without scruples or conscience, agents and producers have found it, according to the stereotype.

Peckinpah's experience with Bresler further jaundiced his view of all producers. Already paranoid, he was even more convinced that producers were not a necessary evil—they were just plain evil. Though he subsequently met a couple with whom he was able to work, his attitudes and behavior were forever affected by *Major Dundee*.

"*Dundee* was one of the most painful things that has ever happened in my life," Peckinpah said. "Making a picture is . . . I don't know . . . you become in love with it. It's part of your life. And when you see it being mutilated and cut to pieces, it's like losing a child or something. When I saw it happening, I went a little crazy. It was my responsibility for going to work under those conditions. You must go in, when you work with a producer, knowing that you're making the same kind of film. Otherwise, it's death."

Unfortunately, Peckinpah would turn around and make the same mistake all over again with his very next film, *The Cincinnati Kid*. And this time, he didn't even get to make the movie.

9

Years in Exile, Part I

PECKINPAH WENT FROM EDITING *Major Dundee* to being fired from *Cincinnati Kid*, a double whammy. The news about his replacement by Norman Jewison on *Cincinnati Kid* hit the trade papers first; then came the disastrous release of *Dundee* and Peckinpah's loud protests about the editing.

Peckinpah's life fell apart on all fronts. He was shut out by the studios, unable to get work. At the same time, his fledgling marriage to Begonia had disintegrated as well. Upset with the violence his drinking brought on and unhappy with the fact that he was also smoking marijuana, Begonia abandoned Peckinpah. There was something wrong with him, she felt, but she had no idea what.

"I couldn't know how hard it was," she says. "But it was like he didn't even see me. He'd say, 'Don't talk to me,' or get mad and throw bottles. I was so confused and so in love."

Things came to a head during the fall of 1964, while he was in preproduction for *Cincinnati Kid*. In an alcoholic rage, during an argument with Begonia, Peckinpah put his arm through the window on a screen door, cutting himself severely. But he seemed not to notice as he grabbed Begonia, smearing his blood on her. Begonia took flight into the Malibu night.

"I started running—there was blood on my nightgown," she says. "I was running and wondering who could help me. I started praying. I was knocking on doors and someone opened up and let me in. They said, 'Oh, we know Sam.' "

Peckinpah wound up in the emergency room to get stitches. He called Begonia's brother, Juan Jose Palacios, who worked for Peckinpah as a driver off and on for twenty years, to come and pick her up.

"At the hospital, he was angry, like this was my fault," Begonia says. "I went back to my brother's house and said, 'I don't want to see him.' But Sam came to get me and was crying, saying he loved me. So I stayed with him. I knew he was hurt in his heart about the movie."

The rapprochement didn't last, however, because the drinking didn't stop. "I started to get afraid of him," Begonia says.

"Begonia was an absolute love," Betty Peckinpah says. "She went through a bunch of awful stuff. He went kind of mad when he was drinking. It was not just an ordinary drunk. It triggered something that was maniacal. He would drink and it would drive him over the edge."

Fearing for her life, Begonia told him she was leaving and had Juan Jose take her back to Mexico. She sued for divorce and went back to work. Their marriage had lasted less than four months.

But Peckinpah wouldn't stay away. At one point in early 1965, he and Jim Silke were hired to turn James Michener's best-seller, *Caravans*, into a screenplay. Peckinpah invited Begonia to New York for meetings on the project, then took her to Spain and proposed to her again.

He also offered to convert to Catholicism. Peckinpah's mother had been Adventist and his father was Catholic; Fern Peckinpah subsequently converted to Christian Science and, to keep her happy, Dave converted as well (though he always kept a bottle hidden in his cabin at the rear of their property).

Peckinpah had never been much of a churchgoer. But the ritualistic, almost mystical nature of traditional Mexican Catholicism appealed to him.

So they returned to Malibu and, in August 1965, married again in a civil ceremony. Shortly afterward, they also were married in a Catholic ceremony. While Peckinpah always referred to the fact that he married Begonia three times, they actually had three wedding ceremonies but only two marriages.

"He wanted to be everything with me, so he was tutored in Catholicism," Begonia says. "Being baptized was very important to him. He told me he felt a bright light in his head. I said, 'Sam, don't kid me.' He said, 'No, Begonia, I have a light in my head.' "

They moved back to Malibu but into a new house at Broad Beach. "I didn't want to be in the same house," Begonia says. "I wanted a new house because of the memories."

Peckinpah brought her brother, Juan Jose, to work for them as a driver, and to keep Begonia company. "Mainly he wanted me to get Begonia acquainted with the United States, to teach her to drive, things like that," Juan Jose says. "I was his driver, doing errands and living in Malibu. He was a very possessive person. You were on call twenty-four hours a day. He was a strong person; I couldn't have a life of my own working with Sam."

Begonia didn't want a life of her own. Having abandoned her career, she wanted to share Sam's life: "I didn't want to work," she says. "I just wanted to have a house and a husband. Everyone would tell me, 'You should fight to work,' but I didn't want to. I just loved him and wanted to understand him."

That was fine at first. Peckinpah would write and Begonia would keep house and cook. "We'd have dinner with candles," she says. "He under-stood Spanish but he would say, 'The verbs are very hard for me. So speak in English.' My English was worse. But we had each other. Sam would say, 'You don't need to talk to understand love.'"

But his drinking continued and so did her loneliness. She had never lived alone and frequently found herself isolated at the house in Malibu, while Peckinpah worked on writing projects with various collaborators.

"Bego and Sam were both very possessive," Juan Jose says. "It's amazing how they couldn't live together. Sam had to do his work. But Bego wanted to be with him all the time. Sam would push her to take classes—to learn English, to continue her career in the United States. But she just wanted to have a married life, to be with Sam."

"He was doing his work," she says, "and I was fighting for my life."

For Peckinpah, doing his work was the same as struggling for survival. Almost overnight, from the time of his firing on December 5, 1964, he found himself persona non grata at all of the studios in Hollywood. He pitched, he pleaded, he pushed, he pulled—but he could not find anyone willing to trust him with a directing assignment. He was thirty-nine and had climbed a pinnacle in his chosen profession, only to be pushed off.

"I couldn't get people on the phone or get through a studio gate," Peck-inpah said. "I was out. I know several people who wanted me for pictures and the studios wouldn't touch me in any way, shape or form."

The perception was that Peckinpah was more trouble than he was worth, says Robert Culp. "That single event [being fired] put a capper on *Major Dundee*," Culp says. "Everybody in the business said, 'Don't touch him.' That's how fast news travels and how someone with that reputation becomes an anathema."

Former head of ABC Pictures Martin Baum says that to refer to Peckinpah as the victim of blacklisting (a term with specific political connotations in Hollywood) or blackballing is a mistake. "Hollywood doesn't blackball," Baum maintains. "When somebody breaks the rules of discipline, the word gets out. Nobody wants to buy trouble. They don't want to hire someone they can't control."

Semantics, however, are cold comfort to the one who is being denied the jobs. Peckinpah ultimately spent all of 1965 and most of 1966 out of work as a director. He was in agony: helpless, impotent, seemingly unable to do anything to make himself attractive to producers or studios. In May 1965, it began to dawn on him that it was more than coincidental that his film projects kept falling apart before they got anywhere. In a letter to his uncle, Wayne Tucker, he wrote: "I have been fighting for my professional life and the issue is still in doubt. I'm starting and cancelling pictures at the rate of one a week and have no idea which one (if any) will go."

L. Q. Jones says, "The thing that crushed him was not that the studios don't call. But if they don't call, he's not going to do his picture and that's where Sam lived. He was double-crushed. I don't think he knew how to adapt. He was close to being totally through with the business he adored."

"He was very angry when he was out of work," his daughter Sharon says. Daughter Kristen adds, "I remember his sitting on the beach and contemplating. He was pretty unhappy and would warn us away from certain people, that they were bad news. He did a lot of writing under other names."

His friends did what they could to land him directing work, mostly without success. Culp, at that time the star of one of the hit TV shows of the period, "I Spy," tried to get Peckinpah an assignment directing an episode. "The only fight I ever had with Sheldon Leonard [the show's producer]," Culp says, "was that I wanted him to hire Sam to direct an 'I Spy.' He just wouldn't do it. Sam was on his ass. He couldn't get arrested."

Lois O'Connor had gone to work for David Susskind and Daniel Melnick, who were producing a TV series called "Run, Buddy, Run," a semi-comic variation of "The Fugitive." O'Connor got Peckinpah a job directing three episodes, but the show was cancelled before he could get behind a camera.

While the inactivity angered him, Peckinpah seemed to draw on untapped reserves of patience and strength during the period, refusing to be sucked into a vortex of frustration and drink, self-pity and self-destruction.

"He seemed to face it rather well," says Walter Peter, his brother-in-law. "He wasn't melancholy or depressed. He was frustrated but he continued working. He was under pressure; he held up well."

"As a worker, the period when he was out of work was his best period," Silke says. "We did more work in those years. We wrote outline after outline. We worked around the clock. That's when I learned to write."

Peckinpah got a number of assignments, on which he and Silke worked. Their routine was fairly constant: They would shop for supplies—bread, peanut butter, ice cream—then sit, eat, talk and rework scripts.

"Sam was the best rewrite man in town," Silke says. "The only work he could get was writing."

They worked on a variety of scripts for TV and film. One was *The Rounders,* a Max Evans novel eventually made into a mild comedy starring Henry Fonda and Glenn Ford ("It pissed him off that he didn't get to direct that," Evans says). Other projects were *Half-Rough,* Evans's *The Hi Lo Country* and *The Scarlet Ladies,* some of which were sold and none of which got made, so their income from all this work was minimal.

"He was always writing, writing, writing," Juan Jose Palacios says. "There would be weeks of getting up, eating and going into the room to write. He just escaped from himself by writing, intensively, for days."

His finances suffered; with little money coming in, he reached the point of bankruptcy. Desperate for cash, he accepted an offer from Levy-Gardner-Laven for his 5 percent share of "The Rifleman." Though it was worth a great deal more (and would have entitled him to residuals from a show that was still being aired in the 1990s), Peckinpah agreed to LGL's offer of $10,000.

"I don't know if he was bitter about it, but nobody put a gun to his head," Arnold Laven says. "At that time, the whole future of TV syndication and what the value of the show would be was really a matter of negotiation. Since then, his 5 percent would have been worth considerably more. Maybe he got angrier with time that his 5 percent buy-out was less fair than it should have been."

The monetary rewards from his writing were small, but the experience was invaluable. Peckinpah relearned how to shape a story, and had ample time to rethink how he would shoot these films, given the chance, as well as how he would shoot the stories he wanted to write.

In July 1965, Peckinpah was hired to do the script for Michener's *Caravans*. He approached it as an exercise with Silke.

"He gave me three pages of legal paper and said, 'Outline this story in three pages and skip every three lines,' " Silke says. "It was to be concise. We did a good job on it. MGM gave the script to David Lean—but he had it rewritten three or four times by other people." *Caravans* ultimately wasn't made until 1978, for television.

If *Caravans* was the biggest potential project Peckinpah worked on during this time, *Castaway* was the closest he came to getting a Peckinpah-directed film into production during the same period. L. Q. Jones had a production company that was looking for a project and asked Peckinpah if he wanted to direct; Peckinpah jumped at the chance and offered his screenplay for Cozzens's *Castaway*, to which he still owned the rights. "Buying that book on terms was like buying a house," Peckinpah once said.

He and Silke devoted six months to reworking the *Castaway* script. "It was the best thing we ever did," Silke maintains. Several months later, after Jones and his partners had raised more than $125,000 to make the film, Jones's lawyer took off with about $75,000 of the money, never to be seen again. That was the end of the project.

"I had to explain it to Sam," Jones recalls. "The next thing I know, Sam is going to sue me. And it was my money that was stolen."

Late in the summer of 1966, a year and a half after *Cincinnati Kid*, Peckinpah got the chance to direct. It was a dramatic program for TV—a step down from features—but it was a directing assignment.

Dan Melnick and David Susskind were successful TV producers, with shows such as "East Side, West Side," "N.Y.P.D.," "Get Smart" and the televised production of "Death of a Salesman" to their credit. Melnick had admired Peckinpah's work since "The Westerner" and thought of him to adapt and direct a Katherine Anne Porter novella to which he owned the rights: *Noon Wine*.

When Melnick called Peckinpah, the director seemed cautious to the point of being defensive. Peckinpah said, "You ought to know I've been black-listed. I've recently been fired from *The Cincinnati Kid*. No one's going to want you to hire me."

As Melnick says now, only partly kidding, "I didn't realize when he told me he was blacklisted that it was because of his personality and work methods." At the same time, it didn't occur to Melnick, though Peckinpah had a reputation for being difficult, that Peckinpah would give him problems "because I'm a good guy and everybody knows I'm a good guy."

When the production was announced in the trade papers, Melnick got several phone calls warning him that he was making a big mistake hiring Sam Peckinpah. "I shouldn't say who from, but a certain amount of thought about the key players in the *Cincinnati Kid* should make it clear who had the strongest emotional hatred," Melnick says. "There was a lot of pressure to bury Sam. The more calls I got, the more stubborn I got."

Noon Wine is the story of a poor farmer in a loveless marriage in turn-of-the-century Texas. Royal Earle Thompson's farm prospers, however, when he hires a hard-working but mysterious stranger, a farmhand named Olaf. Thompson's bubble bursts when a bounty hunter shows up on his farm, claiming jurisdiction over Olaf, who allegedly is wanted for a crime in North Dakota. In a moment of unfocused rage, Thompson kills the bounty hunter with an axe. Olaf runs off, to be killed by a quickly assembled posse. Thompson claims self-defense and is acquitted of the killing. But the town turns him into an outcast because of doubts about his innocence. He tries to justify the killing to himself and his unloving wife in a note, then shoots himself.

For the role of Royal Earle Thompson, Melnick got Jason Robards, fresh from his success in the Broadway and film versions of *A Thousand Clowns*.

"Katy Hepburn and Spencer Tracy were telling me that I had to meet this guy and work with him," Robards says of his introduction to Peckinpah. "They thought he and I would be interesting together."

Robards met with Peckinpah and Melnick, read the script and agreed to play the role. As it turned out, Peckinpah lived just down the beach from Robards at Malibu and the two became friends, meeting to discuss the script, barbecue and drink.

Olivia De Havilland was cast as Thompson's withdrawn, bitter wife. Per Oscarsson, a Norwegian actor, landed the role of Olaf, and Theodore Bikel took the role of the bounty hunter.

When production began in October 1964, Bikel found that Peckinpah hadn't changed significantly in appearance, though he looked thinner. "He was painfully thin, always," Bikel says. "You always had the feeling that this man wasn't long for this world. When I worked with him the second time, I had the feeling that this inexorable progress toward whatever end was going faster than when I originally met him."

Robards took to Peckinpah's methods immediately. For one thing, Peckinpah insisted on two weeks of rehearsal with his cast before beginning the actual shooting of the one-hour show, which was being produced for "ABC Stage 67," an anthology series.

"It was the only time I had the kind of rehearsal you normally don't get on a four- or five-camera show," Robards says. "We could work like it was a play. Rehearsals were very specific, very good. He was particular and rehearsed us well. He was like a good theatrical director: He let us investigate it."

Peckinpah wrote the screenplay himself, adapting it from Porter's novella. But Melnick had to get Porter's approval of the script. He sent it to her and "she wrote this extraordinary letter saying she only hoped she could have been as imaginative and as faithful to the novella if she had written it," Melnick says.

The production was shot in color on videotape and film. Melnick says, "Sam shot *Noon Wine* like a film. He had a very peculiar way of working that took me a while to understand. I realized that though he didn't prepare like many directors do and come in with a shot list, he had a very specific vision. He had specific ideas, but it seemed like he was winging it."

Melnick's line producer for the project was Lois O'Connor, Peckinpah's friend from *Cincinnati Kid*. She says, "He was meticulous about everything he did. He was really so far ahead of everyone in terms of his vision of the story. He understood that hard Texas life."

Peckinpah introduced his old friend O'Connor to his new friend Robards, who was in the process of ending a marriage with Lauren Bacall. The two of them hit it off and eventually married. Peckinpah served as their best man. "He wore a white suit, a black shirt and a gold tie," Robards says. "He had a fresh apple blossom in his lapel and he cried too."

O'Connor eventually introduced Peckinpah to two of his key collaborators in years to come. On *Noon Wine*, she introduced him to composer Jerry Fielding, who would work with him on several subsequent films and become a close friend. A few years later, she steered property master Bobby Visciglia to him; Visciglia became part of Peckinpah's movie-making inner circle. When Robards married her, Peckinpah complained, "You're stealing my good taste."

Peckinpah wouldn't come out and call *Noon Wine* a comeback, but he obviously was anxious to prove that he could still direct, after a two-year layoff.

"There seemed to be a great deal of stress on him by the time of *Noon Wine*," Bikel says. "It was mentioned in passing that he felt this was a grace period for him. Like, 'I've got to do well on this because teacher is watching.' "

"I know he would not acknowledge to anyone outside and only partly acknowledge to himself that this was his opportunity to have another chance," Melnick says. "But it worked that way."

Peckinpah wasn't one to compromise simply because his whole future might be riding on it. He approached *Noon Wine* with the same thoroughness and perfectionism that marked his movie work. That meant that he pushed his crew to reach his own standards of achievement. "He was very tough on the crew, always," Melnick says.

Occasionally, Peckinpah would manipulate actors to draw an emotional response from them off-camera that would bleed into the work they did on film. Some actors resented this; he was trying to elicit emotions that, as actors, they should have been able to create without going through personal turmoil.

"Sam tried to get Olivia De Havilland to be this haggard, worn-down woman on *Noon Wine*," Lois O'Connor says. "The first day in front of the camera, she was getting her hair done and Sam came in and said, 'She looks like she came from a Beverly Hills beauty salon.' He took her and frumped up her hair. He was on her so hard."

Melnick says, "He really beat up on Olivia, because she had difficulty with the last dramatic moment, when the husband blows his head off. Between takes, he kept the cameras running secretly and beat her up emotionally; that moment of devastation and desolation was really the product of something Sam evoked for her in real life. I said, 'Sam, you're really being tough.' And he said, 'Do you want to finish or not?' It wasn't casual meanness but the pursuit of the integrity of the moment."

That integrity translated to a productive working environment for his actors. "My feeling was that this wasn't TV—this was movie-making that happened to end up on TV," Bikel observes. "He didn't do twenty or thirty takes of a scene but he would go nine or ten, until he decided that was it. For the actor, it's a wonderful experience because you know you could shine and he'd give you the opportunity to do it."

Melnick trusted his director's instincts and let him make the film his way. "One of the great things about Sam, which wasn't really appreciated, was that he was a director who knew everything there is to know about film," Melnick says. "I came to realize that if Sam said, 'I know how to make this work,' he did, even if he couldn't fully articulate how to do it."

Melnick apparently was the first producer since Dick Powell who had given Peckinpah the respect and the room he needed to make his film. Peckinpah appreciated that hands-off approach—and let Melnick know it, without coming right out and saying so.

"Sam, in his cryptic way, said, 'We've got to do this again,' " Melnick says. "One night we got drunk and he told me what an extraordinary experience this had been. Over the years we would look back to that as a relatively simple time in our lives."

Still, Peckinpah would try to con even a producer he got along with. Melnick says, "Sam had an ability to convince you that he was the last person, if not on earth, certainly in the film business, with both guts and integrity. In truth, a lot of that was Sam's sense of himself. Sam, like most people in a highly competitive business, made all kinds of decisions out of expediency."

Broadcast in November 1966, *Noon Wine* won good reviews and put a new spin on Peckinpah's career. "The show had an enormous popular reaction," Melnick says. "Sam was a hero again."

Peckinpah received a nomination from the Writers Guild of America for best television adaptation and another from the Directors Guild for best television direction. He didn't win either award, but getting noticed was its own reward.

He also received another directing assignment, still from television, but work was work. This one was for "Bob Hope's Chrysler Theater." Titled "That Lady Is My Life," it starred Bradford Dillman, Jean Simmons and Alex Cord. Peckinpah also cast Begonia, in one of her few acting jobs during their marriages.

Life with Begonia, however, had begun to deteriorate once again. Though he didn't drink as much when he was out of work, once he started directing he would unwind at home with a few drinks. The alcohol made him snaky and unpredictable, violent and abusive.

"At times, it was like he was pushing me away," Begonia says. "We would go to dinner and he would fight with the waiter. I would run away because I couldn't stay with him like that. He said, 'I can't have a wife who runs when I have a fight.' I said, 'Sam, I don't understand why you fight.' When he would work hard, he would drink a lot. He couldn't remember what he did."

But his moods would shift suddenly. "He would invite my family the next day," Begonia says, "and say, 'I love you and I want to drink less.' "

That charismatic side—the thoughtful, intuitive, funny, playful Sam Peckinpah—inspired almost fatal loyalty in his friends and could project a powerful magnetism. Robert Culp recalls, "One morning we were chopping vegetables for a salad at the beach at his house. Now I'm the least gay guy you've ever met but, for no reason, I threw my arms around him and he tensed up. I whispered in his ear, 'You are responsible for me. In a world where you aren't, I don't want to be.' Then I went back to chopping vegetables. Not a word was said about it afterward."

Culp recalls that, in the end, Begonia walked out on him on July 4, 1967, because "she couldn't stand that he had a stash of grass under the house. I think it was because of booze. The day she left him, he wasn't even drunk. He was out on the beach. He went in the house and she was gone."

Begonia recalls that Peckinpah had a loud argument with one of her cousins on July 4 that finally pushed her over the edge. But the fight, says Sam's brother, Denny, came about because Begonia stretched Peckinpah's patience by bringing her family members up from Mexico to live with them.

"He loved Bego—she was a beautiful little gal," Denny says. "But when they got married, the family moved in. I'm not talking about mother and father—I'm talking umpteen brothers and sisters and cousins and nephews. Sam liked them, but when they started running things, it got old in a hurry."

Adds his wife, Betty, "Begonia was his real true love. But the family took advantage of Begonia. She and her brother were supporting the family before Sam married her."

Begonia left in 1967; the divorce became final in 1969. But the two continued to see each other, getting together for a few weeks each year in Mexico. "We'd have a marriage for a time," Begonia says. "But I didn't want to be involved in his work. When he worked that hard, I couldn't be near him."

Peckinpah's work fortunes continued to improve. In the spring of 1967, he sold a screenplay he had been working on for several years, about Pancho Villa's role in the Mexican Revolution. Titled *Villa Rides,* it was produced by Paramount with Buzz Kulik as director.

The title role went to Yul Brynner, the European-born star who, apparently, fancied himself as something of an expert on Mexico.

"Brynner asked for me to be taken off the film because he said I didn't know anything about Mexico," Peckinpah said. "That surprised me because I was then married to a Mexican and I'd been in and out of Mexico for years."

Peckinpah was replaced by Robert Towne, who rewrote most of the screenplay, leaving little of Peckinpah's material and receiving the writing credit. "That was all right," Peckinpah said. "I took the stuff they threw out of that picture and used it in *The Wild Bunch.*"

Peckinpah spent his weeks writing and pitching ideas and his weekends drinking and barbecuing, horsing around with friends in Malibu.

"We had a good time when we'd drink," Jason Robards says. "Lois thought we were big fucking bores because we would stay up and gab all night. Sam would get mad because I'd sing a lot. 'If I Ruled the World,' 'Ivor Novello,' Johnny Cash songs, Irish songs, things like that. It was almost like we were high school or college kids."

Robert Culp recalls, "I would take my kids to his house at the beach with his kids and Walter and Fern Lea's kids—it was kid heaven. Sam would fire up the barbecue and we'd go home in the middle of the night."

Daniel Melnick says, "I was a nondrinker, but Sam delighted in getting me high on margaritas, which I loved. They were the first drink I ever tasted that were as good as an ice cream soda."

It was during this period that Robards introduced Peckinpah to a hobby that would become part of his public persona. "I gave him a set of throwing knives and we did a lot of knife-throwing. He thought he was a great knife thrower."

Peckinpah stuck with the knives, sharpening his proficiency. They became a perennial prop, liable to work their way into a conversation or argument, bringing any discussion to a potentially deadly point.

The one topic that continued to haunt Peckinpah, that obsessed and infuriated him, was producers. No matter how much he had contributed to his own fall from grace in Hollywood, he was convinced that he was the victim of a cabal of producers whose sole goal in life was to make Sam Peckinpah miserable.

Says Robards, "The only thing he ever said to me was, 'Producers are a bunch of assholes. They're peckerheads. They're useless.' He felt that way about most producers."

His daughter Sharon says, "Producers were mean and did some pretty nasty things. Everybody wants to control, everybody wants to have a say-so. Isn't filmmaking about control and power? My father was an artist. He had a vision. It was only luck that his vision was so commercial that he got to do it his way."

To Peckinpah, if it wasn't Marty Ransohoff, it was Jerry Bresler—or Charles FitzSimons or Levy-Gardner-Laven. Producers were his bête noire. What kept him going was the burning desire to direct another movie just to prove them all wrong—and make them pay for it too.

Of course, it was a producer who gave Peckinpah his chance at redemption in the motion picture business. Kenneth Hyman was an American living and working in London, producing pictures for his Seven Arts Ltd. While he was making *The Dirty Dozen* in 1967, Seven Arts merged with Warner Bros. When he finished the film, he went to Hollywood to become vice president in charge of worldwide production—in other words, the man who said yes to movie projects for the Warner studio.

Hyman met Peckinpah in 1966 at Cannes, where Peckinpah had gone to get away and, perhaps, to scout for work. Hyman's film, *The Hill*, directed by Sidney Lumet, was in the competition and, after seeing it, Peckinpah sought out the producer. He introduced himself and told him how much he had liked Hyman's movie. Impressed with the charming American, Hyman did a little research, tracking down a print of *Ride the High Country*.

When Hyman got to Hollywood, he took a house in Malibu before starting at Warner Bros. At dinner one evening, he wound up seated next to the American director who had gone out of his way to meet him in Cannes.

"Ken was an intelligent dude, grounded in all the arts," recalls Robert Culp. "One night at the beach, he was seated next to Sam. Sam was sober and he started to bitch mightily about being out of work, unable to get anything meaningful on. Hyman said, 'Here's my phone number—call me.' "

Hyman says, "I asked him what he wanted to do and he said, 'What's the difference? I'm unemployable.' He showed me a one-page treatment for *The Wild Bunch*. I read it and, a couple of weeks later, I reported for work at the studio. I called him and he came in; when he found out who I was, he threw a chair at me and screamed, 'Why didn't you tell me who you were?' "

Hyman quickly put together a deal for Peckinpah to make *The Wild Bunch*, to be produced by Phil Feldman, who had a deal with Warners. Hyman didn't go into it blind; he knew ahead of time Peckinpah's penchant for ornery behavior.

"His reputation was as a drinker, a brawler, a troublemaker," Hyman says. "But I liked him. We'd both been in the Marines, which was a basis of our relationship. I'd had difficulties too, and knew what that was like."

In February 1968, Peckinpah arrived in Mexico to cast local actors and extras. On March 25, 1968, the cameras rolled on *The Wild Bunch*.

It had been almost four years since Sam Peckinpah had directed a film. He'd been saving up ideas and images—and was about to unleash them in one ground-breaking motion picture.

Part Four

THE WILD BUNCH
1968-1969

I want to be able to make Westerns like Kurosawa makes Westerns.

—SAM PECKINPAH

10

Sex and Violence

THE HOLLYWOOD THAT SAM PECKINPAH RETURNED TO in 1968 was a changed place from the one he'd been booted out of four years earlier.

The general societal turmoil of the Sixties had affected even the entrenched sensibilities in Hollywood. But two factors in particular made this a new, uncharted, off-balance movie industry: the final decline of the old studio system, on which Hollywood had thrived since its beginnings as a motion picture capital, and the death of the Motion Picture Production Code, which was replaced by the new MPAA ratings system in 1967.

Without them, *The Wild Bunch* might not have been made—certainly not in the form that Peckinpah was able to make it.

The mid-1960s wasn't the first time the major studios had teetered on the brink of doom. Things were much worse in 1950, when the film industry was buffeted by twin gales: television, which made home entertainment as interesting as a night at the movies, and the U.S. Justice Department, which found that the motion picture studios—by owning their own chains of movie theaters—constituted a monopoly. The solution was a consent decree in 1950; afterward, the studios could no longer run (or monopolize) movie theaters to show their own films.

Film attendance plunged, from a record high of ninety million paid admissions a week in 1949 to forty-five million weekly in 1952. National film industry income, which was at $1.7 billion in 1946, dipped under a billion dollars annually—way under—and didn't resurface at that magical mark until 1964. In 1952, more than six thousand movie theaters closed.

The studios came back, finding ways to make movies bigger and more spectacular than TV could ever be—Cinemascope, Cinerama, 3-D. This commitment to the blockbuster attraction did draw audiences back. By the mid-1960s, the studios were once again confident of their ability to predict and manipulate the movie-going public.

But the men who ran the studios were getting older and the core audience was getting younger. The studios couldn't foresee that the baby boom was about to make itself felt as a box-office force.

One of the watershed movies of the 1960s was Twentieth Century-Fox's Oscar-winning film of the Broadway musical *The Sound of Music*. Aside from an armload of Academy Awards, *The Sound of Music* earned more than $150 million at the box office.

The message of the movie's success seems obvious enough: People loved Julie Andrews and they loved Rogers and Hammerstein's musical story of the Von Trapp family. Hollywood, however, interpreted this hit as meaning that audiences wanted to see lavish musicals—lots of them.

So many more of them were made—and theater companies built new theaters to house the huge audiences that were supposed to flock to these movies. At the start of 1966, 14,000 theaters and drive-ins were being built.

"I wish *The Sound of Music* had never been made," one studio production chief told *Newsweek* in 1970. "The industry lost sight of reality and thought that budgets didn't matter."

Studios threw caution to the wind and made musical after musical—and each died a more miserable death at the box office than the last one. *Sweet Charity, Star!, Dr. Dolittle, Hello Dolly!, Paint Your Wagon, Goodbye Mr. Chips:* The big-budget musicals of the mid-1960s were dinosaurs and the studios were the tar pits in which they were mired and died. The result was a series of movie studio sales in the mid- and late-1960s. Warner Bros. merged with Seven Arts Ltd., then was sold to Kinney National Services. United Artists, the film company started by Charlie Chaplin, Mary Pickford, Douglas Fairbanks and D. W. Griffith, was purchased by TransAmerica Corporation. Gulf and Western devoured Paramount Pictures.

The change—away from studios run by people who had grown old in the movie industry—was significant. These same studios now were run by businessmen and lawyers, who viewed them as commodities whose value was gauged solely by the figure in the southeast corner of the ledger.

"The day of the mogul was gone," says Martin Baum, who was an agent during those years. "The studios were not owned by the people who ran them; they were owned by conglomerates. The passion and love for film was gone."

The new studio owners took a while to get their bearings but figured out two things: They needed real movie people to lead their new acquisitions and they needed to keep up with the times, which were changing more quickly than Hollywood could reflect.

By the beginning of 1967, there were new young executives—all under forty—in positions of power. Robert Evans, chief of production at Paramount, was thirty-seven. Richard Zanuck, son of famous producer Darryl F. Zanuck, thirty-four, had replaced his father as production chief at Twentieth

Century-Fox. David Picker, vice president for production at United Artists, was thirty-six.

In large part, it was the influence of the youth culture that had burst into being—first with the Beatles, then with Beatles' movies and the rest of rock 'n' roll, finally with movies in general. But kids didn't just want something new—they wanted something more. More freedom. More self-expression. And less censorship.

The film equivalent of rock 'n' roll's long hair and electrically amplified music? The things that hadn't been allowed before: nudity, profanity, violence.

Until the mid-1960s, all of those things were strictly proscribed by the Hollywood Production Code, administered by the Hays Office. The Hays Office had been set up in the 1930s, in response to a public outcry about the increasing sexiness and violence that were luring Depression-era audiences into movies. Several highly visible Hollywood sex and drug scandals also contributed to the impulse to regulate. The code was seen as a way to make it seem that Hollywood was policing itself.

The code forbade the depiction of everything from open-mouthed kissing to adulterers whose bad deeds went unpunished to the mildest cursing. Violence was brief and nonspecific. Sex was chaste and unseen. Nudity was forbidden.

"The old code was designed to forestall government censorship," says film critic Stephen Farber. "But things were getting steadily more liberal under the old code."

By the mid-1960s, the production code was in tatters, a victim of the easing of prohibitions as the times changed. It seemed unrealistic to have movie characters acting as if they were still living in the 1940s, when the 1960s were bubbling all around.

Films continued to push the limits. Sidney Lumet's *The Pawnbroker* dashed the taboo against nudity, intercutting a Harlem prostitute baring her breasts with shots of Jewish women stripped naked in Nazi concentration camps. The final straw may have been Mike Nichols's film of Edward Albee's controversial play *Who's Afraid of Virginia Woolf?*

Released in 1966, it was summarily rejected for code approval because of the racy (for the time) language and the adult subject matter. George and Martha playing "Hump the Hostess" was simply too strong for American viewers, code administrators felt.

But Warner Bros. released the film without the seal of approval. It captured Academy Award nominations in all the major categories.

"When Warners released *Virginia Woolf* without a seal of approval," says Charles Champlin, *Los Angeles Times* entertainment editor and longtime industry observer, "it was clear the old system was dead and the old proscriptions [on] what you could do were set aside."

By the end of 1966, the Motion Picture Association of America had announced a change. The old code was out; a new ratings system, designed to distinguish mature material from that suited for general audiences, would go into effect November 1, 1968.

The new ratings, filmmakers thought, would mean new freedom. "The theory was that any film could now be made and wouldn't have to be cut," Stephen Farber says.

To some extent, that theory was correct. Films from Europe—including such British imports as *Georgy Girl, Blow-Up, Darling* and *Alfie*—attacked contemporary topics with a forthrightness to which Hollywood was unaccustomed. But it took a Hollywood film—Arthur Penn's 1967 film, *Bonnie and Clyde*—to demonstrate the kind of expansion to which the boundaries were subject.

As *Time* magazine wrote in December 1967, "In the wake of *Bonnie and Clyde,* there is an almost euphoric sense in Hollywood that more such movies can and will be made."

Bonnie and Clyde changed everything—and paved the way for *The Wild Bunch.* Penn's use of graphic violence startled and outraged critics and audiences—but it also captivated them. By establishing these likable, bumbling crooks and then showing them committing bloody violence previously unseen on the screen, Penn wrested Hollywood out of the 1940s, placing it square in the latter-day 1960s.

"Under the old code," says Charles Champlin, "you would see somebody be shot but you never saw the body being torn apart. You didn't make the link. *Bonnie and Clyde,* as [reviewer] Joe Morgenstern said, suggested that killing kills, that it's violent and painful. Violence is not an everyday thing without an effect."

Says Joseph Gelmis, critic for *Newsday* at the time, "What changed after that was that you seemed to see bodies actually erupt. There's a division between documentary and fantasy and the line became blurred. What became real was the violence. The question was whether to be shocking to serve a valid purpose or whether to be a showman, to get attention."

Suddenly Hollywood was trying to catch up with the times, to show audience things they'd never seen in ways they'd never seen them. "Hollywood has at long last become part of what the French film journal *Cahiers du Cinema* calls 'the furious springtime of world cinema' and is producing a new kind of movie," *Time* magazine proclaimed at the end of 1967. But *Time* added a cautionary note: "It remains to be seen whether the new thematic and technical freedom is a cause for unrestrained rejoicing; there is the obvious danger that it will be used excessively for the sake of gimmickry or shock."

A month later, critic Judith Crist was bemoaning this same freedom in *Look* magazine. Crist, who would become one of Peckinpah's most strident critics, wrote, "To the horror of the puritans and Neanderthals among us, we're in a no-holds-barred era as far as the content of film is concerned. Inveterate movie-goers (and how more inveterate than see-'em-all movie critics?) are hard-pressed to think of any human aberration, let alone practice, that has not been put on film."

11

Picking the Pefect "Bunch"

As Peckinpah entered preproduction on *The Wild Bunch*, he called in L. Q. Jones, whom he cast as a bounty hunter, for a chat about something else. But he turned the conversation to his own personal devils.

Jones was astonished when Peckinpah asked him, "What's the matter? What is it I do?" He seemed sincerely interested in probing the personality problems that seemed inevitably to trip him. So Jones gave it to him with both barrels.

"Sam, you're a horse's ass, you're stupid and you pick on small people," Jones said. "You don't think and you don't consider other people."

Peckinpah nodded in eager agreement, as though a light bulb had just illuminated his brain. "You're right," he said. "Well, keep an eye on me and if you catch me doing that, point it out to me."

As they were talking, the phone rang on Peckinpah's desk. Picking it up, Peckinpah said, "Why, you unconscious cunt," and reeled off angry obscenities at whoever was on the line for five minutes before hanging up. Then he turned back to Jones as though nothing had happened and continued, "I'm serious. I want you to keep an eye on me," oblivious to what he had just done on the telephone.

The Sam Peckinpah who came back to film work in early 1968 was as different as the Hollywood that welcomed him back. He had a new vision and new ideas about how to create it on film. He also had a festering storehouse of anger and resentment about the ordeal he had just been through and a consuming fire to make this comeback film an effort that no one could ignore.

The script for *The Wild Bunch* originated with Walon Green, a documentary filmmaker, and Roy Sickner, a stuntman.

"I had wanted to do a story about the American railroad and how it treated people abusively," Green recalls. "Sickner had a story in rough outline of the Wild Bunch robbing a town. I wrote the story and the script. I tried it on a couple of people with no success. Then Sickner called me and said Peckinpah liked it and put it under his deal with Warner Bros."

Peckinpah, who was a friend of Sickner's, began rewriting Green's script with Jim Silke. Peckinpah nipped and tucked, reshaped the story, adding scenes and characters to flesh it out.

The material seemed right up Peckinpah's alley. Several years earlier, he had observed, "Up to date, it seems that most of my work has been concerned one way or the other with outsiders, losers, loners, misfits, rounders —individuals looking for something besides security."

It was a theme he discussed frequently:

- In 1969: "The outlaws of the West have always fascinated me. They had a certain notoriety, they were supposed to have a Robin Hood quality about them, which was not really the truth. In a land for all intents and purposes without law, they made their own. I suppose I'm something of an outlaw myself, I identify with them. I've always wondered what happened to the outlaw leaders of the old West when it changed."
- In 1970: "I find color and vitality and meaning in the loser. The outcast is the individualist. I see color, conflict, a wish for something better, in the man who strikes out for himself. I'm talking about people who are not sheep. In a sense, they become outcasts because more and more there's little room for the individual."
- In 1972: "Look, unless you conform, give in completely, you're going to be alone in this world. But by giving in, you lose your independence as an individual. I've got a weakness for losers on the grand scale as well as a kind of sneaky affection for all the misfits and drifters in the world."

So it was with *The Wild Bunch,* a story of a gang of aging outlaws in pre–World War I Texas and Mexico. Led by Pike Bishop and Dutch Engstrom, they try to make one final score, chased by a posse of bounty hunters led by one of their old comrades, Deke Thornton.

"I wasn't trying to make an epic," Peckinpah said. "I was trying to tell a simple story about bad men in changing times. I was trying to make a few comments on violence and the people who live by violence."

As Peckinpah began casting the film, he turned to old friends to fill central roles, only to be stymied for various reasons. He asked Jason Robards to play a role (Robards recalls it as the role of Dutch; casting memos say it was

Sykes, an older member of the gang). But Robards was committed to the Broadway run of Joseph Heller's black comedy, *We Bombed in New Haven.*

Peckinpah also offered a role to James Drury, who had been in *Ride the High Country;* Drury, however, was committed to the TV series "The Virginian" and was unable to accept.

Peckinpah offered the role of Pike Bishop to his friend Lee Marvin, who turned it down twice: first to film John Boorman's *Hell in the Pacific,* then to star in the film musical *Paint Your Wagon.*

According to casting memos, the other actors considered for Pike included James Stewart, Charlton Heston and Gregory Peck. The role finally went to William Holden, and Ernest Borgnine was cast as Dutch, but not before producer Phil Feldman tried to convince Peckinpah to find a younger actor. Glenn Ford was considered for Deke Thornton, but the role eventually went to Robert Ryan.

Rounding out the cast were such Peckinpah stalwarts as L. Q. Jones and Strother Martin as T.C. and Coffer, two scurvy bounty hunters chasing the Wild Bunch with Thornton; Warren Oates and Ben Johnson as the not-exceptionally bright Gorch brothers, who ride with Pike; Jaime Sanchez, a headstrong Hispanic actor cast as Angel, the gang's Mexican member; Edmond O'Brien as Sykes, their aged crony; and Emilio Fernandez, a noted Mexican director who had worked with Peckinpah on *Major Dundee,* as Mapache, the vicious Mexican general who hires the Bunch to steal American Army guns.

Dub Taylor, who had played small roles in other Peckinpah efforts, was cast as a mayor who gives a temperance lecture at the film's beginning, as the Bunch rides into a small Texas town to rob the bank. Taylor had just finished playing Michael J. Pollard's father in *Bonnie and Clyde* and recalls Peckinpah saying, "It'll be better than *Bonnie and Clyde.*"

"Sam loved *[Bonnie and Clyde],*" Gordon Dawson says, "but he said, 'We're going to cut that movie,' " meaning he planned to outdo it in every way he could.

Peckinpah also tried to assemble a crew of key people with whom he had worked before. For his cinematographer, he hired Lucien Ballard, who had shot TV work and *Ride the High Country* with him. Together, they tried to lay out in minute detail the kind of look he wanted for the film.

Ballard recalled, "Sam and I ran everything we could find on Mexico around 1913. We wanted a yellow, dusty feeling. We went down there and everything was green. So I made tests with filters for a week until we finally got pretty much what we wanted."

Lou Lombardo, a TV editor who had worked with him on *Noon Wine,* had confided in Peckinpah his interest in cutting a motion picture. Peckinpah liked his work on *Noon Wine,* for which Lombardo had served as assistant cameraman. Then Lombardo showed Peckinpah some footage he had cut for the TV show "Felony Squad."

"I had this one scene where these cops were firing at Joe Don Baker," Lombardo says. "He's hit and he falls—but it seems like forever because I had triple-printed each frame. That impressed Feldman and Sam too. He said, 'That's how we're going to do *The Wild Bunch*—but not all of it.' "

Gordon Dawson, who had served him so well doing wardrobe on *Major Dundee,* had graduated to writing, leaving costume work behind. But Peckinpah wanted him doing costumes for *Wild Bunch* and wouldn't take no for an answer.

"Phil Feldman called and said, 'Sam wants you,' " Dawson recalls. "I said, 'I'm not doing wardrobe anymore.' I had just sold scripts for 'Cowboy in Africa' and 'Gentle Ben.' But he offered me more and more money until it was ridiculous. He said, 'It'll lead to other things.' Meaning co-producing and writing."

Finally, there was the producer himself: Phil Feldman, who had helped Francis Ford Coppola shepherd his breakthrough film, *You're a Big Boy Now,* to the big screen. He had served as a deciphering analyst during World War II and received a presidential citation for breaking one particularly tough Japanese code.

Peckinpah and Feldman got along because Peckinpah, for all of his idiosyncrasies, believed that Feldman was on his side. And Feldman, though he refused to be steamrolled by the Peckinpah personality, backed his director throughout production.

Says L. Q. Jones, "If it wasn't for Phil Feldman, I don't think Sam would have made anything of consequence. Phil understood that you don't harness a hummingbird."

"Feldman was a power, a sharp guy," Dawson says. "He gave Sam a chance at a comeback. He was really a champion for Sam as long as he lasted. With Sam, it was always us against the suits. Feldman would get between the talent and the suits and did it extremely well. I think Sam knew Phil was for the picture. You could fuck up left, right and sideways if you were for the picture. If you were for the budget or the studio, God help you."

Peckinpah himself said, shortly after concluding production, that Feldman and Ken Hyman were "very creative, very tough, stimulating and damn fine people to work with. I find I work well under these circumstances. I wouldn't want to change a damn thing."

THE WILD BUNCH CAPTURES the final days of a gang of aging badmen, trying to ply their outlaw trade near the border between Mexico and Texas. The film starts with a dazzling double switchback in the audience's expectations, as we see a troop of uniformed American soldiers ride into a dusty little town and head into the local bank. As they do this, figures can be seen scurrying across the rooftops, guns in hand. The impression is that the Army is about to move a valuable cargo—and badmen are waiting to ambush them.

But the soldiers are the robbers in disguise. And the men on the roof are hired killers, paid by the railroad to stop this robbery. As the uniform-clad thieves make their break and the posse begins its assault, a group of temperance marchers, singing "Shall We Gather at the River," parades through the center of town and gets caught in the crossfire. About half of the bank robbers escape; several more are killed, along with bounty hunters and innocent townsfolk.

The posse, it turns out, is being led by Deke Thornton, a furloughed convict. Thornton had been partners with the leader of the bandit gang, Pike Bishop, until the two had been caught by surprise in a whorehouse; Bishop escaped and Thornton didn't. He is being forced to lead a scraggly bunch of trackers after the Wild Bunch, threatened with a return to prison if he fails.

The gang, meanwhile, down to five members, has a rendezvous with a sixth member, Sykes. They decide to divide the loot, only to discover that instead of gold, they have come away with bags filled with washers; the whole robbery has been a setup. Angry and frustrated, they follow Angel, the Mexican member of the gang, to regroup at his native village.

There, they are told that the village has been plundered by the Federales, under the command of a corrupt general named Mapache, who is leading the war against Pancho Villa. Angel's father has been killed; his fiancée has run off with Mapache. After a night in the village, they set off for Agua Verde, Mapache's headquarters, to hunt up some action.

Instead, they wind up in a deal with Mapache, who needs more guns to fight Villa. Mapache's European advisers—a pair of haughty Prussians—enlist Pike, Dutch, the Gorches and Angel to rob an American troop supply train, loaded with munitions. Their reward will be enough money to pull back and get a fresh start in the obviously shifting landscape of the West.

Thornton, knowing how Pike plans, figures out the target and has his men aboard the supply train, along with a group of raw, green soldiers. But Bishop and his group pull the heist with a minimum of fuss, escaping with the train itself and all the guns. Thornton and the bounty hunters pursue them on horseback; Bishop blows up the bridge to Mexico with Thornton and his men still on it.

The Wild Bunch arrives back in Agua Verde, where they see Mapache's newest toy—an automobile, harbinger of an era at its end. But they have something more important to worry about: their pay.

Each of the men is to get a portion of $10,000 in gold for the guns. Angel, however, takes a case of rifles for his pay, giving them to the indigenous tribes of Mexican Indians who are part of the battle against Mapache.

Mapache, learning of this, has his men seize Angel; the Bunch is unable to do anything except leave with their money.

But Pike finally decides to make a stand for what he believes in: sticking with his partners, siding with the men who side with him. He, Dutch and the Gorches march to Mapache's headquarters to demand Angel's return. Mapache, who has tortured Angel, grinningly slits his throat. Pike shoots Mapache and, for one long moment, the hundreds of soldiers who have witnessed the killings are stymied. Instead of shooting the Americans, they stand by helplessly.

Pike and his men realize that this is the moment their lives have led up to: one final, bloody, fatal stand. Pike shoots one of the Prussians and the battle is on—four men against an entire army.

The story is sweeping and multilayered, punctuated by several complicated action sequences: the opening bank robbery, ambush and massacre; three or four large crowd scenes in Agua Verde; the train robbery, including a working locomotive, exploding bridge and dozens of horses; and the final shoot-out, one of the most complicated and graphic gun battles ever filmed.

No script for a Peckinpah film was complete until it had been run through his typewriter. With *Wild Bunch,* that meant adding characters, changing scenes, trimming others—enough overall to earn him a screenwriting credit (and his only Oscar nomination).

According to Walon Green, Peckinpah made a number of noteworthy changes. In the opening shoot-out, Peckinpah added the character of Crazy Lee, a member of the Bunch played by Bo Hopkins. Crazy Lee gets left behind in the bank, under orders from Pike to stay until told otherwise. Long after the others have hotfooted it out of town, Lee is still in the bank. Ultimately he is shot by Thornton's men. Not quite dead, he tells them to "kiss my sister's black cat's ass" and shoots three more men before being killed. He is later revealed to be Sykes's grandson.

"I thought Bo was excessive," Green says, "but I thought what Sam did was just right."

After the opening robbery, the Bunch goes to Angel's village. In Green's original script, Angel went alone for what amounted to five pages of Spanish dialogue with subtitles.

"Sam rewrote it and took the Wild Bunch to the village," Green says. "It made a lot of sense. He took a five-page scene in Spanish and made it an English-speaking scene."

Peckinpah also added a flashback scene with Pike Bishop and Deke Thornton together, when they are ambushed and Thornton is captured. He rewrote a scene in which Bishop, about to go to bed with his Mexican paramour, is interrupted by her jealous husband, who kills her and wounds Bishop. Peckinpah then turned it into a flashback that added depth to Bishop's character.

After the train robbery, Green's script called for the Bunch to cross the river on a cable. Peckinpah rewrote it, changing the cable to a bridge, which is then blown up with Thornton and his men standing on it. Then, near the end of the film, as Sykes is returning from delivering a shipment of guns to Mapache, he is ambushed by Thornton's men and wounded. In Green's script, he does not survive; Peckinpah rewrote it so that Sykes was saved by the Indians who were fighting Mapache.

Green's script ended with Thornton refusing to return to the United States with the bounty hunters after the Bunch has been killed by the Army. Peckinpah brought back Sykes and the Indians to Agua Verde, where they offer Thornton the chance to join them, an offer he accepts. It is a moment that gives the ending particular resonance and closure.

Adds Green, "Of every movie I've written, the most faithful to the script was *The Wild Bunch.*"

Though Green is willing to give credit where it is due, he wasn't about to let Peckinpah grab glory willy-nilly. Green thought it fair that Peckinpah add his name to the screenplay, but he took umbrage when Peckinpah tried to put his name first in the credits. He also took Peckinpah to arbitration with the Writers Guild when Peckinpah tried to add his name to the story credit. Peckinpah's name was removed from the story credit (which went to Green and Sickner). The guild also ruled that Green's name deserved to be the first listed in the screenplay credit.

Peckinpah's attempt to insinuate himself isn't particularly newsworthy. Most writers who rewrite another writer's work have a tendency to overestimate just how crucial their contribution is. As Arnold Laven says, "If you asked three writers their contributions on the same screenplay, each one will say he's contributed between seventy-five and ninety percent of the content and concept. As soon as there is another hand in, the likelihood is they'll downplay the other guy and believe what they are saying."

STILL, THE THEMES WERE quintessential Peckinpah: loyalty to partners, living up to a code, honor among the amoral, men caught in the warp of time. The combination of emotional complexity, scenic grandeur and tough, unstinting action made *The Wild Bunch* the perfect comeback vehicle, a film capable of relaunching the career of the toughest reprobate—even Sam Peckinpah.

It was obvious to him how crucial this coming picture was to his career. He knew that he couldn't make the movie he wanted to by being a yes-man to the producer and the studios. On the other hand, he had an image that could work against him.

"He was regarded as thorny and unpredictable; his reputation was as someone who was hard to get along with," Charles Champlin says. "He was known as someone who drank and was obstreperous when drinking."

As he set off to begin shooting in Parras de Madero, Mexico, Peckinpah knew he had yet to fashion the career he thought he should have had by this point. He was forty-three years old. Others of his contemporaries had directed several films and were well known. One in particular seemed to get his goat.

"He had a love-hate thing for [Stanley] Kubrick," says Gary Weis, who at that point was a young would-be photographer, living with Peckinpah's high-school-aged daughter, Sharon, in Peckinpah's house. "He complained that Kubrick was cold but you could tell that he loved him."

Judy Selland, his former sister-in-law, says, "There was an article in *Esquire* about Stanley Kubrick. I remember Sam being mad that they were paying so much attention to Kubrick and not to him. He felt he was just as good if not better than Kubrick and clearly as important."

12

Wild Adventures

"THE WILD BUNCH WAS THE BATAAN DEATH MARCH," Gordon Dawson says. The eighty-one days spent shooting it in Mexico were grueling and grinding. The work took its toll, both physically and mentally. Much of the wear and tear on bodies and psyches came from being stranded in the middle of the high Mexican desert. But an almost equal amount came from the close contact with Peckinpah himself.

"Nothing in Mexico is smooth to shoot," Dawson says. "But I've never done anything harder. Sam takes you to the asshole of creation to shoot. You fall out of bed at four-thirty and don't get in until twelve at night. Everyone was worried about dying. You're rehearsing with full loads in the guns and horses that are skittish. When you're dealing with thirty or forty horses, a lot of things can go wrong."

Though he loved Mexico, Peckinpah suffered the deprivation of creature comforts with the same bad humor as the rest. Under the best of conditions, Peckinpah was irascible, short-tempered, demanding and dictatorial. Under these conditions, he could drive you crazy.

What was Parras like? Hot, isolated, primitive, with daily sandstorms and the occasional monsoon. The food was bad, the water was worse, the bugs were omnipresent. The kind of wildlife that could be counted on for after-hours distraction on most locations was totally absent.

"Off the set, we spent our time drinking and trying to find good food," Gordon Dawson says. "That's all we did."

"We were out in an area that was so dry the cactus had dried up and the horned toads carried canteens," says Joe Canutt, a stuntman who also had worked for Peckinpah on *Major Dundee*. He recalls his stunt crew going to gruesome lengths to entertain themselves while on location.

"There was a graveyard near where we were shooting that had been looted," says Canutt, son of legendary stuntman Yakima Canutt. "Our only

130

entertainment was going into the graveyard and standing the corpses on end and having our pictures taken with them. One of the guys would put a stiff up against the wall and we'd take his picture."

Usually, Peckinpah would unleash his temper on those who were least likely to fight back. Granted, he was the director, the ultimate boss on the set. But Peckinpah also knew that he didn't have the clout or the power to antagonize stars of the magnitude of William Holden, Robert Ryan and even Ernest Borgnine, without cutting his own throat.

But he'd try—at least once with everyone.

William Holden, for example, disliked the way Peckinpah picked on the actors in smaller parts. On the first day of shooting, a sweltering day in the broiling Mexican sun, he watched Peckinpah give hell to everyone involved in an early scene, in which Holden was not involved. After a few minutes, he got up and started to walk out.

"Where are you going?" Peckinpah asked.

"If that's the way things are going to be on this picture, I want no part of it," Holden said. A couple of days later, when Holden had his first turn before the cameras, Peckinpah was still screaming at the actors—everyone except Holden, that is.

Peckinpah also had a run-in with Robert Ryan, another movie veteran, who was upset at filming only two days in five weeks. Assuming he would not be needed until later in the shoot, he asked Peckinpah if he could get a few days off to go back to the United States to work in the presidential campaign of Sen. Robert Kennedy.

"Can't let you go," Peckinpah said. "I might need you."

Ryan was seething after spending the next ten days in costume and makeup without playing a scene. Finally, he grabbed Peckinpah by the shirt and said, "I'll do anything you ask me to do in front of the camera, because I'm a professional. But you open your mouth to me off the set, and I'll knock your teeth in."

Threats of violence, particularly by large, famous stars, seemed to work wonders with the diminutive director. Ernest Borgnine, for example, was upset that clouds of throat-clogging dust were kicked up on the road leading to location. He tried appealing to Peckinpah as a professional, with little success.

Finally, Borgnine had his driver park by the side of the road and wait. When Peckinpah drove up in his limo, he stopped to ask what the matter was. Borgnine said, "Get this road watered or I'm going to beat the shit out of you." Within minutes, two water trucks appeared and settled the dust.

When Holden asked Borgnine how he had managed it, Borgnine smiled and said, "I just said the magic words."

Yet Borgnine eventually worked with Peckinpah again—apparently happily—on *Convoy*. And Ryan, who once told Peckinpah, "If you turn into

Robert Wise, I'll kill you," said after finishing *The Wild Bunch,* "All the Westerns have been made. The only difference is style and Peckinpah's style is extraordinary."

Says Lou Lombardo, "With time, we became the Wild Bunch. I saw what Holden was doing. He was playing Sam. He was running the Bunch like Sam ran the crew."

PECKINPAH KNEW WHAT HE HAD in the actors he worked with most often: men who understood what he was trying to do as well as he did. "I work well with people who like to work, who think it's a privilege to make a film," he said.

He knew there was only so far he could push most of the actors in his stock company. Men such as Ben Johnson, Warren Oates, L. Q. Jones and Dub Taylor were tough and savvy enough not to put up with the kind of mind games Peckinpah liked to play. But one actor seemed particularly vulnerable to Peckinpah's brand of goading: Strother Martin.

A nervous, high-strung actor, Martin was never a star, except among directors and aficionados of brilliant character actors. He got his start in Hollywood in 1950 in *The Asphalt Jungle* and worked steadily in film and TV. He played a retarded character who was the central character in a "Gunsmoke" Peckinpah wrote and a preacher in *Deadly Companions.*

He brought color and diversity to his characters, earning a permanent place in Sixties film lore for uttering the line "What we have here is a failure to communicate" in 1967's *Cool Hand Luke.* In 1969, he appeared in the year's three most visible Westerns: *The Wild Bunch, True Grit* (in which he played a persnickety horse trader) and *Butch Cassidy and the Sundance Kid* (as an affably grimy mine operator in South America).

In *The Wild Bunch,* Peckinpah teamed Martin with L. Q. Jones as a petty bounty hunter. It was one of Martin's most deliciously oily performances, running the gamut from nasty to childish—arguing over credit for a particular kill, coveting a dead man's boots or assuming a wistful look as he imagined his glory if he actually killed Pike Bishop.

But the production itself was torture for Martin because of Peckinpah, who took great amusement in making life miserable for him. "Strother was like Sammy Davis in the Rat Pack," says Cliff Coleman, who became one of Peckinpah's regular assistant directors. "Peckinpah and his guys were always after Strother."

"Strother was totally petrified of Sam," L. Q. Jones says, recalling an incident from the filming of the opening bank robbery. Martin and Jones were standing behind the door of a building, waiting for their cue to come bursting out into the street.

"Sam said Strother's name, but really soft," Jones says. "Strother's head went up. Sam said his name even quieter. Strother turned around to run out —and slammed right into the door. He caromed back about six feet but his feet never stopped. He hit the door again, bounced back once more and went out the door."

"Sam would ride the shit out of Strother," Lou Lombardo says. "Strother was afraid of horses, for example. Sam gave Strother the tallest horse—and then made him mount on a downhill grade."

"He chewed my ass off every line, every, every one of them," Martin said several years later. "I sensed that he liked me but I wasn't sure."

Shooting a scene in which the bounty hunters come riding up to the camera and deliver some lines, Peckinpah wasn't getting what he wanted from Martin—or not enough of it. As Martin later recalled: "He went about ten takes with me and I was trying to get the smooth canter on my horse and he'd had enough of it. He said, 'Mr. Martin, would you get down off your horse? Would you come under the shade with me so we don't have a sunstroke? Now, Mr. Martin, would you tell me why you want so much to fuck up this picture?' "

It was a story Martin repeated for years; according to his friends, he could do a deadly accurate impersonation of Peckinpah's whispery hiss. To add to the effect, he would put a pair of spoons over his eyes, to mimic the withering Peckinpah gaze made impenetrable by mirrored sunglasses.

"I could never tell if he was joking or being serious," Martin said, "because his voice was completely devoid of emotion and you can't see his eyes because of those goddamned mirrored sunglasses. He never said a compliment to me once until we were going in to loop the picture and he turned to me and he said, 'By the way, you were very good in this picture.' "

Although he did it on *Ride the High Country* and *Major Dundee*, Peckinpah really began to develop his reputation for firing crew members on *The Wild Bunch*. It was an aspect of his working persona that reached a peak with his next film, *The Ballad of Cable Hogue*.

"I make trouble with shoddy workmanship," Peckinpah said, "and with shoddy, shabby people, people who don't do their job, and the whiners and complainers and the bitchers and the sore-asses who talk a good piece of work and never produce. I don't know why the hell they went into motion pictures."

Gordon Dawson says, "As he would fire department heads, I would take over their departments. He fired the prop guy for not having enough ammunition, because Sam would rehearse with full loads. In the middle of the second day, he ran out of ammo. And it's not like you can send it down to Mexico without a lot of permits."

Cliff Coleman, who became a regular on Peckinpah films, recalls getting a call to fly to Mexico to replace the first assistant director on *The Wild Bunch*, Phil Rawlins.

"Phil Rawlins was a tough hand, a cowboy," Coleman says. "As I got there, I saw him walk across the yard of the motel and I said, 'Phil, what the hell are you doing? Why am I down here? Who is this guy?' Phil said, 'You can handle him.' I said, 'What about—?' and he said, 'You've got it,' and walked away."

Joe Canutt says, "We counted. On *Wild Bunch,* he fired 37 percent of the company."

Making a mistake alone wasn't cause for dismissal—though you only got to make so many errors before you were, in Peckinpah's parlance, "on the bus" back to Los Angeles. Peckinpah could tolerate a screwup if it was made in the earnest pursuit of making the movie. But you had to admit it; if you tried to argue with him or put the blame on someone else, you were handed your walking papers.

Peckinpah also couldn't abide anyone whose first allegiance wasn't the director and his movie. On a studio film such as *The Wild Bunch,* however, there were people assigned to the picture who worked directly for Warner Bros. Peckinpah's tolerance level for them was low and he did what he could to get rid of them.

"On location, he was sending guys back all the time and getting new ones," says Max Bercutt, former head of publicity at Warner Bros. "It wasn't too much of my business until the unit publicist called and said Peckinpah wanted him off the location."

Bercutt flew down to Mexico, where he met William Holden, an old friend. "He's crazy," Holden told Bercutt about Peckinpah.

"I'm going to have to have a fight about this," Bercutt told Holden. "This isn't some lighting gaffer. I'm not going to send another guy."

When Bercutt confronted Peckinpah, Peckinpah refused to allow the publicist back on the set. "He doesn't pay attention and he annoys me," the director said. Bercutt insisted; Peckinpah threatened to close the set. Finally, Holden stepped in and said, "You better listen to Max. Let this guy stay or I walk."

"Then Holden winked at me," Bercutt recalls.

Gary Combs, a stuntman on the film, was brought in to play a soldier who gets shot and falls off the train during the hijacking to get weapons for Mapache. When another stuntman who was doubling for Holden was hurt, Combs wound up with that assignment as well.

"By the time I got there, they practically had their own travel agency going," Combs says. "He was firing people like wildfire. He actually fired me one day because I didn't have a beard on."

Combs was part of a scene in which he was supposed to wear a fake beard. But after four days of gluing the beard in place and not being called for the shot, Combs says, "My whole face was red and sore from the glue; it looked like a baboon's behind."

So he refused the beard the next morning in makeup. For the next three days, Combs sat around without being called for a shot. On the fourth day, however, Peckinpah pointed to him—then turned apoplectic when he noticed that Combs was minus his beard.

"He started ranting and raving," Combs says. "I grabbed him by the collar and said, 'All right, you little asshole, if you're going to fire me, then get a car and send me home right now.' And he changed his mind and kept me on."

Many directors might not even have noticed that a stuntman, who was an extra in a scene, was missing his beard, leaving that kind of detail work to continuity people. To Peckinpah, however, the smallest details were as crucial as the broadest strokes.

"It was amazing to see the amount of material that man could keep in his head from scene to scene and sequence to sequence," L. Q. Jones says. "There was that painting that he could see in his head at all times."

Lou Lombardo, echoing the sentiments of many of the people who worked for Peckinpah over the years, says, "He instilled in you to do your best. He challenged you, made you reach down and do better. A lot of people resented that, but he did make it better."

To achieve that moment of perfection in front of the camera required a crew that virtually was capable of reading Peckinpah's mind. It was a trick his closest associates learned over the years.

Every day of shooting a movie is a jigsaw puzzle of logistics right down to the question of where to park the trucks for the equipment, dressing rooms, catering and costumes. Put them in the wrong place and, at literally tens of thousands of dollars a day, it can cost a fortune just to take an hour to reposition them so they aren't in the shot.

"Sam was never the kind of director who could tell you three weeks before, 'Put the transportation here because we'll be shooting this way,' " Gordon Dawson says. "You'd be lucky if you knew the day before. The hardest job was finding out what the first shot of the morning would be. He would say, 'You know what the fuck it is. Have it ready.' Then he'd improvise shit that was brilliant."

Cliff Coleman says, "You'd say, 'Sam, what do you want?' And he'd say, 'Well, think about it and what the fuck we're doing here and why isn't my refrigerator stocked?' So you'd get with the troops and say, 'What can we give him?' We'd figure it out and he'd come in and I'd have the camera in the area I thought would work. He'd look through the camera and I'd walk him through it. Then he'd look at you and say, 'Who the fuck told you to do this?' The reason for the brilliance he got was that he took a collage of exciting people, put them in a bucket, lit a fire under it and started to stir. We all got together and tried to survive."

One person Peckinpah would confer with closely before doing anything was Lucien Ballard, his cinematographer.

"Lucien was an austere tight ass, like an aristocrat," Robert Culp says. "And here he was with Sam."

Their relationship was based in part on their longstanding acquaintance, which went all the way back to Peckinpah's TV days. Ballard had worked on *Ride the High Country* and had forgiven Peckinpah for promising him *Major Dundee* then hiring someone else (after Ballard turned down other work while waiting for *Dundee* to shoot).

Ballard admired Peckinpah's drive, his refusal to settle for anything less than perfection.

"No matter how many hours the rest of us put in, the chances are that Peckinpah will put in more," Ballard said. "He might stop by after a day's shooting to have a few drinks with the boys but long after they've gone to bed, he is up rewriting the script and preparing for the next day's shooting. He's a writer and works like a writer with the camera. He's a twenty-four-hour filmmaker."

Peckinpah and Ballard would, as a matter of routine, drive to and from the location together, planning out the shots for the coming day's scenes.

"A lot of so-called great directors just shoot the script, just eat the pages," Ballard said. "But Sam will work until you take the camera away from him."

One afternoon, as they rode back from location, Ballard mentioned that the upcoming scenes—the meeting between the Bunch and Mapache's advisers about stealing the American guns—might be a bit dull. In the previous scene, Angel had killed his ex-fiancée as she sat in Mapache's lap. Ballard suggested to Peckinpah that the meeting scene might be more interesting visually if it were set at night.

"By the time we were ready to shoot, Sam had an interior dressed for night, filled with candles," Ballard said. "And he worked out a new bit of business that made the scene play: A funeral procession for the dead girl winds its way through Mapache's powwow. 'Get that body out of here,' the drunken Mapache yells as she passes him."

ON *THE WILD BUNCH*, as on other films, Peckinpah's drinking was constant, and occasionally heavy. "Sam found it very difficult to communicate with actors when he was sober and I'd say that 80 percent of the time he was drinking," Cliff Coleman says.

Yet the drinking itself never seemed to interfere with the work—at least at this stage of his career.

"He drank continually, but I never saw him drunk on the set," L. Q. Jones says. "In the evenings, when he drank, you could tell he was under the influence. But he worked a twenty-four-hour day. He never turned it loose."

Alcoholism eventually affects all of the body's systems. In later years, along with his multipack-a-day cigarette habit, alcohol would be one of the causes of Peckinpah's chronic respiratory and heart problems.

Alcoholism also has a deleterious effect on the body's ability to manufacture red blood cells and platelets, crucial in the coagulation of blood and the healing of cuts or abrasions. During *The Wild Bunch,* that caused a serious pain in the ass: a raging case of bleeding hemorrhoids.

"Sam was so tunnel-visioned when he wanted to get something that it could be excruciatingly painful," L. Q. Jones says. "He bled through his pants, on the chair. He was going to finish the picture. When something that bad is after you, you start to lose concentration."

But Peckinpah refused to have the hemorrhoids taken care of, perhaps out of fear that he might be fired. He also had a healthy disrespect for the Mexican medical establishment and had no interest in putting himself at the mercy of a Mexican hospital.

"He'd climb up on the camera and you could see all the way down the side of his leg this red, brown, dusty, bloody, stinking, smelling mess would drain out of him," Warren Oates said later. "But he fucking wouldn't quit."

Producer Phil Feldman, concerned for Peckinpah's health, tried to persuade him to get the problem looked at and, one Sunday, imported a specialist from Los Angeles and convinced Peckinpah to be examined. The doctor recommended that Peckinpah have the hemorrhoid removed, a painful operation that would require, at minimum, a few days for recuperation.

Peckinpah finally said, "If you can take them out in the kitchen by a kerosene lamp, which is the way my granddad had his taken out, and you promise me I can be at work on Monday, I'll do it."

The doctor termed those conditions impossible; a hospital had to figure into the equation somewhere, he said. To which Peckinpah replied, "Nothing doing."

"He went through the whole fucking movie like that," Oates said. "He'd get a shot in the ass for pain and that son of a bitch stuck up there every day."

Alcoholism also disrupts sleep patterns, causing a maldistribution of REM (rapid eye movement) sleep, the period in which the mind unwinds by allowing dreams. REM sleep is a key to the restful quality of slumber, but alcoholics tend to be insomniacs because they have trouble achieving REM and so are condemned to nightmares.

"Sam would stay up all night because he couldn't sleep," Cliff Coleman says. "We'd have long conversations. Then we'd go by in the morning and force him into his clothes and drag him to the set. Through sign language, mumbling and grunting, he'd come around to where he was able to communicate with the actors."

Yet Lou Lombardo, acknowledging that Peckinpah was prone to drink, still says, "Sam was happier on that picture than I'd ever seen him. He was having the time of his life. He had all the paramours he wanted. He was flying girls in and out. He was tan and healthy and happy and working his ass off."

Along with the technical and creative assistance they provided, Peckinpah relied on his crew, particularly his inner circle, to keep him from getting bored on the location. Camaraderie was as much a part of movie-making as exposing film, sometimes more important. Playtime relaxed the demons, satisfied the psyche, kept the world at bay, before it was necessary to jump back into the work the next day. Creating a film was tough, exhausting work and it required an equally disciplined approach to blowing off steam—for everyone except Peckinpah.

"You always had to body-guard him," Gordon Dawson says, "because he'd get drunk and get into trouble. He was a lot of fun to be with until he picked on the biggest bastard in the bar and you had to deal with him."

Adds Lou Lombardo, "He wasn't very big but he had the heart of a lion. He would fight anybody. There was a lot of anger there and a lot of courage. He was a fucker and a fighter and a wild-horse rider."

One Friday afternoon during production, L. Q. Jones and Warren Oates were trying to sneak away from the location early for a weekend of sanity somewhere other than Parras. Peckinpah's habit was to work straight through until Saturday afternoon, then cut loose until Monday morning and start in again. He caught Oates and Jones before they could disappear and shanghaied them into accompanying him on a visit to a female extra who had been hurt during filming and was in the hospital.

"Chalo [Gonzalez, Peckinpah's driver] was playing the guitar and Sam was screaming and dancing around the room," Jones says. "They finally physically threw us out."

As they were driving back to their quarters, Peckinpah made Gonzalez stop the car at a bar "where they'll cut your throat for $1.50," Jones says. After a few hours there, they drove on, until Peckinpah had the car stopped again—"This time, in a part of town where they'll cut your throat to give you $1.50," Jones says.

"We go into a bar filled with people who would absolutely petrify King Kong," Jones continues. "Sam gets a drink and says to the bartender, 'Did you piss in this? 'Cuz that's what it tastes like.' The next thing I know, Warren and I are against the wall fighting for our lives. We nearly got killed. Sam, meanwhile, got in the car and went home."

Work time evoked a "misery loves company" attitude in Peckinpah. Lou Lombardo remembers being immersed in editing at the makeshift facility they had concocted in the clubhouse of a golf course at a retirement home near the location. Peckinpah was shooting at a location thirty miles out in the desert and called Lombardo on the radio phone that linked him to the production offices.

Lombardo, however, refused to take the call and told his assistant to hang up. Peckinpah called several times, finally threatening a secretary with physical harm if she didn't put Lombardo on the phone. When he got the editor, he hissed, "You son of a bitch. Answer the fucking phone. Now come out here and sweat with me."

"That was literally what he wanted," Lombardo said. "I spent two hours in a bouncy car on a bumpy road to sit and sweat and drink beer with him. He demanded camaraderie from anybody he wanted to be tight with. He wanted them with him, wanted them to share his feelings."

Coming from a background in television, Lombardo had the requisite speed to keep up with the mountains of film that Peckinpah was shooting. As Peckinpah shot, Lombardo was editing. Peckinpah would have multiple cameras cranking on the action scenes—some at the normal rate of speed, some much faster to produce the slow-motion imagery that the screenplay called for.

Peckinpah knew he was getting good material. But he was leery of showing anything to anyone before he was completely satisfied with it. He was afraid of being second-guessed, afraid of having the plug pulled based on someone else's interpretation of an incomplete version of any sequence.

So he gave Lombardo a direct order: "Don't show anybody anything you cut until I see it. If Feldman walks in, pull the plug on the moviola."

As Lombardo edited, he was having problems getting one crucial sequence cut together. Peckinpah was in meetings about whether or not to reshoot the sequence, a process that would have been costly and time-consuming. Lombardo was sequestered in his editing cubbyhole.

"Now when I'm involved in editing a sequence," Lombardo says, "I don't know who is in the room. So I'm in the room, really fighting this sequence and I finally got it to work. I look up and the first assistant director is standing there and he says, 'It works.' And I said, 'Yeah, it does.' "

The assistant director ran off to tell Peckinpah. In triumph, Lombardo headed into town for dinner. Before leaving, he mixed himself a martini, his first of the picture, because he had only just gotten hold of a bottle of vermouth. As he drove down the dirt road toward Parras, Lombardo passed Peckinpah running in the opposite direction, with the assistant director on his tail. Lombardo had his driver stop the car because "I thought he'd heard that some dailies had been ruined or something."

Peckinpah came around a corner, his face a frightening shade of red. He approached Lombardo and swung at him with a roundhouse left; he missed the editor but knocked his martini into the nearby golf course.

"Hey, it took me three weeks to get that vermouth," Lombardo protested.

But Peckinpah, now backed up by a half-dozen large stuntmen, was advancing on him, cursing him and finally saying in an accusing tone, "You showed them the film."

"No, I didn't," Lombardo said, talking fast to forestall a beating. Apparently, he was convincing; Peckinpah sheepishly dismissed his phalanx of stuntmen.

Then he turned to Lombardo and said, in quiet disbelief, "It works?"

Peckinpah's paranoia about Warner Bros.' reaction to what he was shooting remained strong. After Lombardo had finished cutting the first ten reels, Peckinpah told him to stop trying to keep up and go back and polish those ten reels.

"Sam, why don't we get it all in one piece first?" Lombardo said.

"No, I've got my reasons," Peckinpah told him. Peckinpah had been tipped off that the Warner brass were going to come down to Mexico to see what he had been shooting. Peckinpah wanted them to see as finished a product as possible, even if it was only a part of the whole film. So Lombardo went over and over the first ten reels (which contain the harrowing bank robbery and shoot-out) in anticipation of showing it to Warner Bros.

A couple of weeks later, Peckinpah got the word to bring the footage he had to Mexico City to show to a contingent of visiting Warner executives. "We showed it to them and they loved it," Lombardo says.

"Sam was kind of on thin ice going in," he continues. "They wanted to see what they had before they gave him any more time or location money. After those ten reels, there was no problem."

PECKINPAH DEMANDED A LOT from his crew for each of the key action sequences. He shot lengthy master shots of the crucial scenes, which meant that, for up to six or seven minutes at a time, everyone—actors, technicians, crew members—had to be on their toes and on their marks. A mental lapse in the final seconds could negate the previous five or six minutes of work.

"I don't think there was a scene with less than a seven-and-a-half-minute master," Cliff Coleman says. "There were cuts through *Wild Bunch* but if you glued them together, you'd get one piece. What he'd demand was to see the whole sequence as he continued to piece it together. That's the way he liked to work. I'd create a bit of life that was scripted right down to the details."

Two sequences in particular were problematic: the scene in which Pike Bishop blows the bridge out from under Deke Thornton and the climactic killing spree, in which the members of the Wild Bunch die, eliminating most of Mapache's forces in the process.

Bud Hulburd had risen to the top of the special-effects crew by attrition.

According to Joe Canutt, Hulburd was not particularly experienced with explosives but got the job because everyone above him had been fired.

When Canutt, who was Robert Ryan's stunt double, examined the bridge before shooting the scene, he found it was rigged to blow sky-high. The eight or ten pilings supporting the center section of the bridge had each been drilled with holes for eight or ten sticks of dynamite—at a 40 percent concentration of nitroglycerine. Enough, in other words, to turn the bridge into kindling and blow the stuntmen back to Hollywood.

When Canutt asked the Mexican effects man what was going on, he said, "Sam said not to tell the stunt guys." So Canutt went to Peckinpah and said, "I've got a flash for you. I don't do things with my eyes shut."

Canutt was not particularly crazy about Peckinpah anyway. "He was a prick; if he could ride someone, he would," Canutt says. Canutt was convinced that Peckinpah was smoking pot, taking peyote and anything else he could lay his hands on. "He was smoking something. Those scenes may not have been slow-motion; maybe that was normal for him."

Peckinpah called a meeting to discuss the scene, angry that Canutt would make an issue out of it. For Canutt's part, he knew that challenging a director could be "the kiss of death, but nobody was going to blow me up."

At the meeting, Peckinpah said, "Joe doesn't want us to cut the timbers with dynamite. Maybe he can tell us how to do it."

Canutt did have a solution: a setup known as a weak knee, which falls like a trapdoor. The bridge would be held by two-by-sixes and a telephone pole, which would be cut by a chainsaw. Eight sticks of dynamite would blow it away—instead of the fifty or sixty that Hulburd had planned. But the image would be the same: a bridge full of men with the ground pulled out from under them, plunging into the river below.

Still, Canutt was not convinced that the stunt was safe. There were charges on both ends of the bridge and one in the water that had to be fired in sequence. But Canutt knew that accidents could happen: If the men on horseback went into the water too early, for example, and the last charge was then ignited, the concussion could kill them.

When he tried to explain this to Hulburd, however, Hulburd was adamant: This was how Peckinpah wanted the charges fired and, no matter what, this was how he would blow them.

So, unbeknownst to Peckinpah and Hulburd, Canutt enlisted Gordon Dawson to stand near Hulburd holding a club behind his back. Dawson's instructions from Canutt were explicit: If anyone goes into the water before Hulburd blows the final charge, hit Hulburd over the head with the club and knock him out before he can set off the last explosive.

Fortunately for everyone, the sequence went off as planned. No one was accidentally blown up or clubbed over the head.

13

The Slow-Motion Leap

THE FINAL SHOOT-OUT, which came to be known among the crew as the Battle of Bloody Porch, required, according to Gordon Dawson, that they kill "15,000 people with 350 Mexican army uniforms."

It was only several hundred soldiers. But with multiple takes—and the fact that it was shot and reshot for eleven days to get all the action from every angle—it probably approximates Dawson's estimate.

Initially, Dawson says, Peckinpah was stumped: "He stepped up on the porch and he was lost. He didn't have a clue. Everyone had to go away, sit down and shut up. He talked with Lucien to figure it out. He knew he had a good picture and that it was important. Eventually, enough footage was shot on that porch for four movies."

Peckinpah worked his way across the veranda, covering about a foot and a half of terrain with each shot. He would shoot the action in the foreground, then restage it to capture the middle ground, then once more to get the background—all of which would eventually be intercut to make the seamless carnival of carnage that would conclude the picture.

But with a limited number of Mexican army uniforms, time was needed between each take to clean up the now-bloody costumes. They also needed to reset the squibs, the tiny explosive charges that blew holes in the condoms full of stage blood under the costumes, sending geysers of gore flying from the bullet wounds.

Blood bags were not an innovation—but showing the blood squirting out of a bullet wound was, shockingly so. For an added touch of realism, Dawson says, Peckinpah had them lay a thin slice of raw steak across the blood bag. Both blood and tissue seemed to be torn loose by bullets.

Eventually, Dawson, Jim Silke and Cliff Coleman set up a kind of assembly line to get the soldiers cleaned up and resquibbed. They'd wash the stage blood off, close up the bullet holes with tape, give the uniform a layer of

khaki paint and dirty it up to look lived in but not yet killed in. After wiring a
new squib, the soldier would be sent back to the front lines.

As Coleman says, "We could squib Mexicans faster than you could shoot
dice."

Many of the Mexican extras were actual members of the Mexican army.
Lou Lombardo had been brought out of the editing room to direct the
second unit while Peckinpah concentrated on the scenes with the principals.

"I was next to the camera, with this plastic shield in front of me,"
Lombardo says. "The wads from the rifles were hitting the shield and the
shield was banging against my head. The prop guy came up and said, 'Did
you know those bandoliers the soldiers are wearing have real bullets?' I said,
'Jesus Christ, get them away from [the soldiers].' I had this image that, in
the heat of the moment, if one of them put a real bullet in, I'd have had a
hole in my head."

PECKINPAH'S DEPICTION OF VIOLENCE in the film—the blood bags, squibs and
pieces of flying meat—set a new standard for eruptive, squirting bloodletting
in Hollywood. It was an area in which Hollywood was still squeamish; until
the 1960s, violence in films consisted of gunshots, followed by images of
people clutching unseen wounds and dropping quietly dead.

The uproar about violence in films had reached a crescendo with *Bonnie
and Clyde*, when the film's title characters are blown away in a hail of machine-gun fire in a brief, partially slow-motion sequence at the film's conclu-
sion. The outcry would grow in volume when more and more filmmakers
began to take their cue from Peckinpah's more gorily realistic, yet still stylized vision of violent death in *The Wild Bunch*.

Peckinpah had an image in his mind for several years before he ever got
the chance to implement it in *The Wild Bunch*. As Joe Bernhard recalls,
Peckinpah focused on a memory from a hunting trip after *Ride the High
Country*, where he had shot a buck.

Bernhard remembers Peckinpah telling him, "The bullet went in the size
of a dime. But the blood on the snow was the size of a salad plate. That's the
way violence is. That's the way death is. And that's what I want to do on
film." Says Bernhard, "He thought if he showed violence the way it really is,
people would shun violence."

Before the introduction of the new rating system in 1968, scripts were
submitted to the production code office before production to get an early
assessment of potential problem areas. On January 30, 1968, Jeffrey Sher-
lock, vice president and director of production code administration at the
Motion Picture Association of America, wrote to Ken Hyman about *The
Wild Bunch*: "In its present form, the story is so violent and bloody and
filled with so many crudities of language that we would hesitate to say that a

picture based on this material could be approved under the production code."

There followed a lengthy list of code violations, along these lines:

· "Page 117: Mapache severs Angel's throat. This is unacceptable."
· "Page 118: The carnage depicted on this page, in which the incredible number of personalized and brutal killings constitute a bloodbath, could not be approved in the finished picture."
· "Page 119: The bloodbath continues unabated on this page and could not be approved as written."

Once the ratings code was implemented, however, the standard of what was unacceptable shifted drastically. Though this was the most violent film to be released up to that point, an X rating was never even a consideration.

"We had an R right from the beginning," Peckinpah said. "I actually cut out more than Warners requested. I cut parts of the violence after we got our rating because I thought they were excessive to the points I wanted to make. I not only want to talk about violence in the film but I have a story to tell too, and I don't want the violence, per se, to dominate what is happening to the people."

Ken Hyman confirms Peckinpah's recollection: "I didn't want to cut it as much as he did."

The only points the ratings administration quibbled with had to do with sex, not violence. In the scene where Lyle and Tector Gorch are cavorting in a wine vat with a trio of Mexican whores, Ben Johnson, as Tector, had ad-libbed a line: "Lookee here, Lyle, nipples as long as your thumb." The line was excised—though not the image of Tector fondling the woman's breast or the words, "Lookee here, Lyle."

IN WRITING HIS SCRIPT, Walon Green had tried to capture the feeling of his favorite action film: Akira Kurosawa's *The Seven Samurai*.

"That had a total of two slow-motion shots in it," Green says. "I thought, wouldn't it be fantastic if the action sequences were in slow motion?"

Others had used similar ideas in the past. Besides *Bonnie and Clyde,* John Derek used slow-motion action sequences in the otherwise forgettable 1965 World War II film, *Once Before I Die.* John Boorman utilized brief slow-motion flashback shots in his 1967 revenge film, *Point Blank.*

Green included the concept in his original script. "Other people said it would have to be taken out," Green says. "Sam was the only guy who read it and thought about keeping it."

While Peckinpah is often credited with virtually inventing slow motion, he only helped innovate its use, together with Lou Lombardo.

Green says, "I wrote it so the whole thing was in slow motion. When they cut it that way, the slow-motion shots played so long that it blew the rhythm of the sequence. Luckily, they shot it both ways. Lou Lombardo saved it. He cut it for the moments in the slow motion, for that one instant. He recut and redesigned the sequence. He saved it."

Lombardo knew going into the editing room what he had, because he'd been behind the camera shooting the second unit. "I had shot about half of it so I knew how I was going to play it. I sketched it out and then Sam came in and told me how to paint it. It was a collaborative thing. He had a great story mind, a great editorial mind."

The resulting film—action sequences that interlaced fierce, bullet-riddled action with stunning inserts that caught the dancelike quality of the violence at peak moments—changed the way people looked at and thought about violence in action films.

Critic Andrew Sarris says that while slow motion was not an innovation for Peckinpah, "he used it better. The combination of frenzied cutting and the slow motion and the blood and balletic grace of people dying carried it to the ultimate level. You had the feeling that it became orgasmic. The way he staged it was very erotic."

Adds critic Michael Sragow, "After Peckinpah, it seemed anyone doing an action movie did slow motion. It became cliché in movies in general, although he tended to do it differently."

The editing of *The Wild Bunch* was complex: more than 3,600 individual cuts, giving the violent-action sequences an almost kaleidoscopic feel, without losing the sense of placing the viewer smack dab in the middle of the action.

Most of the editing work was done in Torreón, near Parras. Having spent the better part of three months shooting there, Peckinpah and Lombardo stayed for another three months editing the rough cut.

After three months of editing in Mexico, Lombardo threatened mutiny if he couldn't get back to Los Angeles and his family. So Peckinpah pulled up stakes and moved back to L.A. in August 1968—where he promptly began preproduction on his next film, *The Ballad of Cable Hogue*. When he started shooting the film, in January 1969, he was still fine-tuning *The Wild Bunch* and would finish editing it during production of *Cable Hogue*.

The first cut of *The Wild Bunch* was five hours long. "We realized that we couldn't release a five-hour picture," Lombardo says. After six months of editing, they had it down to three hours and forty-five minutes, still far too long.

"We got it down to three hours and things started to get anxious," Lombardo says. "He finally told me, 'Lose the footage but don't touch a frame.' " Lombardo worked at it another three months—and got it down to two hours and twenty-four minutes.

Director Paul Schrader, who was a critic for the *L.A. Weekly* and *Cinema* magazine, interviewed Peckinpah at the time. "I saw the 3:45 version and it was absolutely brilliant," Schrader says. "Every time they cut it down, it was less so. But those were good days for him. He had made his masterpiece. Warner Bros. thought it would be the success of his career."

To score the film, Feldman wanted Lalo Schifrin. But Peckinpah convinced him to hire composer Jerry Fielding, who had worked with him on *Noon Wine*. Peckinpah had developed a lasting friendship with Fielding, though the two were as dissimilar as could be imagined.

"Sam was a native Californian from a California political background, while my husband was an intellectual, a Jewish kid from Pittsburgh," says Camille Fielding, the late composer's widow. "They were diametric opposites. Usually at the end of a movie with Sam, Jerry would go to bed exhausted for a month to try to recover. But they wanted to work together. It was hard work, a challenge they both felt with each other."

"Jerry was one of the most aware and concerned people I knew," says Lois O'Connor Robards, who introduced Peckinpah to Fielding. "He was a true humanitarian in every sense of the word. Long before everyone was talking about nuclear disarmament, he was talking about the conflagration. Twenty years or more ago, he was worried about injustices to blacks, about the environment. There was never a night where he didn't come out as you were leaving and say, 'Here's a pamphlet or a book' and tell you you had to read it."

The Peckinpah-Fielding friendship was consistent, if rocky. "My husband got so mad at him once that he threw a chair at him," Camille Fielding says, although that hardly differentiated Fielding from a large group of people whom Peckinpah infuriated.

"Jerry was extremely loyal," says Lois Robards. "He took such abuse from [Sam], yet Jerry admired the son of a bitch."

And Peckinpah admired Fielding's perfectionism. "Jerry sweated every note," Lois Robards says. "He knew what it was supposed to sound like."

Fielding's score was an alternately rousing and evocative work, blending strains of Mexico, the old West and the panoramic sweep of the open territory. "There was more music in *The Wild Bunch* than in *My Fair Lady*," Camille Fielding says. It was the only other aspect of the film to be recognized with an Academy Award nomination.

WHEN PECKINPAH AND LOMBARDO got the film down to a running time of less than 2:30, the film was taken out for previews. Thinking that the themes of loyalty, honor and the closing of the American West would appeal to a middle-American audience, Peckinpah had Warner Bros. schedule the first preview for Kansas City, Missouri, on May 1, 1969.

Max Bercutt, who was on hand as head of Warners' publicity, says, "The house was absolutely full for the preview—on a Wednesday night, at that. And the greatest number of people in the audience were women. Halfway through the picture, I walked into the lobby and about twenty women were there, en masse, saying, 'How dare you show a picture like this?' It turned out that there were four hundred teachers in the audience; there was a teachers' convention in town."

While some of the response was positive, the bulk of the mail-in reaction cards reflected the animosity that the film inspired:

· "The worst potpourri of vulgarity, violence, sex and bloodshed I've seen put together. What a disgusting waste of talent of five good actors."
· "This was the worst movie I've ever seen. It was ridiculous, stupid, with no motive or purpose at all."
· "Do not release this film. The whole thing is sick. To praise everything that is immoral, i.e., brutal death, prostitution, foul language, etc., that [have] made the open sores in our society today. The film is sick, sick, sick."
· "Would suggest you rename it *Bath of Blood*—of course, this would then indicate to future moviegoers that the picture is a horror picture. But truly you didn't intend it as anything else."
· "It is sickening to see so much violence, unnecessary bloodshed and to see innocent children and women killed for no reason."
· "This picture is not fit to be shown to any audience."

Tom Leathers, a writer for the monthly *Town Squire,* from the upscale Kansas City suburb of Shawnee Mission, wrote, "As the film ended, the hissing started in the audience. Then the tired and battered audience filed slowly out. I looked over at the two rows of seats that had been occupied earlier by director Peckinpah, producer Feldman and the rest. But the seats were empty by now. Maybe they realized the attitude of the crowd and feared a lynching. Or maybe they couldn't stand the sight of all that blood and went out for a smoke.

"Out in front of the theater, four black limousines waited to take the Warner Bros. people back to their hotel. The cars had been rented from a local funeral home, the driver said. It seemed a fitting gesture."

Peckinpah was unfazed by the response. He wrote a note to Bercutt saying that, while Leathers "detested the picture, he inadvertently came up with a line that might be of interest: 'Think of a way to kill and it was part of *The Wild Bunch.'* What are your thoughts?"

Peckinpah knew what he had before he went to Kansas City. He described it at one point as "what happens when killers go to Mexico." But he knew it was going to hit people in a way no other film had hit them.

"They're really going to get disturbed about this, I'll tell you," he said. "I'm exhausted when I see it, I'm literally exhausted. And all it is really is a simple adventure story."

Peckinpah's only other response to the preview was to order all of the sound effects—particularly the gunfire—redubbed. He wanted each gun to have a distinctive sound and to be amplified on the soundtrack to make the sounds terrifyingly potent.

Even then, Peckinpah was haunted by the absence of an element that was always glaringly obvious to him—though no one else ever noticed it.

Paul Peterson, an ex-brother-in-law of Peckinpah's who spent most of the late 1970s as one of his running buddies, says, "You couldn't work for Sam if you didn't carry a clipboard to jot down notes. The reason he insisted was that in *The Wild Bunch,* when Sam was editing with Lou, Sam made a comment that he wanted to overlay the sound of flies buzzing in that postbattle scene at the end. But he never remembered to put them in. As a result, he felt *The Wild Bunch* was incomplete."

The film was previewed again, this time in Long Beach, California, but again with unforeseen problems. The theater that was chosen for the sneak preview was showing *The Killing of Sister George,* a film based on Frank Marcus's hit play of the period about a lesbian couple, which had been rated X. As a result, the R-rated *Wild Bunch* was subject to the same restrictions as *Sister George:* No one under seventeen was to be admitted.

Peckinpah had invited several Mexican extras from the film to the preview; they came with children in tow. The manager of the theater, fearing for his license, refused to allow the children into the theater.

When the Mexican family complained, Peckinpah jumped into the fray, trying at first to reason with, then to bully the manager into letting the families in. But the manager was afraid of being shut down for allowing minors into an X-rated film.

Bercutt, who was on hand to monitor this screening as well, asked what the problem was and Peckinpah told him: "I want them in or I'm not going to show the picture."

"Sam, if you let them in, this guy can lose his job," Bercutt said.

"Fuck you, Max," Peckinpah retorted. "We're not running the picture."

Bercutt offered to put the kids into a limousine and take them to another theater, but Peckinpah was adamant: "If they don't go in, the picture doesn't start."

"Fuck you, Sam," Bercutt said, then turned to the manager and said, "Start the picture."

Lou Lombardo, who was standing there at the time, recalls Peckinpah smiling at Bercutt and saying, "Come here a minute," then throwing an arm over Bercutt's shoulder and leading him around a corner.

Bercutt recalls: "Suddenly he turns me around and pulls my hat over my eyes. So I hit him. I must have knocked him three feet. He got up and I knocked him down again. Lou Lombardo ran over and grabbed me. Sam says, 'Hold him,' and he hits me in the mouth."

Lombardo says, "Sam is like on eggshells, wobbly, muttering, 'Mother-fucker, I think I broke my hand.' But he didn't want to go to the hospital."

Says Bercutt, "He turned around and ran down the street to a saloon. I said to hell with it and went into the theater. Afterward, I'm standing there with blood dripping from my mouth and Lou and Sam come back. Sam says, 'You're the fastest guy I ever saw.'"

"Max nearly put Sam out," says Lombardo. "Eventually, I took Sam to the hospital and he had broken his hand."

That was Peckinpah's modus operandi: a sneak attack with a roundhouse left. There was no way Peckinpah could have known that Bercutt, in his college days, had been the welterweight boxing champion at the University of Southern California.

Today, Bercutt says of the encounter, "I felt sorry for him. He was a little man who had to get drunk to do what he wanted. I was sorry I even hit him but I had no alternative. It was strictly a cowboy deal."

14

Unleashing *The Wild Bunch*

WARNER BROS. RELEASED THE COMPLETED FILM in Europe in the spring of 1969 in the 2:24 version, then began screening the film for the American press in advance of the July 1969 release. A press junket in the Bahamas produced a wildly divergent set of reactions, ranging from revulsion to ecstasy.

One critic who saw the film early was Jay Cocks of *Time* magazine, who had gone out to Hollywood in the spring of 1969 to do a story about the Oscars "as an excuse to meet people I'd always wanted to meet."

One was Peckinpah, who, after a lengthy chat, took Cocks to the editing room, where Lombardo was polishing the final gun battle of *The Wild Bunch.*

"He said, 'Take a look at this shit,' " Cocks says. "It was three minutes of the ending of *Wild Bunch*. I had never seen anything like it. It was a screen smaller than a video Walkman but it was atomic in intensity. I couldn't wait to see the movie."

When Cocks was invited to a screening in New York, he took along his friend Martin Scorsese, a film teacher at New York University who was trying to break into features as a director. The two of them sat in the front row of the nearly empty Warner Bros. screening room, which they shared with only two other critics that day: Judith Crist and Rex Reed.

"We were mesmerized by it; it was obviously a masterpiece," Scorsese recalls. "It was real filmmaking, using film in such a way that no other form could do it; it couldn't be done any other way. To see that in an American filmmaker was so exciting."

Reed's and Crist's reaction? "The two of them spent the whole movie screaming and really carrying on, about how dare Warner Bros. release such an atrocity, and so forth," Cocks says. "For Marty and me, it was a great shared experience. We literally turned to each other at the end and were stunned. We were looking at each other, shaking our heads, like we had just come out of a shared fever dream."

Cocks wrote a review in *Time* that came out two weeks before the film opened, in which he referred to it as "a raucous, violent, powerful feat of American filmmaking." He talked about the "sweeping visual panorama of the whole film" and "the extraordinarily forceful acting from a troupe of Hollywood professionals." Calling it "Sam Peckinpah's triumph," Cocks said the film's accomplishments were "sufficient to confirm that Peckinpah, along with Stanley Kubrick and Arthur Penn, belongs with the best of the newer generation of American filmmakers."

Cocks wasn't alone:

· Vincent Canby, *New York Times:* "The first truly interesting American-made Western in years."

· Richard Schickel, *Life* magazine: "*The Wild Bunch* is the first master-piece in the new tradition of 'the dirty Western.' The promise of *Ride the High Country* has finally been fulfilled in what may someday emerge as one of the most important records of the mood of our times and one of the most important American films of the era."

· Stanley Kauffman, *The New Republic:* "[Peckinpah] is such a gifted director that I don't see how one can avoid using the word 'beautiful' about his work. It is a matter of kinetic beauty in the very violence that his film lives and revels in."

But the praises were hardly unanimous. Arthur Knight, in *Saturday Review,* sniped, "I very much doubt that anyone who was not totally honest in his wrongheadedness could ever come up with a picture as wholly revolting as this."

Judith Crist wrote in *New York* magazine, "The film winds up with a shootdown that is the bloodiest and most sickening display of slaughter that I can ever recall in a theatrical film, and quotes attributed to Mr. Holden that this sort of ultra-violence is a healthy purgative for viewers are just about as sick."

Joseph Morgenstern wrote in *Newsweek:* "A chasm yawns and a river of blood flows between what *The Wild Bunch* wanted to be and what it is. Peckinpah could only have intended *The Wild Bunch* to be the last word on violence, but that too was to no avail. It is only the latest word. Several hundred senseless frontier killings don't add up to enlightenment. They only add up to several hundred senseless frontier killings."

Director Peter Bogdanovich, who was still a critic and film historian at the time, says he talked to director Howard Hawks shortly after *The Wild Bunch* was released. Hawks shook his head and said, "I can kill ten guys in the time it takes him to kill one."

But to Peckinpah's friend, critic Pauline Kael, *The Wild Bunch* is "the film that expresses him most fully," she says. "It was so much more complex than his earlier films. It was so devastating. He was ready to make a big Western. *Ride the High Country* was mythologizing. *The Wild Bunch* got the viciousness up there too."

As PECKINPAH WAS SHOOTING *The Wild Bunch* in Mexico, the United States was thrashing about in political turmoil. Martin Luther King, Jr., was assassinated and the cities erupted. Eugene McCarthy challenged President Lyndon Johnson, using the Vietnam War as a moral touchstone—and drove the president from office. As millions of Americans were protesting a war they found unjust and immoral, millions more were about to elect a man president who would prolong the war for an additional six years.

And here was Peckinpah in Mexico, making a movie about amoral badmen who wind up as the heroes of their own life story only at the point at which they lay down their lives. They don't do it because of something they believe in but because it's time—because they have lived by the gun and feel compelled to die by it as well.

They were antiheroes, a reflection of an America in which ideals no longer seemed to hold much meaning, where the government systematically was lying to its people.

Without knowing it—or perhaps knowing it but refusing to articulate it—Peckinpah was making a movie that reflected the times without being about the times. But he tried not to discuss it in those terms.

"He didn't like to talk about what he did," his daughter Kristen says. "There's the fear that, if you name the thing, you diminish it or it won't come back to you."

Adds Gill Dennis, her husband, "He was not trying to show you something that he understood. He was trying to show you things he didn't understand, things you refused to look at or hid from. He thought about things a lot, but he mistrusted talk."

Comedian-satirist Mort Sahl, a longtime Peckinpah acquaintance, says, "He looked around and felt something was missing in America. Sam was interested in areas of social hypocrisy, in people who talk with their head and ignore their heart. He was a Frank Capra 1939 American. He was his own man and belonged to himself. But he worked for people who felt unencumbered by ethics in their dealings with him."

Were it not for the characters created in the Walon Green–Sam Peckinpah screenplay, *The Wild Bunch* would not have struck the kinds of chords it did with critics and audiences alike. Very quickly, these became men that you thought about—and cared about—as they watched an epoch come to a close, rendering them and their way of life extinct.

Without that depth of feeling, the film might have been dismissed as a violent aberration, a negative example of what the new Hollywood freedom had wrought. But there was substance to these characters and their story.

As a result, the startlingly violent, breathtakingly edited action sequences —the initial bank robbery, the train robbery and bridge explosion, the final massacre at Agua Verde—took on new emotional color. There was a cost for this violence, in blood and life. And it was heightened by stylized flourishes that made the action even more frightening, more compelling, more vital.

"It was a Western all of us had written at one point, where the cowboys go in at the end and know they're going to die and shoot it out," Jim Silke says.

Says Martin Scorsese, "What amazed me was the hardness of the characters. There was no attempt to ingratiate them; the audience had to accept them on their own terms. They were no-good bad guys. And when they're all gone—how moving that is. It was savage poetry."

As Peckinpah himself said, "The strange thing is that you feel a great sense of loss when these killers reach the end of the line."

The film became a kind of touchstone, shorthand for graphic violence on the screen. In the ensuing two decades, movies got more and more graphic. Yet *The Wild Bunch* was still the reference point as late as five years after its release when a critic wanted to make a point about the excesses of movie violence.

And it was still engendering debates, or at least attacks from critics who refused to acknowledge its importance, years after its release. When *Action* magazine published a poll in 1975, listing the twelve best Westerns of all time as selected by 250 film critics, Judith Crist felt compelled to respond in a piece in *Take One* magazine, going out of her way to slam *The Wild Bunch* and its inclusion on the list.

"I find this 1969 movie the epitome of the blood-lust slaughter-cult film," she wrote, "two hours of murder and mayhem wherein the innocents are killed by the bad guys who are killed by worse guys. I'd as lief drop in on the local abattoir for entertainment and look to the bloodiest spaghetti western for social significance."

"I think *Wild Bunch* scared people as much as it turned them on," *L.A. Times* entertainment editor Charles Champlin says today. "It made Peckinpah seem like a man who could go over the top in terms of the conventional expectations of this town. It was a film about violence, not just using violence. It was symbolic of a new day in the treatment of violence. This wasn't violence being used as a surrogate for sex. It had a specific gravity, with blood spurting from a cut throat. It was a symbol of freedom and latitude in content."

Peckinpah always took great pride in the film. His favorite moment was the absurdly tense giggle the gang shares, just after Pike has killed Mapache.

By all rights, they should already be dead—but they have buffaloed an entire army. They could walk away, but what would be the point?

James Coburn recalls seeing an early screening of *The Wild Bunch,* at Peckinpah's invitation. Afterward, Coburn said, "All that slow-motion death reminds me of Kurosawa." To which Peckinpah replied, "Thank you."

Peckinpah relished the attention the film drew. After five years of not being able to make a movie, who wouldn't? No one in his situation could be blamed for exercising his ego. Still, Jim Silke, who had been with him through the hardest times, was dismayed by the Peckinpah he saw emerge in the numerous interviews he did.

"He didn't perform well with the press—it was too much attention," Silke says. "I got mad at him. He began to talk about philosophy. And the rule he taught me was: You don't talk about it. You do it. He did interview after interview where he would talk about the importance and the philosophy. I couldn't even use the word 'important' in front of him. It was against his law. He had a sense of appearance and how to present himself but he was not at his best doing that."

PECKINPAH SEEMED CONVINCED that he had a hit on his hands. "The studio seems to share my enthusiasm," he said to one interviewer at the time. To another, he said, "A good picture is usually 70 percent of your intentions. *Ride the High Country* was 60 percent for me. *The Wild Bunch* was about 96 percent."

It turned out to be less, however, when Warner Bros. took it out of theaters after its initial two weeks and trimmed five minutes from the film. The cuts included a scene in which Pancho Villa's forces attack Mapache at a train station, as he learns that the Bunch has successfully stolen the munitions—a moment that showed a different dimension of Mapache.

Peckinpah was in Hawaii, vacationing with his children and editing *Cable Hogue,* he recalled, when he got a call from the producer. "He said they wanted to try it out in one theater, a shorter version," Peckinpah said. "I said, 'Fine—in one theater.' The next thing I knew, it had been cut to pieces all over the country."

Even then, Warner Bros. was not satisfied with the business the film was doing. Warners again called it back for trimming, excising another five minutes—all of the flashbacks that added depth to Pike and Thornton and explained their relationship. At 2:12, the film still didn't perform at the box office—certainly not as well as the old-fashioned *True Grit,* that summer's hit Western.

"We tried to persevere and we fought to preserve the integrity of the movie," Ken Hyman maintains. "But the marketing and distribution people were nervous."

Peckinpah was incensed and blamed Feldman for the cuts. Production memos show that Feldman was upset at the way Warners was playing the film off in second-run houses around the country.

The film had received some positive reviews from important critics. With time, it could build, Feldman thought. This had to be a word-of-mouth movie; it wouldn't immediately draw big crowds based on its star power. But his entreaties to Hyman and the other Warner powers-that-be to rerelease it in the fall—à la *Bonnie and Clyde,* a film that had died quickly, then had been resuscitated by a second release—went unheeded.

Hyman says, "You won't find a producer who doesn't feel his film could be released differently or better. If we were all smart enough, we'd know what the public's attitude will be, but who the hell knows? I would say the company was there to make money, not lose money."

It's ironic to note the other two major American Westerns released in 1969—Henry Hathaway's *True Grit* and George Roy Hill's *Butch Cassidy and the Sundance Kid.* In their own way, both dealt with the same theme Peckinpah did: men whose time had passed them by.

Both films did significantly more business than *Wild Bunch.* Both won Oscars (best actor for John Wayne in *True Grit;* best song, screenplay, score and cinematography for *Butch Cassidy),* while *Wild Bunch* was overlooked.

Look at all three films today, however. *True Grit* looks stilted and dated, mired in sentimental worship of the John Wayne icon it supposedly spoofs. There is no emotional resonance to Butch and the Kid, none of the depth that Pike Bishop and Deke Thornton have. William Goldman's script, which seemed hip and breezy in 1969, sounds jokey and superficial today.

Only *The Wild Bunch* stands the test of time. It still feels utterly contemporary, a film about loyalty and changing times. In the 1990s, with the future obliterating the past on a daily basis, the story of men outliving their time seems, if anything, even more telling, more pertinent to an audience than it did in 1969.

"Peckinpah made people think they could do different things with the Western," critic Michael Sragow says, "that you could use the Western for a different purpose. With Peckinpah, you saw a guy seeming to tear his insides out and show them on the screen—in an articulate way."

Along with another film released in 1969—Dennis Hopper's *Easy Rider,* which changed Hollywood in a very different way—*The Wild Bunch* had a profound effect on the movie industry.

The film changed the way Hollywood looked at violence, for better or worse. Unfortunately, much of the subsequent depiction of realistic violence missed the point. Peckinpah always claimed that he used slow motion to create images of brutality and death that would deter viewers from practicing violence themselves.

"Actually, it's an antiviolence film," he said, "because I use violence as it is. It's ugly, brutalizing and bloody fucking awful. It's not fun and games and cowboys and Indians, it's a terrible ugly thing. And yet there's a certain response that you get from it, an excitement because we're all violent people, we have violence within us. Violence is a part of life and I don't think we can bury our heads in the sand and ignore it. It's important to understand it and the reason people seem to need violence vicariously."

Since the 1968 assassinations of Robert F. Kennedy and Martin Luther King, Jr., the debate had raged about the way violence in films and on television affected society as a whole.

The Wild Bunch was viewed as a symptom of a society that had become increasingly inured to trauma and violence in everyday life. Social critics claimed that people looked to films such as *The Wild Bunch* for kicks, for cheap thrills. Those thrills, in turn, translated into aggressive behavior and an increasing disregard for human life.

"I think his films contributed to the violence of the time," says critic Andrew Sarris. "It added to and reflected it. He glorified it. Showing violence as it is? That's everybody's alibi. Violence is very much a part of the narrative and dramatic art. There is always violence of some kind. The question is, does he come up with anything else? He doesn't show how awful it is; he shows how beautiful it is. Nobody ever gets killed in slow motion. Realism is no excuse for anything."

Peckinpah's vision of brutal, gut-wrenching violence is aped to this day. But most of his imitators merely mimic the spurting bullet hits and slow-motion bloodbaths, with a vision that extends only to box-office grosses.

That misinterpretation had an effect on Peckinpah's career, as well as on people's ideas of what his films were about. Among them was Peckinpah himself, who would spend the latter part of his career trying to recapture that same magic and turning to images of heightened violence in an effort to find it. The violence in *The Wild Bunch* was his salvation and his downfall.

The Wild Bunch made him bankable again. The critical accolades and mild commercial success of the film got him started on his most productive run of work: three years in which he made four of his best films (and his two biggest box-office hits).

But it also branded him. "All they saw," Pauline Kael says, "was the violence. 'Bloody Sam' became his name."

It was all that some people remembered. And it was what no one ever let him forget.

Part Five

1969-1972

The best advice I can give you to be a motion picture director is to learn how to write and spend as much time as you can working with actors. These are the two elements that kept me moving—also living as hard as you can and learning everything about women won't hurt.

—SAM PECKINPAH, IN A 1971 LETTER TO A
HIGH SCHOOL STUDENT WHO WROTE TO
ASK ABOUT HOW TO BECOME A FILM DIRECTOR

15

Butterfly Attack

THE LINE BETWEEN ARTISTIC VISION and sheer craziness can be a thin one; sometimes it is blurred altogether.

So it was with Sam Peckinpah, even at his peak during the years when he made what are arguably his best films.

Peckinpah was too complex—an alcoholic with a poet's soul, an abusive drunk capable of great warmth and deep sentiment, a double-dealer who subscribed to the concepts of honor, loyalty and self-respect in his work—to explain away with a single example. Still, an anecdote about *The Ballad of Cable Hogue,* told by property master Bobby Visciglia, comes close to summing up Peckinpah's weirder impulses, as well as his particular genius.

The cast and crew of *Cable Hogue* were sequestered at the Echo Bay Lodge, a not-yet-open hotel on Echo Bay of Lake Mead, about fifty miles from Las Vegas. Because there was nothing else to do, most days ended up in the hotel bar, where production meetings were held.

Peckinpah had come across a young singer-songwriter named Richard Gillis and had fallen in love with Gillis's syrupy folk song "Butterfly Mornings." He decided to include it in the film, as the musical backdrop for a montage of the characters of Cable Hogue and the prostitute Hildy as they become romantically involved and, among other things, bathe each other in a big tub. "Sam was sitting at the bar with Gordy [Dawson] and Frank [Kowalski]," Visciglia remembers. "And Gordy said, 'Wouldn't it be great if, when he's bathing her in the morning, you see this big swarm of butter-flies?'

"Sam was half-bombed and so was everybody else. Sam leaned over to me and says, 'Visciglia, how soon can you get me one thousand butterflies?'

"I said, 'What the fuck?' He said, 'I want one thousand butterflies.' I said, 'Live?'

"Now this is January in the middle of the fucking desert. The butterflies

159

are all cocoons and don't come out until spring. But Sam says, 'Take a memo,' and he writes one requisitioning one thousand butterflies. That sobered me up pretty good.

"The next day, I called every place. I've got a guy I call John the Snakeman at the University of Arizona and I called him and said, 'I need one thousand butterflies, live.' He said, 'You've got to find them where they are now.' We called a university in South America and talked to a professor there, who said he could get us the butterflies and ship them to us.

"Meanwhile, everybody on the set is saying, 'Visciglia, how are you doing on those butterflies?' Because, with Sam, you had to come up with a plan. When he asked for something, you had to come up with a logical way to do it, no matter how farfetched it was. You had to show him you could do it, whether he used it or not.

"When we finally figured it out, it came out like this: We were going to build a special plastic crate for the butterflies and put that crate in the bomb bay of an Air Force B25. When Sam gave the cue, the B25 would take off from Las Vegas, fly over the set and open the bomb bay. And the butterflies would drop into the set.

"So I laid this all out to Sam and told him I was still waiting to find out how much this was going to cost. I added, 'I'll tell you something else: You get one fucking take. Because as soon as those little sons of bitches hit the cold air, they're going to die.'

"Sam looked me in the eye and said, 'Keep the plan but don't do anything until I tell you to.' And that was the end of the butterflies. I explained to him how we would do it when he was sober on the set, not when he was drunk. Otherwise, he might have said yes.''

16

Composing a "Ballad"

SAM PECKINPAH WAS ON A ROLL, feeling invincible for having shepherded *The Wild Bunch* through production in almost exactly the fashion he had envisioned it. His demons of self-doubt were being kept at bay even as the ones that fueled his sense of omnipotence were being fed.

He was once again a moviemaker who could do anything he imagined—even summon a flock of butterflies from the sky to complement a cinematic moment. Having been denied work for so long, he was ready to remain immersed in it for as long as he could. Every step of the process was an exquisite agony that he couldn't get enough of.

"Sam would prepare for a film until it was absolutely necessary to start shooting," James Coburn says. "Then he wouldn't stop shooting until the camera broke or ran out of film. Then he'd start editing and the only way to get him to stop was to get him another film to do."

"It was sad," Gordon Dawson adds. "When he was on a picture, he had a kingdom and he was the king. When he was off the set, he was a king in exile."

Before *The Wild Bunch* was even out of the editing room, Peckinpah was back in the saddle, ready to start shooting *The Ballad of Cable Hogue*.

Peckinpah almost made another film first, however: *The Diamond Story,* a script that Hyman and Feldman were enthusiastic about. Peckinpah brought in writer Walon Green from *The Wild Bunch* to rework it with him, a process Green says was an exercise in frustration and missed signals.

Peckinpah told him, "I've got a great script that's like *Treasure of the Sierra Madre,* but it needs a rewrite." In reading it, however, Green discovered that the script was "neither great nor *Treasure of the Sierra Madre*" and told Peckinpah so. Undeterred, Peckinpah told him, "We're going to work closely on this," then proceeded to do the opposite.

Green would write pages and submit them; Peckinpah would read them and reject them out of hand. One problem was that Peckinpah wanted to beef up the role of the heroine; however, the script was about a bunch of men robbing a diamond mine in South Africa.

"But he was going with this girl at the time, I think it was Stella Stevens [Stevens denies this], and she was going to be the star and he wanted to develop a part in this that was big for her," Green says. "He kept saying, 'Put her in more scenes.' "

Green continued to submit pages. Peckinpah would say, "I read your stuff and it's no good—and I don't want to talk about it."

"So I finally said, 'Fuck this' to Phil Feldman," Green says. "Feldman tried to smooth it out, so I did a pass at the script and reduced the girl to what I thought she should be. Sam hated it and told Feldman so."

Green went back to documentary filmmaking. Five months later, Feldman called to say that Peckinpah wanted Green to take one more pass at the script —and to remind him that Green owed them two weeks' work. Green, angry to be dragged into it again, agreed to write a beginning. "If you like it, I'll see if you want me to go on," he told Feldman.

"I was really mad. I thought, I'm going to write a beginning that he can't resist," Green says.

The film opened from the girl's point of view. She is passionately making love with a man on a boat in an African lagoon. In the middle of the sex scene, African natives board the boat and there is a shoot-out. The Africans grab the girl and beat her nearly senseless. She bangs her head against the boat, blacks out—and the story shifts into a flashback.

Green sent it off and got an almost immediate return phone call from Feldman, who said excitedly, "Sam loves it!"

"Forget it," Green said. He hung up and never worked with either of them again.

IF *WILD BUNCH* was Peckinpah's vitriolic comment on the way of the world, *The Ballad of Cable Hogue* was his valentine to how he wished it could be. It was his personal favorite among all his films.

"*Hogue* is this wonderful parable about an idealist's view of what the mind can do on its own, of nineteenth-century transcendentalism," critic Michael Sragow says. "You create your own world out of your mind. There's a lot of *The Tempest* in there. It was unique and breathtaking to see that in a movie of that period. *The Wild Bunch* gave you the angry point of view; *Cable Hogue* gave the elegiac, lyrical point."

It wasn't all sweetness and light. There are killings, desertions, vengeance, retribution and the hero dies at the end. Yet it was one of Peckinpah's sweetest efforts, the closest he ever came to a romantic comedy.

"*Cable Hogue,* for me, is an affirmation of life," Peckinpah said.

"It was his most personal film," James Coburn says. "He was Cable."

The script for *The Ballad of Cable Hogue*, written by Edmund Penny and John Crawford (not the same John Crawford who played Mark in "The Rifleman"), had been kicking around for several years. In the mid-1960s, L. Q. Jones had optioned it, hoping to direct it himself.

Jones and Warren Oates gave Peckinpah the screenplay; Oates wanted to play Cable, with Jones as the Rev. Joshua Sloane. Peckinpah worked out a deal with Warner Bros. to produce it himself, with Phil Feldman as executive producer. Though it was envisioned as a low-budget film, Peckinpah felt he needed stronger casting than Oates and Jones (though he did cast Jones as Taggart, one of the film's villains).

According to casting memos, the part of Cable was offered to Jimmy Stewart, who turned it down because he thought it wasn't right for his image. Charlton Heston says he was offered the part but didn't like the script. Peckinpah showed the script to his friend Jason Robards, who agreed to play Cable.

Henry Fonda was interested in playing the Rev. Joshua Sloane, but a deal could not be struck. Then Peckinpah remembered the Karel Reisz film *Morgan*, a 1966 comedy that starred British newcomer David Warner.

Peckinpah contacted Warner about playing the part. After screening *Ride the High Country*, Warner agreed. But the day before he was scheduled to fly to the United States, Warner, a high-strung young actor, had an anxiety attack about flying. He called his agent and said he would have to give up the role because he couldn't bring himself to get on an airplane.

"Six or seven hours later," Warner recalls, "my agent called back and told me I was to take the train to Barcelona. There I was to catch a ship to New York. Once in New York, I would take the Super Chief train to Chicago, and then a train to Los Angeles, where I would be driven to Las Vegas. It would take about two weeks, he said, but Peckinpah was prepared to wait for me.

"I was just an English actor who had done a bit of Shakespeare. My whole feeling for him was colored by that kind of gesture, for an English actor who was not particularly a star. Not to recast the role was quite a wonderful thing."

For the role of Hildy, the prostitute who falls in love with Cable, Peckinpah wanted Stella Stevens, a blond actress who had been stuck playing sexpot roles in films such as *The Silencers*, opposite Dean Martin, and *The Nutty Professor*, opposite Jerry Lewis. Feldman hated the idea—but Peckinpah persuaded him to cast her.

"He came to my house and told me he wanted me above all others," says Stevens, who didn't really know Peckinpah at the time. "I said, 'Sam, I don't know if I'm right for it.' He said to me, 'Stella, you're right for it because I'm writing the part for you right now.'"

Negotiations bogged down over credits and salary, however, and Feldman jumped at the opportunity to try to hire another actress for the part: Joanne Woodward. But Woodward wanted too much money. Stevens used that opportunity to rethink her position and accept the role.

"I had a rough time going through the picture knowing the producer didn't want me," Stevens says. "I had to prove I was not a frivolous sexpot or a bimbo."

"There was a lot of objection by the producer to having her cast," Peckinpah said, "and by almost everybody in the studio. She's a groovy lady. Fine, ballsy, lovely, crazy—major talent. She's finally broken through, not through me necessarily but through herself."

Peckinpah filled the rest of the cast with regulars from his stock company, and a few friends. Taggart and Bowen, the villains who abandon Hogue in the desert without water, were played by L. Q. Jones and Strother Martin, in a nod to their successful pairing in *The Wild Bunch*. R. G. Armstrong was cast as the stage line owner who refuses initially to take Hogue seriously. Peter Whitney, who had played a heavy in "Pericles on 31st Street," was brought in as the banker who gives Hogue his grubstake. Slim Pickens was cast as a stagecoach driver, and Peckinpah gave the role of his sidekick to his old friend writer Max Evans.

Peckinpah hired Gordon Dawson to be his associate producer on *Cable Hogue* and Dawson and Peckinpah rewrote the script, though they didn't receive credit. Peckinpah also enlisted his old buddy Frank Kowalski to serve as script supervisor (he is listed as dialogue supervisor in the credits) for the film, and Kowalski contributed to the script as well.

Says Robards, "Anything that was funny or had real humor, Frank Kowalski did. Frank was invaluable to Sam. He had a mind."

Peckinpah hired Lucien Ballard as his cinematographer and Frank Santillo, who had edited *Ride the High Country,* to cut the film. After his problems with prop men on *Major Dundee* and *The Wild Bunch,* Peckinpah hired a property master who would become part of his inner circle for the rest of his career: Robert Visciglia.

Their meeting was vintage Peckinpah. Visciglia, who had just finished working on the Elvis Presley film *Charo,* ran into an old friend, a production manager, who asked him if he'd ever met Peckinpah. He got Visciglia an appointment at Peckinpah's Warner Bros. office the next day shortly after noon. Peckinpah had been touted to Visciglia by Lois O'Connor.

When Visciglia got to the office, Peckinpah was across the street having lunch at a favored bar. So Visciglia sat in the lobby and read the *Cable Hogue* script while he waited. Suddenly Peckinpah stormed in—his face bruised, his lip cut, his shirt ripped and spattered with blood—and walked straight into his office and closed the door.

A couple of minutes later, he called Visciglia in and asked him how he liked the script. Visciglia expressed his admiration, then added his concern and curiosity about Peckinpah's physical state.

Peckinpah had apparently run into Phil Rawlins, the large cowboy whom he'd fired as first assistant director on *The Wild Bunch*. Peckinpah had challenged him at the bar and Rawlins had picked Peckinpah up and tossed him into a corner. When Peckinpah charged him again, Rawlins punched him. Peckinpah attacked one more time—and Rawlins picked him up and threw him bodily out the front door, into the street.

"But Sam was happy, not pissed," Visciglia says. "He took losses as well as anybody. He said, 'I got a couple of licks in on the son of a bitch.' "

Locations were chosen for the film outside Las Vegas, in the Valley of Fire, north and west of Echo Bay on Lake Mead. The setting, scorched sand and rock surrounded by picturesque mountains, would be ideal for the story of a man who discovers water in the middle of the desert. Exteriors and interiors for the town of Dead Dog would be filmed at Apache Junction, a Western set near Phoenix.

Peckinpah added one other element to the mix: He wanted a documentary shot on the making of *Cable Hogue*. To film it, he tapped Gary Weis, a young still photographer who had never even held a movie camera—and who happened to live with Peckinpah's teen-age daughter, Sharon.

Weis was a case of Peckinpah enlisting accomplices, even as he gave someone new a chance to advance. Throughout his career, Peckinpah would see a spark in someone and try to draw out previously untapped talents. He tried to turn friends into collaborators and accomplices, as if to form his own private crew to eventually serve his vision.

When Weis met Sharon, he was "a beach rat living inside a juice bar in Santa Monica. She was in high school and I was twenty-three." He started living with Sharon at the house she shared with her siblings and her mother, Marie. Eventually, he and Sharon moved out of that house and in with Peckinpah.

Though he had a son, Mathew, Peckinpah treated Weis with paternal regard. He tried to teach him the things he might have passed on to Sharon if she had been male.

"Once Sharon and I were going to take a backpacking trip," Weis recalls. "We were vegetarians and he scoffed at us. 'You have to take bacon,' he said. 'You have to smell that bacon at 18,000 feet.' He had this folksy way about him."

Weis, a pot-smoking product of the times, smoked with Peckinpah, who had been using marijuana since his own hipster days. "He'd forget all about the other business and become very funny, very lighthearted," Weis says. But Peckinpah also was drinking heavily at the time:

"Once or twice, he'd be in bed and he'd start to hyperventilate and he'd call my name," Weis says. "It frightened me. I remember this look on his face."

It was in one such drunken state that Peckinpah hit upon the idea of the documentary. "He's the one who, as he said, turned me out [slang for convincing a woman to become a prostitute]. I can remember him coming home drunk one night and shaking me awake, as Sharon and I were sleeping together," Weis says. "And he said, 'You're going to make movies. You're going to make a film.' The next morning he said, 'You've got to get a camera. You leave in two days.' So he got me a camera and got a cameraman to show me how to load it. I got a Nagra [tape recorder] and we went out to the desert. And I began to shoot a hundred thousand feet of sixteen-millimeter film."

17

Waiting for the Sun

THE BALLAD OF CABLE HOGUE opens with Cable Hogue, a desert-worn prospector, who is left to die without water in the desert by his double-crossing partners, Taggart and Bowen.

Hogue wanders through the desert for four days, sending casual prayers to a seemingly unfeeling God, offering to repent whatever sins he may have committed in exchange for a few drops of water. God apparently ignores him; in the midst of a sandstorm, Hogue collapses, then notices mud on his boot. He digs down into the sand and hits water—and crows triumphantly that it was he, Cable Hogue, and not God who saved him from dehydrated death.

"I found it where it wasn't," Hogue says, in pride and disbelief.

Hogue digs his own well, then notices that his water hole is not far from the stagecoach trail. So he creates a way station where the stage can stop, halfway between Gila City and Dead Dog, charging passersby for his water.

An itinerant preacher, the Rev. Joshua Sloane, passes through. Along with suggesting that Hogue name the place Cable Springs, he points out that Hogue has not filed a claim. So Hogue hurries into Dead Dog and does so. When he tries to get the stagecoach-line owner to underwrite his business, the man laughs him off. But the Dead Dog banker gives him a loan and Hogue establishes himself.

He also falls for Hildy, the town prostitute. When the townsfolk run her off, she moves in with Hogue temporarily. He refuses to leave for San Francisco with her, however, because he wants to get revenge against Taggart and Bowen, whom he is convinced will return.

" 'Vengeance is mine, sayeth the Lord,' " Sloane tells him.

"That's fine with me," Hogue replies, "as long as he don't take too long and I can watch."

"Revenge always turns sour," Hildy says.

"Some things a man can't forget," Hogue responds.

Hildy eventually leaves for San Francisco. Sloane leaves as well and Hogue is left with his enterprise—which has grown into a surprisingly sophisticated spread. One day, the stage pulls up and out step two dandies. It has been three and a half years since he's seen them but Hogue recognizes them immediately as Taggart and Bowen. Hogue affects an air of cordiality and gives them each a drink of water. The stagecoach driver gives Hogue his monthly bag of gold and lets it drop that Hogue doesn't believe in banks. Knowing they will take the bait, Hogue confirms this: He lets it be known that he has his money hidden somewhere on his property. He invites Taggart and Bowen to come back for a visit.

Within hours, they ride up on horses, bent on robbing him. Hogue gets the drop on them and tells them to strip to their underwear and walk into the desert. When Taggart pulls a gun, Hogue kills him. Bowen, in tears, sinks to his knees and says he can't go out there to die and apologizes to Hogue. Despite himself, Hogue forgives him and tells him to bury Taggart.

As Bowen finishes, the stagecoach pulls up. Hogue announces that he has decided to go to San Francisco to find Hildy and to give his way station to Bowen. Almost as soon as the words are out of his mouth, an automobile pulls up—chauffeur-driven, carrying Hildy. She is on her way to New Orleans, she says; Hogue tells her he will join her.

Hogue puts his belongings into the car, accidentally releasing the brake. The car starts to roll toward the unsuspecting Bowen; Hogue shoves him to safety and tries to stop the car himself—but it runs him over.

He is not dead, but he knows he is dying. The Rev. Sloane comes riding up on a motorcycle and Hogue asks him to preach a funeral sermon while he is still around to appreciate it.

"It's not so much the dying you hate," he says. "It's not knowing what they're going to say about you."

Sloane offers final words and, as Hogue is buried, he adds, "Take him, Lord, but, knowing Cable, I suggest you don't take him lightly," as the mourners go in their separate directions, leaving Cable Springs to Bowen and the coyotes.

THE PRODUCTION COMPANY set up camp in the Echo Bay Lodge and, for a week, work on the picture went off without a hitch. It seemed to set the tone for what would be a high-spirited shoot.

It even seemed to bode well for Peckinpah's continued relationship with Phil Feldman, the executive producer, who arrived in Echo Bay the day before shooting was scheduled to begin. The weather had been wet on the weekend; Feldman's plane from L.A. had been delayed because of heavy rains. On the drive to Echo Bay, Feldman proclaimed that he would make the rain go away. The next morning, skies cleared and Peckinpah started on schedule.

The film opened with Cable, knife in hand, face to face with what looked like a Gila monster, a poisonous lizard. He is about to kill it for food when the lizard literally explodes from a bullet from Taggart's rifle.

Visciglia, in breaking down the script, realized he would have to get a Gila monster for a prop. Because the species is protected by law, he settled on Mexican beaded lizards, which look virtually the same. He bought four from a pet shop in Redondo Beach and brought them to Echo Bay, where he kept them in his room.

Gary Weis, who was on location filming his documentary, helped Visciglia feed the lizards and grew attached to them, before he figured out that Peckinpah was planning to blow them up for the camera. He protested to Visciglia, who said, "Nope, we're gonna blow the son of a bitch up."

"Aren't you going to use a dummy?" Weis asked.

"You put a dummy there," Visciglia responded, "and Sam will be able to tell it's not alive. No fucking way. The son of a bitch dies."

It turned into a full-blown, if short-lived, cause célèbre. Weis, who had long hair and a full beard, was nicknamed Gary Good Guy. Gary Liddiard, the makeup man who took Visciglia's side, became Gary Bad Guy.

Weis papered the hotel and the location with mimeographed posters: "Save the Gila!" Visciglia and Liddiard would put notes on each day's call sheet: "Three days to the killing of the Gila monster."

Peckinpah finally spoke to Weis on the set one day and wanted to know what the problem was.

"You're not going to kill it just for the picture?" Weis wanted to know. That, Peckinpah replied, was exactly his intention.

Then he looked at Weis and said, "I tell you what I'll do. That Gila monster will live if you shave your beard and get a haircut." Weis walked away to think about it, then came back.

"Would you still kill the other ones?" Weis wanted to know.

"Sure," Peckinpah said, "but you were only protesting about this one."

The next day, the lizard's last, Weis was told to stay in the hotel because the film was having some union problems.

"I learned later," Weis says, "that Sam didn't want me to see them kill the lizard. That was very sweet, I thought."

Unfortunately, the camera didn't see them kill the lizard the first few times either. Bud Hulburd, who had blown up the bridge in *The Wild Bunch*, used too large a squib on the first lizard. Even with the camera set at high speed, so that it would be seen in slow motion, the lizard didn't explode—it atomized.

"Sam wanted lots of pieces and there weren't any pieces," Visciglia says. "Bud went up to him and said, 'Sam, I've never blown up a Gila monster before.' Sam says, 'What's the difference? You blew up that bridge with all the people on it. What the hell's a little Gila monster?' "

But Hulburd blew up two more lizards without getting the desired effect, though the pieces were bigger after each one. Gill Dennis, who was on the location as an intern from the American Film Institute (and later as co-director of the documentary with Weis), recalls Hulburd shaking his head and saying, "I said, 'Just give me one or two for rehearsal.' "

After the third one, Visciglia collected the pieces of one of the dead lizards. If Hulburd didn't get it right with the last one, Visciglia knew he was on the hook for a replacement.

"I took the pieces of one of the ones that was dead and start sewing the son of a bitch back together with catgut," he says. "I sewed him and taped him. Then I called the standby painter and put paint on him. We put him on a rock and blew him up and Sam loved it. And I don't know if he knew the son of a bitch was dead."

A slow-motion viewing on a videocassette recorder gives it away, if only for a fraction of a second: the image of the lizard, the moment before it explodes, is of a reptile in a comically malformed posture, legs akimbo, head at an unnatural angle—before it is blown to pieces in slow motion. It is one of only a couple of slow-motion shots in the entire film.

During that first week, Peckinpah also shot the initial scenes involving Max Evans, his old drinking buddy, a writer of Western novels and screenplays who had never been in front of a camera before. Peckinpah convinced him to ride shotgun next to Slim Pickens, who played the stagecoach driver.

As they were filming the first encounter between Hogue and the stagecoach, Peckinpah looked at Evans and said to Robards, "What's the matter with him? He's stiff as a board."

The problem, Robards says, is that Evans "was not an actor. He was scared to death." Peckinpah turned to Visciglia and said, "Give him a bottle of Wild Turkey."

Visciglia poured the willing Evans three large tumblers of the potent whiskey. By the sixth take, Evans, who was required to climb down off the stagecoach to utter a couple of lines of dialogue, was seriously inebriated.

"Max is smiling and laughing and still won't move," Robards says. "Sam says, 'What's the matter with him?' I said, 'He's drunk.' So Sam starts yelling at Visciglia and says, 'You're fired. How dare you get an actor drunk?' "

THE STORY OF A MAN who found water where it wasn't (" 'Found it where it wasn't'—that was Frank Kowalski's line," Jason Robards says)—it must have been too much of a temptation for the gods. Here was a Hollywood film crew shooting a movie in the desert, where it hadn't rained literally in decades. And then it started and wouldn't stop.

How long did it rain? It depends on who you ask.

· R. G. Armstrong: "We had eight solid days of rain. We went wild. We didn't know what to do. We were stuck there, restless. It was all fucking and drinking and doing whatever."

· Bobby Visciglia: "Who thought it would rain? But it did, for eleven solid days and nights. We couldn't shoot for eleven days. Then Sam started to improvise. He said, 'I've got to roll the camera.' It got backed up and got pretty tight."

· Max Evans: "The park ranger said that during a specific fifteen days of our shooting, there had been more rain than in the last thirty-one years combined."

· Jason Robards: "We were in the desert and we had twenty-seven days of rain. We'd start to get back on schedule and then the goddamned rain would come. We had to kill growing green stuff in the desert. They were the worst storms in eighty-seven years."

The best estimate is probably in the vicinity of two weeks. It was enough to bring intense pressure from the studio because each rained-out day meant thousands of dollars lost: in salaries, equipment rentals, hotel bills, per diems, transportation costs. It was completely unforeseeable and unpreventable—but, to Warner Bros.' way of thinking, it proved that Peckinpah had problems meeting budgets and schedules. If he couldn't get it to stop raining, he was obviously difficult to work with.

"When it rains," Lou Lombardo says, "they always blame the director. Like he made it rain. It wasn't his fault but, to hear the studio talk, it was."

Peckinpah shot what he could. He had had his crews tear down—board by board—an old wooden whorehouse in Benton Springs, Nevada, ship it to the location and rebuild it for Cable's shack. Then he filmed all of the interior scenes between Cable, Hildy and Joshua that he could. Virtually everything else, however, was to be shot outdoors, in what was supposed to be the blazing sun of the desert.

"We'd sit there all day in the Lizard Lounge and his stomach would be in knots," L. Q. Jones says. "He'd sit there and it would rain and he wouldn't get anything shot."

"Sam finally said, 'We'll shoot in the rain,'" Jason Robards says. "Lucien lit the rain. Sam even wrote a scene about how it was not supposed to rain in the desert. He was just trying to keep things going. But it was useless."

Every morning, Peckinpah, actors and crew would ride the forty bumpy miles to the Valley of Fire and wait for it to stop raining. Every break in the clouds meant a flurry of activity to set up a shot, but by the time the shot was ready, the rain would return, rendering all of the effort pointless.

The result was short tempers all around, but particularly from Peckinpah, who started firing people before shooting even began. Before the production moved to Phoenix to shoot interiors in March, almost three dozen people had been fired. Though there were jokes about the shuttle service between Echo Bay and Los Angeles, the number of firings raised hackles at the various unions in Hollywood, which began to resist requests to send replacements. The film was becoming known as "The Battle of Cable Hogue."

"Sam never fired anyone who didn't deserve it," Visciglia says. "But he fired people to the point that the unions wouldn't send replacements."

Gordon Dawson, the associate producer, says, "How many deserved it? About half. Sam would fly off the handle and say, 'Get that son of a bitch out of my sight.' My deal with him was that he had to say it three times." Dawson, who had to handle the firings, says that Peckinpah would tell him, "Get his replacement in the air before he's on the bus."

But Dawson reveals that, had he fired everyone Peckinpah wanted fired, the casualty level would have been even higher.

"I talked him out of a lot of them," Dawson says. "And a lot of people I moved to Phoenix to prepare for that. Then I brought them back to Las Vegas to strike the set when we moved to Phoenix.

"I had one poor driver who Sam hated. Sam thought I'd fired him. We kept him at the hotel and he'd do our Vegas runs. So the driver is heading out in the desert one day and here comes Sam in his Porsche. The driver just laid down in the seat and let the car drive out into the desert so Sam wouldn't see him. You can't just knock off a Teamster. So we had to keep them out of Sam's sight."

Peckinpah blamed the problems on unions and their refusal to accommodate a film whose budget couldn't handle the expense of the myriad work rules, particularly when rain was playing havoc with schedules.

"*Cable Hogue* is a low-budget picture," Peckinpah said. "But it doesn't make any difference to the unions whether you only have a limited budget or whether you're a multimillion-dollar picture. The same rules go into effect. And I think that's detrimental to the industry. I believe in the unions, but I think they're hurting themselves and they're hurting a lot of us who want to make particular stories that we have to do out of price. We should be encouraged by the unions to do these stories rather than being penalized—perhaps something like deferred payment if the picture makes money."

Still, the number who were fired caused considerable talk in Hollywood. At the end of March 1969, after the production had wrapped, the surviving crew ran an ad in *Variety* that said, "It's been a helluva ball working for Sam Peckinpah. We found it where it was," with forty names appended to it.

"That's where the medals came in," Visciglia says. "I said, 'Anyone who makes it to Arizona deserves a medal.' " Peckinpah agreed and Visciglia had a local jeweler strike a series of medals, which were awarded to anyone who lasted the entire production. They became a tradition on Peckinpah's films.

FOR THE MOST PART, Peckinpah reserved his wrath for crew people and the bit players. Once again, Strother Martin came in for his share of abuse.

At one point, Martin had the inspiration to walk around Hildy's automobile and kick the tire. But he fretted about actually asking Peckinpah to let him do it.

"He walked a slight path in the carpet in my hotel room, worrying about asking Sam about it, talking it out," L. Q. Jones says. "That was how much he feared Sam. Sam was a great manipulator. He got exactly what he wanted from Strother."

Yet Peckinpah would go out of his way for a few hours of company—and to keep from having to let go of the picture. After *Cable Hogue* wrapped in Phoenix, for example, Peckinpah decided he needed to reshoot part of the opening scene back in the Valley of Fire, in which Taggart and Bowen ride off, leaving Hogue to die.

He got Martin, then arranged for Jones, who had already moved on to another picture, to be flown directly from the set where he was shooting to Echo Bay. From there, Jones was driven by limousine (in which he changed into costume) to the location to get the shot before sunset.

"We rush out to the set," Jones says, "and the sun is going down. We shoot it and Strother fucks up. We do it again—this is the last chance before we lose the sun. And I fuck up. As we come back, Sam comes out screaming at Strother, 'You cocksucker, I'm going to see that you never work again.' Strother is a basket case and Sam is going on in this manner. I say, 'Um, Sam—' and he snaps, 'Keep your nose out of this, L. Q.', and turns around and starts in on Strother. I finally say, 'Sam, I was the one who fucked up.' Sam didn't even stop. He turns back to Strother and starts in all over: 'You stupid son of a bitch, you let me make an ass of myself like that without telling me it was L. Q.'s fault? You'll never work again!' "

"I learned to read Sam through Gordy Dawson and Frank Kowalski," Visciglia says. "Kowalski would say to me, 'Fuck him, he's trying to fuck around with you to get to so-and-so.' He always picked on the people closest to him, never on strangers. He knew he could depend on us not to take it seriously or turn on him. He'd push on one person because he was mad at another. So he took it out on that other person. You had to understand that; otherwise, you'd think, What the hell is he picking on me for? He can stick this picture in his ass. And you'd be gone in a week."

Dawson says, "As associate producer, I'd take an ass-chewing for the guy standing next to me. I was trying to save the guy's job."

It was also a way to kill a little time while he figured out how to deal with a problematic scene, Dawson adds. "There would be a bunch of Indians sitting on a ridge during *Dundee* and he'd say, 'Look, that uniform on that guy way up there—it's too clean. How can I shoot that?' So you'd take care of it. Actually, he was buying time. He needed an hour to get his act together and he was using you to get it for him. On *Cable Hogue*, he had Bobby Visciglia moving sand dunes for him."

Despite his cynicism and personally jaundiced approach to life, Peckinpah put deeply personal moments into the film. The most striking comes as Hogue finally gets the stagecoach-line manager to give him the way-station franchise. The stagecoach driver, played by Slim Pickens, steps up to Hogue and hands him a package.

Hogue opens it, says, "Well, if that don't beat all," and unfurls an American flag, for which he promptly builds a pole. He raises and lowers the flag several times during the film, without a trace of sarcasm—merely as an expression of heartfelt patriotism.

Critic and film historian Paul Seydor says, "He makes a great violent epic poem [*The Wild Bunch*] at the peak of the antiwar movement. Then he has Cable raise a flag in 1970 and he doesn't treat it ironically. Patriotic is probably the correct description: like Emerson and Thoreau. He's radically patriotic in the sense of going back to origins. He was declaring independence from the worst of what America was becoming, trying to get to the most decent parts of himself."

PECKINPAH BENT OVER BACKWARD to keep some of his *Cable Hogue* stars happy. In the case of Jason Robards, that meant setting him up in a mobile home away from the Echo Bay Lodge.

"Lois and I had a trailer, so I'd have a semblance of a home," says Robards, a recovering alcoholic who was still drinking at the time. "If I'd been staying at the motel, I'd have been in trouble. I never would have made the film. I would have been hauled away."

But O'Connor wasn't on hand for the whole production. Visciglia recalls, "I stayed drunk with Jason Robards for five days; that was one of my duties. I had to make sure he didn't take off. Jason and I were sitting there in his trailer listening to Johnny Cash records, drinking out of a broken bottle of J & B and eating two-day-old stew out of an iron pot."

David Warner presented a different problem. The young Englishman was far from home, in a part of the world the likes of which he'd never seen, working on a picture in which, for the first four weeks, he didn't even get in front of a camera.

"David Warner was an agoraphobic," Robards says. "He'd get out in the open and he'd cry. Sam was very kind to him; he treated him with kid gloves. The remoteness would make you go crazy."

Max Evans recalled taking Warner for a ride in the desert. "David had withdrawn more and more," Evans said. "The enormity of the desert had him scared, really scared. He wouldn't even look out the window at its limitless beauty. The entire trip he remained hunkered down as low in the seat as he possibly could and stared straight ahead."

"For me, personally, the desert was like being on the moors," Warner says. "As an Englishman, I was not sure what it would do to me. There was nothing to do except go to the bar; it was really weird. I didn't drive. So I'd listen to the Bee Gees and I went fishing. In fact, I caught the champion bass of the season in Lake Mead."

Stella Stevens was another matter. Stevens, initially elated to finally have landed a serious role in a film, arrived in Echo Bay to discover that she was one of only a few women on location. And Peckinpah was not at all the kind of director she expected.

"I thought his major hold on people was their being unsure of whether he was crazy or sane at any moment," she says. "You never knew what he would do or what mood he'd be in."

(Affirms Dawson, "I came to realize that he was an off-balance individual. His game plan was to keep everyone more off-balance. He was full of a lot of fear. To get stabilized, he had to keep everyone else more unstable.")

Peckinpah had wooed Stevens for the part. On her first day of shooting, he hugged her and said, "Welcome to the place of love."

"He would say things like that," Stevens says, "but he didn't always behave that way."

Visciglia recalls that, on Stevens's first day on the set, she had a cooking scene and began to make demands for period cooking utensils.

"She said, 'I want a pot and some kind of cutter for biscuits,' " Visciglia says. "Now my truck is three hundred yards up the hill. And she wanted this thing and it had to be from the right period. And Sam is yelling, 'Bobby, get what Stella wants.' He knew it was taking the pressure off her and laying it on someone else, even though he was pissed at her. I got a tin can and cut the ends off and she thought it was just perfect. She says, 'Where did you get that?' I said, 'What the hell do you think I've got—a Von's supermarket up the road?' "

Stevens found Peckinpah uncommunicative and unresponsive. "The hardest part was trying to make sense with Sam," she says. "I didn't know what he wanted or expected from me. I said, 'Who is she?' and he said, 'She's you.' That frightened me at first. But we all had tremendous trepidations [in trying]to please him. You never knew if something would make him angry or extremely happy."

For example, as a whore in a remote Western town, Stevens decided that her character might own a curling iron but wouldn't wear makeup. But when she asked Peckinpah if she could wear no makeup, he wouldn't answer.

In one of the first scenes she shot, she had to take off her clothes and put on a nightgown. "That meant I had to strip naked in front of the crew," she says. "I spent an extra hour doing a total body makeup. I said good morning to Sam and he said, 'Get that goddamned makeup off.' So I had to go back to my trailer, where I only had cold water. I was so mad, I was ready to quit. I said, 'Get yourself another size eight.' "

("The next thing I knew," Dawson says, "her luggage was lined up in the lobby and she was going home. My job was to keep her happy.")

Stevens says, "He had a cruel streak that delighted him. Instead of encouraging me to do my best, he battered and belittled me. Anything he could do to throw you off, he would. It was like working with a wounded rattlesnake. It's not an enjoyable way to work."

"It was hard because Sam was a man of different temperaments and it was very hard for him to express what he wanted," David Warner says. "He was sometimes impossible and sometimes vague. You would instinctively do what you felt he wanted but sometimes it was frustrating because he couldn't say."

Peckinpah spoke his own language. He was hard to hear because he spoke quietly. And he would express things in cryptic, elliptical ways.

"He talked in code, in such a low tone and such a confusing way," Visciglia says. "Then he'd say, 'You misunderstood me.' He'd put you at a disadvantage. He'd challenge you with misleading words and his writing was illegible. He'd say, 'Can't you read?' He'd show it to you and you couldn't tell what it was."

Dawson says, "I think alcohol put him more in his shell. He needed people to communicate with him but he was giving cryptograms to you and you had to decipher them. There was a scene in *Cable Hogue* he wanted me to write. So he tells me, 'Give me something about fucking and God and mother. You know what I want.' "

"He spoke a kind of second-generation imagery," Gary Weis says. "Like people who are a little afraid that what they're going to say isn't that interesting. I don't know if it was drinking or if he was afraid that he would not appear smart. And he was an oddball, let's face it. But part of it was fear. He wasn't an articulate, verbal, easygoing guy. Some people think he was a big prick and I'm sure that's the way he was with people he felt frightened of or uncomfortable about."

Gill Dennis, who eventually married Peckinpah's second daughter, Kristen, got a firsthand view as an intern for the American Film Institute. He had specifically requested to work with Peckinpah ("Who is Sam Peckinpah?"

George Stevens, Jr., the AFI head, had asked him) and had met with Jim Silke, who was working for AFI at that point.

Silke told him, "The only thing I'll tell you is don't ever make an excuse. If he asks you to do something, you work all night to do it. You make every effort. If you can't do it, you tell him."

But Peckinpah was still suspicious of Dennis, unsure whether he was a sycophant, a studio spy or just one more person to get in his way. Dennis tried to play the invisible man, watching everything while staying out of the way. Finally, one day, Dennis felt a tap on the shoulder. It was Peckinpah, who said, "You don't ask enough fucking questions."

The next day, Peckinpah approached him again and said, "Isn't it interesting how the emphasis is changing?" and walked away again.

"I figure this is a cue," Dennis says, "so I go up to him and say, 'How is the emphasis changing?' And Sam says, 'That's a fucking good question.' Gordy Dawson told me I'd learned a good lesson: When somebody asks you a question, you ask a question right back."

Dennis got an even closer look at the production than he'd anticipated. Frank Kowalski was the script supervisor on the film, in charge of keeping track of when, what and how long each take of each shot was. But Kowalski "was drinking a lot, so he wasn't getting all his paperwork done," Dennis says. "Frank looked around and said, 'Come here, you.' So I was doing his paperwork. That puts you right up by the camera."

As long as the work was getting done, Peckinpah didn't care. Just so the picture was getting made—that was Peckinpah's purest passion.

"Can I see myself doing anything other than making movies?" Peckinpah said. "No, I love it. I've lost two marriages and my family because of it. Not through being away from home. No. Just because I was making love to a thirty-five-millimeter camera."

After dailies one day, Gary Weis recalls, "Sam came up to me and put his arm around me warmly, looked me in the face and gestured toward the screen where the dailies had just been and said, 'That's where it's at.' It was so corny."

Says Visciglia, "With Sam, it was twenty-four hours a day. The closer you were to Sam, the more he depended on you. If anything was wrong, if it was his mistake (which he'd never admit), he blamed three or four of us. Me, Walter Kelley, Frank Kowalski, Gordy Dawson. He'd say, 'Hey, assholes, who's watching the store?' "

He didn't demand more from others than he demanded of himself. "I'm up at four in the morning looking at my day's work," Peckinpah said, "which I've already sketched in before. I try to know every single possible approach and then I pick the one I want. I always prepare. That's why I lose fifteen to twenty pounds on every picture. It's like an endurance race or something."

Peckinpah saw the director as being a monarch, on or off the set. And rank had its privileges. During filming in the Valley of Fire, Peckinpah was approached by an emissary for director Michelangelo Antonioni, who was shooting his first American film, *Zabriskie Point*, in the same desert. Peckinpah had the permit for the entire stretch of desert; Antonioni was asking permission to drive through to get to his next location.

But Peckinpah held a grudge: Antonioni had acted high-handed several years before, refusing to let Richard Harris off the set or Peckinpah on during production of *Red Desert*, when Peckinpah wanted to talk to Harris about *Major Dundee*. So Peckinpah forced Antonioni to come to him personally and ask for permission.

Then he turned him down.

Actor R. G. Armstrong, who watched the transaction, recalls, "He drove up and Sam was waiting by the camera. He was playing with the guy. He said, 'No, you can't. I'm shooting here and I was here first.' After he left, Sam said, 'He doesn't know that you never introduce yourself to someone when you're in trouble.' "

As he was trying to shoot *Cable Hogue* each day, he was still editing *The Wild Bunch* each night. Lou Lombardo set up his editing equipment in a laundry room at the Echo Bay Lodge, where Peckinpah would spend his evenings going over *Wild Bunch* footage.

(Lombardo wound up as co-editor on *Cable Hogue* because of his presence in Echo Bay. Frank Santillo, who had been hired for the job, was cutting sequences for *Hogue* as Peckinpah shot them, but Santillo had another job lined up, which was being threatened because of the rain delays. So he convinced Lombardo to take over the film.)

"We'd come in from shooting," Visciglia says, "and I'd go to the bar and get two big pitchers of martinis. Then we'd walk across to the laundry room and drink them dry while he went over the film with Lombardo."

Those editing sessions, however, usually were preceded by impromptu production meetings in the hotel bar, before anyone had a chance to shower or change clothes. "Sam would point to certain guys and we would follow him to the Lizard Lounge for a meeting," Visciglia says. "A lot of times we'd sit under the bar with a candle. Sam would say, 'Fuck this bar. Let's sit down on the floor.' Just to be different.

"There was usually business discussed. At those times, we never drank for drinking's sake; we drank for business's sake. When it was for business's sake, with other people around, you drank out of a glass. When you drank for drinking's sake, you drank out of the bottle."

There was a lot of drinking for drinking's sake, because of the delays and rain-outs. The company was subject to serious bouts of cabin fever, a malady exacerbated by the location: a deserted hotel in the middle of nowhere.

Peckinpah had chosen it in part because it was the closest accommodation to the locations he wanted. But he also told Robards, "I'm going far enough away from these bastards that they can't find me." Though Feldman was there the first week, Peckinpah didn't allow him on the location for the rest of the production.

So the cast and crew found itself confined—by circumstance and weather —to the Echo Bay Lodge and, in particular, the hotel bar. In the wake of the Great Gila Protest, the bar had been rechristened the Lizard Lounge. Most survivors of the picture credit Robards with the name. Robards says, "After the lizard became a cause célèbre, we would meet in the lounge. Frank Kowalski talked about lounge lizards and then transposed it to Lizard Lounge."

At one point, Peckinpah and Robards were sitting under a table drinking with their friend photojournalist John Bryson, who had come out for a visit. Apropos of nothing, Peckinpah leaned over to Bryson and said, "You're not tough enough for this business. You have to be so tough that they have to kill you to get at you."

Yet, as Visciglia notes, "Sam would always get out of the Lizard Lounge on time. He'd get everything stirred up. When he left, we'd spend hours hashing out what he said and how we'd do it the next day, when we were fifty miles from nowhere. And that was his production meeting."

To fill the time, once the alcohol had started to flow, the actors and crew would do virtually anything that came to mind. There were fistfights between stuntmen and, one evening, a contest between Richard Gillis and David Warner to see who could do the most convincing fall—without using arms or hands to break the descent—on the dance floor. There were also tackle football games in the Lizard Lounge, using large glass ashtrays for footballs.

"One night I got drunk," Gill Dennis says. "Sam was not around so it was Kowalski, Robards and some guy who used to play pro football, a friend of Robards. We're playing football with the big glass ashtrays and the football guy is on my team. I guess I didn't like his looks because I knocked the guy down, he landed on a chair and smashed it into a million pieces. The next morning, Sam walks up and says, 'Welcome to the Wild Bunch.' From then, he had me up there with him all the time."

Peckinpah wasn't immune to the alcoholic revels. The production was having problems, for example, with the National Park Service rangers, who were trying to keep the film company from driving across protected desert lands. One evening, a park ranger came to the hotel to complain about a particular transgression. Peckinpah saw him coming, stood up on the balcony of a room, and urinated on him.

"He was in charge of letting us use the whole park," Gordon Dawson says. "That took a few days to clear up."

Another night, assistant director Cliff Coleman, who departed the picture early on, got a phone call at 2 A.M. The woman at the front desk was screaming, "Help, they're tearing the lobby to bits! They're going to kill me!" Coleman put on a pair of jockey shorts and went downstairs, where he found Peckinpah and Robards, both deeply drunk.

"Peckinpah was pissing into a potted plant," Coleman says. "Robards was drinking out of a gallon tequila bottle—and they were yelling and screaming at each other. They'd pass the bottle and knock down furniture and rush at each other in mock battle. They were dangerous. Jason staggers up to Sam and gives him a big push. Sam fell backwards and then got up and pushed Jason. The bottle went flying across the room. Jason charged Sam and pushed Sam and Sam fell backward.

"I finally stepped in and said, 'Cool it.' Before I could say any more, Sam got off the floor and hit me in the side of the head with a left hook and knocked me out. Then he felt very bad. I got up and then I could start to deal with them."

A number of waitresses and maids wound up in bed with members of the company; one woman passed along a venereal disease that made its way through a large percentage of the crew.

For good measure, Peckinpah imported whores to Echo Bay, prostitution being legal in Nevada. But even that was no guarantee of tranquility.

David Warner, Visciglia recalls, had been sitting around doing nothing for weeks, waiting for his first scene to be shot. The day before his first scene, Warner was nervous, on edge, seemingly on the verge of flipping out.

"He was going bananas," Visciglia says. "Sam came to me at 4 P.M. and said, 'We've got to get Warner fucked. Get me a couple of hookers. Get me three.' So I get them, at $200 a girl, and get the money from the production accountant. Warner takes one girl, Sam takes one and Kowalski takes one. I go to bed, figuring I've done good. At 3 A.M., I get a phone call from Kowalski, saying Sam's beating the shit out of one of the girls because, after she had fucked him, she had fucked Kowalski. Sam figured the three whores were for him, that they should be in love with him, that it was his party. He came to me and said, 'Don't pay them. Fuck 'em.' I said, 'Sam, you pay a whore up-front.' He says, 'Why'd you give them the fucking money?' "

The women fled into the night, where they ran into Slim Pickens and Max Evans returning from a night out. Evans recalled, "One of them was sobbing almost hysterically. The other two were also obviously upset. One blubbered out, 'I'm just not used to being treated like that!' "

The next day, as Gordon Dawson walked through the lobby of the hotel, a stranger—the women's pimp—came up to him, angry about the way they had been treated.

"He said, 'Are you Sam Peckinpah?' and stuck a .38 in my stomach," Dawson says. "I managed to convince him I wasn't and steered him away."

Still, Gill Dennis says, "Sam never missed a day's shooting during *Cable*.

The guy was unbelievable, the energy he had. He'd drink all night, work all day. And it was hard work."

Peckinpah saved some of his most eccentric behavior for after-hours poker games. He was a terrible gambler: impulsive, inattentive, quick to crow, quicker to anger—and a poor loser to boot.

"We detested playing poker with Sam," L. Q. Jones says.

His favorite game was liar's poker, a game in which two players create poker hands out of the combined serial numbers on their own dollar bills—one of which they can't see.

"He refined it," Gill Dennis says, "to the point where it was Zen liar's poker, played with imaginary bills. He would always lose and just be furious."

One notable evening, Peckinpah wheedled his way into a card game in Jones's room, involving Jones, Strother Martin, Max Evans, Frank Kowalski, Bobby Visciglia, actor Gene Evans and a couple of stuntmen. Before long, there were several thousand dollars on the table, the culmination of a long-running game throughout the production.

Peckinpah, however, lost all of his cash in short order. "He was pissing and moaning," Jones says. "The game goes on and he tries to borrow money from me. I tell him to fuck off. He tries to borrow from Strother and I said I won't let him lend Sam the money either."

According to Jones, Peckinpah then grabbed the cards, said, "Ante $100," grabs his ante from Jones's pile, and deals two cards each.

"Eventually, there's almost all the money in the center," Jones says. "He deals the last card and says, 'Shit, you win it all, Max.' Now, he had never announced the rules. You'd think if he was going to do that, he'd at least say, 'I win.' Nobody knew quite what to do."

The money sat there for a couple of minutes, Jones says. Peckinpah went to the phone, called the front desk to order more money, then yanked the phone out by the roots.

Without warning, he scooped up all the cash, walked over to the window, tore the money into pieces and threw it out the window.

"Then he stood up on the air conditioner and pissed out the window on the money," Jones says.

In the middle of the night, Gill Dennis was awakened by a phone call from Kowalski, informing him that the card players had opened the bar and telling him to get down there.

Dennis says, "To them, Sam had finally gone too far. They were all in there, plotting to kill Sam on the way to the location the next day. I spent an hour and a half talking them out of it."

The next day, production assistants were dispatched to pick up the pieces of money that now littered the hotel grounds. The pieces were brought in to the production manager's office, where they were washed in a large vat. The pieces were dried with an iron on an ironing board. And the assistants were put to work with Scotch tape, fitting pieces of currency together like valuable little jigsaw puzzles.

BECAUSE OF WEATHER PROBLEMS, *The Ballad of Cable Hogue* went almost a month over schedule, wrapping near the end of March 1969. Peckinpah returned his attention to putting the finishing touches on *The Wild Bunch*, while his cast and crew scattered.

"I went to Hawaii to get as far away from Sam Peckinpah as I could," Gordon Dawson says. "After a week, I got a phone call: 'I'm at the airport. Pick me up; we're cutting the picture here.' "

Peckinpah brought his children along as a vacation for them but spent his time working with Dawson and Lombardo, who was completing the editing that Frank Santillo had started.

"I cut *Cable Hogue* pretty standard, like it played," Lombardo says. "Sam would say, 'Let's do a *Wild Bunch* number here, where they meet in the middle of the street, but let's speed the film up here.' We sped the film up to expedite the situation. I thought it was kind of hokey but it worked. Sam, for all his anger and violence, was really a pussycat. He loved the 'moments.' 'Give me another moment,' he'd say. He loved all that background stuff, the looks back and forth, the camaraderie, the love."

Ballad of Cable Hogue had its stylized moments, using speeded-up motion (for comic effect) in a couple of scenes. After Cable's first encounter with Hildy, Peckinpah had Lombardo insert several leering subliminal cuts back to her cleavage as Cable fixated on it. When Cable considers using his newly borrowed cash for a visit to Hildy, the Indian head on the money gives him a knowing smile.

The dialogue in several sequences intercut moments from different scenes into a single conversation, compressing time without losing meaning. Peckinpah also employed the momentarily trendy technique of split-screen imagery, showing four or five different scenes in the same frame: in the opening credits, as Cable wanders in the desert, and during a montage in which Cable builds his shack.

But the problems with Warner Bros. and Feldman over the release—and cutting—of *The Wild Bunch* began to erode Peckinpah's relationship with Feldman. Feldman, to be sure, was less than thrilled with the cost overruns on *Cable Hogue*, though the weather was the obvious cause. But the fact that Peckinpah had kept him away from the set and the bad publicity in the industry over the numerous firings stretched his patience.

On May 22, 1969, he wrote a memo to Peckinpah, taking him to task for the nose-thumbing gesture of giving medals to the survivors on *Cable Hogue*. "I think you have got to start thinking for your next picture about these facts," wrote Feldman. "People work for a living. They don't need the living that badly that they will suffer some of the indignities which I, and hopefully you, may have to be exposed to because we have more than a living involved in the project."

Peckinpah, in a gracious mood, responded on May 24: "The truth is, doing two pictures almost back to back has left me emotionally exhausted and I am afraid that I have taken out my needless impatience upon people close to me, and you are one of those people. We have both worked long exhausting hours doing the best we know how. I think the end result will be something we can be proud of even if I am not proud of some of my remarks to you.

"Maybe that's what a friend is for: to chew your ass out when you need it. Phil, I hope this is not the end of the line. I hope it is the beginning if it can still be. I want you to know if it means anything anymore I wouldn't have it any other way."

Gill Dennis says, "Renoir said that evil in Hollywood isn't greed; it's desire for perfection. A lot of unpleasantness comes from that. Phil Feldman said to me at one point, 'Sam has 90 percent of what it takes. He needs my 10 percent.' But what happens in movies is you don't get 100—you get a 90. You don't say, 'I wish there was more of Ibsen in Strindberg.' If you bring in Ibsen to rewrite Strindberg, you might only get a 75. But in the writing and the editing stage, everybody feels they can fix it."

So it was with *The Wild Bunch* and the ever-growing number of minutes that were being taken out of it as it was dropped into American theaters and then yanked out again. When Peckinpah found out what was being done, he wrote Feldman a memo on June 16, 1969: "The fact that I take issue with you does not necessarily mean that you were wrong, but the fact that you overrule me in certain areas means that you think I am wrong. This happens to be the field in which I consider myself a professional.

"I once sent you a memo saying I'd go with you. This evidently was not enough. I accept it now with regret because at the present time we can't seem to reachieve the understanding we once had.

"I know you have protected me from myself but I beg of you with the deepest kind of affection to please look at the other side of the coin."

The war of words continued, with Feldman convinced that Peckinpah was making him the fall guy. "Phil was weary," Gordon Dawson says. "It was hard working with Sam."

Feldman finally responded on July 2, 1969: "If we ever associate someday it must be predicated upon deeds done voluntarily by you that indicate to me I would have pleasure in associating with you and I would get some fun out of anything we attempted together and that we'd really partner an adventure. I think your memo is doing what you have done for an awful long time and I'll not have you do it to me or to yourself. You are building walls and setting up straw men which you can use later in defense of your own actions."

As the release of *Cable Hogue* approached, Peckinpah and Feldman were barely on speaking terms. Peckinpah began to bad-mouth Feldman in the press for allowing *Wild Bunch* to be both trimmed and badly released.

"Feldman let those rotten sons of bitches at Warners chop out twenty minutes [of *The Wild Bunch*] so they could hustle more popcorn," he said.

Then Peckinpah found out that Feldman had allowed Warner Bros. to show a rough cut of *Cable Hogue* to distributors—a version thirty minutes longer than the finished film, without a finished soundtrack or score. That showing convinced them the film would not do much business; it came and went from theaters, without any major first-run bookings, in two weeks in March 1970.

"Warner Bros. wrote off *Cable Hogue* after one weekend as a tax loss," Peckinpah said. "That was the end. That's corporate dealings in Hollywood and there's nothing you can do about it, unless you buy a print or steal one."

Later in the year, in a letter he wrote to director Francis Ford Coppola on behalf of actor Joe Spinell (who wanted a role in *The Godfather*), Peckinpah added, "If you have any Mafia connections, kindly inform me. I would like to make out some contracts regarding key Warner Brothers personnel."

Peckinpah finally cut off relations with Feldman, a split that obviously caused Feldman a great deal of pain. In a handwritten note to Peckinpah from the end of 1969, he said: "I have tried to be the best partner I know how to be. Sometimes you may not have agreed with me. You told me that last week and I respect your right so to do. You have every right and should satisfy yourself in discontinuing any relationship. I have, however, tried to protect the film you made. Sometimes it may have seemed contrary to your own wishes, but that is when I believe it will be to your own ultimate benefit. I have never hidden anything from you. And yet chemistry is what should certainly govern you.

"I believe I am the best partner one could wish for. Whatever you decide on any score, be assured that I am only and always trying for the best film and for your own ultimate best."

"Peckinpah burned his bridges," says critic Michael Sragow. "When I was at NYU film school, Phil Feldman brought *Cable Hogue* for us to see and he was still talking highly of Peckinpah. With Feldman he made two of his best films. Maybe [Peckinpah] shouldn't have blamed him for all his problems. Peckinpah didn't know how to save important friendships to keep him in the business. He was more interested in people who couldn't do him any good —cinematographers, actors."

WHEN *CABLE HOGUE* was released in March 1970, *Time* magazine said Peckinpah "makes shooting a movie look as easy as whittling" and called the film "quiet, lyrical, bawdy, funny and sad in almost equal portions, exactly as a good back-room yarn should be. With this film, Peckinpah unmistakably becomes the successor to John Ford, not only as a director of westerns but as an American film artist."

Richard Schickel, who had championed *The Wild Bunch,* wrote in *Life* magazine, "I think [*Cable Hogue*] is less than his best work—but a great deal better than about 90 percent of the stuff we are ordinarily subjected to at the movies. We come to love it as we might a child's playhouse, not for its perfect symmetry, but for the open way it expresses the feeling of its creator."

Newsweek's Joseph Morgenstern, who had frowned on *The Wild Bunch,* referred here to Peckinpah's "lyrical direction. The director is clearly in a mood to please, which is a good mood for him to be in."

On the other hand, Stanley Kaufmann, writing in *The New Republic,* called the film "a disaster." He referred to Stevens as having "very much less appeal than, but all the talent of, Kim Novak," and said that Robards was, from his first appearance "physically phony," an actor who "turns this intended folk ballad into ham salad."

The film became one of the lost films of 1970. Stevens, who was counting on it to jump-start her career, wound up sorely disappointed. "I felt like this would be one big break," she says. "But I was not offered any other roles. There was never any direct relation between my getting work and this film. It turned out to be a little film that a few people saw on TV."

"*Cable* was Sam's answer to *The Wild Bunch,*" says Joe Bernhard. "He was saying, 'There's this part of us here and this part of us there.' When *Ballad of Cable Hogue* failed, it destroyed him."

Peckinpah said, "I hope I don't go back to Westerns at all. That's a thing that ends with me with *Cable Hogue.* I'll never go back to that: men who lived out of their time, et cetera. I've played that out."

Peckinpah's publicist, Joel Reisner, arranged a retrospective of Peckinpah's work at the Los Angeles County Museum of Art. Called "A Profile of Sam Peckinpah," it featured the premiere of *Cable Hogue* on March 8, 1970, as well as showings of *Ride the High Country* and *The Wild Bunch.*

After the honorific evening, Peckinpah sent a letter to Phillip Chamberlain, who had curated the retrospective for the museum, and praised "the spirit and dedication" of the event. Then he wrote: "Regretfully, I must withdraw my offer to contribute to your archives my personal collection of prints, even though I feel strongly that this is an honor. I withdraw this offer because of the shameful way my work was projected during your film event. I don't know whether it was the equipment or the maintenance, but it was haphazard, to say the least. I simply cannot allow you to chew up my life's work and, consequently, am accepting the offer of the Museum of Modern Art in New York City to contribute my films to their archives."

Though this encounter was not publicized, it fit into the public image he was slowly developing. The people who knew him understood that he could be unpredictable and vindictive, sometimes doing something frightening or infuriating just to get a rise out of people, to see how they would respond to different stimuli.

"He would pick on you, try to make you angry, just to needle you," says John Bryson. "He was a constant student of human behavior. He was constantly watching how people reacted to situations and emotions. He loved to stir things up and see what happened."

Gill Dennis says, "Gordon Dawson used to say, 'Don't think just because you got drunk with him that you're friends.' "

Joel Reisner told several people the story of the afternoon he was talking to Peckinpah at Peckinpah's office. A boa constrictor lay digesting a mouse in a cage on Peckinpah's desk. A second mouse was also in the cage, quaking in the corner, seemingly aware of its fate once its cousin was digested. Peckinpah beamed at Reisner and asked, "Who do you think will win?"

To which Reisner replied, "You will, Sam."

18

Casting About, Casting Off

THOUGH HE HAD NOW MADE TWO FILMS IN A ROW that had not been big commercial hits, Peckinpah had shown that he could work within the studio system, get a picture finished and earn critical plaudits at the same time.

He was bankable. He was in demand. Even Warner Bros., despite the conflicts over marketing decisions on these two films, was willing to work with him again.

Yet he found himself limited by his image as an action director, a maker of Western films. He wanted to expand his horizons. One project that intrigued him was *Play It As It Lays,* a brooding and cynical story of the suicidal wife of a self-absorbed film director in modern Hollywood.

The novel was written by Joan Didion, the ranking queen of modern literary angst. Didion and her husband, writer John Gregory Dunne, were eager to have Peckinpah do the screen adaptation. In April 1970, Didion wrote to Peckinpah: "My agent at William Morris wants to take *Play It As It Lays* to a studio and make a deal before publication, which is July something. A lot of people have asked for it but I told Morris not to show it to anyone until I found out what you want to do—whether, on reflection, you still want to do it, and if so what studio you would want us to take it to. I hope you still want to do it. Obviously I want you to—you are the only person John and I can see taking it beyond where it is and bringing back a picture of the very edge."

When Peckinpah read the galleys and discussed it with Dunne and Didion, they were further convinced that he was the perfect director for the project. He told them, "To me, this movie is about the third man through the door," referring to the standard Hollywood photograph of the star, his wife —and the faceless third person who always seems to be holding the door for them.

"That image has stayed with me," Dunne later said. "Though we always admired Sam's talent, that image helped convince us that Peckinpah should make the movie."

They, apparently, were the only ones who thought so. No one else could see "Bloody Sam" Peckinpah behind the camera on a neurasthenic film about Hollywood.

"He would have been ideal for *Play It As It Lays,*" Pauline Kael says. "But if you make Westerns, you're thought of as a Western director."

At the same time, another project presented itself: an opportunity to work with Robert Culp, who was still trying to cross over from acting into writing and directing. Culp put Peckinpah together with writer-director Lee Pogostin. The three of them would collaborate on a script Culp had written called *Summer Soldiers.*

Summer Soldiers was set in an unspecified Central American country in 1970. A group of American college students, led by their professor, arrives in the country and heads for the hills to fight for the revolutionaries, who are at war with the government. One of the rebel leaders is an American mercenary, the college professor's older brother.

The idea jibed with Peckinpah's view of the world at the time. "We're in the midst of a revolution," he said. "I don't think that you can say during a revolution whether anything specific will happen. It's a total dissatisfaction with the morality of the past. In fact, it looks like the next picture I'll be doing will be a script with Lee Pogostin and Bob Culp, concerning literal revolution that meshes with this humanist revolution. Actually, I'm not political—but I am concerned. I'm concerned with us."

His daughter Kristen says, "Anything that became politicized tended to get his hackles up." Gill Dennis adds, "He'd say, 'I don't know what I know, but I have a nose for dogma.' "

To Culp and Pogostin, it seemed like an ideal project: a chance to work with friends and make a script they believed in. They worked it over during the end of 1969 and into the beginning of 1970.

"We had an open-door policy twenty-four hours a day because we were working together on the script," Pogostin says. "I remember him coming into my beach house one morning at 3 A.M. with a gun. I said, 'Is it loaded?' He said, 'Yeah.' 'Well, take the bullets out,' I said, and he did. If he was going to play Sam Peckinpah with me, I didn't want a loaded gun in the house while we were working together.

"One time I was on the beach with him and Culp and the waves were coming in. Sam looks at the waves and says, 'Those are big.' So he swims out a ways, then bodysurfs onto the top of a wave in the most perfect way, walks up and towels off. I didn't know whether to be impressed or what. He was a warm, wonderful human being with me, never nuts."

Mutual friends warned Culp that Peckinpah could be treacherous, but Culp had been frustrated too often to back away from the project.

Culp says, "I was told many times, 'You shouldn't trust this guy. He'll betray you.' I said, 'He'll never do it to me.' "

Culp was riding high. His TV series, "I Spy," a major hit of the 1960s, had just gone off the air; he apparently had made the successful leap to motion picture stardom in Paul Mazursky's *Bob & Carol & Ted & Alice.*

"I was at the peak of my game, really cooking," Culp says. "I said, I'm going to put the deal together, we'll go to Warner Bros. and make the deal."

Peckinpah would direct, Culp would play the college professor and George C. Scott was signed to play the mercenary older brother. They had Pogostin do a rewrite of Culp's script, which both Culp and Peckinpah found dissatisfying and reworked, melding it with Culp's original.

Peckinpah left for Europe, with an invitation from Ingmar Bergman to lecture film students in Stockholm. Culp proceeded: He had a green light, offices at Warners and a start date. Peckinpah would do his brief tour of the continent, then stop in New York to pick up George C. Scott and head back to Hollywood to start the film.

According to John Calley, the *Cincinnati Kid* co-producer who had taken over as head of production at Warner Bros. after Ken Hyman left, the deal eventually just fell apart: "It had momentum and then it died."

But Culp says that Calley called him and Pogostin into his office at Warners and said, "I don't know how to tell you this but you're fired. Your partner Peckinpah stopped in London and gave a press conference, where he told the press that the sales department at Warner Bros. were inept, incompetent fools who did not know how to sell a picture. That was why *Cable Hogue* did not succeed and *Wild Bunch* did not succeed either. Then he went to Paris and did the same thing. And to Stockholm and did the same thing. The guys from New York called and said, 'We've made two pictures back-to-back with him. Fuck him. Fire them all.' "

Culp was so furious he sent Peckinpah a letter asking to buy back the rights to the script. Peckinpah wrote back, saying they were worth about twenty-five cents. Culp sent him a quarter taped to a piece of cardboard.

The script was never filmed. The two friends didn't speak again for five years.

"I was so mad at the bastard I could have killed him," Culp says. "To shoot us all down with a childish stunt. Any twelve-year-old knows what's going to happen. It would have changed everybody's life if he'd kept his mouth shut."

Peckinpah's hostile relations with Warner Bros. continued that year when he expressed interest in directing the film of James Dickey's novel, *Deliverance.* Calley says there was never a chance that Peckinpah could have made the movie, but not for personal reasons. "I bought it specifically for John Boorman," Calley says.

Still, Peckinpah corresponded with Dickey about the project, writing to him on September 3, 1970: "I would still like to direct the film. Like hell, I would love to direct the film, but I don't know what to do because, as you know, I am suing Warner Bros. for breach of good faith, which has a tendency to make their assholes pucker like a splash of turpentine."

In December, he wrote to Dickey again: "My situation with Warner Bros. remains the same: Unless someone with clout leans on them, they won't let me direct traffic through the men's room."

19

A "Straw" Is Born

By THAT TIME, HOWEVER, Peckinpah had committed to a new film. Even while he, Culp and Pogostin were maneuvering to get *Summer Soldiers* before the cameras, Peckinpah had been talking to producer Daniel Melnick about Melnick's upcoming maiden effort at film production.

David Susskind, Melnick's partner, had acquired the rights to a British potboiler, a novel called *The Siege at Trencher's Farm*, by Gordon Williams. But the scripts he commissioned didn't seem to click. So Melnick took a shot at it, getting Peckinpah interested in the idea. He sold the idea to ABC Pictures president Martin Baum, with the proviso that Peckinpah be allowed to direct. Baum was cautious: He knew Peckinpah only by reputation. Still, he knew and trusted Melnick's judgment.

"I had heard stories about his drinking and his general tumultuous behavior," Baum says. "I was very nervous. Dan asked me to meet him and I found him to be a soft-spoken gentleman, utterly disarming in demeanor. He had excellent ideas as to what *Straw Dogs* could be. Melnick's faith led me to hire him."

Peckinpah didn't have time to write a new screenplay and, frankly, wasn't interested in doing the first draft. So Melnick hired writer David Z. Goodman to adapt the book as a script.

The novel was the story of a professor of English who, with his young wife, returns to her native village near Cornwall. The book culminates in an armed attack on their home, where they are sheltering an escaped criminal who is accused of murdering a girl. The timid academic rises to the occasion of defending his home, killing all of the attackers in the process.

Goodman made the academic an American on sabbatical, an astromathematician involved in deep theoretical research. He is trying to escape the violence and insanity of the political upheavals in the United States. But he runs afoul of the neighborhood brutes, who rape his wife and then mount an attack on his house to seize a local child molester who has accidentally killed a teen.

The film played to Peckinpah's strength, not to mention his newfound critical reputation as the cinematic poet of violent death.

"It's about the violence within us all," Peckinpah said, "the violence which is reflecting on the political conditions of the world today. It serves a dual purpose. I intend it to have a cathartic effect. Someone may feel a sick exultation at the violence but he should then ask himself, 'What is going on in my heart?' I want to achieve a catharsis through pity and fear."

The theme—a peaceful man provoked to violence in defense of his family and home—spoke to ideas that Peckinpah had been toying with since Strother Martin had given him Robert Ardrey's books *African Genesis* and *The Territorial Imperative*. A sociological anthropologist, Ardrey wrote at length about the instinctive violence that lurks just beneath the surface of civilized man. Cues in the present could easily trigger instincts and impulses that were thought to be buried beneath hundreds of generations of evolution.

Several of Ardrey's observations struck a chord with Peckinpah when he was considering *The Siege at Trencher's Farm:*

· "Territory, in the evolving world of animals, is a force perhaps older than sex."

· "Males compete for real estate, never for females."

· "Evil is not inherent in human nature, it is learned. Aggressiveness is taught, as are all forms of violence which human beings exhibit."

· "Territory is like a rubber disc: the tighter it is compressed, the more powerful will be the pressure outward to spring it back into shape. A proprietor's confidence is at its peak in the heartland, as is an intruder's at its lowest. Here the proprietor will fight hardest, chase fastest."

DURING THE SUMMER OF 1970, Melnick and Peckinpah worked over the screenplay. At one point, Peckinpah spent a weekend at Melnick's house in Pound Ridge, a tony suburb north of New York City in Westchester County. It was Melnick's first hint that Peckinpah had a problem with alcohol.

"I realized he started the morning with coffee with brandy," Melnick says. "After a number of those, he moved on between the end of breakfast and lunch to drinking white wine. Then he had real drinks with lunch and would drink all afternoon."

If he hadn't seen him do the actual drinking, however, Melnick might not have tumbled to it. Peckinpah seldom evinced any overt signs of drunkenness. "He'd become more taciturn but he wouldn't slur his words," Melnick says. "He was one of those people about whom people say they didn't know he was a drunk until one day he showed up sober. I remember being shaken up by my own feelings of responsibility to the people who were writing the checks and by my own fundamental uncomfortableness with people who are drunk."

He finally confronted Peckinpah with his concerns, although in a diplomatic way. Peckinpah disarmed him by agreeing with him. "You're right," he said. "I know I have a problem and I'm drying out. By the time we do the show, I won't be drinking."

But, as Melnick later discovered, "Sam's drying out meant drinking only wine—and in prodigious quantities."

Melnick need only have asked Peckinpah's nephew David, whose perceptions of his uncle were altered by an incident earlier that same year. David, seventeen at the time, had come down to Los Angeles to look at UCLA as a possible place to go to college.

"Sam had a driver pick me up," David says. "We went to the studio and he was drinking and all these attractive young ladies were coming into his office. We were going to go to a screening of *Fellini Satyricon*. By the time we got to the banquet, he was completely shitfaced. He was dressed as though he was in costume for an appearance. He had a bandana around his head and a tuxedo and a .38 in a shoulder holster. He was like an actor preparing himself for a performance.

"We got there and the movie had already started. They wouldn't let us in. Sam was furious. So we're standing in the lobby and there are these huge buffet trays covered with food. He started making little packets and stuffing them in his pocket. A chef comes out and tells him to stop. It quickly escalated into a yelling match and the security guards came. Before I know it, Sam had left. He left me standing there.

"Gill Dennis took me under his wing and took me back to his apartment in Westwood. He took me to UCLA the next day and I finally rendezvoused with Sam for the weekend at his beach house, which was forty-eight hours of drunken debauchery. I left thinking, 'I don't want to do this.' "

AT VARIOUS POINTS, Baum, Melnick, Peckinpah and David Goodman all had input into the script for *Straw Dogs*, with each rewrite refining the revisions of the last person. Peckinpah moved to London in the fall of 1970 to begin preproduction. At that point, he submitted the screenplay to playwright Harold Pinter with a suggestion that he might be interested in taking a pass at it.

Pinter, the modern master of implicit and unspoken menace, did not take kindly to this tale of explicit and howling violence. "Dear Sam Peckinpah," he wrote. "I enjoyed our meeting very much a while ago, but I'm sorry you've asked me for my comments on the script. I have to tell you I detest it with unqualified detestation. It seems to me totally unreal, obscene not only in its unequivocal delighted rape and violence but in its absolute lack of connection with anything that is recognizable or true in human beings and in its pathetic assumption that it is saying something 'important' about human beings.

"How you can associate yourself with it is beyond me. However, that's your business. I can only say I consider it an abomination."

Melnick's original idea for casting the film centered on Dustin Hoffman, as the tortuously pragmatic and self-absorbed American mathematician. Hoffman was one of the most sought-after young actors in America, with Oscar nominations for *The Graduate* and *Midnight Cowboy*. But Hoffman, who had developed a reputation for being strong-minded about scripts, dug in his heels until the *Trencher's Farm* screenplay was in suitable shape.

So Peckinpah and Melnick started looking at other actors: Elliott Gould, Beau Bridges, Stacy Keach, Donald Sutherland. Eventually, Hoffman came around, signing in October 1970 for just under a million dollars.

For the part of the wife, several of the brightest young lights in British cinema were auditioned, among them Judy Geeson and Carol White. Peckinpah decided on Susan George, despite protests from Melnick and Hoffman, who didn't feel she was right for the role.

The local working-class men—who turn into the mob that launches the siege—were cast from the British stage and screen. To play Henry Niles, the feeble-minded child molester, Peckinpah turned to David Warner, as much because he wanted to help the unfortunate Warner as because he felt he was right for the role.

Warner, who was still suffering from various phobias and insecurities after finishing *Cable Hogue,* had gone to Italy, where he had had an accident, in which he had jumped or fallen out of a window, landing upright and smashing the bones in his feet. It was reported in the press as a suicide attempt, though Warner claims it wasn't.

Doctors only gave Warner a fifty-fifty chance of ever being able to walk again. Peckinpah called him and said, "What you need is to work in front of a camera."

Because of the accident, however, Warner was considered uninsurable by the studio. When Warner mentioned this to Peckinpah, he said, "Not insurable? Fuck 'em. I'll be responsible for you."

(Several weeks after production started, when Baum and other studio executives showed up on location, a bout of flu had so decimated the company and crew that the only member of the production well enough to greet them at the railroad station was the uninsurable David Warner.)

As he worked on finding locations and other preproduction details, Peckinpah made two connections that would be lasting ones. One was with a former secretary for Richard Harris, Joie Gould, whom Peckinpah met and began to romance. The other was also with a British secretary: Katy Haber, who wound up as his secretary, personal assistant, lover and conduit to the rest of the world for the better part of the next eight years.

Peckinpah found Haber accidentally. He mentioned that he needed a secretary to a producer friend, who knew Haber was looking for work. The producer put the two of them together by telephone. But the first two times they spoke, Peckinpah said, "Can you be here in ten minutes?" Both times, when Haber said, "Well, I'm an hour away," Peckinpah said, "Forget it."

A week or so later, Haber was visiting the mutual friend, who took her into an adjoining office and introduced her to Peckinpah. "I suppose you want me to give you another chance," Haber joked.

"Sit down, shut up and start typing," Peckinpah replied. He gave her the rape scene from *Trencher's Farm* and had her typing around the clock for three days, until the script was finished.

"I'd never met anyone like him," says Haber, now director of development for a production company. "I was a nice Jewish girl who had led a sheltered life in London. And I met Wyatt Earp."

Though he was involved with Joie Gould, Peckinpah became romantically entangled with Haber within two weeks. He was forty-five; she was twenty-six. "It was very romantic," she says of the relationship that became part of life on location in Cornwall.

PECKINPAH WASN'T OVERWHELMED by the title of the book and hit upon an alternative, thanks to yet another person who, with *Straw Dogs,* became part of his inner working circle. Walter Kelley was an actor, writer and producer who had fled Hollywood in the early 1960s to live in France. He had known Peckinpah slightly during Peckinpah's TV days and bumped into him in a London restaurant, which he had walked into by mistake.

Peckinpah immediately shanghaied Kelley, moving him into the director's flat to write and live together during preproduction. Fresh blood—a new accomplice. They would stay up writing, trying to figure out how to end the story in a way that made sense and was still satisfying.

Kelley gave him a key to the story by providing a quotation from the Tao Te Ching by the Chinese philosopher Lao-tse: "Heaven and earth are ruthless and treat the myriad creatures as straw dogs. The sage is ruthless and treats the people like straw dogs."

Peckinpah loved it. The marketing people at ABC Pictures were less thrilled. They toyed with titles such as "The Square Root of Fear." They also tested the titles they had and variations on them. Research showed that audiences thought "The Siege at Trencher's Farm" sounded like a Western. "Siege at Trencher's" sounded like a war story.

"Straw Dogs," people told researchers, sounded like a comedy.

In *STRAW DOGS,* David and Amy Sumner have returned to Amy's native village in the north of England. David is on a sabbatical from his position at an American college, to do research. But he is also trying to escape the political turmoil that has swept college campuses in America and the country at large.

Once they have moved into Trencher's Farm, however, their lives begin to deteriorate. Amy, feeling neglected by David, flirts with Charlie Venner, her old boyfriend. Venner offers to help other local workmen who are rebuilding their garage. Rapidly, the workmen become an oppressive presence, invading the Sumners' privacy, going so far as to kill their cat and leave it hanging in their closet as an act of terror and arrogance.

But the cerebral David refuses to confront the workmen. Instead, he accepts their invitation to go hunting. They leave him in a field while Venner and Scutt, another of the workmen, double back and rape Amy.

Attending a church social that evening, Amy falls apart under the trauma of the rape. In another part of the town, a disturbed local man, Henry Niles, who has a history of child molesting, accidentally kills a flirtatious young girl. When David starts to drive Amy home, his car hits Niles and David takes him back to their house.

A mob, which has formed to look for Niles and the girl, discovers that Niles is at David's house. When they try to capture Niles, however, David refuses to let them in, feeling he is responsible for Niles's well-being. The mob, made up of the workmen and a couple of their friends, gets progressively drunker, then mounts a violent assault on the house. David, pushed to his limit, finally makes a stand and kills them all.

Location filming for *Straw Dogs* began in January 1971 near Cornwall. The weather was damp and chilly, about what you'd expect from January in the English heath.

Peckinpah and Hoffman hit it off, though neither was ever quite sure what the other was talking about. As Jason Robards says about Peckinpah, "He didn't give you a lot of acting lessons. It was just, 'Cut a look here, then put it on the money.' I don't like all this research where you examine your navel until you can't find any more lint. He wanted none of that shit and that's why I liked to work with him."

Or, as Peckinpah said, "Don't give me any of those Charley Star assholes."

Hoffman, on the other hand, is well known for that kind of self-absorption, losing himself in a role. He expects to collaborate with a director in developing a synergy between the character and the movie. But Peckinpah didn't speak that language.

"Sam worked entirely intuitively and didn't have Dustin's acting vocabulary to communicate with," Melnick says. "When Dustin would talk to him about an intention or a beat in the script or what an emotional truth was, Sam would slap him on the shoulder and say, 'Just get in there and do your number.' And Dustin would look at me and roll his eyes and mouth the words, 'Do my number?' Dustin and I would have dinner night after night and talk about the character. I told Sam what Dustin needed. Sam said, 'Kid, you're a producer. Earn your money. Talk to him and get him to the set on time.' I think Dustin had a combination of respect, adoration and frustration with Sam."

"Working with Dustin Hoffman was an experience, indeed," Peckinpah wrote to his friend, critic Jan Aghed. "He is undoubtedly one of the most talented and conscientious artists I have worked with. His dedication and love of his work was a joy to behold and sometimes a pain in the ass."

Or, as he told Begonia when she stopped in London for a brief visit during production, "I'm working with an actor who is crazier than I am. I love it."

Hoffman was tactful in describing Peckinpah to reporters at the time. Putting on the best spin possible, he said, "Sam's like a fight trainer. He shapes you up, he psyches you, he draws everything out of you. He's subtle, though, yet baroque and I want to get into the baroqueness. Like the other day, during a scene in which I was supposed to be answering a door and registering surprise. Well, it was the end of the day and I wasn't acting very surprised, so he smashes a beer bottle down behind me, right out of camera range. I mean, Christ, I nearly jumped out of my skin. But he got what he wanted."

He also said, "Sam Peckinpah is a man out of his time, a gunfighter in an age when we're going to the moon."

In the end, however, he said, "Don't ask me what the real Sam Peckinpah is like. Because I have no idea."

There were various problems once the production started at the location. The first few days' dailies were ruined, Melnick discovered, because the cinematographer, whose wife had recently died, had shot blank film the first two days and was having a nervous breakdown. So a new cinematographer, John Coquillon, was brought in.

The production also had a problem with the film's editor, who kept issuing panicked bulletins to executives at ABC about the awfulness of Peckinpah's footage.

"The editor kept saying, 'This isn't going to work,' because Sam's shooting technique was very unlike [that of] an English classicist," Melnick says. "Sam would do a take and know what thirteen seconds he wanted from it, but the editor had no idea." The editor called in the studio executives, so Melnick fired him.

Because of English guild laws, Peckinpah was restricted to a single American on his crew. Exercising his option, he tried to hire Lou Lombardo to edit the film. But by the time he called, Lombardo was in the midst of cutting *McCabe and Mrs. Miller* for Robert Altman in Vancouver.

Instead, the three editor's assistants—Roger Spottiswoode, Tony Lawson and Paul Davies—were given the job jointly. Peckinpah brought in American editor Bob Wolfe (who had worked on *The Wild Bunch*) and gave him the title "editorial consultant."

Spottiswoode recalls being hired without meeting Peckinpah and being asked to assemble a Pinteresque tea-party scene at the center of the film as his first task. Then, at a production meeting, Peckinpah put the young editor on the spot.

"I'd only just met him," says Spottiswoode, now a veteran director. "The room was full of the whole crew and he said, 'Who's got some cut footage for me to look at?' Nobody did, so he said, 'Come on, I hear you've got a scene, Spottis-woodie.'

"I said I didn't really want to show it because it wasn't really done. Sam said, 'Tough shit,' and nudged Katy. She always carried a shopping bag of drinks for him. She poured an entire tumbler of Scotch and gave it to Sam, who handed it to me and said, 'Drink this, doctor.' Then we ran the scene."

At the end of the scene, there was complete silence as everyone tried to gauge Peckinpah's reaction. He sat quietly, then finally said, "Shit." The atmosphere chilled instantly, until he added, "Great, great shit."

"He sure enjoyed my agony when he said, 'Shit,' " Spottiswoode says. "Just because he knew he was putting me through agony didn't stop him from having a laugh at my expense."

Peckinpah would shoot by day, then retire to his rented cottage in Cornwall by night, to drink and work with Walter Kelley and Frank Kowalski, who was also on hand, on an idea for a screenplay that Kowalski had (which would become *Bring Me the Head of Alfredo Garcia*).

He also had his daughter Kristen living with him for a while; now seventeen, she was trying to decide whether to quit school and study ballet.

"I think I realized something about him there, with his anger," Kristen says. "He was fairly well eaten up with this rage. He could really work himself over. Drinking would set it off. I finally figured out that I could be there at the wrong time and get it directed at me. Especially when you're in the middle of working and things are not going particularly well. There are times just to walk away from this guy because it's not an argument you could win."

The chill damp of the English countryside, combined with late hours and overzealous drinking, gradually wore down Peckinpah's health. A *New York*

Times reporter who visited the location for a story described him as speaking "in a dried-out voice, more parched by alcohol than by the desert."

Kristen says, "After *The Wild Bunch,* when he became well known, there was a period where the drinking got heavy. You can't do that for a long time without it affecting you."

Always a victim of upper-respiratory ailments because of his alcohol and tobacco intake, Peckinpah began to deteriorate physically—into flu and finally into walking pneumonia. The ill health took its toll on his work. His concentration was spotty and it began to show up in the film he was making.

"Attending dailies," Martin Baum says, "I saw that the work he was doing was erratic, rambling, lacking in focus. I did a little checking. I found out the coffee he was drinking in the morning was laced with brandy at breakfast. The fruit juice he was drinking during the day was fortified by vodka. He was dehydrated from alcohol."

Four weeks into shooting, Peckinpah's health seemed to be failing as fast as his work was deteriorating. So Melnick and Baum agreed that the picture should be shut down temporarily while Peckinpah was hospitalized to recover from the virus that was debilitating him.

"I expect you during this time to really dry out," Melnick told him. "As close as we are, if you have another drink during the working day, I'll replace you."

"You never would because you're my friend," Peckinpah said.

"I would because you are my friend," Melnick replied.

There was pressure from ABC Pictures to fire Peckinpah and finish the film with another director. The effect on his career would have been devastating. Baum told him so in no uncertain terms when he visited Peckinpah in the hospital.

"I pointed out that if he were fired for cause, the stain on his career would be difficult to overcome," Baum says. "I told him that there was pressure to fire him, that he'd got to curb his alcoholism because whatever he was doing was sufficient to put him in the hospital. He was frightened. He didn't want to get fired. If I gave him a chance I had to have his word of honor that the drinking would stop. He agreed to stop drinking."

Though the threat to replace him became publicly known, the publicized cause was his pneumonia, not his drinking. It was a charade in which he was happy to participate; there was still a big difference between being known as a hard-drinking maverick and having a reputation as a drunk.

So he took pains to gloss over the incident as simple ill health, the result of overwork. To Jim Silke he wrote, "They tell me at the hospital I will soon be over my pneumonia. Having been raised in Burbank, the lack of smog causes serious complications."

Later, he angrily wrote to David Susskind when he heard that Susskind was telling stories about his drinking problem: "I was astonished and dismayed to hear from Ken Hyman that he had received a phone call from Peter Bart at Paramount saying that you had stated that 'the big problem on *Straw Dogs* was getting Peckinpah out of bed every morning because he was drunk.'

"I must tell you, David, it is not only a malicious lie, it is slander and I take a dim view, as do my attorneys, of this kind of verbal diarrhea.

"If there is any more of this unfounded bullshit, I will be forced to take personal issue with you. I might even go as far as locking you in a cell with Shelley Winters for your Easter vacation.

"Seriously, what the hell is this nonsense all about?"

The British press put a different spin on his departure from Cornwall. On April 12, 1971, the London *Evening News* ran an article by William Hall that alleged that Peckinpah and Dustin Hoffman "had their problems on the film early on. During the locations in Cornwall, relations between director and star grew so strained that at one point Peckinpah left the unit and came up to London reportedly threatening to quit."

Peckinpah immediately dispatched a letter to his barrister, Michael Simkins, in London to begin action: "I have over one hundred witnesses that will vouch for the fact that I returned to London due to an illness and was ordered by the doctor to spend five days at the London Clinic.

"This statement is enormously damaging to me, and I would therefore like to take legal action against Mr. Hall and the *Evening News* on the grounds of libel.

"When Mr. Melnick rang Mr. Hall on this point, he told him that he had obtained the story from at least three different people on the set when he visited the studio some weeks ago. I'd like to find out who these people were, taking action against them for defamation of character."

The threat of a suit apparently was enough. The *Evening News* eventually printed not one but two separate retractions of the story.

When Peckinpah recovered, he returned to finish the location shots in Cornwall, then moved the production to Twickenham Studios in London to shoot the interiors for the film. Still stung by nearly being fired, Peckinpah also had to contend with Susan George's increasing lack of cooperation with his demands.

George suffered a blossoming anxiety throughout the production because of the way Peckinpah and Hoffman had treated her. The events of the plot cause the characters of Amy and David to become more and more estranged. Hoffman and Peckinpah mirrored that alienation in their treatment of George.

"There was an unconscious pact between Sam and Dustin," Melnick says. "In the beginning, Susan was treated like a princess, and Dustin and she were together all the time. Since we did the picture essentially in sequence, when we got to the point in the film where Dustin's character started getting angry with her, he and Sam became increasingly cold and hostile to her. Sam did a version of what he did with Olivia De Havilland in *Noon Wine*. He got the performance by provoking her into it."

Katy Haber confirms this: "He made life difficult for Susan George to get a performance from her. He did cruel things."

George's fears centered on the rape scene itself. The script called for Amy to be abused and sexually attacked by Charlie Venner, her old boyfriend, while David is off on a snipe hunt with the rest of the local ruffians. When Venner finishes, Amy seems less violated than satisfied—until she spots Venner's mate, Norman Scutt, waiting his turn. He threatens to kill her, then flips her over to take her from behind.

During contract negotiations, George had agreed to do the rape scene, but had asked to use a body double for the nudity, a point that Peckinpah refused. Still, once actual filming of the scene approached, George began to balk at the deal she had made. She turned to Melnick for sympathy, much to Peckinpah's chagrin.

"This afternoon when we discussed the rape scene and Susan George's relationship to it, I was stunned," Peckinpah wrote in a March 15, 1971, memo to Melnick. "I told you that she was becoming very bitchy about showing any part of her body and that if she continued we should be prepared to get a photographic double for the scene. I also thought your suggestion to discuss the matter with her agent and her lawyers was excellent; in the event of her refusal or stalling, to be prepared to sue. You told me today that you had discussed the matter with her and let her feel that she would not have to do the rape scene. I repeat, I was stunned.

"Every effort should be made to let her know that if she holds us up, we are prepared to get a photographic double and file suit. I do not want this highly emotional and gifted young lady to destroy any chance we have of coming in on or under budget.

"As you know, I have no intention of being salacious. I have no intention of coming anywhere near anything faintly smelling of pornography. Pussies and penises do not interest me. The emotional havoc that happens to Amy is the basis of our story."

By that point, however, George was terrified, Melnick says. "She didn't trust Sam and a couple of the actors, who were quite primitive in their art, not to really rape her. I didn't want to devastate her and didn't think it was worth having a huge drama about. But Sam insisted."

The only way Melnick could reassure George was by promising to be on the set himself during the filming of the rape scene. When he told Peckinpah, the director said accusingly, "You don't trust me."

"It's not that I don't; she doesn't," Melnick said. Then he added, "Between you and me, I think you really would have someone fuck her."

Peckinpah paused a moment, then said, "I'd only do it if it were really necessary."

Melnick spent the two days of filming sitting atop a ladder on the set, visible to George but otherwise unobtrusive to the shooting, which went off without incident.

As filming wound down, the film's ending still could not be resolved to anyone's satisfaction. The shooting script, as written, called for the village children to converge on Amy and David in their house after the siege, implying that the offspring of the dead would now take up the cudgel of instinctive and ruthless violence.

"I've had hassles all the way through this thing from CBS [sic]," Peckinpah told one reporter. "They want a nice love story."

Discussions of the ending provided the subtext of the other frustrations that Peckinpah was having with Melnick. He would inundate Melnick with lengthy memos, filled with complaints, accusations and breast-beating.

"One of Sam's great defenses was to play 'Gotcha!' " Melnick says. "He loved to find something wrong with the production that would give him justification for being late or for something else. We had adjacent offices and I'd hear him dictate memos to his lawyer—and he'd send me a copy— saying, 'On such and such a date, this and this and this weren't prepared properly and this mistake cost me eleven minutes and twenty-three seconds.' You see the line of paranoia and self-justification.

"I remember saying, 'Sam, who do you think reads all of this?' And Sam said, 'Well, you've got to be thorough.' I said, 'No one ever reads this junk. It's only running up your legal bills. If the picture is good, we'll be heroes. And if it's not, we'll be bums.' "

But Peckinpah continued his compulsive memo writing, dictating his fevered thoughts to Katy Haber, who dutifully typed and distributed them. On March 25, 1971, for example, angered that Dustin Hoffman had left the set to do dubbing without Peckinpah knowing it, he wrote to Melnick: "I know you have other responsibilities but mine is to get the best film I can in the time allotted me. I need more help and to be perfectly frank, I am not getting it.

"To be even more perfectly frank, part of the burden rests on my shoulders so it might be a good idea for everybody to eat my ass for a while because I'm going to start eating everybody's, as of this date."

On April 1, 1971, increasingly beset by doubts about the ending and the impending end of production, Peckinpah gave vent again in another memo to Melnick: "Despite the fact that you do not like memos, they seem to be a necessity as I cannot reach you in the evening by phone. I have now worked from 8:30 to 11:15 in the evening straight through with twenty-two minutes off for sauna and shower and lunch and since you were not available after shooting I have just tried to call you again and there was no answer.

"I cannot make my time for a conference to fit yours. I do not have the luxury of going out to dinner, I do not have the luxury of going out—period. As you know, I am now sleeping at the studio. Don't expect me to take the time from shooting and cutting to fit your schedule. Please, I repeat, please try and understand that if I am picking up time, it's because I am spending time. Please, I repeat, please give me a little more of yours. If you think I am uptight, you are right."

Melnick couldn't resist responding in kind: "Re your memo of April 1, 1971: Since you indicate that you wrote it at 11:45 P.M., I can but hope that you were merely getting in under the wire for an April fool's joke.

"Sam, I have tried to reach you more than halfway from the time we first worked together on *Noon Wine*. I have continued to do so and will continue to do so but I confess that I have a frustrating feeling that every time I take a step toward you, you take two steps away.

"Our relationship has been long, basically good and certainly never dull. The tough part is almost over—let's hang in together and deliver a flick of which we can be proud."

To which Peckinpah immediately replied: "Being a congenital and pathological liar, your memo was, of course, no surprise.

"You spoke of the heavy load I carry. I am only attempting to alleviate it and put it where it really belongs, on your broad, supple and somewhat shifty shoulders.

"It might come as a surprise to you but I have been shooting a film, not sitting with my thumb up my ass barking at the moon.

"I know you are busy with your myriad projects but I am busy with one. I suggest with utmost humility that if you use the name producer, why don't you start to produce?

"You were a line producer on *Noon Wine* and the best I ever worked with. What happened to the Dan Melnick of yesteryear?

"I ask for one simple thing: help and cooperation and attention. And the answer I get is the same old Dan Melnick ego trip, which is becoming a bore to a lot of people, me included.

"I have told you before and I will tell you again, the tough part is not almost over, it's just beginning. Needless to say, I look forward to your next memo."

"Nobody manipulated guilt better than Sam, including my mother," Melnick says. "He had the ability to convince you that if you didn't do or deliver exactly what he wanted, whether you were capable of doing it or thought it was a good thing to do, somehow not only were you letting him —this man of great integrity—down, but you were letting down the side of freedom, democracy and the Bill of Rights, everything you held dear."

For his part, Peckinpah said, "Producers are often only administrators, and they're too interested in defending their own prerogatives. I've got a temper and I can't stand stupidity, so I'm always at war with these cats. I want control of everything and if I don't get what I want from people, I put them on the bus. The trouble with producers is you can't do that to them."

With almost everything else completed, Peckinpah, Melnick and Baum hashed through the various ideas for the ending, narrowing their choices to three alternatives. None of them seemed satisfying, as Melnick outlined them in an April 8 memo:

"1. Amy and David together (emotionally if not necessarily physically after the carnage).
"2. Bobby Hedden and kids entering after siege and menacing David and Amy.
"3. (which I guess is an extension of 1.) David ultimately leaving Amy alone and walking out the door ambiguously."

Melnick added: "I will attempt to get approval to shoot all three with the understanding we will give each one its best shot."

At one point, concerned because they had not been able to agree, Melnick called Peckinpah to the studio for a Sunday meeting. They met in Peckinpah's office and argued, with Peckinpah drinking steadily throughout. In the middle of the discussion, Peckinpah changed the subject and brought up a still-festering wound.

"You tried to ruin my career by putting me in the hospital," he said.

Melnick replied, "Would you rather I let you die in the middle of a picture? You had walking pneumonia."

"Well, it will be bad for my career," Peckinpah said.

"Not as bad as death," Melnick countered.

Seething at his inability to persuade Melnick of his own rightness, Peckinpah finally tipped his desk over in anger and frustration. Rather than rise to the bait, Melnick stood and said, "We'll continue this conversation when you're sober."

As he turned, Melnick saw Peckinpah pick up the throwing knife he kept on his desk as a paperweight. Melnick had seen Peckinpah use it on the set during off moments, sticking it into anything solid and wooden he could throw it at. And he knew Peckinpah was about to throw it again.

"I knew that, if he wanted to hit me, he could, but I was convinced he wouldn't," Melnick recalls. "As the knife whizzed by my head, I made a pact with a god whose existence I was less than convinced of if he would not give [Peckinpah] the satisfaction of letting it stick in the wall and do one of those reverb things. It hit the wall and fell. I picked it up and tossed it to him underhand and said, 'Some days, you can't do anything right.' "

The production went right down to the final day of shooting. Peckinpah was left with this: Having killed all of the attackers in the siege, having defended a wife who had to think hard before defending him, David Sumner walks out of his house, leaving his wife behind, accompanied by Henry Niles, the child molester.

As they drove off into the fog in David's car, Henry's line was "I don't know my way home." Peckinpah had Warner and Hoffman improvise with the scene for a few minutes and inspiration struck.

"I don't know my way home," Niles says.

"That's okay," David replies. "I don't either."

The finished film is a startling exercise in tension and discomfort, a story that starts out edgy and moves rapidly, with increasingly violent outbursts—a broken glass in the pub, the dead cat, the dual rape, the final nightmarish battle—to bloody madness.

Yet, while the elements of Ardrey's "territorial imperative" are apparent ("This is my house . . . This is me," David says), Peckinpah ultimately has crafted a story about a man who cannot cope with the physical reality of anything, except by overreacting.

David Sumner is a man totally ill at ease with the life outside of the mind. David's work—theoretical and ethereal—is real to him, while life is abstract. His concept of marriage is as abstract as his misreading of his wife is actual.

Though there is tough, realistic violence in *Straw Dogs,* much of the film's edge comes from that sense of a man constantly unable to get his balance. Most of that is achieved with the editing. The final battle, though it contains strong images of bloodshed and physical brutality, is as effective as it is less because of splattering blood than because of the breathless pace at which the images are cut together.

How one responds to it depends, in large part, on whether one can get past that surface revulsion to the more painful emotional issues that Peckinpah deals with. *Straw Dogs* is never a likable film, but it is always a compelling and highly effective one.

20

Dogged by Violence

PECKINPAH OVERSAW EDITING ON THE FINAL BATTLE while production was still going on in London. Bob Wolfe and the other editors completed a rough assemblage before filming had even finished—a version of the battle scene that, by itself, was one hundred minutes long.

"During *Straw Dogs,* he would come into the bar and say he was having trouble with the last reel," David Warner recalls. "He came in one night and said, 'I think I've made my statement on violence.'"

Before he could begin to seriously get the film into shape, however, Martin Baum was back, offering him the chance to direct another film for ABC Pictures. The catch was that *Junior Bonner* had to begin shooting at the end of June in Prescott, Arizona.

"I'm rather pleased with my film, as are the big bosses evidently," Peckinpah wrote to Jan Aghed on May 19, 1971. "They want me to leave England with my editors to start a picture with Steve McQueen next month."

The film, about an aging rodeo star, used the Prescott Frontier Days Rodeo as its backdrop. In order to be able to shoot during the actual rodeo, Peckinpah had to head back to the United States almost immediately to start preproduction.

So Peckinpah, who had offered producer Daniel Melnick so much antagonism during the production of *Straw Dogs,* reverted to Dr. Jekyll.

"Sam came to me and, with his wonderful, seductive, sentimental aspect, we sat and had a beer," Melnick says. "He said, 'Dan, you're the only creative producer I've worked with or heard of in the business and the only man I know with taste and guts and integrity.' Then he said, 'Dan, you're the only man in the world I'd trust with my film.' He started to go on and I started to laugh. I said, 'Sam, what you're going to tell me is that you've

Peckinpah progenitor: Peckinpah's maternal grandfather, Denver S. Church, a noted California jurist and congressman, once appointed himself defense attorney to an unrepresented defendant on a case for which he was also serving as judge. Church the judge then granted a motion by Church the defense counsel to dismiss charges. *(Courtesy Fresno City and County Historical Society Archives)*

The Boss and his bosss: Peckinpah's parents, David Peckinpah and Fern Church Peckinpah, ca. 1930. Though he was a Lincolnesque attorney, beloved by children, friends and neighbors, she was the unseen force, manipulating her children and husband alike. *(Courtesy of Kristen Peckinpah)*

Horse sense: Young D. Sam Peckinpah at age 7 or 8. He spent his summers at Bass Lake, Calif., and the rest of the year in Fresno, though he tended to exaggerate his cowboy upbringing in later years. *(Courtesy of Kristen Peckinpah)*

It's a man's world: Sam Peckinpah, age 16 (bottom left), with his hand on the shoulder of his father, David Peckinpah, and, behind them, grandfather Denver Church (left) and brother Denver Peckinpah (right). *(Courtesy of Kristen Peckinpah)*

A man in uniform: Always proud of his hitch in the U.S. Marines, Peckinpah (right, with unidentified service buddy) was posted to China at the end of World War II but, to his frustration, never saw combat. *(Courtesy of Kristen Peckinpah)*

A secretive existence: Peckinpah (standing, left) and first wife Marie Selland (standing, farthest right) were secretly married for a month before deciding to tell their parents. Also pictured, ca. 1947: (standing) Fern and David Peckinpah, Sam's parents; (on stool) Fern Lea Peckinpah, Sam's sister; (seated) Louise and Denver Church, Sam's maternal grandparents. *(Courtesy of Kristen Peckinpah)*

Fading glory: Gil Westrum (Randolph Scott, standing) and Steve Judd (Joel McCrea) get ready to face their last showdown in *Ride the High Country*. The film was the last for both of the aging cowboy stars. *(Courtesy of Museum of Modern Art/Film Stills Archive)*

Still on friendly terms: Before they finished making *Major Dundee,* Peckinpah (left) would provoke the usually unflappable Charlton Heston to charge at him on horseback, with saber drawn. *(Courtesy of Museum of Modern Art/Film Stills Archive)*

When killers go to Mexico: The Wild Bunch walks the last mile to a showdown that will change the way Hollywood thinks about movie violence. From left: Ben Johnson, Warren Oates, William Holden, Ernest Borgnine. *(Courtesy of Museum of Modern Art/Film Stills Archive)*

The last straw: Pike Bishop seals his fate by killing the vicious Mexican general, Mapache. From left: Emilio Fernandez, William Holden, Ernest Borgnine. *(Courtesy of Museum of Modern Art/Film Stills Archive)*

The Battle of Bloody Porch: Sam Peckinpah (right) examines the plaza where he will shoot the bloody finale of *The Wild Bunch.* *(Courtesy of Museum of Modern Art/Film Stills Archive)*

He found it where it wasn't: Cable Hogue (Jason Robards) was Peckinpah's perfect hero: a loner who carved his own niche, only to get caught in the transition of times. *(Courtesy of Museum of Modern Art/Film Stills Archive)*

The perfect foil: Strother Martin (left) was a constant target for Peckinpah's teasing. Peckinpah, who teamed Martin with L.Q. Jones in *The Wild Bunch,* put them together again here in *The Ballad of Cable Hogue. (Courtesy of Museum of Modern Art/Film Stills Archive)*

Positive identification: Peckinpah seemed to take on protective coloration based on the film he was making. It's hard to tell Peckinpah (left) from Jason Robards on the location for *The Ballad of Cable Hogue.* *(Courtesy of Museum of Modern Art/Film Stills Archive)*

. . . but the grizzled prospector is transformed into the college professor by the time Peckinpah (right) directs Dustin Hoffman in *Straw Dogs.* *(Courtesy of Museum of Modern Art/Film Stills Archive)*

Encountering controversy: Ken Hutchison (left) confronts Dustin Hoffman (center) and Del Henney (right) as Susan George looks on in *Straw Dogs,* a Peckinpah film which became a touchstone for critics of screen violence for years to come. *(Courtesy of Museum of Modern Art/Film Stills Archive)*

Life imitates art: Peckinpah (right) cast Ali MacGraw as Steve McQueen's wife in *The Getaway,* then watched in amusement as McQueen ignited an off-screen romance with MacGraw, to the chagrin of MacGraw's husband, Paramount Pictures head Robert Evans. *(Courtesy of Museum of Modern Art/Film Stills Archive)*

Earn while you learn: Ali MacGraw, who had never fired a gun or driven a car, was cast as a gun-toting, getaway-car-driving bank robber's wife. It was up to prop master Bobby Visciglia (left, rear) and Steve McQueen (center) to make MacGraw look like she knew what she was doing. *(Courtesy of Museum of Modern Art/Film Stills Archive)*

"What if we let him live?": At one point, during the troubled production of *Pat Garrett & Billy the Kid,* Peckinpah considered rewriting myth and history by letting Billy (Kris Kristofferson, prone) survive his encounter with Pat Garrett (James Coburn, standing). Cooler heads prevailed. *(Courtesy of Museum of Modern Art/Film Stills Archive)*

Heads up: Warren Oates seemed to be doing an extended imitation of Peckinpah, playing a loser looking for one big score (and toting a head around in a bag) in *Bring Me the Head of Alfredo Garcia*. *(Courtesy of Museum of Modern Art/Film Stills Archive)*

In the barrel: On *Cross of Iron*, Peckinpah (right, coaching two actors) had to cope with a producer who was running one step ahead of his European creditors, even as he was hustling to find the cash to finish the picture. *(Courtesy of Museum of Modern Art/Film Stills Archive)*

Winging it: In the end, Peckinpah ran out of funds and was unable to give *Cross of Iron* the kind of finale he had hoped. Maximilian Schell (left) and James Coburn wound up improvising the last scene while the cameras rolled. *(Courtesy of Museum of Modern Art/Film Stills Archive)*

Road to ruin: Peckinpah (left) often told his actors, including Burt Young (center) and Ernest Borgnine, to write their own dialogue during his wildly erratic production of *Convoy,* his penultimate film. He wouldn't get behind a camera again for almost five years. *(Courtesy of Museum of Modern Art/Film Stills Archive)*

been offered another gig and you want me to finish the editing and post-production.' So we just reversed the normal role of producer and director."

According to Melnick and Spottiswoode, the footage was shipped back to Hollywood from London. The two of them holed up in the editing room while Peckinpah took off for Arizona.

Although he wasn't there on a day-to-day basis, Peckinpah's vision guided the editing process. Melnick, Spottiswoode and Wolfe would assemble film in the way they imagined Peckinpah would, then fly to Prescott for weekly screenings of what had been cut. Peckinpah would watch and give them extensive notes before they cut it further.

"He shot so much film that he always had two or three people editing, because it would have been impossible for one person to cope with," Spottiswoode says. "But you don't feel that it was cut by two or three different people; you always feel it's a Peckinpah film. He gave his editors a great deal of freedom within the canvas he painted. And that canvas wasn't always a reflection of what you saw in dailies."

The encounters with Peckinpah weren't conducive to good work, yet managed to produce constructive change.

"We'd go on Sunday night and he'd be three sheets to the wind," Spottiswoode says. "We'd have two or three hours a week with him. But he was very perceptive. He'd look at a reel and help shape it. He was involved enough that the film was very much him, though he only saw it once a week."

The finale—the siege itself—went from being one hundred minutes in its roughest cut down to thirty minutes and finally to eighteen minutes.

"Taking it from thirty minutes to eighteen minutes—that was difficult," Spottiswoode says. "Shots that had been six feet long became four frames. We didn't take anything out—we just compressed it. Each time we'd shorten something 50 percent or more. It became a very different animal. It turned from an exciting but standard battle into this strange, otherworldly scene."

The editing also had to take the rating into consideration. With only minuscule changes, the film won an R in the United States. In England, on the other hand, Melnick had to do some extensive explaining about the second half of the rape scene.

"I remember sitting over a moviola with this venerable member of the aristocracy," Melnick says, "explaining to him by looking at the rape scene that what was going on was rear entry, not sodomy. By British standards, rear entry was acceptable but sodomy was not."

When *Straw Dogs* was released in December 1971, it became Peckinpah's most commercially successful film to that point—and sparked a long-lasting debate about the effect of graphic violence in films on the audiences that watch them.

In that respect, it was lumped together with a pair of films released at the same time—appropriately enough, *Dirty Harry,* directed by Peckinpah's mentor, Don Siegel, and *A Clockwork Orange,* directed by Stanley Kubrick. Both films brought shocked responses, Kubrick's film for its nihilistic view of a future society in which violence is a form of currency, Siegel's for its hawkish depiction of a society in which liberal thinking has given criminals more rights than their victims.

But *Straw Dogs* touched the newly sensitive nerve of violence toward women, sexual and otherwise. Even as he was being celebrated for exploring the primal instinct let loose, Peckinpah was being reviled for showing a woman who seemed to be enjoying rape.

"Sam said he was making a film about violence and the senselessness of it and how we all can be moved to it," Melnick says. "As far as I was concerned, we were making a film about the violence inherent in all of us and how accessible it was to us, [that] we were all capable of rage that could lead us to kill."

People couldn't even agree on who the villains were in *Straw Dogs,* let alone what it was about. John Bryson, after seeing the film, said to Peckinpah, "Where'd you get the heavies? They were incredible," referring to the beefy British actors.

Peckinpah narrowed his eyes, gave Bryson one of his reptilian smiles and said, "They weren't the heavies. The husband and wife were the heavies."

The film's creators were often amused and appalled at audience response to the grisly battle that consumed the film's last eighteen minutes.

"At the screening of *Straw Dogs* at the North Point Theater in San Francisco," Melnick recalls, "the audience had this wild reaction. I hoped people would be devastated and shocked and horrified by the siege. Suddenly I heard six hundred people shout, 'Kill him, get him!' I thought, My God, what have we unleashed?

"At one point right after, Sam, Roger, David [Goodman], Marty and I were standing in the lobby discussing the film and a guy came up to the group. 'Who's responsible for this picture?' he said. He was clearly angry. Sam pointed at me and the guy said, 'That's the most disgusting thing I've ever seen. I'm a pacifist and I'll kill you for making it.' "

Peckinpah's brother, Denny, attended the opening of *Straw Dogs* in Fresno, as close to a Hollywood social event as Fresno usually came. "We were sitting in pretty good seats, with some little old ladies sitting behind us," Denny says. "And during that scene when Dustin Hoffman is killing the guy behind the couch, a little old lady jumps up and screams, 'Hit him again! Hit him again!' "

In *Newsweek,* Paul D. Zimmerman wrote, "It's hard to imagine that Sam Peckinpah will ever make a better movie than *Straw Dogs.* It flawlessly expresses his primitive vision of experience—his belief that manhood requires rites of violence, that home and hearth are inviolate and must be defended by blood, that a man must conquer other men to prove his courage and hold on to his woman."

Jay Cocks, who praised *A Clockwork Orange* in the same issue of *Time,* called it Peckinpah's "first film to challenge the very ideal of heroism around which his work so far has been built. *Straw Dogs* is a brilliant feat of movie-making . . . so cold, so unsparing, that our natural impulse is to resist it. It is a measure of Peckinpah's skill that, in giving voice to his own despair, he came to make this nightmare seem like our own."

Arthur Knight, writing in *Saturday Review,* said, "The last two reels of *Straw Dogs* become a demonic ballet, a frenetic jousting with death. It is tremendous movie-making. It is also tremendously sick-making."

Atlantic's David Denby wrote, "A hateful but very exciting movie . . . as brilliant as *The Wild Bunch,* but a lot harder to defend."

Richard Schickel, one of the champions of *The Wild Bunch,* attacked Peckinpah's intellect in *Life* magazine: "*Straw Dogs* is literally sophomoric. It resembles the horrified reaction of an adolescent to the discovery that evil really exists in the world and his brief, if passionate, contemplation of the possibility that it might be universal. The trouble with *Straw Dogs* is that Sam Peckinpah really means it. Unable to question either [Peckinpah's] craft or the sincerity of his motives, one must question his intelligence and perception."

Peckinpah couldn't let that go unchallenged and fired back a letter to Schickel: "I thought of anybody in the world you would have understood what I was trying to say, but instead you did a half-gainer, dipping into Pauline and Judith Crist and coming out with something that makes me realize that I have failed.

"You missed all I was trying to get across (thank God, some British critics and some people in the States got it) but then you reviewed it and I feel I have fallen on my ass. If I am at fault, part of it is because I expected too much, my vision of morality is certainly not yours, but I damn you for having the bad taste to speak of me as you did of my life in conjunction with my film.

"I obviously overestimated your perceptiveness of my own vision. If you are judging my intelligence, on what basis is it? If it's mine, what makes you so right? If it's yours, what in Christ's name makes you so right? Not that I want you to stop doing what you do, but I would like you to see the film again and perhaps discuss why it affected you so strongly or perhaps discuss it as a film, because, Dick, that's all it was.

"If you really want to see a great film, go to see *The Last Picture Show* and play critic to that crashing bore, or is that the criteria that New York critics live by these days?"

Peckinpah made the point to Schickel that he made at several other times:

that, with *Straw Dogs*, he had taken a submediocre piece of material, the novel *The Siege at Trencher's Farm*, and improved it beyond all expectation into a solid piece of challenging popular entertainment.

"It became a kind of trademark," Walter Kelley says. "He'd take inferior material and he'd make something better out of it."

If Schickel's review angered him, Pauline Kael's in the *New Yorker* stung him to the quick. Though she started out appreciatively ("Sam Peckinpah is the youngest legendary American director"), she quickly got down to the crux of her argument: "The vision of *Straw Dogs* is narrow and puny, as obsessions with masculinity so often are; Peckinpah's view of human experience seems to be no more than the sort of anecdote that drunks tell in bars."

Even as she praised the artistry, she denigrated the vision, until she finally summed up: "What I am saying, I fear, is that Sam Peckinpah, who is an artist, has, with *Straw Dogs*, made the first American film that is a fascist work of art."

After Peckinpah saw that, he remarked to Joe Bernhard, "Geez, she must never have seen *Birth of a Nation*."

She mitigated it slightly two paragraphs later, saying, "I realize that it's a terrible thing to say of someone whose gifts you admire that he has made a fascist classic." But the label was on the table: fascist, a highly charged word in any season. In early 1972, with a Republican in the White House who was eavesdropping electronically on opponents he had placed on a secret "enemies" list, it was positively incendiary.

Kael's line is the one that stuck with the film ever after, the easy-to-remember description that forever tagged *Straw Dogs* (though Kael professes not to be aware of how widely quoted her description was).

Furious, Peckinpah dashed off a letter that began "Dear Pauline": "I read your review. Its ambivalence was complete, although I was distressed that you didn't pick up that David was inciting the very violence he was running away from. I appreciate your concern and involvement, but I don't appreciate the description of the film as a fascist one, because it has connotations which to me are odious.

"Shall I discuss this with my lawyer or are you prepared to print in public the definition of the film? Simply I think the term is in incredible bad taste and I intend to take issue with it. What do you suggest? How you could identify any element of my work in terms of fascism is beyond my belief."

In another letter to her a couple of years later, Peckinpah, in a much friendlier mood, still smarted from the criticism and brought it up again: "Fascist, God how I hate that word, but I suppose every director in his way is a fascist. *Straw Dogs* was about a bad marriage and the subtle incitement of violence by David Sumner. It was a funny thing, but I know that couple, which means knowledge has nothing to do with art. As I evidently failed. In a way I made it for you and [Schickel], with all the integrity I could and missed the boat.

"One thing I don't understand is how a great novel like *Deliverance* can be made into such a shitty film and be nominated for three awards. I don't like your town but Hollywood is really a dunghill."

For her part, Kael says that people put more weight on the word "fascist" than she ever intended when she was writing the review.

"I meant sexual fascism and I used the term loosely," she says. "But he was very pissed. He made fun of me in print. I had assumed that the wife had reacted so violently to the second rape because he was indicating that she was being sodomized. He said she wasn't. I still don't believe him. It was a movie I disliked."

Kael was referring to an August 1972 *Playboy* interview with Peckinpah in which several questions dealt with her review of his film. At one point, Peckinpah said, "Doesn't Kael know anything about sex? Dominating and being dominated: the fantasy too of being taken by force is certainly one way people make love."

At another juncture, he said, "I like Kael; she's a feisty little gal and I enjoy drinking with her—which I've done on occasion—but here she's cracking walnuts in her ass."

Peckinpah seemed to be of two minds about how to view the growing controversy. On the one hand, his image as the visionary of violence, the macho man exploring his bloodiest fantasies on film, sold a lot of tickets. And it was an easy part to play: Peckinpah loved putting on roles and this one was a persona he could slip into without effort.

But it was a trap as well. He got hemmed in by the way other people perceived him and that meant lost opportunities. His experience with *Play It As It Lays* already reflected that.

So he tried to explain himself in interviews—rationally, at first, then with increasing rancor when it became obvious no one was interested.

- 1971: "Everybody seems to deny that we're violent. We're violent by nature. We're going to survive by being violent. If we don't recognize that we're violent people, we're dead. We're going to be on some beach and we're going to drop bombs on each other. I would like to understand the nature of violence. Is there a way to channel it, to use it positively? Churches, laws, everybody seems to think that man is a noble savage. But he's only an animal, a meat-eating, talking animal. Recognize it. He also has grace and love and beauty. But don't say to me we're not violent. It's one of the greatest brainwashes of all times."
- 1972: "Violence? They were ragging me about all the violence in *The Wild Bunch*. And four months later they sprang My Lai on us."

- 1972: "You can't make violence real to audiences today without rubbing their noses in it. We watch our wars and see men die, really die, every day on television, but it doesn't seem real. We don't believe those are real people dying on that screen. We've been anesthetized by the media. What I do is show people what it's really like. When people complain about the way I handle violence, what they're really saying is, 'Please don't show me; I don't want to know.' "
- 1974: "I really think we show violence as it is, and people will recognize it as it is. I don't put violence on the screen so that people can enjoy it. I want them to understand what it is but unfortunately most people come to see it because they dig it, which is a study of human nature and which makes me a little sick."

Yet he would undercut his own credibility over and over again, just to see how far he could stretch the line.

"I'm like a good whore—I go where I'm kicked," he said on more than one occasion. Or: "I'm a whore—but I'm a good whore." Asked what interested him most about the script that eventually became *Straw Dogs,* he said, "What really turned me on was the amount of money I was given to do it. You start with the money and after you get that into focus, you try to figure out what the hell you're doing."

Still, that's not as disingenuous as it seems. According to Jim Silke, "He said that when I met him [in 1962]. He felt that's the way it is. It's a huge industry with lots of money involved and huge egos and incredible talent. He had said it privately for years. But he began to say it in public."

While Peckinpah would talk reflectively about violence, he would be boorish and posturing about women: "There are two kinds of women. There are women and then there's pussy. One of the advantages of being a celebrity is that a lot of attractive pussy that wasn't available to you before suddenly becomes available. I ignore women's lib. I'm for most of what they're for but I can't see why they have to make such assholes of themselves over the issue. I consider myself one of the foremost male lesbians in the world."

But his kidding-on-the-square and posing undercut the impact of the sober-minded words he had to say about his work and his vision. Which were you supposed to take seriously: the thoughtful philosophizing or the seemingly stewed self-parody?

A CRITIQUE OF A DIFFERENT SORT was delivered by the satirical group Monty Python's Flying Circus, which spoofed Peckinpah in a sketch titled "Sam Peckinpah's Salad Days." In the sketch, a film critic introduced what purported to be an excerpt of Peckinpah's follow-up to *Straw Dogs,* then rolled a clip of a group of English twits in tennis togs:

"LIONEL: I say, anyone for tennis?
JULIAN: Oh, super!
CHARLES: What fun.
JULIAN: I say, Lionel, catch.
He throws the tennis ball to Lionel. It hits Lionel on the head. Lionel claps one hand to his forehead. He roars in pain as blood seeps through his fingers.
LIONEL: Oh gosh.
He tosses his racket out of frame and we hear a hideous scream. The camera pans to pick up a pretty girl in summer frock with the handle of the racket embedded in her stomach. Blood is pouring out down her dress."

The sketch took the idea to hilarious extremes, ending with the host himself being riddled with machine-gun fire.

Ultimately, the impact and image of *Straw Dogs* grew out of proportion to anything Peckinpah ever intended. He was making a statement about violence in man, about tapping primal rage—but people saw it as much more.

Before they were finished, the film had become a metaphor for violence in film, synonymous with gore and brutality, though the actual graphic images were never as specific or detailed as their reputation. The title—along with that of *A Clockwork Orange*—was used by groups and writers concerned about the increasing realism of screen violence as shorthand to conjure up an unflattering image of the movie industry as a whole.

The furor reached its height shortly after *Straw Dogs* came out, with the release of the U.S. Surgeon General's report, "Television and Growing Up: The Impact of Televised Violence." The study reported a causal relationship between the amount of violence on TV and increases in aggressive behavior in children who watch a lot of TV.

In writing about the surgeon general's report, *Newsweek*'s Joseph Morgenstern took Peckinpah to task for irresponsibly inciting his audience.

"A film like *Straw Dogs* may put us in touch with our primal emotions, but that's no great trick," Morgenstern wrote. "The Nazis did it constantly." Morgenstern quoted Peckinpah as saying that though he was sickened by his own film, "somewhere in it there is a mirror for everyone."

"Maybe so," Morgenstern noted, "but the mirror is framed in right-wing gilt. It shows the stereotyped liberal intellectual as a cowardly contemptible nerd who won't take a stand until the barbarians are inside his own house."

Like all such crusades against violence, this one eventually fizzled. As 1972 rolled on, with the insurgent candidacy of George McGovern, the escalating protests against the war in Vietnam and the administration-led conspiracy against civil liberties, *Straw Dogs* eventually faded from memory, about the time it played out its second-run bookings and disappeared.

But its name alone retained the power to shock. When a particularly vio-

lent movie would become momentarily popular, the same antiviolence cru-
saders would invoke the name of Sam Peckinpah and his film *Straw Dogs* to
bolster their case. Chief among these was TV personality and critic Gene
Shalit, who made a habit of resurrecting *Straw Dogs* to thump the antiviolence tub.

"I don't know which was more disheartening, the fact that *Straw Dogs*
was made or the fact that audiences found such pleasure in it," Shalit wrote
in the April 1974 *Ladies' Home Journal,* two years and four months after the
film was released.

"Shouldn't we blame ourselves? Because while the vicious *Straw Dogs* was
sad and *Marathon Man* sadder still, can we be sure the American public is
not the sadist of all?" Shalit wrote in the January 1977 *Ladies' Home Journal*
—more than five years after the movie came out.

It turned out to be the film that Peckinpah had to explain and justify,
whose image he had to fight, from that point on.

21

Way Out West Again

When Peckinpah got back to the United States to film *Junior Bonner*, however, that was all still in the future. This "master of violence," as Max Evans's unfortunately titled account of the making of *Cable Hogue* referred to him, followed *Straw Dogs* with his least violent effort: *Junior Bonner*, in which no one gets killed. Aside from one sucker punch and a barroom brawl, there's no violence to speak of (outside of the competitive violence of the rodeo ring).

Four films in a row all on the same theme—men out of sync with the times around them. Yet each could not have been more dissimilar from its predecessor.

Junior Bonner is an easygoing (some critics would say slow-moving) portrait of an aging rodeo star. His champion days behind him, Junior Bonner returns to his hometown for the annual rodeo. There, he finds that his younger brother, a rich property developer, has bought the family homestead out from under his parents. His father, a charismatic but unlucky speculator, is looking for the money to go to Australia to prospect for gold. But the brother won't give it to him—and Junior doesn't have it to give.

It's easy to imagine Peckinpah envisioning the script, written by Jeb Rosebrook, as Tennessee Williams in chaps. The boorish businessman brother with no respect for the father's dreams; the father with his head in the clouds, one foot in the poorhouse and no sense of what his whims have cost his family; the wandering son who follows a dream not that far removed from the father's. Minus the psychosexual Sturm und Drang of Williams, it is still potentially a touching and affecting family drama of the sort Peckinpah loved.

Peckinpah could have avoided paying American taxes on his *Straw Dogs* earnings had he stayed in England another two months. Instead, he came back to get *Junior Bonner* ready for a quick start and lost the tax advantage of working abroad.

The script had been around for a couple of years. Rosebrook was a screenwriter who had built his story around the annual Prescott rodeo he remembered from summers as an asthmatic child spent in the relatively pure air of Arizona.

"I was originally asked to direct *Junior Bonner* and I turned it down because I didn't quite know what to do with it," says director-editor Monte Hellman, whose film *Two-Lane Blacktop* made him a momentarily hot director at the time. "I was amazed at how Sam transformed a not-good script into a quite-good movie."

Peckinpah, who liked to become firmly entrenched in a movie before he even started shooting, had to hit the ground running for this one. From the time he arrived back in Los Angeles until the first day of shooting in Prescott, he had less than six weeks to prepare the entire film.

"You can do anything if you put your mind to it," says Joe Wizan, who produced the film. "We cast it and scouted locations and were shooting in five weeks. We had to shoot because that was the day of the parade. We weren't going to stage it. Working that fast didn't hurt the picture one iota."

After working with strong producers who sought to be artistic collaborators, Peckinpah took to Wizan's hands-off approach. A former agent producing his second film, Wizan would argue about budgets and schedules, but he also seemed to know how much he didn't know.

"Joe Wizan left him alone—and to Sam, leaving him alone was a sign of respect," says Katy Haber, who was summoned to America to work for Peckinpah on the film a week after she finished her work on *Straw Dogs*. "Sam had this built-in dislike of producers because he felt they never contributed. Joe was an absentee producer; he was doing *Kansas City Prime*, so we hardly ever saw him."

Their relationship, however, wasn't always pacific. "Sam drank a lot and yelled a lot and had big temperamental fits," Wizan says. He would also write Wizan the same kind of memos he had written to Melnick and Feldman. Inevitably, he started out polite but took a sharp turn when things weren't as thoroughly taken care of as he expected.

"I know that memos are a bore," he wrote to Wizan during preproduction in June 1971, "but since I have no memory, can we put as much on paper as possible so that I can use it as a referral and, as a favor to me, will you please sign the enclosed copy and return it?"

Six weeks later, under the pressure of production, the tone was saltier: "I once again came to see dailies and found them to be out of order and unsynched. Once again the master shot was missing on one of the scenes.

"I thank you for all your efforts on our behalf. This really is a vote of confidence.

"I have no intention of seeing any more dailies until you advise me that this prolifera of incompetence has been taken care of.

"If I submitted such a shambles, I'd be fired on the spot."

"I loved the guy and I hated him," Wizan says. "He drove me crazy. He was great to argue with. It was fun because he was passionate. He had no agenda; it wasn't about ego. He would argue about what he felt was right and wrong. Sure, there were times when I wanted to beat him up, but he would apologize afterward."

For the film, Peckinpah assembled the now not-inconsiderable group of regulars who populated the crews of his films. Lucien Ballard would shoot it; Bobby Visciglia would be the prop man; Frank Kowalski would shoot second unit; Jerry Fielding would do the music and Katy would return as assistant, secretary, translator and all-around girl Friday.

The film also reunited Peckinpah with Ted Haworth, the film's art director, with whom Peckinpah had worked under Don Siegel in the 1950s. Haworth had been living in Europe for fifteen years; Peckinpah, who had been a gofer when he left, was now the man in charge and had obviously changed.

"He'd aged a lot," Haworth says. "Don Siegel told me he had been at a theater and run into Sam. 'This guy came up to me in a dark theater, this old desert rat—and it turned out to be Sam Peckinpah.' "

Haworth found that while Peckinpah didn't talk much, he communicated what he wanted and inspired his crews to break their backs to get it for him.

"He got the best out of you with a minimal effort," Haworth says. "Sometimes I'd go through a whole conversation about the set and there wouldn't be a dozen words between us. A day or two later, I'd come back with the sketches and he'd say, 'Pure gold.' He brought out of you whatever uniqueness you might have."

The cast also had a couple of Peckinpah regulars: Dub Taylor (who played the bartender at the saloon where everyone hung out), and Ben Johnson, who was cast as the rodeo promoter and cattleman who controls Junior's destiny. Peckinpah cast Robert Preston as Junior's scalawag of a father, classy Ida Lupino as Junior's long-suffering mother and burly, surly Joe Don Baker as his grasping brother Curly.

For Junior, Peckinpah had Steve McQueen, still one of the most prominent stars in Hollywood. A hit as an action star, McQueen had taken on *Junior Bonner* for the chance to do something of a gentler nature than *Bullitt* or *The Thomas Crown Affair*.

It was Peckinpah's first film with McQueen since *The Cincinnati Kid,* when McQueen had agreed to let Peckinpah be fired. So there was a certain amount of tension that was natural going in but it passed quickly.

"*Junior Bonner* is turning out to be an interesting little flick," Peckinpah wrote to Jan Aghed shortly before production began. "Steve McQueen is one hell of an actor and we seem to be getting it on pretty well. Robert ("Seventy-Six Trombones") Preston is also playing one of the starring roles and is a delight to be with."

For his part, McQueen admitted that the studios weren't overly fond of him because "I've always been a perfectionist, and that means I give head-aches to a lot of people. Sam's got a bad rep too. He's a prime hell-raiser. Him and me, we're some combo. The studio is buying a lot of aspirin."

As it turned out, McQueen was the one who needed the aspirin. Though common sense dictated that he couldn't do his own stunts, he got close enough to horses and bucking bulls to sprain a finger, gash his nose and nearly break his wrist. "Jeez, this is more dangerous than Le Mans," he said, "and a hell of a lot less enjoyable."

One newcomer to the Peckinpah crew was assistant director Newt Arnold, who came into the picture late after another A.D. had been fired. Arnold wound up working on most of Peckinpah's subsequent films, trading off as first assistant director with Cliff Coleman and Ron Wright, another Peck-inpah regular.

What struck Arnold immediately about Peckinpah, aside from his com-mand of filmmaking, was his sense of humor. On *Junior Bonner,* he got a look at it right away. Arnold, who wears an eyepatch, was working with the crowd of extras at the rodeo for cutaway shots of the audience during the various competitions. The cameras were pointed at the extras, and Arnold ran around the rodeo ring to direct their focus and reaction.

"Sam said, 'Newt, would you mind being the bull and running back and forth?' " Arnold says. "I started to do it. At one point, he gestured for me to go beyond the farthest camera. When I got there, he yelled, 'Cut,' be-cause it was the end of the shot. I came back and said, 'What's your pleasure, Sam?' His head came up and he was wearing an eyepatch. A dozen other people in the crew were wearing them too."

The production itself was a relatively smooth one, though Peckinpah did have his pet peeves. One was actor Joe Don Baker, who, for some reason, rubbed Peckinpah the wrong way immediately.

"Sam hated Joe Don Baker—just didn't like him," says prop man Bobby Visciglia, who was in charge of making sure Peckinpah and the stars had chairs with their names on them on the set. "He said, 'Fuck him, he's an asshole. Take his chair away. Let him stand up.' It was Joe Don's first big movie role. He'd come to me and say, 'Where's my chair?' And I'd always say, 'I'm getting it fixed.' After three weeks, he knew he wasn't going to get a chair."

Peckinpah cast his son, Mathew, as one of Curly's children in the film, and hired his daughter Sharon, then twenty-two, to handle second-unit continuity. Her father "had a set of standards and, in his own words, he could be a mean son of a bitch," she says. "He would bend over backward to help people do things, people he didn't even know. He'd help you if you paid your dues. But his own children had to pay twice. It wasn't just working. You were his daughter and he expected a certain decorum. You were supposed to act a certain way because it was a reflection on him. It was like that line William Holden said in *The Wild Bunch:* 'Either you learn to live with it or we'll leave you.'"

Most of Matt Peckinpah's scenes were handled by the second unit, though Peckinpah himself directed a dinner-table scene with the Bonner family. "He had a hell of a time getting me to properly deliver the line, 'Gee, Uncle Junior, you can ride anything with hair on it,'" Matt says. "I also remember the scene on the float during the parade. My dad, with Steve McQueen nearby, was trying to explain to me what I was supposed to be doing and I began to lose my attention and look around and not listen to what my dad was saying. All of a sudden, Steve McQueen poked me in the chest and said, 'Listen to what your dad is telling you.'"

Otherwise, Matt remembers that his on-location relationship with his father was expected to be a professional one. "It was adamantly understood that I was not to act like a little god on the set," he says. "And if I wanted to know what was going on, I would always ask somebody other than my dad. It was very important that I not act privileged or have any unearned privilege granted to me."

Part of Sharon's job, as she soon found out, was taking care of eleven-year-old Mathew in the evenings, a duty she hadn't bargained on. "My work didn't end with the movie," she says. "I was staying at his house and had to take care of my brother, so I was constantly on call."

Ultimately, it meant taking care of her father as well.

"On the set, he was very much in control," she says. "Only later in the privacy of the house did I see him get out of control. Either he wouldn't show up at night or if he did, he'd be dead drunk."

Though the serious drinking took place after work, the sexual adventuring wasn't confined to his off-set hours. He had Katy Haber on hand, though he still had a relationship going with Joie Gould, the British secretary with whom he'd become involved during *Straw Dogs*. But he didn't stop there.

Several scenes in the film were shot at the Palace Bar in Prescott, an aging landmark of Western authenticity that had a large apartment on the second floor, which Peckinpah had also rented for the production. Bobby Visciglia says: "The apartment was one big room. Sam was fooling around with this redhead who worked in the bar. There was also this big Indian broad. So while they were setting up a shot one day, we had these waitresses and Katy up in the apartment. Sam is popping amyl nitrates into the waitresses. We'd pop the amyl nitrates into the Indian's nose and she'd say, 'Give me more of that white man's medicine.' Sam had Katy and the redhead in the bathroom and I had the Indian broad out in the living room.

"But Sam could be vicious with women. He'd hit them. This time, he punched Katy and knocked her down the steps. Katy had a big black eye for a week."

Haber says, "McQueen asked me what happened and I said I had fallen upstairs. He said, 'I suppose if somebody pushes you hard enough, you can fall up stairs.' "

Peckinpah had no major production problems on the film. But he did fire Frank Kowalski, causing a rift that lasted almost four years. Still, the firing had one of the best punchlines of any incident in Peckinpah's career.

The set-up occurred seven months earlier, when Peckinpah was shooting *Straw Dogs* in London and Kowalski was writing *Bring Me the Head of Alfredo Garcia*. "He'd come back from shooting each day and read my pages and tell me they were never good enough," Kowalski says. "So we were drinking one night and I was telling him I miss my wife and kids and my friends. And Sam says, 'You don't need friends.' And I said, 'You'll have trouble finding six to take you to your hole.' "

On *Junior Bonner*, Kowalski was directing the second unit. After watching dailies one evening, Kowalski slept in the next day, only to be awakened by a call from Katy Haber. "Mr. Peckinpah requests your presence at dailies," Haber said. Kowalski said he'd seen them and went back to sleep. So Visciglia knocked on the door and told him that Peckinpah wanted him at dailies.

"Fuck him—I've seen that footage a hundred times," Kowalski said. Haber called again and Kowalski said to tell him he was IFD: ill from drink.

"Finally the phone rings again and it's Sam," Kowalski says. "He says, 'You coming to dailies?' I said, 'No.' He says, 'Then I suggest you pack. You're on the bus.' "

So Kowalski did. But first he went to the bar and wrote Peckinpah a note and had it delivered to Peckinpah on the set. Peckinpah read it and said to Visciglia, "Come here." He showed him the note, which said: "Dear Sam, Scratch one pallbearer. Frank."

JUNIOR BONNER lacks the headlong plotting that marks most of Peckinpah's films. It is a kind of miniature, a slice of life that examines the details of that life. Warm and funny, bittersweet but optimistic, it is, like most of Peckinpah's films, the story of a loser who doesn't know when to quit.

Some might call it slow; studied is probably a better adjective. There is little about the plot or characters that is surprising and yet nothing that rings false. In its own way, it is honest and poetic, a valentine to the loners and drifters who are part of the rodeo circuit.

Edited by two Peckinpah veterans, Bob Wolfe and Frank Santillo, the film does make use of its crisp cutting to lend excitement to the rodeo competition scenes. The intercutting of slow-motion and real-time footage during the bronco- and bull-riding convey the beauty and the challenge of these animals and the bravery and skill of the riders.

Peckinpah probably is too sentimental for some tastes in two key scenes: the confrontation between Junior and his father, Ace, in a deserted train station where Junior tells him he doesn't have the money to send him to Australia; and the encounter between Ace and his estranged wife Ellie on the back steps of the Palace Bar, in which they manage to strike sparks of love once more. Peckinpah gives them emotional resonance by letting facial expressions and timing accentuate the feelings that run so strongly beneath the surface.

The two moments were among Peckinpah's favorite scenes in his own work. Writer Jim Hamilton recalls a party at San Francisco's Fairmont Hotel in the wake of the premiere of *The Killer Elite,* two days of room service and drinking. Hamilton finally stepped outside to get some air, then returned to Peckinpah's suite, "which was knee deep in styrofoam cups and crab-leg shells," to find the director transfixed by an airing of *Junior Bonner* on a local TV station. It happened to be the scene between Junior and Ace; Peckinpah was watching raptly.

When it was over, Peckinpah murmured, almost to himself, "That's one of the best pieces of film I ever made in my life."

Pauline Kael appreciated the effort to show another facet of his talent but found films such as *Cable Hogue* and *Junior Bonner* "a little too reverential," she says. "There was something in his mythmaking about the West—and it was mythmaking. He loved the idea of the upright Westerner. He loved the idea of the upright man. He wanted to be that. He loved acting the part. But he was a terrible person, in many ways. There was nothing in the way he behaved that lived up to that."

STRAW DOGS was released Christmas 1971 to wildly disparate reviews and big business. *Junior Bonner* opened six months later, to mixed reviews and slim box office. McQueen blamed the film's failure on ABC Pictures' decision to open in a lot of theaters at once. He felt that a limited release, to allow it to build by word of mouth, might have given it more than a fighting chance.

But ABC wanted to cash in on McQueen's and Peckinpah's box-office clout (despite the fact that this was an atypical film for both). The fact that *Junior Bonner* happened to be the third rodeo film released in the space of a month didn't help. (The others were *J. W. Coop* with Cliff Robertson and *The Honkers* with James Coburn. None of them caused a box-office stampede.)

"It was a gentle Western and the word 'Western' was anathema at that time," says producer Joe Wizan. "There was no action, no shooting, no guns. It didn't do much business. But it was Steve's favorite film."

"It was a distinguished piece of work," Martin Baum says. "Although it was not a giant hit at the box office, it was successful for the company."

Among the critics, Richard Schickel said in *Life*, "Sam Peckinpah, having temporarily purged his evil demons in *Straw Dogs*, in a loose, nice shaggy-dog mood. Very easy riding." And other critics cast votes of approval:

    · Penelope Gilliatt, *New Yorker:* "We often say of this country that it is the place with no past, but it has one in Peckinpah's movie. The film has a harsh laugh buried in it, like an enduring old boozer's cackle; much robustness, much technical grasp; and moments of piercing expansiveness typical of the best of Peckinpah's work."

    · Arthur Knight, *Saturday Review: "Junior Bonner* is a sober, thoughtful and ultimately moving film."

    · Vincent Canby, *New York Times:* "Peckinpah in the benignly comic mood that, I suspect, is much more the natural fashion of this fine director than is the gross, intellectualized mayhem of his recent *Straw Dogs. Junior Bonner*, which looks like a rodeo film and sounds like a rodeo film, is a superior family comedy in disguise."

But there were exceptions:

    · Paul D. Zimmerman, *Newsweek:* "A ponderously slow tale. Peckinpah gets sandbagged by his tiresome macho ethic, exemplified by a barroom brawl in which the men do their thing . . . a screenplay by Jeb Rosebrook that would break the spirit of lesser men."

    · Jay Cocks, *Time:* "Lackluster stuff. Peckinpah tries to make it work by underplaying everything, which is like turning down the volume on a bad record instead of switching it off."

THE END OF 1971 was a crazed time, with Peckinpah caught up in the whirlwind of controversy surrounding *Straw Dogs*. He was on a roll, able now to put together projects that appealed to him.

One such project was *Jeremiah Johnson*, a tough tale of a legendary mountain man that Joe Wizan was producing. At one point, Peckinpah was supposed to direct the John Milius screenplay, with Clint Eastwood in the title role. Then the part was given to Robert Redford, who decided he wanted Sydney Pollack to direct.

"What a different movie that would have been," Milius says.

Peckinpah was also attached to a screenplay called *Emperor of the North Pole*, an action picture set in the Depression, built around the struggle between hoboes and railroad companies. The story centered on the battle between A-No. 1, the champion hobo at riding the rails, and Shack, a sadistic train conductor who specialized in keeping hoboes off his train.

The script was written by Christopher Knopf. Peckinpah had rewritten it and spent three years trying to get it produced. He found an interested party in Kenneth Hyman, the former head of Warner Bros., who was now an independent producer. Hyman sold it to Robert Evans, then head of production at Paramount.

According to Peckinpah's memory of it, Evans agreed to have Paramount produce "Emperor of the North Pole," if Peckinpah would first direct a film of Jim Thompson's novel *The Getaway*. But when Peckinpah and Evans agreed, Peckinpah said, Hyman fired Peckinpah as director of "Emperor of the North Pole," paying him $10,000 for his rights to the script. To add insult to injury, Paramount then dropped *The Getaway*, leaving Peckinpah with nothing.

Kenneth Hyman, however, says, "I bought the rights to ['Emperor'] and Sam was going to direct it. We had a deal for him to direct and Sam was doing a rewrite. [Unfortunately,] Sam decided to do another picture first and I couldn't wait. We had a bit of a falling out. Sam was somewhat bitter about that."

In February 1972, Peckinpah wrote to his friend Clive Wilkinson in England, saying: "I fully intended to do 'Emperor of the North Pole' but I guess Ken changed his mind. Why I do not know as I'm only dealing with his lawyers, but I must say that my ass is beginning to turn a little red at this point in what I term politely as 'this lack of communication.' "

"Emperor of the North Pole" wound up as a project for director Robert Aldrich, to whom Peckinpah also wrote in February 1972. "I have been deeply involved in 'Emperor of the North Pole' for the last few years," said Peckinpah. "I cannot say that I am happy about not doing it but I can say that I'm very happy that you are in charge. I have been a devoted fan of your pictures over the years and I feel that my adopted baby is in very good hands."

22

"We Cut a Fat Hog"

WHEN PARAMOUNT DROPPED *THE GETAWAY,* Steve McQueen was eager enough to make it that he had his own company, First Artists, take it over.

(First Artists had been formed a couple of years earlier by McQueen, Paul Newman, Dustin Hoffman, Barbra Streisand and Sidney Poitier, in an effort to gain control over their careers and have input into the films they were making. Like United Artists before it, the running of the film company fell to others with more experience and business acumen than the titular artists. First Artists eventually disbanded without producing a noteworthy body of work.)

Even as he was preparing to direct *The Getaway,* Peckinpah was also getting ready to make a third woman Mrs. Sam Peckinpah: Joie Gould, the British secretary he had wooed during *Straw Dogs* and lived with intermittently afterward.

"Joie was a nice woman," says Peckinpah's daughter Sharon. "She bit off more than she could chew. She was very young; there was at least fifteen years between them. My take on it was that she was kind of swept away by the romance of the situation."

"They were very happy," says Cliff Coleman, "except he got drunk and beat the shit out of her in the hotel in London once."

Apparently out of remorse for the incident, he convinced her to come to the United States and marry him. He started shooting *The Getaway* in February 1972, with Joie by his side; they were married in Juarez, Mexico, on April 9, 1972. She was given the credit "assistant to the producer" on the film.

"Joie was about five-foot-two and she had been with Richard Harris before Sam," Gordon Dawson says. "They had some terrific fights. But he married her."

The marriage obviously upset Katy Haber, with whom he had also been involved. But she stayed on as his assistant on *The Getaway*—until he fired her.

"The day before the wedding, I was sitting in some dive with Katy, just sitting at the bar," Dawson says. "I'm sure it couldn't be easy for her."

"Katy wanted to marry Sam," says Bobby Visciglia, "and Sam married everyone around her just to piss her off. She started fooling around with a camera assistant on *The Getaway* and he found out and fired her. She would be complaining to me, 'I never get laid,' and Sam's lying in bed with someone else."

"Why did I stay? I asked myself that question over and over," Haber says. "I loved him. He was the most interesting, most intense man in my life. Somehow the man was infectious. Did I want to marry him? No."

As for her dismissal, she says, "I was fired when he married Joie. Joie left and he called and I came back."

The marriage lasted less than six months. Joie filed for divorce in August 1972, and it was granted the following year. His abusiveness and drinking were part of the problem.

"He was married to Joie long enough for it to get real expensive," his brother Denny says. "He brought Joie up to meet us. He was getting ready to shoot *The Getaway*. I said, 'Sam, she's a lovely girl but don't hurry here.' He said, 'What do you mean?' I said, 'You're going to make a lot of money on this movie. If you want to share it with her, fine. But don't con yourself into thinking you can give her a couple of grand and then tell her goodbye.' He still got off easy, for about $25,000."

"Joie would come to the office [on *The Getaway*] with a black eye," recalls Sharon, who worked on the film. Says Jim Silke, "He married Joie on *Getaway* but, before it was over, he was back with Begonia."

Joie herself refuses to discuss the marriage. "I have a husband and children and a life," she says. "I haven't even discussed it with my closest friends. Why would I talk about it to a complete stranger?"

At the time, however, she said, "All of my friends told me not to marry Sam. If you wanted to get involved, that was one thing. But nothing permanent. I said I thought I could handle it. It turned out they were right, and I was wrong."

When the divorce was finalized in 1973, Peckinpah sent a telegram to her parents in London, Rachel and Coleman Gould: "Sorry it didn't work out, but Joie has what she always wanted, money in the bank. I would like to ask you as a favor to request her not to use my name in any way, shape or form or I will be forced to take further legal action. Again, I must say I'm sorry but happy that the one thing I ever did in my life was helping you to visit America. Some day I hope we can sit down and talk about this. Unfortunately, right now I am as bitter as she and with just as much reason."

Joie eventually married a producer and moved to Australia, where she now lives. Apparently Peckinpah kept track of her whereabouts and circumstances: When she was in the hospital in Australia having her first child, he sent a large basket of flowers.

THE GETAWAY IS THE STORY of Carter "Doc" McCoy, a convicted bank robber serving a prison term in Huntsville Prison in Texas. Denied parole after serving four years of a ten-year sentence, he tells his wife Carol to agree to a deal offered by a member of the parole board, Jack Benyon, a San Antonio banker.

Benyon helps McCoy get a parole. In return, McCoy agrees to mastermind a bank robbery for Benyon. The objective is an oil company payroll in a small-town bank; the robbery will also help cover the financial shenanigans of Benyon's brother, one of the bank's directors.

Benyon insists that McCoy work with two of his men: Rudy and Frank. But the robbery is a setup for a double cross. Benyon and Rudy, independent of each other, plan to kill McCoy and take the money.

Instead, McCoy shoots Rudy and leaves him for dead. Carol kills Benyon, and she and McCoy take off together, heading for El Paso, where they will cross into Mexico.

The rest of the story is a cat-and-mouse game as Doc and Carol elude the police, while being stalked by Rudy. It ends with a shoot-out in an El Paso hotel between Doc and Carol, Rudy and Benyon's goons. Doc and Carol are the only ones to emerge alive, escaping into Mexico with the profits of the robbery.

On *The Getaway,* Peckinpah's producer, David Foster, left him alone. "Foster just said, 'Make the movie,' " Gordon Dawson says. "There was no studio to fight. There was nobody meddling in the day-to-day, trying to handle Sam's idiosyncrasies."

Says Newt Arnold, "Foster told him, 'This is one of my first experiences in producing. I need your help and I hope I can help you.' That was exactly the right thing to say."

Everything went the way it was supposed to and the film finished without serious problems. As to his mood: "He was in love with Joie on that one," Dawson says. Adds Visciglia, "If Sam was in love, we didn't see too much of him at night during a production. So we tried to get him to fall in love so he would leave us alone."

His crew was crackling: "Everybody just did their job," Newt Arnold says. "We knew what Sam wanted. If we didn't, we'd ask him. Logistically, it was a demanding picture. There were a lot of moves. We were all over the place. But it all just flowed."

Adds Dawson, "It was the best experience we ever had. We came in under schedule, under budget. We cut a fat hog on that one."

Peckinpah brought in his favorite crew people: Gordon Dawson as associate producer and second-unit director, Lucien Ballard as cinematographer, Bobby Visciglia to handle props, Newt Arnold and Ron Wright as assistant directors, Ted Haworth as art director, Bob Wolfe and Roger Spottiswoode to edit, Bud Hulburd to do special effects and Jerry Fielding to do the music. The screenplay was written by an up-and-comer, Walter Hill, who later directed several action-thrillers that owed a debt to Peckinpah, including *The Long Riders* and *Southern Comfort.*

The film reunited Peckinpah with McQueen for the second picture in a row. Peckinpah filled out the cast with several members of his stock company: Slim Pickens, Dub Taylor, Ben Johnson, Bo Hopkins. He picked newcomer Sally Struthers, who had just made a splash on television in "All in the Family," and Jack Dodson, a regular on "The Andy Griffith Show," to play a veterinarian and his wife who are kidnapped by one of McCoy's duplicitous accomplices. He filled another small role with his friend photojournalist John Bryson, who had not acted before.

One key role was Rudy, the gunman who is part of the double cross. Peckinpah's original choice for the role was Jack Palance. Peckinpah discussed the role with him, thinking he would be perfect for the snaky character. But the budget only allowed $50,000 for that role, half of Palance's usual salary.

Peckinpah wanted him badly enough that he convinced Foster and McQueen to up the salary to $65,000 and to throw in three percent of the net profits (one each from Peckinpah, McQueen and Foster). Palance turned it down. Peckinpah then tried to make up the difference out of his own money to come up with $100,000 for Palance. But Foster finally said it just wasn't going to work.

During the negotiations, Peckinpah ran into producer Al Ruddy, who was in the midst of postproduction on *The Godfather.* When Peckinpah mentioned his problem in signing Palance, Ruddy says, "I told him I had a heavy he had to see and showed him footage of Al Lettieri playing Sollozzo in *The Godfather.* He ran right out and made a deal to give Al the part of Rudy."

Palance, however, thought he had an oral contract for the film. When Peckinpah cast Lettieri, Palance filed suit, claiming breach of contract. After depositions were taken, the suit was dismissed.

The role of Carol, Doc's wife, went to model-turned-actress Ali Mac-Graw, who had appeared in *Goodbye, Columbus,* and *Love Story.* MacGraw arrived at the Texas location to play half of a bank-robbing team—the half that drove the getaway car. And she promptly announced that she didn't know how to drive.

"I said, 'Have you ever driven a car before?' " Visciglia recalls. "She said, 'No, I don't have a license.' When she was a model, she used to take the bus

or cabs. I said, 'Didn't you read the script?' She had to drive all these cars.
And they were all stick-shifts."

Gordon Dawson says, "Sam cried when he heard she couldn't drive. Then
he said, 'What the fuck are you telling me for? Get her to driving class.' "

Never much of an actress, MacGraw did generate heat with McQueen.
But it wasn't acting: Though MacGraw was married to Robert Evans, the
Paramount production chief, she and McQueen rapidly fell into a love affair
on the set. Eventually, she divorced Evans and married McQueen.

To Peckinpah, it was justice for what he saw as Evans's double-dealing on
"Emperor of the North Pole" and *The Getaway*.

"Evans is a liar, a cheat and a thief," Peckinpah said. "I got even. I had a
long talk with Bobby in Juarez, Mexico. Then I got Ali and Steve married.
What that says, I guess, is don't mess with Sam Peckinpah."

Gordon Dawson recalls, "We were playing at hiding Steve and Ali when
Bob Evans came to town." Peckinpah said later, "Evans walked into Juarez
and said, 'Where's Ali?' and I said, 'Just don't fuck with my picture.' "

Peckinpah's daughter Sharon once again joined the crew, this time as
dialogue director. "I was interested in filmmaking," she says, "and I was
interested in having a father. So I tried that. It didn't work. He wasn't fun to
be around on the set."

Sharon lasted a few weeks before finally having a blowup with her father.
"He fired me three times in the same night," she says. "I couldn't keep my
mouth shut. I started to get tired of him being mean to me. I'm not a good
doormat. He'd take your ego, throw it on the ground and stomp on it. Then
he'd do it over and over. I got sick of it so I'd talk back in front of the crew.
I'd yell at him. So he fired me—three times."

Asked about it later in the production, Peckinpah said, "That's correct. I
did fire my daughter off the production. Her attitude was punk. She wasn't
doing her work, so I canned her and she went off to Mexico with some long-
haired guy."

Sharon's mother, Marie, felt the fallout of the blowup: "It hurt Sharon
wretchedly, terribly, when he fired her. She always felt very angry with him. I
can understand why he fired her; I'm sure he was disappointed in her. But
being fired by [her] own father without a reasonable explanation of what he
expected her work to be—she felt this great sense of disrespect for him and
he felt exactly the same. He was hurt she wouldn't come through for him.
He was real hard on [his children]. He was very nonsupportive of their
talent."

THOUGH PRODUCTION OF *The Getaway* went like clockwork, there were moments that stood out during filming. The film's opening scenes, of Doc
McCoy in prison, were filmed at Huntsville State Penitentiary, near San

Marcos, Texas. McQueen, costumed in prison garb, was mixed in with a group of real convicts for several shots. One of these was a shot in the exercise yard, involving McQueen and about fifty actual prisoners.

"On our first afternoon there, when the scene was wrapped and Sam yelled 'Cut!' I took off toward my dressing room for some coffee," McQueen recalled. "Well, here I was, in prison duds, splitting away from the other cons—and suddenly I'm running like hell, because this pack of hounds are snappin' at my ass. They'd been trained to go after any con who broke ranks and nobody had bothered to tell them this was a movie. I barely made it out of that yard in one piece. I almost got my ass chewed off."

Kent James and his wife Carol were costumers on the film who were newcomers to the Peckinpah sphere. "When I was introduced to him, I knew everyone he'd fired," Kent James says. "I said, 'Sam, under tension and pressure, I pass out. So I won't hear a word you say.' He had a good sense of humor as long as you did your job and could play good."

At one point in *The Getaway*, several people in raincoats were blasted with shotguns. To do multiple takes, the Jameses had to be cleaning off the stage blood and patching the raincoats for the next shot.

"[Peckinpah] turned to me at one point and said, 'Give me that last raincoat,' " Kent James says. "I said, 'I cleaned it already.' He said, 'What? Goddamn it, I told you—' and I dropped to the ground."

Peckinpah had great intuitive powers, on and off the set. "He had a psychic sense of what was going on with people," his daughter Sharon says. "He knew what was happening before it happened. It was scary, and I mean that in the funny sense. He knew what people were thinking almost."

John Bryson, who was around for the entire production of *The Getaway*, said, "He always knows who's having troubles, who's sleeping with who, the whole ball of wax. It gets downright eerie. Like in my case, there was something that had to do with my personal life that nobody in the world could've known about, but then Sam said to me, 'John, don't do such-and-such.' I nearly fell over dead. I said, 'Holy shit, this scares me beyond belief. How could you know anything about that?' And Sam just smiled that Jesus-like smile of his and said, 'I always know everything that happens in my company.' "

The Getaway brought back unexpected echoes of *Ride the High Country* when, during editing, someone suggested that a TV in the background of one scene be playing the old Peckinpah film. But, as Peckinpah wrote in an October 16, 1972, letter to Joel McCrea: "I considered it briefly and agreed, but in thinking it over and realizing the quality of the two pictures and what their intentions were, I cancelled the idea.

"*Ride the High Country* does not belong in *The Getaway*. It's a different kind of class. It's not that I think *The Getaway* is a bad picture, it's just that what it has to say doesn't measure up to *High Country* and all the things we believed in when we made it."

McCrea responded: "It was good to hear from you and to know that we feel the same about *Ride the High Country*. It's good to know that, with all your talent, you also have integrity, rare these days."

Still in the thick of the controversy over his treatment of women in *Straw Dogs* while shooting *The Getaway,* Peckinpah one day was shown a clipping of an Associated Press story in which he had been voted one of the Sourpuss Awards by a New York feminist group called the Pussycat League. The honor itself was called the Kinky Machismo Award.

"Shit, I showed a guy eating pussy in *Straw Dogs,*" he said. "What do they think about that? What in hell is the Pussycat League, anyway? Sounds like a bunch of dumb cunts. I'll bet Judith Crist belongs to that outfit."

Near the end of the production, the shooting schedule started to get backed up while filming the final shoot-out in the Laughlin Hotel in El Paso. The sequence is a series of shots of men firing shotguns and automatic weapons at each other in hotel corridors, with the attendant explosions of plaster and wood.

"They had seven effects guys squibbing the walls in the hotel," Bobby Visciglia says. "They'd worked all night long squibbing the walls. Then a gun would jam and they'd have to start all over."

The machine guns Visciglia had for the henchmen seemed to give a couple of actors particular trouble. They would jam the guns, the squibs would explode holes in the walls—and then production would have to halt while someone replastered, squibbed, painted and aged the walls to make them match the previous shots. It was a time-consuming process that threatened to put them behind schedule.

Finally, Visciglia made a suggestion to Peckinpah: He would lead a second-unit crew to the various points in the hotel where the action was being filmed. The actors would do their part—ducking behind a wall just before the squib was supposed to go off. Then Visciglia would clear the floor of actors and, with the crew, shoot the walls with actual shotgun shells.

"We kept everyone else two floors away," he says. "It was just me and a second-unit crew. In one day, I picked up six days on the schedule firing real ammo, which is kind of unheard of now."

When the film was finished and Jerry Fielding had finished the score, McQueen, whose company had backed the venture, eliminated Fielding's soundtrack and replaced it with a jazzier score by Quincy Jones.

"That was a big bitch with Sam—but it was Steve's company," says Camille Fielding. "Sam took out a full-page ad in *Variety* to say it was against his will."

The ad, which ran in *Daily Variety* on November 17, 1972, said:

"Dear Jerry,

I know you will be pleased that the second preview of *Getaway* was as great as the first. In fact, it was even more enthusiastically received. Which is surprising since it was attended mostly by industry people.

I want to thank you for the beautiful job you did with the music. I have heard many marvelous comments, particularly on the second showing. Possibly because no one there had impaired hearing and we had no problem with malfunctioning equipment.

Once again, congratulations. I am looking forward to the next one.

Best regards,
Sam Peckinpah"

Actor Al Lettieri attended one of the screenings and found, to his dismay, that, in recutting the film for the soundtrack, McQueen had also removed certain bits of comic business that he had interpolated into the film. But Lettieri assumed it was producer David Foster who had excised his work.

"I stepped into the hall after the studio screening," says Gill Dennis. "There was Joan Didion smoking a cigarette. I hear the crash of the door and here comes Al Lettieri, with two guys holding him back. He's outraged at the producer for having trimmed his part. He goes booming into the screening, very insulting, a lot of people there. And Sam is trying to calm everybody down. Frank Kowalski said that was the only time he saw Sam trying to break up a fight."

THE GETAWAY WAS PECKINPAH's least personal movie to that point, a technically well-crafted film, entertaining and exciting, but without particular heart or soul. It was the story of criminals battling other criminals but unlike *The Wild Bunch,* Doc and Carol McCoy were not people living out a credo or code. They were just bank robbers trying to escape from double-crossing partners and the law with stolen money.

Peckinpah always claimed that he meant the film as a satire of the genre. At three different points in the film, characters make the observation, "It's just a game."

"The Getaway, despite my first attempt at satire, turned out to be a mildly entertaining film, at least according to the distributors, who figure it will do about $15 million," Peckinpah wrote in October 1972 to his friend Jan Aghed.

Whatever satire there may be is thoroughly masked by the conventions of the action-thriller. It was easy to admire the mechanics of the film—the breathless editing of the bank robbery and getaway and the brutal but exciting shoot-out at the finale—but wonder why Peckinpah would apply his talents to a movie he could make in his sleep.

In *Time,* Jay Cocks said, "It has lately become Peckinpah's ironic pleasure to refer to himself in interviews as a 'whore,' and, appropriately, *The Getaway* works on that same kind of disinterested, mechanical level. There are a great many scenes of action and bloodletting, professionally handled and exciting. But the viewer is always aware that he is being manipulated very coolly and cynically."

Pauline Kael summed it up in the *New Yorker,* saying, "There's no reason for this picture—another bank heist—to have been made. This is the most completely commercial film Peckinpah has made, and his self-parasitism gives one forebodings of emptiness."

If the critics were tough with Peckinpah, they were absolutely vicious to MacGraw who, in truth, walked through the film looking like she'd been shot with a stun gun before most scenes.

· Said Pauline Kael: "Miss MacGraw communicates thought by frowning and opening her mouth. Last time I saw Candice Bergen, I thought she was a worse actress than MacGraw; now I think that I slandered Bergen."

· And from Jay Cocks: "As a screen personality, MacGraw is abrasive. As a talent, she is embarrassing. Supposedly a scruffy Texas tart, MacGraw appears with a designer wardrobe and a set of Seven Sister mannerisms."

· Joseph Gelmis of *Newsday* wrote: "Part of what is wrong with *The Getaway* is that the rest of the cast isn't strong enough to carry Ali's insipid performance. A quiver, a model's profile, a sweet face, is no substitute for the inner life of neurotic drive that makes a star. Ali is all face."

Peckinpah took enough umbrage to write MacGraw a commiserative note on February 21, 1973: "I was incensed by the reviews. It seems to me they had a personal vendetta against you. I thought you were damn good outside of a couple of little mannerisms that were taken out and then put back in. You're a much better actress than anyone else gives you credit for, including yourself. I think you are a natural and do not need to be taught."

The film was the most commercially successful of Peckinpah's career, grossing almost $20 million in the United States—big box office in 1973 dollars.

After the success of *The Getaway,* Peckinpah's brother Denny told him, "Goddamn it, Sam, you talk about your dad and Denver Church and me. But your work is seen and your name is known by millions of people. You have achieved more in a single go-round than the rest of us put together, but you don't feel you've done anything."

Peckinpah shook his head and said, "It's not what you've done. It's what you're going to do that counts."

PECKINPAH'S DRINKING VARIED according to the level of tension on a set. The fewer problems, apparently, the less restraint he placed on himself. It didn't seem to get in his way on *The Getaway,* but it created a false sense of security about the drinking itself. He was drinking even more than usual yet seemed to get more work done more efficiently than ever before (thanks to a crack crew).

"On that picture, I had rigged this hawker's tray with a bucket of ice in the center and vodka, Campari and soda," Bobby Visciglia says. "I hung it around my neck on the set and carried it around. Whatever I would mix for Sam, I would mix for myself, so I could keep track of what he was drinking. We were shooting in San Marcos and Marty Baum had flown in to talk to Sam. So they had this meeting at Sam's house and Marty says, 'Do you know that your property master is drinking all day long?' And Sam looked him straight in the eye and said, 'It's in his contract, Marty.' "

"I think he was in hot pursuit of the feeling of being more alive," his daughter Sharon says. "At the same time, he wanted to kill the pain. Drinking was a good way to do that. And I say that ironically. This was somebody who was so sensitive. I think he drank for millions of reasons, but one was to kill the shame. I think he was brought up with shame. It was in his core, that shame. He was a very shy man. He had this enormous gifted fertile imagination. I'm sure it drove him nuts sometimes."

It was apparent to those who were observant that he was drinking heavily even before production began on *The Getaway.* Actress Mariette Hartley, who hadn't seen Peckinpah since making *Ride the High Country* a decade earlier, went in to audition for the role of Carol McCoy and was startled by what she found.

"When I met him for *Getaway,* he was another person," she says. "It was like a ghost of who he was. There was a grayness to his skin. I confronted him and said, 'What's wrong? What's going on?' I said, 'Do you know about the twelve-step program?' I gave him a number and told him to call. There was a moment when I almost thought he might bite. There's that moment when the scales go from the eyes. I was very straight with him. I felt he had respect for my honesty. There was no way he could hide."

Peckinpah's nephew David says, "Sam would say, 'I'm a functioning alcoholic.' It makes me wonder if, just for a while, he could have made one picture without drinking. If he'd had twelve months of sobriety, what would his view of life have been? He did not see life the way most of the world does. That's the part of the myth that's so damaging, this ingrained belief that self-destructiveness is linked to the creative process. That's bullshit."

Part Six

PAT GARRETT AND BILLY THE KID 1972-1973

Pat Garrett and Billy the Kid *is beginning to smell good to me. I look forward to being back in Old Mex again. As a matter of fact, I look forward to anything that is out of this town.*

—SAM PECKINPAH IN A LETTER TO JAN AGHED,
OCTOBER 16, 1972

I am so sick that someone else is finishing this picture for me. There is only one thing I can say . . . stay away from MGM and the major studios, which is exactly what I'm going to do from now on.

—SAM PECKINPAH IN A LETTER TO JAN AGHED,
JANUARY 31, 1973

23

"Feels Like Times Have Changed"

PART OF PECKINPAH'S ANNUAL ROUTINE was a hunting trip each fall to the mountains north and west of Fresno. He would pack his car, pick up his brother-in-law Walter Peter, drive up to Fresno to rendezvous with his brother Denny and other hunting buddies and head into the mountains to stalk deer.

As the 1970s started and Peckinpah became increasingly involved in film-making, he made it to Fresno for the hunting trips less and less often, eventually stopping altogether. But for most of the 1950s and 1960s, it was almost a sacrament to him: a time to shake off the pressures and tensions of Hollywood and return to the kind of experiences that reminded him of the simplicity of his youth.

"He loved to go camping," Peter remembers. "On the first day out, he'd make phone calls. On the second day, we'd be in the bowels of Nevada. And on the third day, almost to Utah, he was a delight. It was like he was losing weight with each 500 miles from Hollywood he got. He loved to play poker and spend a lot of time in whorehouses. He'd become more relaxed and laugh more easily."

His group of hunting buddies became known as the Walker River Boys because of an incident in 1960. The group—Peckinpah, Denny and their father, Dave; Bud Williams and his father, Claude; and Blaine Pettitt had headed for its usual destination near Ely, Nevada. Someone had heard that there was good hunting near Hawthorne, Nevada. But after some serious drinking, they got lost on the pitch-dark ribbons of mountain roads, most of which have only minimal identifying markings even today. In the dark, they found a river and set up camp. The next morning they determined from maps that they were at the Walker River.

"It was like an oasis," Pettitt says. "We were lucky we ended up anyplace.

We were all laughing at ourselves for getting sucked into a deal of finding this place. We never did find the place we were supposed to go."

The Walker River Boys made the trip an annual event. "One year, the Walker River Boys went hunting at night in a pickup and shot a farmer's prize bull," says Susan Peckinpah. "Truly, it was a straggly old steer, but in the farmer's eyes, there was money to be made from these guys."

When he got old enough, they would take along Denny's oldest son, David. "The hunting trips were alcohol-fueled marathons," David recalls. "Lots of rough talk and wild stories. It was pretty romantic for a twelve- or thirteen-year-old. As they progressed, Sam would bring more and more of what my dad called Hollywood people."

Still, David carries some tender memories: "When I was sixteen, I was crippled in a car crash," he says. "My dad took me on the hunting trip, but I had a wheelchair and braces and crutches. I remember waking up once at four A.M. and Sam was out there in the campsite with a Coleman lantern, raking the campsite so the wheelchair wouldn't hang up on anything."

It was also a time of reckless merriment, usually enlivened by alcohol. Denny recalls a posttrip drink at a saloon in Bass Lake. A loudmouth at the bar started smarting off to Peckinpah, who refused to take the bait. The troublemaker finally said, "Kiss my ass."

Peckinpah responded, "Mark off a square, you son of a bitch, because you're all ass to me."

"That ended the fight," Denny says.

On another memorable trip, Peckinpah and Walter Peter were in the cab of a truck with a camper cap on the bed. Denny, who was riding in the camper, pounded on the window to indicate that he needed to stop to relieve himself. Peckinpah and Peter laughed and ignored him. A few miles further down the road, Denny knocked again, this time with more urgency. Again, Peckinpah and Peter laughed and kept driving.

Suddenly, the windshield exploded. To make his point, the angry Denny had taken a rifle and blown a hole through the window of the camper and the cab, taking out the windshield in the process.

Peckinpah slammed on the brakes. He and Peter dove out opposite sides of the truck, rolling into the high grass and lying there for several long minutes before they were convinced that Denny didn't mean to shoot them as well.

Because Denny was a California Superior Court judge at the time, the incident went unreported to any form of constabulary. Indeed, to this day, Denny feigns ignorance of the incident.

"As Sam got busier and the pressure of the life-style got heavier," Denny says, "we didn't see him as much. He began missing the hunting trips because of other commitments."

"I saw him change as he got progressively deeper into his own shit,"

David Peckinpah says. "It was like he had to continue the film-set mentality. It used to be when he got up there, he was able to just relax, kick back, sit by the fire and swap lies. After a while, he wasn't able to stop playing the part of Sam Peckinpah."

24

Approaching Familiar Territory

THERE WERE TWO WATERSHED FILMS in Peckinpah's career. *The Wild Bunch* lifted him out of exile and back into the business for the most successful years of his life. *Pat Garrett and Billy the Kid* was the other landmark—the film that sent him into a tailspin, both personally and professionally, from which his career never recovered.

By the time of *Pat Garrett and Billy the Kid*, playing the part of Sam Peckinpah was practically a full-time job, even when he was directing.

"There were a handful of people in Hollywood who were figures of myth," says John Bryson, "including Sam and John Huston. Sam was Sam. There was nobody like him. He became a figure of legend. And he realized that if he was the real himself, it furthered the legend. After a while, he began trying to live up to the legend."

His brother Denny would read the interviews in which Peckinpah spouted off on various topics and think, "Sam's up to his old tricks."

"He succeeded pretty well at creating an image," Denny says. "I'd call him and he'd say, 'Oh, Denny, you've got to give them what they're looking for.' But you give them what they're looking for and pretty soon that's what they're looking for."

Coming off the smooth production of *The Getaway*, Peckinpah had no reason to believe he would not have a similar experience with his next film. More important, he was about to film a story that was close to his heart.

The tale of Billy the Kid was one of the seminal legends of the old West: romantic, dangerous, exciting and tragic—no matter what the truth of William Bonney's story might actually be.

To Peckinpah, the story was emblematic. He felt particularly close to it because it had been the source of his first screenplay, what eventually became *One-Eyed Jacks*. To his mind, however, Marlon Brando had spoiled his script

240

and sullied the myth to boot. Now Peckinpah finally had a chance to tell the story his way, with all of his mythologizing touches.

If you buy the notion of Billy the Kid as a romantic hero, at odds with a changing West and the encroachment of business interests into daily life on the frontier, then his demise is a tragic tale.

In that sense, Peckinpah's production of *Pat Garrett and Billy the Kid* is similarly tragic. Having made his maverick approach work successfully within the system on five successive films, Peckinpah ran out of luck the sixth time around. He ran into a studio head even more ruthless than he was and a studio more than willing to trample his work to get what it wanted—not a film created from an artist's vision but a product that could be marketed with Peckinpah's name (if not his vision) attached to it.

The script for *Pat Garrett and Billy the Kid* had been around for a couple of years, since producer Gordon Carroll, who made such films as *Cool Hand Luke* and *The April Fools,* had hired writer Rudolph Wurlitzer to write it in 1970.

Wurlitzer was an East Coast novelist who had written the screenplay for *Two-Lane Blacktop* for director Monte Hellman. Released in 1971, *Two-Lane* was an existential car race movie that starred Warren Oates and rock stars Dennis Wilson (of the Beach Boys) and James Taylor. Hailed by critics, it failed to attract audiences, becoming a film that was all word of mouth and no box office.

Pat Garrett and Billy the Kid was sold to MGM with the idea that Hellman would direct it based on the critical reception for *Two-Lane Blacktop.* When MGM's bottom-line-conscious executives saw the anemic grosses, however, they changed their mind.

Carroll shopped the script to other studios, with no takers. Wurlitzer rewrote it and it wound up back at MGM, where Peckinpah saw it and agreed to do it.

Peckinpah, of course, wanted to rewrite to suit himself, a process that upset Wurlitzer at the time. There was another force at work as well: MGM, which wanted a Sam Peckinpah picture awash with action.

"Most of the rewrites were a compromise between him and the studio," Wurlitzer says. "They wanted more violence and action. Three or four scenes were added on afterward, mostly of violence. My initial script was a little more existential.

"At that point," Wurlitzer adds, "I didn't know anything about what happens to a script, and how battered a writer can be. I was upset that Sam hadn't dealt with it until he started to shoot. I don't think he read it more than once. I see now it was an extension of him; he inhabited it in a way I was not aware of at the time. I was unprepared for the process."

It was Peckinpah's usual method: Break the script down, then build it back.

"It was a perfect script," says James Coburn, who appeared in the film. "But perfect to Sam is too mechanical, too ordered. He wanted to fuck it up, make it more real. Rudy thought Sam screwed it up."

"Rudy just died," says Gordon Dawson, who served as second-unit director on the film. "It was an awful experience for him."

Wurlitzer expressed his anger in the introduction to the published version of the screenplay, which combined his original and Peckinpah's version of the shooting script. Writing in the third person, Wurlitzer said:

> "The writer went back to Hollywood to work with the director. Finally they had two or three conversations about the director's past sexual exploits and about the savage, warlike rigors of the celluloid trail. The script was never discussed . . . the director hadn't read it yet. The writer and director went to Mexico to scout locations and work on the script. The director, who by this time had skimmed the first few scenes, became suddenly thrilled by his own collaborative gifts. In the writer's version, Billy and Garrett never met until the final scene, when Garrett killed him. The director wanted their relationship in front, so that everyone would know they were old buddies. Rewriting was imposed with the added inspirational help of some of the director's old TV scripts. The beginning was changed completely. Extraordinary lines about male camaraderie made a soggy entrance into the body of the script."

PECKINPAH'S VERSION OF *Pat Garrett and Billy the Kid* opened in 1908, with an aged, crotchety Garrett riding on his land, arguing with John Poe about the sheep Poe has let graze on Garrett's land. They argue about the lease and the Sante Fe Ring, for whom Garrett used to work. As Garrett rails at Poe, an ambush is launched and three men—including Poe—shoot Garrett, who falls to the ground.

As he falls, the scene flashes back to Fort Sumner, New Mexico, in 1881. Billy the Kid and his compatriots are taking target practice, shooting at the heads of chickens, which have been buried up to their necks. Garrett rides up and joins in, then invites Billy to come for a drink.

In the saloon, he tells Billy that he has accepted the job of sheriff of Lincoln County and that his first job is to rid the territory of Billy. As an old friend, he has come to warn Billy to leave the area and head for Mexico or face the consequences.

Billy, taking the news in stride, says, "So you sold out to the Sante Fe Ring. How's it feel?"

"It feels," Garrett says, "like times have changed."

Garrett arrests Billy a week later after a shoot-out and takes him back to

Lincoln to hang. But Billy kills Garrett's deputies and escapes. Billy goes back to Fort Sumner and debates whether to make a run for Mexico.

Garrett, meanwhile, must track down his old friend. The two circle each other in concentric, violent rings. Garrett has run-ins with Gov. Lew Wallace and the cattle baron Chisum, while trying to maintain his integrity. Billy shoots several of Chisum's men when they kill his friends. He decides to stand his ground and not to go to Mexico.

In the end, Billy and Garrett end up in Fort Sumner on the same night. Garrett kills him—the last thing he flashes back to before the film returns to 1908 and the moment of Garrett's death.

THE SCRIPT CAUSED CONSTERNATION in the MGM front office. The studio was under the control of James Aubrey, who, as head of CBS from 1959 to 1965, had been nicknamed "the Smiling Cobra" for the pleasure he seemed to derive from taking the budgetary axe to programs and careers.

Aubrey was hired at MGM in 1969 to stem the tide of red ink that was threatening to sink the studio. MGM was losing $35 million for the year. More than $80 million in debt, it faced $70 million in write-offs for bad films.

Aubrey immediately canceled fifteen films that were in progress, including director Fred Zinnemann's production of André Malraux's *Man's Fate*, on which MGM already had spent $3 million. By 1970, MGM was only $30 million in debt and was showing a profit of $8.1 million for the first nine months of the year.

In the next four years, Aubrey sliced the MGM staff from 6,200 to 1,200 and sold off everything from MGM's record division to studio real estate to its storehouse of props—including Ben Hur's chariot.

The price was artistic integrity. The studio of Irving Thalberg was being run by an administrator who thought nothing of recutting a director's work to suit his own commercial vision. Even before he worked with Peckinpah, he had a reputation among many directors as a philistine.

Daniel Melnick, who had moved from independent production to become head of production at MGM, remembers Aubrey's outrage over one scene in particular during a script meeting for *Pat Garrett and Billy the Kid*.

Garrett, sitting alone on a riverbank, hears gunfire and sees a raft filled with people and possessions drifting down the river. A boy on the raft throws empty bottles into the river; his father shoots at them as target practice. Garrett picks up his gun and tries his luck at one of the bottles. The father turns and shoots at Garrett, missing him. Garrett points his gun at the father; the father points at Garrett. After a moment of standoff, he goes back to shooting at the bottle.

BLOODY SAM

Aubrey read the script and said, "What the fuck is that scene with Pat Garrett and the guy floating down the river on a raft?"

Melnick tried to explain in terms that would soothe Aubrey, but Saul David, the literary editor on the film, spoke up: "That's a piece of existential violence."

Aubrey exploded, throwing them both out of his office. As they left, he shouted after them, "Existential fucking violence? What are you talking about? Don't ever let me hear that phrase again."

The relationship between Aubrey and Peckinpah only got worse. Melnick says, "Sam provoked Jim to his deepest core. Jim thought Sam was immoral and irresponsible. Sam thought Jim was the ultimate businessman running an enterprise and not smart enough to see what the public wanted, someone who certainly didn't care about the integrity of the project. I think they were both right. And they were convinced they were right."

That raft scene, James Coburn adds, "was one of the reasons [Sam and I] both wanted to do the film." They shot it, then found that the film was out of focus, a recurring problem early in the production. Aubrey refused to okay the time or money to reshoot the scene. So Peckinpah got his crew to sneak it in at the end of a day when they had finished early.

"It infuriated Aubrey," Coburn says. "Instead of making up time and moving on, we were using the time to reshoot things."

As CASTING BEGAN, hopes ran high that a new Sam Peckinpah Western could attract some high-profile talent. Peckinpah offered the role of Garrett to Charlton Heston, who turned him down. The others on the list for Garrett (all of whom proved either uninterested, unavailable or overpriced) included Paul Newman, Henry Fonda, Robert Mitchum and Rod Steiger, as well as James Coburn. The part finally went to Coburn, working with Peckinpah for the first time since *Major Dundee*.

Most of the hot young actors of the moment were considered for Billy the Kid: Peter Fonda, Jon Voight, Malcolm McDowell, Marjoe, even a newcomer named Don Johnson. Then Peckinpah saw a singer-songwriter named Kris Kristofferson in a low-budget drama called *Cisco Pike*. Kristofferson was obviously raw, but Peckinpah liked what he saw.

After catching the singer's act at the Troubadour in Los Angeles, Peckinpah offered him the role. "There were a lot of people they wanted to cast before Kris," Wurlitzer says. "Kris wasn't even the fifth choice." For good measure, he hired members of Kristofferson's band to play Billy's gang.

Peckinpah filled out the cast with some of the most recognizable faces in Hollywood: Jason Robards, Barry Sullivan, Katy Jurado, Jack Elam, Richard Jaeckel, Harry Dean Stanton, Elisha Cook, Jr. There were the usual suspects from Peckinpah's stock company: R. G. Armstrong, L. Q. Jones, Emilio

Fernandez, Dub Taylor. And there were even a few throwbacks to the early part of Peckinpah's career: Paul Fix, who had played the marshal on "The Rifleman" and Chill Wills, who was in *The Deadly Companions.*

The biggest casting coup, however, was for the role of Alias, a quirky member of the gang who echoed most of Billy's lines. Bo Hopkins and rock singer Jackson Browne were initially considered. Johnny Crawford, who had played Mark on "The Rifleman," auditioned and was turned down.

Then rock superstar Bob Dylan, a friend of Wurlitzer's, heard about the project and dropped by Wurlitzer's place in New York. "Would you like to be in it?" Wurlitzer asked. Gordon Carroll jumped at the prospect, seeing Dylan as box-office bait for the youth audience, although Dylan had never acted.

Wurlitzer and Dylan went to Durango, Mexico, where the production was headquartered, to meet Peckinpah. "Everyone was intimidated by Dylan, even Sam, because Dylan's legend was bigger than Sam's," Wurlitzer says. "I think that pissed Sam off. Sam didn't know what to make of Dylan. But for sure, Sam wanted to be the main man."

Dylan later recalled, "Rudy needed a song for the script. I wasn't doing anything. Rudy sent the script and I read it and liked it and we got together and he needed a title song. So I wrote that song real quick and played it for Sam and he really liked it and asked me to be in the movie."

But Peckinpah wasn't really sure who Dylan was or what he stood for. Peckinpah, after all, was the man who considered Richard Gillis's "Butterfly Mornings" a model of the songwriting form.

"Rudy said, 'Dylan has written a couple of songs. He'd like to be part of this,' " Coburn says. "Sam said, 'Bob who? Oh yeah, my kids listen to him.' "

When Dylan arrived, Peckinpah tried to impress him by telling him, "I'm a big Roger Miller fan myself." They had an elaborate dinner, with goat's head soup and tacos, tequila and mescal, marijuana and cocaine. Afterward, Peckinpah said to Dylan, "Okay, kid, let's hear what you got." Dylan took out his guitar, and he and Peckinpah adjourned to another room. Peckinpah sat in a rocking chair, Dylan sat on a footstool.

After a couple of tunes, Peckinpah came back to the dining room, tears coursing down his cheeks, obviously moved, muttering, "That son of a bitch. That cocksucker," in admiration. He cast Dylan as Alias, had Wurlitzer expand the part and signed Dylan to write the score.

Peckinpah wasn't the only one who wasn't really sure who Dylan was. Bobby Visciglia, who was in charge of props as well as playing a small part in the film, recalls that Kristofferson told him to have a chair made up with Dylan's name on it. The next day, Visciglia showed up with a chair with "Bob Dillon" printed on the back of it.

"Kris goes crazy when he sees it," Visciglia says. "What the fuck did I know? But right behind him is Dylan. And he says, 'Don't you dare change it. When I'm done here, I want it.' ''

BECAUSE MOST OF THE SCREENPLAY was set in New Mexico, Peckinpah wanted to shoot there, to gain the added verisimilitude. But MGM vetoed the idea, suggesting areas near Durango, Mexico. So Peckinpah sent Gordon Dawson down to scout and arrange locations and line up facilities, lodging, catering, equipment, horses and livestock, laborers and the rest of the support material that would be needed.

Dawson arrived to find that John Wayne was also planning a location shoot in Durango for his film *Cahill, U.S. Marshal*. Wayne was Durango's favorite son, because he used the town for so many of his Westerns.

Dawson says, "There were only so many facilities, hotels and caterers in town and Wayne owned the town. We were fighting with his production company on everything and not winning. My preproduction report was more optimistic than things really were."

At one point in that report, from August 1972, Dawson wrote: "We began our search for production offices, warehouses, wardrobe facilities, etc. TILT! Guess who'd tied up all of the desirable places? Yep, the dreaded one-lunged runaway patriot had struck again and hind tit ruled our menu at every door."

In scouting areas that would serve for various towns in the script, Dawson found one, El Arnal, thirty minutes south of Durango. He wrote in his report: "I think you'll like it, Sam—hopelessly impoverished, desolate, lifeless earth, bleak desperation, and a street just loaded with shit, flies, ants, scorpions, scrawny dogs and sharp rocks—all of the Peckinpah ingredients."

Dawson scouted four or five available hotels for cast and crew, and found that one refused to rent to movie people and one "I couldn't bring myself to ask any enemy to live in." Of the others, Dawson observed that one had a restaurant that supposedly ranked with the best in Durango "which doesn't mean shit because they held a 'ten best restaurants' contest there and nobody even made the semifinals."

For Coburn, *Pat Garrett* was his fourth film that year. He arrived in Durango from filming *The Last of Sheila* on the French Riviera.

"It was like going from the sublime to the asshole of the world," Coburn says. "I got off the plane from opulence into Durango. It was fall and winter and cold. We were living like aliens in the atmosphere. The food was terrible; it was an old cow town, with 4,000 years of cowshit swirling in the air. I'd walk around all the time with this slight fluish, feverish burning."

25

Shooting *Billy the Kid*

"SAM WAS A VERY BAD BOY ON FILM LOCATIONS," says his nephew David Peckinpah. "It was his kingdom. He was above the law of God and nature. When you're successful, you can get away with saying and doing things ordinary folks can't. On top of that, he was a jet-fueled maniacal alcoholic, who landed in a business that not only tolerated it but encouraged it."

"I think being on location was the only time he felt alive," Gordon Dawson says.

As production began in November 1972, Peckinpah had high expectations for *Pat Garrett and Billy the Kid*—expectations that quickly were dashed when he started getting the wrong answers from his producer, Gordon Carroll. Once things started to go wrong, Peckinpah immediately perceived the situation as an all-out assault on his artistic intentions and fought back—less by trying to make the movie his way than by trying to find ways to screw the studio, to prove he was the biggest skunk in this particular pissing match.

The initial problem seemed minor, but it quickly took on major proportions. Peckinpah had asked for a camera mechanic to be on staff at the location, a request MGM turned down to cut costs. Because all of the film was being sent to Los Angeles for processing and printing, there was often more than a week's lag between the time footage was shot and the time Peckinpah and his crew could look at the assembled dailies.

What no one realized until too late was that one of the Panavision lenses was slightly damaged. "It turned out the right side was .002 or .003 of an inch out of whack," says Newt Arnold, one of Peckinpah's assistant directors on the film. "Everything on the right-hand margin was out of focus. You never like to go back and reshoot, but it happens."

But it took a while to narrow down what the problem was. Until someone realized it was the lens itself, footage kept being shot and returning from Los

Angeles out of focus. Garth Craven, the sound editor on *Straw Dogs* whom Peckinpah had moved up to help edit *Pat Garrett,* says, "You're on location, you're not in a perfect projection booth, so you're never sure if it's the camera or the projector."

Peckinpah grew increasingly frustrated with the problem. One evening, in the middle of watching dailies in the hotel ballroom, Peckinpah stood, carried a chair in front of the screen, stood up on it and peed a giant "S" right in the middle of the screen.

Then he hissed, "I can at least expect some fucking focus," and stomped out of the room.

The lens was eventually located and repaired. But MGM, through Carroll, was against reshooting. Instead, Carroll tried to get Peckinpah to work around the spoiled footage and patch the film together without it. Peckinpah insisted on recapturing as much of it as he could, putting the production behind schedule and over budget.

"He demanded a lot of his crews," Coburn says. "He challenged them daily. If you were not interested in making movies more than in your personal life, he didn't want you around. He was like a mad general. For three hours a day, he was a genius."

"He would never know what to do until he walked on the set," Katy Haber says. "The environment would suddenly make him walk off to the side and come back with a stroke of genius. New people found it hard to work with him because they couldn't anticipate him. He would come up with fantastic ideas. If you weren't one step ahead of him, he'd go crazy."

You had to know how to handle him, however. The wrong response to one of Peckinpah's bad moods could end up costing a day's shooting—or your job. The best way to defuse it, most found, was with humor.

Newt Arnold recalls a day when they were supposed to film the bar scene in which Garrett shoots the character of Holly, played by Richard Bright. Peckinpah, who had been arguing with producer Carroll and other MGM officials, showed up on the set with a black cloud over his head.

He gathered cinematographer John Coquillon, Gordon Dawson and Arnold into a semicircle, then began to pace back and forth and announced, "I'm going to shut this down. I'm not going to shoot." He went on, giving an increasingly vitriolic speech against the studio.

Arnold, for some reason ("I don't know why," he says), had spent the production carrying a baby's rubber pacifier in his pocket. On an impulse, he pulled it out, popped it into his mouth and began sucking it vigorously. Peckinpah saw it and did a double take. Absolute silence. Then, slowly, Peckinpah's lip began to quiver and he burst out laughing. End of crisis.

"I call that the $50,000 pacifier," Arnold says. "That's what the day would have cost. You had to break through the anger and pull him back to the positive."

Peckinpah also responded to anyone who refused to back down in the face of his aggressive anger. One who wouldn't was art director Ted Haworth. "One day on the set, when I asked him to look at something he said, 'Fuck off,' " Haworth says. "I said, 'Wait a minute—' and he said, 'I'm talking to the producer. Now fuck off.' I said, 'I started in this business when I was twelve and I have never learned to fuck off. But if I want to learn, I'll come to you because you're the biggest fuck-off I know.' Sam burst out laughing and said, 'Do you know how many guys would have the guts to say that?' "

PECKINPAH RARELY TOLD ACTORS what to do, letting them find their moments themselves. He would also manipulate them in ways that would provoke offscreen responses that would alter their performances.

The major scene for R. G. Armstrong, who played Bible-thumping deputy Bob Ollinger, called for Ollinger to erupt in anger at Billy's smart-mouthed cracks. Peckinpah filmed a take, then yelled at Armstrong, "I don't believe a goddamned thing you're saying or doing."

"I was in a rage," Armstrong says. "I thought, 'How dare he!' I went back and sat down to do it again. I was so full of rage that when I went for Kris, I was ready to spit fire. I knocked him right on his ass. Sam said, 'God damn, print that.' He'd gotten the rage he wanted."

"I never saw him walk into a scene and take an actor aside and whisper in his ear," Bobby Visciglia says. "If necessary, I would transmit information from Sam to the actor. Sam would mutter, 'Why'd that fucking asshole do that? Tell the cocksucker to wait until the door is open before he moves.' I'd go into the scene and adjust the actor's gunbelt or something and say, 'Next time, try waiting until the door opens.' "

Midway through the production, an epidemic of influenza struck the company, devastating many of them—including Peckinpah.

Katy Haber, who had joined the company midway through the production (after being fired from *The Getaway*), says, "Everyone was so sick that they used to line up for B_{12} shots. One day, Sam was so sick, he forgot he shot a scene. The next day, he said, 'Let's shoot it,' and someone had to tell him he shot it already."

(Haber had learned to administer B_{12} shots on *Straw Dogs*. Peckinpah, who may have known about vitamin B_{12}'s ability to stave off anemia in alcoholics, took them regularly. "When I first started," Haber says, "he had an Indian doctor who came every day for five pounds a day. I said, 'I could do that,' and did.")

Peckinpah kept filming for as long as he could from behind a haze of illness, probably to the detriment of the film. L. Q. Jones, who had flown in to play the outlaw Black Harris for a couple of days, says, "When I got there, I heard this feeble sound and there was Sam. He looked so bad that the next day, if someone had said he'd died, it would not have been a surprise. But they couldn't get him away from the camera. That's admirable, but it's also kind of stupid. When you're that weak, you're not thinking straight."

Peckinpah finally took to his bed to try to recover. "I have been sick in bed with the worst case of flu I have ever had with a temperature of 104," he wrote to Jim Silke. "Don't let it get you and if it does, stay down and don't move till it's over."

He deputized Gordon Dawson and Newt Arnold to shoot for him, a decision that didn't sit well with Carroll.

"Gordy and I took over the first unit," Arnold says. "Sam insisted we do it. Carroll was not happy."

"We'd gather around Sam's bed and he'd tell us what to shoot," Dawson says. "Gordon Carroll would try to defy us to do it. The studio thought he had a director out of control, but he just didn't have Sam's respect."

In Carroll's defense, the producer was caught in the middle. On one side was Peckinpah, demanding to be supported and left alone to make his movie his way; on the other side were Aubrey and MGM, pressuring Carroll to rein the director in, to cut corners wherever possible, even if it meant treating the director like a hired hand.

"Gordon was in an unfortunate position," Wurlitzer says. "Gordon was the one who had gotten the script and worked with me. He had contributed considerably. I think he had a totally traumatic time."

Newt Arnold says, "I found Gordon Carroll to be responsible and extremely intelligent and very dedicated to shepherding the picture through to success. But the two men were just in conflict. Gordon had a difficult bag to carry. He was representing the upper echelons of the studio and was beholden to them to follow through on certain things they were demanding. Sam had a conflict with the upper echelon that automatically transferred to Gordon."

A good producer can act as a buffer between his director and the studio. He runs interference, soothes jangled nerves and absorbs the shocks so that the director can concentrate on the myriad details that he confronts every day he shoots.

"Lew Rachmil and Melnick and the group at MGM were on Sam like stink on shit," Dawson says. "But Gordon Carroll did not protect him. If anything, he joined in the attacks."

"Sam couldn't stand Gordon Carroll," Katy Haber says. "You couldn't even mention his name."

The more Carroll tried to control him, the more Peckinpah went in the opposite direction. Stuntman Gary Combs says, "We just got further and further behind. Nobody was going to tell Sam what to do. The minute he fell behind, the producer would want him to speed up. Before long, there was a war going on. The more they would push, the slower Sam would go."

MGM wanted blood and guts, hell and high water on horseback. Peck-inpah, however, wanted to do something different. He'd already done *The Wild Bunch;* he didn't want to repeat himself. Instead, he was angling for a more studied effect, as purposefully slow as the Sergio Leone spaghetti Westerns but less self-conscious, mythic and poetic without being obvious about it.

"It was a huge switch in Sam," Jim Silke says. "This is a lyric poem. It's not like most of his film work. It works on an entirely different basis. He had a strong vision of the West and he had a vision of change."

That vision extended as far as literally changing the ending. "At one point," James Coburn says, "he said, 'You know, let's not kill Billy. Let's create a new myth.'" That notion didn't get far with the MGM brass.

Nothing seemed to. Every idea Peckinpah broached was shot down or discouraged—but he did it anyway. The rumor swept the company that Aubrey himself was about to descend on Durango and personally terminate Peckinpah, but it didn't happen.

The conflict goaded Peckinpah to push farther and farther, to see how far he could provoke the authorities controlling the picture.

"On the last night of *Pat Garrett,*" recalls Walter Kelley, who had a small role in the film, "he made me sit down and said, 'Walter, we'll never forget this.' He liked creating his own life as a general does in a war."

"They gave him an enormous amount of rope and he kept pushing," Rudy Wurlitzer says. "There was always a great deal of cunning and shrewd-ness in Sam's rage at authority. I began to realize that, in some demented way, he was in control. He was relatively smart about people and how far you could push them and when to stop. His nature was to be confronta-tional but he was not compulsive about it."

Wurlitzer recalled his experiences on *Pat Garrett* a decade later in his 1984 novel, *Slow Fade.* He says the character of self-destructive film director Wesley Hardin (named, perhaps, after the outlaw John Wesley Hardin) was inspired by Peckinpah, though not strictly based on him.

Still, in one of the book's early scenes, it's hard not to see an exchange between Hardin and his producer as an echo of similar encounters between Peckinpah and Gordon Carroll:

> "You're five million over, Wesley," the producer said evenly. "No one cares about excuses when you're five million over."
>
> "Is that why you're flying off to L.A. tonight to sabotage me?"
>
> "I'm keeping the studio off your back, which necessarily involves not telling you everything."
>
> "That must be why you didn't tell me about the memo you sent them yesterday on my age, drinking habits, and all-around perversity."

"You are an obnoxious man," the producer yelled suddenly. "An unholy cocksucker of the first rank."

The producer's impulsive attack was unexpected and left Wesley's lower lip quivering with rage. As he reached for the tequila bottle, he saw Walker watching him from the rear of the trailer.

"Betrayal, cowardice, deceit," he muttered, breaking the bottle over the edge of the kitchenette's Formica counter and advancing toward the producer, who quickly retreated out the door.

IN PART, DRINKING PROVOKED Peckinpah to test the limits. It certainly inspired some harebrained ideas. In one bit of drunken inspiration, he decided that, in order to get the desired effect of a horse being shot out from under a rider, he would literally kill the horse, actually shoot him, while a stuntman sat on its back.

Stuntman Gary Combs was scheduled to be on this particular horse. Concerned, he went to stunt coordinator Whitey Hughes.

"This won't work," he said to Hughes. "First of all, what if he misses? And second, he's going to kill this horse."

Hughes, however, was intimidated by Peckinpah and not about to contradict him. So Combs waited until the day before the scene was to be shot. Then he went out to the place Peckinpah would go nightly to watch the sun go down and drink a bottle of wine.

"I hear you're going to shoot a horse," Combs said.

"That's right," Peckinpah replied.

"You ever see a horse get shot in the eye?" Combs asked.

"No. What happens?" Peckinpah asked.

"He drops to his knees and that's it," Combs said. Now that he had Peckinpah's attention, he explained how he could rig a horse with hobble cables on a sheet of plywood and topple the animal for a more spectacular fall, without shooting it. Fortunately for Combs, Peckinpah agreed to try it —and it worked.

"I could just see him putting a bullet through the head of that horse and having it come out its neck and go through me," Combs says. "If somebody hadn't had the guts to stand up to him, he would have gone through with it."

Combs apparently caught Peckinpah at a more sober moment. Juan Jose Palacios, his former brother-in-law and driver, says, "He would have a cooler in the back of the car. Emilio Fernandez used to say that, by the time Sam got to the set, nobody knew how drunk or not he was."

Rumors were rife in Hollywood that *Pat Garrett* was a runaway production, helmed by a hopeless drunk who was out of control. Katy Haber says, "At one point, after it was reported in the trades that he was having drinking problems on the set, he was brought on the set with booze being given to him intravenously. He was on a stretcher and I was dressed as a nurse. Then we took a picture of it and put it in an ad in *Variety*."

Most of the drinking, however, was not that jovial. "On *Straw Dogs*, he had started to drink a lot," says editor Roger Spottiswoode. "On *Junior Bonner*, he was really drinking. On [*The Getaway*], he was a drunk. By the time of *Pat Garrett*, he was so steeped in alcohol that he never even saw the whole thing at a preview."

Blaming all of his bad behavior on his alcoholism would be too simplistic. More than one person has suggested that before he had even completed the film, Peckinpah was looking for an excuse, in case it wasn't as good as he hoped.

"When he was not at his best, a lot of Sam's fears overwhelmed him," says critic Paul Seydor. "On *Pat Garrett*, Sam was extremely destructive. He was afraid of the film. There was so much riding on him that he arranged a safety valve. He would arrange his excuses and, eventually, something happened."

Time magazine critic Jay Cocks, who saw an early screening of Peckinpah's rough cut, says, "It dawned on me after a while that Sam had collaborated in his own destruction. I think he needed a heavy to blame if he fucked up. He wanted to be able to pass it along. I feel it in my soul that he needed to establish a mechanism so he could say, 'Those fuckers did it.' He'd never say, 'I fucked up.' "

He had already started to put the pieces into place by the time Roger Spottiswoode arrived to begin cutting the film.

"I remember him calling me in England and telling me to come to Mexico," Spottiswoode says. "I met him on the first day of shooting and said, 'I like the script.' He said, 'Don't worry about it. I'm just doing this one for the money. It's the next one that counts.' But this was the one he had talked about on the previous one. Now he didn't give a shit. To arrive in Durango and have him say he was just doing this one for the money, that it was *Bring Me the Head of Alfredo Garcia* that counted—he was on the slide at that point."

Adding to the confusion was the on-again, off-again presence of his ex-wife, Begonia Palacios, whom he still saw on an annual basis. She came to Durango and stayed a few days. Inevitably, however, Peckinpah would start drinking after a day on the set, then turn abusive. They'd have screaming fights and, usually, Begonia would flee the scene.

"One of the biggest fights was in Durango," Juan Jose Palacios says. "My mother called, crying, and said, 'Do you know what your sister did? She had a fight with Sam, ran out, got in a taxi and came all the way back to Mexico City.' "

Quite a taxi ride: about 500 miles as the crow flies.

26

The Death of *Pat Garrett and Billy the Kid*

DESPITE THE SETBACKS, WHEN PECKINPAH FINISHED shooting—twenty-one days over schedule in March 1973—he felt good about what he had captured on film. He was convinced he had a movie that would vindicate all of the problems that had been attributed to him, whether for drinking, stubbornness or whatever. He wrote to Pauline Kael in February 1973: "It is a strange story which I thought I could waltz through but I became involved in it and it became a lot tougher than I expected. Strange cast with Bob Dylan and Kris Kristofferson in the same picture. Won't know how it will look for a couple of months until I have a rough cut. But it smells good. If it doesn't come out, it will all be my fault, because I had some of the world's greatest character actors come out. Quite an experience going from cameo to cameo at the same time directing Bob Dylan in his first picture and Kris in his second."

But things got dicey almost as soon as the cameras stopped rolling. Peckinpah's plan was to cut the film at Churubusco Studios in Mexico City. Shortly after shooting was finished, Garth Craven and Roger Spottiswoode, who had been editing during production, assembled a long rough cut, which Peckinpah screened in March for Daniel Melnick, who had flown down to see it.

Then MGM told Peckinpah that the studio had already booked the film to open its first-run engagement on Memorial Day. Peckinpah and his editors would have to come back to Hollywood to finish cutting the film. That gave him less than two months to fine-tune what he envisioned as an epic.

"It was completely chaotic," Roger Spottiswoode says. "We were in Mexico for six weeks and finished a cut to show the studio. We flew back to L.A. to run it for the studio. It was a very charged situation."

When Peckinpah resumed editing in Hollywood, the American film editors' union put its foot down and barred Spottiswoode and Craven, who were both British, from physically editing film in the United States.

"The studio wanted us to work in secret behind locked doors, but neither Roger nor I thought that was a wise plan," Craven says.

So Peckinpah brought in Robert Wolfe and a handful of assistants. "We were running from cutting room to cutting room, looking over people's shoulders and saying, 'Cut there,' " Craven says. "It all heightened the general sense of mayhem." In the end, six editors were credited.

Still, the studio thought the film was too long and didn't have enough action. Peckinpah began to bridle at the suggestions, unaware that he was about to walk into a buzzsaw named James Aubrey.

Aubrey had his own pressures. The MGM Grand Hotel, which was being built in Las Vegas, was behind schedule and over budget. The studio had cash-flow problems and needed product in the theaters quickly to bring in money. So Aubrey was more than willing to throw *Pat Garrett* at the public, ready or not.

"It was like Aubrey was consciously trying to destroy the studio, to make films with big names, usurp power and cut their balls off," says James Coburn.

Aubrey was a voracious studio executive, willing to sacrifice anyone's work at the twin altars of the bottom line and his own ego. And Peckinpah was overly cocky about just how much clout he had in this bargain. He overestimated the importance that would be given to artistry and integrity in a Hollywood business decision.

"The Wurlitzer script was beautiful—but I kept saying to Sam, 'Why do it here? Aubrey is going to fuck it up,' " Coburn says. "Sam said, 'Don't worry. I bought one share of MGM stock. I'll sue as a stockholder.' That's so naive. He thought he could hold him off with Tinkertoys."

Garth Craven says, "Sam's relationship with the producer and the studio was always a mystery; it was very acrimonious. I'm not sure whether he had no interest in dealing with them or whether he totally misread them. He was shooting brilliant footage and it seems his head-on tactics weren't going to protect his back at all. Maybe nothing would have."

Melnick tried to intervene, to use his history with Peckinpah to persuade the director of the wisdom of doing it Aubrey's way.

"They were clearly headed for a mortal shoot-out," Melnick says. "I tried to head it off as long as possible."

"Danny probably told Aubrey he could handle Sam because they were buddies," Katy Haber says. "He tried to impose MGM's judgment on Sam. Danny wanted more action and less poetry."

That was the MGM company line. It was repeated over and over again in notes about editing from Aubrey that were sent to the editors. "Aubrey issued edicts that boggled the mind," Garth Craven says. "As far as Aubrey was concerned, if it was not plot or action, out it went. There was a growing animosity between Sam and the studio. Melnick came to represent the studio, so he was on the wrong side of the fence."

The longer the process went on, the more recalcitrant Peckinpah became. At studio screenings, Craven says, "Sam would say, 'If so-and-so is in the room, I'm not going to be in the room.' So Sam stalks out and sits in the hall. Everybody is embarrassed. No work gets done because egos are clashing."

Peckinpah and his editors got the film down to two hours and twenty minutes, a length that was still too long for the studio.

"Sam pushed Aubrey until he had to take it away," Rudy Wurlitzer says. "At the end, Sam was drinking a lot, making demands that the film be a lot longer than it could be."

Roger Spottiswoode says that the film was bloated and incohesive at that length. "There was no narrative thrust," he says. "It didn't work at 2:20. We ran it for the executives and the film didn't work." Peckinpah, however, had stormed out of the screening because of the presence of people he perceived as enemies. Though he refused to sit through the film, he also refused to listen to the criticisms of executives who had.

"The studio was incensed," Spottiswoode says. "He was never at any of the screenings all the way through. He would only speak to these people on the phone. Part of him completely believed in the battle. He could only see the fight. They were attacking his film and he was defensive. The fact that the film needed work was not something he was coming to grips with. We tried to get him to improve it but he never ran enough of it to realize that it didn't play."

Jay Cocks was in Los Angeles with Martin Scorsese and arranged for the two of them to visit Peckinpah on the MGM lot, where he was cutting *Pat Garrett*. They showed up at 11 A.M. on a Sunday morning to find Peckinpah behind his desk, slumped down so low that "his chin was four inches off the desk," Cocks says. "There was a long row of syringe bottles and a huge tumbler of ice water."

As they talked, Peckinpah drank five or six large tumblers of the "ice water" and seemed to revive; as Cocks later discovered, the tumblers were full of vodka. The more animated Peckinpah became, the more he railed against the studio and the producer. Finally, he took them over to the screening room and showed them the film. Halfway through, Pauline Kael walked in and watched with them.

"We saw a rough cut and it was brilliant," Scorsese says. "For me, it was as important as *The Wild Bunch*."

Kael wasn't as overwhelmed by what she saw that day. "It was unfinished, very rough," she says. "It didn't have the kind of editing excitement. It was still pretty literal-minded. There were long scenes that sort of drifted around."

They wound up back in Peckinpah's office—Cocks, Kael, Scorsese, Peckinpah—with Carroll, who had the bad luck to show up at that point.

"Sam started railing at the guy in front of us," Cocks says. "Obviously, what Sam was doing was using me, Marty and Pauline as a crowbar against Gordon Carroll. To rank him out in front of the critics from *Time* and the *New Yorker* was really balls-to-the-wall tough shit. Carroll withstood it better than I would have. That pissed Sam off because he couldn't get a rise out of him."

When Peckinpah began to talk about taking off and leaving the film behind to make a personal appearance at a college on the East Coast, Kael lit into him. "She said, 'You dumb bastard, you stay here and fight and get this movie finished,'" Cocks says. "Sam sat back and sipped ice water. He really liked to mix it up with her."

Adds Scorsese, "I think she was tougher than he was."

"*Pat Garrett* needed editing," Kael says. "It was going to be cut by the studio. He was trying to spite the producer. I thought it was important for him to stay and finish editing the film. They needed him to tell them what to do. But he was abandoning his movie when it needed him. He had worked like a fiend on that movie. Now he was doing himself in over what others were doing to him. It was a crazy, sadomasochistic thing."

Whether because of Kael or because of simple common sense, Peckinpah stayed. But when it came to the preview of his cut mandated by his contract, Peckinpah still refused to take any studio counsel.

"The film still didn't work; the audience was restless," Spottiswoode says. "The studio asked what he was going to do. He said, 'I'm going to cut twelve seconds.' They later learned he hadn't even shown up at the screening. He was asking to be attacked. He incited them."

Aubrey finally took the step everyone had warned Peckinpah he would take. Without telling Peckinpah, Aubrey set up a team of his own editors elsewhere at MGM and began using duplicates of Peckinpah's footage to recut the film his own way.

John Bryson was living in Malibu at the time and got a call from Peckinpah, summoning him to Culver City to his office at MGM. Peckinpah took him outside because he was convinced that MGM had his office bugged.

"I've just learned," he told Bryson, "that, even as I'm cutting this picture, Aubrey has set up a cutting room in another building and they are cutting my film. I want you to get on a plane to Mexico City. Get El Indio [Emilio Fernandez]. Get a couple of *pistoleros*. I'll fly them up here first class and they'll kill Jim Aubrey."

Pistoleros, Bryson points out, are hired guns; in Mexico, he says, "it's an honorable profession. They don't come back to blackmail you or anything. And you can hire them to shoot someone."

Aghast, Bryson refused. "I can't do that, Sam," he said. "That makes me an accessory if they kill the head of MGM."

Peckinpah gave him a cold stare and said, "I thought you were a friend of mine."

Today, Bryson says, "I don't know to this day if Aubrey knows how close he came to being killed."

"They were not nice people," Spottiswoode says of MGM, "and Sam was a drunk. Plus he was a large-scale employer. He gave people lots of jobs. Those people didn't dare say, 'Sam, you're an alcoholic. You've got to get straightened out.' For about a year there, no one was willing to say, 'We're dealing with a drunk. Let's ignore him.' It became a battle between him and a voracious studio. He was a drunk and the studio were a bunch of mean bastards, even though they were right about some things. There's no clear-cut answer. The studio was wrong. Sam was wrong. There was no easy moral."

Was there anything Peckinpah could have done to save his film at that point?

Given the corner he had painted himself and the studio into, probably not. In trying to take the moral and artistic high ground without ever acknowledging that anyone else might have a point, he had alienated everyone —ally and enemy alike—within MGM. Justified or not, Aubrey could make a convincing case that he was doing what had to be done in the best interest of the studio and the film.

So he took the film away from Peckinpah and slashed it, cutting it down to a collection of action scenes strung together with minimal texture or connective tissue. "They cut it according to what they thought the audience would take rather than what the artist wanted to give the audience," James Coburn says.

"It was wide and big and breathless, at least what Sam had in mind," Bob Dylan said, "but it didn't come out that way. I saw it in a movie house one cut away from his and I could tell it had been chopped to pieces. Someone other than Sam had taken a knife to some valuable scenes that were in it."

What started out to be a character-driven Western that explored the nature of myth and its effect on the men who were mythologized was turned into a substandard oater full of shoot-outs and blood squibs, a jangly, disconnected mess.

There are disputes over whether Peckinpah ever truly completed the film, given his intransigent stance toward the studio. In the late 1980s, what was billed as "the restored director's cut" was shown on the Z Channel in Los Angeles and, in 1989, at the Film Forum in New York. It was subsequently released on videocassette, at a running length of 123 minutes.

Those versions restored some missing scenes (including the framing scenes set in 1908, at the moment of Garrett's killing) and gave the film a more fluid feeling than the choppy, stunted MGM version (also available on videocassette). But a couple of scenes are still missing. One is an encounter between Garrett and his wife; the other is the full scene between Garrett and Chisum (played by Barry Sullivan). A portion of it is included, but lacks their discussion of money Chisum has loaned Garrett.

That 123-minute version is probably close to what Peckinpah had in mind. That's still seventeen minutes shy of the 140-minute version Roger Spottiswoode talks about. But it plays more smoothly than the 106-minute version MGM released Memorial Day weekend in 1973. The math is right; in an appearance at the Seattle Film Society in July 1978, Peckinpah said, "They took seventeen minutes out and destroyed the film." Which would square with the 106-minute version that was released.

There are differences of opinion, however, on the quality of Peckinpah's original cut because so few people saw it before the studio took its cleaver to the footage.

Roger Spottiswoode says emphatically that Peckinpah's version meandered and wandered. So does Rudy Wurlitzer.

"The so-called Sam's version had some things that were not as good as the Aubrey version," he says. "I think Sam's was too long, sentimental at the end, with scenes of gratuitous violence."

Garth Craven, who was in on the editing process all the way through, says, "Sam's cut was far better than anything the studio did. It was a far more interesting film than the one that was released. They never got their version. They got a watered-down version of Sam's version."

Peckinpah tried to take rearguard actions to save the film. He filed a $2.5-million suit against MGM charging breach of contract over final cut. And he sued MGM when it was announced that MGM had sold the TV rights to CBS, without Peckinpah's consent and without providing for his input in editing it for television.

"I was trying to beat 'em down and I failed," he said. "I sued them with everything I had, which was very little, and it dribbled away and lost. Failed."

Pat Garrett and Billy the Kid was released on schedule, with Peckinpah's name but without his input or approval. Though there were still traces of Peckinpah's lyrical approach, the film was disjointed and insubstantial, eviscerated in order to get it out in a hurry—and at a length that would allow one more showing a day.

"[Aubrey's] particular evil nature, I mean, the thing that he got his kicks off of [was] destroying films that other people made," James Coburn said. "You can't imagine, you really can't imagine the kind of ability that this cocksucker has. For a man to deliberately destroy a film . . . What happens is that we all take the blame for it."

But they didn't all—only Peckinpah. Unfortunately, though Peckinpah tried to get the word out that his film had been manhandled, such complaints usually are not given much credence. Everyone is willing to take credit for a hit but no one wants to take the blame for a flop.

Pat Garrett barely lasted in theaters through July 4. Critics were not kind. Stanley Kauffman wrote in the *New Republic:* "This stale saga is dull, slow, and sillily portentous. What a lot of loutish, cretinous, degenerate layabouts they all are, supposed to be epic because once in a while or oftener, they kill one another."

From *Newsweek's* Paul D. Zimmerman: "The question remains: Did the studio ruin an interesting film, or did it merely try to salvage a hopelessly muddled one? Whatever the case, the movie is a misshapen mess. This is Peckinpah country without the salvation of style—without the consistently tight, brilliant editing and compelling crescendos of tension that made a film as atavistic as *Straw Dogs* work. And, shorn of style, Peckinpah's adolescent machismo stands nakedly ridiculous."

But Jay Cocks wrote in *Time:* "Peckinpah's original version has been altered, shortened and generally abused by MGM. The changes ordered by the studio are mostly stupid but not disastrous. Even in the maimed state in which it has been released, *Pat Garrett and Billy the Kid* is the richest, most exciting American film so far this year. The film has a parched, eerie splendor that no one could really destroy."

Parched splendor, however, was hardly what audiences were seeking in that year of *The Exorcist, The Sting* and *American Graffiti*. The damage was done. *Pat Garrett and Billy the Kid* had been shot in the back—by MGM and, in a sense, by Peckinpah himself.

As L. Q. Jones says, "Sam screwed up a monumental opportunity just to be Sam on that one."

When Peckinpah later filed a suit over the fact that MGM reissued the film as *Sam Peckinpah's Pat Garrett and Billy the Kid,* one of MGM's contentions in court was that if there was any damage to his reputation, it had already been done.

The experience left him bitter and sad. His nephew David says, "I sat with him in his office after the screening and he was beaten. It was a real creative gutting. He cared a lot. *Pat Garrett* broke his heart. He started dying ten years before he died. When he lost that passion, everything else overtook him."

On the other hand, David says, "He made so few pictures that turned a profit that he wore people out. If he had made three *Getaway*s in a row, he could have strung producers up in effigy on the lot. But an old dog that can't do new tricks can't bite the hand of the trainer. It's a cruel business.

No matter how much you love the business, it doesn't love you back. It'll keep you young up to a point—and then it kills you."

Even as the film was suffering its abbreviated commercial fate, Peckinpah had already made a deal to go back to Mexico to make his next movie. But the fallout from *Pat Garrett* continued, in unexpected ways.

One was a memo Peckinpah received in September 1973 that began:

"TO: Sam Peckinpah

"FROM: James Aubrey

"SUBJECT: Future projects for you

"Possibly you've heard that MGM was going out of the motion picture business and will concentrate on TV films. However, we have not announced that we are also going into production shortly of the old-fashioned serials; in a period where the public is very taken with nostalgia, we feel this could be a real breakthrough in commercial entertainment.

"For one of the series, we are planning, in fifteen weekly parts, *Pat Garrett and Billy the Kid.* In view of your closeness to this subject and the fact that we'll be using a great many of your outtakes on it, we wonder if you would be interested in directing this project.

"If this does not interest you, we're also planning one based in Biblical times on a transvestite chariot race, to be titled *Ben Her.* We feel you would be a natural for this."

The memo was written by John Bryson, shortly after Aubrey had announced that MGM was getting out of film distribution and cutting its film production to fewer than six a year. With the drain on MGM reserves by the still-unfinished MGM Grand Hotel in Las Vegas and the poor performance of MGM films in 1973—including *Pat Garrett and Billy the Kid* and *The Man Who Loved Cat Dancing*—Aubrey was himself given the axe in November 1973.

ON JANUARY 13, 1974, an article in the *New York Times* by T. F. D. Klein on the mistreatment of animals in films included this paragraph: "Though John Wayne has always abided by [American Humane Association] guidelines, using only trained horses in his films, directors like Sam Peckinpah prefer to take the easy way out. Peckinpah's most recent, *Pat Garrett and Billy the Kid,* got an unacceptable rating for both the trip-wiring of horses and casual use of chickens, buried in the ground up to their necks for target practice."

The article triggered a flood of mail to Peckinpah's office, including this one dated February 5, 1974, signed by an entire class of students from a Guilford, Connecticut, high school: "We, the undersigned, protest the inhumane treatment of animals in *Pat Garrett and Billy the Kid, The Ballad of Cable Hogue, The Wild Bunch*. We intend to boycott those movies and request that you cease to kill and cause unnecessary suffering to animals for art's sake in movies. We do not believe that shooting chickens, using trip wire, shooting a Gila monster or setting a scorpion on fire is justifiable."

It took the letter a while to reach Peckinpah, who was spending time in Mexico. Never one to resist an argument, Peckinpah fired back a letter on May 7, 1974: "It might interest you to know my father was the founding president of the SPCA in Fresno, California.

"Those chickens were taken out of a slaughterhouse assembly line and given three extra days of life on the finest feed and water and killed instantly without pain. They were then given to the local villagers, who ate them with mucho gusto and appreciation.

"Millions of sheep, cattle and chickens are driven into line to die daily at slaughterhouses the world over. Several branches of science have proven that plants have feelings of pain and fear. Imagine if you will the chilling horror of trillions of stalks of greens, as monstrous machines bear down, cutting, shredding, mutilating them. Oh, how they must suffer as their seeds are ground into flour and baked into bread to fill the bloated bellies of starving children.

"Think of the billions of poor carrots, turnips, onions ripped from the earth, their delicate roots severed, shivering in silent pain to be fried, boiled, chewed, swallowed and defecated, all in the stupid name of human survival. Think of it.

"Every single day hundreds of female lions stalk beautiful zebra, graceful impala, even the stately giraffe, hunting them down and hurling them against the ground to be torn apart by all members of the pride under the guise of animal survival. Think of it.

"Finally, I'd wager I have adopted more stray dogs, cats and kids than you've ever seen.

"P.S. What were your efforts against defoliation in Vietnam? The fire bombs that scarred children on both sides of the stupid goddamn tragedy and stupid war!? As far as I'm concerned, your own self-pitying form of Watergate that permits the slaughter of human beings while crying wolf for things that don't exist is a great waste. I know where I'm at, do you?

"P.S.S. The iguana in *The Ballad of Cable Hogue* died of an overgluttony of eggs and milk, thus his body was used instead of the prepared mock-up."

THE EXPERIENCE ON *PAT GARRETT AND BILLY THE KID* changed Peckinpah. It soured him completely on producers and studios—which put him in a bind because he relied on them for financing and support.

His reaction was to try to find a way to bite the hand, even while he coaxed it into feeding him, to use the people he hated without hating himself. But it didn't work; Peckinpah grew increasingly bitter, vindictive, and self-destructive. His drinking increased, even as his emotional investment in his projects plummeted.

Making a movie became a game. The object was to see how far he could push, how deeply he could gouge and how audaciously he could screw the people who were giving him the chance to pursue his art. The winner—and the loser—of that game inevitably was Sam Peckinpah.

Part Seven

1973-1977

I hope you've enjoyed the films. I trust they'll get better but if they don't, kiss my ass.
> —SAM PECKINPAH AT THE SAN FRANCISCO FILM FESTIVAL,
> QUOTED IN THE *College of Marin Times,*
> October 27, 1974

Thank you for being here to see my films. I trust they will get better. And if they don't, kick my ass.

> —SAM PECKINPAH AT THE SAN FRANCISCO FILM FESTIVAL,
> QUOTED IN THE *San Francisco Chronicle,*
> October 30, 1974

27

"Heads" and Tales

TWO NOTIONS HAD INTRIGUED FRANK KOWALSKI for several years as possible fodder for a screenplay. One was bartenders, whom Kowalski thought "lead the most colorful lives going. They live fast and get broads and, the next thing they know, they're forty-five or fifty and it's all over. It's a strange life cycle, like a moth."

The other was the case of Caryl Chessman, the convicted rapist who, after winning numerous appeals over twelve years, was finally executed in California in 1960. "He used to rape girls at gunpoint and then take off," Kowalski says. "That idea intrigued me and Sam: What if someone was raping your girl and you had to stand and watch?"

Well, you'd take it as long as you could. Then, in the Peckinpah universe, you would somehow wind up with a gun in your hand, plugging the rapist full of slugs, while your girl watched.

Thus was *Bring Me the Head of Alfredo Garcia* spawned.

Peckinpah had been developing *Alfredo Garcia* with Kowalski, Gordon Dawson and Walter Kelley for almost three years, since preproduction on *Straw Dogs*. Kowalski had written an outline, which Peckinpah gave to Kelley to work on. It passed to Dawson, who wrote the script. Peckinpah subsequently rewrote it, sharing credit for the screenplay with Dawson and for the story with Kowalski.

"When you wrote for Sam, you wrote a first draft," Jim Silke says. "Nobody could finish for Sam. He was not a classicist. He was trying to find a way that would not occur to anyone and shoot it that way."

After the debacle with *Pat Garrett*, Peckinpah wanted to get the hell out of Hollywood in a hurry. Not just that—he wanted to rub the noses of everyone who had ever double-crossed him in something as extreme as possible.

He thought he had the perfect vehicle in the script for *Alfredo Garcia*, the story of a down-and-out American lounge entertainer in Mexico. The story was also Peckinpah's way of thumbing his nose at America, a reflection of Peckinpah's disgust with the course his country was taking.

"I'm a Mexican resident," he said. "When Nixon was elected president, I said, 'I'm getting the fuck out, this cocksucker is going to ruin this country.' I campaigned against Nixon every time he ran for office in California. When they reelected him president, I thought, 'Those idiots, they'll never learn.' And I left."

Peckinpah set up a deal at United Artists for himself to direct and produce, with Dawson as associate producer and Martin Baum and Helmut Dantine as executive producers. Baum, the former head of ABC Pictures (which had collapsed at that point), had become an independent producer. He was brought into the project by David Picker, then the head of United Artists, because he had worked with Peckinpah in the past.

Baum says, "I read it and said, 'I'm a nice Jewish boy from the Bronx. Why would you send me to Mexico to do a picture about a man who carries a severed head in a potato sack the length and breadth of Mexico?' " But Picker convinced him.

Though Peckinpah was glad to be working in Mexico again, those who knew him closely felt his heart wasn't in the project. "He wasn't his former self," Dawson says, "Not as forceful or natural. I don't think he believed in the picture. He was a very exciting man when he had that belief. But whatever that passion you've got to have was, that passion had been snuffed out."

To play Bennie, the down-and-out American at the film's center, Peckinpah cast about among friends and acquaintances. He discussed it with James Coburn, while they were still filming *Pat Garrett*.

"I said, 'I hate this,' " Coburn says. "I said, 'Why would you want to do this?' "

Peter Falk also had discussions with him. "I can see Sam in the kitchen at my house, explaining the opening shot of the film," Falk says. "He tells me he sees this guy going around in a car. And the camera comes up and slowly reveals that there's a head sitting in the passenger seat. As an afterthought, he said, 'Maybe I'll have some flies buzzing around it.' It got your attention." Falk says he probably would have done the picture, but it quickly became apparent that Peckinpah's schedule would conflict with the season's shooting for "Columbo," Falk's hit TV series.

Peckinpah finally settled on Warren Oates, who had worked with him on *Ride the High Country*, *Major Dundee* and *The Wild Bunch*.

"I think he made *Alfredo Garcia* for Warren just because Warren had been involved in *Cable Hogue* and had wanted to play Cable," Gill Dennis says. "Sam felt he had to do something for Warren."

The idea of casting an archetypal character actor such as Oates in a leading role struck some as quixotic and quirky, others as misjudgment.

Pauline Kael says, "He was very sweet to Warren Oates—he tried to make him a star. Warren was a great character actor but I don't think he had it in him to be a star. If you were in a room with Warren and Sam, you knew who the star was. I think Warren was imitating Sam in the picture because that was his idea of how to be a star."

Dawson kiddingly conceived the role as a send-up of the director himself. "Tongue-in-cheek Peckinpah," Dawson says. "Then Sam and Warren went ahead and made it that way. It was all camp Sam in a way. Nobody sets out to make that. I can't believe we made that movie."

For other roles, he convinced Helmut Dantine, a star of the silent era, to play the majordomo to El Jefe, the Mexican who initiates the contract on Alfredo Garcia. Kris Kristofferson and Donnie Fritts, a member of his band, were on hand to play two bikers who waylay Benny and his girlfriend. Peckinpah signed his friend Mort Sahl to play Quill, the head thug who goes hunting for Alfredo and, eventually, connects with Benny.

Oates became ill, postponing production a couple of weeks. Sahl had already booked a series of sixty-five college concert dates. "The colleges threatened a class-action suit if I didn't perform," Sahl says. "I couldn't postpone it so I had to drop out."

According to one report, Peckinpah and Sahl had a shouting match on the phone about his decision to quit. Peckinpah supposedly sent Sahl a bouquet of yellow roses a couple of weeks later to make up; Sahl allegedly responded with a black wreath bearing the message "Drop dead," an act he today denies. To replace him, Peckinpah cast Gig Young as Quill, with Robert Webber as his assistant.

Though the role of El Jefe was a small part, it was a crucial one. Once again, Peckinpah turned to his old friend Emilio Fernandez, the noted Mexican director who had won the Cannes Film Festival grand prize in 1946 for his film of John Steinbeck's *The Pearl*. In addition, Fernandez, known as El Indio, was to direct the film's second unit.

Fernandez was the perfect Peckinpah co-conspirator. Rumored to have killed a number of men in duels, he was Mexico's most famous director and one of its most notorious characters. As hard-drinking as Peckinpah, he was also an inveterate womanizer and brawler, married a number of times, with connections to everyone from the Mexican government to the Mexican underworld (which, not infrequently, were one and the same). In short, a character not that far removed from El Jefe or Mapache, the character he had played in *The Wild Bunch*.

"Fernandez was a wild man," says Alex Phillips, Jr., the Mexican cinematographer on *Alfredo Garcia*. "With women, he was extremely jealous. He liked girls and parties. He was like a playboy who was always broke but never saw that he had no money. He always carried a gun."

Katy Haber says, "Emilio was a poet, a writer, a director, a womanizer, a drinker and a murderer. He was Hemingway, Huston and Peckinpah wrapped into one and turned into a Mexican."

"Emilio would take out his .38s and start blowing the art off the walls," Dawson says. "He'd pistol-whip people just to watch them bleed. Sam was not an evil man like this guy was."

Peckinpah originally thought he would give the female lead to actress Aurora Clavel, with whom he was having an affair. But he tested a half-dozen actresses, including Mexican film star Isela Vega.

"The part was very small in the script," Vega says. "I wanted to work with this man, but I was disappointed because the character didn't really exist. At the audition, when he asked if I liked the part, I said, 'What part?' As soon as I said it, I went, Uh-oh, I shouldn't have said that, there goes another part. But he laughed. Later, I had a screen test with Warren. Alex Phillips, who had seen the other girls, said, 'I think you'll get the part.'" She did.

Aside from Dawson, editor Garth Craven, property master Alf Pegley, an Englishman who had worked on *Straw Dogs,* and producers Dantine and Baum, Peckinpah used an all-Mexican crew. There was one other American on the crew: his daughter Sharon, who signed on as production assistant and wound up credited as dialogue director.

"I was never going to talk to him again after *The Getaway,*" she says. "Then something would come up and I'd think, 'I need to get to know him better and maybe I was wrong.' It was pure nepotism, the perfect way to learn the film industry. He was an easy in. But it wasn't easy once you got there, let me tell you. Still, I managed to get through *Alfredo Garcia.*"

Production started in September 1973 in Mexico City. Within a week, there was another American on the crew, a Texas college student named Dan York. A sophomore at the University of Texas film school, York had wangled an introduction to Gordon Dawson during production of *The Getaway.* He invited himself down to Mexico City as an observer; because he could speak fluent Spanish, he was hired on as a production assistant.

"I worked a month before Sam paid me any mind," says York, now a producer. "He walked over, wearing mirrored sunglasses, and said, 'Learning anything?' I said, 'Two things. Your equipment isn't worth shit and you can't trust anyone.' He laughed and said, 'You've learned a lot.'"

BRING ME THE HEAD OF ALFREDO GARCIA centers on Bennie, an American who lives in Mexico and supports himself by playing piano in a tourist-trap piano bar in Mexico City.

Bennie is approached by underlings for El Jefe, a provincial power whose daughter has been impregnated by a man named Alfredo Garcia. El Jefe is offering a large reward for Garcia's head. Bennie has his own grudge against Garcia, for Garcia's dalliance with Bennie's girlfriend, Elita. Bennie sees the bounty as his opportunity to pull himself out of the low life once and for all.

When Elita tells him that Garcia has been killed the previous week in a drunk-driving incident, Bennie assumes his task will be even easier. But the closer he gets to the head, the more his life begins to fall apart. He kills two bikers, after they pull guns on him and rape Elita. El Jefe's goons, who are following them, knock Bennie out, kill Elita and steal the head.

Bennie is forced farther and farther into a hellish world of gun battles and dead bodies, as he resolutely tries to deliver the head and collect the reward. In the end, however, he opts for a suicidal last stand, killing El Jefe and his henchmen, after deciding too many good people have died for the sake of this head.

BY PECKINPAH STANDARDS, production was smooth, though not without incident. At one point, shooting in a poor and dangerous section of Mexico City, Peckinpah had just finished filming one of Vega's nude scenes with Vega and Oates.

"There were hundreds of people standing around outside," Alex Phillips says. "Isela was a huge star and sex symbol. Sam finished the scene and came downstairs to prepare for the next shot. He tells Isela she's finished and goes outside. There are all these people standing around out there and Isela leans naked out of the second-floor window and yells, 'Hey, Peckinpah, what are we going to do next?' Police came. Husbands and other men were outraged. Sam was shocked that she would come out naked. The men were going crazy. He was going crazy. This broad was crazy."

While he was filming, Peckinpah got a crank letter that was odd enough for him to stick it in his files for posterity. It was written by a man in rural Pennsylvania who purported to have come up with a system—which he called "medianalysis"—that could produce ranks and cross references in the arts by a system of qualitative analysis by quantitative means.

Peckinpah, this fervent fan said, had scored in the highest mathematical range of his system, which placed him at a level called "Canon XVIII." The man enclosed a list for Peckinpah's edification and the names on it included: Ingmar Bergman, Eugene O'Neill, Sophocles, Ernst Lubitsch, T. S. Eliot, Walt Disney, Frank Capra, Charles Chaplin, Sam Peckinpah, Orson Welles, Walt Whitman, Ezra Pound, Picasso, Cézanne, Rembrandt, Mozart, Samuel Beckett and Euripides.

IN A SATISFIED MOOD during filming, Peckinpah confined his drinking mostly to evenings and weekends when he would grow mellow and reflective.

"One night near the end, Sam was staying in a motor home and he invited me over," Dan York recalls. "We drank and drank and drank. We went outside and the stars were so bright and we were both drunk. We were standing out there talking and we were both taking a piss, leaning back to look at the stars. I hear this thump and it was Sam hitting the ground. He was awestruck by the sky—and he was lying there peeing like a fountain."

For Gordon Dawson, however, the experience was unsatisfying; something was missing. He had co-screenwriter credit, he was working as associate producer with the director who had helped shape his career—and yet it was strangely unfulfilling because Peckinpah had so obviously changed. It was the last time they worked together.

"He would call me his protégé and tell me I could be a great director," Dawson says. "I really liked the guy. He was a unique son of a bitch, unpredictable. He got the best out of me. He made me climb mountains I'd never have tried. It was like combat; we went through wars together. I saw the shit he went through. He was a tormented man.

"I was sad about the way it ended up. I only saw him a few dozen times after that. But I wanted to stop signing checks 'Son of Sam.'"

AS WAS HIS CUSTOM when in Mexico, Peckinpah reunited with Begonia Palacios. He had been sharing a hacienda with Katy Haber and his daughter Sharon, where he would throw knives into the doors for fun and shoot holes in the walls of his bedroom for sport. When Begonia moved in, the other women moved out.

Begonia had tried during their marriages to have children but had had gynecological problems that caused her to miscarry twice. The problem was corrected by surgery and, during *Pat Garrett,* she had become pregnant.

"When I got pregnant, I felt this was my big chance to be Sam's woman," Begonia says, "to be his wife. I felt in love. I was lucky to have Sam's daughter. She was born prematurely. He went to see her and said, 'I'm proud of you, Begonia. You have what you want.'"

Lupita Palacios was born September 23, 1973. But Begonia and Peckinpah quarreled after living together for a while and Begonia finally moved out, taking Lupita with her.

"They couldn't stay together long," says Juan Jose Palacios. "When Lupita was born, Begonia was afraid that Sam, with his money and power, would take her away. So she never registered Lupita under his name. Sam tried to convince her that he wanted to legitimize Lupita but Begonia would say, 'I'm afraid.'"

PECKINPAH FINISHED SHOOTING *Alfredo Garcia* in December 1973 and returned to Los Angeles to cut and finish the film. In the midst of postproduction, he took an evening off to attend an American Film Institute tribute to James Cagney in March 1974. He invited Isela Vega, who was in town for dubbing.

He sent a limousine for her, which then stopped to pick him up at the Beverly Hilton, where he was staying. "He came out looking great in a tux but he was very drunk," Vega says.

As they pulled up at the event, the paparazzi swarmed around Peckinpah and Vega. Feeling puckish, Peckinpah grabbed the front of Vega's dress and yanked it down, exposing her breasts. When she barked at him to stop, "he got mad at my tone and tried to rip my dress," she says. "I thought he was going to rip it off. Then we went inside and he kept drinking."

They were seated at a table with, among others, Steve McQueen, Mick and Bianca Jagger, Paul Newman and Joanne Woodward. Peckinpah had the waiters bringing him drinks until "there were four or five lined up in front of him," Vega says.

The program itself consisted of film clips and laudatory speeches. Peckinpah finally lost his patience while Shirley MacLaine and Jack Lemmon exchanged banter about the honoree. Lemmon, in particular, seemed to provoke him, as he went on at length about Cagney's stature in the industry.

"Lemmon was drunk and on the podium," says Jim Silke, who was at the dinner as an AFI program director. "Shirley MacLaine gave him six or eight closing lines to get him off, but he kept going."

Peckinpah couldn't take any more. "Let the man speak for himself!" he thundered. "Get off the stage!"

The room went quiet, though MacLaine and Lemmon tried to laugh off Peckinpah's outburst.

"Good, tell him more," Paul Newman said to Peckinpah.

"What kind of party is this? What are you guys doing up there?" Peckinpah yelled.

"Everyone was looking at him," Vega says. "I wanted to crawl under the table."

Lemmon finally took the hint and brought his remarks to a close. Cagney was brought on and the evening wound down to postbanquet drinking and dancing.

Peckinpah concentrated on the drinking—and wound up in a fight. Well into his cups, he had fixated on a dark-complected waiter and started speaking Spanish to him. When the taciturn waiter refused to respond, Peckinpah began throwing fists. Security guards stepped in and removed Peckinpah from the hall.

"Sam told me later, 'This asshole—I knew he was Mexican,' " Juan Jose Palacios says. "He said, 'I started speaking to him in Spanish and he wouldn't answer me.' So Sam hit him. He said to me afterward, 'How was I supposed to know he was Hawaiian?' "

The dustup earned a three-picture panel in *People* magazine a couple of weeks later. "A film directed by Sam Peckinpah," the accompanying caption read, "is good for at least one scene of gratuitous violence. An evening out with Peckinpah seems to contain some of the same ingredients. Attending a film industry tribute to James Cagney, the director treated his date to a suggestion that they streak naked through the audience (which she declined), then interrupted the festivities and got himself thrown out of the main ballroom. As a finale, Peckinpah found his way to the bar and there had a few words with the bartender. Fists were waved, but a uniformed guard arrived in time to yell, 'Cut.' "

FROM THE DISTANCE OF almost two decades, an argument can be made for *Alfredo Garcia* as an underrated film, a poignant if nihilistic tale of a loser trying to salvage a shred of dignity at the end of his life. Its brutal quality has an undertone of sadness and regret. It also has a vein of black humor built around the image of the head in the sack.

But when it was released in August 1974, it was regarded as an unmitigated horror: a confrontationally ugly film about mean-spirited people pointlessly wreaking havoc across a savage landscape.

Had he made almost any other film in his canon (with the exception of *Convoy*) with the ease and discipline that *Alfredo Garcia* was completed, Peckinpah might have shaken the stigma left from *Pat Garrett*. Instead, Peckinpah was confirmed as a certifiable wildman, one only interested in exploiting violence and brutalizing women.

Mike Medavoy, then a newly appointed production executive at United Artists and now head of TriStar Pictures, recalls attending a preview of the film at the Writers Guild building. "As I was sitting in the theater, [during] a scene where Warren is carrying around this head in the burlap bag with the flies buzzing around it, someone yelled out, 'Bring me the head of Eric Pleskow!' [Pleskow was the head of UA.] It wasn't exactly one of the great hits of all time. What was the thinking at United Artists at the time it was released? It was, 'Take cover!' "

Peckinpah didn't help matters by traveling to New York on a publicity trip to meet the press and discuss the film. He spent the lion's share of his time in Manhattan with a drink in his hand, conducting interviews from his hotelroom bed. In his alcoholic candor, he discussed everything from hitting women to his own romantic problems.

Publicity tours are calculated to arouse interest in a movie, to make people want to see what you've got to sell. But Peckinpah was a peculiar salesman, touting his film with such quotes as:

· "Finally, finally, somebody gets pissed off with all this bull, and takes a gun and shoots a lot of people and gets killed. He's Everyman, Peckinpah's Everyman."

· "I said to Lee Marvin, 'I really hate actors,' and he said, 'Every actor does, baby.' "

· "Somebody asked if I hit women and I said, 'Of course I do. I believe in equal rights for women.' If you study and live with something at all, you find that tenderness and violence sometimes go hand in hand."

· "I'm afraid to walk the streets of New York or Los Angeles. I have a gun in my home and I'm prepared to use it. I don't feel like killing anybody but if anyone breaks in my house, they're going to be met with as much force as I can muster."

INTERVIEWER: "The female lead in your new movie belongs to a whole Peckinpah line of women who enjoy rape."
PECKINPAH: "Well, most women do."
INTERVIEWER: "You'll get differences of opinion on that."
PECKINPAH: "Not from women."

It was tightrope act for Peckinpah. He hit people square in the face with *Alfredo Garcia,* his darkest vision of mankind. He said outrageous things. But he did it while employing his most seductive personality. Here was the big bad film—and here was the thoroughly engaging director, making you like him in spite of everything.

One by one, reporter by reporter, he seemed to pull it off. No matter what they thought of the movie itself—and many of them were horrified by its offhanded brutality—they were taken in by Peckinpah. From Barbara Walters on the "Today" show to Joseph Gelmis at *Newsday,* from his suite at The Sherry Netherland to the Russian Tea Room, Peckinpah cut a wide swath with his candid talk and his sense of humor.

"I remember being essentially charmed by him," Gelmis says. "You couldn't get mad at him. There was no sense of him thinking of himself as an elite artist with a reason to be a snob. He thought of himself like a trail boss. He was pragmatic, proud to be self-reliant."

Jay Cocks wound up at New York's elite Russian Tea Room with Peckinpah, Isela Vega and John Bryson: "He walks in like 'Sam Takes the Town,' " Cocks says. "It was really stimulating. It amused me but it was also poignant, like he was acting too big for his britches."

At least one friend in the press, however, didn't like what she was seeing. Pauline Kael showed up at the hotel for a dinner date; instead, she went in to his bedroom and talked to him for about two hours.

"She gave him a lecture because of his machismo," recalls Isela Vega, who was on hand, "and the way he treated women in his movies and all the killing. He said, 'Nobody has died who didn't deserve it.' "

Kael says, "We spent a long time alone talking. He was lying on his bed stewed. If you saw him on TV, you saw how impossible he could be. He talked almost inaudibly. He would play hard to get and use one- or two-word answers to force them into asking more questions. He was showing his contempt for interviewers and the fact that they didn't know his work, which, in the case of TV interviewers, was probably true. He was making it hard for them, and so he made it hard on himself."

The reviews for the film were almost unanimously negative. Though a few critics praised it ("A strange, weird masterpiece that will turn off a lot of people," Roger Ebert wrote in the *Chicago Sun-Times*), its journey into dread and death was more often assessed with outrage and anger. "There's a smell of Peckinpah surrounded now by yes-men who tell him that his every burp is immortal," wrote Stanley Kaufmann in the *New Republic*.

Peckinpah's friend Jay Cocks wrote in *Time: "Alfredo Garcia* is full of fury and bile. It is like a private bit of self-mockery, a sort of ritual of closet masochism that invites, even challenges, everyone to think the worst. Many will. That is part of what Peckinpah was after, and his success in getting it is the most disturbing element in this strange, strangled movie."

The film had its critical admirers, but they were neither timely nor influential enough to save it from a quick commercial death. Those opinions were a distinct minority for a film that made many more critics' ten-worst lists in that year.

Yet it was one of the films on which he had the least interference, says Katy Haber: "*Alfredo Garcia* and *Cross of Iron* were the closest he came to final cut." Peckinpah said the same thing in October 1974, when he showed up for a tribute to his career at the San Francisco Film Festival.

John Bryson, who loved jokes at Peckinpah's expense, recalls an afternoon at Malibu, shortly after the release of *Bring Me the Head of Alfredo Garcia*. Peckinpah was gone for the day, and Bryson and Jason Robards were having a barbecue; as they drank the afternoon away, they smoked a suckling pig. After nightfall, with the pig thoroughly cooked and the cooks thoroughly sloshed, they paid a surreptitious visit to the trailer at Paradise Cove where Peckinpah lived for the last decade of his life.

That night, when Peckinpah returned home, he opened his trailer and stumbled over the head of a pig, sitting on the floor. As he wiped his boot off and cursed loudly, he came across a card thoughtfully left behind by the invaders: "IN HONOR OF ALFREDO GARCIA."

28

A Cure for Drinking

DURING HIS INTERVIEWS FOR *ALFREDO GARCIA*, Peckinpah made what was one of his occasional public confessions about drinking.

"I try to stick to light drinks," he said. "Campari with water or something like that. I'm an alcoholic. There's no question about that. I'm a working alcoholic. And it's just about got me whipped."

Peckinpah had no real interest in giving up alcohol. Even his periodic attempts at going on the wagon meant only that he would confine himself to wine, beer or both.

Rather, it was a defensive gesture, one calculated to play to the notion that acknowledging your problem is the first step toward solving it. Peckinpah never progressed beyond his "Yeah, I've got to do something about this drinking problem" phase. Instead, he traded on it for sympathy, without losing alcohol as an excuse for bad behavior.

After *Alfredo Garcia*, Peckinpah went back to Hollywood, where he was scheduled to direct *The Insurance Company* for Joe Wizan at Twentieth Century-Fox. Dan York, who had asked him for a job during *Alfredo Garcia*, followed him back to Los Angeles and went to work in his office at the Fox studio. *The Insurance Company*, an action-thriller about a right-wing conspiracy by a group of police, fell apart after several months of preproduction, because of casting problems.

York, meanwhile, persuaded Peckinpah to check into a hospital because of a persistent cough. "The doctor told him that if he didn't stop drinking, he'd be dead in six months," York recalls. "Sam said, 'I guess that leaves me with wine.' The doctor said, 'That leaves you with nothing.'"

To York, Peckinpah was an unpredictable boss, as likely to charm you as to call you at 2 A.M. and lecture you on your shortcomings as a human being. York worked for him on and off for two years before quitting to go back to school. Working for Peckinpah, York adds, meant drinking with Peckinpah.

"I finally became a teetotaler when I quit working for Sam—after drinking a half-bottle of Scotch a day."

Even as Peckinpah resisted the urgings of others to quit drinking, he must have had moments of clarity when he saw the havoc that alcohol was playing —if not with his work, then with the rest of his life. There had to have been hangover mornings, unsettling encounters and angry phone calls that made him think it was finally time to stop. But the discipline that he brought to his work never seemed to translate to his personal habits.

To some extent, he was probably afraid of who he might be without alcohol. To other people, however, he expressed it as a craving for excitement that only alcohol could provide.

"I asked him late in life why he drank," Jim Silke says. "He said, 'Boredom.' "

Similarly, Isela Vega says, "I used to say, 'If you quit drinking, you'd live longer.' He said, 'But it would be boring.' "

Yet there was the impulse to quit—if only an easy way could be found, one that wouldn't require any particular discipline or effort. What Peckinpah sought was a drug that would make him feel the same way alcohol did, but without the side effects.

During *Alfredo Garcia,* Warren Oates introduced him to what seemed to be just that substance. It gave him the same lift without the hangover, at least initially. It made him feel stronger, more energized than alcohol ever did, with a sense of well-being that approached euphoria.

Best of all, it was not addictive. It was a drug with few side effects and little potential for serious problems—at first.

Cocaine was that way for a lot of people in Hollywood. Getting started with cocaine was always a seductive, upbeat sensation. How could a drug that made you feel so completely on top of your game ever hurt you?

In 1973, *Time* magazine wrote about how fashionable cocaine had become. It quoted a government study that concluded that cocaine use had surpassed heroin use in the United States and noted: "A New York advertising firm is said to impress clients by giving out small samples. A Hollywood film editor says that some movie and record companies pay for the stuff out of their operating budgets because 'people won't work without their wake-up calls.' Most important to new users is coke's current status as an 'in' drug. 'It's the height of fashion,' says a well-heeled snow freak, 'because it shows success.' "

The *New York Times Magazine* in 1974 said: "Cocaine is now showing the same tendency toward upward mobility that marijuana demonstrated during the late 1960s. Once the nearly exclusive province of pimps and prostitutes—street people of the night—the drug has spread into widening circles, if not into the light of day. Its users encompass all social and economic categories but are particularly concentrated among what one drug-abuse specialist calls 'the glitter people': a who's who of Hollywood and Hollywood on the Hudson that includes actors, models, athletes, artists, jazz musicians, designers and ad men."

While the *Times* article brought up the question of cocaine's addictive powers, it ultimately left the matter up in the air. Some experts cited a tendency toward psychological addiction among chronic users but that term —"psychological addiction"—seemed benign compared to the fright-movie visions of heroin addiction and withdrawal. By comparison, a cocaine habit seemed no more threatening than being hooked on nicotine, and didn't carry the risk of lung cancer.

"Because it is not physiologically addicting, [cocaine users] rarely turn up at hospitals and drug clinics," the *Times* wrote. "What's more, many of today's cocaine aficionados are hardly types to appear on police registers·or in public hospitals. Unlike heroin, there is no drain on state resources in the form of cocaine-treatment centers, since the drug is not addicting, at least in a physiological sense. Many users simply drop the stuff when the money runs out."

That perception changed, of course, once the 1970s turned into the 1980s and the long-term effects of cocaine could truly be seen. Cocaine use spread into the general population and, with increased exposure and use, it began to show its more insidious side.

In that mid-1970s era of Watergate, however, cocaine was regarded the same way as marijuana: yet another example of government dissembling about the danger of so-called dangerous drugs. It was another example of government hysteria about what was obviously a harmless and even beneficial drug.

As Sam Peckinpah began dabbling, it seemed like the perfect substitute for —and complement to—drinking. What could the harm be?

"Coke," says Peckinpah's friend, Joe Bernhard, "makes you think you're doing good when you ain't doing good."

29

Bad Behavior by the Bay

BY THE TIME HE FINISHED *ALFREDO GARCIA,* Peckinpah's salary was about $400,000 a picture. But, says Kip Dellinger, his former business manager, Peckinpah was less interested in the salary than in the expense money he would receive. "I don't have to pay a percentage on that," he would say.

Peckinpah would demand the expense money in cash in advance. He would then endeavor to bill whatever he could (his housing, his meals, his transportation) to the production—to the producer and the studio—instead of paying for it out of his expense money.

"I said, 'Sam, you may become the only director to do a picture for scale, plus $375,000 in expenses,' " Dellinger says.

PRODUCER ARTHUR LEWIS had been developing *The Killer Elite* for two years with writer Reginald Rose, based on a novel by Robert Rostand (written under a pen name). Lewis convinced Martin Baum to show it to Peckinpah and, at the end of 1974, Peckinpah agreed to do the picture, with Baum and Lewis co-producing.

The deal was set up with United Artists. The story, about American agents in England who provide safe transport for an African revolutionary leader back to his own country, was topical and timely. It was also expensive, requiring London and African locations. But United Artists considered it worth the risk, because it would have the Peckinpah touch.

When James Caan was signed to play the lead American agent, Lewis suddenly was told the story had to be changed. Caan had just finished shooting *Rollerball* in London and wanted his next picture to be set in the United States, preferably in California. United Artists production executive Mike Medavoy asked the producers to make the necessary changes in the script.

The impression was that Caan had pulled a star trip on Medavoy: If I can't make the movie in the United States, I won't make the movie. But Caan says now, "I can't remember saying that about the location. I might have voiced it, but I don't think I said it like Hitler. That's not my style."

Lewis says, "Caan told Marty Baum that he'd been playing poker and he told Medavoy that he'd prefer to do his next film in California. Caan also told Baum that if there was serious resistance, he'd have done it in England. But the way United Artists was functioning at that time, anything that was done in the United States came under Medavoy's supervision. So there was a kind of political motivation. Medavoy didn't resist Caan's desire to do it in California."

Lewis didn't argue because he was a relative newcomer to films, with a background in theater in London and New York. "I was just delighted to have the eminent Sam Peckinpah to direct my movie," he says.

Rose, who was British, wasn't considered appropriate to Americanize the screenplay, so Marc Norman, author of the novel *Oklahoma Crude,* was brought in to do a rewrite. His version of the script didn't work, so Baum asked a favor of a former client of his, writer Stirling Silliphant.

Silliphant, a successful writer-producer in television, had received his break in features through Baum, who had gotten him the job of writing *In the Heat of the Night.* Silliphant's script won the Oscar and he went on to write *The New Centurions* and *The Towering Inferno,* among others.

"I had to change it from London to San Francisco and the political figure to Asian and provide him with a daughter," Silliphant says. "You couldn't just change nationalities without major structural changes. It required a rewrite to give it some content beyond, 'Cover the rear; I'll go in the front door.' "

Silliphant and his wife, Tiana, were both active students of Eastern martial arts, disciples of the late Bruce Lee. Silliphant had heard about Peckinpah's penchant for sucker punches, landing the first blow before his opponent knew the brawl was on. So he went into his rewriting sessions with Peckinpah in a slightly defensive posture.

His only previous acquaintance with Peckinpah had been at the Writers Guild strike meetings in 1960. Now, fifteen years later, he showed up at Peckinpah's office at Samuel Goldwyn Studios for a 10 P.M. meeting to find someone who "looked like an old man to me—and I was older than he was. He looked like shit. I didn't have a good feeling. We had a lot of work and only a little time. We had to shoot in only two weeks."

Silliphant was further unnerved when Peckinpah pulled out a large throwing knife and began tossing it at a target on the wall between sips of brandy. Silliphant decided that a confrontational approach was best.

"You and I had better have a mano a mano," he said. "I've heard bad stories about you. I understand you have a drinking problem."

"What cocksucker told you that?" Peckinpah growled, taking the brandy glass away from his lips.

"Well, it's obvious from the way you're drinking tonight that this is something you do every night. Now it's very distracting for you to be throwing that knife. Are you trying to tell me something?"

"No, no, no," Peckinpah said. "You're reading too much into this."

To which Silliphant said, "I'll give you a clue. I've been studying with Bruce Lee and I know I can beat the shit out of you. So if you take a shot, you better keep working on me because if you don't kill me, I'm going to get up off the floor and destroy you. I'll flatten your nose. I'll close your windpipe. I'll ruin your kidneys. Let's be clear. If you take a shot at me, it had better be terminal because if it's not, I'm going to kill you."

Peckinpah stared at him, then gave him an innocent smile. "Whoa, you're really filled with hostility," he said.

"No," Silliphant replied, "I'm filled with love. I just want you to know what will happen."

Peckinpah smiled again, put away the knife and they went to work. But Peckinpah seemed to be resisting the process; Silliphant finally asked if there was more going on than met the eye.

"I don't want to shoot this thing," Peckinpah said. He opened his drawer and showed Silliphant another script.

"He wanted to take this cast and budget and put them into this other script," Silliphant says. "His secret ambition was that I would fail with the rewrite and he would slide his in. Once he told me, he dropped the idea and never mentioned it again. I never knew what it was and always wondered. I don't know how serious he was."

THAT FEBRUARY, PECKINPAH CELEBRATED his fiftieth birthday. With his brother Denny and Kip Dellinger, he was driven to composer Jerry Fielding's house for a celebratory drink with a few friends.

Instead, he walked into a surprise party of 250 people—but not before he and Denny had stopped outside the darkened house to take a leak in the bushes. Telling Dellinger that it was bad manners to ask for a bathroom as soon as you entered someone's house, they watered the shrubbery in full view of the guests, who were milling about in the dark.

The party was particularly touching for Peckinpah, who assumed that you couldn't put that many people together who'd still talk to him.

"He was surprised that the people there had come because of him," says his cousin Wanda Justice, who flew down from Vancouver for the party. "By that time, he was thinking people licked his boots because they wanted to get into pictures. Any real show of affection or expression of gratitude amazed him."

There were plenty of gag gifts and rousing toasts. Stella Stevens, who hadn't seen Peckinpah since *Cable Hogue,* showed up with a blow-up sex doll. "Here's a woman you can get along with," she said, getting a big laugh.

As the party rolled on, Fielding and Dellinger, who had been the principal instigators, looked on with amusement. Fielding watched Peckinpah for a while, then turned to Dellinger and said, "Don't you see what you've done? By doing this, you give this man the tacit approval to be the asshole that he is."

As Silliphant continued rewriting, Peckinpah took off to attend a retrospective of his work at Clemson University in Clemson, South Carolina. Critic Andrew Sarris was at Clemson to speak the day before Peckinpah's appearance and was convinced to stay on to serve as moderator for Peckinpah's retrospective. But Peckinpah, who apparently was familiar with Sarris's critical opinion of his work, wouldn't allow Sarris on the same stage with him. Sarris had already missed his plane, so he stayed around for the program and reported in the *Village Voice:* "He was much older and wearier than I had remembered him four years earlier. But his routine had not changed in the slightest. It was a shrewd mixture of the bang and the whimper, the aggression and the apology.

"A surly questioner from Campus Crusade for Christ so exasperated Peckinpah that he retorted rudely, 'What I really like is a pompous ass who makes value judgments.' When a girl was ordered by a media stooge to stand up when she was asking a question, Peckinpah chimed in with, 'You can take off your bra, honey.' I couldn't tell whether Peckinpah was putting down the media person or the girl, but it was easy with either or both. His answers to questions alternated between surly indistinctness and remorseful intensity."

THE KILLER ELITE is about Mike Locken and George Hansen, longtime partners who work for COMTEG, a private security company that subcontracts for the CIA.

Hansen sells out to the other side in the middle of a mission. Rather than kill Locken, he cripples him, shooting him in the elbow and knee. Locken's COMTEG bosses tell him he is finished but Locken vows to rehabilitate himself back into action and does.

COMTEG is hired by the CIA to shepherd a Japanese dissident leader safely back to Japan from the United States. Hansen is part of the team trying to kill him, so COMTEG's top boss decides to give the assignment to Locken. But when Locken finally comes face to face with Hansen, he finds out that he and Hansen are still working for the same man: One of the COMTEG management people is a double agent.

Locken finishes his assignment and shoots his double-dealing superior.

Rather than take the man's job, as offered, he turns his back on the profession and sails off into the sunset.

Silliphant finished the rewrite on schedule and *Killer Elite* got under way, shooting on location in and around San Francisco. Because Peckinpah routinely rewrote, he took a pass at Silliphant's script. But his vision for the rewrite was similar to the one he had for *The Getaway:* to turn it into a satire of action films.

"That was just kind of a fun-and-games film and everybody took it so seriously," he said later. "I couldn't figure that out. I don't know why people took it so grim."

It may have been because Peckinpah's notions of satire were odd and unfunny: political speeches and throwaway one-liners, some directed at his nemesis, MGM.

Bobby Visciglia, who was on hand to handle props once again, says, "Stirling would write at night and Sam would change it during the day. It was a tough script to understand."

"He had private jokes in the movie for twenty or thirty of his pals," James Caan says.

Lewis and Baum were upset with the rewrites. Unable to get Peckinpah to stop, they brought Medavoy in to crack the whip. Medavoy called Peckinpah, telling him to stop whatever writing he was doing on the script. Peckinpah responded on January 27, 1975, with a memo to Medavoy: "As per our conversation of January 24, it is my understanding that you have instructed me to do no writing on the script. However I feel that we both agreed that I should proceed along the lines that a hyphenate could, as defined by the Writers Guild of America and the Directors Guild. Would you please confirm this memo because this is the road that I am taking."

Medavoy responded on January 28, 1975, with a memo of his own: "I'm confirming to you per your note of January 27 that you are not to do any writing on the script.

"Of course we are not intending to foreclose you from any of the customary functions of a director as described or permitted by the agreements with the Directors Guild and the Writers Guild."

Peckinpah took both memos and had them printed on T-shirts, front and back, and distributed them to his cast and crew.

"I thought it was funny," Medavoy says now. "I was trying to control him and he was saying, 'I'm going to do what I want,' but in a respectful way. He'd 'yes' you to death until there was no way you could do anything and then he'd do what he wanted."

Word of the tensions reached the media in Hollywood. On April 22, 1975, *L.A. Times* gossip columnist Joyce Haber reported: "*Elite* is already showing the slow hand of Peckinpah. A three-minute scene of James Caan that takes place in North Beach's topless joint, El Cid, took seven and a half hours to shoot. The company was, additionally, five hours late in arriving at the club. Needless to say, the owner lost all his business that night. But director Peckinpah—maybe to avoid a tangle with sometime cowboy, strapping star Caan—bought the cast and crew drinks. His tab: $15,000. That's cheaper than brown-belting it, Sam, with your overworked star.''

Peckinpah fired off a letter to Haber on April 25: "Somebody's giving you some very bad information. On the day in question, we concluded filming in one location at 3 P.M. and Jimmy Caan was dismissed for the day. I then moved the whole crew to the El Cid nightclub location and, with travel, rehearsal and lighting, the first shot was in the can at 5:30 P.M. I then proceeded to complete a sequence that was scheduled for one day by 9:30 that night. If you want proof, I can send you call sheets and progress reports that show that a complete day was gained on the schedule.

"Unless you are deliberately trying to put me in the barrel, I would appreciate your putting this straight."

Haber responded almost a month later, on May 22, with a column item that included a reprint of Peckinpah's letter and ended: " '[Someone seems to be] deliberately trying to put me in the barrel.' Not me, Sam. I'm no Harold Pinter. So there."

PECKINPAH AND BAUM had a solid relationship of long standing, but *Killer Elite* strained it considerably. Baum had initiated Medavoy's involvement in the controversy about rewriting. In anger, Peckinpah went to the studio and tried to get Baum fired from the picture.

"I was backed by the studio and we proceeded to shoot the Silliphant script," Baum says. "But Sam continued to change scenes daily. I felt *Killer Elite* never reached its full potential because of discord between the producer and director over material."

There were other disputes as well. In an ill-thought-out cost-cutting measure, the producers issued a memo saying there was no money for coffee or food at staff meetings or crew parties, one of the perquisites of filmmaking. Peckinpah responded by offering to cover the cost of these items himself— then having this memo printed on a T-shirt as well.

"When I showed up, everyone had the memo on a T-shirt," Baum says. "It was certainly colorful. But I was pissed."

"One of the pieces of lagniappe on a production is that you get good coffee and doughnuts in the morning," Silliphant says. "Sam offered to pay for them himself but rather than make the gesture quietly, he proclaimed it with T-shirts. That only creates a deeper schism between the crew and the producers. His whole nature was to be divisive."

Lewis felt a kind of helplessness in working with Peckinpah: "I didn't consider myself his enemy. I was just a nonperson on the movie. There was never any way to win."

Baum finally called in the powers that be from United Artists, in hopes of showing Peckinpah who was really in charge. The group that journeyed to the set in San Francisco included Medavoy and his United Artists bosses: Eric Pleskow, Bill Bernstein and Arthur Krim. Once they arrived, however, all Pleskow was interested in was getting the photographer to take a group picture.

"This was supposed to be a meeting to say, 'Stop fucking around,' " Baum says. "As we're leaving after the picture, Arthur Krim goes and pats Sam on the cheek and says, 'Be a good boy.' And that was it."

The tensions on the set of *Killer Elite* seem to have been derived as much from the producers' own insecurities as from Peckinpah's urge to question their authority. Newt Arnold, one of the assistant directors on the film, says, "There were three producers [the third was Helmut Dantine] and all three felt compelled to exert themselves. Sam finally said to them, 'If you guys want me on the set, you leave me alone when I'm on the set.' "

"If there was tension with the producers, we actors never felt it," Caan says. "Sam did. But he never pushed it on the actors. I think he liked to give the appearance that he didn't give a fuck."

Just as it is hard to pin down how much of the director-producer tension could be blamed on each side, it is also tough to decipher how much of Peckinpah's erratic and irascible behavior could be attributed to his personality alone—and how much of it should be ascribed to his increasing cocaine use.

"*Killer Elite* is when the cocaine started to get heavy," Bobby Visciglia says. "He started falling apart."

"I don't know where he was going with that film," Katy Haber says. "I don't think he was much in control."

The cocaine use usually translated into megalomaniacal behavior that would cost time on the set. One day at Suisun Bay, while shooting on a large ship that was part of the Mothball Fleet, the camera was set up at one end of the deck, while the crew members operating the generator were at the far end, hidden behind some superstructure. Peckinpah sat and rehearsed a scene and then, just before he was to shoot, he held up a hand and brought everything to a halt. He got up and slowly walked the length of the deck to the generators. There, he found the generator operators quietly playing cards.

"Nobody plays cards on my set," he said. "I want total attention. If it happens again, you're out of here." Then he slowly strode all the way back, the king demonstrating dominance of his domain. But location shooting costs $50,000 a day; his gesture ate up a solid ten minutes, when ten seconds with a bullhorn would have achieved the same end.

Cocaine wasn't the only drug he used. He was a hypochondriac who was constantly getting doctors to prescribe for him. He had trouble sleeping, so he had prescriptions for Quaaludes, the prescription version of the hypnotic, methaqualone. He had prescriptions for drugs to help him wake up from the sleeping pills. And he had a constant supply of vitamins, including B_{12} shots, to try to maintain his health.

"Sam was a chronic," Visciglia says. "Every time he wanted some time to get his thoughts together or evaluate a situation, he'd get hurt. He was a nut for pills. He'd wake the medic up for pills twenty-four hours a day. He took B_{12} shots every day. He'd drop his drawers on the set or on the street."

During a dinner one evening with Katy Haber and Kip Dellinger, Peckinpah grew increasingly drunk until Haber made a remark he didn't like. He reached across the table and slapped her. Haber grabbed his hand and bit him.

At 1:30 A.M., Peckinpah woke Dellinger and said, "Katy's got to be fired." Dellinger tried to talk him out of it, to which Peckinpah said, "She should know better than to bite the hand that feeds her."

Peckinpah called up Silliphant, who was renting a house in Tiburon, and said, "Come right over—and bring your wife." Silliphant and his wife jumped into their car and drove to Peckinpah's rented house in Sausalito. Peckinpah, who had obviously been drinking heavily, let them in and said, "I want you to hear something."

He got on the phone to Haber and, once he got her on the line, began to abuse her: "You're fired. Get the fuck off my movie, get the fuck off my set, get the fuck out of my life." Embarrassed, Silliphant and his wife left in the middle of the conversation. The next day, Silliphant says, Haber was not on the set; she didn't return for two weeks.

PRODUCTION CONCLUDED with the filming of interiors in Los Angeles. Before editing began, Peckinpah decided that he needed an impromptu vacation.

"We'd had a wrap party," recalls Bobby Visciglia, "and after about three hours, I was feeling pretty good. Sam asked what I was going to do and I said, 'I'm going to run away and hide.' He tells me he has these free tickets on Western Airlines and says, 'Let's go to Hawaii.' "

Peckinpah had his secretary call and make reservations for seats and hotel reservations. Even as she was doing it, someone else in the group spoke up and asked if he had ever flown on Continental Airlines. This person launched into what must have been such a ringing endorsement that Peckinpah, though he had free tickets on another airline, changed his mind and decided to fly Continental. He and Visciglia made plans to meet at the Continental VIP Lounge at Los Angeles International Airport that evening.

When they rendezvoused at LAX, Visciglia says, "Sam was still half-drunk." They had a drink in the lounge and then were told they could board. Once on the plane, "they kept giving us some purple drink in first class to get us in the mood for Hawaii."

That preflight happy hour, however, expanded until they actually had been sitting on the plane for an hour. "The steward kept saying, 'We're having a little problem. It'll just be fifteen minutes,' " Visciglia says.

After three or four such delays, Visciglia turned to Peckinpah and said, "I don't think I'm going to take this plane."

"Why?" Peckinpah asked.

"Because they keep saying they're fixing it," Visciglia says. "But we've got to fly in it for 3,000 miles. There are a lot of other planes leaving for Hawaii that are okay. I've got guys waiting for us with limos and hookers."

When they started to get out of their seats, the steward came running up and told them they couldn't leave. When Visciglia and Peckinpah insisted, the steward called the airport police. When they responded, the steward told them that the pair was causing a disturbance. To which Visciglia said, "We've been sitting for over an hour and we decided we don't want to fly on the son of a bitch. We want to get off." The officer agreed and they disembarked—and were promptly met by a Continental public-relations man, Steve Jackson, who asked what the problem was.

"We want to get off the fucking plane," Peckinpah replied.

Jackson walked them up the ramp, familiarly putting his arm around Peckinpah's shoulder ("A fucking no-no," Visciglia says). At the top of the ramp, Visciglia asked where their luggage was. Jackson laughed and pointed out the window: "On that plane that just took off for Hawaii."

Peckinpah turned red, dropped the briefcase he was carrying—and let fly with the invisible left hook that was an ever-present threat. He connected with Jackson's chin, knocking Jackson to the ground.

Three ticket agents came around from behind the Continental counter and charged toward them. Visciglia, a short bull of a man, put his head down and barreled into them, knocking them into the counter. Out of the corner of his eye, Visciglia saw two more figures coming at him; he lowered his head again and knocked them down as well.

But the last two were the airport police officers who had helped them off the plane. They got up laughing, then slapped the handcuffs on Peckinpah and Visciglia and drove them to the Venice Police Station, where they were formally booked and jailed. Visciglia's bail was $500; Peckinpah's, $250.

"I'm sitting in jail and Sam is signing autographs for the Mexicans," Visciglia says.

Composer Jerry Fielding eventually came and gave Visciglia a ride home. Peckinpah's friend Dr. Bob Gray, a chiropractor, picked him up.

"We went out for a few belts," Gray says. "We had to soak his ring finger in ice water to get it off where he belted the guy."

Steve Jackson filed a complaint that read, in part: "Defendant was behaving in such a loud, rude and obnoxious manner as to become so annoying and upsetting to the passengers that it became necessary to ask defendant to leave the plane. Stewardesses, in the most tactful, courteous and pleasant manner, finally were able to persuade defendant to leave said plane. After defendant complained, plaintiff, in his capacity as an employee of Continental Airlines, had attempted to placate defendant. Some conversation ensued and defendant, after a period of time, apparently quieted down and started to behave more rationally. And then to plaintiff's complete surprise, defendant dropped the case he was carrying onto plaintiff's feet and as plaintiff knelt to pick it up, the defendant then and there wantonly, willfully, viciously, maliciously and deliberately struck the plaintiff in the face with his fist."

Visciglia's case was eventually thrown out of court. Jackson, who was transferred to Hawaii, sued Peckinpah for $50,000 in general damages and $250,000 in punitive damages. After two years, he settled for $30,000.

"Sam was not an easy guy to go anywhere with," Visciglia says. "He never had a bodyguard. But he needed one."

THE KILLER ELITE editing room was set up at MGM Studios in Culver City, where United Artists' offices were located. Peckinpah used the opportunity to settle an old score.

He filled a truck with crew members from Killer Elite and armed them with automatic weapons loaded with blanks. Then he mounted an armed assault on the Irving Thalberg Building, home of MGM's main offices. His target: the office of Daniel Melnick, still head of MGM production, in retaliation for Melnick's perceived betrayal on Pat Garrett.

But Melnick had been tipped off. He got a dummy, dressed it in his clothes and hung it from the light fixture with a note that said, "I can't face the disgrace of capture." Then he hid in an adjoining office and watched Peckinpah's troops storm the office.

Later, Peckinpah called Melnick and said, "You son of a bitch. You topped me again. Why couldn't you let me have my little victory?"

Peckinpah turned the film over to editor Garth Craven, who had also done most of the editing on Alfredo Garcia. But he was unhappy with Craven's work on the kung-fu scenes that dotted the film. So he brought in Monte Hellman, who took the fight sequences and started from scratch.

Hellman had directed a couple of cult Westerns for Roger Corman in the 1960s that starred Jack Nicholson (The Shooting, Ride in the Whirlwind) and Two-Lane Blacktop. He'd also worked as a film doctor, helping to shape Sergio Leone's A Fistful of Dollars, among others.

Hellman's description of working with Peckinpah is distinctly at odds with those of Baum, Lewis and Silliphant—probably because he was not in any kind of power struggle with the director. He was an employee, there to contribute to the director's vision, and Peckinpah appreciated it.

"He had the quietest way of talking of anybody I know," Hellman says. "It forced you to lean in until he had your undivided attention. It was a theatrical trick. The way he stimulated his editors was fascinating. He would never come out and criticize you directly. He would always work around it. It was the way a good director works with actors.

"Just to see how his mind worked was fascinating to me. One fight sequence I recut and thought was good—he looked at it and had the idea to intercut it with a dialogue scene. It was incredible, the way it turned out. I wouldn't have thought to do that."

There was concern that the film would get an R rating. UA was banking on a PG, which meant bigger box office. In June, Lewis sent Peckinpah a memo about a party scene in a brothel: "I'm sure you are aware of the broad guidelines for the use of nudity vis-à-vis our PG rating. However, the following has been pointed out by the United Artists' legal department:

"1. The nudity cannot be sex-related.
"2. It is permissible to use side shots if the lady's nipples are not too prominently displayed.
"3. Frontal nudity must be fast and fleeting with virtually no repetition.

"The MPAA, of course, will reserve final judgement until viewing the cumulative effect in the finished film."

Baum maintains that there was never pressure on Peckinpah to come up with a PG-rated film. But Lewis says, "The studio thought the difference between a PG and an R was a lot of gross. Nobody thought it would be any problem until the MPAA started to react to the movie. You can be pretty darn violent and still get a PG. They were reacting to Peckinpah's reputation."

Questions about the rating were less pressing than those about the ending. "They rewrote the ending four times and we shot the ending three different ways," Bobby Visciglia says.

Actually, it was two—but they were diametric opposites. As the script was written, Locken and his two assistants, Miller (Bo Hopkins) and Mac (Burt Young), face off against the corrupt CIA forces at the Mothball Fleet. Locken emerges victorious but Miller is killed in the battle. Locken and Mac get on their boat and sail off.

Peckinpah's second version seemed to be part of his vision of the film as satire: Everything was the same as the first version, except that, as the boat sailed off, Miller, who had been killed, could be seen laughing and drinking a beer on the boat with Mac and Locken.

The producers tried politely to tell him that it wouldn't work. When he persisted, they put their foot down and said that it wasn't the way the film would end. When he inserted it anyway into a print that was shown for a preview in San Francisco, they were furious.

"He wanted to do a very abstract ending that made no sense at all," Lewis says. "He turned the whole movie at the last instant into a fantasy. It only existed for the very moment the movie ended. Again, it was a matter of his perversity. When we went to San Francisco to do the preview, he put his ending on it. If we didn't like it, it was all Sam."

On October 31, 1975, Lewis sent Peckinpah a memo, laying out the producers' decision: "Marty and I have been instructed by Eric Pleskow and Mike Medavoy to inform you that only one ending needs to be added, scored, dubbed and used in the final cut of the film, the one, as in scene 415 in the final shooting script, where it is clearly indicated that Miller is killed and that in the actual ending as in the script only Locken and Mac among the principals would go off in the ketch."

Peckinpah replied with a memo on November 6: "The basic fact is that all of us are pulling for you but you have not yet reached the level of being totally incompetent. I appreciate your efforts and hope that you try harder. If we're all lucky, someday you might make it and go on to greater heights. Possibly one day you might become just a simple pain in the ass."

To which Lewis responded, on November 11: "About becoming a pain in the ass, it's always mind-busting to be recognized by a master. As you are one of the few child prodigies in this field, I am grateful for your generous encouragement."

DURING THE EDITING PROCESS, Peckinpah nearly drowned in an incident he later claimed led to his heart attack in 1979.

"He was staying at the Beverly Hilton in a room by the pool," says actor Seymour Cassel. "One night he decided to jump in and he never came up. I think the shock of hitting the water rendered him unconscious for a minute or so. Ron Wright [one of the *Killer Elite* assistant directors] saved his life. If [Ron] hadn't been with him, he wouldn't have lived."

Peckinpah was a strong swimmer, a body surfer and scuba diver. How could a simple jump into a hotel pool knock him out?

"He was drunk and he'd been taking Ludes [Quaaludes]," Cliff Coleman says. "He jumped into the water and when Bitsy and Ron Wright looked down, he didn't come up. He stopped doing everything and sank like a rock. Ron pulled him out and hit him on the chest two or three times and that was that."

The thumps on the chest and artificial respiration were necessary because he had aspirated water and his heart had stopped. So Peckinpah was taken to the hospital for observation and then released. But Peckinpah always believed that the measures that saved his life also contributed to the arrhythmia that led to his heart attack four years later.

THE THEME OF GOVERNMENT CORRUPTION in *Killer Elite* echoed Peckinpah's own feelings about the American government, after the revelations of CIA involvement in everything from Watergate to the overthrow and assassination of Salvador Allende in Chile.

The people who knew Peckinpah disagree on what his politics were. Even his children are at odds: Sharon, a liberal, thought of him as a conservative, while Matt, a conservative, thought he was extremely liberal.

The one consistent feature was his antipathy for Republican presidents. "He hated Nixon—and Reagan," Sharon says. "He thought they were hopeless; he thought they were liars."

"He was mostly apolitical," Matt says, "but what political convictions he did hold were the old-line liberal ideas from the Democratic party."

Blaine Pettitt, his old hunting companion and a Republican party activist, says, "Sam was a Republican but he took great joy in harassing me about Nixon." Around the time of Watergate, Peckinpah sent Pettitt a gift that exemplified his view.

"It was a carving of two elephants in wood," Pettitt says, "and the elephants were in the love embrace. It was a joke about the GOP, I think. Of course, my wife would never let me display it. She didn't even want me to keep it. She said, 'What if you died and they found it among your effects?' "

THE KILLER ELITE was hustled into theaters to compete with the Christmas trade in December 1975, against such seasonal heavy-hitters as Stanley Kubrick's *Barry Lyndon, Funny Lady* (also with James Caan), *The Sunshine Boys* and *One Flew Over the Cuckoo's Nest*. It didn't get lost in the shuffle, but it wasn't one of the must-see pictures of the year-end release frenzy. "It recouped its money," Mike Medavoy says. "It did better than I thought it would."

The reviews were mixed; the most common reaction was typified by Jack Kroll's review in *Newsweek:* "Even in a throwaway flick like *Killer Elite,* he can't help but display some signs of talent and sensibility—a lean, hard rhythm and a positively carnal feeling for the film image. But he's moving like a tired fighter as he mines the current cliché about the sinister, double-crossing CIA."

Pauline Kael saw within *Killer Elite* a subtext that used the plot as a not-too-subtle metaphor for Peckinpah's own career. In "Notes on the Nihilist

Poetry of Sam Peckinpah," a *New Yorker* piece that summed up her feelings about his work, she wrote, "Sam Peckinpah is a great 'personal' filmmaker; he's an artist who can work as an artist only on his own terms. He likes to say that he's a good whore who goes where he's kicked. The truth is he's a very bad whore; he can't turn out a routine piece of craftsmanship—he can't use his skills to improve somebody else's conception.

"Peckinpah's vision has become so scabrous, theatrical and obsessive that it is now controlling him. His new film, *The Killer Elite*, is set so far inside his fantasy-morality world that it goes beyond personal filmmaking into private filmmaking. Increasingly, his films have reflected his war with the producers and distributors, and in *The Killer Elite*, this war takes its most single-minded form.

"It would be too simple to say that he has been driven out of the American movie industry, but it's more than half true. No one is Peckinpah's master as a director of individual sequences; no one else gets such beauty out of movement and hard grain and silence. The images in *The Killer Elite* are charged, and you have the feeling that not one is wasted. Peckinpah has become so nihilistic that filmmaking itself seems to be the only thing he believes in. He's crowing in *The Killer Elite*, saying, 'No matter what you do to me, look at the way I can make a movie.' The bedevilled bastard's got a right to crow."

For Arthur Lewis, one of the people he apparently was crowing at, the experience was a painful one.

"When a man directs a movie, there's no way to inhibit him," Lewis says. "It was not a matter of clashing with him. Nobody rolled up their sleeves and got into a fight with him. It was a matter of watching a guy go down the drain and being pragmatic enough to know nothing could be done."

Even as the film was being readied for release, Lewis sent a final memo to Peckinpah on December 11, 1975:

"Dear Sam,

"You're a talented man.

"Too bad you're not a gracious one.

"I have no idea why you singled me out as an adversary but I think I helped you a lot.

"I got us a PG and Eric Pleskow thinks it's worth a million and a half over whatever our gross would have been as an R. If that's so, next Christmas I'll buy you a drink—either here or in the South of France. Even if it isn't, I'll buy you a drink.

"I'm glad it's over. However, it was an experience I'll always remember, an experience unlike any I've ever had and believe me, I've been there, man.

"Anyway, good luck on your next one. Make *Sgt. Steiner [Cross of Iron]* a hit and don't be too harsh on my old and good friend Julie Epstein."

To which Peckinpah replied: "My problem is I do not suffer fools graciously and detest petty thievery and incompetence. Other than that, I found you charming and, on occasion, mildly entertaining. Thank you for the GP [sic]. Everyone is proud of you."

Peckinpah also had T-shirts printed and distributed to his closest associates to wear to the film's premiere in San Francisco: "The only preparation we ever had on this picture—was Preparation H."

30

"Cross" the Line

PECKINPAH SPENT THE LAST HALF OF 1975 alternating between Los Angeles and
a Sausalito apartment he had taken a two-year lease on at the beginning of
Killer Elite. As was his habit when he was not working on a picture, he
began to drink more heavily.

But cocaine was also now a regular component in his life.

"Sam used cocaine to get off liquor," says Paul Peterson, his ex-brother-
in-law who was his constant companion for the last half of the 1970s.
"That's really how it started. When he was doing cocaine, he would drink
one glass of sherry a night. He felt he had his drinking problem licked. What
he never realized was that he had a bigger problem."

Jim Hamilton, a San Francisco writer who met Peckinpah during *The
Getaway*, renewed his acquaintance with him during *Killer Elite*. After the
film was finished, he began to run into Peckinpah in a Sausalito pub and
started to spend time with him.

"He was so physically run down and debilitated that conventional conversations were sort of rare," Hamilton says. "When I met him, he had started
around the bend, in terms of his morale and personal methods. He was
getting heavily into cocaine about that time. After he got into coke, he just
got strange and unpredictable. He was uneasy most of the time."

During this same period, Peckinpah acquired his own personal archivist: a
former rock musician named Don Hyde. Hyde, a longtime Peckinpah fan,
lived in nearby Mill Valley and owned one of the Bay Area's first privately
owned video postproduction facilities. Aware that Peckinpah was living in
the area and eager to meet him, Hyde decided to offer to put all of his films
on three-quarter-inch videotape for him, a luxury that few directors had at
their disposal in that pre-VCR era.

Hyde presented himself at Peckinpah's door one day at 10 A.M., gifts in hand, to volunteer his services. It was not an auspicious hour at which to meet.

"He'd been up all night partying and had crashed on the couch with his clothes and his boots on," Hyde says. "He stumbled to the door and he's real pissed. He says, 'What the fuck do you want?' I told him I had some things I wanted to give him. He said, 'Come back in an hour.' "

Hamilton, who was there at the time, recalls, "Hyde was this guy in classic hippie attire. Long hair, Indian poncho, white cowboy boots. In his hands he had what looked like a rug. And in a very formal pose, he made a speech: 'Mr. Peckinpah, as a token of my esteem, I want to present this to you.' And it was this beautiful Indian rug and an original Curtis Indian print. At a glance, he looked like a classic camp follower and idolater, but he wasn't. And Sam was very touched."

Hyde would get together with Peckinpah to run his films on videotape; at one point, he and Peckinpah reedited *Alfredo Garcia* to Peckinpah's satisfaction on video. Hyde eventually joined Peckinpah's circle of caretakers: people who would be drawn into a close relationship in which they would serve alternately as playmate and parent to Peckinpah.

Hamilton, a sometime longshoreman, became another of Peckinpah's frequent companions, someone with whom Peckinpah would drink and talk, someone he could count on to watch his back and keep him out of trouble. Sometimes, the company was extremely convivial.

"He had an irresistible kind of energy," Hamilton says. "When he was having fun, he was truly grand, extremely generous. He could walk in any room and take over."

One evening, Peckinpah handed Hamilton a script.

"What is this you're doing?" Hamilton asked.

"It's a war film called *Cross of Iron*," Peckinpah replied. "I can't make sense out of the script."

Hamilton realized that, in his own way, Peckinpah was asking him to sort the script out. Hamilton, in a roundabout way, said he'd be interested in trying to do just that.

Peckinpah had been offered the film by a German producer, Wolf Hartwig, who had assembled money from American, German and Yugoslavian investors to make a film based on Willi Heinrich's novel, *Cross of Iron*. The original screenplay had been written by Julius Epstein, a Hollywood veteran whose credits included *Casablanca*. Peckinpah had turned it over to Walter Kelley for a rewrite, then passed it along to Hamilton for a further reworking.

"The original was a disjointed piece of work that looked as though sections had been lifted straight out of the novel," Hamilton says. "I found a remaindered copy of the novel and rewrote it in twenty-nine days. I got it to the studio the day before he was leaving for Yugoslavia. He had two secretaries typing. Sam was lying in bed with a jug of Henry McKenna whiskey. I sat there all night while they typed and he and I drank. The next day he got in a limo and headed for the airport.

"The script was 160 pages. I had no chance to rewrite or polish the dialogue. What I gave him was structure. The only thing we worked out together was one night when I told him my war experience. Sam was not in combat. I told him that there was a kind of tenderness in an unlikely situation between infantrymen."

Even as he accepted *Cross of Iron*, Peckinpah turned down two other directing offers. One was the Salkind brothers' production of *Superman* (which was eventually directed by Richard Donner). The other was Dino de Laurentiis's remake of *King Kong* (later directed by John Guillermin).

"I turned down *King Kong* to do *Cross of Iron* because I didn't feel I was competent enough to deal with puppets," Peckinpah later joked.

Peckinpah took off for London and then Yugoslavia in January 1976 to do research and preproduction for *Cross of Iron*, which was to begin shooting in March. Even before he got started, he was at odds with Hartwig, a German producer whose main experience had been in soft-core skin films that starred his wife.

Hartwig was a small-timer desperately trying to climb into the big time, using Peckinpah as his stepping-stone. He was able to raise funds on the strength of Peckinpah's name and the names of the actors in the international cast: American James Coburn, Brits James Mason and David Warner, Germans Maximilian Schell and Senta Berger.

But Hartwig never had all the money together at any one time. He'd get it together in increments, spend it on production—pinching pennies to make it go farther—then run off to other parts of the continent to scare up more funds to keep the production afloat.

"We called him Wolf the Bagman," says Bobby Visciglia. "Wolf had this big red Cadillac. He'd come back from a trip with a bag of German marks and we'd keep shooting. He was selling distribution rights as we were filming. It was a constant battle for money."

"Wolf promised us everything, gave us half and charged us double," Coburn says. "Sam said, 'If he wasn't who he was, we'd have had to invent him.' "

Hartwig kept trying to scale back the production, as Peckinpah tried to prepare this story of a German unit at the Russian front in 1943, trying to keep themselves alive as the war effort starts to stall and fail. Even as Peckinpah was doing research, he was fending off lengthy memos from Hartwig about how to cut costs. On January 12, 1976, he wrote to Hartwig: "Your comments on the story are absolutely horseshit. If you cannot read English, get someone who can." He never sent that memo.

The battles with Hartwig over money continued all through filming.

Hartwig wanted a film with Peckinpah's vision, but without a Peckinpah budget. So he scrimped where he could and fought with Peckinpah when Peckinpah protested his pettiness.

On March 3, 1976, Peckinpah wrote a letter to his lawyer, Norma Fink: "People are killing themselves to meet a totally impossible start date due to Mr. Hartwig's incredible lack of foresight and professionalism. I have never seen a budget or a breakdown or a written confirmation of the actors' availabilities.

"I have sent numerous memos to Mr. Hartwig trying to help him anticipate the problems of a major international picture, of which this is his first, but he seems to take no heed whatsoever and I am really getting desperate."

Visciglia recalls, "Sam would say, 'I need ten tanks' and Wolf would say, 'Can you do it with four?' "

The tanks were a constant source of irritation. Aside from Hartwig's cheapness, there was a simple question of availability. There were only so many vintage World War II tanks in working order available in Europe. Most of them had been spoken for by Sir Richard Attenborough, who was shooting *A Bridge Too Far* in the Netherlands.

As a result, for a crucial scene in which the Germans elude Russian tanks, Peckinpah only had two tanks at his disposal. Only one of them moved. It's a testament to his craft and editing ingenuity that this shortage is never apparent in the tense, seamless tank chase.

There were problems in all departments, due to Hartwig's spit-and-baling-wire approach to financing: a lack of qualified stuntmen, substandard costumes, and on and on. Peckinpah's American crew, including Kent James and his wife Carol, Ron and Bitsy Wright, Cliff Coleman, Visciglia, Katy Haber and Walter Kelley, made the best of what they had at hand to give *Cross of Iron* as much realism and grit as they could.

Frustration built on a day-to-day basis. Occasionally, Peckinpah would take it out on the people around him.

"Toward the end, Sam asked for a very difficult instant set," recalls Ted Haworth, the production designer on the film. "I managed it in about three hours. He showed up with the crew, set up and called me to come back to the set. 'Do you mind getting that damn rope from in front of the lens?' he said. I took a stick and raised the rope about three feet and wedged it in. Then I turned around and said loudly, 'You've got a crew of grown men. Never call a boy to do a man's job.' Sam just glared at me. I started up some freshly dug steps and Sam said, 'Don't let the door hit you in the ass on the way out.' I stopped, looked down at the group and said, 'The biggest ass is on the other side of the door.' "

Haworth walked away. Five minutes later, there was an arm around his shoulder; it was Peckinpah, who put his head in close by Haworth's and said, "Jesus, I thought you left me, partner."

"At the rate you're going, Sam," Haworth replied, "you'll leave me before I leave you."

More often, the target of frustration was Wolf Hartwig—for Peckinpah and everyone else.

"He beat Wolf to a pulp," assistant director Cliff Coleman says. "He would go out of his way to insult him and make his life miserable. They turned Wolf into an individual under total stress."

Kent James, the head of wardrobe, cut a furball out of some skins and tied it to a rope. Then he dragged it around behind him, parading in front of the crew as he kicked the furball and called it "Wolfie."

"The Yugoslavians in the crew loved it," James says. "They'd fall on the floor laughing. Wolfie himself didn't like it."

At one point, when Hartwig was late with the payroll, James dressed up as a German soldier, commandeered the tank and stuck the barrel of its gun through the window of a building where Hartwig was in a meeting.

Later in the production, there was a mild earthquake in Zagreb, Yugoslavia, where the company was staying. Hartwig came running out of his hotel room in his underwear with his money stuffed in a suitcase.

"So we would pound on the wall of his room and yell, 'Earthquake,' and he'd come running out every time," James says. "Then he'd look at me and say, 'I do not like this boy.'"

The problems with the payroll were manifold. In April, Ron Wright wrote to Tara Poole, a secretary of Peckinpah's in L.A.: "There are still money problems. Sam still hates Wolf, just a bit too much more than is necessary, and I truly don't feel secure about the picture being finished."

When Coburn's agent told him that he wasn't being paid, Coburn refused to work until the money was forthcoming. Every payroll date was a potential crisis, as Hartwig scrambled to keep the film afloat.

As the situation worsened, Peckinpah called his old friend Frank Kowalski, imploring him to fly over and lend a hand. Kowalski made the trip from L.A. to London, where he met Peckinpah. Once he got there, he discovered Peckinpah had exaggerated the salary he was able to pay him, as well as the general state of the production.

"I get to the hotel and Sam is drunk," Kowalski says. "On the plane to Yugoslavia, all he wants to do is play liar's poker. In Zagreb, I got to my room and, the next morning, everyone is saying how everything is all screwed up. So I got on a plane and went home that day. I should have killed him that night."

On March 25, 1976, Peckinpah sent a telegram to producer Alex Winitzky and lawyer Norma Fink: "As of today the situation is still deteriorating. Certain people have not been paid for four weeks, some for two weeks, and they are getting sick of it. Someone must pay the people that are here or we close down until they are paid, as of tomorrow."

On March 26, Peckinpah followed up with a telegram to Hartwig: "No one works until everyone is paid."

Hartwig came up with the money and production proceeded. On April 11, Peckinpah cabled Alex Winitzky: "Situation deteriorating. Seventy-two-day schedule impossible. Now four days behind."

On April 15, he sent a telegram to Norma Fink: "Situation very serious. Cannot reach you by phone. Hartwig laying blame of four and a half days over schedule totally on me. Please try and call here tonight."

"*Cross of Iron* was a nightmare," Fink says. "The problem was this producer just didn't have the money. Sam called me literally every night. It was one disaster after another."

Katy Haber says, "[Wolf] walked around saying he'd been in a panzer division in World War II and had a bullet in the ass to prove it. The rumor was that Wolf ran brothels for the Germans in Paris during the war."

One victim of Peckinpah's increasingly combative stance was his daughter Sharon, who had signed on at Peckinpah's invitation to shoot a documentary about the making of *Cross of Iron*.

"He said, 'You have to come up with a camera and your own transportation to Yugoslavia,' " Sharon says. "He'd try to help and then he'd pull the rug out from under you. That was our relationship. There was the seed of a parent who wanted to help me out. And there was Mr. Hyde."

Peckinpah, who found it simple to assume the public persona of tough-talking, mythical director Sam Peckinpah for interviews, did just that whenever Sharon turned her camera on him.

"There was a little reality to that image the media created but it wasn't the whole picture," she says. "The macho tough-guy image really disguised this very sensitive, fragile person. It also romanticized his alcoholism. It made it easy for him to continue in the public eye. He didn't have to hide it. It was part of his legend, this hard-drinking guy."

Knowing that and getting him to admit it, however, were two different things. Peckinpah refused to sit down and honestly discuss his work with her on film. In frustration, she finally quit the project.

In a letter to Tara Poole in April 1976, Ron and Bitsy Wright wrote, "Sharon's documentary went down the drain—not sure why—not the easiest person to get along with, and Sam wouldn't let her film him having a fit because there was no coffee on the set, or the electricity in his trailer wasn't hooked up, so he couldn't wash his hands."

"That's when I finally gave up," Sharon says. "There was no way I could ever be a filmmaker. It was too crazy."

Sharon wasn't the only one to leave. In a letter later in the production to friends in the States, Ron Wright wrote, "Sam, in his infinite wisdom, has given us our walking papers in the most gentle of ways: We didn't have to quit and he didn't have to fire us. So this is my last day. His line to me is indelible in my mind, but I think it should be committed to his files: 'The picture business has fucked up more of my relationships than I care to remember and I don't want to see it happen to two of the people I love most in the world.' As much as I care for Sam and his project, my relationship with my wife is too important to jeopardize, so my response was a simple, 'Okay, Sam, and thank you.' "

Even as Peckinpah struggled to make do with Hartwig's rickety budget, he was also coping—as usual—with his own ill health. Early on in the production, he fell and punctured his leg. His body was so deteriorated from drinking that cuts seldom healed easily or quickly. This one festered until he could barely walk; he had to be driven around in the sidecar of a motorcycle by Coleman.

"I ended up physically carrying him around," Coleman says. "I'd go in and pick him up and carry him to the set. But then, I couldn't get him out of his trailer when he had two good legs."

Fearful about crossing international borders, Peckinpah hadn't tried to bring cocaine to Yugoslavia. But he assumed that his handy doctor's bag of prescription drugs—vitamins, sleeping pills and the like—would easily clear customs. Instead, border officials confiscated all of his pills to test them as he entered the country, and didn't return them for two months.

So Peckinpah began drinking more; that, combined with his cigarette habit—two packs a day of filterless Camels and Pall Malls—further weakened his resistance to colds and respiratory infections.

"For someone so afraid of dying, he was amazingly self-destructive," Katy Haber says.

Haber is convinced that Peckinpah suffered a mild heart attack in Yugoslavia that went undiagnosed, a precursor to the one that would nearly kill him in 1979.

"He had chest pains," she says. "He was in terrible pain. We drove to a hospital in the middle of nowhere. It was like out of an English horror movie. One doctor came wafting down the corridor every few hours. They finally gave him nitroglycerine."

To help him recuperate, Haber and Coburn put Peckinpah on a plane and flew with him to Venice for a weekend break from the set. On Saturday morning, Peckinpah, who liked to spend his weekends lounging in bed, told Coburn and Haber to go shopping and find things he'd like, which he'd go see after lunch. In the lobby of the hotel, they ran into Federico Fellini, the Italian cinematic master, whom Coburn had met previously.

Coburn told him they were there with Sam Peckinpah and asked if he would mind coming up to meet him. Fellini agreed.

Peckinpah, who was napping, was testy at being awakened when Coburn knocked on the door. "Who is it, goddamn it?" he barked.

"We've got a surprise for you," Coburn said.

"I hate surprises," Peckinpah growled. But when Coburn entered the room with Fellini in tow, Peckinpah sat bolt upright, like a child awakened from a sound sleep to find Santa Claus standing in his bedroom.

"Oh, Mr. Fellini," Peckinpah said, taking the maestro's hand between his, "thank you for all the wonderful films you've given us."

IN SPITE OF ALL THE CORNER-CUTTING and half-measures that Hartwig inflicted, *Cross of Iron* stands as a hard-edged, grim picture about the hell of war from the point of view of a soldier, one who has a job to do but no particular flag to wave.

That soldier is Corporal Steiner, leader of a reconnaisance platoon in the Taman Peninsula during the retreat from the Russian front in 1943. As the film opens, he and his group are behind enemy lines, taking out a gun emplacement and making an assessment of the coming offensive.

They return to their headquarters to find they have a new commanding officer, Captain Stransky, a Prussian martinet. Stransky tells Steiner that his goal is to win the Iron Cross. But when a Russian offensive is launched, Stransky cowers in his bunker, rather than lead the counterattack.

Steiner receives a concussion and ends up in a hospital, where he is supposed to receive a medical discharge. Instead, he returns to the Russian front. There, he rejoins his old platoon. Stransky asks Steiner to verify him for the Iron Cross for leading the counterattack. Steiner refuses.

When their commanding officer, Colonel Brandt, asks Steiner to testify against Stransky at a court martial for falsifying his own heroism, Steiner also refuses. Brandt, who had defended Steiner's unorthodox methods in the past, can't understand Steiner's refusal. "Do you think because you are more enlightened that I hate you less? I hate all officers," Steiner tells him.

When a major Russian assault looms, German forces are told to retreat, with no rear guard. But Stransky double-crosses Steiner's platoon, failing to notify them of the retreat. They awake to find themselves overrun by Russian troops and tanks.

They escape, eluding tanks and making their way through miles of Russian-held territory to the German lines. When they radio that they are coming through the lines, however, Stransky orders his troops to open fire. Most of Steiner's men are killed but Steiner gets through and kills Stransky's adjutant, then confronts Stransky himself. Instead of killing him, he forces Stransky to join him in the continued retreat from the Russian forces.

CROSS OF IRON wrapped production in the summer of 1976—but not before nearly being shut down one more time for lack of funds. Hartwig enticed the British company EMI Films to provide completion funds in exchange for a percentage of the gross.

Peckinpah moved his operation to London for postproduction work at EMI Studios—along with more acrimony directed at Hartwig over the budget. At one point, he wrote a memo to Hartwig accusing him of pinching pennies to the point of outright theft: "This has been your constant approach to the picture, stepping over a thousand dollars to steal a dime."

They had a particularly heated exchange during editing, leading Peckinpah to send Hartwig a memo on June 30, 1976: "On two separate occasions, you have made direct and indirect threats on my life. I want you to know that I have taken out an insurance policy on myself and it is in your best interest that I stay alive for the next two years."

His health continued to decline as his drinking increased during the editing in London. Peckinpah had taken an apartment and after dinner one evening with Coburn, the two of them decided to walk home.

"Sam was drunk and he fell down five times within a hundred feet," Coburn says, "three times crossing the street. The third time, I left him lying there. I said, 'I'm not picking you up again. I know someone who can help you. You can come up to my apartment and see them—or fuck you. I don't want to watch you destroy yourself.'"

Peckinpah showed up at Coburn's apartment the next day with a bottle of sherry and apologized. Coburn told him, "I can take you to somebody who can save your ass. Otherwise, you're going to blow our friendship by killing yourself."

Peckinpah agreed and Coburn took him to see Norman Thatcher, a British specialist in aikido and shiatsu. Thatcher examined Peckinpah and said, "You're almost too late." He put Peckinpah on a more nutritious diet and told him to stop drinking.

"It probably added five or six years to his life," Coburn says.

Jason Robards had seen Peckinpah around the same time and expressed his concern to Coburn.

"I was doing *Julia* in London and I had lunch with Sam," Robards says. "He looked well but he was shaking hard. It was a hard road back to health. It was very sad not knowing what to do for him. Jimmy stuck by him."

During the same period, Peckinpah reconnected with an old friend who was also struck by the way he looked and acted at the time. Robert Culp arrived in London to act in a TV movie at 5 A.M. one morning, only to reach his hotel and have his phone ring immediately. A British voice said, "This is the secretary to the princess at the palace. We wish to have a retrospective of old outtakes of 'Trackdown' and wondered if you might be able to arrange it."

"Who the fuck is this?" Culp said.

"Hold for Mr. Peckinpah," the voice said.

"I hadn't spoken to him in five years," Culp says now. "But it was like nothing had happened."

The next day, Culp, who was shooting on the same lot where Peckinpah was finishing up some scenes for *Cross of Iron,* went over to meet him and found him effusive and lively, completely sober.

"He wanted me to see the picture," Culp says. "When I saw it, I was bowled over. But Sam was terrified of releasing it. The subject matter would not find an audience unless you begged them into the theater with a set of dishes."

Culp and Peckinpah had dinner shortly after that and Culp remembers Peckinpah being so drunk and weary by the end of the evening "that he put his head on his hands to keep it up."

He wasn't too drunk to offer some startlingly clear-eyed career advice. Culp still wanted to make the transition from actor to director. On this evening, he was holding forth about a picture he was going to direct.

Head on hands, eyes closed, Peckinpah mumbled in a drunken stupor, "You're not ready."

Culp bristled and said, "The fuck I'm not."

Without opening his eyes, but with all trace of alcohol now gone from his voice, Peckinpah said evenly, "Don't you understand? They'll never take you seriously until you stop acting first."

CROSS OF IRON took its toll on Peckinpah, physically and artistically. It was tough, unforgiving material that could have been a significant film, given strong production values and a less chaotic production in general.

"By the time of *Cross,* Sam was already into the dark side," Jim Silke says, "and they ask him to make a movie about Nazis. It was too hard for him. He wanted to say something at the end to make it all right."

Instead, the film's ending was a virtual afterthought, the result of on-camera improvisation when time and money ran out; it ultimately didn't do the rest of the film justice. But Peckinpah once again was clashing with Hartwig, trying to get the time to shoot it correctly and the money to pay the actors to do it.

He got mild revenge while looping the film. When Steiner returns to his platoon after being in the hospital, he walks through the bunker, past the latrine, where a man is just pulling up his trousers. "Hartwig, caught with your pants down again, eh?" a voice says from off-camera.

The film received a spotty release in the United States and equally spotty reviews. Stanley Kaufmann, in the *New Republic,* wrote, "All that Peckinpah seems eager about is making sure that his trademarks are noted. What he doesn't give us is the picture we might have expected from him eight years after *The Wild Bunch.*"

Penelope Gilliatt, in the *New Yorker*, wrote that the film "has unlikably right-wing political prejudices" and called it "as gross and crude a picture as Peckinpah—who is capable of burly lyricism—has made since *Straw Dogs.*"

In *Time*, Christopher Porterfield said, "Peckinpah, haranguing us from the front of the bus about the horrors of war, lends a grisly authenticity to some of the scenes, but he cannot make it all fresh enough to justify the long, grueling trip."

But Jack Kroll, reviewing in *Newsweek*, said, "Peckinpah reminds you of Hemingway in his effort to touch the besieged sweetness at the eye of a storm of violence. This grim, unrelenting film has a brooding power unique to Peckinpah. *Cross of Iron* is another ravaged film by a mysteriously ravaged artist, but it has a genuine heart—you feel its muffled beat somewhere inside the mud and metal of its artificial hell."

Though the film only had a brief run in the United States, it was a commercial hit in Europe and elsewhere in the world. EMI even put together a sequel—involving none of the principals from the original—and rushed it out in Europe. The sequel was never released in the United States.

Peckinpah never complimented Jim Hamilton directly for his contributions to the script. But he said to him a year or so after the film had opened, "Listen, asshole, I had a telegram from Orson Welles and he said he thought it was the best antiwar film since *All's Quiet on the Western Front.*"

31

Convoy to Oblivion

SANDY PECKINPAH, WHO IS MARRIED TO Peckinpah's nephew David, recalls being awakened at 4 A.M. one morning late in 1976. It was Peckinpah calling from London.

"Do you know what my next picture is going to be?" he said over the long-distance link. Then he held a tape player up to the receiver and played a recording of C. W. McCall's song "Convoy," the CB hit that had swept the American charts in 1975.

"We thought he was kidding," Sandy says.

"We hoped he was kidding," adds David. "But Sam was always so frightened that he wouldn't get another picture that he'd take whatever was offered. I don't care if he hired Kurosawa to direct the second unit, *Convoy* still would be a piece of shit."

Convoy effectively called a halt to Peckinpah's career for five long years. His penultimate film set his reputation in cement as a profligate director who would burn money and shoot miles of film on a whim. He was viewed as a crazed, combative drug abuser and drunk, pursuing some chemically induced vision, no matter what the cost to someone else.

Having tried to quit drinking, Peckinpah was using cocaine instead, perhaps not in the same volume as alcohol but certainly at the same level of regularity. It affected his judgment, made him paranoid and led him to test (and, in many cases, sever) his closest friendships.

And he did it while trying to lend depth and meaning to a script he saw as a 1970s version of *The Wild Bunch*—what was in reality a lame trucker comedy built on the brief success of a novelty tune.

C. W. McCall's song had stayed at the top of the charts for several months in 1975. Producer Robert Sherman was riding in his car with his daughter when it came on the radio. Sherman immediately thought the song had movie possibilities and secured the rights. The record was a tall tale about a convoy of semi trucks led by a driver called Rubber Duck, cannonballing across the South to protest the fifty-five-mile-per-hour speed limit, communicating with each other on citizen's band radios.

Writer B. W. L. Norton had the same impulse after hearing the song. When he found that Sherman already owned the rights, he approached him about writing a screenplay. Norton wrote a comedy, and he and Sherman got a deal to produce it with EMI. EMI, which was paying for the completion of *Cross of Iron* at the same time, offered the script to Peckinpah.

"We had a meeting while he was finishing *Cross of Iron*," recalls Michael Deeley, president of EMI. "We discussed *Convoy* and he said he wanted to do it. I thought it was inspirational, the fact that it was this outdoorsy type of show and that there was an obvious analogy to be drawn between the long-distance truck driver and the lone cowboy."

"His decision-making process was odd," says David Wardlow, Peckinpah's agent at the time. "He committed to do it on the basis of a song. He said, 'Make the deal,' and he was more concerned about his expense account than the cash compensation on his gross. The buyers for the film were concerned about his attitude toward schedules and budgets. They offered him $100,000 bonus if he brought it in on schedule and budget."

Norton set out to write a comedy that paid tongue-in-cheek homage to *The Wild Bunch,* one of his favorite films. So he was initially pleased that a director he so admired would be directing his script.

"When he was hired," Norton says, "he said, 'This is the most commercial screenplay I've ever gotten my hands on, and I expect it to be a big hit.' "

But Peckinpah tended to exaggerate his enthusiasm to others (and probably to himself) during preproduction. Once filming started, he said, "I don't have the opportunity of turning down pictures. I have three ex-wives and five children."

Coburn, who was with him in London when he made the decision to do *Convoy,* says, "He took it to get him to stop editing *Cross of Iron*. He knew he couldn't do anything with *Convoy* but whatever turned out would all be created by him."

EMI knew that audience interest in the subject of truckers and CB radios was probably short-lived. But the company felt it might have a chance to be the first film to capitalize on the fad.

Deeley didn't go into the film with blinders on about Peckinpah. "I knew he'd been a drinker," Deeley says. "I had heard the usual amount of talk about his resistance to what some thought were the normal disciplines of a filmmaker. One knew the risk with Sam Peckinpah. But one knew the equal possibility of something special."

Almost immediately, however, Peckinpah began trying to shift the balance of power, consolidating as much as possible for himself by agitating to get rid of Bob Sherman, the producer.

"There were decisions that had to be made right away, but I had a lot of difficulty in pinning Sam down," Deeley says. "Sam seemed determined to get Robert Sherman off. He was very cruel to Sherman."

"He thought Bob Sherman was baggage, a deal-maker," Wardlow says. "He had no respect for him. He perceived Deeley as a bureaucrat, and the enemy."

Even as he was trying to get Sherman fired, he had started to rewrite the script with Norton.

"Rewriting with Peckinpah consisted of driving out to scout locations," Norton says. "He'd start passing cocaine around. He had a secretary with a tape recorder. He'd start blithering dialogue. And she'd type it up and tell me to put it in the script. It just got worse and worse."

Actual writing sessions were "pretty superficial," Norton says. "He would say, 'Let's write dialogue for the background characters.' I had written characters I called Cop One and Cop Two. I remember him telling me, 'You've got to give those people names. Actors respond better to names.'

"When I got tired, they brought a couple of other people in and the script changed dramatically. Originally it was a funny script but it got out of control. At one point, Sam brought Mort Sahl in to lend his wit, but I don't know if Sam used any of what Mort did. With Mort, he tried to lend a larger political motivation to the truckers' strike."

Norton never intended much more than a truck-crashing comedy, built around a kind of *Captains Courageous* idea: a trucker with wives at both ends of his route. He has to drive faster to make more money to support both ends, but runs into trouble when the fifty-five-mile-per-hour speed limit cuts into his ability to keep up.

Peckinpah had cocaine-fueled visions of a tale about the struggle of the little guy in modern society. These weren't just truckers; they were the modern equivalent of the cowboy driving his cattle to market to make a living. They were talking the real language of real Americans, doing it on CB radios.

He continued to rewrite even as the film went into production from a base in Albuquerque, New Mexico, in the spring of 1977. But the script never really got better—just longer and more confused.

"The script was a bad script," says comedian Franklyn Ajaye, who played the trucker Spider Mike in the film. "I compared it to being in a World War II movie where you don't really act. They just showed you in your truck."

At one point during production, Peckinpah decided he needed more of the spirit of the real trucker in the script. He sent James Coburn, who was co-directing the second unit, and Mort Sahl, who was there to work on the script, into truckers' cafés with tape recorders to interview truckers and record conversations.

"What did they object to? Interstate regulations," Coburn says. "There was no conflict. They didn't know what the fuck was going on. Fifty-five miles an hour? Is that what it was all about? He had to invent stuff to make the convoy an entity, to see it as a unit."

Graeme Clifford, the film's supervising editor, says, "On the one hand, he was trying to make a political statement. On the other, it was a basic action-adventure. Sam was trying to graft on political views. To a certain extent, it worked; to a certain extent, it didn't."

In his various efforts to give the script authenticity and depth, he even turned to the actors to write their own parts.

"By the time I got to Albuquerque," says Frank Kowalski, "Sam had convinced the cast their parts were good but needed some rewrites."

"He had me write the governor's speech and then filmed it with nine cameras," says actor Seymour Cassel, who, as the New Mexico governor, had to eulogize Rubber Duck as a metaphor for the American working man.

"The feeling began to emerge," Michael Deeley says, in something of an understatement, "that he would make a different film. He sought to turn a simple story into a film with social significance. The point was that it was a simple story. Neither the nature of the film nor the cast merited a significant statement."

Convoy was about Rubber Duck, an easygoing trucker who gets into an escalating feud with Dirty Lyle, an Arizona sheriff who sets up speed traps and then forces truckers to pay bribes to avoid speeding tickets.

After one such encounter, Duck and two friends, Spider Mike and Pigpen, wind up in a fight at a truck stop with Lyle and a couple of highway patrolmen. They escape but Lyle gives chase. Eventually, through the network of CB radios, Duck's plight turns him into a folk hero. Even as Lyle is enlisting law enforcement aid from neighboring jurisdictions, including New Mexico and Texas, Duck's group is growing, until he is leading a convoy of a hundred trucks across the Southwest.

They finally stop in New Mexico, where the governor, trying to hype his own campaign for the U.S. Senate, offers his help. Spider Mike, who has gone on ahead to be with his wife, who is having a baby, is jailed in Texas and beaten. When Duck, who feels he is being turned into a political pawn, gets the word, he walks out on the New Mexico governor and goes to rescue Mike.

Duck and the truckers spring Mike, then take off for Mexico. Lyle sets up a roadblock on a bridge, with tanks and soldiers to stop them. Duck barrels straight into the assault; his truck explodes and falls off the bridge into the river below.

At a mass open-air funeral in New Mexico, a female journalist who has been Duck's companion on this trip discovers that Duck is still alive and in disguise, as the truckers roll out onto the highway in the never-ending convoy.

PECKINPAH WAS TOO CAGEY to let on to his producers or his studio the extent of his cocaine use. Even he probably was not aware of how it was distorting his judgment and his personality. But the people close to him were aware that cocaine made him unpredictable, paranoid and irritable.

Katy Haber says, "When you're basically paranoid to begin with, all you need is substance abuse to push you over the [edge]. Sam lost perspective and thought everyone was deceiving him. It was depressing to stand around and watch him do it to himself. There he was, destroying his life."

"On Convoy, the cocaine was bad," Bobby Visciglia says. "The story line got lost. Convoy was the big blowout."

Says his nephew David Peckinpah, now a writer-producer, "It was a very Elvis-like situation. Everyone knew he was a drug addict."

Except they still didn't think of it in those terms, because cocaine was so common: "Convoy was a heavy drinking and coking crew," Cliff Coleman says. "Everybody was a coker—it was as simple as that. That was back when they said coke wasn't habit-forming."

In mid-1970s Hollywood, it was only beginning to become apparent just how damaging cocaine could be. Attitudes about coke use were still relatively benign; if not tolerated, cocaine use was certainly ignored.

"Ideas about coke were different in those days," Kip Dellinger says. "Nobody had any idea it was as devastating or addictive as it is. It was prevalent in Hollywood. That didn't mean it was right. But it was considered an okay thing to do."

"Cocaine was so popular," Frank Kowalski says, "I assumed that if people drank martinis, they would do cocaine."

PECKINPAH CAST THE FILM with a couple of old friends: Kris Kristofferson, who was to play Rubber Duck, and Ernest Borgnine, who was to play Dirty Lyle. Other truck-driving roles were filled by Burt Young, Madge Sinclair and Franklyn Ajaye. Seymour Cassel was to play the governor of New Mexico, while Cassie Yates was cast as a waitress with whom Rubber Duck dallies. Ali MacGraw was given the role of the photojournalist who starts out as a hitchhiker in Duck's truck and winds up as his lover.

Peckinpah rounded up as many of the old crew as he could get. Visciglia handled props, and Kent and Carol James did wardrobe. Walter Kelley co-directed second unit with Coburn; Sass Bedig, who had done special effects on Cross of Iron, was hired as well. Otherwise, the producers tried to limit the number of Peckinpah veterans on the crew, on the theory that Peckinpah loyalists would insulate the director and give him more power.

Within the first two weeks of production in the spring of 1977, *Convoy* fell seriously behind schedule. Peckinpah had effectively frozen out producer Robert Sherman. The initial crew was in disarray, morale was low and Peckinpah veterans were being summoned from Los Angeles and elsewhere.

Says Katy Haber, "Robert Sherman was someone Sam was able to overwhelm."

"Sam ate these people like candy bars," Cliff Coleman says. "He did what he wanted to do."

Peckinpah spent a week and a half filming a slapstick fight sequence that was scheduled for three days. That kind of delay put the film over budget and behind schedule immediately.

Gary Combs, who had moved up from stuntman to stunt coordinator for this picture, says, "The production manager scheduled it for three days: two fights in the same room with eleven people. On a normal film, that would be about right. A week and a half later, we were still trying to get it done."

"That fight was supposed to be the catalyst, the scene that justified the movie," says actor Franklyn Ajaye, who was part of the scene. "But if you watch it, you don't know if we're playing it serious or for laughs."

Concerned that his film was spinning out of control before it was barely started, Deeley came to the location to function as the line producer, supplanting Sherman.

"I found a situation where the producer and the director were not on speaking terms," he says. "By the time I got there, there was not a script a person could read. It was a two-camp situation: the sensible filmmaker and the Peckinpah aficionados."

Peckinpah was incensed at Deeley's presence, convinced that it was a vote of no confidence: "Michael [Deeley] is a rock and that angered Sam," Haber says. "Sam couldn't get control and it angered him no end."

But Deeley couldn't quite get control either. The film ended up shooting for almost four months. Scheduled to conclude in July, filming went over schedule, causing a conflict with a concert tour Kristofferson had booked. So *Convoy* closed down for the month of August while Kristofferson went on the road.

To Deeley, Peckinpah's methods were arrogantly wasteful. He was filming the truck crashes with multiple camera setups, with cameras rolling at different speeds to get slow-motion effects.

"It was a shotgun approach," Deeley says. "If he set up seven cameras, he had to have something magical in one of them, he said. The counterargument is that he was not concentrating on the shot that would have the most dramatic effect. It was difficult to see it as other than a lazy way to shoot."

Ajaye says, "The movie has a lot of wasted scenes of trucks going through sand. How many of those can you see?"

Gary Combs remembers sitting in the shade under a truck, while waiting for a shot in Needles, California, when Deeley walked by. Deeley stopped and said to Combs, "You've done a lot of pictures with Sam. Is he doing abnormally poorly?"

"No," Combs said. "This is about average. Did you do any research on him?"

"*Convoy* was a total fiasco every day," Combs says. "Nobody knew what they were doing. It was a total zoo. You always had to interpret what Sam was talking about. You could not get a direct answer out of the man. He'd talk in riddles. He'd tell me one thing and do another."

Franklyn Ajaye says, "He treated the actors with respect but the crew was treated bad. He worked them to death and did it in a disdainful way. One day, they had to shoot coming from Albuquerque to Santa Fe. I went to Santa Fe earlier and that night I'm in the hotel when the crew came in. A bunch of them went straight to the phones in the lobby and started calling their agents, quitting right there on the spot. He had worked them all day with no lunch."

To BE FAIR, there were logistical problems on *Convoy*. As Katy Haber points out, "We were dealing with 150 trucks, five cameras, a helicopter. Ninety percent of the truckers were bit players. Just to coordinate them was a nightmare."

Peckinpah took advantage of whatever the fates threw his way. When a truck overturned on its way to the set, a cameraman, shooting up the end of a roll of film to get extra truck footage, caught it on film. Peckinpah found a way to write the overturned truck into the story so he could use the crash.

"This is a million-dollar stunt that we could never afford," Peckinpah said. When another stunt went awry—a car that was supposed to fly through the roof of a barn seriously overshot the mark—Peckinpah just smiled and said, "Great, we'll use it."

But Peckinpah's behavior, altered by cocaine and alcohol, became more and more erratic. Michael Deeley didn't know what the reason was; he only knew that his director made less and less sense each day.

"He became increasingly eccentric," Deeley says. "I felt as though he was resentful of a lot of things in life. He seemed to create absurd difficulties to his own smooth passage as part of his personal torment."

That torment ranged from strange calls to friends in other parts of the country to bouts of intense paranoia.

"He called me in a coke psychosis from Albuquerque," David Peckinpah says, "saying he was convinced they were going to kill him. I said, 'Who?'

He said, 'Steve McQueen and the Executive Car Leasing Company.' I didn't realize how crazy he had become."

Robert Culp says, "All you have to do is look at the movie and it's not a Sam Peckinpah–directed movie. Nothing worked in the movie."

As David Peckinpah says, "You can't do substances and have a cohesive vision. You've got to have those wires connected. He'd lay out these elaborate setups, then walk away—and when he came back, he had no idea what he'd said."

A *Time* magazine reporter who visited the set for a story described him as a beleaguered figure, not quite able to withstand the onslaught of other people's needs on the set: "The trusty old dog, bastard, genius, otherwise known by his own CB handle, 'Iguana,' is besieged by his staff every time he walks out of the hotel or his air-conditioned trailer," he wrote. "Most of the questions he simply ignores or shrugs off, however, his head shrinking toward his collar like a turtle putting out the 'Out to lunch' sign. Short, hunched, with deep lines across his face, Peckinpah looks older than his fifty-two years. He always gives the impression that he is being stalked by some monster who is about to gobble up him and all his progeny."

Rudy Wurlitzer, the *Pat Garrett* screenwriter, happened across the *Convoy* company while driving to Albuquerque. So he stopped and poked his head into Peckinpah's trailer to say hello.

"He was half-naked, getting a B_{12} shot," Wurlitzer says. "There was a live goat and a .38 with a pulled-back hammer. He said, 'Where the fuck have you been?' He looked fairly ravaged, like he'd aged a bit. It was shocking in a way. He aged very fast in the last four or five years. You could see he had one foot over the cliff, that he was on the edge of the wedge in some way. I could feel this helplessness around him and there was nothing anybody could do."

Filming a long run of the convoy on the highway one day, Peckinpah showed up several hours late. At lunch hour, Peckinpah announced that his helicopter needed to be refueled. "He took off and the first assistant director didn't know whether to break for lunch or not," Gary Combs says. "It was probably two hours before Sam came back. Then he wanted to shoot so we were on meal penalty all day. Then he decides he wants to take the whole convoy of a hundred trucks through the streets of Las Vegas, New Mexico, without warning them.

"Frank Kowalski had been on the wagon the whole picture but he got drunk that day," Combs continues. "He had a recording of Hitler and he started playing it over the two-way radio. Sam could hear it and says, 'Who the fuck is doing that?' Kowalski says, 'Where are you taking this convoy?' Sam says, 'I might be going to take a shit.' Kowalski says, 'That's where you're taking the whole picture.' Sam said, 'Yeah, well, you're fired.' "

When the first assistant director quit midway through the film, the pro-

ducers hired Newt Arnold to come in and ramrod the film back on track —
even though they had rejected Peckinpah's request before the film began to
hire Arnold, because he was a Peckinpah veteran.

"I ended up in Albuquerque with a picture that was out of control,"
Arnold says. "My head was spinning with what I saw."

The production may have reached its nadir the day Peckinpah was supposed to film the funeral sequence for Rubber Duck. A large racetrack had
been rented and the grandstand filled with 3,000 extras. There were more
than a hundred trucks circled on the track itself, and almost all of the principal actors in the film were on hand.

But Peckinpah refused to come out of his trailer. He sat in the trailer the
entire day, while groups huddled to figure out how to get him to come and
direct the sequence. Whether he was sitting in there snorting cocaine, suffering an attack of paranoia or upset at some imagined slight by the producer,
no one knew.

"Everything was ready, everything was in place," Newt Arnold says. "The
second assistant director goes to get Sam, then comes back and says, 'He
won't come out.' "

"He sat in his trailer from 7 A.M. to 7 P.M. and refused to come out,"
Haber says. "I forgot what aggravated him. He had 3,000 people standing
around, 150 trucks, and he didn't shoot until 7 P.M. How many excuses can
you make?"

Finally, at the end of the day, Arnold went in and confronted him. "I
don't know what's going on," he told the director. "You're a talented man.
The shot is ready. All it needs is your eye and your command. Now I want
you on the set."

"Gee, Newt, don't get angry," Peckinpah said. A few minutes later, he
came out and got the shot.

That night, trying to get Peckinpah to commit to the next day's setups,
Arnold finally said in exasperation, "Do you have less respect for yourself
than I do?"

"Gee, Newt," Peckinpah said again, "don't get so angry. What do you
want?"

"Sam, if you don't give me the first shot of the morning tonight," Arnold
said, "I want you at crew call to give us that first shot. Let's shoot the movie.
That's all I want. I'd sure like it if you could give me the information the
night before. It will save you time and it will save us time."

"It was a long conversation," Arnold says now, "about stuff I knew he
knew. The next morning, he came out and did it. And he did it for one day.
The following day, he was back to the same old thing. He wouldn't or
couldn't do it. I don't know which.

"It unfortunately reached a level where I said, 'I'm sorry. I need to help
you but I can't work this way.' I asked to be relieved of the picture. I was

there for a month. I'm sure he felt great disappointment with me. The problems were too great to correct."

Between the last months of *Convoy* and the time of Peckinpah's heart attack in 1979, he systematically alienated most of his closest friends in bizarre tests of their loyalty. He would push them to the limits of friendship, then push them one step farther. If friends gave up on him at that point, it proved to him that they had never been true friends to begin with. Haber says, "It was always, 'Are you loyal or disloyal? Are you willing to lay your life down? If not, I don't want you around.' He was always hardest on the people closest to him."

Along with Newt Arnold, Walter Kelley was among the relationship casualties on *Convoy*. Kelley, who had been with Peckinpah as long as Haber, had an argument with Peckinpah over the way he was treating people and quit. "I didn't speak to him again until after he had his heart attack," he says.

Peckinpah's ongoing disintegration ultimately caused a split between him and Haber. "I'd run out of excuses for him sitting in his trailer all day not coming out," she says. "I couldn't live for him anymore. I didn't have the strength to keep him standing. He was losing control and I was going down with him. I had no self-respect. For my own mental attitude, I felt it would be better to get out. But it's very difficult to leave someone who needs you that much."

Peckinpah made it easier on her: He fired her.

"He told me to go back to L.A. and to take some stuff to Kip and Norma during the hiatus [while Kristofferson was on tour]," she says. "Then I got a call that Sam did not want me around and that I had better leave. So I went to London. Sam called and said, 'What are you doing in London?' I said, 'You know damn well.' He was jealous. I was having a relationship with a camera operator. He was very possessive about people around him."

Shortly afterward, Michael Deeley called and offered her a job with EMI, working on *The Deer Hunter*. Haber accepted—and never spoke to Peckinpah again.

For all of Peckinpah's personal problems, of course, the film had other troubles as well. Peckinpah had reduced the script to a series of scenes that alternated between truckers driving in a convoy and truckers talking politics, with the occasional shot of one vehicle crashing into another. Even with a coherent script, it would have been tough to make much of it, given the casting.

Kristofferson was more of a presence than an actor. In *Pat Garrett*, Peckinpah had surrounded him with the cream of Hollywood's character actors and just let Kristofferson react to them. In *Alfredo Garcia*, he only had a rape scene to handle. But in *Convoy*, Kristofferson was expected to carry the action, to be the catalyst.

He wasn't that kind of actor. Neither was Ali MacGraw.

Together, the two of them were like cinematic black holes, draining the energy out of any scene they played together. Sitting in the cab of that truck, driving down the highway, there was nowhere for the two leads to hide and nothing to do except keep on trucking.

"Everybody knew these were two low-key actors with nothing happening between them," says Gordon Dawson, who turned down Peckinpah's offers to come help.

The feeling was strong on the set that though they had signed up to work with the legendary Sam Peckinpah, what they had gotten was the legend in decline, a man of great facility whose control of his powers had slipped from his grasp.

"I'm a huge fan of Peckinpah," writer B. W. L. Norton says. "So it was something of a letdown to see this guy I admire fuck up this movie."

"You can't do what he did to himself and not destroy yourself," Gary Combs says. "He got old real fast. I hated to see him destroy himself."

"I felt I had come in and worked with a genius on his way down," Franklyn Ajaye says. "Sam was in control of the set. Was he in control of his skills? Judging by the finished product, I'd say no."

As the production shut down for the month of August to accommodate Kristofferson's concert tour, there were rumors that EMI was going to step in and have someone else finish the production. Deeley says now that EMI never had any intention of taking such a step.

"Replacing him would have been normal studio behavior," Deeley says. "The idea may have come up. The fact is I had undertaken to deliver a picture directed by Sam Peckinpah and I was going to, if humanly possible."

But those rumors made their way back to Peckinpah, who began sifting his own conversations with Deeley to see if there were any veiled threats. A paranoid man anyway, Peckinpah had no trouble finding all the evidence he needed to convince himself that a coup was imminent.

Always convinced that he would be fired, Peckinpah began readying his story for the point when the film was taken away from him, to escape responsibility for a movie that didn't work. He also began making noises about quitting if EMI didn't stop pressuring him.

"I have heard recently suggestions that you would prefer to leave and hand over the picture to somebody else," Deeley wrote in an August 19, 1977, memo. "EMI has spent so far $9.5 million on the incomplete *Convoy* and I have personally supported you stalwartly through all the failures and adversities of this production. Now it is time some effective support comes from you and you do the detailed work required to prepare the completion of this."

Peckinpah replied by telegram, on August 23, 1977: "I do not know what you've heard about my preferring to leave. I do know I was informed that you were considering replacing me and took this information directly to you.

We met in my trailer, as you recall. When I brought it up, you replied it was under consideration. I replied, 'Perhaps someone else could get the job done faster.' You instantly asked me if I had anyone in mind. By that time, I did have something in mind. I had in mind that you and Tony Wade and obviously Bob Sherman wanted me off the picture. Maybe you are right, Michael, but regardless of whether you are right or not, I do not want off the picture.

"I don't intend to quit, neither do I intend to change my style or destroy my work or my reputation by doing less than my best. It is your decision as to whether you want a Sam Peckinpah picture and I intend to keep trying to make one, regardless of adversity, stupidity, incompetence and lack of organization that we both have witnessed."

Deeley responded by telegram on August 25: "Any thoughts about replacing you on *Convoy* emanated entirely from your remarks to Tony Wade and subsequently to me that in your opinion we would be better off having another director finish the picture. Had you chosen to quit, clearly, we would need to have another standby arrangement. In any event I am absolutely delighted by your assurances you do not wish to go. For whatever reasons, there have been many script changes, some of which I knew the reasons for and some of which I did not. Now that we have a picture which is unfinished and $2.5 million over budget, it is inappropriate for there to be any undisciplined approach to completion. We have already shot nearly fourteen weeks on a picture scheduled for eleven.

"Obviously, we all want the best picture, but your reference to changing your style and destroying your work and your reputation have to be reconciled to professionalism and propriety."

CONVOY ENDED UP two months behind and almost $3 million over budget. Before production was finished, *Smokey and the Bandit*, starring Burt Reynolds, was released. It became one of the surprise hits of the summer of 1977, which otherwise had been dominated by *Star Wars*. That took the shine off *Convoy* as an action-comedy about a dispute between truckers and the highway patrol.

But *Convoy* still wasn't complete. After coming back from hiatus and shooting another couple of weeks, Peckinpah had to go back and shoot still more footage a month after that.

"At one point, I told him he had another week and then I was pulling the plug," Deeley says. "He came up with a list of shots that would have added six weeks to the production. He had six pages of scenes that would have extended the film to four hours. We shot for two weeks."

The delays didn't end when the camera stopped rolling. "The editing was torturous," Deeley says. "There were two editors working with him. We missed four deadlines. His cut had a scene of Ali MacGraw running across the screen upside down. He had his cut three times over and that was it."

Editing took so long because, using his slow-motion, multicamera setups, Peckinpah had shot more than a million feet of film—closer to 1.25 million feet, nearly enough to stretch from Hollywood to Las Vegas.

"Working with him was difficult because he used so much film," editor Graeme Clifford says. "He was the kind of director who wanted to try everything. He was never satisfied until you had cut a scene sixteen million different ways from Sunday. And it was a pretty excessive amount of film to condense into a regular-length movie."

B. W. L. Norton says, "I eventually saw a screening of the director's cut. It was about two hours long and it covered, in terms of my script, up to page sixty or seventy. Then there was the card 'SCENE MISSING.' Then it cut to the end. It was a complete disaster."

"Sam sensed they were going to take the picture away," Robert Culp says. "Sam had a bunker mentality anyway. He called me and said, 'Get over here.' I went to his office and he was so high you couldn't reach his toes. He was whispering. He explained the walls were bugged. I said, 'What are you talking about?' 'They're going to take the picture away and I've got to stop them,' he said.

"There was a meeting in the screening room. They stood up, the producer and everyone else, and stripped him of all remaining power in front of everybody. It was like breaking the guy's sword in front of the troops."

Paul Peterson, the ex-brother-in-law who was Peckinpah's constant companion, says, "It was very important to Sam to believe he was a victim. When he knew he was going to be fired from *Convoy,* he stayed up all night working on a speech that he wanted to seem impromptu."

PECKINPAH ALWAYS INSISTED that he didn't have the opportunity to finish *Convoy* the way he wanted. "We ran eight reels of supposedly the director's cut," he said. "My first cut and that's all I've ever seen. At one point, I thought it had the chance of being one of my best movies, but then it was jerked away from me by idiots and the movie I was making went out the window. I never saw it all. If I had, I might have gone looking for unregistered arms to commit some act of violence."

In a letter to Ernest Borgnine in September 1979, Peckinpah wrote: "The truth was, they stalled me until my contract time ran out and then kicked my ass out. I haven't seen the film and don't intend to. I am damned sure you came off fine and in any case made some money."

Peckinpah was pressing EMI to give him eight months for the editing. As it was, with the various delays, the film wasn't released until late summer 1978; the added months might have meant holding it until 1979.

Deeley says, "He didn't want it to be seen and he didn't want to sit around. We finally took it away from him and it was edited by Graeme Clifford."

David Wardlow, Peckinpah's agent at the time, confirms: "He was way overdue with his cut. He was living at Goldwyn. They had a release date and they were afraid he wasn't going to make it. As an incentive, they proposed a sizable amount of cash to buy him out of the film, which he elected to do."

But Clifford says, "The fact that the film was taken away was built into a whole event when it was really a nonevent. Sam was still involved, although it was officially taken away. We were in communication throughout. I was trying to cut according to his wishes. It was pretty well finished by the time he left."

EMI offered to buy back his profit participation in the film for $700,000. Peckinpah took the deal, losing money he would have earned if he'd been fired outright. Despite its quality, *Convoy* was a hit in the southern United States and abroad, eventually earning $11 million in the United States and $35 million in foreign dates. If Peckinpah had been fired and had retained his profit participation, his cut would have been around $1 million.

Even the buy-out ended with a Peckinpah touch. During production, Peckinpah had collected all of his expense money in cash, then charged all of his meals to the production. EMI had withheld his last three paychecks. Peckinpah decided to dispute the expenses and took Kip Dellinger, his business manager, with him.

"It was a joke—Sam had to get a leg up on somebody," Dellinger says. "We negotiated and got them to the point that he was going to get half the money. I was going to make the deal for 50 percent and I said, 'Sam, is that okay?' He said, 'No.' They said, 'What would make you happy?' He said, 'Can you throw in a case of Cristal champagne?' They said okay. He said, 'How about two?' They did—and he thought he got the better part of the bargain."

CONVOY WOUND UP as a plodding, tendentious effort, a failed comedy devoid of wit. What value there is can be seen in the editing, which lends excitement to an otherwise mundane script, enhancing material that can never rise beyond the level of mediocrity.

Pauline Kael tried to be kind, scolding the film's most vocal critics by saying the film should be taken for what it was: a bumptious yarn with a cornpone sense of humor.

But Frank Rich wrote in *Time:* "*Convoy,* which seems to be Sam Peckinpah's uncalled-for remake of *Smokey and the Bandit,* is roughly as much fun as a ride on the New Jersey Turnpike with the windows open. It not only numbs the brain but also pollutes the senses. This time the director doesn't even bother to reward his hardcore fans with some gratuitous violence or mean-spirited sex."

Variety wrote, "Scores of craft personnel assisted in setting up the unmotivated crashes and such; it's not their fault there's nothing in the story to really justify such a cynical waste of time and money."

And David Ansen, in *Newsweek,* said, "Director Sam Peckinpah imprints his name on every frame of *Convoy,* and his name is mud. The spectacle of his continuing skid is a sad one."

Ansen's phrase—"his continuing skid"—was more than apropos for what was to come in the next half-decade, as Peckinpah scuffled for work.

"With *Convoy,* he forfeited his credentials as a serious director," David Peckinpah says. "It's one thing for Hal Needham to make that movie. But important directors don't do movies based on CB songs."

The effect on his career, his nephew adds, was predictable: "Film directors rarely bottom out and come back," he says. "An actor's heat is like flash paper. A writer's heat is like cast iron. But directors don't retain heat at all. Sam pissed off a lot of people on *Convoy.* The word got around."

Part Eight

1978-1982

I'm really curious to know what you think you're involved in, because I'm beginning to think I have no idea.

—Line from *Convoy*

Comfort yourself with the thought that you never did have a choice. It's usually the case.

—Line from *The Osterman Weekend*

32

Years in Exile, Part II

DURING THE PRODUCTION OF *CONVOY*, Warren Oates showed up on location unannounced one day and stayed "for a three-day drunk," according to Bobby Visciglia. Before he left, however, he'd gotten Peckinpah involved in a real-estate deal.

Oates owned about six hundred acres in the mountains outside of Livingston, Montana, where he had built a cabin. He was having trouble making the payments and offered to sell half of the land to Peckinpah, on which Peckinpah could build a cabin of his own.

Peckinpah sent his brother Denny with Oates up to Livingston to check out the property. "We were sitting on the deck looking over the mountain," Denny recalls. "It was spring and we counted about twenty-five head of elk and an equal number of deer feeding on the mountain. You could see them from the deck; it was all part of the ranch. I knew Sam would be wild for it."

Peckinpah made the deal and immediately ordered the construction of a cabin of his own on the property, several miles from Oates's and about forty miles outside of Livingston. While he was waiting for it to be built, he went back to Sausalito, living with Paul Peterson, using him as a right-hand man, writing partner and running buddy.

Immediately after *Convoy*, Peckinpah flew off to Italy, to appear in the film *China 9, Liberty 37*, as a favor to director Monte Hellman. But because of the delays on *Convoy*, he wound up with a different part than Hellman originally intended.

"We actually had several roles pinpointed for him," Hellman says. "Each time he was supposed to come and didn't, the role would be cast with someone else. There was one last role on the last day of shooting and I was amazed when he got off the plane. He played a newspaper writer and he was terrific. He was a born actor. I joked, 'How did you learn to act?' and he said, 'I've been doing it all my life.' "

Peckinpah shot in Rome for a day. That evening, he and Hellman and Jerry Harvey, the picture's producer, got together. Peckinpah decided he wanted Harvey to get hold of Fellini for him. Harvey dialed the number wrong and reached the hotel restaurant instead.

Peckinpah took the phone and, thinking he had Fellini on the line, said grandly, "Maestro." The maître d', assuming Peckinpah was addressing him, carried on a conversation for several minutes. When he began to suggest possible entrées for dinner, Peckinpah finally realized who he was talking to. He calmly made dinner reservations—before hanging up and tongue-lashing Harvey for making him look foolish.

Once back from Italy (and a cameo in another Italian film, *The Visitor,* for which another voice was eventually dubbed for his), Peckinpah settled with Peterson into a routine of cocaine, travel and debauchery, all ostensibly while trying to write scripts and get another picture to do. They traveled a circuit from the San Francisco Bay Area to Mexico City to Livingston, promoting projects that never got made.

They spent several months in Mexico City to establish Peckinpah's Mexican residency, so that he could set up a production company with Emilio Fernandez, actor Jorge Russek, Isela Vega and Alex Phillips, Jr. Peckinpah figured that, with his own company, he would be free of the prying hands of studio executives. The company would raise money and produce films that Peckinpah wanted to make in Mexico.

During the residency period, Peckinpah and Peterson moved back and forth between Mexico City and Cuernavaca. In Mexico City, he would visit Begonia and try to establish a relationship with his daughter Lupita. But most of his time was devoted to drinking, cocaine and chasing women.

"We rented a place in Cuernavaca and hid out," Peterson says. "The typical day, we'd sleep until noon, or not at all, depending on the cocaine supply. Then we'd get up. Somebody would come to the house, a Mexican actor or whoever, and the drinking would start early. We basically did nothing; we squandered our lives. We just spent a lot of time in the house."

When there was cocaine, they did cocaine. When there wasn't, they would drink.

"He hated to make drinks," Peterson says. "Frankly, it was easier if I made them because he'd screw them up. But one day he insisted. We were in Mexico, during this period where we were drinking Camparis. There was no cocaine around so we sat around for a couple of hours drinking these Camparis he was mixing and my mouth went numb. I had no feeling in it. It turned out we had just drunk two bottles of Lavoris. So the numbness was a normal feeling."

Occasionally, Peckinpah would find a whore who pleased him, only to end up mistreating her before the evening was through. Peterson says, "We were at the El Presidente in Mexico City and he had this whore who he just wanted to give him head. She made the mistake of glancing at the TV and he caught her. He pounded her on the head with a roll of toilet paper; she wasn't giving him her full attention."

It wasn't the only such encounter Peterson was party to. "I think Sam had a contempt for whores at the same time that he really believed they were as honest as women could be," Peterson says. "He was a misogynist. He believed he'd been screwed over by women. He didn't have to worry that a whore would do that. That gave him a feeling of security.

"He'd always hassle the whores, though. He didn't want to pay them. Everything was a struggle with Sam. No matter where we were, you always worried about whether they were going to come and arrest you for something Sam did."

The residency period wound up as a bust. While Peckinpah was granted residency, the production company never got off the ground. Peckinpah said, "I tried to set up a production company in Mexico and we went broke. Finances are not my forte."

"We talked about points one night and what we each would do for the company," Phillips says. "But it never happened. We had two screenplays but we were never able to put the money together. We didn't have the money to produce a Peckinpah movie."

Peckinpah's interest in spending more time with Lupita was thwarted by Begonia, who worried that he would steal her and take her back to L.A. Peckinpah's friends who saw him worried about his health. He seemed on the verge of some kind of collapse, but no one was willing or able to convince him that he was killing himself.

"Jason [Robards] and his wife called me from Connecticut to say Sam was in bad shape," Daniel Melnick says. "Sam was drinking a lot and finding it very hard to get work. Twice I made trips to Mexico to get him straight, into AA or something. The first day, I'd show up and he'd embrace me and get teary and say, 'By God, to have friends like you and Jason.' By the night, he'd be saying, 'You cocksucker. I'll do what I want to do. Don't be a Salvation Army band leader.'"

Peckinpah and Peterson headed back to Sausalito, commuting to Livingston to see how work was coming on his cabin. There was the occasional expression of interest in Peckinpah from the outside world, but no offers of work.

One inquiry came from the Seattle Film Society, which invited him to be guest of honor at a tribute to his work. Peckinpah accepted and went to Seattle for the weekend of July 19, 1978. The hosts for the society were critics Richard Jameson (now editor of *Film Comment*) and his wife, Kathleen Murphy. Peckinpah was aware of Murphy because she was one of the few women to favorably review *Straw Dogs*.

Arriving in Seattle, Peckinpah repaired to the airport bar with Jameson and other members of a welcoming committee. Peckinpah announced that he was on the wagon, then ordered port and sack. Jameson ordered a bourbon and, after a few minutes, realized that his and Peckinpah's glasses had been switched.

"I believe I have your drink," Jameson said.

"Oh really?" Peckinpah said. "What are you drinking?"

Jameson said, "Wild Turkey." Peckinpah picked up the glass in front of him, drained about half of it and then handed it to Jameson: "I believe you're right, partner."

Expecting to be confronted with a hostile audience at the tribute, Peckinpah instead found an adoring one, which asked sympathetic questions about studio interference and other problems he had faced. "I think he really began to feel he was among friends," Jameson says.

"He seemed pleased at the respect he got," Murphy says. "He was very responsive to that. There was a gallantry and an intensity in his courtesy to people. He was supposed to be the Bad Boy of Hollywood. So it was interesting to see him as an old-fashioned gentleman."

Having decided Jameson and Murphy were all right, Peckinpah took Jameson aside the first evening, pulled out a vial of cocaine and said, "Do you ever do this? Would you like to try?"

"It was one of the few times I ever tried cocaine," Jameson says. "We had a party for him at our house and, when my wife was rearranging the cushions afterward, she found a rolled-up $100 bill."

Always in search of new accomplices, Peckinpah decided Jameson and Murphy were ripe for temptation and offered them a chance. "He started talking about a treatment for a film that he had which was hopeless in its present form," Jameson says. "He started saying, 'You and Kathleen will write a new treatment and change it and make it 1,000 percent better. You'll come down to Sausalito. And I'll pay you $500.' We were astonished."

"We read it fast and wrote it fast and gave it to him," Murphy says.

The story was called "The Door in the Jungle." "There were pieces of *Treasure of the Sierra Madre* but it was in South America," Jameson says. "There was a lot of hot fucking with dusky women. We played around with it a lot."

In Sausalito, they stayed at Peckinpah's apartment, a little place on the edge of the water. But they never actually got to work with Peckinpah because, shortly after their arrival, a woman friend of Peckinpah's, Marcy Blueher, whom he'd met while filming *Convoy*, came for a visit with her three children. So Jameson and Murphy moved out.

Jameson recalls spending an evening smoking grass with Paul Peterson and others on the balcony overlooking the bay. "There were boats moving and we could see their lights," Jameson says. "One boat was coming in in a kind of snaky fashion. Paul deadpanned, 'I don't like the way that boat is moving around.' He was pretending there was someone sneaking in; it was a joke. But there was no question that they had this locked-in, embattled mentality. The door was immediately locked any time it was opened. It was like somebody was going to get in or somebody might attack."

The evening they did stay, Murphy says, she woke up in the middle of the night and heard music, which she recognized as the theme from *The Wild Bunch*. "It seemed to be coming in over the water," she says. "I assumed I was hallucinating. It turned out that Sam was in his bedroom, watching *The Wild Bunch*."

PECKINPAH UNDERSTOOD that he couldn't handle alcohol, Peterson believes. "Between us, Sam knew his drinking was a problem. He wasn't a fool. Sam was a bona fide alcoholic. Denial was part of the process. No true alcoholic lives up to it. He knew he was a naughty boy but he couldn't accept that. He could articulate it at 3 A.M. but the next day, when he'd have a run-in with a producer, to his mind the producer was a prick."

So he leaned on the cocaine to help him give up drinking. He liked cocaine, obviously, for the feeling it gave him—the sense of invulnerability and indefatigable energy. But he also liked the risk of it, the chance to flout the rules, to be an outlaw and live on the edge.

"We would pack coke into capsules to take on planes," Peterson says. "He had an obsession with fingerprints so we would spend literally hours wiping fingerprints off a vial of coke and then burying it in a deserted location in Montana. It was that element of danger he lived for. Every time he got away with it, he was like a little kid."

When he did cocaine, he turned a disapproving eye on people who drank. He saw them as weaklings who relied on alcohol, an obviously debilitating substance, when cocaine was obviously so much less detrimental to the health.

"When he stopped using grass," says Joe Bernhard, "then everybody who used it was an asshole. When he gravitated to cocaine, then all his drinking buddies were the enemy."

John Bryson recalls giving a party for British star Trevor Howard at Bryson's Malibu house during this period. Peckinpah was invited because he was Bryson's friend but also because Howard wanted to meet him.

Howard, a serious drinker with a large nose made red and outsized by years of alcoholic indulgence, held court on the deck of Bryson's house. Peckinpah retired to a back bedroom with friends, snorting cocaine through $100 bills. Finally, Bryson intruded on Peckinpah's privacy to ask him to please make the gesture of meeting Howard.

"Sam, for Christ's sake, come out to the back deck," Bryson said. "Trevor is dying to visit with you. This is a party in his honor."

Peckinpah did another toot, looked at Bryson and growled, "I can't stand drunks."

PECKINPAH AND PETERSON would work sporadically, writing scripts and discussing film, a process that made the four or five years he devoted to Sam Peckinpah worth the time, Peterson says. He doesn't blame Peckinpah for the state of dissolution they both eventually reached.

"We were both hard on ourselves," Peterson says. "I was doing cocaine with him. I wasn't suffering under his weight. It was mutual. The fact that we did it mutually was the reason I spent so much time.

"My duties ranged from baby-sitting to being a gofer to actually writing. We wrote two scripts. Probably more than anything, I was there because he wanted me to be there. If he wanted me to wax his car, that was good enough for me.

"We were inseparable. There was not a day that we weren't with each other twenty-four hours. It was a dependency. Sam couldn't stand to be alone. When we'd go to hotels, we either stayed in the same room or adjoining rooms. I happened to be the person he chose to hang around with all the time. Some days felt like they lasted a hundred years.

"I loved Sam. Even at his worst, the bottom line was that I loved him. For all the bad, bad days or months or years, there were moments that were the absolute essence of creativity, when I got to see him at his best. I kind of lived for that. The high point was working on those scripts.

"We'd start out just talking, talking about a character. We'd pick out a scene and imagine it, go into great detail, down to the boots the guy was wearing. When we finished that scene, we'd go on to a subsequent scene, not necessarily in sequence. We might start at reel fifteen and go backwards. I would sit and type and he'd critique my output.

"He taught me that producers don't read scripts. He had this trick: You rub a little rubber cement on the corners of a few pages in the middle. When you get the script back, if that seal isn't broken, you can safely assume they haven't read it. On the first script we worked on, I did that to Sam. The next day he gave it back to me and he'd scribbled on the title page, 'This is a piece of shit. Redo it.' But the seal wasn't broken. So I didn't touch it but I kept it a day. Then I gave it back to him. And he loved it. He figured you were a good student if you put one over on him."

But you also had to be willing to suffer the same fate at his hands. As Allen Keller, a rodeo cowboy and stuntman who had tagged along with Peckinpah as an unofficial bodyguard at times, put it, "He was my friend—and Sam loved to fuck his friends."

"I once lived with a wonderful man in Mexico," Peckinpah said. "He was the most trustworthy man I have ever met. I would have done anything for him. I would have put my family in his care. He took me for every cent. A true friend is one who is really able to screw you."

"Sam had a death wish for his friends," says L. Q. Jones. Joe Bernhard adds, "He torpedoed everybody who ever did anything with him. Why do you fuck with loyalty? He always did it."

While the cabin in Montana was being finished, Peckinpah and Peterson decided to make a clean break with Hollywood and start living their lives in Livingston. So Peckinpah began severing even more relationships in Hollywood, pushing everyone away from him.

He fired Kip Dellinger as his business manager and split with attorney Norma Fink. He also became estranged from his sister Fern Lea and her husband, Walter Peter. Fern Lea disapproved of Peckinpah's drug use and said so.

"There were a lot of values in *The Wild Bunch* that I could relate to," Dellinger says. "That was Sam's film. I expected those values to be Sam's. But it was like he gave lip service to those values. Sam might address them but he didn't live by them."

In Livingston, Peckinpah spent much of his time living at the Yellowstone Motor Inn and the Murray Hotel. His cabin, now completed, was too far into the wilderness to have electricity or indoor bathroom facilities. While he loved the idea of the cabin, he wasn't as enamored of actually staying there as he thought he would be.

With his notoriety and his visibility, as well as his drug habit, he became a target for scam artists and hustlers. Peckinpah, sharply perceptive at reading new people normally, was ruled by paranoia, focusing on the imagined forces he was sure were seeking his downfall.

"In his mind, everybody was trying to screw Sam," Peterson says. "The IRS, the Mexican government, the American government—they were all out to get him. He used bad judgement. He got taken advantage of by a lot of people. He let it happen. He was always being hustled by people. Everybody had a deal for Sam."

Still, Peckinpah found a real friend in a lawyer he hired in Livingston to handle his various affairs there. Joe Swindlehurst had never seen anyone like Sam Peckinpah, at least not in person, before Peckinpah walked into his office one afternoon in 1977.

"He was dressed up in a scarf and this funny little hat, a cap with a bill that you'd expect to see in Great Britain," Swindlehurst says. "And he had a woman with him who wrote down everything he said. I had difficulty understanding what he was talking about. If I didn't understand something, I'd ignore it. If it was important, Sam would say it three or four times."

Swindlehurst earned Peckinpah's loyalty when he successfully defended him against an assault charge pressed by some college students who had been staying at Peckinpah's cabin. They were there as fans and film students;

in the course of an evening of drinking, Peckinpah took umbrage with the way one of the young men was handling a knife and pulled a pistol on him, going so far as to smack him with it.

"Sam allegedly cleaned the earwax out of some guy's ear with a pistol," Swindlehurst says. "I got him out of it. There were a group of college students staying with him in his cabin. One of them said Sam went berserk and attacked him with a pistol because he was sleeping in Sam's bed. They claimed Sam had brandished a pistol and Sam said they'd attacked him with a knife. They had him arrested, but he got off."

Peckinpah became a regular guest at the Swindlehurst house for dinners with Swindlehurst and his then wife, Carolyn. Contrary to the Hollywood image of the wild, rough and legendary film director, Carolyn Swindlehurst says, "He was a very shy man. That's something I feel very strongly about. It's not a commonly held feeling but it was mine. He was a very gentle and sensitive man. We were good friends and he would talk about his work, about his feelings, about his children. He loved and cared and thought and worried and wondered about his children."

STILL FASCINATED BY COCAINE, Peckinpah was also intrigued with the whole cocaine subculture. Robert Sabbag chronicled it in an early 1980s book, *Snowblind;* Peckinpah looked into the possibility of making a film of the book.

"A great story," he said at one point. "It tells a lot about the subculture of the United States in the late 1960s and early 1970s."

Peckinpah took a trip to Bogotá with actor Seymour Cassel, ostensibly to do research for the film. Their true purpose remains sketchy, but, at one point, Peckinpah and Cassel wound up under arrest in the South American cocaine capital.

Cassel says, "It got pretty scary. We didn't know how scary because we were having a good time. The way to be protected was to have the Colombians know what you were doing. They kept offering us guns but we knew if we had them, we'd have to use them. I introduced him to some people down there. They wanted to do a movie about grass but he said, 'Coke,' because of the anger and the craziness.

"This was 1978 and it got a little crazy. I saw a guy get shot in the ass with his own gun in the airport. They had an interview with Sam in the newspaper and called it 'Messiah of Violence.' He didn't have a visa, because it had run out coming in on the plane. So we had eight days to stay. In Bogotá, I left the hotel, went out and got fourteen hookers but they wouldn't let me bring them in. So Sam moved out to this country club and I moved into this house by myself. He took my passport and ran off. So I couldn't leave the country until my wife brought me down a new passport."

When he came back, Peckinpah became more paranoid and increasingly isolated, Peterson says, spending long periods of time holed up in the hotel in Livingston and in his cabin. He kept Peterson constantly by his side, no matter what the circumstance.

"One night in Montana, I had to watch him go down on a 400-pound woman for four hours," Peterson says. "She was obese. But Sam was screwing everything. He had a penchant for unattractive women in particular. That was his paranoia. Sam felt safe with people like that. He didn't feel they would take advantage of him. He could have screwed any starlet with a casting-couch promise but he didn't. He'd just as soon get a whore off the street in Mexico."

The drinking and cocaine use increased. "It got so bad that one night in Montana, at the peak of Sam's paranoia, he saw lights off in the distance," Peterson says. "It was minus forty degrees and we were staying at Warren Oates's place. We were convinced they were flying saucers. We were so convinced that we called the sheriff. He came out and looked at us like we were crazy. We loaded all the rifles. We were convinced that aliens had nothing better to do than invade Montana when it's forty degrees below zero."

His daughter Kristen was invited to visit Livingston in January 1979 and was alarmed at what she found. Peckinpah had not been sleeping, driving himself with a steady intake of alcohol and cocaine. Emaciated and gray-skinned, he had haunted eyes and was talking about government conspiracies. He was sleeping with a loaded shotgun in his bed, with the muzzle pointed toward his head. Shaken, she called Gill Dennis, who called Jim Silke.

"He was on the mountain and was either going to kill himself or freeze to death," Silke says. "Kristen called and said, 'Jim, what would you do?' I finally said there was only one thing she could do. I said, 'You've got to go and take over. You just have to take over. When you come through the door, he'll know it.' "

She drove back up to the cabin and found Peckinpah in a frightening state.

"He was convinced the phone was bugged. He kept telling me he wanted me to leave because he didn't want me to get hurt. It was extremely alarming. I didn't know if this was self-dramatization or how much of it he truly believed. Or whether he was just trying to make an impression on me."

After listening to him rant, she walked over to him, looked him in the eye and said, "Dad, I want you to come back down to the hotel with me."

He looked at her and said, "Okay, honey," and went without an argument. "He had the room next to mine and I'd listen to him talking to himself, into a tape recorder," Kristen says.

33

Heart Attack

ON MAY 15, 1979, PECKINPAH WAS IN HIS ROOM at the Yellowstone Motor Inn, talking on the phone to his friend Dr. Bob Gray back in Beverly Hills.

"You know, Bob, I'm not feeling so good," Peckinpah said, describing the symptoms of a heart attack. Gray told Peckinpah to sit still for a moment, put him on hold and called the hotel, to alert them that Peckinpah was having a heart attack. Swindlehurst, who was calling the hotel at the same time, was given the news.

Fortunately for Peckinpah, a group of nurses were gathered in a meeting room at the Yellowstone Motor Inn to discuss a possible walkout at the local hospitals. The switchboard alerted the nurses; some went to Peckinpah's room, while others alerted the hospital to send an ambulance.

Swindlehurst drove straight to the hospital, where he found Dr. Dennis Noteboom, who handled Peckinpah in the emergency room.

"I don't think this guy's going to make it," Noteboom told him. "He's had a heart attack and he has hardly any blood pressure. He's shocky—cold, pale, sweaty."

But they managed to stabilize him and determine that he was suffering from coronary blockage complicated by an arrhythmia. (Alcohol, a solvent, tends to dissolve fat in tissues, which flows through the blood and accumulates in the arteries and heart.) Peckinpah would require an extended hospital stay as well as a heart pacemaker.

But Peckinpah was a difficult patient. It wasn't just the restrictions inherent in hospitalization; he was also going through withdrawal and detoxification from alcohol, cocaine, cigarettes, Quaaludes and everything else he'd been taking.

"He was definitely in withdrawal for about ten days," Noteboom says. "That didn't help the heart attack situation any. He was a person who was living a high-stress life. He took life that way. The drugs and alcohol were a reflection of the amount of stress."

He made life hell for both the nurses at the hospital and for the friends and family who converged on Livingston to be with him.

"He attracted slightly psychotic people and when he was in the hospital, he had six lawyers there," Kristen says. "Uncle Denny finally arrived and told them they weren't needed. The waitress from the hotel restaurant got into his hospital room by saying she was his niece. She started reading to him from the Tibetan Book of the Dead."

Denver Peckinpah, who had suffered a near-fatal coronary of his own that forced him to retire from the bench, had gone to Livingston to try to take care of his brother. But the only help Peckinpah wanted was aid in escaping from the hospital. He called the Livingston police and had them come to the hospital, insisting to them he was being held there against his will.

"They had him in tethers, tied to the bed," Denny says. "He was telling me to get my camera and photograph these people so he could sue them. When I had my heart attack, it scared hell out of me. It took me a long time to get well. But Sam didn't take his seriously. He was saying, 'Get me some cigarettes, goddamnit, and some vodka. I need a drink.' "

Noteboom says, "He wanted to get out, but he was in no shape to. He felt that legally we were holding him against his will. But it would have been suicide for him to leave. He was in the hospital for four to six weeks."

They put a temporary pacemaker in, then replaced it with a permanent model. The pacemaker device is put in a pouch of skin on the chest wall. The wire is inserted into a large vein below the collarbone and into the heart, where it can regulate the rhythm.

Installing a pacemaker is a fairly routine procedure. But there was little that was routine about Sam Peckinpah; putting in his permanent pacemaker was no exception. Noteboom refers to the incident as "one of my more frightening moments in medicine."

Noteboom had to put in the permanent pacemaker first and then remove the temporary. The wires got tangled and Noteboom accidentally pulled out both sets. He says that Peckinpah, lying on the table, suddenly faced the alarming sight of his own heart monitor, registering no heartbeat—a flat line. Jim Silke was walking in the front door of the hospital at that moment.

"I could see Sam," Silke says. "He's having the permanent pacemaker put in and he's screaming at the doctor, 'I'm dying, you son of a bitch! Here I go!' And he went. Bells started ringing. They all rushed in to put in the pacemaker and save his life."

Silke found Peckinpah was detoxing badly. "I tried to explain to the doctor that he was on coke," Silke says. "They were giving him a quarter of a Quaalude. But there were more Quaaludes in Sam's apartment than there were in the hospital. A quarter of a Quaalude didn't mean anything to his body."

When Peckinpah was released from the hospital at the end of June,

Noteboom told him that he'd had a close call and would have to be responsible for making sure he didn't have another one. That meant giving up cigarettes and drinking, getting regular exercise and eating and sleeping properly. He also warned Peckinpah not to jar the pacemaker.

Joe and Carolyn Swindlehurst picked him up at the hospital and took him back to the Yellowstone Motor Inn. In the lobby, he took a right turn and marched straight into the lounge, with the Swindlehursts in tow. He strode up to the bar and ordered a Ramos Fizz, a drink with sloe gin and an egg. Once it was set in front of him, he took a long, long gulp, emptying the glass in a single swallow.

If the next moment had been in one of his films, it would have happened in slow motion: Peckinpah, who was sitting on a tall barstool, sat bolt upright, clutched at his chest, then fell over backward. He hit the floor with a thud and lay there motionless.

Carolyn Swindlehurst screamed, then burst into tears. A smile slowly flickered across Peckinpah's lips, and then he started to laugh. It was a joke and it had had the desired effect.

"It was an amazing maneuver," Carolyn says now, "considering that he had just had a pacemaker put in. It easily could have been dislodged."

Just how seriously he took the heart attack, how much it worried him or affected his outlook on life—after an experience that proved how easily life could be cut short without warning—is a matter of debate. The people closest to him believe it delivered a fundamental shock to his system that frightened him to the core. To others, he seemed to shrug it off, either out of lack of concern or an arrogant willingness to play roulette with his own life.

"It scared him for about two weeks," says David Wardlow, his agent at the time. "He had this wonderful lady taking care of him and she had rationed him to one glass of wine a day. Shortly thereafter, he was back to quite a bit of wine."

"He would talk about death a lot after that," Carolyn Swindlehurst says. "He was very frightened by death. I think he acted with great bravado, but my impression was that he was deeply affected by the heart attack."

"If anything, the heart attack fueled the addiction," David Peckinpah says. "It was just an inconvenience to him. His denial system was so strong."

"The heart attack did slow him down," Matt Peckinpah says. "But unfortunately I don't think it made him afraid because he did not quit smoking or working under very stressful conditions."

Peckinpah had no fear of going back to cocaine after the heart attack—but he was afraid to spend much time at his cabin, because of the elevation and the remoteness. He feared being stuck up on the mountain and suffering another heart attack. At one point, he got up there and then locked his keys in his car.

So he lived at the Murray Hotel in Livingston, letting his friends take care of him while he tried to shake the perception that he was damaged goods so he could find another job.

"We spent three weeks going through his files and papers," says Don Hyde, his archivist, who stayed with him during this period. "We started getting this mess of papers in order. We started to flesh out a script he had been commissioned to do, *The Texans*."

Hyde was yet another in the string of accomplices Peckinpah talked into writing with him—anything to avoid doing a first draft himself. Hyde, who freely admits that he is not a writer, says, "He used people like tubes in a radio. He'd stick you in until you burned out. Then he'd discard you and put someone else in. He'd come up with a scenario and you would write it and he would pick it apart and use about one-tenth of it. It was exhilarating and frustrating. If you were around him, he'd try to use you. He tried to get whatever he could out of you."

Hyde would run videocassettes of current hit movies for Peckinpah, reveling in the director's analysis and eye for detail. Peckinpah would frequently surprise him with what he liked and what he didn't.

"You could never nail him down," Hyde says. "I showed him *Midnight Express* and I didn't think he'd like it but he thought it was a good film. He liked *The Duellists*. He didn't like *Blade Runner*."

He continued to drink and use cocaine, which, in itself, was not a threat to his condition. While cocaine causes an increase in the heart rate and can do heart damage, Noteboom says it isn't particularly threatening to pacemaker patients such as Peckinpah.

"His coronary arteries were going to block off again," Noteboom says. "Cocaine does do damage to the heart and probably contributed to an earlier demise, but it wasn't particularly dangerous with the pacemaker."

During this period, Peckinpah accepted an invitation from his old friend Bobby Visciglia, who was handling the props for a Western being shot near Peckinpah's Livingston hideout: *Heaven's Gate*, which was being directed by the recent Oscar-winner Michael Cimino.

Visciglia had called Peckinpah because Cimino wanted him to. "Cimino told me he used to sit in the cutting room at Goldwyn and study Sam's rushes while he was working on *The Getaway*. During *Heaven's Gate*, Cimino asked me, 'Did Sam use this much ammo?' I said, 'No, Michael, you're the fucking king.' He shot something like a million and a half rounds.

"I talked to Sam. I didn't know he'd had a pacemaker put in. I said, 'How would you like to do second unit for the battle sequence in *Heaven's Gate*?' He hadn't worked in a while and it whetted his appetite. When I found out he had the pacemaker, I realized he couldn't handle it. Cimino wanted him to do it but, medically, he wasn't ready to.

"But Sam came to visit in Kalispell and everybody wanted to meet him, at lunch at the Outlaw Inn. The place was mobbed, like they were seeing a god. Cimino and Peckinpah were at the same table. It was the first time they'd ever met. Sam loved it. They all worshipped him. He stayed for four days and we went to all the whorehouses."

Allen Keller was working on the film and saw Peckinpah during his stay. "Sam wasn't very fucking impressed," Keller says. "He figured Cimino was wasting money. He said, 'It's because of guys like that that I can't get the money to do a picture.' "

Peckinpah got the deal shortly after that for *The Texans,* a script John Milius had written in the late 1960s, which now belonged to producer Albert Ruddy.

The story dealt with an aging oil executive who, just before retirement, decides to act on his fantasy of driving a herd of cattle up the old Chisholm Trail. He gets his Ivy League son and most of his junior executives to sign on for the drive. Ruddy was interested in having Peckinpah rewrite the screenplay and direct the finished product.

"We felt he had the potential and talent to make a great movie, if he could get himself together," Ruddy says.

Ruddy had lunch with Peckinpah in Los Angeles to discuss the project. "You expect this robust, ballsy character," Ruddy says, "and he was this pale, white, pasty guy. But he said he was getting back in shape. We discussed at length his ability to shoot a contemporary cattle drive. I was convinced that if he said he could do it, he could and would be in shape to do it."

In April 1980, as he worked on *The Texans,* Peckinpah was given the John Ford Award at the Cowboy Hall of Fame in Oklahoma City, Oklahoma. He was to be inducted along with Tex Ritter and James Michener. He rounded up his brother Denver and Denver's son David and headed to Oklahoma City.

"He was flying in from Japan, from meeting Kurosawa," recalls Denny. "We were going to meet Sam at the Beverly Wilshire. He and I and David all flew to Oklahoma City and they had the carpet rolled out for us."

To David, a recovering alcoholic, the trip is one blurry nightmare. "I had been sober for a while," he recalls. "I hadn't had a drink in a long time. But once we hooked up with Sam, I was drunk by the time we got on the plane and I was in a blackout by the time we got to Oklahoma. I'm told that Sam and I were having wheelchair races in the lobby of the hotel."

Peckinpah pleaded jet lag when they got to Oklahoma City and sent Denny and David to the opening banquet as his emissaries. They took the limo to the barbecue at the Hall of Fame, where David began drinking sherry. He and Denny separated to mingle. A little while later, Denny saw the driver of their limo standing at the edge of crowd, looking for him.

David had decided he wanted to go back to the hotel. When he couldn't find the limo driver, he had found the limo instead and taken it. In trying to pull out, he had hit each of the handful of cars and limos in the lot.

"There were only a couple of vehicles in the parking lot, but I managed to hit them all," David says. "The next day, Sam was introducing me as his driver. This was real power drinking."

But Peckinpah was truly honored at the award and at sharing the podium with Michener and Ritter. At one point, he sidled over to Michener, shook his hand and said, "I'm pleased to meet you. I've been stealing from you for years."

Peckinpah went back to Montana to start writing *The Texans*, even as he attempted to cope with the marriage into which he had jumped only a couple of months before. He found himself trying to do research and write while integrating himself into a household that not only included a wife but three kids, two dogs, cats and rabbits.

Her name was Marcy Blueher and Peckinpah had wooed her initially while filming *Convoy* in Albuquerque. He met her when her house was recommended as one he might rent during production. Fascinated by his entrance (he arrived in a helicopter) and an immediately felt connection ("He began sending flowers the next day," she says), she arranged for him to rent the house across the highway so she could stay in her home for the summer.

Blueher was thirty-eight and a widow with three children. Peckinpah began calling on her, trying to involve her in the film by soliciting her opinion on sets and enlisting her to help him round up extras and secure permits.

After *Convoy*, Peckinpah went back to Sausalito and tried to convince Blueher to move with him, but she wouldn't. Instead, she had taken her kids and moved. Her first stop was London. Peckinpah had sent her there on business a few months earlier and at the urging of a Peckinpah friend, she had decided to move her children there for six months ("I wanted them, while they were still young, to experience living overseas").

After that, she moved to San Diego. Peckinpah kept in touch, calling every few months to tell her to get a babysitter and meet him in Los Angeles or Mexico City or Sausalito.

When Peckinpah moved to Livingston, he called and asked her to come up there and she did. Then he had his heart attack; Blueher was one of those who took care of him after the pacemaker was inserted.

"From the first time we started going out, we talked about feeling so comfortable and knowing we belonged together," she says. "But marriage was the most irrational thing we could have considered. At one point, he asked me please not to let him marry me. He said, 'This is a relationship that could be deep.' He had a history of abuse. It was something he feared.

"He felt in a way that he was a monster. It concerned him. He seemed to set traps for himself and for others: 'You don't care about me. You can't care about me because look how terrible I am.' He definitely wanted closeness but he was so afraid of it."

After three years of the relationship, "it seemed like if we were ever going to complete whatever we were going to be, marriage had to be part of it," she says. "It was make or break."

Her children, who were still in San Diego, were loaded into a car and driven to Livingston by Peckinpah's daughter Melissa and her boyfriend. "We didn't want them to come up here and start school with us not being married," Marcy says. "So we went to a justice of the peace in Livingston and were married in January 1980."

They had a prenuptial agreement to keep their property separate. The document was Marcy's choice, to keep her finances separate from his.

"I had my own money and my own way of taking care of myself," she says. "I didn't want anything from his finances. That bothered him. 'That's what I'm about,' he said. 'You have to want something.' If you didn't, he felt he wasn't giving."

Once the family arrived, it quickly became apparent that Peckinpah had made a serious mistake. Used to his own rhythms and the freedom of solitude, he suddenly had to curtail his activities to accommodate a household. Though he still lived at the Murray Hotel, he felt compelled to devote time to Blueher and her children. He couldn't get started on his writing and took it out on those around him.

"He was not physically able to work," Marcy says. "The phone was ringing constantly. I bought a house and he made a commitment not to come up for air until he finished the script.

"It was like he had two separate lives. One was completely stable in one place. The other involved going off to spend intense, creative days and nights in discussions without thinking of answering phones or eating. He never lived both lives together.

"It was awful because we argued quite a bit. He couldn't understand another person having needs. For two people with obligations, there was no way it could have worked, especially when one is physically drained.

"He was afraid he would hit me. Once, while he was drinking, he did. I reacted by putting my fist through every one of the windows in the French doors. It was so absurd, but it was the only thing I could do to bring a little ridiculousness to the situation.

"He didn't understand recuperation, or sleeping eight hours and eating three meals a day. That was outside his frame of reference. He would push things as far as they could possibly go.

"He had poor health and he was working long hours. So he used every trick to stay awake and alert to be physically capable of handling the work. He took such an entourage of medication. He was a substance abuser. He took things to make him sleep, things to make him wake up."

The fights continued. Peckinpah would feel repentant, going so far as to write poetry for her:

> "Loneliness is a thin line
> My gift
> But not for you
> For me and mine"

The marriage lasted a month: "It was make or break—and it was too much to handle," she says. "It didn't last. We made a mutual decision to have it annulled. We were bitter that we couldn't work it out."

34

The Cocaine Depths

"PSYCHOSIS IS STILL A VERY RARE EVENT for an intranasal user, but we do see people becoming paranoid with high-dose, intranasal use of cocaine," Dr. Ronald K. Siegel, a research psychopharmacologist from UCLA, said in a 1982 *People* magazine article. "The users tend to progress through three stages. The first encounters tend to be euphoric. With increased dosages and increasing frequency of use, this euphoria gives rise to dysphoria, depression marked by melancholy, sadness, inability to pay attention and concentrate, insomnia, anorexia and lack of sexual interest. As cocaine dosages increase or stay the same over time, the dysphoria is replaced by paranoia, which can be accompanied by hallucinations and other elements of psychotic thinking."

"After Sam had his pacemaker put in," Paul Peterson says, "he was convinced that the pacemaker was a CIA plant, that it could be detonated at any time. The last few months in Montana were horrendous. He was in absolute terror and misery most of the time. He would stay in his bedroom for days on end. That got worse as long as he did coke. The more intense the paranoia got, the more reclusive he became.

"He had a drug, Enderil, to regulate his arrhythmia and he wouldn't take it. No matter how hard I reminded him, he wouldn't take it. And no matter how hard I tried to make sure he couldn't get cocaine, he could always find it. Even after his heart attack, somebody would always find cocaine for him. He had no problem finding sycophants."

Peckinpah developed an interest in English mysticism and brought in a British healer named Rose Gladden to exorcise him. "It was Begonia, Sam, Rose Gladden and I," Peterson says. "I was in the outer office. Sam thought he was possessed and that Rose would take this demon out of him. He wanted Begonia and me to witness it. He made these incredible animalistic noises. Then he felt pretty good for a while. It freaked Begonia out."

"The coke made him paranoid, but mellow about it," Jim Silke says. "He was paranoid about Begonia being a magician and working curses on him."

Peckinpah's work on the screenplay for *The Texans* fell two, then three months behind the scheduled delivery date. Albert Ruddy went to visit him shortly after he had started writing, then again when the first draft was three months overdue. On the second visit, he found Peckinpah had taken over an entire floor of Livingston's venerable Murray Hotel because he was afraid to spend time at his cabin.

"It was very sad, that meeting in Montana," Ruddy says. "He was living in this second-rate hotel and it was like something out of a bad Western. He was walking around at the hotel in flannel pajamas, a bathrobe and slippers, looking very pale.

"We had lunch and he had written 130 pages. But he said it was half of the screenplay. When I finally got the remainder, it was an additional 120 or 130 pages."

Jim Silke says, "He showed me the first draft and the opening scene was sixty pages of six people in a helicopter. It was unbelievable for him. I said so and he said, 'You don't know how I'm going to shoot it.' It was people arguing about the world, this unwieldy thing to try and deal with."

When he turned in the final pages, Peckinpah also turned in bills for $16,000 in expenses he had incurred while researching and writing the screenplay. Ruddy and Golden Harvest, the production company behind him, complained about the expenses—which included trips to Mexico and Bogotá—but ultimately paid most of them.

"Sam was sending Ruddy these strange expense reports for cigars and four Xerox machines, the rental of a truck," David Wardlow says. "Al was outraged and rightly so. But he kept approving them on the basis of getting the script."

Ruddy balked, however, at paying Peckinpah for the screenplay itself. For one thing, Peckinpah had written an entirely new script. "Sam read Milius's original and didn't care for it," Wardlow says. "Originally, it was supposed to be a rewrite. Sam had his own idea and so his was an original screenplay. Al kept saying, 'It's not an original, it's an adaptation.' "

Then there was the question of the length. The average four-hour miniseries has a script of 180 to 190 pages. Peckinpah had turned in 250 pages for a feature film—and six months late, at that.

"If we had shot this as written, it would have been four and a half hours long," Ruddy says. "It had some of the most memorable scenes I've ever read, but it was way overwritten. And he didn't even want to address the issue of cutting it."

Peckinpah took the matter to the Writers Guild for arbitration, saying that Ruddy and Golden Harvest had reneged on their agreement. The WGA found in favor of Ruddy and Golden Harvest, saying that Peckinpah had breached his contract by failing to keep the deadline.

"*The Texans* was the first time in my experience," Wardlow says, "that a producer refused payment based on the length of the screenplay. Al acknowledged that half the screenplay was as good as anything he'd read. But they were outraged by the length."

Peckinpah quickly got a deal for another writing project. He called Jim Silke to come work on a script for an Elmore Leonard book, *City Primeval,* which they were calling *Hang Tough.*

"The opening scene the producers liked," Silke says. "But the writing wasn't good. Then the writers' strike came and he didn't want to work. I did the first draft and he'd rewrite. We fought because he was back on coke and wanted cash. So he kept changing our deal to get cash. It ended up that I owed him $2,500. *Hang Tough* was a good script but it got caught when there were three management changes at United Artists."

Upset that these deals had fallen through, unable to recognize his own culpability, Peckinpah fired Wardlow as his agent. "I believe the reason was that I solicited *The Texans* for him," Wardlow says. "He painted me with the same brush he painted Al Ruddy."

Then Peckinpah called Martin Baum, who had gone back to the agenting business after his work as a producer and studio executive. Baum had started his own agency, then merged it with the on-the-rise Creative Artists Agency, where he became a partner.

"There were disappointments in the past, but I still felt he was doing me an honor," Baum says.

Among the first things that came his way was a TV movie, to which producer Ely Landau and actor Richard Harris were attached. They sent the script to Peckinpah, who immediately expressed his interest. He met with Harris at the Westwood Marquis to discuss the project.

"I said, 'Would you really work with me?' " says Harris, who by that time had similarly trashed his own reputation with wild drinking, drug binges and erratic behavior.

Peckinpah said that he would be glad to. As Harris poured himself a drink, Peckinpah unbuttoned his shirt and showed Harris the spot where his pacemaker was. Then he said, "You really ought to quit drinking. That stuff will kill you."

Harris allowed that he was probably right. Peckinpah shook out a small pile of cocaine onto a mirrored table and cut it into lines. "This stuff is much better for you," he told Harris.

But the financing fell through on the project. Peckinpah continued to cast about, even going so far as to have discussions with producer Martin Ransohoff about a possible film based on Edward Abbey's *The Monkey Wrench Gang,* an adventure story about eco-guerrillas battling a power company.

"Sam's agent went to a couple of studios," Ransohoff says, "who were not wildly excited about the idea of spending $8 or $9 million making a picture with Sam and me." End of idea.

Meanwhile, Peckinpah kept seeing his name in the trades, attached to this film and that. Here was a note in *Variety* saying he had been signed to direct a film called *King of Nothing* for a producer named Martin Cohen. There was a news item in *Variety* saying he was about to direct Mariette Hartley in a film called *Medicine Woman*. And Rona Barrett had just gone on TV to say that Peckinpah was going to be at the helm of a remake of *For Whom the Bell Tolls*.

Peckinpah was frustrated and angry. Someone was raising production money on the basis of his name—and he wasn't getting a dime of it. Even worse, if other producers thought he was busy on these speculative projects, they wouldn't offer him any real work. So Peckinpah sent a letter to Marty Baum: "I am asking your advice which obviously I need very bad. I do not feel any of this is helping Sam Peckinpah get a suitable picture to direct, or even an unsuitable one. I think some action should be taken but I don't intend to blow my top again without discussing it fully with you."

AT THE END OF 1980, Peckinpah's son Mathew, twenty, enlisted in the Marine Corps. Mathew suffered from dyslexia, a learning disability, and had never been an accomplished student. He finally enlisted in the Marines after high school. His mother Marie assumed that it was because Peckinpah had spoken so glowingly all of his life about his tour of duty in the Marines. But Mathew told her he wanted to give his life the structure and discipline the military—particularly the Marines—could offer.

The day Matt entered the Marines, Peckinpah wrote him a long letter, addressing the kind of father-son sentiments he had difficulty expressing otherwise. The letter amounts to an instructional guide on how not to make the same mistakes Peckinpah had made as a young (and older) man.

"I am proud of you and I am proud to be your father," he wrote. "As my brother once said, Peckinpahs have a tendency to mature late in life and their learning process is slow. Now yours will really begin as it did with me.

"You have nothing to prove—you have everything to learn—just as I did, and still do. You are clever, quick and caring in many ways. In other ways, you are slow and careless and lazy.

"Keep the first to yourself—don't volunteer information or opinions unless asked, and then, very carefully.

"The questions you ask so often are things you should have studied—you should have read. They are careless questions. The corps has no room for carelessness in actions, or in questions. You have no one to beat. You have only to do your best. And to do your best, you must *learn to read* and *understand what you read*. And more important, you must learn to love it—because in that path lies knowledge.

"Try to associate with people who are brighter than you, and *listen*—I repeat, listen.

"Don't ask careless questions, because so many times you pay no attention to the answers.

"You are part of a team and *the team comes first—not you*.

"The corps and I expect you to learn, to take responsibility and to follow it through.

"When you make a mistake, do something dumb—make a jackass out of yourself—Stop! And I really mean stop berating yourself, or turning it on others. Think it over—write it down. Repeat: Write it down, then remember what caused the problem, how you can fix it and why it won't happen again. Chances are it will—many times. Each time, the lesson will go a little deeper, until finally it will be instinctive.

"Most important, don't forget how to laugh—especially at yourself and the devil—not at other's misfortunes.

"Forget completely any obvious attempts to display superiority to your fellow man. It only demonstrates how little you know. If you have nothing to brag about, don't. If you have something to brag about, it's even more important to keep your *Goddamned mouth shut*.

"There are weaknesses in the corps—but it is not your place to comment on them. Learn from them. Learn to do better. Above all else, stay loose—*stay easy. If you try too hard, then you'll break yourself.*

"Sometimes homesickness, loneliness, will become almost unbearable. But know, as I did, that your Dad is right there with you. For the next three years, you've got a new family. You belong to them and they belong to you. But you've got people who love you—who care about you—and they'll be close.

"Remember: Boot camp is only the beginning. After that it gets rough. I was proud to leave Parris Island as a marine, and I still look back at those weeks as the most exhilarating, productive part of my life. Godspeed—good luck—and, as we say in the corps, old buddy, Semper fi, motherfucker!"

IN MID-1981, PECKINPAH BECAME a grandfather at the age of fifty-six, when his daughter Sharon had a son. In anticipation, Peckinpah wrote a letter to his son-in-law, actor Richard Marcus: "You are now marked on a path that is irrevocable—despair, trauma, value judgements, regrets—all trivial compared to the gladness and joy that will never match any experience in your life.

"To become a father is an enlightening, terrifying and rewarding experience—it was to me—I'm sure it will be to you—but—

"After my initial elation at the knowledge that I was to become a grandfather, I began to, and still do, wonder about my obligations, privileges and role, so to speak.

"My own grandfather saved my life at least a dozen times. I attempted to kill him twice, once when I was four and once when I was six.

"I can only say, I guess, that I'm very proud that you're my son-in-law and the knowledge that I learned late in life—your responsibility will not only be to the baby (girl or boy—it's bound to be one or the other)—but to your wife. But you can never show it—show that innate sense of responsibility. Marriage and parenthood, I think, are the ultimate tests of learning to become a man. In my case, it was a difficult task indeed—and it hasn't ended.

"I hear a thousand times a week people saying in different languages, in different ways—'All I want to do is be happy.' The only way that I ever found happiness was sharing my children's laughter and occasional love.

"I believe it was Ustinov who once wrote 'parents are the bones that the children sharpen their claws on.' And when all is said and done, you grow up to realize it's a privilege.

"Knowing a little about Sharon, who was born after twenty-seven hours of labor, like a rose—unmarked and beyond any concept of the beautiful baby syndrome—I wait with fear and trepidation, delight, anticipation and joy, the birth of your child. My daughter, my daughter's child. I'm looking forward to becoming a grandfather.

"I know now why my father spent so many hours walking the hospital corridors with me. I wish my children had known their grandfather and I pray to God Almighty that yours will know theirs.

"I'll always be there when needed (keeping a low profile) and, like now, wishing you Godspeed, good luck and sending my love, all of it, to both of you.

"Signed,

"The Old Iguana

"P.S. Despair is the only unforgivable sin—and it's always reaching for us —despair and my old friend, remorse, and that insidious, beckoning finger of self-pity—how well I know them. But they can always be banished by the ongoing love of life, laughter and carefully chosen immorality. Onward!"

"He was very proud of having grandchildren," Sharon says. "I didn't have the heart to tell him I wouldn't trust my child to be alone with him. When I had a first birthday party for my son, he called and I told him that if he wanted to come, I wanted him sober. He didn't get pissed off. He said, 'That's tough but I hear it.' And he didn't show up."

35

Working on the "Weekend"

PECKINPAH FINALLY GOT SOME WORK that was meaningful to him in 1981, when his old mentor, Don Siegel, called and asked if he'd be interested in directing the second unit for a picture he was making, originally called *The Edge*, whose title prophetically had been changed to *Jinxed*.

The production itself was a troubled one. There were numerous stories in the *L.A. Times* about the clashes between Siegel and his star, Bette Midler, making her first film since her Oscar nomination for *The Rose*. Siegel, in ill health and behind schedule, called on his old protégé for assistance.

Peckinpah snuck in and out for about two weeks of uncredited second-unit direction. "It was wonderful to be back under the gun and to work with Don," he said. "Remember, I'd started as a gofer on one of his early pictures and I'd been dialogue director on several others. He'd always encouraged me."

Walter Kelley, who went along as Peckinpah's assistant, says, "The first day, he went to shoot and he was like a nervous Nellie. I was surprised. I had set it all up with Polaroids. But it gave him a great boost. It was a great time to do that."

Knowing that Siegel had suffered reams of adverse publicity on the project, Peckinpah took out an ad in the *Hollywood Reporter* on November 19, 1981, an open letter to Siegel: "I wish to express my appreciation for the opportunity you gave me to work on your latest film . . . not as a gofer, but after twenty-two years, as a second-unit director.

"When I look back, Mr. Siegel, I feel you can take a lot of credit and most of the blame (I wish) for what I've done since you took it upon yourself to make me a motion picture director.

"Our deal was that you permit me to shoot second unit for you only if you could shoot second unit for me."

346

PECKINPAH WAS CUTTING BACK on his drinking and cocaine. Perhaps it was a reflection of becoming a grandparent or the chance to once again get behind the camera. Perhaps it was a sense of reflection that had dawned because of both of those, or from the departure of Paul Peterson.

"We couldn't seem to correct our lives when we were together," Peterson says. "I probably just quit because of my own self-preservation. I couldn't do it anymore. It wasn't healthy for either of us. I knew one of us was going to die. He was destroying himself. Because of the age difference between us, [roughly 20 years] I had the chance to clean up my act. If I was Sam's age, we'd be dead together."

Whatever the reason, Peckinpah straightened himself up enough to look at work again. He pursued and was pursued for a couple of projects, all of them Westerns: *The Last Running, The Red-Headed Stranger, Songwriter* (the latter two of which would have teamed him with Willie Nelson).

But as hard as Martin Baum pushed his client, none of the films seemed to come together. "I found to my dismay that studio doors were closed to him," Baum says. "He wasn't wanted. I was determined to find him work. He needed a picture badly and I found one: *The Osterman Weekend.*"

BILL PANZER AND PETER DAVIS were low-budget producers with big-budget aspirations when they got ahold of the rights to Robert Ludlum's thriller, *The Osterman Weekend.* Their most visible and legitimate production up to that point had been a 1981 TV movie, *St. Helens,* starring Art Carney.

The producers had an *Osterman* screenplay written, and then rewritten. The last writer to take a crack at it was Alan Sharp, an Englishman with credits such as *Ulzana's Raid, The Last Run* and *Night Moves.* Sharp reworked the material, but Ludlum's plot resisted coherence.

"The script never worked," Sharp says. "I never anticipated from the script I wrote that they'd ever get it made. It wasn't a satisfactory job. Ludlum leaves a lot to be revealed later and you find yourself saying, 'How could that happen?' When you've got to simplify for a script, you've got to throw out about 60 percent. And there are gaps and jumps in logic."

Sharp's final script apparently was enough to satisfy Panzer and Davis, who began looking for a director with whom to sell the film. Though he hadn't directed anything since the ill-fated *Convoy* in 1977, almost five years earlier, Sam Peckinpah's name found its way onto their short list. The producers approached Baum, who got Peckinpah the job.

"Everyone said we were crazy to do this," Panzer says. "It was helpful to the deal to have him and, if he had his act together, he could do interesting things. At that point, he had a reputation for filling his liver and his nose, for being grotesquely irresponsible about budget and schedule. Most of it was due to *Convoy* and *Cross of Iron*. We said he probably wouldn't be the easiest to work with but we'll try. Was it a step up for us? Absolutely. This was Robert Ludlum and Sam Peckinpah."

The disagreements started before he'd even formally accepted the film. In May 1982, Peckinpah wrote to Martin Baum: "Nobody's watching the store. Nobody cares. I have completed my obligations and they have money still owing for contractual and guild laws. I do not believe they ever intended to make this picture—with or without me.

"There is no use in wasting all our energies when I feel they are in breach by making offers to actors [and] production people and not paying their obligations to contract and guild specs.

"Gentlemen, I suppose my problem is my love for the casual poetry and not the petty, and I mean very petty, cash."

Davis, not wishing to tip this applecart before it had a chance to do business, wrote a placating note to Peckinpah's attorney, Harold Friedman: "We are not adversaries. We presently have over $400,000 invested in *The Osterman Weekend* and Sam Peckinpah. Time is growing short. We should all be working toward the common goal of providing the means and support by which Sam can make a very successful film for us all."

Despite his irascibility, Peckinpah had cut back on his cocaine use and, in an interview before production started, claimed to have quit drinking.

"After thirty years, I decided I'd had enough," he said. "And the odd thing is I don't even miss it. Though now and again the thought of a couple of dry martinis does cross my mind."

Dennis Hopper, who was almost at the nadir of his own struggle with alcohol and cocaine, was cast in the film as one of the Osterman weekend participants. "I was trying to sober up, trying to clean up," Hopper recalls. "But I was doing a lot of coke. Everybody in the picture was trying to clean up. None of us had, though. It looked as if Sam had cleaned up. We were doing little things; actually, I was doing a lot of coke and he was doing a little. I think it was hard for him to be sober. He was white-knuckling it the whole way."

ASKED HOW HE PROTECTED HIMSELF against producer interference Peckinpah said, "I pray a lot." He'd have been better off investigating his new employers.

While Panzer and Davis had checked on Peckinpah's reputation, he hadn't bothered to do the same with them. If he had, he would have been told that they were small-time guys with penny-pinching ways, ready to cut a corner to save a buck. In other words, exactly the kind of producers guaranteed to piss him off.

"Davis and Panzer are hacks who try to put money together to make bucks," Alan Sharp says. "They're brash and young and had no track record in terms of quality. I had no respect for their taste. I was amazed that Sam would get drawn in."

"It seemed like Sam was always fighting producers, maybe in some cases not righteously," says Dave Rawlins, who edited *Osterman*. "In this case, he was right, because these guys were snakes."

Everyone agreed that the script had problems—everyone except Panzer and Davis, who were happy with it just the way it was. Peckinpah asked for a chance to rewrite with Sharp. At script conferences with the producers, Peckinpah recorded every word that was said.

"It was the first and last time we had a meeting with a director who pulled out a tape recorder," Panzer says.

Adds Sharp, "He'd come in with typed transcripts, a 240-page document of all this rubbish. I asked why and his assistant said, 'Sam likes to have it down because he's had a lot of experience with producers who say one thing and do another.' It was paranoia of a level I was never aware of. I wondered why he put his energy into it."

Panzer and Davis agreed to let Peckinpah take a pass at the script. "Sam did some rewriting and it was rejected," Panzer says. "It was off the mark. He wanted a try so we gave him one. I don't think anybody was pleased with the result. I was happy with the shape the script was in."

Says Sharp, "The script was irredeemably imperfect."

At one point, Peckinpah complained about the script to his friend Jason Robards. "Ludlum is a neighbor of mine," Robards says, "and he came by the house and said, 'My God, I'll rewrite it for free.' But Sam couldn't change anything."

"Sam talked angrily about the fact that they wouldn't let him change the script," Pauline Kael says. "He kept insisting that the book did not make sense. They insisted he stick with the book. He was very angry. He had hopes of doing a decent picture. He felt that, once again, executives were crippling him."

The producers also attempted to do what the producers of *Convoy* had had such a notable lack of success with. They prohibited Peckinpah from hiring the core group of production department heads he'd relied on for so many other films.

"We heard that a Peckinpah movie was like plutonium," Panzer says. "It achieved critical mass and got totally out of control. We tried not to pack the crew with good old boys who had been down in Mexico with rattlesnakes, a .45 and a bottle of tequila. We did not want to create an environment that would not let him do himself his best personal service."

Katy Haber says, "It was stupid not to hire his people on *Osterman Weekend*. What was wrong about it was that they weren't yes-men. The people closest to him were the only ones who could stand up to him. He said, 'I don't believe in the auteur theory. I'm only as good as the people who work for me.' "

He was able to hire British cinematographer John Coquillon and production designer Ted Haworth. Walter Kelley was on hand as an assistant and was given a small role as a CIA spook working for John Hurt. He wanted to hire Lou Lombardo to edit but the producers said no. So he hired Dave Rawlins, whose brother, Phil, he had had a combative relationship with, and talked his daughter Kristen into taking the job of dialogue director.

"But I think he just wanted me to be around, to make him lunch and take care of him," she says.

IN ITS FINAL SCRIPTED FORM, *The Osterman Weekend* was turned into an indictment of the CIA and the manipulative nature of media. It dealt with a CIA operation to expose a ring of spies in the United States. But its central premise—about a network TV interviewer whose friends may be Soviet agents—was a confusing double-cross. As it turns out, there are no spies; the entire operation is a setup by a rogue CIA agent seeking vengeance against the head of the agency, using innocent people as his pawns.

For his cast, Peckinpah hired Dutch émigré Rutger Hauer, a curious choice for John Tanner, the Mike Wallace–style TV talk-show host. His wife was played by Meg Foster, while his friends were played by Hopper, Craig T. Nelson and Chris Sarandon.

Cassie Yates, who had worked for Peckinpah in *Convoy*, played Sarandon's wife and Helen Shaver played Hopper's. Burt Lancaster was signed to do a high-profile cameo as the head of the CIA, a man with presidential aspirations, and British actor John Hurt was signed to play Fassett, the rogue CIA agent. The film mostly was shot using the old Robert Taylor estate in Mandeville Canyon as Tanner's house.

Peckinpah was obviously a sick and tired man as he began production. Panzer remembers scouting locations with Peckinpah in a car on the winding roads of the Hollywood and Malibu hills.

"After a couple of hours, Sam stopped the car, opened the door, stepped onto the pavement and was violently ill," Panzer says. "One of the guys in the car says, 'Hmmm, so old Blood-and-Guts gets carsick.' He laughed. He loved it if you got him.

"The first morning of production, we were shooting video stuff that would be surveillance footage. We were somewhere near MacArthur Park and it's seven in the morning. Sam trips over a cable; he nearly falls into the street and almost gets hit by a truck. He looks around and says, 'There goes your whole package, baby.' He pauses and adds, 'Ah, but you're probably insured.' "

"He was this little pale, translucent man who clearly didn't have the juice," Alan Sharp says. "I got a sense he had a certain amount of energy to get through the day. He was this mild, elderly, unwell man who had a convalescent air to him."

Lou Lombardo dropped by the Taylor estate to visit Peckinpah and was surprised by what he found. "He was kind of beaten down," Lombardo says. "He wasn't the Sam I knew. He was always bronze and sweaty; at this point, there wasn't any flash left in his eyes. He had a gray pallor."

Though hypochondriacal, Peckinpah wasn't about to play the invalid. A good showing here and the offers might start up again. He still had a name, the last few pictures aside.

"Marty Baum said to Sam, 'If you do this without fucking up, you'll be back in the million-dollar director circle,' " Walter Kelley says.

Anne Thompson, a film industry observer for *Variety* who worked on the film as unit publicist, says, "I think everyone felt that it was the comeback he hoped for. We were genuinely trying to make a good movie under the worst circumstances. With the budget, he had to compromise at every level just to make a film."

Still, as he was starting production, Peckinpah sent a mailgram to Baum, in appreciation for getting him the chance to work again: "Marty, I am surrounded by memories. Memories of laughter and anger, memories of despair and accomplishment, memories of always being pushed to do a little better, memories of what it means to be a professional.

"We shared part of it.

"I hope you understand what I'm trying to say because you are the only one who can."

PECKINPAH'S PATIENCE GREW SHORT very quickly as production of *The Osterman Weekend* got under way. Despite a script that called for extensive, expensive video-surveillance sequences, Panzer and Davis were determined to bring the film in for less than $5 million. They scrimped in all of the ways that proved to Peckinpah that they were out for themselves, not for his picture.

The producers had hired an insurance guarantor who kept a man on the set to monitor Peckinpah's health and progress. It amounted to constant second-guessing, the kind of thing Peckinpah couldn't stand. He had a bad script and needed the elbow room to stretch out, tear it apart and put it back together in coherent form. But the producers wouldn't give him the latitude to try. And, say those who knew him, he just wasn't physically up to it.

"Directing a picture is a very difficult task," Marty Baum says. "You have to be an engineer, an electrician, a psychological expert. It calls upon many areas of human endeavor. Your faculties need to be sharp and to be responsible. But his hands shook; there was no color in his face. Alcohol did him in."

"He mistrusted the producers," Kristen says. "He felt they were using him. Dad stayed pretty calm. But he felt the producers were pretty half-assed."

According to Panzer, it's all part of the game in maximizing the effectiveness of a low-budget production.

"In fairness, the financial limits were more severe than on most films," he says. "What it takes to get a film started sometimes puts you in a situation where you purposely underestimate how long it may take; you do that to get the money. Eventually, the director goes along with you and does in eight weeks what he thought would take him ten."

To Dennis Hopper, the stress was reflected in Peckinpah's attitude on the set. Hopper, who had known Peckinpah almost thirty years earlier, says, "He had developed this style of being Sam Peckinpah. He could be very harsh and cutting. It would be done with a certain playfulness but it wasn't playful. That was the way he dealt with everything."

The tension on the set was obvious to reporters who visited to do stories on Sam Peckinpah's return to film.

"He was three or four years older than the last time I'd seen him but he looked ten [years older]," says Richard Jameson, who was writing a location story for *Film Comment*. "He was a hired director, considered to have a useful name. But Sam seemed to have the total loyalty and commitment of the crew and cast. His cottage was like a fortress. He was not real happy but he was working on a film. 'It's the least objectionable of the options I'd have signed to direct,' he said."

Hopper would occasionally sit in Peckinpah's trailer or dressing room, reminiscing about old times and old friends. "We'd both known a lot of people who were really cool who were now dead, who would tell him about me or me about him," Hopper says. "People like Steve McQueen and Lenny Bruce and a lot of jazz musicians and actors. We'd talk about our times in Mexico; we both loved it. There's an unfortunate streak in me, but I find great poetry in poverty and he had the same feelings."

Critic Michael Sragow visited the location, doing a story for *The Movies* magazine and also found the atmosphere on the *Osterman* set tense. One of the days that he was hanging around for his story, an issue of *Sight and Sound* magazine came out, carrying the selections of several dozen critics of the top ten films of all time. Sragow, one of the critics polled, had put *The Wild Bunch* at the head of his list.

"Sam had ignored me the whole time I was there," Sragow says. "The day after the magazine came out, he sidled over and said, 'Thanks for the pick.' This was not a shrinking ego here."

PECKINPAH WAS REPEATEDLY STYMIED by his basic differences with Panzer and Davis over what the final film should be.

"He saw the picture as less of a mystery and more of a mindfuck for the audience," Panzer says. "He wanted them to feel the same confusion everyone in the movie felt as they were being manipulated and knew nothing about it. But as they used to say about Antonioni, it's one thing to convey the idea of boredom but you don't have to bore me to do it."

"The producers kept saying, 'It doesn't make sense,' " recalls Dave Rawlins. "And Sam would say, 'Of course it doesn't make sense.' "

Bad weather played havoc with shooting exteriors; shooting inside the house was equally time consuming. The conditions made Peckinpah snappish but didn't rob him of his sense of humor, as an encounter with production designer Ted Haworth showed.

"He nailed me right in front of the crew—'Where are those location photographs I asked you to take?' " Haworth says. "I stopped dead and said, 'I gave them to you a week ago.' 'You're a damn liar,' Sam roared. I was really put out. I pointed my finger in his face and said, 'You were lying in your trailer and I handed them to you. Now I'm going to the trailer and find them and if I do find them, you're apologizing to me in front of everyone.'

"I went to the trailer, pulled out the daybed and there were all the photos. So I took them back to the set. Everyone saw me storm in, walk up to Sam and throw about two hundred photos at him. Then I turned and started for home. 'No, you don't get off that easy,' Sam yelled. 'Not until I apologize in front of the whole crew like you always force me to.' "

Peckinpah also hadn't lost his needling relationship with authority. Early on in the production, Panzer and Davis told Peckinpah that they had arranged a trade-out with an airline to get free airline tickets. In exchange, "all we needed to do was have a commercial for the airline play on the TV in the background of a scene," Panzer says.

The trade was worth about $55,000 to the producers. Peckinpah said it wouldn't be a problem to shoot. "Then he shot it in such a way that if we'd used it, we couldn't have cut the scene together," Panzer says. "It sounds amusing now but we had to pay $55,000 to the airline. It was like Sam said, 'If you tell me I've got to, I won't.' "

Peckinpah managed to contain his temper for much of the production. The penny-ante approach finally got to him near the end, while he was filming part of the climactic battle. Rutger Hauer and Craig T. Nelson were to run across the pool deck, in front of a set of poolhouse windows. They jump into the pool to escape machine-gun fire, which was supposed to blast out the windows of the poolhouse.

According to Panzer, Peckinpah had been shooting the scene for several nights and, finally, concerned about budget constraints, the production manager told him, "That's the last take."

"Why?" Peckinpah asked.

"Because you're taking so much time and all this glass costs money," he was told.

Panzer says, "There was lots of glass leaning against the side of the building and Sam proceeded to smash every one of the pieces."

Peckinpah's daughter Kristen says that Peckinpah was forced to shoot the scene without breakaway glass because the producers hadn't budgeted for it.

"The producers decided they weren't going to pay for breakaway windows, but they didn't tell him," she says. "So they spent the night setting up this shot and then they shot it—and the windows didn't break. He was furious. Finally someone told him the producers wouldn't pay for them. He got pale, walked over and kicked out the windows. Then he felt bad because this was somebody's house and these were these people's windows. A camera operator walks across the set, shakes his hand and says, 'Welcome back, Sam.' "

Production concluded at the end of 1982; when the editing began, Peckinpah encountered still more trouble with the producers. His vision of the film, obviously at odds with that of Panzer and Davis, continued to produce disputes during postproduction.

"They threw in a lot of violence because evidently that is what people pay for," Peckinpah said. "I took out a lot but they put some back in. I shot some under protest. I was more interested in the characters. Gratuitous violence has never been my bag. And there was a good deal more humor before the producers had their lick at it. I felt the picture should have been a little more fun because logically it makes no sense at all. Neither does the book. The problem is I'm afraid people might take it too seriously."

"Sam was a realist," editor Dave Rawlins says. "At the beginning of the film, he felt it was a new beginning. When he realized how the work was going, he got bitter. At the end, he didn't have enough strength to fight off the wolves."

He also was drinking more during the summer, as the editing proceeded. "In the editing room," Panzer says, "there was a lot of Gatorade that, on closer inspection, turned out to be Pernod and water."

Panzer and Davis, as part of the production deal, had retained final cut. They let Peckinpah edit as long as they felt it was feasible, then pulled the plug and took over the film themselves.

"We didn't change it much," Panzer says. "We made it a few minutes shorter. We all had trouble with exactly what was happening with the John Hurt character and why he was doing it. One of the mistakes we made was that the opening scene with John Hurt and Burt Lancaster was incredibly important exposition but was never shot face on. The audience didn't get it. It was not a mistake we had time to rectify."

Peckinpah did what he could to convince the producers to give him more time. He even called in James Coburn to screen the unfinished version for him, with the producers present.

"Afterward, he said, 'I'm trying to get them to come up with more money to finish editing it,'" Coburn says. "He was walking with a cane at that point. I said, 'The first two-thirds is great but that last part doesn't make sense.' He turned to the producers and said, 'You hear?'

"We walked out and Sam's limping and I said, 'Sam, the other leg.' He was playing a game, trying to get something for his picture. He didn't fight for money or fame. He fought for the film."

"We had a screening of his cut," Panzer says. "At the beginning was a title card that said, 'This is the authorized and official Sam Peckinpah version of this film,' this great long card. The audience was not excited about the film. They were confused. People don't mind being mystified or tricked but they don't like to be confused because it makes them feel stupid. That was part of Sam's idea: 'Fuck 'em if they don't get it.'"

Peckinpah did what he could to retain control of the film. He disputed the date his cut actually began, hoping to gain a few more days under his contract. Memos flew back and forth in the summer of 1983 as the producers tried to ready the film for release.

"We are extremely concerned both creatively and economically with the main title sequence," Panzer and Davis wrote to Peckinpah in a production memo in July 1983. "At this juncture, we question whether the effect we all were so enthusiastic about will in fact work.

"In addition, we feel that the side angle cuts of Fassett's wife masturbating will have the effect of turning off a substantial portion of our audience unnecessarily.

"Economically, the sequence has just gotten out of hand. To further complicate this matter, the titles must be finished for the preview on the nineteenth of July."

Peckinpah wrote back: "This sequence was approved enthusiastically by both of you. If it has gotten out of hand, where [are] Bill Panzer and Peter Davis? I have no understanding of your statement, 'The titles must be completed by the nineteenth of July.' What preview? Whose preview? For whom? And why? It has nothing to do with my contract. Once again, you have made a unilateral decision without discussing anything with me. I am particularly disturbed by your total change of face from absolute enthusiasm to anger and a negative value judgment on a piece of film that has yet to be viewed by us."

Panzer says, "Any film can always be better. Choices have to be made. A director should be the one who makes them. Very few films can roll on until they're finished in the director's opinion. But Sam didn't want to stop editing. Maybe he knew the shape better than anyone else."

Released at the end of 1983, *The Osterman Weekend* benefited from the

press's interest in Peckinpah's return. He did a number of interviews about
the film and, while he didn't rave about it, he didn't go out of his way to
bad-mouth it, aware that prospective employers would be reading these stories.

"I had no creative control," he said. "But they let me have a damned
good cast and a damned good crew and that means a lot. Tight budget,
tight schedule, which is good, and a lot of material. I think it'll be good. I
think it'll be entertaining. Whether it will be a Sam Peckinpah picture when
it gets to the screen, I have no idea."

"When we chatted on *Osterman*," says Charles Champlin, "he was a
captive of all this technology. I think he took a certain kind of pride in
bringing off a technically difficult film with an ambiguous, intricate plot. But
he was a hired gun. There was very little he could bring except compe-
tence."

But he showed his true feelings in a letter to his old friend Joe Bernhard:
"Well, *The Osterman Weekend* is finally fucking over and I'm delighted. I'm
less suicidal, most of the time; livid hatred, carefully concealed paranoia and
the constant diarrhea are abating. I'm again taking up my Biblical studies
and, at the same time, working on a new project, a preteen porn, nothing of
which is the corruption of adults by children."

Isela Vega recalls phoning Peckinpah on what turned out to be the opening night for *Osterman Weekend*: "He was sitting home by himself," she
says. "He was a lonely man."

The film was released in December 1983. Though it was a large step
above *Convoy*, it was a confused and confusing film, with too little too late
about CIA corruption, a topic Peckinpah had handled seven years earlier in
Killer Elite.

Stanley Kaufmann, in the *New Republic*, wrote, "A dreary occasion . . .
I've seen sillier spy thrillers than *The Osterman Weekend*, but they weren't
made by Peckinpah and thus were less depressing."

Even the positive reviews were tepid, damning the film with faint praise
and left-handed compliments. They weren't the kind of notices that would
draw people to the box office or producers to Sam Peckinpah's door.

David Ansen wrote in *Newsweek*, "If one can overlook a great deal of
narrative nonsense—a lot to ask, admittedly—there remains the somewhat
decadent pleasure of watching Peckinpah flex his dormant muscles again.
He's still an ace choreographer of mayhem, an edgy observer of domestic
tension, an action painter of great if often misused gifts. Once again he gives
us some terrific brushwork on a rotten canvas. A sad and familiar story, but
'Bloody Sam' has never had it easy in Hollywood."

The film did little business in the United States though it did moderately
well overseas, where it also received better reviews. To support the film,
Peckinpah flew to Europe, where the film opened before its American pre-

miere. Though he had virtually stopped drinking in September, he drank until he could barely stand up on the flight over, but only seemed to push himself deeper into despair.

Attorney Joe Swindlehurst, who accompanied him on the trip, says, "On that trip over, he was drinking to the point that his health was almost failing. I thought he wouldn't live much longer. He was getting old, he was short of money. He had made a movie that was not going to be a success and he probably knew it."

Part Nine

1983-1984

I'm older now and I've already had the chance to make Noon Wine, The Wild Bunch, Straw Dogs, Junior Bonner—*lots of good pictures.*

—SAM PECKINPAH, 1983, ON THE SET
OF *The Osterman Weekend*

36

Further Adventures on the Comeback Trail

By 1983, HOLLYWOOD HAD CHANGED SUFFICIENTLY that Sam Peckinpah virtually had to start over. The studio suites were full of baby moguls and young turks, former agents and lawyers who had been raised on movies and were now making them.

They had little sense of film history, except recent box-office trends. Their cinematic education began with Lucas and Spielberg, *Star Wars* and *E.T.* Westerns were virtually dead and the men who had made them were all but forgotten (except by the men making movies who stole from and paid homage to them).

A story from that period, probably apocryphal, centers on a meeting between one such shortsighted newcomer and the great director David Lean, whose career included such milestones as *Dr. Zhivago, Lawrence of Arabia* and *The Bridge on the River Kwai*. Attempting to get a project going in the early 1980s (his last film having been 1970's *Ryan's Daughter*), Lean had a meeting with an extremely young studio executive.

"So, tell me what you've done," the ignorant young exec said.

Lean smiled and said, "No, you first."

Still, Peckinpah's name meant something. It got him a look at scripts and enough momentum to keep him going. He took meetings, had lunches, met people and pitched to them—many of the activities he liked least in the movie business.

But from the time he was taken off the editing of *The Osterman Weekend* in the late summer of 1983 until his death the next year, Peckinpah never got back on a movie set.

It wasn't that he hadn't partially rehabilitated his reputation with *Oster-*

man: "His behavior was impeccable," Martin Baum says. "I felt that, if nothing else, it showed he could still make a picture on budget, on time."

But nothing concrete came his way. There were possibilities, always possibilities, but none that reached a meaningful stage of commitment. It was frustrating for the newly sober Peckinpah.

"I'll be in Mexico on Monday and for the next six weeks but can be reached through my office in case anything might turn up—or has that become a bad joke?" he wrote to Baum in June of 1984. "I was wondering if you might come up with a little work—or have I been prematurely retired without benefit of counsel?"

Dan York, Peckinpah's one-time assistant, had gone to work for Baum at the beginning of 1984 and found himself taking Peckinpah's calls on an almost daily basis.

"Sam was a high-maintenance client," York says. "He had a lot of complaints, most of them not justified. Marty didn't want to deal with the day-to-day Sam.

"Sam would complain about not getting material and about the quality of the material he got. When I'd get him a job, he'd say, 'Why did you get me that job? Why didn't you get me this other job?' There was that wonderful little evil, hotfoot personality. It was a direct barometer of how he felt about the work. If he was secure, then he said, 'What about the next job?' If he was nervous, he said, 'You're not helping me much here.' "

In June 1983, Peckinpah's mother, Fern Church Peckinpah, died. She had spent the last nine years of her life in a nursing home sinking into schizophrenic madness.

She had lived alone since her husband, Dave Peckinpah, had died in 1960. A few years after his death, she was operated on for uterine cancer, a condition she ignored until it was so advanced that she was dehydrated and hemorrhaging.

She survived the cancer, only to begin to lose her mental facilities in the early 1970s. "People were afraid of her," says Susan Peckinpah, Peckinpah's youngest sister, who stayed in Fresno looking after her. "She would leave the phone off the hook and when the telephone repairman would come, she'd pull her guns on him. She was a crack shot. I heard stories about her walking the fence line with a shotgun at night."

Susan finally had her put into a rest home, where she remained until her death.

"Sam went to see his mother in the nursing home and she didn't recognize him," Marcy Blueher says. "He was really morose about that visit. He thought that was how he would end up."

Peckinpah and his sisters, Fern Lea and Susan, attended the funeral in Fresno. Their oldest brother, Denver, refused.

WHILE WORKING ON *Osterman Weekend,* Peckinpah had become involved with Carol O'Connor, a young legal secretary and accountant, a divorced mother of a small boy, who was moonlighting as a makeup artist. He had originally met her in 1980, after his heart attack, through Walter Kelley. They began dating and, for all practical purposes, living together. They spent almost every day together from the fall of 1983 until he died.

At that point, she says, he had stopped drinking. "I never realized what a heavy drinker he had been," she said. "He told me he wasn't a pretty drunk. He drank Perrier and diet Coke."

He also claimed to have cut down on his smoking. "But he smoked several different brands, according to his mood," she says. "Camels, Winstons, Marlboros, Luckys. When I bought cigarettes for him, I felt like I was buying cigarettes for a poker game."

As with most of the women in his life, O'Connor quickly settled in, not just as a lover but as assistant, helper and all-around girl Friday.

"He was very disorganized when it came to paperwork," she says. "He didn't want to deal with it. He couldn't. I only worked full-time for him for a couple of months, but it was always full-time. There were artistic files, research, correspondence. I never gave up my outside job completely because I wanted a little independence."

She watched as Peckinpah would pull himself together and go out to try to charm someone into giving him a movie deal.

"On *Red-Headed Stranger,* which was going to have a European theatrical release, he said, 'Don't they realize how big I am in Europe?' " she says. "He hated not being offered jobs and being run through the mill. He went on so many interviews for so many projects. He put so many hours in. He was willing to play with it as much as anybody. He'd do the dance."

Even when he wasn't being paid for it, Peckinpah was always working, always writing. He and O'Connor would take off for Sausalito or Hawaii together. He still carried a script to work on: the now-dog-eared *Castaway,* from the James Gould Cozzens novel.

"He always felt that was his ace in the hole," O'Connor says. "When there was nothing else, he would pull that out and work on it. When we were in Hawaii, he asked me once how I would do it. When I told him, he threw it in the sand and said, 'Son of a bitch, you do it.' "

Among Peckinpah's affectations was a small stuffed doll that looked like a monkey. It had been given to him as a Christmas gift by Joe Swindlehurst (who had a stuffed monkey of his own), and Peckinpah had named it Simon (pronounced as though it were Spanish). He carried it in a basket and took it everywhere he went.

"The monkey was a discussion point, a prop," Swindlehurst says. "The monkey could say and do things that you or I never could."

"The monkey represented Sam's addictions, I think," says Dave Rawlins, the editor on his last film. "Sam had an arrangement. Before he did anything rash, he had to have a talk with the monkey. He told me one time that he and Joe were flying to Europe first class and they had bought seats for their monkeys too. The plane was full and [the airline] wanted the seat the monkey was in, even though it was paid for. Sam wouldn't give it up."

Gill Dennis says, "I remember talking to him and the monkey was sitting on the edge of the bed next to him. I was telling him a story about a job that fell through and he reached over and tipped the monkey sideways and said, 'See? The monkey knows.' The monkey always knew when things were good. And when things were bad, he'd fall over."

Wherever Peckinpah went, the first things he unpacked were the monkey, his Bible and his crucifix. Then he'd place the monkey somewhere in his room and see how long it took O'Connor to find it.

"To him, the monkey was a person," she says. "It wasn't a childlike thing. It didn't seem unusual. It was his alter ego. If he was shy, he'd say, 'Well, Simon's happy to see you.' "

Occasionally, Peckinpah would be able to show off a little of his old fame (or notoriety): "He beamed when people recognized him or talked about his work," O'Connor says. "He was almost shy about it. He'd thank them and kiss their hand."

He was invited to attend a retrospective of his films at Rice University in Houston. "That retrospective was important to him," says O'Connor, who attended with him. "He prepared for weeks. He made me do research about the retinal retention factor, things like that. Then hardly any students asked those kinds of questions. He didn't find out until after he arrived that Rice didn't have a film department."

They became close enough that Peckinpah began to talk about marriage. He told O'Connor that if he hadn't had such a bad track record, he'd have married her from the start of their relationship.

"What makes you think I'd marry you?" she responded tartly, an answer that amused Peckinpah.

He would cook for her and admonish her not to reveal that he did. "He was a great cook, but he'd say, 'Don't tell anyone. It would hurt my image.' "

She, in turn, tried out new-age treatments on him. "Someone had told me about the healing power of cayenne pepper. A tablespoon in a big tumbler of water. So he tried it and he got beet red. He sputtered, 'You're trying to kill me.' But then he said he could feel every pore in his skin."

He sent her yellow roses and she would pamper him by waiting on him around her apartment. He urged her to try writing and tried to teach her about film as well. One evening, to provoke an argument, he said, "You're an independent-thinking woman. What's your favorite Western?"

"It was a no-win situation," O'Connor says. "If I said, *The Wild Bunch*, he'd say I was condescending to him. If I said, *Butch Cassidy and the Sundance Kid*, I'd never see him again. So I said, *Citizen Kane*. He thought that was wonderful."

Peckinpah saw arguing as a facet of any romantic relationship. "He'd start a fight and this was how he worked things out emotionally," she says. "He'd say, 'I don't believe you love me unless you fight with me.' It was as strong an emotion as love to him. He said, 'I want to hear you raise your voice.'"

37

Second-Generation Rock

MARTIN LEWIS WAS IN TROUBLE. A brash young Brit in his early thirties, he had been a promoter and producer, working on *The Secret Policeman's Other Ball* concert film for Amnesty International.

In mid-1984, hustling for work in New York, he had run into Tony Stratton-Smith, the head of Charisma Records in London. Stratton-Smith had just signed Julian Lennon to a recording contract. Lewis had convinced Stratton-Smith that he would be the perfect choice to produce a documentary film on Julian. The film would introduce young Lennon to the public in his own right, out of the shadow of his late father, John Lennon.

But here it was, July 1984; the project was scheduled to be shot after Labor Day. And Lewis was suddenly without a director.

His original choice for the project had been Alan Rudolph, who turned him down. He had been able to sign Robert Altman but after six weeks of preparation, Altman backed out. Lewis had three days to find someone else.

A friend suggested Sam Peckinpah. Figuring he had nothing to lose, Lewis called Martin Baum at CAA.

"I expected to be shrugged off," Lewis says. "But Dan York, Marty's assistant, said he'd call me back. Five minutes later, I get the call: Sam's interested."

Lewis reached Peckinpah by phone and they agreed to meet in San Francisco, where Peckinpah was negotiating to direct a film called *On the Rock,* for which a San Francisco group was offering financing.

"He couldn't have been nicer or more interested in the project," Lewis says. "He was lively, almost chirpy, flirting with the waitress and expressing great interest. Don Hyde was with him and we drove up to Sonoma for the weekend. The upshot was that he wanted to do it."

They worked out a deal calling for $100,000 for Peckinpah: $25,000 to start, $25,000 upon completion, $25,000 upon release and 25 percent of the net profit.

366

"I couldn't work out why he was interested," Lewis says, "except that he obviously needed it."

"Sam was desperate for a job," Dan York says. Adds Marty Baum, "He did the Julian Lennon thing for the money. He always needed money."

Lewis flew back to New York. After discussions with Lennon and Phil Ramone, who was producing Lennon's first album, Lewis decided that he, Peckinpah and Lennon should sit down for a weekend of talks to come up with a concept and an outline for the documentary. When Lewis called Peckinpah to ask if New York was okay, Peckinpah said, "I'm a whore. I'll go wherever you want me to."

They converged on the Port Royal Inn in Montauk, Long Island, on Labor Day weekend, 1984. Besides the three of them, Lennon was accompanied by Dean Gordon, a schoolmate who had convinced Lennon to let him manage him.

Lennon was a pleasantly vague young man who floated through life as nonchalantly as possible—the perfect tool for a climber like Gordon. Gordon, on the other hand, had a few limited notions about how to launch Lennon's career and seemed to take great pleasure in vetoing the ideas that Peckinpah and Lewis came up with. Peckinpah started getting impatient with Lennon, who was hard to engage and who left all decisions to Gordon.

Gradually, over the weekend, Peckinpah and Lewis fashioned an idea to shoot the film as a pseudodocumentary along the lines of *A Hard Day's Night* or *The Rutles*.

"If we had put Julian on tape in too raw a state, it would have been unfair," Lewis says. "We decided to create a character who stands between Julian and the audience, this character pursuing Julian. It would be a film about making a film. Sam was convinced that I should play that character. In effect, I should play myself: someone trying to put Julian over but trying a little too hard."

After the weekend, they headed back to New York, to look at home movies of Lennon in the recording studio and refine the idea. While there, they hit upon another notion: Rehearse Lennon, then put him on stage in a bar in a small town performing for locals. The idea was shot down by Lennon and Gordon, who said, "We don't want to have Julian go on stage until he's perfect."

Peckinpah, who was staying at the Algonquin Hotel, started watching MTV to get a clearer idea of what he was involved with. The all-music TV network had been on the air for more than two years but it was new to him. He also was seeing old friends, including Jason Robards, with whom he had lunch. By that point, he had begun to see the potential for music videos.

"He had been watching MTV and he was telling me that this was going to be a big thing and make a lot of money," Robards said.

After a few days in New York, Peckinpah grew uneasy about Lewis's laissez-faire approach. To Lewis, the project was an idea that was developing by free-form evolution. To Peckinpah, Lewis was simply unprofessional and disorganized, with no writer, no guiding idea and no one in a position to make a firm artistic decision.

"I was finding him more acerbic," Lewis says. "My producing abilities were more entrepreneurial, rather than being able to marshal forces. Sam was saying the whole operation needed to be more professional."

In New York, Peckinpah seemed like a fish out of water. Julie Mann, who had been hired as his assistant while he was in Manhattan, says, "He couldn't do anything for himself and he hated to be alone. He wanted to be treated like a king. He took limos everywhere. He had a lot of pills and he used to give himself shots every day. He said they were B_{12}. He made me watch him and I thought it was gross. He took pills to calm down."

"Sam carried a little pharmacy, all his prescriptions," says Robin Chambers, who took over as Peckinpah's assistant for the subsequent video shoot. "I think he was debilitated by his pacemaker and was feeling the effects of it. That was frightening to a man like Sam. It probably went against his whole life-style."

He continued to watch MTV, as research for what he was about to do. "He was excited about breaking into a new field," Mann says. "It was kind of an honor that this particular artist wanted him."

Still, Mann says, "For all his gruffness and medication you could tell that this man was terrified of being alone."

With stasis setting in, the decision was made to take a break and rethink the project. Peckinpah went back to L.A. and Lewis went to London.

The original plan had been to have the documentary coincide with the release of Lennon's first album, but time had gotten away from them. The album was due out at the end of October. At the end of September, it was decided to put the documentary on hold. The first order of business needed to be videos to promote the album's release.

Lewis was still keen on using Peckinpah for the videos and made an offer of $10,000. He closed the deal in a conference call with Baum and Peckinpah, who agreed to come back to New York to shoot them. "He also expressed the hope that things would be more professional," Lewis says.

Lewis hung up from the conference call, then picked up the receiver to make another call. But he found that the connection with Baum and Peckinpah had not been broken. They were still on the line, discussing matters between themselves. Eavesdropping for a minute, Lewis heard Peckinpah say, "If I go there, I'm gonna need some muscle. Otherwise, that Martin Lewis will get me in a corner and fuck me to death."

"I was dead thrilled to hear that," Lewis says, with a note of pride.

"Martin was a charming fellow," Dan York says. "Sam once complained that, with Martin, he felt charmed by a bullshit artist."

They decided to film very simple performance videos of Lennon singing in a recording studio and selected Beartracks in Suffern, New York. Peckinpah asked Lewis to hire John Coquillon as cinematographer. When he wasn't available, Peckinpah asked for—and received—Alex Phillips, Jr. He also asked Lewis to hire Walter Kelley as an assistant director.

Both Phillips and Kelley arrived ahead of Peckinpah and went up to get things organized in Suffern. Lewis was slightly wary when he saw who he'd be working with.

"Alex arrived in New York and he was a crazy man—five-foot-four or so, mid-forties," Lewis says. "He was knocking back tequilas and chasing women from the moment he came to New York. Then Walter Kelley arrived, this Lorne Greene–type character with white hair."

"Walter knew Sam," says Robin Chambers. "He was like a security blanket; Sam felt comfortable with him. He was a buddy."

Peckinpah, however, was late. Given a first-class ticket, he had cashed it in to get two coach tickets, so he could bring Carol O'Connor along. Then they had missed the flight. Once in the air, he had a message sent to Lewis that he had been taken ill on the plane. Lewis had a wheelchair waiting to meet Peckinpah—who had himself wheeled into the airport gift shop to purchase a hunting knife.

"We finally got to the hotel room upstate and, with no warning or reason, this knife whistled within an inch of my head and buried itself in the wall behind me," Lewis says. "Walter Kelley later told me, 'He's the world's worst knife thrower. He has no idea what he's doing.' "

Once they reached Suffern, the plan was to spend a day of rehearsal in the studio, during which they'd develop ideas for the two videos to be shot— "Too Late for Goodbyes" and "Valotte." "I had never shot a video, but I had faith something would evolve," Lewis says.

Lewis had not counted on Peckinpah's bottom-line pragmatism. The day of the rehearsal, Lewis went to Peckinpah's room and found him still in bed, nursing a bad attitude.

"Where's my check?" Peckinpah demanded. Lewis, ready for the question, whipped a check from Charisma Records out of his pocket.

"It's not certified," Peckinpah said, after studying it for a few seconds. Lewis tried to reason with him, pointing out that a major record label would hardly pass a bad check, but Peckinpah dug in his heels.

"I'm not getting out of bed until I have cash in my hand," he said. Walter Kelley, on hand to try to keep Peckinpah on an even keel, couldn't dissuade him.

"He was always apprehensive that he'd get a check that would bounce or that he would get in a fight and have them stop payment on the check," Kelley says. "He didn't like the idea that there was a chance of him blowing it and not getting paid."

Lewis, ever the entrepreneur, got on the phone and tried to find a way that Peckinpah could get his payment in cash that very day. While it was morning in New York, it was already afternoon in London, where the main office was, and still pre-dawn in Los Angeles, where the other office was located.

Lewis was able to strike a deal whereby the record company would wire the funds to a local bank in upstate New York. An account would be opened for Peckinpah and he would be given the passbook, so he could withdraw the money himself. The whole process—of working out the deal and then getting Peckinpah the money—took three hours.

Finally ready to head to the recording studio, Lewis got everyone into the car to drive the ten minutes to Beartracks. Peckinpah, who had a bad cold, asked Chambers to get him some soup. She ran into a nearby store and came out with a cup of cream of broccoli.

As he sipped it, he said, "There are too many people in the car. DGA [Directors Guild of America] regulations say a director is supposed to have a car to himself and his assistant."

"Sam was in the backseat with two people and I was in the front seat with the driver," Lewis says. "So I said, 'We're only going ten minutes up the road. Now just drive.' "

As the driver took off, Peckinpah growled, "You're in trouble with the DGA," and kept grousing.

Finally pushed to the limit, Lewis snapped, "Where does it say in the DGA regulations that I have to spend the morning opening a bank account for you?"

Peckinpah said, "Right here, partner"—and dumped the cream of broccoli soup in Lewis's lap.

"It was such an aggressive act and in such a confined space," Chambers remembers. "I grabbed the back of Sam's shirt and yanked him back and said, 'Sit down, Sam.' "

There was a moment of stunned silence. In that moment, Lewis thought to himself, "Is this grounds to punch somebody?" and then thought, "Careful, he's testing you."

With impeccable timing, Lewis looked up from his soggy lap and said, "Sam, I think if you look in the DGA regulations, if you throw soup at a Jewish producer, it has to be chicken soup."

And nothing more was said. "It was like a storm had broken," says Lewis, who spent the rest of the day walking around with a large, wet stain on his pants.

"It was a childish thing for him to do," Kelley says. "Martin was a brash music person who didn't have the sense to back off. Sam would react violently and physically if somebody pushed him."

At the studio, a brainstorming session was in progress. Meanwhile, Lennon sat at the piano, practicing the songs.

"Sam loved Julian," Chambers says. "He thought he was an enormous talent. Julian was delighted to be around Sam. The clackers for the video said, 'J. Lennon.' Sam made them change it to 'Julian L.' Sam was getting emotional about how much Julian sounded like his father."

Peckinpah, tired from the day, demanded a masseuse. One was brought in and he received a massage. Then he stood up and said, "Let's not rehearse. Let's catch it now. Let's shoot it today."

Peckinpah retired to a back room to lie down and nurse his cough. He slept for three hours while Lewis's crew set up lights, cameras and the rest of the equipment needed to film the video. Finally, around 6 P.M., Peckinpah arose and came out to survey the studio.

Then he announced that he didn't like the setup and that he didn't feel like shooting that day after all. "If I shoot anymore, I'll collapse," he said and went back to lie down.

Furious, Lewis threw a tantrum at Kelley, about the fact that everything had been in a continual state of flux for the entire day to suit Peckinpah's whim—only to have him cancel shooting at the last minute.

Kelley went in to talk to Peckinpah, who finally relented. They wound up working on the "Too Late for Goodbyes" video until 3 A.M.

"Once we actually started shooting, it went beautifully," Chambers says. "But Sam was very intimidating. It was like a steam roller. You don't stop it. He was a movie person and these were music video people."

The next day, they shot "Valotte." "It was Sam's idea to put [choreographer] Moses Pendleton in," Lewis says. "Sam had ordered these large mirrors for the studio. He was twenty million leagues ahead of us. He was thinking visually and had it all in his head."

With shooting completed in the allotted two days, they headed back to Manhattan to edit the videos, which had to be finished and readied for airplay. Peckinpah shuttled back and forth between two editing rooms in the same building, supervising the work of two editors on electronic video editing equipment.

"It was fabulous to watch him work," Lewis says. Adds Chambers, "He was really hands-on. He took the job as seriously as any film job. He was pushing and demanding from everyone around him."

The finished products were striking yet simple, nonnarrative videos with an elegant mood and a moving camera that gave the music a graceful feeling. They captured a winning personality but also a searching and sensitive soul, an image that Lennon was hoping to build upon.

When the videos were completed, Lewis sent Peckinpah a memo that said, "For a whore, you're sure a great fuck." The crew had a wrap party; Peckinpah made an appearance and Lewis, who had been drinking, made a speech hailing Peckinpah and referring to havoc, mayhem and soup. The crew presented Peckinpah with a satin tour jacket with the legend "Too Soon for Goodbyes."

"We were clearly making more of a fuss over Sam than Julian," Lewis says.

Peckinpah couldn't leave it at that, however. Within forty-eight hours, he had called Tony Stratton-Smith, the head of Charisma Records, to complain about Lewis. Stratton-Smith called Lewis, who, though he did his best to counter Peckinpah's charges of lack of professionalism, hung up the phone convinced his career was over.

Within minutes, Peckinpah was on the phone with Lewis, chipper and cheery. "How's everything going, partner?" he asked.

"Fine, Sam, couldn't be better," Lewis said through gritted teeth. "I wasn't going to give him the satisfaction," Lewis says now.

When they hung up, Lewis called his co-producer, Michael Owen, to complain about how Peckinpah had slammed him to Stratton-Smith. Five minutes later, Owen called back to say he had just spoken to Peckinpah, who was brokenhearted at the way Lewis had treated him on the phone. Owen had jumped to Lewis's defense, contending that Lewis was extremely upset with the way Peckinpah had trashed him to the head of the record company.

At which point Lewis figured it out: Peckinpah had made the call to Stratton-Smith as a prank, though Stratton-Smith had taken him semiseriously. While Peckinpah hadn't been able to get a rise out of Lewis when he called him, he'd accomplished his goal: to rile up Martin Lewis. And he had confirmation of it from Michael Owen.

"I'm sure he was in seventh heaven," Lewis says.

The documentary never went any further. Lewis hired Graham Chapman, formerly of the Monty Python comedy troupe, to write a script for a documentary. But Peckinpah critiqued the script with corrosive sarcasm. "I couldn't see any spirit of compromise in his critique," Lewis says. "I couldn't get anything constructive from him. So it was left unresolved and we decided to leave it to the new year."

38

Last Trip to Mexico

PECKINPAH CONTINUED TO LOOK FOR A MOVIE PROJECT that was worthy of him. He got as far as actually being hired to rewrite *On the Rock* for a group of investors in San Francisco. "He was hired to rewrite it in the hopes that he could be seduced into directing it," O'Connor says. He worked over the script, then called his old writing partner Jim Silke.

"He talked me into coming out to the trailer in Malibu," Silke says. "The principal characters in the script were essentially Dave Blassingame and Burgundy Smith, but he was calling them Sam and Silk. He was flattering me but he was also conning me. But it was all right. So I broke the script down for him and it was a mess. I took it out to him a week later. We went shopping in Point Dume and did exactly what we had done all those years ago. I got peanut butter and bread and he got ice cream. I set up the trailer for us to work a script. I sat and told him what was wrong and he listened. I leveled with him and told him it was a mess."

The project finally fell apart. But Peckinpah was already being considered for something else: *The Shotgunners,* an original script by horror-meister Stephen King.

"Ironically, it was the Julian Lennon video that brought Sam to Stephen King's attention," Dan York says. "He had a screenplay he wanted Sam to direct. Sam did meet him. It was a surreal sort of horror-action piece with a tremendous amount of gunplay and violence."

The film dealt with a modern suburb being terrorized by mystery vigilantes. Eventually, it turns out that these are specters from the past and that the ancestors of the people who live on this block were responsible for a lynching one hundred years earlier.

"Nobody liked it except Peckinpah," King said. "Peckinpah loved it. He flipped and said he wanted to do it. We sat down and he knew exactly what to do. He was a great guy and he knew it would've been a great movie."

Even as he was trying to reestablish himself professionally, Peckinpah was also mending fences in his personal life. During the final year of his life, he repaired relations with a number of old friends and family members he had so pointedly kissed off during the period before his heart attack.

He attended his mother's funeral in Fresno, where he made amends with his sister Fern Lea, whom he had angered and alienated with his drug use. In May 1984, he returned to Fresno for the funeral of his Aunt Jane Visher, his father's adoptive sister. During most of his visits to Fresno in the previous decade, for Peckinpah family reunions on Peckinpah Mountain, he had been drunk and obstreperous, the famous family alcoholic. But this trip he was cold sober, aged and quiet.

"We met at my house before the funeral," says his cousin, Bob Peckinpah, who had taken care of Aunt Jane in her declining years. "I had heard he was off the booze but everyone was concerned about him. He saw me looking at the glass he was drinking from and said, 'Would you believe this is tea?' And it was. He looked tired, but he was pretty relaxed."

He tried to soothe the old wounds with his daughter Sharon as well. He came for dinner in late October 1984 and was too feeble to carry a VCR into the house. "He brought some presents," Sharon says. "He brought my son, who was three, a Polaroid. Then he said to him, 'Use this like a pro.' That was his perfectionism. You already had to be a professional. You never had time to make mistakes. Add water and be an instant grown-up.

"There was something about that visit; I knew he wasn't going to last. I spontaneously hugged him, which I never did, and after he left, I had this feeling of enormous sadness. I said to my husband that I had a feeling I would never see him again and I never did."

His nephew David had had a run-in with Peckinpah in early 1982. Because they had the same name—David Peckinpah—the Writers Guild had sent a residual check to Sam instead of David.

"It was a check for $5,000," David says, "and he called me up and said, 'I've just finished a very good bottle of brandy that I bought with your check. If you've got a problem, talk to the guild.' And I was broke at the time. He was very amused at being able to get one up on anybody."

But David found a changed person at the dinner at Sharon's: "He was sober, clean, not smoking cigarettes," he says. "I said, 'Who is this man and what have you done with Sam?'"

"That last year, he went to see people," says his daughter Kristen. "He made up with Fern Lea and went to visit Mama Ceil, my mother's mother. At a certain point, you weren't going to see him if you didn't go."

Peckinpah extended himself in other ways. When his friend Don Levy was suffering from prostate cancer and facing an operation that could render him impotent and incontinent, Peckinpah recommended a specialist. That doctor removed Levy's cancer, without the drastic side effects.

Lying in the hospital in Los Angeles, Levy awoke in the middle of the night to find Peckinpah there.

"The place is dark—it's one or two in the morning—and in comes Sam," Levy says. "Sam had a bandana on his head and cowboy boots. He said, 'I brought you a book.' It was Nietzsche's *Antichrist*. Then he said he wanted to teach me a game: two-handed poker. After a while, he said, 'I have to go to a meeting.' And I believed him."

Bobby Visciglia, whose son, Bob, Jr., had worked for him doing props on *Convoy*, says that, a couple of years later, Bob, Jr., wound up in the medical center at UCLA with a serious illness.

"My son calls me and says, 'Dad, guess who came to visit me today? Sam Peckinpah,' " Visciglia says. "He spent an hour. And he visited him two or three times. How he found out that my son was in the hospital, I don't know."

AT THANKSGIVING 1984, Peckinpah was invited to Fern Lea's for dinner. But at the appointed hour, he hadn't shown up. So a posse was deputized to head for his trailer at Paradise Cove and bring him back alive.

By that point, most of his friends and family were used to the fact that he loved to lie around in bed all day. He ate, talked on the phone, wrote, dictated, smoked, watched TV, drank, received company and had sex there. The bed was the throne from which he routinely held court.

But on Thanksgiving, he just lay there looking gray and wan, without energy or spirit. Walter Peter, Joe Bernhard and Max Evans visited him and tried to get him to come back for the feast but couldn't rouse him.

"Sam's looking at us and he just wants friends," Bernhard says. "He's really beat. Max wanted to talk about movies. Sam was supposed to come up and eat with us but he finally said he just couldn't."

IN DECEMBER 1984, Peckinpah had a fight with Carol O'Connor and stopped seeing her. He worked on the Stephen King script until Christmas, then decided to take off. "Whenever we'd have a fight, he'd go to Mexico," O'Connor says.

The day before Christmas, he had himself driven to San Diego, where he checked into the San Diego Hilton. From there, he tried to call Juan Jose Palacios, who was married and living in San Diego, to drive him down to Mexico. But Palacios was out of town. Peckinpah left a message on his answering machine, accusing him of being a deserter and telling him he was flying down to Puerto Vallarta for some relaxation.

Two days later, Begonia Palacios got a call in Mexico City from Peckinpah. She knew he was in Puerto Vallarta; she had plans to meet him there for her birthday on the twenty-eighth.

"Begonia," he said, "I feel very cold. I don't want you to come, but pray for me."

"I thought he was joking," she says. "He was always saying, 'Begonia, I'm dying.' But I got this feeling. He asked me to pray to God not to forget him. When I finished work, I went home and Lupita was crying, saying, 'My daddy is dying.' He had called her to say, 'I love you,' and sounded so bad that my mother called Juan."

The next call Juan Jose received was from a government hospital in Puerto Vallarta: Peckinpah had been admitted in bad shape, complaining of chest pains and vomiting blood. But the Mexican doctors didn't want to touch him because they weren't sure how to treat the pacemaker. They needed a way to get him back to a hospital in the States.

After a couple of hours of trying to track down the money, Juan Jose arranged an ambulance plane to take Peckinpah from Puerto Vallarta back to Los Angeles. By this time, Begonia had flown there to accompany him back. The attendants loaded Peckinpah onto the plane and he headed for Los Angeles.

"He looked very sick," she says. "His face was completely white and he was coughing up blood. He told me he didn't want to see me cry. On the plane, he was saying, 'Begonia, why did God do this to me? I stopped drinking for a year. I was good. And now look at me.' "

An ambulance met them at Los Angeles International Airport. His condition was considered grave enough that rather than risk the traffic to Century City Hospital, where his own doctor was waiting, he was driven straight to Centinela Medical Center in Inglewood, less than a mile from the airport. He was admitted a little after 2 P.M. on Dec. 27; Begonia registered him as a Catholic because she knew he wanted last rites.

Begonia found herself in a side room "praying and signing papers" as doctors worked to stabilize Peckinpah. "He was fighting like a lion," Begonia says. "I stayed at the hospital, not thinking he was dying. Sam looked at me and said, 'Do you know the last film I made was five minutes long?' "

Doctors took him away to treat him. Begonia sat and talked to Peckinpah's sister, Fern Lea, who had been summoned.

"It's your birthday tomorrow," Fern Lea observed, as December 27 moved into the early-morning hours of December 28. "I'm sorry this is happening."

Begonia recalls that "Sam used to say to me, 'What do you want? You live with a great director in Malibu with a car and a house. What do you want?' I'd say, 'Sam, I want peace. Can you give it to me?' "

Now, as he was being attended to in desperate efforts to save his life, he turned to his ex-wife and said, "I'm learning some of the peace you talk about. You have the light inside you. I know that peace you want."

As doctors continued to work on Peckinpah in an unseen emergency chamber, Begonia finally fell asleep, only to be awakened an hour or so later by a nurse, who said, "They need you downstairs."

Peckinpah had started to have breathing problems and the nurses and doctors tried to get him on a respirator around 6:30 A.M. As they did, he went into cardiac arrest. He could not be revived. He was pronounced dead at 9:45 A.M. on Dec. 28, 1984, two months shy of his sixtieth birthday.

"There was a priest; I was sitting with Fern Lea and they told me he was dead," Begonia says. "I saw Sam and kissed him. He was at peace."

THE OBITUARIES RANGED FROM the terse, in *Time* and *Newsweek,* to the more complete in *Variety* and the *New York Times.*

Time referred to him as a "maverick action-film director whose best work combines an obsession with the ubiquity of violence and a surgeon's skill at bloodletting." It said that he "had a gift for antagonizing producers; he was unable at times to get financing, and only a handful of his films were released in their original versions." The best of his films "bitterly depict the death of the Old West, with macho heroes increasingly at odds with the march of progress; the worst sink in a sea of sadistic, superfluous gore."

Newsweek was even less sentimental, dwelling on the mid-1960s period of being blackballed, mentioning that *The Wild Bunch* was denounced for its violence and recalling Pauline Kael's "fascist" remark about *Straw Dogs.* It quoted Peckinpah as saying "I'm a student of violence because I'm a student of the human heart."

The *New York Times* also focused on the violence of Peckinpah's films and his rebellious nature. "Mr. Peckinpah's work was characterized by a machismo that mirrored his own hard-drinking, hard-living style of life," Leslie Bennetts wrote. The obituary also noted that Peckinpah started out making Westerns, then made films set in modern times. Those films "transposed the scenes of rape and slaughter to more contemporary settings, but the notorious Peckinpah spectacles of blood and gore continued to shock many while winning critical praise for the directorial skill with which they were filmed."

The most detailed obituary ran in *Variety,* where writer Todd McCarthy appreciatively mentioned Peckinpah's more lyrical films as well as the controversy of his violent vision. McCarthy also gave Peckinpah credit for a complete rewrite of *Invasion of the Body Snatchers,* perpetuating that myth, and spelled Marie's name Sellen instead of Selland.

All of the obituaries referred to heart failure or cardiac arrest as the cause of death. But the autopsy performed by Dr. Lakshmanan Sathyavagiswaran, deputy medical examiner of Los Angeles County, showed that Peckinpah's heart failure was not caused by his preexisting cardiac problems.

Rather, the pneumonia that sent him into arrest was created by blood clots breaking off from his heart and rushing up the pulmonary artery into his lungs. These clots, the autopsy showed, were caused by staphylococcal tricuspid valve endocarditis—a staph infection that rapidly broke down the tricuspid valve.

That kind of staph infection usually is found only in intravenous drug users. But the autopsy turned up no needle track scars. It also showed no trace of alcohol, cocaine, barbiturates or drugs other than those administered to him at the hospital.

PECKINPAH WAS CREMATED and his ashes were spread in the waters of the Pacific Ocean at Paradise Cove, near his trailer in Malibu.

His will left his property to his children: the ranch in Montana, his trailer and a few paintings that he had invested in that he still owned.

But the paintings—three Picassos, a Paul Klee and a Matisse drawing— were sold to pay taxes. So was most of the acreage in Montana. Peckinpah's children and the heirs of Warren Oates ultimately settled their debt by ceding five hundred of the six hundred acres on which the cabins were situated to the U.S. Forest Service. The Peckinpahs and the Oateses each got to keep their cabin and about fifty acres.

The will also recognized Lupita Palacios as his daughter, an inclusion that meant she would have dual citizenship in the United States and Mexico. Her portion of the estate was put into trust until she turned eighteen.

"The money he made could have gone a lot further, as far as supporting him," says his brother Denny, co-executor with daughter Kristen. "At one point, this guy comes up with a note for $50,000 and there was no doubt he had loaned it to Sam. We finally had to pay him $25,000 or $30,000."

In going through his effects, Walter and Fern Lea Peter came across a small briefcase. After examining the contents, they called Carol O'Connor and gave it to her.

When she opened it, she found packets of letters she had written to Peckinpah, collected together in chronological order, tied into bundles with ribbons.

Part Ten

EPILOGUE

Sam was tough on his enemies and tougher on his friends. He wasn't an easy man—but nothing good comes easy.

—WALTER PETER, AT THE JANUARY 1985 TRIBUTE TO PECKINPAH

Epilogue

In early January 1985, two weeks after his death, friends, associates and relatives gathered at the Directors Guild of America building on Sunset Boulevard in Hollywood for a tribute to Sam Peckinpah.

Organized by his family, it included a selection of film clips put together by Kristen and Gill Dennis and a roster of well-known friends as speakers, with Walter Peter as the master of ceremonies.

Joe Bernhard was sitting next to Max Evans, who turned to him at one point and said, "I never thought I'd make sixty."

Bernhard replied, "If we thought we'd live this long, we'd have taken better care of ourselves."

Martin Lewis, the brash young producer from the Julian Lennon videos, convinced Charisma Records to send him to the tribute. Peckinpah had died two months after completing the videos and Lewis was still suffering the effects of his final prank.

"I had all these unresolved feelings about him," Lewis says. "It was a rite of passage for me to work with him. The DGA tribute was the most cathartic experience."

The gathering of the hundreds of people who had known, loved, hated, worked, fought and played with Sam Peckinpah created an intense and unique sense of camaraderie. It was as if a huge club was convening for the first time for its members to share their communal status as Peckinpah veterans.

"Being on a Peckinpah film was a badge of recognition that you had been through something extraordinary," David Warner says. "I feel I have a camaraderie with Ernest Borgnine, even though I've never met him. The first time I met Kris Kristofferson, I knew that we both shared this same secret, of having worked with Sam. I feel something slightly special to have worked for him, something you only get working with Peckinpah."

"As I sat there at the tribute," Martin Lewis says, "I felt I was part of a community of people who had been touched by this man—and what a glorious thing it was. The notion that a man can be so complex, such a glorious mess of contradictions of big, happy memories and yet be so enraging. That's the contradiction. All my unresolved feelings resolved themselves. He made me deliver; he forced me to work harder. By creating hysteria, he forced everyone to do their best work. There was a method to his madness."

"You felt with Sam that you were part of a tribe," Jim Hamilton says. "That's what the DGA ceremony was, a gathering of a tribe."

"WE HAVE GATHERED TO SHARE a few recollections of a uniquely talented man," Walter Peter began. Noting that he never had the privilege of working with his brother-in-law, Peter talked instead about the side of Peckinpah that many people never saw.

"Spending a vacation with Sam was a unique experience," Peter said. "His sense of humor would be in full flower and his capacity for sheer fun and nonsense was without equal. Among his less well-known talents, he was a concerned parent, a babysitter par excellence, a friend in need and, God love him, he was never dull."

They were there, Peter said, to honor Peckinpah as one of the breakthrough artists in American film. "A Peckinpah location was no day at the beach," he observed, to laughter from the crowd. "It was a complex survival drill, grueling and exhilarating. You survived, battered and bloodied, swearing you'd never work for him again and hoping you'd get the chance. You were willing to face the fire to get a taste of his magic.

"Sam was tough on his enemies and tougher on his friends. He wasn't an easy man—but nothing good comes easy. He cared passionately about his work. He cared about stimulating an audience—to think, to react, to feel.

"Sam was one of the world's worst poker players. He opened strong, hoping to separate the gamblers from the ribbon clerks. He was the same way with people. He had to put up with the ribbon clerks but the gamblers were his friends.

"Being Sam's friend was like working the center ring with the big cats. The raw dangerous beauty of his talent was hypnotic and the potential for all hell breaking loose was there in a split second.

"I saw him in the mountains. White Levi's, a sweat-stained cowboy hat, his coat buttoned against a high canyon wind, a deer rifle over his shoulder and his eyes searching the mahogany thickets. We're ten miles from camp, losing daylight and it's starting to spit snow. He wouldn't have it any other way.

"I won't talk about the films he left behind, but I like to think about the one he's making now. He got a start date a couple of weeks ago. A hell of a cast: Steve McQueen, Robert Ryan, Bill Holden, Warren Oates, Slim Pickens, Strother Martin. Bruce Geller is collaborating on the screenplay and Jerry Fielding is doing the score. There's no studio, no producer, no schedule, no budget and a million miles of film. The first assistant is pounding on the trailer door: 'We're ready on the set, Sam.'

"I expected him to live forever. I'm shocked, saddened and pissed off that he didn't. Now when the phone rings at 3 A.M., I'll have to wonder who it is.

"Adios, Sam. We love you and miss you. Shalom."

Director Don Siegel, Peckinpah's mentor in his first days in film, told the story about Peckinpah and the warden of Folsom Prison on *Riot in Cell Block Eleven* and recalled Peckinpah's initial job interview with him, arranged by producer Walter Wanger.

"He said he wanted to go to work for me and I said, 'Doing what?' " Siegel said. "He said, 'Anything—I don't care.' I asked if he belonged to the union or the guild and he said, 'No, sir.' I studied him and observed his excitement and his sense of fun. I liked his wit and his pleasant manner, his politeness and his burning ambition.

"So I said, 'I've never worked with a gofer before.' He said, 'What's that mean?' I said, 'A gofer is a fellow who goes for things: toothpicks, coffee, girls.' He said, 'Girls? That's the job for me.'

"There is a wonderful legacy of films that he made," Siegel said. "Already, some of them are classics. I'm very proud of Sam's work. And I'm very proud that I was a good, close friend of Sam's."

James Coburn described Peckinpah as a director "who pushed me over the abyss and then jumped in after me. He took me on some great adventures."

But Coburn said he most remembered Peckinpah's vulnerability. He recounted the story of taking Federico Fellini to visit Peckinpah in his Venice hotel room, with Peckinpah sitting straight up in bed and saying, "Oh, Mr. Fellini, thank you for giving us all those wonderful films."

"Well, Sam Peckinpah, thank you, for all those films and the chance to work with you," Coburn concluded.

L. Q. Jones strode on stage and, before telling the *Cable Hogue* story about Peckinpah cussing out Strother Martin for Jones's error, said, "You can tell this is a Peckinpah production. We got started late and nobody knows what's happening."

Taking a survey of the room, Jones offered a wolfish smile and said, "God's gonna be sorry, folks." The audience burst out laughing, as Jones continued: "If you've ever tried to be in charge of something and Sam comes along . . . well, He's gonna be sorry."

Mariette Hartley, obviously shaken, said, "I wish Sam had written this and told me how to do it." She offered warm recollections of *Ride the High*

Country and observed, "My time with Sam was short and absolutely without pain. I don't know how many memories I have like that."

She quoted her three favorite lines from the film, concluding with Steve Judd's ambition "to enter my house justified."

"Well, you have, Sam," she said.

Robert Culp traced his friendship with Peckinpah, calling him "the most seductive human being I have met in my life." Observing that many people were mourning the films Peckinpah never got to make, Culp said, "The miracle of Sam was that he got any of them done at all, given the odds against a creative force constantly and diametrically opposed to the establishment. It's amazing that there is a *Wild Bunch*. Let's just think about that incredible, savage, iron-burning will; that he got them done and that we knew him."

Brian Keith recalled a drunkenly philosophical discussion of the nature of the universe he and Peckinpah had, in which they concluded that they were born about a hundred years too late. They'd deduced from this that, if there is an afterlife, the individual gets to pick it for himself.

"So I don't think Sam is making a movie," Keith said. "He's on a mountainside, on an Appaloosa horse, with an Indian maiden and a bow and arrow and he's sniffing the snow as it starts to fall. And I hope he holds a place for me."

Lee Marvin told the audience about a monument to RAF flyers in Great Britain, on which was printed the apostle Paul's letter to Timothy, 4:7: "I have fought a good fight. I have finished my course. I have kept the faith." Having recited this, Marvin added, "Sam Peckinpah."

Peckinpah "taught me to drive, he taught me to shoot and he taught me to shoot tequila," Ali MacGraw said. "What he began to teach me was what sort of person I wanted to be when I grew up. Because nobody ever nailed my stuff faster than Sam Peckinpah. And I loved him for it."

The tribute finished up with Richard Gillis singing "Butterfly Mornings," a collection of film clips and a song by Kris Kristofferson.

But they were preceded by Jason Robards, who walked up to the podium and recited Prospero's speech from Shakespeare's *The Tempest*:

> "Our revels now are ended. These our actors,
> As I foretold you, were all spirits, and
> Are melted into air, into thin air.
> And, like the baseless fabric of this vision,
> The cloud-capped towers, the gorgeous palaces,
> The solemn temples, the great globe itself—
> Yea, all which it inherit—shall dissolve
> And, like this insubstantial pageant faded,
> Leave not a rack behind. We are such stuff

As dreams are made of, and our little life
Is rounded with sleep."

Robards remembers sitting between Lee Marvin and Mariette Hartley at the tribute, with Hartley clutching his arm as she dissolved in tears. Afterward, as the tribute let out on to a crisp, sunny January day, a group of people headed for Camille Fielding's house.

Robards walked to his car in the sunshine, glancing around at the Hollywood neighborhood where he had spent several childhood years.

"I looked up and there was a chicken hawk flying around," Robards recalls. "When I was a kid growing up three blocks from there, my friend and I bagged a chicken hawk and had it stuffed. But nowadays, there aren't any hawks left. They're all gone.

"But here was one. He flew in a circle over us three times. I thought, 'Maybe he's right there after all.' "

An unidentified observer, apparently reading Robards's mind, looked at the hawk a moment, then said, "If he shits on us, we'll know it's Sam."

Sam Peckinpah Filmography

1. THE DEADLY COMPANIONS (1961)

A Carousel production, released by Pathe-America. Rereleased in 1965 as *Trigger Happy*. Running time: 90 minutes, cut to 79 minutes.

Producer: Charles B. FitzSimons. Screenplay: A. S. Fleischman, based on his novel *Yellowleg*. Director of photography: William H. Clothier. Music: Marlin Skiles. Song: "A Dream of Love" by Skiles and FitzSimons, sung by Maureen O'Hara. Editor: Stanley Rabjohn, assisted by Leonard Kwit. Sound: Robert J. Callen and Gordon Sawyer. Makeup: James Barker. Special Effects: Dave Kohler. Production manager: Lee Lukather. Wardrobe: Frank Beetson Sr. and Sheila O'Brien.

Cast: Kit Tilden: Maureen O'Hara. Yellowleg: Brian Keith. Billy: Steve Cochran. Turk: Chill Wills. Parson: Strother Martin. Doctor: Will Wright. Mead: Billy Vaughan.

2. RIDE THE HIGH COUNTRY (1962)

Metro-Goldwyn-Mayer. Released in Great Britain as *Guns in the Afternoon*. Running time: 94 minutes.

Producer: Richard Lyons. Screenplay: N. B. Stone, Jr. Director of photography: Lucien Ballard. Art directors: George W. Davis, Leroy Coleman. Set decorations: Henry Grace, Otto Siegel. Music: George Bassman. Sound: Franklin Milton. Makeup: William Tuttle. Editor: Frank Santillo. Assistant director: Hal Polaire.

Cast: Gil Westrum: Randolph Scott. Steve Judd: Joel McCrea. Heck Longtree: Ron Starr. Elsa Knudsen: Mariette Hartley. Billy Hammond: James Drury. Joshua Knudsen: R. G. Armstrong. Judge Tolliver: Edgar Buchanan. Elder Hammond: John Anderson. Sylvus Hammond: L. Q. Jones. Henry Hammond: Warren Oates. Jimmy Hammond: John David Chandler. Kate: Jenie Jackson.

3. MAJOR DUNDEE (1965)

Jerry Bresler Productions, released by Columbia Pictures. Running time: Originally released at 134 minutes, cut to 120.

Producer: Jerry Bresler. Screenplay: Harry Julian Fink, Oscar Saul and Sam Peckinpah, from a story by Fink. Director of photography: Sam Leavitt. Assistant directors: John Veitch, Floyd Joyer. Assistant director-Mexico: Emilio Fernandez. Second-unit director: Cliff Lyons. Production manager: Francisco Day. Art director: Al Ybarra. Music: Daniele Amfitheatrof. Title song: "Major Dundee March," music by Amfitheatrof, lyrics by Ned Washington. Sung by Mitch Miller's Sing Along Gang. Sound: Charles J. Rice, James Flaster. Costumes: Tom Dawson. Special effects: August Lohman. Makeup: Ben Lane, Larry Butterworth. Editors: William A. Lyon, Don Starling, Howard, Kunin.

Cast: Major Amos Dundee: Charlton Heston. Capt. Benjamin Tyreen: Richard Harris. Lt. Graham: Jim Hutton. Samuel Potts: James Coburn. Tim Ryan: Michael Anderson Jr. Teresa Santiago: Senta Berger. Sgt. Gomez: Mario Adorf. Aesop: Brock Peters. O. W. Hadley: Warren Oates. Sgt. Chillum: Ben Johnson. Rev. Dahlstrom: R. G. Armstrong. Arthur Hadley: L. Q. Jones. Wiley: Slim Pickens. Linda: Begonia Palacios.

4. THE WILD BUNCH (1969)

A Phil Feldman production, released by Warner Bros.-Seven Arts. Running time: 144 minutes, cut to 134 minutes. Academy Award nominations for screenplay and music.

Producer: Phil Feldman. Screenplay: Walon Green, Sam Peckinpah, from a story by Green and Roy Sickner. Director of photography: Lucien Ballard. Associate producer: Roy Sickner. Second-unit director: Buzz Henry. Assistant directors: Cliff Coleman, Fred Gammon. Production manager: William Faralla. Art director: Edward Carrere. Music: Jerry Fielding. Music supervision: Sonny Burke. Sound: Robert J. Miller. Wardrobe supervisor: Gordon Dawson. Special effects: Bud Hulburd. Makeup: Al Greenway. Editor: Lou Lombardo. Associate editor: Robert Wolfe.

Cast: Pike Bishop: William Holden. Dutch Engstrom: Ernest Borgnine. Deke Thornton: Robert Ryan. Freddy Sykes: Edmond O'Brien. Lyle Gorch: Warren Oates. Angel: Jaime Sanchez. Tector Gorch: Ben Johnson. Mapache: Emilio Fernandez. Coffer: Strother Martin. T. C.: L. Q. Jones. Harrigan: Albert Dekker. Crazy Lee: Bo Hopkins. Mayor Wainscoat: Dub Taylor. Lt. Zamorra: Jorge Russek. Herrera: Alfonso Arau. Don Jose: Chano Urueta. Aurora: Aurora Clavell. Teresa: Sonia Amelio.

5. The Ballad of Cable Hogue (1970)

A Latigo-Phil Feldman Production, released by Warner Bros.-Seven Arts. Running time: 121 minutes.
Producer: Sam Peckinpah. Executive producer: Phil Feldman. Screenplay: John Crawford, Edmund Penney. Director of photography: Lucien Ballard. Associate producer: Gordon Dawson. Co-producer: William Faralla. Assistant director: John Gaudioso. Art director: Leroy Coleman. Set decorator: Jack Mills. Music: Jerry Goldsmith. Songs: "Tomorrow Is the Song I Sing," music by Jerry Goldsmith, lyrics by Richard Gillis; "Wait for Me Sunrise," music and lyrics by Gillis (both sung by Gillis); "Butterfly Mornings," music and lyrics by Gillis. Sound: Don Rush. Costumes for Stella Stevens: Robert Fletcher. Makeup: Gary Liddiard, Al Fleming. Special effects: Bud Hulburd. Unit production manager: Dink Templeton. Dialogue supervisor: Frank Kowalski. Property master: Robert Visciglia. Editors: Frank Santillo, Lou Lombardo.
Cast: Cable Hogue: Jason Robards. Hildy: Stella Stevens. Rev. Joshua Sloane: David Warner. Bowen: Strother Martin. Taggart: L. Q. Jones. Ben Fairchild: Slim Pickens. Cushing: Peter Whitney. Quittner: R. G. Armstrong.

6. Straw Dogs (1971)

Co-production of Talent Associates Films and Amerbroco Films, distributed by Cinerama Releasing Corp. An ABC Pictures Presentation. Running time: 118 minutes, cut to 113 for U.S.
Producer: Daniel Melnick. Screenplay: David Z. Goodman, Sam Peckinpah, from the novel *The Siege of Trencher's Farm* by Gordon Williams. Director of photographer: John Coquillon. Editors: Roger Spottiswoode, Paul Davis, Tony Lawson. Editorial consultant: Robert Wolfe. Associate producer: James Swann. Assistant director: Terry Marcel. Assistant to director: Katy Haber. Production designer: Ray Simm. Production design consultant: Julia Trevelyan Oman. Art director: Ken Bridgeman. Set decorator: Peter James. Music: Jerry Fielding. Sound: John Bramall. Sound editor: Garth Craven. Wardrobe: Tiny Nicholls. Makeup: Harry Frampton. Special effects: John Richardson. Continuity: Pamela Davies. Production supervisor: Derek Kavanagh. Property master: Alf Pegley.
Cast: David Sumner: Dustin Hoffman. Amy Sumner: Susan George. Tom Hedden: Peter Vaughan. Major Scott: T. P. McKenna. Charlie Venner: Del Henney. Norman Scutt: Ken Hutchison. Rev. Hood: Colin Welland. Chris Cawsey: Jim Norton. Janice Hedden: Sally Thomsett. Henry Niles: David Warner (uncredited).

7. Junior Bonner (1972)

A Joe Wizan-Booth Gardner production, in association with Solar Productions for ABC Pictures, distributed by Cinerama Releasing Corp. Running time: 103 minutes.

Producer: Joe Wizan. Screenplay: Jeb Rosebrook. Director of photography: Lucien Ballard. Editors: Robert Wolfe, Frank Santillo. Associate producer: Mickey Borofsky. Assistant directors: Frank Baur, Malcolm Harding, Newt Arnold. Production manager: James C. Pratt. Production assistants: Raymond Green, Betty Gumm, Katy Haber. Art director: Ted Haworth. Set decorator: Gerald Wunderlich. Music: Jerry Fielding. Songs: "Bound to Be Back Again," words and music by Dennis Lambert and Brian Potter, sung by Alex Taylor; "Arizona Morning," "Rodeo Man," words, music and sung by Rod Hart. Costumes: Eddie Armand. Makeup: Donald Robertson, William Turner. Special effects: Bud Hulburd. Property master: Robert Visciglia. Technical advisor: Casey Tibbs.

Cast: Junior Bonner: Steve McQueen. Ace Bonner: Robert Preston. Elvira Bonner: Ida Lupino. Buck Roan: Ben Johnson. Curly Bonner: Joe Don Baker. Charmagne: Barbara Leigh. Red Terwiliger: William McKinney. Del: Dub Taylor. Nurse Arlis: Sandra Deel. Tim Bonner: Mathew Peckinpah.

8. The Getaway (1972)

A Solar/Foster-Brower production for First Artists Production Co., distributed by National General Pictures. Running time: 122 minutes.

Producers: David Foster and Mitchell Brower. Screenplay: Walter Hill, from the novel by Jim Thompson. Director of photography: Lucien Ballard. Editors: Robert Wolfe; assistants: Mike Klein and William Lindemann. Editorial consultant: Roger Spottiswoode. Associate producer and second-unit director: Gordon Dawson. Assistant directors: Newt Arnold, Ron Wright. Assistant to the producer: Joie Gould. Art directors: Ted Haworth, Angelo Graham. Set decorator: George R. Nelson. Music: Quincy Jones. Harmonica solos: Toots Thielemans. Sound: Chuck Wilborn, Garth Craven, Richard Portman, Joe von Stroheim, Mike Colgan. Costumes: Ray Summers. Makeup: Al Fleming, Jack Petty. Special effects: Bud Hulburd. Property master: Robert Visciglia.

Cast: Doc McCoy: Steve McQueen. Carol McCoy: Ali MacGraw. Jack Benyon: Ben Johnson. Fran Clinton: Sally Struthers. Rudy Butler: Al Lettieri. Cowboy: Slim Pickens. Thief: Richard Bright. Harold Clinton: Jack Dodson. Laughlin: Dub Taylor. Frank Jackson: Bo Hopkins. Accountant: John Bryson.

9. PAT GARRETT AND BILLY THE KID (1973)

A Gordon Carroll-Sam Peckinpah production for MGM. Running time: 123 minutes, cut to 106 minutes for release.

Producer: Gordon Carroll. Screenplay: Rudolph Wurlitzer. Director of cinematography: John Coquillon. Editors: Roger Spottiswoode, Garth Craven, Robert Wolfe, Richard Halsey, David Berlatsky, Tony De Zarraga. Second-unit director: Gordon Dawson. Assistant directors: Newt Arnold, Lawrence Powell. Art director: Ted Haworth. Set decoration: Ray Moyer. Music: Bob Dylan. Sound: Chuck Wilborn, Harry Tetrick. Wardrobe: Michael Butler. Makeup: Jack Wilson. Special effects: A. J. Lohman. Unit production manager: Jim Henderling. Mexican production manager: Alfonso Sanchez Tello. Mexican assistant director: Jesus Marin Bello. Property master: Robert Visciglia.

Cast: Pat Garrett: James Coburn. Billy the Kid: Kris Kristofferson. Alias: Bob Dylan. Sheriff Kip McKinney: Richard Jaeckel. Sheriff Baker: Slim Pickens. Mrs. Baker: Katy Jurado. Alamosa Bill: Jack Elam. Chisum: Barry Sullivan. Lemuel: Chill Wills. Gov. Lew Wallace: Jason Robards. Bob Ollinger: R. G. Armstrong. Black Harris: L. Q. Jones. Poe: John Beck. Holly: Richard Bright. Eno: Luke Askew. J. W. Bell: Matt Clark. Maria: Rita Coolidge. Paco: Emilio Fernandez. Pete Maxwell: Paul Fix.

10. BRING ME THE HEAD OF ALFREDO GARCIA (1974)

An Optimus-Latigo-Estudios Churubusco Co. production for United Artists. Running time: 112 minutes.

Producer: Martin Baum. Screenplay: Gordon Dawson, Sam Peckinpah, from a story by Peckinpah and Frank Kowalski. Director of photography: Alex Phillips, Jr. Supervising editor: Garth Craven. Editors: Robbe Roberts, Sergio Ortega, Dennis Dolan. Executive producer: Helmut Dantine. Associate producer: Gordon Dawson. Executive production manager and assistant director: William C. Davidson. Assistant to the director: Katy Haber. Art director: Augustin Ituarte. Set dresser: Enrique Estevez. Music: Jerry Fielding. Sound: Manuel Topete, Mike Colgan, Harry Tetrick. Wardrobe: Adolfo Ramirez. Makeup: Rosa Guerrero. Special effects: Leon Ortega, Raul Fabmir, Federico Farfan. Property master: Alf Pegley. Unit production manager: Carlos Terron Garcia. Mexican assistant director: Jesus Marin Bello. Dialogue director: Sharon Peckinpah.

Cast: Bennie: Warren Oates. Elita: Isela Vega. Sappensly: Robert Webber. Quill: Gig Young. Max: Helmut Dantine. El Jefe: Emilio Fernandez. Paco: Kris Kristofferson. John: Donnie Fritts. Frank: Don Levy.

11. THE KILLER ELITE (1975)

An Arthur Lewis-Baum/Dantine production of an Exeter/Persky-Bright Feature, distributed by United Artists. Running time: 122 minutes.

Producers: Martin Baum, Arthur Lewis. Screenplay: Mark Norman and Stirling Silliphant, based on the novel by Robert Rostand. Director of photography: Philip Lathrop. Supervising editor: Garth Craven. Editors: Tony De Zarraga, Monte Hellman. Executive producer: Helmut Dantine. Production manager: Bill Davidson. Second-unit director: Frank Kowalski. Assistant directors: Newt Arnold, Ron Wright, Jim Bloom, Cliff Coleman. Assistant to the director: Katy Haber. Production designer: Ted Haworth. Set decorator: Rick Gentz. Music: Jerry Fielding. Sound: Fred Brown, Chuck Wilborn, Richard Portman. Wardrobe designer: Ray Summers. Makeup: Jack Wilson, Jack Petty. Special effects: Sass Bedig. Property master: Robert Visciglia.

Cast: Mike Locken: James Caan. George Hansen: Robert Duvall. Cap Collis: Arthur Hill. Jerome Miller: Bo Hopkins. Yuen Chang: Mako. Mac: Burt Young. Lawrence Weyburn: Gig Young. Vorodny: Helmut Dantine.

12. CROSS OF IRON (1977)

A co-production of Anglo-EMI Productions, London; Rapid Film, Munich; and Terra Filmkunst, Berlin; an ITC Entertainment, distributed by Avco-Embassy.

Producers: Alex Winitsky, Arlene Sellers. Screenplay: Julius Epstein, Walter Kelley, James Hamilton, based on the novel by Willi Heinrich. Director of photography: John Coquillon. Editors: Tony Lawson, Murray Jordan, Michael Ellis. Executive producer: Wolf Hartwig. Associate producer: Pat Duggan. Second-unit director: Walter Kelley. Assistant directors: Cliff Coleman, Bert Batt. Production supervisor: Dieter Nobbe. Assistant to the director: Katy Haber. Production designer: Ted Haworth. Art director: Veljko Despotovic. Music: Ernest Gold. Sound: David Hildyard, Bill Rowe, Jerry Stanford, Rodney Holland. Wardrobe supervisors: Kent James and Carol James. Makeup: Colin Arthur. Special effects: Sass Bedig, Richard Richtsfeld, Zdravko Smojver. Property master: Robert Visciglia. Stunt arranger: Peter Brayham. Military advisors: Maj. A. D. Schrodek and Claus Von Trotha.

Cast: Cpl. Steiner: James Coburn. Capt. Stransky: Maximilian Schell. Col. Brandt: James Mason. Capt. Kiesel: David Warner. Kruger: Klaus Lowitsch. Sister Eva: Senta Berger. Zoll: Arthur Brauss. Kern: Vadim Glowna. Lt. Triebig: Roger Fritz. Anselm: Dieter Schidor. Dietz: Michael Nowka.

13. CONVOY (1978)

EMI Films, distributed by United Artists. Running time: 110 minutes.
Producer: Robert Sherman. Screenplay: B. W. L. Norton, based on the
song by C. W. McCall. Director of photography: Harry Stradling, Jr. Supervising editor: Graeme Clifford. Editors: John Wright, Garth Craven. Executive producers: Michael Deeley, Barry Spikings. Second-unit directors: Walter Kelley, James Coburn. Assistant directors: Tom Shaw, Richard Wells,
Pepi Lenzi, John Poer, Cliff Coleman, Newt Arnold, Ron Wright. Production managers: Tony Wade, Tom Shaw. Production designer: Fernando
Carrere. Art director: J. Dennis Washington. Set decorator: Francis
Lombardo. Music: Chip Davis. Sound: Bill Randall, Don Mitchell, Bob Litt,
Steve Maslow. Costumers: Kent James and Carol James. Makeup: Steve
Abrums, Jim McCoy. Special effects: Sass Bedig, Marcel Vercoutere, Candy
Flanagin. Property master: Robert Visciglia. Stunt coordinator: Gary
Combs.
    Cast: Rubber Duck: Kris Kristofferson. Melissa: Ali MacGraw. Lyle Wallace: Ernest Borgnine. Pig Pen: Burt Young. Widow Woman: Madge Sinclair. Spider Mike: Franklyn Ajaye. Chuck Arnoldi: Brian Davies. Gov. Haskins: Seymour Cassel. Violet: Cassie Yates. Hamilton: Walter Kelley. Texas
governor: John Bryson.

14. THE OSTERMAN WEEKEND (1983)

A 20th Century-Fox release of a Michael Timothy Murphy and Guy Collins
presentation of a Davis-Panzer production. Running time: 102 minutes.
    Producers: William Panzer, Peter Davis. Screenplay: Alan Sharp; adaptation by Ian Masters, based on the novel by Robert Ludlum. Director of
photography: John Coquillon. Editors: David Rawlins, Edward Abroms. Executive producers: Michael Timothy Murphy, Larry Jones, Marc Zavat. Associate producers: Don Guest, E. C. Monell. Production manager: Don
Guest. Second-unit director: Rod Amateau. Assistant director: Win Phelps.
Art director: Robb Wilson King. Set decorator: Keith Hein. Music: Lalo
Schifrin. Sound: Richard Bryce Goodman, Bayard Carey. Key costumer:
George Little. Makeup: Robert Sidell. Special effects: Peter Chesney. Property master: Douglas Madison. Stunt coordinator: Thomas Huff.
    Cast: John Tanner: Rutger Hauer. Lawrence Fassett: John Hurt. Bernie
Osterman: Craig T. Nelson. Ali Tanner: Meg Foster. Betty Cardone: Cassie
Yates. Joseph Cardone: Chris Sarandon. Virginia Tremayne: Helen Shaver.
Richard Tremayne: Dennis Hopper. Maxwell Danforth: Burt Lancaster.

Chapter Notes

Prologue

Information about:
Cincinnati Kid, from interviews with Martin Ransohoff (interviewed in Beverly
  Hills, Calif., 6/90), Lois O'Connor (interviewed in Southport, Conn., 7/90); L.
  Q. Jones (interviewed in Hollywood, Calif., 6/90), Jim Silke (telephone interview
  7/90), John Calley (telephone interview 10/90), Daniel Melnick (interviewed in
  West Hollywood, Calif., 6/90), Martin Baum (interviewed in Beverly Hills, Calif.,
  6/90).
Letter to Robert Weitman from Peckinpah archive.

Peckinpah quotes:
"I spent four months," from *Films & Filming,* 10/69.
"We had a little," from *Movietone News,* 2/5/79.
"I had a feeling," from *Sight & Sound,* Autumn 1969.
"I got angry," from *Cinema,* Fall 1969.

PART ONE: To 1958

Peckinpah quote:
"My people are all crazy," from *Rolling Stone,* 5/13/71.

CHAPTER ONE: FROM PECKINPAUGH TO PECKINPAH

Peckinpah quote:
"I had a great aunt Jane," from *Films & Filming,* 10/69.
Genealogical material from "Peckinpaughs, Pickenpaughs, Beckenbaughs, Peckinpahs and Peckenpaughs: Descendants of John Adam and Anna Maria Beck-
  enbach," compiled by Edwin T. and Atha Peckenpaugh, Brace Gateway Press,
  1984.

Information about:

Charles Peckinpah, from interview with Bob Peckinpah (interviewed in North Fork, Calif., 6/90).

Denver Church, from interview with Denver Peckinpah (interviewed in Monterey, Calif., 3/90).

Courtship of Dave Peckinpah and Fern Church, from interviews with Denver Peckinpah and Susan Peckinpah (interviewed in Fresno, Calif., 6/90).

Fern Peckinpah, from interviews with Marie Selland Taylor (interviewed in Portland, Ore., 3/90, and subsequent telephone interviews).

Family relationships, from interviews with Denver Peckinpah, Susan Peckinpah, Bob Peckinpah and Betty Peckinpah (interviewed in Monterey, Calif., 3/90).

Denver Church court case, from *Fresno Past & Present: Journal of the Fresno City and County Historical Society,* Spring 1990.

Birth and childhood of Sam Peckinpah, from interviews with Denver Peckinpah and Kristen Peckinpah (interviewed in Portland, Ore., 3/90).

Peckinpah and Denver Church, from interviews with Denver Peckinpah, Joe Bernhard (interviewed in Clovis, Calif., 6/90).

Fresno, from interview with Joe Bernhard.

Dave Peckinpah, from interviews with Bob Peckinpah, Susan Peckinpah.

William Saroyan excerpt from *A Bicycle Rider in Beverly Hills.*

Dave Peckinpah, from interviews with Denver Peckinpah, Blaine Pettitt (interviewed in Fresno, Calif., 6/90), Bob Peckinpah.

Fern Peckinpah, from interviews with Denver Peckinpah, Bob Peckinpah, Susan Peckinpah, Katy Haber (interviewed in West Hollywood, Calif., 7/90).

Dave and Sam Peckinpah, from interviews with Denver Peckinpah, Wanda Justice (telephone interview 5/90).

Family life in Fresno, from interviews with Bob Peckinpah, Susan Peckinpah, Sharon Peckinpah (interviewed in Los Angeles, Calif., 4/90).

Peckinpah's childhood, from interviews with Betty Peckinpah, Blaine Pettitt.

Peckinpah and Fern Peckinpah, from interviews with Marie Selland Taylor.

Childhood fighting, from interview with Joe Bernhard.

Peckinpah as a teen, from interviews with Betty Peckinpah, Joe Bernhard, Bob Peckinpah, Don Levy (telephone interview 6/90).

Fraternity hazing and military school, from interviews with Joe Bernhard, Betty Peckinpah, Denver Peckinpah.

Peckinpah and the Marines, from interviews with Denver Peckinpah, Joe Bernhard, Marie Selland Taylor.

Peckinpah and school, from interviews with Denver Peckinpah, Bud Williams (interviewed in Bass Lake, Calif., 6/90).

Marie Selland and Peckinpah, from interviews with Marie Selland Taylor, Don Levy.

Peckinpah in Mexico, from interviews with Marie Selland Taylor, Joe Bernhard.

Seiki Sano, from interview with Isela Vega (interviewed in Beverly Hills, Calif., 7/90).

Peckinpah and Marie marry, from interviews with Marie Selland Taylor.

Tell their parents, relations between Peckinpah and Arthur Selland, from interviews with Marie Selland Taylor, Judy Selland (interviewed in Portland, Ore., 3/90).

Marriage license, from Peckinpah archive at Academy of Motion Picture Arts and Sciences library, Beverly Hills, Calif.

Peckinpah at USC, early married life, from interviews with Marie Selland Taylor, Denver Peckinpah, Bud Williams, Don Levy.

Peckinpah quotes:

"My earliest memory," "I was a tagalong kid," "My father believed in the Bible," "I went back to school," "I learned more," from *Playboy Interview,* Playboy, 8/72.

"I was very much a loner," from *Movietone News,* 2/5/79.

"I was nine years old," and "When I was a kid," from *Sight and Sound,* Autumn 1969.

"I was sixteen," from *Newsday,* 8/25/74.

"It never felt like," from *Rolling Stone,* 10/12/72.

"One of the longest split seconds," from *"Peckinpah: A Portrait in Montage,"* by Garner Simmons, University of Texas Press, 1982.

"I was shot," from *New York,* 8/19/74.

"That's what people say," from *Los Angeles Herald-Examiner,* 11/82.

"Another marine told me," from *Life* magazine, 8/11/72.

"Maybe the only thing," from *Films & Filming,* 10/69.

CHAPTER TWO: STAGE, SCREEN AND TELEVISION

Information about:

Peckinpah at Huntington Park Civic Theater, as father, at KLAC-TV, from interviews with Marie Selland Taylor, Betty Peckinpah.

Firing at KLAC, from interviews with Marie Selland Taylor, Walter Peter (interviewed in Beverly Hills, Calif., 4/90 and 5/90) and from *Films & Filming,* 10/ 69.

Master's thesis, from Peckinpah archive.

CHAPTER THREE: A GOFER MOVES IN

Information about:

Peckinpah's meeting with Walter Wanger and Don Siegel, from interviews with Denver Peckinpah, Marie Selland Taylor.

Don Siegel, from an interview with Ted Haworth (telephone interview 7/90).

Daniel Mainwaring letter from Peckinpah archive.

Don Siegel quotes about *Riot in Cell Block Eleven,* from tape recording of Sam Peckinpah memorial at Directors Guild of America, January 1985.

Peckinpah and "Gunsmoke" from interviews with Ted Haworth, Gordon Dawson.

Effect on family of first TV writing success, from interviews with Sharon Peckinpah, Marie Selland Taylor, Joe Bernhard.

Malibu fire, life in Malibu, from interviews with Joe Bernhard, Kristen Peckinpah, Sharon Peckinpah, Walter Peter.

Family tensions and Peckinpah's drinking, from interviews with Joe Bernhard, Kristen Peckinpah, Sharon Peckinpah, Walter Peter, Susan Peckinpah, Judy Selland, Betty Peckinpah.

One-Eyed Jacks, from interview with James Coburn (interviewed in Sherman Oaks, Calif., 6/90); *Movietone News,* 2/5/79.

Early TV work, from *Film Heritage,* Winter 1974–75.

Glory Guys, working with Levy-Gardner-Laven, from interviews with Arnold Laven (telephone interview 6/90), Jules Levy (telephone interview 6/90), Denver Peckinpah, Joe Bernhard.

"The Rifleman," from interview with Arnold Laven.

Peckinpah quotes:

"Don Siegel and Walter Wanger," from *Film Quarterly,* Winter 1963–64.

"I played different parts," "It took me five months," "There was one scene," from *Films & Filming,* 10/69.

"One of my first film jobs," from *Rolling Stone,* 10/12/72.

"I'd like to clear up," from interview with Barbara Baskin, BBC, 1982, from Peckinpah archive.

"It was hell," "Marlon screwed it up," from *Playboy,* 8/72.

"It was a damn good script," "I worked with Marlon," from *Movietone News,* 2/5/79.

"They liked the scripts," *Sight & Sound,* Autumn 1969.

"Every time I started a show," "Christ, it was five," from *New York Times Magazine,* 10/31/71.

PART TWO: 1958–1963

Peckinpah quote:

"It is not a good world," from letter 10/23/60 from Peckinpah archive.

CHAPTER FOUR: "THE RIFLEMAN" AND "THE WESTERNER"

Information about:

"The Rifleman" success, from *Complete Directory of Prime Time Network Shows, 1946–Present,* by Tim Brooks and Earl Marsh, Ballantine Books, 1979; interviews with Arnold Laven, Dennis Hopper (telephone interview 9/90), R. G. Armstrong (interviewed in Sherman Oaks, Calif., 7/90), Don Levy.

Peckinpah directing "Rifleman," from interviews with Arnold Laven, Jules Levy, Johnny Crawford (telephone interview 5/90), Robert Culp (interviewed in Beverly Hills, Calif., 7/90).

Problems on "The Rifleman," quitting to do "Westerner," *The Glory Guys,* from interviews with Arnold Laven, Jules Levy, Johnny Crawford.

1960 Writers Guild Strike, from interview with Stirling Silliphant (interviewed in New York, 7/90).

Development of "The Westerner," from Film Heritage, Winter 1974–75, *Complete Directory of Prime Time Network Shows, 1946–Present,* interviews with Joe Bernhard, Dub Taylor, Walter Peter, Robert Culp, Denver Peckinpah, Arnold Laven, James Coburn.

CHAPTER FIVE: PERSONAL PROBLEMS AND *Deadly Companions*

Information about:
Peckinpah and Marie marital problems, from interviews with Marie Selland Taylor, Robert Culp, Kristen Peckinpah, Sharon Peckinpah, Betty Peckinpah, Susan Peckinpah.
Letters from Peckinpah archive.
David Peckinpah death and funeral, from interviews with Susan Peckinpah, Denver Peckinpah.
Deadly Companions, from interviews with Charles FitzSimons (telephone interview 4/90).
William Clothier quote, from *Five American Cinematographers,* by Scott Eyman, Scarecrow Press, 1987.
Divorce from Marie, from interviews with Marie Selland Taylor, Kristen Peckinpah, Sharon Peckinpah, Mathew Peckinpah (questions answered in letter, 8/90), Joe Bernhard.
Life at the Bird House after divorce, from interviews with Kristen Peckinpah, Sharon Peckinpah, Joe Bernhard, Betty Peckinpah.

Peckinpah quotes:
"It was Brian Keith," from *Playboy,* 8/72.
"It was all based," "All I can say is," "It's a brutal," "It was cut," from *Film Quarterly,* Winter 1963–64.
"Every time I'd volunteer," "Brian had enough sense," "I defy anyone," from *Films & Filming,* 10/69.

CHAPTER SIX: ELEGY FOR THE *High Country*

Information about:
Origins of *Ride the High Country,* from interviews with Paul Seydor (interviewed in Los Angeles, Calif., 5/90), Joe Bernhard.
Casting *Ride the High Country,* from interviews with Robert Culp, James Drury (telephone interview 5/90), Mariette Hartley (telephone interview 5/90).
Production of *Ride the High Country,* from interviews with James Drury, Mariette Hartley, L. Q. Jones.
Joel McCrea letters from Peckinpah archive.
Lucien Ballard quote from *Behind the Camera: The Cinematographer's Art,* by Leonard Maltin, Dover Publications, 1978.
Response to *Ride the High Country,* from interview with James Drury, Andrew Sarris (interviewed in New York, 5/90), Pauline Kael (telephone interview 9/90), Jim Silke (telephone interview 7/90).
"Pericles on 31st Street" and "Dick Powell Theater," from *Film Heritage,* Winter 1974–75, interviews with Harry Mark Petrakis (telephone interview 7/90), Theodore Bikel (telephone interview 4/90), Robert Culp.
Little Britches, from *Film Heritage,* Winter 1974–75.
Bachelor life, from interviews with Marie Selland Taylor, Sharon Peckinpah.

Peckinpah quotes:
"It's very difficult," "He wanted a rewrite," from *Film Quarterly,* Winter 1963–64.
"MGM saw," from *Playboy,* 8/72.
Interview excerpt from *Cinema* magazine, June–July 1962.

PART THREE: 1963–1968

CHAPTER SEVEN: A "MAJOR" PROJECT

Information about:
Castaway, by James Gould Cozzens, originally published by Harcourt Brace Jovanovich, 1934.
Letter to Samuel X. Abarbanel from Peckinpah archive.
Major Dundee, from interview with Charlton Heston (telephone interview 8/90).
Journal excerpts from *Charlton Heston: The Actor's Life,* by Charlton Heston, E. P. Dutton, 1978.
Production of *Major Dundee,* from interviews with Jim Silke, Joe Canutt (telephone interview 8/90), James Coburn, Charlton Heston, L. Q. Jones, R. G. Armstrong, Peter Bogdanovich (interviewed in New York, 9/90), Gordon Dawson (interviewed in Sherman Oaks, Calif., 7/90).
Casting memos, Heston letter to Jerry Bresler, from Peckinpah archive.
Heston quote, "There are directors," from *Filmmakers on Filmmaking: The AFI Seminars on Motion Pictures and Television, Vol. 2,* edited by Joseph McBride, J. P. Tarcher Inc., 1983.
Romance with Begonia Palacios, from interview with Begonia Palacios (interviewed in Mexico City, 7/90).

Peckinpah quotes:
"Very simply," from *Film Quarterly,* Winter 1963–64.
"Jerry Bresler gave," "It was a very," "It gives me shivers," from *Films & Filming,* 10/69.
"One night I ended up," from *Rolling Stone,* 5/13/71.

CHAPTER EIGHT: DONE IN BY *Dundee*

Information about:
Editing *Major Dundee,* from interviews with Charlton Heston, James Coburn, Jim Silke, Kristen Peckinpah.
Memos to Jerry Bresler and Evarts Ziegler; memo from Jerry Bresler; letters to *Hollywood Reporter, Newsweek* from Peckinpah archive.
Journal excerpts from *Charlton Heston: The Actor's Life,* by Charlton Heston, E. P. Dutton, 1978.

Peckinpah quotes:
"At two hours," *"Dundee* was," from *Sight & Sound,* Autumn 1969.
"Where it fails," from *Films & Filming,* 10/69.

CHAPTER NINE: YEARS IN EXILE, PART ONE

Information about:
Marital problems with Begonia, from interviews with Begonia Palacios, Juan Jose
Palacios (interviewed in San Diego, Calif., 5/90), Betty Peckinpah, Jim Silke.
Being blackballed, from interviews with Begonia Palacios, Robert Culp, Martin
Baum, Jim Silke, L. Q. Jones, Kristen Peckinpah, Lois O'Connor, Walter Peter,
Max Evans (telephone interview 8/90), Juan Jose Palacios.
Selling residual rights, from interview with Arnold Laven.
Working on *Caravans* and *Castaway,* from interviews with Jim Silke, L. Q. Jones.
Letter to Wayne Tucker from Peckinpah archive.
Noon Wine, from interviews with Daniel Melnick, Lois O'Connor, Jason Robards
(interviewed at Southport, Conn., 7/90), Theodore Bikel.
Deterioration of marriage, from interviews with Begonia Palacios, Robert Culp, Den-
ver Peckinpah, Betty Peckinpah, Juan Jose Palacios.
Villa Rides, from *Peckinpah: A Portrait in Montage.*
Life in Malibu, from interviews with Jason Robards, Robert Culp, Daniel Melnick,
Sharon Peckinpah.
Peckinpah and Kenneth Hyman, from interviews with Kenneth Hyman (telephone
interview, 6/90), Robert Culp.

Peckinpah quote:
"Brynner asked," from *Los Angeles Times,* 12/9/79.

PART FOUR: *The Wild Bunch* 1968–69

Peckinpah quote:
"I want to be able," from *Film Quarterly,* Winter 1963–64.

CHAPTER TEN: SEX AND VIOLENCE

Information about:
Film attendance from *Saturday Review,* 12/28/68.
National film industry income, *The Sound of Music,* increase in theaters, from *U.S.
News and World Report,* 10/17/66.
Studio sales, from *Newsweek,* 2/2/70.
Changes in studio heads, from *Time,* 4/12/68, author's interview with Martin
Baum.
Changes in rating system, *Time,* 9/30/66, *Newsweek,* 10/9/67, interviews with
Stephen Farber (telephone interview 8/90), Charles Champlin (telephone inter-
view 8/90), Joseph Gelmis (interviewed in New York, 5/90).

Quotes:
"I wish 'The Sound,' " from *Newsweek,* 2/2/70.
"In the wake of," "Hollywood has at long last," from *Time,* 12/8/67.
"To the horror of the puritans," from *Look,* 1/9/68.

CHAPTER ELEVEN: PICKING THE PERFECT "BUNCH"

Information about:
Peckinpah introspection, from interview with L. Q. Jones.
Wild Bunch screenplay, from interviews with Walon Green (telephone interview 5/90), Jim Silke.
Casting, from interviews with Jason Robards, James Drury, Charlton Heston.
Bonnie and Clyde, from interviews with Dub Taylor, Gordon Dawson.
Assembling crew, from interviews with Gordon Dawson, Lou Lombardo (telephone interview 4/90).
Phil Feldman, from interviews with L. Q. Jones, Gordon Dawson, *Sam Peckinpah, Master of Violence,* by Max Evans, Dakota Press, 1972.
Lucien Ballard quote from *Behind the Camera: The Cinematographer's Art,* by Leonard Maltin. Dover Publications, 1978.
Casting memos from Peckinpah archive.
Peckinpah's rewrites, attempts to steal credit, from interviews with Walon Green, Arnold Laven.
Peckinpah's personality, from interview with Charles Champlin.
Stanley Kubrick, from interviews with Judy Selland, Gary Weis (telephone interview 5/90).

Peckinpah quotes:
"The outlaws of the West," "I wasn't trying to make," "Very creative, very tough," from *Film Quarterly,* Fall 1969.
"I find color," from *Adam Film World,* 3/70.
"Look, unless you conform," from *Playboy,* 8/72.

CHAPTER TWELVE: WILD ADVENTURES

Information about:
Conditions in Mexico, from interviews with Gordon Dawson, Joe Canutt, Lou Lombardo.
William Holden, Robert Ryan, Ernest Borgnine quotes and anecdotes from *Golden Boy: The Untold Story of William Holden,* by Bob Thomas, St. Martins Press, 1983.
Robert Ryan quotes: "If you turn into," from Paul Seydor; "All the Westerns," from *Action,* May–June 1970.
Strother Martin, from interviews with L. Q. Jones, Lou Lombardo, Cliff Coleman (telephone interview 8/90).
Strother Martin quotes from *Film Comment,* January–February 1981.
Firing crew members, from interviews with Gordon Dawson, Cliff Coleman, Joe Canutt, Max Bercutt (telephone interview 5/90), Gary Combs (telephone interview 5/90).
Peckinpah's perfectionism and preparation, from interviews with L. Q. Jones, Lou Lombardo, Gordon Dawson, Cliff Coleman.
Peckinpah and Lucien Ballard, from interview with Robert Culp.
Peckinpah's drinking, from interviews with Cliff Coleman, L. Q. Jones, Martin Baum, Lou Lombardo.

Peckinpah's hemorrhoids, from interviews with L. Q. Jones, Lou Lombardo.

Lucien Ballard quotes: "No matter how many hours," from *Action*, 5–6/70; "A lot of so-called," "By the time we were," from *The Movies*, 10/83.

Warren Oates quotes from *Film Comment*, 1–2/81.

Facts on alcoholism from Dr. Hugo Kierszenbaum, director, Alcohol Treatment Services, Psychiatric Institute, Westchester Medical Center, interviewed 8/90.

Peckinpah off-set activities, from interviews with Gordon Dawson, Lou Lombardo, L. Q. Jones, Dub Taylor.

Editing in Mexico, from interviews with Lou Lombardo.

Filming *Wild Bunch* bridge sequence, from interviews with Cliff Coleman, Joe Canutt, Gordon Dawson.

Peckinpah quotes:

"I work well with," from *Adam Film World*, 3/70.

"I make trouble," from *Film Quarterly*, Fall 1969.

CHAPTER THIRTEEN: THE SLOW-MOTION LEAP

Information about:

Filming "Battle of Bloody Porch," from interviews with Gordon Dawson, Lou Lombardo, Cliff Coleman, Jim Silke.

Peckinpah's image of violence, from interview with Joe Bernhard.

Wild Bunch cuts, from *Sight & Sound*, Autumn 1969, interview with Ken Hyman.

MPAA report from Peckinpah archive.

Use of slow motion, from interviews with Walon Green, Lou Lombardo, Andrew Sarris, Michael Sragow (interviewed in San Francisco 3/90).

Editing *Wild Bunch,* from interviews with Lou Lombardo, Paul Schrader (telephone interview 7/90).

Scoring *Wild Bunch,* friendship with Jerry Fielding, from interviews with Camille Fielding (telephone interview 5/90), Lois O'Connor.

Kansas City preview, from interview with Max Bercutt.

Editing *Wild Bunch* sound, from interview with Paul Peterson (telephone interview 4/90).

Long Beach preview, from interviews with Max Bercutt, Lou Lombardo.

Excerpts from preview cards, Town Squire review, Peckinpah memo from Peckinpah archives.

Peckinpah quotes:

"We had an R," "What happens when," from *Cinema*, Fall 1969.

"Actually, I went back," from *Sight & Sound*, Autumn 1969.

"They're really going," from *Film Quarterly*, Fall 1969.

CHAPTER FOURTEEN: UNLEASHING *The Wild Bunch*

Information about:

Wild Bunch release, from interviews with Jay Cocks (interviewed in *New York*, 6/90), Martin Scorsese (telephone interview 2/91), Peter Bogdanovich, Pauline Kael.

Peckinpah themes, from interviews with Kristen Peckinpah, Gill Dennis (interviewed in Portland, Ore., 3/90), Mort Sahl (interviewed in Studio City, Calif., 6/90), Jim Silke, Martin Scorsese, Charles Champlin, James Coburn.

Judith Crist quote from *Take One*, 12/75.

Cuts to *Wild Bunch* after release, from interviews with Ken Hyman, Lou Lombardo.

Production memos by Phil Feldman from Peckinpah archive.

Wild Bunch impact, from interviews with Michael Sragow, Andrew Sarris, Pauline Kael.

Peckinpah quotes:

"The strange thing," "Actually, it's an antiviolence film," from *Film Quarterly*, Fall 1969.

"The studio seems," from *Films & Filming*, 10/69.

"A good picture," from *Cinema*, Fall 1969.

"He said they wanted," from *Movietone News*, 2/5/79.

PART FIVE: 1969–1972

Peckinpah letter from Peckinpah archive.

CHAPTER FIFTEEN: BUTTERFLY ATTACK

Information about:

Butterflies and *Cable Hogue,* from interview with Bobby Visciglia (interviewed in Thousand Oaks, Calif., 4/90).

CHAPTER SIXTEEN: COMPOSING A "BALLAD"

Information about:

Peckinpah's trouble finishing a film, from interviews with James Coburn, Gordon Dawson.

The Diamond Story, from interviews with Walon Green, Ken Hyman.

Peckinpah's approach to *Cable Hogue,* from interviews with Michael Sragow, James Coburn.

Cable Hogue script, from interview with L. Q. Jones.

Casting and staffing, from interviews with Jason Robards, David Warner (interviewed in Beverly Hills, Calif., 5/90), Stella Stevens (telephone interview 6/90), Gordon Dawson, Bobby Visciglia.

Documentary, from interviews with Gary Weis, Gill Dennis.

Casting memos from Peckinpah archive.

Peckinpah quote:

" 'Cable Hogue,' for me," from *Adam Film World*, 3/70.

CHAPTER SEVENTEEN: WAITING FOR THE SUN

Information about:
The weather, from *Sam Peckinpah, Master of Violence.*
Gila monster, from interviews with Bobby Visciglia, Gary Weis, Gill Dennis.
Max Evans' scenes, from interviews with Max Evans, Jason Robards.
Rainy weather and its impact, from interviews with R. G. Armstrong, Bobby Visciglia, Max Evans, Jason Robards, Lou Lombardo, L. Q. Jones.
Peckinpah firing people, from interviews with Bobby Visciglia, Gordon Dawson.
Medals, from interview with Bobby Visciglia.
Strother Martin, from interview with L. Q. Jones.
Chewing people out, from interviews with Bobby Visciglia, Gordon Dawson.
Peckinpah's patriotism, from interview with Paul Seydor.
Keeping actors happy, making actors nervous, from interviews with Jason Robards, Lois O'Connor Robards, Bobby Visciglia, David Warner, Stella Stevens, Gordon Dawson.
Peckinpah talking in code, from interviews with Bobby Visciglia, Gordon Dawson, Gary Weis.
Working with Peckinpah, from interview with Gill Dennis.
Peckinpah's passion for film, from interviews with Gary Weis, Bobby Visciglia.
Encounter with Antonioni, from interviews with Gordon Dawson, R. G. Armstrong.
Editing *Wild Bunch,* from interviews with Lou Lombardo, Bobby Visciglia.
Drinking after work, from interview with Bobby Visciglia.
Max Evans quotes from *Sam Peckinpah, Master of Violence.*
Life at Echo Bay, from interviews with Jason Robards, Bobby Visciglia, Gill Dennis, Gordon Dawson, Cliff Coleman.
Poker game, from interviews with L. Q. Jones, Gill Dennis.
Editing *Cable Hogue,* from interviews with Gordon Dawson, Lou Lombardo.
Problems with Phil Feldman, from interview with Gill Dennis.
Peckinpah, Feldman memos from Peckinpah archive.
Split with Phil Feldman, from interview with Michael Sragow.
Letter to Coppola, memos from Phil Feldman from Peckinpah archive.
Response to *Cable Hogue,* from interviews with Joe Bernhard, Stella Stevens.
Psychological games, from interviews with John Bryson (interviewed in New York, 3/90), Gill Dennis, Paul Schrader.
Letter to L.A. County Museum of Art, from Peckinpah archive.

Peckinpah quote:
"*Cable Hogue* is a low-budget," "I'm up at four," from *Film Quarterly,* Fall 1969.
"Can I see myself," from *Newsday,* 5/23/70.
"You're not tough enough," from *American Film,* 4/85.
"Feldman let those," from *Rolling Stone,* 10/12/72.
"Warner Bros. wrote off," from *Movietone News,* 2/5/79.
"I hope I don't go back," from *Adam Film World,* 3/70.

CHAPTER EIGHTEEN: CASTING ABOUT, CASTING OFF

Information about:
Play It As It Lays, from interview with Pauline Kael.
Peckinpah's politics, from interviews with Kristen Peckinpah, Gill Dennis.
Summer Soldiers, from interviews with Robert Culp, Lee Pogostin (telephone interview 5/90), John Calley.
Joan Didion letter, letters to James Dickey from Peckinpah archive.
John Dunne quote from *The Movies,* 10/83.

Peckinpah quote:
"To me, this movie," from *The Movies,* 10/83.

CHAPTER NINETEEN: A "STRAW" IS BORN

Information about:
Preproduction of *Straw Dogs,* from interviews with Daniel Melnick, Martin Baum.
The Territorial Imperative, by Robert Ardrey, Atheneum, 1966.
Peckinpah and alcoholism, from interviews with Daniel Melnick, David Peckinpah (interviewed in Westlake Village, Calif., 5/90).
Script development, casting *Straw Dogs,* from interviews with Daniel Melnick, Martin Baum, David Warner.
Meeting Katy Haber, from interview with Katy Haber.
Meeting Walter Kelley, from interview with Walter Kelley (interviewed in Malibu, Calif., 4/90).
Harold Pinter letter, casting memos, marketing research from Peckinpah archive.
Peckinpah's style with actors on *Straw Dogs,* from interviews with Jason Robards, Daniel Melnick.
Problems with cinematographer, editor, from interviews with Daniel Melnick, Lou Lombardo.
Meeting Peckinpah, from interview with Roger Spottiswoode (telephone interview 4/90).
Peckinpah after hours, from interviews with Walter Kelley, Kristen Peckinpah, Frank Kowalski (interviewed in Van Nuys, Calif., 6/90).
Drinking problems on location, from interviews with Kristen Peckinpah, Katy Haber, Martin Baum, Daniel Melnick.
Letters to Jan Aghed, Jim Silke, David Susskind, Michael Simkins from Peckinpah archive.
Dustin Hoffman quotes: "Sam's like a fight trainer," from *Rolling Stone,* 5/13/71; "Sam Peckinpah is a man," "Don't ask me," from *New York Times Magazine,* 10/31/71.
Problems with Susan George on *Straw Dogs,* from interview with Daniel Melnick, Katy Haber.
Finding an ending to *Straw Dogs,* from interviews with Gordon Dawson, Daniel Melnick, David Warner.
Memos to and from Melnick from Peckinpah archive.

Peckinpah quotes:
"It's about the violence," "Don't give me," "I've had hassles," from *Rolling Stone*, 5/13/71.
"Producers are often only," from *Playboy*, 8/72.

CHAPTER TWENTY: DOGGED BY VIOLENCE

Information about:
Editing *Straw Dogs*, being offered *Junior Bonner*, from interviews with David Warner, Martin Baum, Daniel Melnick, Roger Spottiswoode.
Letter to Jan Aghed from Peckinpah archive.
Response to *Straw Dogs* violence, from interviews with Daniel Melnick, John Bryson, Denver Peckinpah, Walter Kelley.
Reaction to Kael's "fascist" review, from interviews with Daniel Melnick, Joe Bernhard, Pauline Kael.
Peckinpah's image, from interview with Jim Silke.
Kael review quoted from *New Yorker*, 1/29/72.
Letters to Richard Schickel, Pauline Kael, from Peckinpah archive.
"Sam Peckinpah's Salad Days," quoted from *Monty Python's Flying Circus: Just the Words, Vol. 2*, Pantheon Books, 1989.
Joseph Morgenstern quoted from *Newsweek*, 2/14/72.

Peckinpah quotes:
"Doesn't Kael know," "I like Kael," "You can't make violence real," "I'm like a good whore," "What really turned me on," "There are two kinds of women," from *Playboy*, 8/72.
"Everybody seems to deny," from *New York Times Magazine*, 10/31/71.
"Violence? They were ragging," from *Life*, 8/11/72.
"I really think we show violence," from *New York*, 8/19/74.

CHAPTER TWENTY-ONE: WAY OUT WEST AGAIN

Information about:
Developing *Junior Bonner* script, from interviews with Monte Hellman (telephone interview 6/90), Joe Wizan (telephone interview 6/90).
Working with Joe Wizan, from interviews with Katy Haber, Joe Wizan.
Memos to Joe Wizan from Peckinpah archive.
Peckinpah's condition, from interview with Ted Haworth; working with Peckinpah, from interviews with Newt Arnold (interviewed in Encino, Calif., 7/90), Bobby Visciglia.
Working with his kids, from interviews with Sharon Peckinpah, Mathew Peckinpah.
Sexual adventuring, from interview with Bobby Visciglia.
Violence toward women, from interviews with Bobby Visciglia, Katy Haber.
Firing Frank Kowalski, from interviews with Frank Kowalski, Bobby Visciglia, Katy Haber.
McQueen quotes from *McQueen*, by William F. Nolan, Congdon & Weed, 1984.
Letter to Jan Aghed from Peckinpah archive.

Peckinpah's favorite scenes, from interview with Jim Hamilton (interviewed in San Francisco 3/90), Pauline Kael.

Release of *Junior Bonner,* from interviews with Joe Wizan, Martin Baum.

Jeremiah Johnson, from interview with John Milius (telephone interview 1/91); *Emperor of the North Pole,* from interview with Kenneth Hyman.

Letters to Clive Wilkinson, Robert Aldrich from Peckinpah archive.

CHAPTER TWENTY-TWO: "WE CUT A FAT HOG"

Information about:

Marriage to Joie Gould, from interviews with Sharon Peckinpah, Cliff Coleman, Gordon Dawson.

Peckinpah and Katy Haber, from Katy Haber, Gordon Dawson, Bobby Visciglia.

Divorce from Joie Gould, from interviews with Denver Peckinpah, Jim Silke, Joie Gould (telephone conversation 7/90), John Bryson.

Telegram to Joie Gould's parents from Peckinpah archive.

Joie Gould quote, "All of my friends," from *Peckinpah: A Portrait in Montage,* Garner Simmons, University of Texas Press, 1982.

Getaway production, from interviews with Gordon Dawson, Bobby Visciglia, Newt Arnold.

Casting, from interviews with Albert Ruddy (telephone interview 8/90), Bobby Visciglia, Gordon Dawson.

Firing Sharon, from interviews with Sharon Peckinpah, Marie Selland Taylor.

Casting information, Palance suit from Peckinpah archive.

Working with Peckinpah, from interviews with Kent James (telephone interview 8/90), Sharon Peckinpah, Bobby Visciglia.

Musical score, from interview with Camille Fielding.

Screening fight with Al Lettieri, from interview with Gill Dennis.

Letters to, from Joel McCrea, from Peckinpah archive.

McQueen quotes from *McQueen,* by William F. Nolan, Congdon & Weed, 1984.

John Bryson quotes from *Rolling Stone,* 10/12/72.

Peckinpah's response to commercial success, from interview with Denver Peckinpah.

Letters to Jan Aghed, Ali MacGraw from Peckinpah archive.

Peckinpah's drinking, from interviews with Bobby Visciglia, Sharon Peckinpah, Mariette Hartley, David Peckinpah.

Peckinpah quotes:

"Evans is a liar," from *Newsday,* 8/25/74.

"Evans walked into Juarez," from *New York,* 8/19/74.

"That's correct," "Shit, I showed a guy," from *Rolling Stone,* 10/12/72.

PART SIX: "Pat Garrett and Billy the Kid" 1972–1973

Letters to Jan Aghed from Peckinpah archive.

CHAPTER TWENTY-THREE: "FEELS LIKE TIMES ARE CHANGING"

Information about:
Hunting trips from interviews with Walter Peter, Denver Peckinpah, Blaine Pettitt, Bud Williams, Susan Peckinpah, David Peckinpah.

CHAPTER TWENTY-FOUR: APPROACHING FAMILIAR TERRITORY

Information about:
Peckinpah's public image, from interviews with John Bryson, Denver Peckinpah.
Development of *Pat Garrett* script, from interviews with Rudolph Wurlitzer (telephone interview 6/90), James Coburn, Gordon Carroll.
Excerpt from *Pat Garrett and Billy the Kid* introduction, Signet Books, 1973.
James Aubrey at MGM, from *Time,* 2/9/70 and 11/12/73.
Aubrey and Peckinpah, from interview with Daniel Melnick.
Raft scene, from interview with James Coburn.
Casting, from interviews with Rudolph Wurlitzer, James Coburn, Gordon Dawson.
Casting Bob Dylan, from interviews with Rudolph Wurlitzer, James Coburn, Bobby Visciglia.
Bob Dylan quote from *Rolling Stone,* 3/15/73.
Casting memos from Peckinpah archive.
Locations, from interviews with Gordon Dawson, James Coburn.
Location report, courtesy of Gordon Dawson.

CHAPTER TWENTY-FIVE: SHOOTING *Billy the Kid*

Information about:
Peckinpah on location, from interviews with David Peckinpah, Gordon Dawson.
Technical problems on *Pat Garrett,* from interviews with Newt Arnold, Garth Craven (telephone interview 6/90).
Peckinpah's demands on crews, from interviews with James Coburn, Katy Haber.
Handling Peckinpah, from interviews with Newt Arnold, Ted Haworth.
Peckinpah working with actors, from interviews with R. G. Armstrong, Bobby Visciglia, Don Levy.
Flu outbreak, from interviews with Katy Haber, L. Q. Jones, Gordon Dawson, Newt Arnold.
Gordon Carroll as producer, from interviews with Rudolph Wurlitzer, Gordon Dawson, Newt Arnold, Katy Haber, Gary Combs.
Peckinpah's vision, from interviews with Jim Silke, James Coburn.
Conflict with MGM, from interviews with Walter Kelley, Rudolph Wurlitzer.
Excerpt from *Slow Fade,* by Rudolph Wurlitzer, Alfred A. Knopf, 1984.
Peckinpah's drinking, from interviews with Gary Combs, Juan Jose Palacios, Katy Haber, Roger Spottiswoode.
Making excuses, from interviews with Paul Seydor, Jay Cocks, Roger Spottiswoode.
Relations with Begonia Palacios, from interviews with Begonia Palacios, Juan Jose Palacios.

CHAPTER TWENTY-SIX: THE DEATH OF *Pat Garrett and Billy the Kid*

Information about:
Editing *Pat Garrett,* from interviews with Roger Spottiswoode, Garth Craven.
Struggle with Aubrey and MGM from *Time,* 11/12/73, interviews with James Coburn, Garth Craven, Daniel Melnick, Katy Haber.
Peckinpah's cut of *Pat Garrett,* from interviews with Rudolph Wurlitzer, Roger Spottiswoode, Jim Silke, Jay Cocks, Martin Scorsese, Pauline Kael.
Previews, from interview with Roger Spottiswoode.
Hiring *pistoleros,* from interview with John Bryson.
MGM cutting *Pat Garrett,* from interviews with James Coburn, Roger Spottiswoode, Rudolph Wurlitzer, Garth Craven.
Bob Dylan quote from liner notes to "Biograph," by Cameron Crowe, Columbia Records, 1985.
Letter to Pauline Kael from Peckinpah archive.
Release of *Pat Garrett,* from interview with L. Q. Jones.
Lawsuit, from interview with Norma Fink (telephone interview 7/90).
Effect on Peckinpah, from interviews with Katy Haber, David Peckinpah.
Aubrey's firing, from *Time,* 11/12/73.
Information on lawsuit, fake Aubrey memo from Peckinpah archive.
James Coburn quote, "Aubrey's particular evil nature," from *Take One,* 12/75.
Letters about animal cruelty from Peckinpah archive.

Peckinpah quote:
"They took seventeen minutes," "I was trying to beat," from *Movietone News,* 2/5/79.

PART SEVEN: 1973–1977

CHAPTER TWENTY-SEVEN: "HEAD" AND TALES

Information about:
Origins of *Alfredo Garcia,* from interviews with Frank Kowalski, Walter Kelley, Gordon Dawson, Jim Silke.
Developing *Alfredo Garcia,* from interviews with Martin Baum, James Coburn, Peter Falk (interviewed in New York, 4/90).
Casting Warren Oates, from interviews with Gill Dennis, Pauline Kael, Gordon Dawson.
Changes in Peckinpah, from interview with Gordon Dawson.
Casting, from interview with Mort Sahl.
Emilio Fernandez, from interviews with Alex Phillips, Jr. (interviewed in Mexico City, 7/90), Katy Haber, Gordon Dawson, Dan York (telephone interview 7/90).
Casting Isela Vega, from interview with Isela Vega.
Hiring his daughter and Dan York, from interviews with Sharon Peckinpah, Dan York.

Shooting in Mexico City, from interview with Alex Phillips, Jr.

"Medianalysis" letter from Peckinpah archive.

Peckinpah's drinking, from interviews with Dan York, Gordon Dawson.

Begonia's pregnancy, from interviews with Begonia Palacios, Juan Jose Palacios.

AFI Cagney tribute, from interviews with Isela Vega, Jim Silke, Juan Jose Palacios, David Peckinpah.

Caption from *People*, 4/1/74.

Response to *Alfredo Garcia*, from interview with Mike Medavoy (telephone interview 8/90).

Peckinpah and the press, from interviews with Joseph Gelmis, Pauline Kael, Isela Vega, Jay Cocks.

Peckinpah's cut, from interview with Katy Haber.

Pig head, from interview with John Bryson.

Peckinpah quotes:

"I'm a Mexican resident," "Finally, finally," "I said to Lee Marvin," "Somebody asked if I hit," "I'm afraid to walk," from *New York*, 8/19/74.

"The female lead," from *Newsday*, 8/25/74.

CHAPTER TWENTY-EIGHT: A CURE FOR DRINKING

Information about:

"Insurance Company," from interviews with Dan York, Joe Wizan.

Drinking, from interviews with Dan York, Jim Silke, Isela Vega.

Introduction to cocaine, from interview with Robert Culp.

The spread of cocaine use, from *Time*, 4/16/73; *New York Times Magazine*, 9/1/74; interview with Joe Bernhard.

Peckinpah quote:

"I try to stick," from *Newsday*, 8/25/74.

CHAPTER TWENTY-NINE: BAD BEHAVIOR BY THE BAY

Information about:

Peckinpah and expense money, from interview with Kip Dellinger (interviewed in Brentwood, Calif., 6/90).

Development of *Killer Elite*, from interviews with Arthur Lewis (telephone interview 7/90), James Caan (telephone interview 8/90), Martin Baum, Mike Medavoy.

Reworking *Killer Elite* script, from interviews with Martin Baum, Arthur Lewis, Stirling Silliphant.

Confronting Peckinpah, from interviews with Stirling Silliphant, James Caan.

Peckinpah's fiftieth birthday party from interviews with Kip Dellinger, Wanda Justice, Stella Stevens.

Peckinpah appearance at Clemson, from interview with Andrew Sarris.

Peckinpah rewriting *Killer Elite*, from interviews with Bobby Visciglia, James Caan, Arthur Lewis, Martin Baum, Stirling Silliphant, Mike Medavoy.

Andrew Sarris quote, "A surly questioner," from the *Village Voice*, 1/27/75.

Script memos, Joyce Haber letter from Peckinpah archives.

Tensions with Peckinpah, from interviews with Martin Baum, Stirling Silliphant, Arthur Lewis, Newt Arnold, James Caan.

Cocaine on *Killer Elite,* from interviews with Bobby Visciglia, Katy Haber.

Mothball Fleet incident, from interview with Stirling Silliphant.

Peckinpah as hypochondriac, from interviews with Bobby Visciglia, Katy Haber.

Peckinpah mistreating Katy Haber, from interviews with Kip Dellinger, Stirling Silliphant.

Peckinpah fight at L. A. Airport, from interviews with Bobby Visciglia, Dr. Bob Gray.

Legal complaint from Peckinpah archive.

Attack on Melnick's office, from interviews with Daniel Melnick, Arthur Lewis.

Editing *Killer Elite,* from interviews with Monte Hellman.

PG rating, from interviews with Arthur Lewis, Martin Baum.

Killer Elite ending, from interviews with Bobby Visciglia, Arthur Lewis, Mike Medavoy.

Arthur Lewis memos from Peckinpah archive.

Near-drowning, from interviews with Seymour Cassel (interviewed in W. Los Angeles, Calif., 6/90), Cliff Coleman, Denver Peckinpah.

Peckinpah's politics, from interviews with Sharon Peckinpah, Kristen Peckinpah, Mathew Peckinpah, Blaine Pettitt.

Killer Elite release, from interviews with Mike Medavoy, Arthur Lewis.

Pauline Kael review, from *New Yorker,* 1/12/76.

Memos from Peckinpah archive.

Peckinpah quote:
"That was a kind of," from *Movietone News,* 2/5/79.

CHAPTER THIRTY: "CROSS" THE LINE

Information about:
Sausalito and cocaine, from interviews with Paul Peterson, Jim Hamilton, Don Hyde (interviewed in Healdsburg, Calif., 3/90).

Cross of Iron script, from interview with Jim Hamilton.

Peckinpah's involvement, from interview with Katy Haber.

Wolf Hartwig, from interviews with Bobby Visciglia, Katy Haber, James Coburn, David Warner.

Research for *Cross of Iron,* from interview with James Coburn.

Struggles over budget, tormenting Hartwig, from interviews with James Coburn, Bobby Visciglia, Cliff Coleman, Ted Haworth, Kent James.

Production problems, from interviews with Frank Kowalski, James Coburn, Katy Haber, Norma Fink.

Documentary, from interview with Sharon Peckinpah.

Peckinpah's health, from interviews with Cliff Coleman, Katy Haber, James Coburn.

Meeting Fellini, from interview with James Coburn.

Production memos, telegrams, letters to Tara Poole, from Peckinpah archive.

Peckinpah's drinking, from interviews with James Coburn, Jason Robards, Robert Culp.

Production memos from Peckinpah archive.

Completing *Cross of Iron*, from interviews with Robert Culp, James Coburn, Jim Silke.

Reaction to *Cross of Iron*, from interviews with James Coburn, Jim Hamilton.

Peckinpah quote:
"I turned down *King Kong*," from *Movietone News*, 2/5/79.

CHAPTER THIRTY-ONE: "CONVOY" TO OBLIVION

Information about:
Origins of *Convoy*, from interviews with Sandy Peckinpah (interviewed in Westlake Village, Calif., 5/90), David Peckinpah, B. W. L. Norton (telephone interview 5/90), Michael Deeley (telephone interview 7/90), David Wardlow (interviewed in Beverly Hills, Calif., 6/90), James Coburn.

Peckinpah's reputation, power games, from interviews with Michael Deeley, David Wardlow.

Rewriting *Convoy*, from interviews with B. W. L. Norton, Mort Sahl, Franklyn Ajaye (telephone interview 8/90), James Coburn, Graeme Clifford (telephone interview 9/90), Frank Kowalski, Seymour Cassel, Michael Deeley.

Cocaine use, from interviews with Katy Haber, Bobby Visciglia, David Peckinpah, Cliff Coleman, Kip Dellinger, Frank Kowalski.

Production problems, fight scene, from interviews with Katy Haber, Cliff Coleman, Gary Combs, Michael Deeley, Franklyn Ajaye.

Logistical problems from *Time*, 7/4/77, interview with Katy Haber.

Peckinpah's erratic behavior, from interviews with Michael Deeley, David Peckinpah, Robert Culp, Rudolph Wurlitzer, Gary Combs, Newt Arnold.

Split with Katy Haber, from interview with Katy Haber.

Alienating friends, from interviews with Katy Haber, Walter Kelley, Newt Arnold, Gordon Dawson.

Acting quality, from interview with Gordon Dawson.

Peckinpah as legend in decline, from interviews with B. W. L. Norton, Gary Combs, Franklyn Ajaye.

Replacing Peckinpah, from interview with Michael Deeley.

Memos, telegrams from Peckinpah archive.

Completing *Convoy*, from interviews with Cliff Coleman, Michael Deeley.

Editing *Convoy*, from interviews with Michael Deeley, Graeme Clifford, B. W. L. Norton.

Removing Peckinpah from editing, from interviews with Robert Culp, Paul Peterson, David Peckinpah.

Final cut on *Convoy*, from interviews with Michael Deeley, David Wardlow, Graeme Clifford, Kip Dellinger.

Letter to Ernest Borgnine, from Peckinpah archive.

Effect of *Convoy* on career, from interview with David Peckinpah.

Peckinpah quotes:
"I don't have the opportunity," "This is a million-dollar," from *Time*, 7/4/77.
"We ran eight reels," from *Movietone News*, 2/5/79.

PART EIGHT: 1978–1982

CHAPTER THIRTY-TWO: YEARS IN EXILE, PART II

Information about:
Cabin in Livingston, from interviews with Bobby Visciglia, Denver Peckinpah.
"China 9, Liberty 37," from interview with Monte Hellman.
Life on the road, from interview with Paul Peterson.
Mexican production company, from interviews with Isela Vega, Alex Phillips, Jr.
Friends' efforts to save him, from interview with Daniel Melnick.
Trip to Seattle Film Society, screenplay, visit to Sausalito, from interviews with Richard Jameson (interviewed in New York, 4/90), Kathleen Murphy (telephone interview 7/90).
Alcohol and cocaine, from interviews with Paul Peterson, John Bryson, Joe Bernhard.
Working on scripts, from interview with Paul Peterson.
Screwing his friends, from interviews with Alan Keller (telephone interview 5/90), Joe Bernhard, Jim Hamilton.
Severing relationships, from interviews with Kip Dellinger, Norma Fink, Walter Peter.
Life in Livingston, from interviews with Paul Peterson, Joe Swindlehurst (telephone interview 3/90), Carolyn Swindlehurst (telephone interview 3/90).
"Snowblind," Bogotá trip, from interview with Seymour Cassel.
Cocaine paranoia, from interview with Paul Peterson.
Peckinpah in decline, from interviews with Kristen Peckinpah, Jim Silke.

Peckinpah quotes:
"I tried to set up," from *Los Angeles Times,* 12/19/82.
"I once lived with," from *Cinema,* Fall 1969.

CHAPTER THIRTY-THREE: HEART ATTACK

Information about:
Heart attack, from interviews with Dr. Bob Gray, Joe Swindlehurst, Dr. Dennis Noteboom (telephone interview 4/90).
Recovery, from interviews with Kristen Peckinpah, Denver Peckinpah, Dr. Noteboom; pacemaker, from interviews with Dr. Dennis Noteboom, Jim Silke.
Leaving the hospital, from interviews with Joe Swindlehurst, Carolyn Swindlehurst.
Effect on Peckinpah, from interviews with David Wardlow, Carolyn Swindlehurst, Joe Swindlehurst, David Peckinpah, Mathew Peckinpah.
Post–heart attack period, from interviews with Paul Peterson, Don Hyde, Dr. Dennis Noteboom.
Visiting the set of *Heaven's Gate,* from interviews with Bobby Visciglia, Allen Keller.
The Texans, from interviews with Don Hyde, Paul Peterson, Albert Ruddy.

Cowboy Hall of Fame, from interviews with Allen Keller, Denver Peckinpah, David Peckinpah.

Marriage to Marcy Blueher, from interview with Marcy Blueher Ellis (telephone interview 5/90).

Prenuptial agreement, from Peckinpah archive.

Poem courtesy of Marcy Blueher Ellis.

CHAPTER THIRTY-FOUR: THE COCAINE DEPTHS

Information about:

Continued cocaine use, from interviews with Paul Peterson, Jim Silke.

Problems with *The Texans,* from interviews with Paul Peterson, Albert Ruddy, David Wardlow, Jim Silke.

Hang Tough, from interview with Jim Silke.

Firing his agent, from interviews with David Wardlow, Martin Baum.

TV movie, from interview with Richard Harris (interviewed in New York, 12/90).

The Monkey Wrench Gang, from interview with Martin Ransohoff.

Memo to Martin Baum, letter to Mathew Peckinpah, letter to Richard Marcus from Peckinpah archive.

Peckinpah as grandfather, from interview with Sharon Peckinpah.

CHAPTER THIRTY-FIVE: WORKING ON THE "WEEKEND"

Information about:

Jinxed, from interview with Walter Kelley.

Splitting with Paul Peterson, from interview with Paul Peterson.

Trouble finding work, from interview with Martin Baum.

Development of *Osterman Weekend,* from interviews with Bill Panzer (interviewed in Hollywood, Calif., 7/90), Alan Sharp (telephone interview 6/90).

Peckinpah and sobriety, from interview with Dennis Hopper.

Peckinpah, Davis memos from Peckinpah archive.

Panzer-Davis, from interviews with Alan Sharp, Dave Rawlins (telephone interview 6/90).

Script rewrites, from interviews with Alan Sharp, Bill Panzer, Jason Robards, Pauline Kael.

Choosing his crew, from interviews with Anne Thompson (telephone interview 6/90), Bill Panzer, Katy Haber, Kristen Peckinpah, Walter Kelley.

Peckinpah's health, from interviews with Bill Panzer, Alan Sharp, Lou Lombardo, Walter Kelley, Kathleen Murphy.

Comeback, from interviews with Walter Kelley, Anne Thompson.

Memo to Martin Baum from Peckinpah archive.

Budget problems, from interviews with Bill Panzer, Martin Baum, Kristen Peckinpah.

Production problems, from interviews with Dennis Hopper, Richard Jameson, Michael Sragow.

Disagreements over what the film should be, from interviews with Bill Panzer, Dave Rawlins.

The production, from interviews with Ted Haworth, Bill Panzer.

Breaking glass, from interviews with Bill Panzer, Kristen Peckinpah.

Editing *Osterman Weekend,* from interviews with Dave Rawlins, Bill Panzer, James Coburn.

Production memos from Peckinpah archive.

Release of *Osterman,* from interviews with Charles Champlin, Isela Vega, Joe Swindlehurst.

Peckinpah quotes:

"It was wonderful to be back," "After 30 years," "I pray a lot," from *Los Angeles Times,* 4/1/82.

"They threw in a lot," from *Los Angeles Herald-Examiner,* 11/82.

"I had no creative control," from *Los Angeles Times,* 12/19/82.

PART NINE: 1983–1984

Peckinpah quote from *The Movies,* 10/83.

CHAPTER THIRTY-SIX: FURTHER ADVENTURES ON THE COMEBACK TRAIL

Information about:

Trying to get another movie, from interviews with Martin Baum, Dan York.

Memo to Martin Baum from Peckinpah archive.

Death of Fern Church Peckinpah, from interview with Susan Peckinpah, Marcy Blueher Ellis.

Relationship with Carol O'Connor, from interview with Carol O'Connor (interviewed in Beverly Hills, Calif., 6/90).

The monkey, from interviews with Carol O'Connor, Gill Dennis, Joe Swindlehurst, Dave Rawlins.

CHAPTER THIRTY-SEVEN: SECOND-GENERATION ROCK

Information about:

Martin Lewis and Julian Lennon documentary, from interviews with Martin Lewis (interviewed in Hollywood, 5/90), Martin Baum, Dan York.

Peckinpah in New York, shooting video at Suffern, from interviews with Martin Lewis, Jason Robards, Julie Mann (telephone interview 6/90), Robin Chambers (interviewed in New York, 7/90), Walter Kelley, Alex Phillips, Jr., Carol O'Connor, Pauline Kael.

CHAPTER THIRTY-EIGHT: LAST TRIP TO MEXICO

Information about:

On the Rock, from interviews with Carol O'Connor, Jim Silke.

The Shotgunners, from interview with Dan York.

Mending fences, from interviews with Bob Peckinpah, Sharon Peckinpah, Kristen Peckinpah, David Peckinpah, Don Levy, Bobby Visciglia.

Stephen King quote from *Cinefantastique,* February 1991.
Thanksgiving 1984, from interviews with Gill Dennis, Joe Bernhard.
Trip to Mexico, heart attack and death, from interviews with Begonia Palacios, Juan Jose Palacios.
Autopsy report, courtesy of Los Angeles County Medical Examiner.
Cremation from interview with Kristen Peckinpah.
Will, from interviews with Denver Peckinpah, Kristen Peckinpah.
Letters, from interviews with Carol O'Connor, John Bryson.
Peckinpah will, courtesy of Kristen Peckinpah.

PART TEN: Epilogue

Walter Peter quote, from tape recording of Sam Peckinpah memorial at Directors Guild of America, January 1985.

Information about:
Reaction to tribute, from interviews with Martin Lewis, Joe Bernhard, David Warner, Jim Hamilton, Jason Robards.
All quotes from Peckinpah memorial from tape recording of the event, courtesy of Walter Peter.

INDEX

419